EVERYMAN,
I WILL GO WITH THEE,
AND BE THY GUIDE,
IN THY MOST NEED
TO GO BY THY SIDE

MARCEL PROUST

IN SEARCH OF LOST TIME

VOLUME 4

THE FUGITIVE
TIME REGAINED

TRANSLATED FROM THE FRENCH
BY C.K. SCOTT MONCRIEFF
AND TERENCE KILMARTIN
(THE FUGITIVE)

ANDREAS MAJOR AND
TERENCE KILMARTIN
(TIME REGAINED)

REVISED BY D.J. ENRIGHT

WITH AN INTRODUCTION
BY HAROLD BLOOM

EVERYMAN'S LIBRARY

250

First included in Everyman's Library, 2001
Translation copyright © Chatto & Windus and Random House, Inc.,
1981
Copyright in the revisions to translation © D. J. Enright, 1992
Introduction (in volume 1) originally appeared as 'Proust:
The True Persuasion of Sexual Jealousy' in *The Western Canon* by
Harold Bloom, Macmillan, 1995, and is reprinted by permission of
Macmillan Publishers Ltd.
Bibliography and Chronology © Everyman's Library, 2001
Typography by Peter B. Willberg

ISBN 978-1-84159-899-4

A CIP catalogue record for this book is available from the
British Library

Published by Everyman's Library,
Northburgh House, 10 Northburgh Street,
London EC1V 0AT

Distributed by Random House (UK) Ltd.,
20 Vauxhall Bridge Road, London SW1V 2SA

Printed and bound in Germany by GGP Media GmbH, Pössneck

IN SEARCH OF
LOST TIME

———

CONTENTS OF VOLUME FOUR

Numerals in the text refer the reader to explanatory notes, while asterisks indicate the position of textual addenda. The notes and the addenda follow the text.

THE FUGITIVE

CHAPTER ONE

GRIEVING AND FORGETTING

"MADEMOISELLE ALBERTINE has gone!" How much further does anguish penetrate in psychology than psychology itself! A moment before, in the process of analysing myself, I had believed that this separation without having seen each other again was precisely what I wished, and, comparing the mediocrity of the pleasures that Albertine afforded me with the richness of the desires which she prevented me from realising, I had felt that I was being subtle, had concluded that I no longer wished to see her, that I no longer loved her. But now these words: "Mademoiselle Albertine has gone," had produced in my heart an anguish such that I felt I could not endure it much longer. So what I had believed to be nothing to me was simply my entire life. How ignorant one is of oneself. My anguish must be made to end at once; tender towards myself as my mother had been towards my dying grandmother, I said to myself with that genuine wish that one has to relieve the suffering of a person one loves: "Be patient for a moment, we shall find something to take the pain away, don't fret, we're not going to allow you to suffer like this." It was in this category of ideas that my instinct of self-preservation sought for the first balms to lay upon my open wound: "None of this is of the slightest importance, because I'm going to bring her back at once. I shall have to think how, but in any case she will be here this evening. Therefore it's useless to torment myself." "None of this is of the slightest importance"—I had not been content merely with giving myself this assurance, but had tried to convey the same impression to Françoise by not allowing her to see my suffering, because, even at the moment when I was feeling it so acutely, my love did not forget how important it was that it should appear a happy love, a mutual love, especially in the eyes of Françoise, who disliked Albertine and had always doubted her sincerity.

Yes, a moment ago, before Françoise came into the room, I had believed that I no longer loved Albertine, I had believed that I was

3

leaving nothing out of account, like a rigorous analyst; I had believed that I knew the state of my own heart. But our intelligence, however lucid, cannot perceive the elements that compose it and remain unsuspected so long as, from the volatile state in which they generally exist, a phenomenon capable of isolating them has not subjected them to the first stages of solidification. I had been mistaken in thinking that I could see clearly into my own heart. But this knowledge, which the shrewdest perceptions of the mind would not have given me, had now been brought to me, hard, glittering, strange, like a crystallised salt, by the abrupt reaction of pain. I was so much in the habit of having Albertine with me, and now I suddenly saw a new aspect of Habit. Hitherto I had regarded it chiefly as an annihilating force which suppresses the originality and even the awareness of one's perceptions; now I saw it as a dread deity, so riveted to one's being, its insignificant face so incrusted in one's heart, that if it detaches itself, if it turns away from one, this deity that one had barely distinguished inflicts on one sufferings more terrible than any other and is then as cruel as death itself.

The first thing to be done was to read Albertine's letter, since I was anxious to think of some way of bringing her back. I felt that this lay in my power, because, as the future is what exists as yet only in the mind, it seems to us to be still alterable by the intervention, at the eleventh hour, of the will. But at the same time, I remembered that I had seen forces other than my own act upon it, forces against which, even if I had had more time, I could never have prevailed. Of what use is it that the hour has not yet struck if we can do nothing to influence what will happen when it does? When Albertine was living in the house I had been quite determined to retain the initiative in our parting. And then she had gone. I opened her letter. It ran as follows:

"My dear friend,

Forgive me for not having dared to say to you in person what I am now writing, but I am such a coward, and have always been so afraid in your presence, that however much I tried to force myself I could not find the courage to do so. This is what I should have said to you: Our life together has become impossible; indeed you must have realised, from your outburst the other evening, that there had been a change in our relations. What we were able to patch up that night would become irreparable in a few days' time. It is better for us, therefore, since we have had the good fortune to be reconciled, to part as friends. That is why, my darling, I am sending you this line, and I beg you to be kind enough to forgive me if I am causing you a little grief when you think of the immensity of mine. Dearest one, I do not want to become your enemy; it will be bad enough to become by degrees, and all too soon, a stranger to you; and so, as I have absolutely made up my mind, before sending you this letter by Françoise I shall have asked her to let me have my boxes. Good-bye: I leave you the best of myself.

ALBERTINE"

"All this means nothing," I told myself, "it's even better than I thought, for as she doesn't mean a word of what she says, she obviously wrote it only in order to give me a shock, to frighten me, to stop me behaving unbearably towards her. I must think of something to do as soon as possible, so that Albertine will be back here this evening. It's sad to think that the Bontemps are unscrupulous people who make use of their niece to extort money from me. But what does that matter? Even if, to have Albertine here this evening, I must give half my fortune to Mme Bontemps, we shall still have enough left, Albertine and I, to live in comfort." And at the same time I calculated whether I had time to go out that morning and order the yacht and the Rolls-Royce which she coveted, quite forgetting, all my doubts having vanished, that I had decided that it would be unwise to give them to her. "Even if Mme Bontemps's agreement isn't enough, if Albertine refuses to obey her aunt and makes it a condition of her return that she shall enjoy complete independence, well, however much it may distress me, I shall let her have it; she shall go out by herself, as and when she likes. One must be prepared to make sacrifices, however painful they may be, for the thing to which one attaches most importance, which is, in spite of everything I decided this morning on the strength of my precise and absurd arguments, that Albertine shall continue to live here." Can I say moreover that to grant her that freedom would have been altogether painful to me? I should be lying if I did. Already I had often felt that the anguish of leaving her free to misbehave far away from me was perhaps less acute even than the sort of misery which I used to feel when I sensed that she was bored in my company, under my roof. No doubt at the actual moment of her asking me to let her go somewhere, allowing her to do so, with my mind obsessed by the idea of organised orgies, would have been agonising for me. But to say to her: "Take our yacht, or the train, and go away for a month, to some place which I have never seen, where I shall know nothing of what you're doing"—this had often appealed to me, because of the thought that, by force of contrast, when she was far away from me, she would hanker after my society, and would be happy when she returned. "Besides, it's certainly what she herself wants; she doesn't in the least demand that freedom on which moreover, by offering her every day some new pleasure, I could easily succeed in imposing day by day some further restriction. No, what Albertine wanted was for me not to go on behaving insufferably to her, and above all—like Odette with Swann—for me to make up my mind to marry her. Once she is married, her independence will cease to matter to her, we shall stay here together, in perfect happiness." No doubt this meant giving up any thought of Venice. But the cities for which we have most longed (and *a fortiori* the most agreeable hostesses, the most pleasurable diversions—even more than Venice, the Duchesse de Guermantes or the theatre), how pale, insignificant, dead they become when we are tied to another's heart by a bond so painful that it prevents us from tearing ourselves away! "Besides, Albertine is perfectly right about our marriage. Mamma herself was saying that all this procrastination was ridiculous. Marry her, that's what I ought to have done long ago, that's what I must do now, that's what made her write her letter without meaning a word of it; it's only to bring about our marriage that she has postponed for a few hours what she must desire as keenly as I do: her return to this house. Yes, that's what she wanted, that was the purpose of her action," my compassionate reason assured me; but I felt that, in doing so, my reason was still basing itself on the same hypothesis which it had adopted from the start. Whereas I was well aware that it was the other hypothesis which had invariably proved correct. No doubt this second hypothesis would never have been so bold as to formulate in so many words the notion that Albertine could have been on intimate terms with Mlle Vinteuil and her friend. And yet, when I had been overwhelmed by the impact of that terrible revelation, as the train slowed down before stopping at Incarville station, it was the second hypothesis that had been confirmed. This hypothesis had subsequently never conceived the idea that Albertine might leave me of her own accord, in this fashion, without warning me and giving me time to prevent her departure. But all the same, if, after the immense new leap which life had just caused me to make, the reality that confronted me was as novel as that which is presented to us by the discovery of a scientist, by the inquiries of an examining magistrate or the researches of a historian into the hidden aspects of a crime or a revolution, this reality, while exceeding the puny predictions of my second hypothesis, nevertheless fulfilled them. This second hypothesis was not an intellectual one, and the panic fear that had gripped me on the evening when Albertine had refused to kiss me, or the night when I had heard the sound of her window being opened, was not based upon reason. But—and what follows will show it even more clearly, as many episodes must have indicated it already—the fact that our intelligence is not the subtlest, most powerful, most appropriate instrument for grasping the truth is only one reason the more for beginning with the intelligence, and not with an unconscious intuition, a ready-made faith in presentiments. It is life that, little by little, case by case, enables us to observe that what is most important to our hearts or to our minds is taught us not by reasoning but by other powers. And then it is the intelligence itself which, acknowledging their superiority, abdicates to them through reasoning and consents to become their collaborator and their servant. Experimental faith. It seemed to me that the unforeseen calamity with which I found myself grappling was also something that I had already known (as I had known of Albertine's friendship with a pair of lesbians), from having read it in so many signs in which (notwithstanding the contrary affirmations of my reason, based upon Albertine's own statements) I had discerned the weariness, the loathing that she felt at having to live in that state of slavery, signs that had so often seemed to me to be written as though in invisible ink behind her sad, submissive eyes, upon her cheeks suddenly inflamed with an unaccountable blush, in the sound of the window that had suddenly been flung open. Doubtless I had not dared to explore them fully or to form explicitly the idea of her sudden departure. I had thought, with a mind kept in equilibrium by Albertine's presence, only of a departure arranged by myself at an undetermined date, that is to say a date situated in a non-existent time; consequently I had had merely the illusion of thinking of a departure, just as people imagine that they are not afraid of death when they think of it while they are in good health and are actually doing no more than introduce a purely negative idea into a healthy state which the approach of death would of course precisely alter. Besides, the idea of Albertine's departure on her own initiative might have occurred to my mind a thousand times over, in the clearest, the most sharply defined form, without my suspecting any the more what, in relation to myself, that is to say in reality, that departure would be, what an unprecedented, appalling, unknown thing, how entirely novel a calamity. I might have gone on thinking of that departure (had I foreseen it) unceasingly for years on end, without all those thoughts, placed end to end, having the faintest connexion, not merely in intensity but in kind, with the unimaginable hell the curtain of which Françoise had raised for me when she said: "Mademoiselle Albertine has gone." In order to picture to itself an unknown situation the imagination borrows elements that are already familiar and, for that reason, cannot picture it. But the sensibility, even in its most physical form, receives, like the wake of a thunderbolt, the original and for long indelible imprint of the novel event. And I hardly dared say to myself that, if I had foreseen this departure, I would perhaps have been incapable of picturing it to myself in all its horror, or indeed, with Albertine informing me of it, and myself threatening, imploring her, of preventing it. How far removed from me now was the desire to go to Venice! Just as, long ago at Combray, had been the desire to know Mme de Guermantes when the moment came at which I longed for one thing only, to have Mamma in my room. And it was indeed all the anxieties I had felt ever since my childhood which, at the bidding of this new anguish, had come hastening to reinforce it, to amalgamate themselves with it in a homogeneous mass that suffocated me.

To be sure, the physical blow which such a parting administers to the heart, and which, because of that terrible capacity for registering things with which the body is endowed, makes the pain somehow contemporaneous with all the epochs in our life in which we have suffered—to be sure, this blow to the heart which—so little compunction do we feel for the sufferings of others—she who wishes to give the maximum intensity to the regret she causes, whether because, her departure being only a sham, she merely wants to demand better terms, or because, leaving us for ever—for ever!—she desires to wound us, or in order to avenge herself, or to continue to be loved, or (with an eye to the quality of the memory that she will leave behind her) to destroy the web of lassitude and indifference which she has felt being woven about her—to be sure, this blow to the heart is something we had vowed that we would avoid, assuring ourselves that we would part on good terms. But it is seldom indeed that one does part on good terms, because if one were on good terms one would not part. And then the woman to whom we show the utmost indifference nevertheless obscurely feels that in growing tired of her, by virtue of an identical force of habit, we have grown more and more attached to her, and she reflects that one of the essential elements in parting on good terms is to warn the other person before one goes. But she is afraid, by warning, of preventing. Every woman feels that the greater her power over a man, the more impossible it is to leave him except by sudden flight: a fugitive precisely because a queen. True, there is an extraordinary discrepancy between the boredom which she inspired a moment ago and, because she has gone, this furious desire to have her back again. But for this—over and above those which have been given in the course of this work and others which will be given later on—there are reasons. For one thing, her departure occurs as often as not at the moment when her companion's indifference—real or imagined—is greatest, at the extreme point of the swing of the pendulum. The woman says to herself: "No, this can't go on any longer," precisely because the man speaks of nothing but leaving her, or thinks of nothing else; and it is she who leaves him. Then, the pendulum swinging back to the other extreme, the distance is all the greater. In an instant it returns to this point; once more, apart from all the reasons that have been given, it is so natural! The heart still beats; and besides, the woman who has gone is no longer the same as the woman who was with us. Her life under our roof, all too well known, is suddenly enlarged by the addition of the lives with which she is inevitably to be associated, and it is perhaps to associate herself with them that she has left us. So that this new richness of the life of the woman who has gone retroacts upon the woman who was with us and was perhaps premeditating her departure. To the sequence of psychological facts which we are able to deduce and which form part of her life with us, our too evident boredom in her company, our jealousy too (and the effect of which is that men who have been left by a number of women have been left almost always in the same way because of their character and of certain always identical reactions which can be calculated: everyone has his own way of being betrayed, as he has his own way of catching cold), to this sequence that is not too mysterious for us there doubtless corresponded a sequence of facts of which we were unaware. She must for some time past have been keeping up relations, written, or verbal, or through messengers, with some man, or some woman, have been awaiting some signal which we may perhaps have given her unwittingly ourselves when we said: "X called yesterday to see me," if she had arranged with X that on the eve of the day when she was to join him he was to call on me. How many possible hypotheses! Possible only. I constructed the truth so well, but in the realm of possibility only, that, having one day opened by mistake a letter addressed to one of my mistresses, a letter written in a prearranged code which said: "Still awaiting signal to go to the Marquis de Saint-Loup's; please inform tomorrow by telephone," I reconstructed a sort of projected flight; the name of the Marquis de Saint-Loup was there only as a substitute for some other name, for my mistress did not know Saint-Loup, but had heard me speak of him, and moreover the signature was some sort of nickname, without any intelligible form. As it happened, the letter was addressed not to my mistress but to another person in the building who bore a different name which had been misread. The letter was written not in a code but in bad French because it was from an American woman, who was indeed a friend of Saint-Loup, as he himself told me. And the odd way in which this American woman formed certain letters had given the appearance of a nickname to a name which was quite genuine, only foreign. And so I had on that occasion been utterly mistaken in my suspicions. But the intellectual structure which had linked these facts, all of them false, together in my mind was itself so strict and accurate a model of the truth that when, three months later, my mistress (who had at that time been meaning to spend the rest of her life with me) left me, it was in a fashion absolutely identical with that which I had imagined on the former occasion. A letter arrived, containing the same peculiarities which I had wrongly attributed to the former letter, but this time it was indeed meant as a signal.

The present calamity was the worst that I had experienced in my life. And yet the suffering that it caused me was perhaps even exceeded by my curiosity to learn the causes of this calamity: who Albertine had desired and gone to join. But the sources of great events are like those of rivers; in vain do we explore the earth's surface, we can never find them. Had Albertine been planning her flight for a long time past? I have not mentioned the fact (because at the time it had seemed to me simply affectation and ill-humour, what in the case of Françoise we called "a fit of the sulks") that, from the day when she had ceased to kiss me, she had gone about as though tormented by a devil, stiffly erect, unbending, saying the simplest things in a mournful voice, slow in her movements, never smiling. I cannot say that there was any concrete proof of conspiracy with the outer world. True, Françoise told me later that, having gone into Albertine's room two days before her departure, she had found it empty, with the curtains drawn, but had sensed from the atmosphere of the room and from the noise that the window was open. And indeed she had found Albertine on the balcony. But it is difficult to see with whom she could have been communicating from there, and moreover the drawn curtains screening the open window could doubtless be explained by the fact that she knew I was afraid of draughts, and that even if the curtains afforded me little protection they would prevent Françoise from seeing from the passage that the shutters had been opened so early. No, I can see nothing apart from one trifling fact which proves merely that on the day before her departure she knew that she was going. For during that day she took from my room without my noticing it a large quantity of wrapping-paper and packing-cloth which was kept there, and in which she spent the whole night packing her innumerable negligées and dressing-gowns so that she might leave the house in the morning. This is the only fact; that was all. I cannot attach any importance to her having repaid that evening, practically by force, a thousand francs which she owed me; there is nothing extraordinary in that, for she was extremely scrupulous about money.

Yes, she took the wrapping-paper the night before, but it was not only then that she knew that she was going to leave me! For it was not resentment that made her leave but the decision, already taken, to leave me, to abandon the life of which she had dreamed, that gave her that air of resentment. A resentful air, almost solemnly cold towards myself, except on the last evening when, after staying in my room longer than she had intended, she said—a remark which surprised me, coming from her who had always sought to postpone the moment of parting—she said to me from the door: "Good-bye, little one, good-bye." But I did not take any notice of this at the time. Françoise told me that next morning when Albertine informed her that she was going (but this may be explained also by exhaustion, for she had not undressed and had spent the whole night packing everything except the things she had to ask Françoise for, as they were not in her bedroom or her dressing-room), she was still so sad, so much more erect, so much stiffer than during the previous days that Françoise thought, when Albertine said to her: "Good-bye, Françoise," that she was about to fall. When one is told a thing like that one realises that the woman who appealed to us so much less than any of the women whom one meets so easily in the course of the briefest outing, the woman who makes us resent having to sacrifice them to her, is on the contrary the one we would a thousand times prefer. For the choice lies no longer between a certain pleasure—which has become by force of habit, and perhaps by the mediocrity of its object, almost null and void—and other pleasures which tempt and thrill us, but between these latter pleasures and something that is far stronger than they, compassion for suffering.

When I vowed to myself that Albertine would be back in the house before night, I had proceeded as quickly as possible to cover with a fresh belief the open wound from which I had torn the belief I had lived with until then. But swiftly though my instinct of self-preservation had acted, I had, when Françoise spoke to me, been left helpless for an instant, and for all that I now knew that Albertine would be back that same evening, the pain I had felt during the instant in which I had not yet assured myself of her return (the instant that had followed the words: "Mademoiselle Albertine has asked for her boxes; Mademoiselle Albertine has gone"), this pain reawoke in me of its own accord, as sharp as it had been before, that is to say as if I had still been unaware of Albertine's imminent return. However, it was essential that she should return, but of her own accord. On any assumption, to appear to be taking the first step, to be begging her to return, would be to defeat my own object. True, I lacked the strength to give her up as I had given up Gilberte. Even more than to see Albertine again, what I wanted was to put an end to the physical anguish which my heart, less robust than of old, could endure no longer. Then, by dint of accustoming myself not to use my will-power, whether it was a question of work or of anything else, I had become more cowardly. But above all, this anguish was incomparably more intense for a number of reasons of which the most important was perhaps not that I had never tasted any sensual pleasure with Mme de Guermantes or with Gilberte, but that, not seeing them every day, and at every hour of the day, having no opportunity and consequently no need to see them, there had been lacking, in my love for them, the immense force of Habit.

Perhaps, now that my heart, incapable of willing and of voluntarily enduring suffering, could think of only one possible solution, that Albertine should return at all costs, perhaps the opposite solution (a deliberate renunciation, a gradual resignation) would have seemed to me a novelist's solution, improbable in real life, had I not myself opted for it in the case of Gilberte. I knew therefore that this other solution might be accepted also, and by one and the same man, for I had remained more or less the same. But time had played its part, time which had aged me, time which moreover had kept Albertine perpetually in my company while we were living together. But at least, without giving her up, what survived in me of all that I had felt for Gilberte was the pride which made me refuse to be to Albertine a despicable plaything by begging her to return; I wanted her to come back without my appearing to care whether she did or not. I got up, in order to lose no more time, but my anguish made me pause; this was the first time that I had got out of bed since Albertine had left me. Yet I must dress at once in order to go and make inquiries of Albertine's concierge.

Suffering, the prolongation of a spiritual shock that has come from without, keeps aspiring to change its form; one hopes to be able to dispel it by making plans, by seeking information; one wants it to pass through its countless metamorphoses, for this requires less courage than keeping our suffering intact; the bed on which we lie down with our grief appears so narrow, hard and cold. I therefore put my feet to the ground, and I stepped across the room with infinite care, placing myself in such a way as not to see Albertine's chair, the pianola on the pedals of which she used to press her golden slippers, or a single one of the things which she had used and all of which, in the secret language that my memories had taught them, seemed to be seeking to give me a translation, a different version, for a second time to tell me, of her departure. But even without looking at them I could see them: my strength left me; I sank down on one of those blue satin armchairs, the glossy surface of which an hour earlier, in the dimness of my bedroom anaesthetised by a ray of morning light, had made me dream dreams which then I had passionately caressed but which were infinitely remote from me now. Alas, I had never sat in one of them until this minute except when Albertine was still with me. And so I could not remain sitting there, and stood up again; and thus, at every moment, there was one more of those innumerable and humble "selves" that compose our personality which was still unaware of Albertine's departure and must be informed of it; I was obliged—and this was more cruel than if they had been strangers and did not share my susceptibility to suffering—to announce to all these beings, to all these "selves" who did not yet know of it, the calamity that had just occurred; each of them in turn must hear for the first time the words: "Albertine has asked for her boxes"— those coffin-shaped boxes which I had seen loaded on to the train at Balbec with my mother's—"Albertine has gone." Each of them had to be told of my grief, the grief which is in no way a pessimistic conclusion freely drawn from an accumulation of baneful circumstances, but is the intermittent and involuntary reviviscence of a specific impression that has come to us from without and was not chosen by us. There were some of these "selves" which I had not encountered for a long time past. For instance (I had not remembered that it was the day on which the barber called) the "self" that I was when I was having my hair cut. I had forgotten this "self," and his arrival made me burst into tears, as, at a funeral, does the appearance of an old retired servant who has not forgotten the deceased. Then all of a sudden I remembered that, during the past week, I had from time to time been seized by panic fears which I had not confessed to myself. At those moments, however, I had debated the question, saying to myself: "No need, of course, to consider the hypothesis of her suddenly leaving me. It's absurd. If I were to confide it to a sensible, intelligent man" (and I would have done so to set my mind at rest, had not jealousy prevented me from confiding in anyone) "he would be sure to say to me: 'Why, you're mad. It's impossible.' (And, as a matter of fact, during these last days we had not quarrelled once.) People leave you for a reason. They tell you the reason. They give you a chance to reply. They don't run away like that. No, it's perfectly childish. It's the only really absurd hypothesis." And yet, every day, on finding her still there in the morning when I rang my bell, I had heaved an immense sigh of relief. And when Françoise handed me Albertine's letter, I had at once been certain that it referred to the one thing that could not happen, to this departure which I had somehow perceived several days in advance, in spite of the logical reasons for feeling reassured. I had told myself this, almost with self-satisfaction at my perspicacity in my despair, like a murderer who knows that he cannot be found out but is nevertheless afraid and all of a sudden sees his victim's name written at the top of a document on the table of the examining magistrate who has sent for him.

My only hope was that Albertine had gone to Touraine, to her aunt's house, where after all she would be under some sort of surveillance and could not do anything very serious before I brought her back. My worst fear was that she might have stayed in Paris, or have gone to Amsterdam or to Montjouvain, in other words that she had escaped in order to pursue some intrigue the preliminaries of which I had failed to observe. But in reality, when I said to myself Paris, Amsterdam, Montjouvain, that is to say several places, I was thinking of places that were merely potential. And so, when Albertine's concierge informed me that she had gone to Touraine, that place of residence which I had thought desirable seemed to me the most dreadful of all, because it was real, and because for the first time, tortured by the certainty of the present and the uncertainty of the future, I pictured Albertine starting on a life which she had deliberately chosen to lead apart from me, perhaps for a long time, perhaps for ever, a life in which she would realise that unknown element which in the past had so often troubled me, even though I enjoyed the good fortune of possessing, of caressing what was its outer shell, that charming face, impenetrable and captive. It was this unknown element that formed the core of my love. As for Albertine herself, she scarcely existed in me save under the form of her name, which, but for certain rare moments of respite when I awoke, came and engraved itself upon my brain and continued incessantly to do so. If I had thought aloud, I should have kept on repeating it, and my speech would have been as monotonous, as limited, as if I had been transformed into a bird, a bird like the one in the fable whose song repeated incessantly the name of her whom it had loved when a man. One says the name to oneself, and since one remains silent it is as though one were inscribing it inside oneself, as though it were leaving its trace on one's brain, which must end up, like a wall on which somebody has amused himself scribbling, by being entirely covered with the name, written a thousand times over, of the woman one loves. One rewrites it all the time in one's mind when one is happy, and even more when one is unhappy. And one feels a constantly recurring need to repeat this name which brings one nothing more than what one already knows, until, in course of time, it wearies us. I did not even give a thought to carnal pleasure at this moment; I did not even see in my mind's eye the image of that Albertine who had been the cause of such an upheaval of my being, I did not perceive her body, and if I had tried to isolate the idea—for there is always one—that was bound up with my suffering, it would have been, alternately, on the one hand my doubt as to the intention with which she had left me, with or without any thought of returning, and on the other hand the means of bringing her back. Perhaps there is something symbolical and true in the infinitesimal place occupied in our anxiety by the one who is its cause. The fact is that her person itself counts for little or nothing; what is almost everything is the series of emotions and anxieties which chance occurrences have made us feel in the past in connexion with her and which habit has associated with her. What proves this clearly is (even more than the boredom which we feel in moments of happiness) the extent to which seeing or not seeing the person in question, being or not being admired by her, having or not having her at our disposal, will seem to us utterly irrelevant when we no longer have to pose ourselves the problem (so otiose that we shall no longer take the trouble to consider it) save in relation to the person herself—the series of emotions and anxieties being forgotten, at least so far as she is concerned, for it may have developed anew, but transferred to another. Before this, when it was still attached to her, we supposed that our happiness was dependent upon her person; it depended merely upon the cessation of our anxiety. Our unconscious was therefore more clairvoyant than ourselves at that moment, when it made the figure of the beloved so minute, a figure which we had even perhaps forgotten, which we might have been comparatively unfamiliar with and thought mediocre, in the terrible drama in which seeing her again in order to cease waiting for her could be a matter of life and death for us. Minuscule proportions of the woman's form; logical and necessary effect of the manner in which love develops; clear allegory of the subjective nature of that love.

Outside the door of Albertine's house I found a little poor girl who gazed at me with huge eyes and who looked so sweet-natured that I asked her whether she would care to come home with me, as I might have taken home a dog with faithful eyes. She seemed pleased at the suggestion. When I got home, I held her for some time on my knee, but very soon her presence, by making me feel too keenly Albertine's absence, became intolerable. And I asked her to go away, after giving her a five-hundred-franc note. And yet, soon afterwards, the thought of having some other little girl in the house with me, of never being alone without the comfort of an innocent presence, was the only thing that enabled me to endure the idea that Albertine might perhaps remain away for some time. The spirit in which Albertine had left me was similar no doubt to that of nations who pave the way by a demonstration of their armed force for the exercise of their diplomacy. She must have left me only in order to obtain from me better terms, greater freedom, more luxury. In that case, of the two of us, the one who prevailed would have been myself, had I had the strength to await the moment when, seeing that she could gain nothing, she would return of her own accord. But if at cards, or in war, where victory alone matters, we can hold out against bluff, the conditions are not the same as those created by love and jealousy, not to mention suffering. If, in order to wait, to "hold out," I allowed Albertine to remain away from me for several days, for several weeks perhaps, I was ruining what had been my sole purpose for more than a year: never to leave her by herself for a single hour. All my precautions would be rendered fruitless if I allowed her the time and the opportunity to be unfaithful to me to her heart's content; and if in the end she capitulated, I should never be able to forget the time when she had been alone, and even though victorious in the end, nevertheless in the past, that is to say irreparably, I should be the vanquished one.

As for the means of bringing Albertine back, they had all the more chance of success the more plausible the hypothesis appeared that she had left me only in the hope of being summoned back on more favourable terms. And of course to the people who did not believe in Albertine's sincerity, certainly to Françoise for instance, it was indeed plausible. But my reason, to which, before I knew anything, the only explanation of certain bouts of ill-humour, of certain attitudes, had appeared to be that she had planned to leave for good, found it difficult to believe that, now that her departure had occurred, it was a mere feint. I say my reason, not myself. The hypothesis of a feint became all the more necessary to me the more improbable it was, and gained in strength what it lost in probability. When we find ourselves on the verge of despair and it seems as though God has forsaken us, we no longer hesitate to expect a miracle of him.

I realise that in all this I was the most apathetic, albeit the most anxious of detectives. But Albertine's flight had not restored to me the faculties of which the habit of having her watched by other people had deprived me. I could think of one thing only: employing another person to search for her. This other person was Saint-Loup, who agreed. The transference of the anxiety of so many days to another person filled me with joy and I jigged about, certain of success, my hands becoming suddenly dry again as in the past, and no longer moist with the sweat in which Françoise had soaked me when she said: "Mademoiselle Albertine has gone."

It will be remembered that when I decided to live with Albertine, and even to marry her, it was in order to guard her, to know what she was doing, to prevent her from returning to her old habits with Mlle Vinteuil. It had been in the appalling anguish caused by her revelation at Balbec, when she had told me, as a thing which was quite natural, and which I succeeded, although it was the greatest sorrow I had ever experienced in my life, in appearing to find quite natural, the thing which in my worst suppositions I should never have been bold enough to imagine. (It is astonishing what a want of imagination jealousy, which spends its time making petty suppositions that are false, shows when it comes to discovering what is true.) Now this love, born first and foremost of a need to prevent Albertine from doing wrong, this love had thereafter preserved the traces of its origin. Being with her mattered little to me so long as I could prevent the fugitive creature from going to this place or to that. In order to prevent her, I had had recourse to the vigilance, to the company, of the people who escorted her, and they had only to give me at the end of the day a report that was fairly reassuring for my anxieties to dissolve into good-humour.

Having given myself the assurance that, whatever steps I might have to take, Albertine would be back in the house that same evening, I had granted a respite to the pain which Françoise had caused me when she told me that Albertine had gone (because at that moment my mind, caught unawares, had believed for an instant that her departure was final). But after an interruption, when under the momentum of its own independent life the initial pain revived spontaneously in me, it was just as agonising as before, because it pre-existed the consoling promise that I had given myself to bring Albertine back that evening. My suffering was oblivious of this promise which would have calmed it. To set in motion the means of bringing about her return, once again I was condemned—not that such an attitude had ever proved very successful, but because I had always adopted it since I had been in love with Albertine—to behave as though I did not love her, as though I was not hurt by her departure; I was condemned to continue to lie to her. I could be all the more energetic in my efforts to bring her back in that personally I should appear to have given her up for good. I proposed to write Albertine a farewell letter in which I would regard her departure as final, while at the same time I would send Saint-Loup down, as though without my knowledge, to put the most brutal pressure on Mme Bontemps to make Albertine return as soon as possible. No doubt I had had experience with Gilberte of the danger of letters expressing an indifference which, feigned at first, ends by becoming genuine. And this experience ought to have restrained me from writing to Albertine letters of the same sort as those I had written to Gilberte. But what we call experience is merely the revelation to our own eyes of a trait in our character which naturally reappears, and reappears all the more markedly because we have already once brought it to light, so that the spontaneous impulse which guided us on the first occasion finds itself reinforced by all the suggestions of memory. The human plagiarism which is most difficult to avoid, for individuals (and even for nations which persevere in their faults and indeed intensify them), is self-plagiarism.

Knowing that Saint-Loup was in Paris, I summoned him there and then; he hastened round at once, swift and efficient as he had been long ago at Doncières, and agreed to set off at once for Touraine. I suggested to him the following arrangement. He was to take the train to Châtellerault, find out where Mme Bontemps lived, and wait until Albertine had left the house, since there was a risk of her recognising him. "But does the girl in question know me, then?" he asked. I told him that I did not think so. This plan of action filled me with indescribable joy. It was nevertheless diametrically opposed to my original intention: to arrange things so that I should not appear to be seeking Albertine's return; whereas by so acting I must inevitably appear to be seeking it. But this plan had the inestimable advantage over "the proper thing to do" that it enabled me to say to myself that someone sent by me was going to see Albertine, and would doubtless bring her back with him. And if I had been able to see clearly into my own heart at the outset, I might have foreseen that it was this solution, which was hidden in the shadows and which I thought deplorable, that would ultimately prevail over the alternative course of patience which I had decided to adopt, from lack of will-power. As Saint-Loup already appeared slightly surprised to learn that a girl had been living with me through the whole winter without my having said a word to him about her, as moreover he had often spoken to me of the girl he had seen at Balbec and I had never said in reply: "But she's living here," he might have been offended by my lack of trust. It was true that Mme Bontemps might talk to him about Balbec. But I was too impatient for his departure, and for his arrival at the other end, to be willing or able to think of the possible consequences of his journey. As for the risk of his recognising Albertine (whom in any case he had resolutely refrained from looking at when he had met her at Doncières), she had, everyone said, so changed and put on weight that it was hardly likely. He asked me whether I had a picture of Albertine. I replied at first that I had not, so that he might not have a chance of recognising Albertine from her photograph, taken at about the time of our stay at Balbec, though he had had no more than a glimpse of her in the railway carriage. But then I realised that in the photograph she would be already as different from the Albertine of Balbec as the living Albertine now was, and that he would recognise her no better from her photograph than in the flesh. While I was looking for it, he laid his hand gently on my forehead, by way of consoling me. I was touched by the distress which the grief that he guessed me to be feeling was causing him. In the first place, however final his breach with Rachel, what he had felt at that time was not yet so remote for him not to have a special sympathy, a special pity for sufferings of that kind, as one feels closer to a person who is afflicted with the same illness as oneself. Besides, he had so strong an affection for me that the thought of my suffering was intolerable to him. Hence he conceived a mixture of rancour and admiration for the girl who was the cause of it. He regarded me as so superior a being that he felt that for me to be in thrall to another creature she must be quite out of the ordinary. I quite expected that he would think Albertine pretty in her photograph, but since at the same time I did not imagine that it would produce upon him the impression that Helen made upon the Trojan elders, as I continued to look for it I said modestly: "Oh, you know, you mustn't get ideas into your head. For one thing it's a bad photograph, and besides there's nothing startling about her, she's not a beauty, she's merely very nice."

"Oh, but she must be wonderful," he said with a naïve, sincere enthusiasm as he sought to form a mental picture of the person who was capable of plunging me into such despair and agitation. "I'm angry with her for hurting you, but at the same time one can't help seeing that someone who's an artist to his fingertips as you are, someone who loves beauty in all its forms and with so passionate a love, that you were predestined to suffer more than an ordinary person when you found it in a woman."

At last I had found the photograph. "She's bound to be wonderful," Robert was still saying, not yet having seen that I was holding out the photograph to him. All at once he caught sight of it, and held it for a moment between his hands. His face expressed a stupefaction which amounted to stupidity. "Is this the girl you love?" he said at length in a tone in which astonishment was curbed by his fear of offending me. He made no comment, but he had assumed the reasonable, prudent, unavoidably somewhat disdainful air which one assumes in front of a sick person—even if he is a man of outstanding gifts, and your friend—who is now nothing of the sort, for, raving mad, he speaks to you of a celestial being who has appeared to him, and continues to behold this being where you, being sane, can see nothing but a quilt on the bed. I at once understood Robert's astonishment, realising that it was the same as that which the sight of his mistress had provoked in me, the only difference being that I had recognised in her a woman whom I already knew, where he imagined that he had never seen Albertine. But no doubt the difference between our respective impressions of the same person was equally great. The time was long past when I had all too tentatively begun at Balbec by adding to my visual sensations when I gazed at Albertine sensations of taste, of smell, of touch. Since then, other more profound, more tender, more indefinable sensations had been added to them, and afterwards painful sensations. In short, Albertine was merely, like a stone round which snow has gathered, the generating centre of an immense structure which rose above the plane of my heart. Robert, to whom all this stratification of sensations was invisible, grasped only a residue which it prevented me, on the contrary, from perceiving. What had struck Robert when his eyes fell upon Albertine's photograph was not the thrill of wonderment that overcame the Trojan elders seeing Helen go by and saying:

One single glance from her eclipses all our ills[1]

but precisely the opposite impression which may be expressed by: "What, it's for this that he has worked himself into such a state, has grieved himself so, has done so many idiotic things!" It must indeed be admitted that this sort of reaction at the sight of the person who has caused the suffering, upset the life, sometimes brought about the death of someone we love, is infinitely more frequent than that of the Trojan elders, indeed to all intents and purposes the habitual one. This is not merely because love is individual, nor because, when we ourselves do not feel it, finding it avoidable and philosophising about the folly of others comes naturally to us. No, it is because, when it has reached the stage at which it causes such misery, the edifice of the sensations inter-posed between the face of the woman and the eyes of her lover—the huge egg of pain which encases it and conceals it as a mantle of snow conceals a fountain—is already raised so high that the point at which the lover's gaze comes to rest, the point at which he finds his pleasure and his sufferings, is as far from the point which other people see as is the real sun from the place in which its refracted light enables us to see it in the sky. And what is more, during this time, beneath the chrysalis of grief and tenderness which renders the worst metamorphoses of the beloved object invisible to the lover, her face has had time to grow old and to change. With the result that, if the face which the lover saw for the first time is very far removed from that which he has seen since he has loved and suffered, it is, in the opposite sense, equally far from the face which may now be seen by the indifferent onlooker. (What would have happened if, instead of the photograph of one who was still a girl, Robert had seen the photograph of an elderly mistress?) And indeed, in order to feel this astonishment, we have no need to see for the first time the woman who has caused such ravages. Often we know her already, as my great-uncle knew Odette. So the difference in optics extends not only to people's physical appearance but to their character, and to their individual import-ance. It is more likely than not that the woman who is causing the man who loves her to suffer has always behaved good-naturedly towards someone who was indifferent to her, as Odette, who was so cruel to Swann, had been the kind, attentive "lady in pink" to my great-uncle, or indeed that the person whose every decision is computed in advance by the man who loves her, with as much dread as that of a deity, appears as a person of no consequence, only too glad to do anything he asks, in the eyes of the man who does not love her, as Saint-Loup's mistress had appeared to me who saw in her merely that "Rachel when from the Lord" who had so repeatedly been offered to me. I recalled my own amazement, the first time I met her with Saint-Loup, at the thought that anybody could be tormented by not knowing what such a woman had been doing one evening, what she might have whispered to someone, why she had desired a rupture. And I felt that all this past existence—but, in this case, Albertine's—towards which every fibre of my heart, of my life, was directed with a throbbing and importunate pain, must appear just as insignificant to Saint-Loup, and would one day, perhaps, appear so to me; I felt that I might gradually pass, so far as the insignificance or gravity of Albertine's past was concerned, from the state of mind in which I was at the moment to that of Saint-Loup, for I was under no illusion as to what Saint-Loup might be thinking, as to what anyone else than the lover himself may think. And I was not unduly distressed. Let us leave pretty women to men with no imagination. I recalled that tragic explanation of so many lives which is furnished by an inspired but not lifelike portrait such as Elstir's portrait of Odette, which is a portrait not so much of a mistress as of the distortions of love. All that it lacked was—what so many portraits have—the fact of coming at once from a great painter and from a lover (and even then it was said that Elstir had been Odette's). The whole life of a lover, of a lover whose folly nobody understands—the whole life of a Swann—goes to prove this disparity. But let the lover be embodied in a painter like Elstir and then we have the clue to the enigma, we have at last before our eyes those lips which the common herd have never perceived, that nose which nobody has ever seen, that unsuspected carriage. The portrait says: "What I have loved, what has made me suffer, what I have never ceased to behold, is this." By an inverse gymnastic, I who had made a mental effort to add to Rachel all that Saint-Loup had added to her of himself, I now attempted to subtract the contribution of my heart and mind from the composition of Albertine and to picture her to myself as she must appear to Saint-Loup, as Rachel had appeared to me. But how much importance does all this have? Would we give credence to these differences, even if we could see them ourselves? When, in the summer at Balbec, Albertine used to wait for me beneath the

arcades of Incarville and jump into my carriage, not only had she
not yet "thickened," but, as a result of too much exercise, she had
lost weight; thin, made plainer by an ugly hat which left visible
only the tip of an ugly nose and, at a side-view, pale cheeks like
white slugs, there was very little of her that I recognised, enough,
however, to know, when she sprang into the carriage, that it was
she, that she had been punctual in keeping our appointment and
had not gone somewhere else; and this was enough; what we love
is too much in the past, consists too much in the time that we have
wasted together for us to require the whole woman; we wish only
to be sure that it is she, not to be mistaken as to her identity, a thing
far more important than beauty to those who love; her cheeks may
grow hollow, her body thin, even to those who were originally
proudest, in the eyes of the world, of their domination over a
beauty, and yet that little tip of nose, that sign which epitomises
the permanent personality of a woman, that algebraical formula,
that constant factor, is sufficient to prevent a man who is courted
in the highest society, and was once fond of it, from having a single
evening free because he spends his time combing and uncombing,
until it is time to go to sleep, the hair of the woman he loves, or
simply sitting by her side, in order to be with her, or in order that
she may be with him, or merely in order that she may not be with
other men.

"Are you sure," Robert asked me, "that I can offer this woman
thirty thousand francs just like that for her husband's election
committee? She's as dishonest as all that? If you're right, three
thousand francs would be enough."

"No, I beg of you, don't be cheeseparing about a thing that
matters so much to me. This is what you're to say to her (and it's to
some extent true): 'My friend had borrowed these thirty thousand
francs from a relative for the election expenses of the uncle of the
girl he was engaged to marry. It was because of this engagement
that the money was given him. And he had asked me to bring it to
you so that Albertine should know nothing about it. And now
Albertine has left him. He doesn't know what to do. He's
obliged to pay back the thirty thousand francs if he doesn't
marry Albertine. And if he *is* going to marry her, then if only to
keep up appearances she ought to return immediately, because it
will make a very bad impression if she stays away for long.' You
think I've deliberately made all this up?"

"Not at all," Saint-Loup assured me out of kindness, out of tact, and also because he knew that circumstances are often stranger than one supposes.

After all, it was by no means impossible that in this tale of the thirty thousand francs there might be, as I assured him, a large element of truth. It was possible, but it was not true, and this element of truth was in fact a lie. But we lied to each other, Robert and I, as in every conversation when one friend is genuinely anxious to help another who is unhappy in love. The friend who is being counsellor, prop, comforter, may pity the other's distress but cannot share it, and the kinder he is to him the more he lies. And the other confesses to him as much as is necessary in order to secure his help, but, precisely in order to secure that help, perhaps, conceals many things from him. And the happy one of the two is, when all is said, he who takes trouble, goes on a journey, carries out a mission, but has no inner anguish. I was at this moment the person Robert had been at Doncières when he thought that Rachel had left him.

"Very well, just as you like; if I get a snub, I accept it in advance for your sake. And even if it does seem a bit queer to make such an undisguised bargain, I know that in our world there are plenty of duchesses, even the stuffiest of them, who if you offered them thirty thousand francs would do things far more difficult than telling their nieces not to stay in Touraine. Anyhow, I'm doubly glad to be doing you a service, since it's the only thing that will make you agree to see me. If I marry," he went on, "don't you think we might see more of one another, won't you regard my house as your own? . . . "

He suddenly stopped short, the thought having occurred to him (as I supposed at the time) that, if I too were to marry, Albertine might not be a suitable friend for his wife. And I remembered what the Cambremers had said to me about the probability of his marrying a niece of the Prince de Guermantes.

He consulted the time-table, and found that he could not leave Paris until the evening. Françoise inquired: "Am I to take Mlle Albertine's bed out of the study?" "On the contrary," I said, "you must make it for her." I hoped that she would return any day and did not wish Françoise to suppose that there could be any doubt of this. Albertine's departure must appear to have been agreed between ourselves, and not in any way to imply that she loved me less than before. But Françoise looked at me with an air, if not of incredulity, at any rate of doubt. She too had her alternative hypotheses. Her nostrils flared, she scented a quarrel, she must have felt it in the air for a long time past. And if she was not absolutely sure of it, this was perhaps only because, like myself, she hesitated to believe unconditionally what would have given her too much pleasure. Now the weight of the affair no longer rested on my overtaxed mind but on Saint-Loup. I was buoyed up with gladness because I had made a decision, because I told myself: "I have answered quick as a flash."

Saint-Loup could scarcely have been in the train when I ran into Bloch in my hall. I had not heard his ring, and was obliged to let him stay with me for a while. He had met me recently with Albertine (whom he had known at Balbec) on a day when she was in a bad mood. "I met M. Bontemps at dinner," he told me, "and as I have a certain influence over him, I told him that I was grieved that his niece was not nicer to you, and that he ought to have a word with her about it." I choked with rage; these remonstrances and complaints would destroy the whole effect of Saint-Loup's intervention and involve me directly in the eyes of Albertine, whom I now seemed to be imploring to return. To make matters worse, Françoise, who was lingering in the hall, could hear every word. I heaped every imaginable reproach upon Bloch, telling him that I had never authorised him to do anything of the sort and that, besides, the whole thing was nonsense. From then on, Bloch never left off smiling, less, I think, from joy than from embarrassment at having annoyed me. He laughingly expressed his surprise at having provoked such anger. Perhaps he said this in the hope of minimising in my eyes the importance of his indiscreet intervention, perhaps because he was of a cowardly nature and lived gaily and idly in an atmosphere of falsehood, as jelly-fish float upon the surface of the sea, perhaps because, even if he had been a man of a different kind, other people can never see things from our point of view and therefore do not realise the magnitude of the injury that words uttered at random can do us. I had barely shown him out, unable to think of any remedy for the mischief he had done, when the bell rang again and Françoise brought me a summons from the head of the Sûreté. The parents of the little girl whom I had brought into the house for an hour had decided to bring a charge against me for abduction of a minor. There are moments in life when a sort of beauty is born of the multiplicity of the troubles that assail us, intertwined like Wagnerian leitmotifs, and also from the notion, which then emerges, that events are not situated in the sum of the reflexions portrayed in the wretched little mirror which the mind holds in front of it and which it calls the future, that they are somewhere outside and spring up as suddenly as a person who comes to catch us in the act. Even when left to itself, an event becomes modified, whether frustration amplifies it for us or satisfaction reduces it. But it is rarely unaccompanied. The feelings aroused by each one of them contradict one another, and fear, to a certain extent, as I felt on my way to see the head of the Sûreté, is an at least temporary and fairly efficacious counter-irritant for sentimental miseries.

At the Sûreté, I found the girl's parents, who insulted me and with the words "We'd rather starve" handed me back the five hundred francs which I did not want to take, and the head of the Sûreté who, setting himself the inimitable example of the judicial facility in repartee, seized upon a word in each sentence that I uttered for the purpose of concocting a witty and crushing retort. My innocence of the alleged crime was never taken into consideration, for that was the sole hypothesis which nobody was willing to accept for an instant. Nevertheless the difficulty of proving the charge enabled me to escape with this castigation, which was extremely violent for as long as the parents were in the room. But as soon as they had gone, the head of the Sûreté, who had a weakness for little girls, changed his tone and admonished me as man to man: "Next time, you must be more careful. Good God, you can't pick them up as easily as that, or you'll get into trouble. Anyhow, you'll find dozens of little girls who are better-looking than that one, and far cheaper. It was a perfectly ridiculous amount to pay." I was so certain that he would fail to understand me if I attempted to tell him the truth that without saying a word I took advantage of his permission to withdraw. Every passer-by, until I was safely at home, seemed to me an inspector appointed to spy on my every movement. But this leitmotif, like that of my anger with Bloch, died away, leaving the field clear for that of Albertine's departure.

The latter resumed on an almost joyous note now that Saint-Loup had set out. Since he had undertaken to go and see Mme Bontemps, my sufferings had been dispelled. I believed that this was because I had acted, and I believed it sincerely, for we never know what is concealed in our hearts of hearts. But what really made me happy was not, as I supposed, that I had unburdened my indecisions on to Saint-Loup. I was not in fact entirely mistaken; the specific for curing an unfortunate event (and three events out of four are unfortunate) is a decision; for it has the effect, by a sudden reversal of our thoughts, of interrupting the flow of those that come from the past event and prolong its vibration, and breaking it with a counter-flow of thoughts from the outside, from the future. But these new thoughts are most of all beneficial to us (and this was the case with the thoughts that assailed me at this moment) when from the depths of that future it is a hope that they bring us. What really made me so happy was the secret certainty that Saint-Loup's mission could not fail and that Albertine was bound to return. I realised this; for not having received any word from Saint-Loup on the following day, I began to suffer anew. My decision, my transference to him of plenipotentiary powers, was not, therefore, the cause of my joy, which in that case would have persisted; its cause was rather the "Success is certain" which had been in my mind when I said "Come what may." And the thought, aroused by his delay, that after all his mission might not prove successful, was so hateful to me that all my gaiety evaporated. It is in reality our anticipation, our hope of happy events that fills us with a joy which we ascribe to other causes and which ceases, plunging us once more into misery, if we are no longer so certain that what we desire will come to pass. It is always an invisible belief that sustains the edifice of our sensory world and deprived of which it totters. We have seen that it created for us the merit or the nullity of other people, our excitement or boredom at seeing them. It similarly creates the possibility of enduring a grief which seems to us trivial simply because we are convinced that it will presently be brought to an end, or its sudden intensification to the point where a person's presence matters to us as much as, sometimes even more than, life itself.

One thing finally succeeded in making my heartache as acute as it had been in the first instant and (I am bound to admit) no longer was. This was when I re-read a sentence in Albertine's letter. However much we love people, the pain of losing them—when in our isolation we are confronted with it alone, to which our mind to a certain extent gives whatever form it chooses—is endurable and different from that other pain, less human, less our own—as unforeseen and unusual as an accident in the moral world and in the region of the heart—which is caused not so much by the people themselves as by the manner in which we have

learned that we will never see them again. I could think of
Albertine while weeping gently and accepting the fact that
I should not be seeing her tonight any more than I had yesterday;
but to re-read "my decision is irrevocable" was another matter; it
was like taking a dangerous drug which had given me a heart
attack from which I might never recover. There is in inanimate
objects, in events, in farewell letters, a special danger which
amplifies and alters the very nature of the grief that people are
capable of causing us. But this pain did not last long. I was, when
all was said, so sure of Saint-Loup's skill, of his eventual success,
Albertine's return seemed to me so certain, that I wondered
whether I had been right to wish for it. Nevertheless, I rejoiced
at the thought. Unfortunately, although I had assumed that the
business with the Sûreté was over and done with, Françoise came
in to tell me that an inspector had called to inquire whether I was
in the habit of having girls in the house, that the concierge,
supposing him to be referring to Albertine, had replied in the
affirmative, and that since then it seemed as though the house was
being watched. Henceforth it would be impossible for me ever to
bring a little girl into the house to console me in my grief, without
risking the shame of an inspector suddenly appearing and of her
taking me for a criminal. And in the same instant I realised how
much more important certain longings are to us than we suppose,
for this impossibility of my ever taking a little girl on my knee again
seemed to me to strip life of all its value; but what was more,
I realised how understandable it is that people will readily refuse
wealth and risk death, whereas we imagine that pecuniary interest
and the fear of dying rule the world. For, rather than think that
even an unknown little girl might be given a bad impression of me
by the arrival of a policeman, I should have preferred to kill
myself! Indeed there was no possible comparison between the
two degrees of suffering. Yet in everyday life people never bear in
mind that those to whom they offer money, or whom they
threaten to kill, may have mistresses, or merely friends, whose
respect they value even if they do not value their own. But all of a
sudden, by a confusion of which I was not aware (for it did not
occur to me that Albertine, being of age, was free to live under my
roof and even to be my mistress), it seemed to me that the charge
of corrupting minors might apply to Albertine also. Thereupon
my life appeared to me to be hedged in on every side. And
reflecting that I had not lived chastely with her, I saw, in the

punishment that had been inflicted upon me for having dandled an unknown little girl on my knee, that relation which almost always exists in human sanctions, whereby there is hardly ever either a just sentence or a judicial error, but a sort of compromise between the false idea that the judge forms of an innocent act and the culpable deeds of which he is unaware. But then when I thought that Albertine's return might involve me in an ignominious charge which would degrade me in her eyes and might perhaps even do her some damage for which she would not forgive me, I ceased to look forward to her return, it terrified me. I wanted to cable her to tell her not to come back. And immediately, a passionate desire for her return overwhelmed me, drowning everything else. The fact was that, having envisaged for a moment the possibility of telling her not to return and of living without her, all of a sudden I felt on the contrary ready to abandon all travel, all pleasure, all work, if only Albertine would return!

Ah, how my love for Albertine, the course of which I had imagined that I could foretell on the basis of my love for Gilberte, had developed differently from the latter, indeed in perfect contrast with it! How impossible it was for me to live without seeing her! And with each of my actions, even the most trivial, since they had all been steeped beforehand in the blissful atmosphere which was Albertine's presence, I was obliged time after time, at renewed cost, with the same pain, to relive the first experience of separation. Then the competition of other forms of life thrust this new pain into the background, and during those days which were the first days of spring, as I waited until Saint-Loup had managed to see Mme Bontemps, I even enjoyed a few moments of agreeable calm in imagining Venice and beautiful, unknown women. As soon as I was conscious of this, I felt within me a panic terror. This calm which I had just enjoyed was the first apparition of that great intermittent force which was to wage war in me against grief, against love, and would ultimately get the better of them. This state of which I had just had a foretaste and had received the warning was for a moment only what would in time to come be my permanent state, a life in which I should no longer be able to suffer on account of Albertine, in which I should no longer love her. And my love, which had just seen and recognised the one enemy by whom it could be conquered, forgetfulness, began to tremble, like a lion which in the cage in which it has been confined has suddenly caught sight of the python that will devour it.

I thought of Albertine all the time, and Françoise, when she came into my room, never said to me "There are no letters" quickly enough to curtail my anguish. From time to time I succeeded, by letting some current or other of ideas flow through my grief, in freshening, in airing to some slight extent the vitiated atmosphere of my heart; but at night, if I succeeded in going to sleep, then it was as though the memory of Albertine had been the drug that had procured my sleep and the cessation of whose influence would awaken me. I thought all the time of Albertine while I was asleep. It was a special sleep of her own that she gave me, and one in which, moreover, I was no longer at liberty, as when awake, to think of other things. Sleep and the memory of her were like two substances which one must mix together and take at one draught in order to sleep. When I was awake, meanwhile, my suffering went on increasing day by day instead of diminishing. Not that oblivion was not performing its task, but by that very fact it encouraged the idealisation of the lamented image and thereby the assimilation of my initial suffering to other analogous sufferings which intensified it. At least that image was endurable. But if all of a sudden I thought of her room, of her room in which the bed stood empty, of her piano, of her motor-car, all my strength left me, I shut my eyes and let my head droop on my shoulder like someone who is about to faint. The sound of doors being opened hurt me almost as much because it was not she that was opening them. When it was possible that a telegram might have come from Saint-Loup, I dared not ask: "Is there a telegram?" At length one did come, but brought with it only a postponement, with the message: "The ladies have gone away for three days."

No doubt, if I had endured the four days that had already elapsed since her departure, it was because I said to myself: "It's only a matter of time. By the end of the week she will be here." But this consideration did not alter the fact that for my heart, for my body, the action to be performed was the same: living without her, returning home and not finding her in the house, passing the door of her room (as for opening it, I did not yet have the courage to do that) knowing that she was not inside, going to bed without having said good-night to her—such were the tasks that my heart had been obliged to perform in their terrible entirety, and for all the world as though I was not going to see Albertine again. But the fact that my heart had already performed this daily task four times proved that it was now capable of continuing to perform it. And soon, perhaps, the consideration that was helping me thus to go on living—the prospect of Albertine's return—would cease to be necessary to me; I should be able to say to myself: "She will never come back," and go on living all the same as I had already done for the last four days, like a cripple who has recovered the use of his legs and can dispense with his crutches. No doubt when I came home at night I still found, taking my breath away, suffocating me in the vacuum of solitude, the memories, placed end to end in an interminable series, of all the evenings on which Albertine had been waiting for me; but already I also found the memory of last night, of the night before and of the two previous nights, that is to say the memory of the four nights that had passed since Albertine's departure, during which I had remained without her, alone, through which none the less I had lived, four nights already forming a strip of memories which was very slender compared with the other, but which would be filled out, perhaps, by every day that went by.

I shall say nothing of the letter conveying a declaration of affection which I received at this time from a niece of Mme de Guermantes who was considered to be the prettiest girl in Paris, or of the overtures made to me by the Duc de Guermantes on behalf of her parents, resigned, in their anxiety to secure their daughter's happiness, to the inequality of the match, to an apparent misalliance. Such incidents which might prove gratifying to one's self-esteem are too painful when one is in love. One might have the desire but not the indelicacy to communicate them to her who has a less flattering opinion of one, an opinion which moreover would not be modified by the knowledge that one is capable of inspiring a quite different one. What the Duke's niece wrote to me could only have irritated Albertine.

From the moment of waking, when I picked up my grief again at the point where I had left it before going to sleep, like a book which had been shut for a while but which I would keep before my eyes until night, it was invariably to some thought concerning Albertine that I related every sensation, whether it came to me from without or from within. The bell would ring: it must be a letter from her, or she herself perhaps! If I felt well and not too miserable, I was no longer jealous, I no longer had any grievance against her, I wanted to see her at once, to kiss her, to live happily with her ever after. The act of telegraphing to her "Come at once" seemed to me to have become a perfectly simple thing, as though my new mood had changed not merely my attitude, but things external to myself, had made them easier. If I was in a sombre mood, all my anger with her revived, I no longer felt any desire to kiss her, I felt how impossible it was that she could ever make me happy, I sought only to harm her and to prevent her from belonging to other people. But the outcome of these two opposite moods was identical: it was essential that she should return as soon as possible. And yet, whatever joy I might feel at the moment of her return, I sensed that very soon the same difficulties would recur and that to seek happiness in the satisfaction of a desire of the mind was as naïve as to attempt to reach the horizon by walking straight ahead. The further the desire advances, the further does real possession recede. So that if happiness, or at least the absence of suffering, can be found, it is not the satisfaction, but the gradual reduction and the eventual extinction of desire that one should seek. One seeks to see the beloved object, but one ought to seek not to: forgetfulness alone brings about the ultimate extinction of desire. And I imagine that if an author were to publish truths of this sort he would dedicate the book that contained them to a woman with whom he would thus take pleasure in striking up a relationship, saying to her: "This book is yours." And thus, while telling the truth in his book, he would be lying in his dedication, for he will attach to the book's being hers only the importance that he attaches to the stone which came to him from her and which will remain precious to him only so long as he is in love with her. The bonds between ourselves and another person exist only in our minds. Memory as it grows fainter loosens them, and notwithstanding the illusion by which we want to be duped and with which, out of love, friendship, politeness, deference, duty, we dupe other people, we exist alone. Man is the creature who cannot escape from himself, who knows other people only in himself, and when he asserts the contrary, he is lying. And I should have been so afraid of being robbed (had anyone been capable of so robbing me) of this need of her, this love for her, that I convinced myself that it was a precious necessity in my life. To be able to hear, without being charmed and pained by them, the names of the stations through which the train passed on its way to Touraine would have seemed to me a diminution of myself (for no other reason really than that it would have proved that I was becoming indifferent to Albertine). It was right, I told myself, that by incessantly asking myself what she could be doing, thinking, wishing, at every moment, whether she intended, whether she was going to return, I should keep open that communicating door which love had opened up in me, and feel another person's life flooding through open sluices to fill the reservoir which must not again become stagnant.

Presently, as Saint-Loup's silence persisted, a subordinate anxiety—my expectation of a further telegram or a telephone call from him—masked the first, my uncertainty as to the result, whether Albertine was going to return. Listening for every sound in expectation of the telegram became so intolerable that I felt that, whatever its contents might be, the arrival of the telegram, which was the only thing I could think of at the moment, would put an end to my sufferings. But when at last I received a telegram from Robert in which he informed me that he had seen Mme Bontemps but that in spite of all his precautions Albertine had seen him, and that this had upset everything, I burst out in a torrent of fury and despair, for this was what I had wanted at all costs to avoid. Once it came to Albertine's knowledge, Saint-Loup's mission gave me an appearance of needing her which could only dissuade her from returning and my horror of which was moreover all that I had retained of the pride that my love had boasted in Gilberte's day and had since lost. I cursed Robert, then told myself that, if this scheme had failed, I would try another. Since man is capable of influencing the external world, how could I fail, by bringing into play cunning, intelligence, money, affection, to abolish this terrible fact: Albertine's absence? We believe that we can change the things around us in accordance with our desires—we believe it because otherwise we can see no favourable outcome. We do not think of the outcome which generally comes to pass and is also favourable: we do not succeed in changing things in accordance with our desires, but gradually our desires change. The situation that we hoped to change because it was intolerable becomes unimportant to us. We have failed to surmount the obstacle, as we were absolutely determined to do, but life has taken us round it, led us beyond it, and then if we turn round to gaze into the distance of the past, we can barely see it, so imperceptible has it become.

From the floor above I could hear one of the neighbours playing some tunes from *Manon*. I applied their words, which I knew, to Albertine and myself, and was stirred so deeply that I began to cry. The words were:

> Alas, most often at night
> The bird that flees from what it felt was bondage
> Returns to beat at the glass in desperate flight,

and the death of Manon:

> Then, Manon, answer me!—The one love of my soul,
> Never till now did I know the goodness of your heart.

Since Manon returned to Des Grieux, it seemed to me that I was to Albertine the one and only love of her life. Alas, it is probable that, if she had been listening at that moment to the same tune, it would not have been me that she cherished under the name of Des Grieux, and, even if the idea had occurred to her at all, the memory of me would have prevented her from being moved by this music which, though subtler and better-written, was very much of the kind that she admired. As for me, I had not the heart to abandon myself to the comforting thought of Albertine calling me her "soul's one love" and realising that she had been mistaken over what she had "felt was bondage." I knew that one can never read a novel without giving its heroine the form and features of the woman one loves. But however happy the book's ending may be, our love has not advanced an inch and, when we have shut it, she whom we love and who has come to us at last in its pages, loves us no better in real life.

In a fit of fury, I telegraphed to Saint-Loup to return as quickly as possible to Paris, in order to avoid at least the appearance of an aggravating persistence in a mission which I had been so anxious to keep secret. But even before he had returned in obedience to my instructions, it was from Albertine herself that I received the following message:

"My dear, you have sent your friend Saint-Loup to my aunt, which was foolish. My dearest, if you needed me, why did you not write to me direct? I should have been only too delighted to come back. Do not let us have any more of these absurd approaches."

"I should have been only too delighted to come back"! If she said this, it must mean that she regretted her departure, and was only waiting for an excuse to return. I had only to do what she said, to write to her that I needed her, and she would return. So I was going to see her again, her, the Albertine of Balbec (for since her departure this was what she had once more become for me; like a sea-shell to which one ceases to pay any attention when it is always there on one's chest of drawers, and once one has parted with it, either by giving it away or by losing it, one begins to think about again, she recalled to me all the joyous beauty of the blue mountains of the sea). And it was not only she that had become a creature of the imagination, that is to say desirable, but life with her had become an imaginary life, that is to say a life freed from all difficulties, so that I said to myself: "How happy we are going to be!" But, now that I was assured of her return, I must not appear to be seeking to hasten it, but must on the contrary efface the bad impression left by Saint-Loup's intervention, which I could always disavow later on by saying that he had acted on his own initiative, because he had always been in favour of our marriage.

Meanwhile, I read her letter again, and was after all disappointed to be reminded of how little there is of a person in a letter. Doubtless the characters traced on the paper express our thoughts, as do also our features; it is still a thought of some kind that we are confronted with. But even so, in the person, the thought is not apparent to us until it has been diffused through the corolla of the face opened up like a water-lily. This modifies it considerably, after all. And it is perhaps one of the causes of our perpetual disappointments in love, this perpetual displacement whereby, in response to our expectation of the ideal person whom we love, each meeting provides us with a person in flesh and blood who yet contains so little trace of our dream. And then, when we demand something of this person, we receive from her a letter in which even of the person very little remains, as in the letters of an algebraical formula there no longer remains the precise value of the arithmetical figures, which themselves do not contain the qualities of the fruit or flowers that they enumerate. And yet "love," the "beloved," her letters, are perhaps nevertheless translations (unsatisfying though it may be to pass from one to the other) of the same reality, since the letter seems to us inadequate only while we are reading it, but we sweat blood until its arrival, and it is sufficient to calm our anguish, if not to appease, with its tiny black symbols, our desire which knows that it contains after all only the equivalent of a word, a smile, a kiss, not those things themselves.

I wrote to Albertine:

"Dear friend, I was just about to write to you. Thank you for saying that if I had been in need of you you would have come at once; it is good of you to have so exalted a sense of loyalty to an old friend, and my regard for you can only be increased thereby. But no, I did not ask and I shall not ask you to return; our seeing each other again—for a long time to come—might not perhaps be painful to you, a heartless girl. To me, whom at times you have thought so cold, it would be most painful. Life has driven us apart. You have made a decision which I consider very wise, and which you made at the right moment, with wonderful prescience, for you left me on the day when I had just received my mother's consent to my asking for your hand. I would have told you this when I awoke, when I received her letter (at the same time as yours). Perhaps you would have been afraid of hurting me by leaving there and then. And we might perhaps have linked our lives together in what (who knows?) could have been unhappiness. If that was what was in store for us, then I bless you for your wisdom. We should lose all the fruit of it were we to meet again. This is not to say that I should not find it a temptation. But I claim no great credit for resisting it. You know what an inconstant person I am and how quickly I forget. Therefore I am not greatly to be pitied. As you have told me often, I am first and foremost a man of habit. The habits which I am beginning to form in your absence are not as yet very strong. Naturally, for the moment, the habits which I shared with you and which your departure has disturbed are still the stronger. They will not remain so for very long. For that reason, indeed, I had thought of taking advantage of these last few days in which our meeting would not yet be for me what it will be in a fortnight's time, perhaps even sooner, a . . . (forgive my frankness) an inconvenience—I had thought of taking advantage of them, before oblivion finally comes, in order to settle certain little material questions with you, in which you might, as a kind and charming friend, have rendered a service to him who for five minutes imagined himself your future husband. Since I never doubted my mother's approval, and since moreover I desired that we should each of us enjoy all that liberty of which you had too generously and abundantly made a sacrifice which was acceptable for a few weeks' living together but would have become as hateful to you as to myself now that we were to spend the rest of our lives together (it almost pains me as I write to you to think that this nearly happened, that we came within a few seconds of it), I had thought of organising our existence in the most independent manner possible, and to begin with I wished you to have that yacht in which you could go cruising while I, not being well enough to accompany you, would wait for you in port (I had written to Elstir to ask for his advice, since you admire his taste); and on land I wished you to have a motor-car to yourself, for your very own, in which you could go out, could travel wherever you chose. The yacht was almost ready, it is named, after a wish that you expressed at Balbec, the *Swan*. And remembering that you preferred Rolls-Royces to any other cars, I had ordered one. But now that we are never to meet again, as I have no hope of persuading you to accept either the boat or the car (to me they would be quite useless), I had thought—as I had ordered them through a middleman, in your name—that you might perhaps by countermanding them yourself save me the expense of the yacht and the car which are no longer required. But this, and many other matters, would have needed to be discussed. And I find that so long as I am capable of falling in love with you again, which will not be for long, it would be madness, for the sake of a sailing boat and a Rolls-Royce, to meet again and to jeopardise your life's happiness since you have decided that it lies in your living apart from me. No, I prefer to keep the Rolls and even the yacht. And as I shall make no use of them and they are likely to remain for ever, one in its dock, dismantled, the other in its garage, I shall have engraved on the . . . of the yacht (Heavens, I'm afraid of calling it the wrong thing and committing a heresy which would shock you) those lines of Mallarmé which you used to like:

> A swan of olden times recalls that he,
> Splendid yet void of hope to free himself,
> Had left unsung the realm of life itself
> When sterile winter glittered with ennui.

You remember—it's the poem that begins: 'The lively, lovely, virginal today.' Alas, today is no longer either virginal or lovely. But those who, like me, know that they will very soon make of it an endurable 'tomorrow' are seldom *endurable* themselves. As for the Rolls, it would deserve rather those other lines of the same poet which you said you could not understand:

> Say then if I am not joyful
> Thunder and rubies at the axle
> To see in the air pierced by this fire
>
> With every scattered palatine
> Dying as though in purple of Tyre
> The wheel of my chariot vespertine.

Farewell for ever, my little Albertine, and thank you once again for the enjoyable drive which we went for together on the eve of our separation. I retain a very pleasant memory of it.

PS. I make no reference to what you tell me of the alleged suggestions which Saint-Loup (whom I do not for a moment believe to be in Touraine) may have made to your aunt. It's pure Sherlock Holmes. What do you take me for?"

No doubt, just as I had said in the past to Albertine: "I don't love you," in order that she should love me, "I forget people when I don't see them," in order that she might see me often, "I have decided to leave you," in order to forestall any idea of separation, now it was because I was absolutely determined that she must return within a week that I said to her: "Farewell for ever"; it was because I wished to see her again that I said to her: "I think it would be dangerous to see you"; it was because living apart from her seemed to me worse than death that I wrote to her: "You were right, we would be unhappy together." Alas, in writing this sham letter in order to appear not to need her (the only vestige of pride that survived from my former love for Gilberte in my love for Albertine), and also to enjoy the pleasure of saying certain things which were only capable of moving me and not her, I ought to have foreseen from the start that it was possible that it would invite a negative response, that is to say, one which substantiated what I had said; that this was indeed probable, for even had Albertine been less intelligent than she was, she would never have doubted for an instant that what I said to her was untrue. Indeed, without pausing to consider the intentions that I expressed in this letter, the mere fact of my writing it, even if it had not been preceded by Saint-Loup's intervention, was enough to prove to her that I desired her return and to prompt her to let me become more and more inextricably ensnared. Then, having foreseen the poss-ibility of a negative reply, I ought also to have foreseen that this reply would at once revive in its fullest intensity my love for Albertine. And I ought, still before posting my letter, to have asked myself whether, in the event of Albertine's replying in the same tone and refusing to return, I should have sufficient control over my grief to force myself to remain silent, not to telegraph to her "Come back," not to send her some other emissary—all of which, after I had written to her to say that we would never meet again, would make it perfectly obvious that I could not do without her, and would lead to her refusing more emphatically than ever, whereupon, unable to endure my anguish for another moment, I would go down to her myself and might, for all I knew, be refused admission. And doubtless this would have been, after three enormous blunders, the worst of all, after which there would be nothing left but to kill myself in front of her house. But the disastrous way in which the psychopathological universe is constructed has decreed that the clumsy act, the act which we ought most sedulously to avoid, is precisely the act that will calm us, the act that, opening before us, until we discover its outcome, fresh avenues of hope, momentarily relieves us of the intolerable pain which a refusal has aroused in us. So that, when the pain is too acute, we dash headlong into the blunder that consists in writing to, in sending somebody to intercede with, in going in person to see, in proving that we cannot do without, the woman we love.

But I foresaw none of all this. The probable outcome of my letter seemed to me on the contrary to be to make Albertine return to me at once. And so, with this outcome in mind, I had felt a sweet pleasure in writing the letter. But at the same time I had not ceased to shed tears while writing it; partly, first of all, in the same way as on the day when I had acted a pretence of separation, because, as the words represented for me the idea which they expressed to me although they were addressed to a different end (uttered mendaciously because my pride forbade me to admit that I loved), they carried their own load of sorrow, but also because I felt that the idea contained a grain of truth.

As this letter seemed to me to be certain of its effect, I began to regret that I had sent it. For when I pictured to myself Albertine's return and what an easy matter it was after all, suddenly all the reasons which made our marriage a thing disastrous to myself returned in their fullest force. I hoped that she would refuse to come back. I was in the process of calculating that my liberty, my whole future depended upon her refusal, that I had been mad to write to her, that I ought to have retrieved my letter which, alas, had gone, when Françoise brought it back to me (at the same time handing me the newspaper which she had just brought upstairs). She was not certain how many stamps it required. But immediately I changed my mind; I hoped that Albertine would not return, but I wanted the decision to come from her, so as to put an end to my anxiety, and I handed the letter back to Françoise. I opened the newspaper. It announced a performance by Berma. Then I remembered the two different ways in which I had listened to *Phèdre*, and it was now in a third way that I thought of the declaration scene. It seemed to me that what I had so often recited to myself, and had seen and heard in the theatre, was the statement of the laws which I was to experience in my life. There are things in our hearts to which we do not realise how strongly we are attached. Or else, if we live without them, it is because day after day, from fear of failure, or of being made to suffer, we put off entering into possession of them. This was what had happened to me in the case of Gilberte, when I thought that I was giving her up. If before the time comes when we are entirely detached from these things—a time long subsequent to that in which we believe ourselves to be detached from them—the girl we love becomes, for instance, engaged to someone else, we are driven mad, we can no longer endure the life which appeared to us to be so mournfully calm. Or else, if the thing is already in our possession, we feel that it is a burden, that we should be only too glad to be rid of it; and this was what had happened to me in the case of Albertine. But let a sudden departure remove the unwanted person from us, and we can no longer bear to live. Now, did not the "argument" of *Phèdre* combine these two cases? Hippolyte is about to leave. Phèdre, who until then has gone out of her way to court his enmity, from qualms of conscience, she says (or rather the poet makes her say), but really because she does not see that it can lead anywhere and feels that she is not loved, Phèdre can endure the situation no longer. She comes to him to confess her love, and this was the scene which I had so often recited to myself:

> They say a prompt departure takes you from us.

Doubtless Hippolyte's departure is a secondary reason, one may feel, compared to the death of Thésée. And similarly when, a few lines further on, Phèdre pretends for a moment that she has been misunderstood:

> Would I have cast off all care for my honour?

we may suppose that it is because Hippolyte has repulsed her declaration:

> Do you not remember,
> Lady, Theseus is your husband, and my father?

But if he had evinced no indignation, Phèdre, her happiness achieved, might have had the same feeling that it did not amount to much. Whereas, as soon as she sees that it still eludes her grasp, that Hippolyte thinks he has misunderstood her and makes apologies, then, like myself when I decided to give my letter back to Françoise, she decides that the refusal must come from him, decides to stake everything on one last throw of the dice:

> Ah, cruel! You have understood me all too well.

And even the very harshness with which, I had been told, Swann had treated Odette, or with which I myself had treated Albertine, a harshness which substituted for the original love a new love composed of pity, tenderness, the need for an outpouring of emotion which was merely a variant of the first, is to be found also in this scene:

> You hated me the more, I did not love you less.
> Your misfortunes lent you further and fresh charms.

What proves that it is not to the "care for her honour" that Phèdre attaches most importance is that she would have forgiven Hippolyte and turned a deaf ear to Oenone's advice had she not learned that Hippolyte was in love with Aricie. For jealousy, which in love is equivalent to the loss of all happiness, outweighs mere loss of reputation. It is then that she allows Oenone (who is merely a name for the baser side of herself) to slander Hippolyte without taking upon herself the "burden of his defence" and thus sends the man who will have none of her to a fate the calamities of which are moreover no consolation to herself, since her own suicide follows immediately upon the death of Hippolyte. Thus at least it was that, reducing the part played by all the "Jansenist" scruples, as Bergotte would have put it, which Racine ascribed to Phèdre to make her appear less guilty, I saw this scene, as a sort of prophecy of the amorous episodes in my own life. These reflexions had, however, in no way altered my resolve, and I handed my letter to Françoise so that she might post it after all, in order to carry into effect that approach to Albertine which seemed to me to be essential now that I had learned that my former attempt had failed. And no doubt we are wrong when we suppose that the fulfilment of our desire is a small matter, since as soon as we believe that it cannot be realised we become intent upon it once again, and decide that it was not worth our while to pursue it only when we are quite certain that our attempt will not fail. And yet we are right also. For if that fulfilment, if the achievement of happiness, appears of small account only in the light of certainty, nevertheless it is an unstable element from which only sorrows can arise. And those sorrows will be all the greater the more completely our desire will have been fulfilled, all the more impossible to endure when our happiness has been, in defiance of the law of nature, prolonged for a certain time, when it has received the consecration of habit. In another sense, too, these two tendencies, in this particular case that which made me anxious that my letter should be posted, and, when I thought that it had gone, that which made me regret the fact, have each of them a certain element of truth. As regards the first tendency, it is only too understandable that we should go in pursuit of our happiness—or misery—and that at the same time we should hope to keep before us, by this latest action which is about to involve us in its consequences, a state of expectancy which does not leave us in absolute despair, in a word that we should seek to convert into other forms which, we imagine, must be less painful to us, the malady from which we are suffering. But the other tendency is no less important, for, born of our belief in the success of our enterprise, it is simply an anticipation of the disillusionment which we should very soon feel in the presence of a satisfied desire, our regret at having fixed for ourselves, at the expense of others which are necessarily excluded, this particular form of happiness.

I gave the letter back to Françoise and asked her to go out at once and post it. As soon as it had gone, I began once more to think of Albertine's return as imminent. The thought did not fail to introduce into my mind certain pleasing images which neutralised to some extent the dangers I foresaw in her return. The pleasure, so long lost, of having her with me was intoxicating.

Time passes, and little by little everything that we have spoken in falsehood becomes true; I had learned this only too well with Gilberte; the indifference I had feigned while never ceasing to weep had eventually become a fact; gradually life, as I told Gilberte in a lying formula which retrospectively had come true, life had driven us apart. I remembered this, saying to myself: "If Albertine allows a few months to go by, my lies will become the truth. And now that the worst moments are over, isn't it to be wished that she will allow this month to elapse? If she returns, I shall have to renounce the true life which certainly I am not in a fit state to enjoy as yet, but which as time goes on may begin to offer me attractions while my memory of Albertine grows fainter."

I do not say that the process of forgetting was not beginning to operate. But one of the effects of forgetting was precisely—since it meant that many of Albertine's less pleasing aspects, of the boring hours that I had spent with her, no longer figured in my memory, ceased therefore to be reasons for my wanting her not to be there as I used to when she was—that it gave me a more concise impression of her enhanced by all the love that I had ever felt for other women. In this particular form, forgetfulness, although it was working towards inuring me to separation from her, nevertheless, by showing me a sweeter and more beautiful Albertine, made me long all the more for her return.

Often, since her departure, when I was confident that I showed no trace of tears, I had rung for Françoise and said to her: "We must make sure that Mademoiselle Albertine hasn't forgotten anything. See that you do her room so that it's nice and tidy for her when she comes." Or simply: "Only the other day Mademoiselle Albertine was saying to me, let me think now, it was the day before she left . . ." I wanted to diminish Françoise's detestable pleasure at Albertine's departure by giving her the impression that it was not to be prolonged. I wanted, too, to show Françoise that I was not afraid to speak of this departure, to proclaim it—like certain generals who describe a forced retreat as a strategic withdrawal in conformity with a prearranged plan—as deliberate, as constituting an episode the true meaning of which I was concealing for the moment, but in no way implying the end of my friendship with Albertine. I wanted, finally, by repeating her name incessantly, to introduce, like a breath of air, something of her into that room in which her departure had left a vacuum, in which I could no longer breathe. Besides, one seeks to reduce the dimensions of one's grief by fitting it into one's everyday talk between ordering a suit of clothes and ordering dinner.

While she was doing Albertine's room, Françoise, out of curiosity, opened the drawer of a little rosewood table in which my mistress used to put away the ornaments which she discarded when she went to bed. "Oh! Monsieur, Mademoiselle Albertine has forgotten to take her rings, they're still in the drawer."

My first impulse was to say: "We must send them after her." But this would make me appear uncertain of her return. "Oh well," I replied after a moment's silence, "it's hardly worth while sending them to her as she's coming back so soon. Give them to me, I shall see about them."

Françoise handed me the rings with some misgiving. She loathed Albertine, but, judging me by her own standards, she reckoned that one could not give me a letter in my mistress's handwriting without the risk of my opening it. I took the rings.

"Monsieur must take care not to lose them," said Françoise. "They're real beauties, they are! I don't know who gave them to her, whether it was Monsieur or someone else, but I can tell it was someone rich, who had good taste!"

"It wasn't me," I assured her, "and besides, they don't both come from the same person. One was given her by her aunt and the other she bought for herself."

"Not from the same person!" Françoise exclaimed. "Monsieur must be joking, they're exactly the same, except for the ruby that's been added to one of them, there's the same eagle on both, the same initials inside . . ."

I do not know whether Françoise was conscious of the pain she was causing me, but a smile began to flicker across her lips and thereafter never left them.

"What do you mean, the same eagle? You're talking nonsense. It's true that the one without the ruby has an eagle on it, but the other has a sort of man's head carved on it."

"A man's head? Where did Monsieur see that? I had only to put on my specs to see at once that it was one of the eagle's wings. If Monsieur takes his magnifying glass, he'll see the other wing on the other side, and the head and the beak in the middle. You can count every feather. Oh, it's a fine piece of work."

My intense anxiety to know whether Albertine had lied to me made me forget that I ought to maintain a certain dignity in Françoise's presence and deny her the wicked pleasure that she felt, if not in torturing me, at least in harming Albertine. I almost gasped for breath as Françoise went to fetch my magnifying glass. I took it from her, and asked her to show me the eagle on the ring with the ruby. She had no difficulty in making me pick out the wings, stylised in the same way as on the other ring, the relief of the feathers, the head. She also pointed out to me the similar inscriptions, to which, it is true, others were added on the ring with the ruby. And on the inside of both was Albertine's monogram.

"But I'm surprised that it should need all this to make Monsieur see that the rings are the same," said Françoise. "Even without examining them, you can see that it's the same style, the same way of turning the gold, the same shape. As soon as I looked at them I could have sworn they came from the same place. You can tell straight away, just as you can tell the dishes of a good cook."

And indeed, to the curiosity of a servant fanned by hatred and trained to observe details with terrifying precision, there had been added, to assist her in this expert criticism, her natural taste, that same taste, in fact, which she showed in her cookery and which was sharpened perhaps, as I had noticed on the way to Balbec in the way she dressed, by the coquetry of a woman who has once been pretty and has studied the jewellery and dresses of other women. I might have picked up the wrong bottle of pills and, instead of swallowing a few veronal tablets on a day when I felt that I had drunk too many cups of tea, might have swallowed as many caffeine tablets, and my heart would not have pounded more violently. I asked Françoise to leave the room. I would have liked to see Albertine immediately. My horror at her lie, my jealousy of the unknown donor, was combined with pain at the thought that she should have allowed herself to accept presents. I gave her even more, it is true, but a woman whom we are keeping does not seem to us to be a kept woman as long as we are unaware that she is being kept by other men. And yet, since I had never ceased to spend a great deal of money on her, I had taken her in spite of this moral baseness; I had encouraged this baseness of hers, I had perhaps increased, perhaps even created it. Then, just as we have the faculty of making up stories to soothe our anguish, just as we manage, when we are dying of hunger, to persuade ourselves that a stranger is going to leave us a fortune of a hundred million, I imagined Albertine in my arms, explaining to me without the slightest hesitation that it was because of the similarity of its workmanship that she had bought the second ring, that it was she who had had her initials engraved on it. But this explanation was still fragile, it had not yet had time to thrust into my mind its beneficent roots, and my pain could not be so quickly assuaged. And I reflected that many men who tell their friends that their mistress is very sweet to them must suffer similar torments. Thus it is that they lie to others and to themselves. They do not altogether lie; they do spend in her company hours that are genuinely delightful; but the sweetness which she shows her lover in front of his friends and which enables him to preen himself, and the sweetness which she shows him when they are alone together and which enables him to bless her, conceal all too many unrecorded hours in which the lover has suffered, doubted, sought everywhere in vain to discover the truth! Such sufferings are inseparable from the pleasure of loving, of delighting in a woman's most trivial remarks, remarks which we know to be trivial but which we perfume with her fragrance. At that moment, I was no longer capable of delighting, through memory, in the fragrance of Albertine. Shattered, holding the two rings in my hand, I stared at that pitiless eagle whose beak was rending my heart, whose wings, chiselled in high relief, had borne away the trust that I still retained in my mistress, in whose claws my tortured mind was unable to escape for an instant from the incessantly recurring questions concerning the stranger whose name the eagle doubtless symbolised though without allowing me to decipher it, whom she had doubtless loved in the past, and whom she had doubtless seen again not so long ago, since it was on the day, so peaceful, so loving and so intimate, of our drive together through the Bois that I had seen, for the first time, the second ring, the one in which the eagle appeared to be dipping its beak in the bright blood of the ruby.

If, however, from morning till night, I never ceased to grieve over Albertine's departure, this did not mean that I thought only of her. For one thing, her charm having for a long time past spread gradually over things which had since become quite remote from her, but were none the less electrified by the same emotion as she gave me, if something made me think of Incarville, or of the Verdurins, or of some new part that Léa was playing, a sudden flux of pain would overwhelm me. For another thing, what I myself called thinking of Albertine meant thinking of how I might get her back, how I might join her, how I might discover what she was doing. With the result that if, during those hours of incessant torment, a pictogram could have represented the images that accompanied my sufferings, it would have shown pictures of the Gare d'Orsay, of the banknotes offered to Mme Bontemps, of Saint-Loup stooping over the sloping desk of a telegraph office filling in a telegram form to me, never the picture of Albertine. Just as, throughout the whole course of one's life, one's egoism sees before it all the time the objects that are of concern to the self, but never takes in that "I" itself which is perpetually observing them, so the desire which directs our actions descends towards them, but does not reach back to itself, whether because, being unduly utilitarian, it plunges into the action and disdains all knowledge of it, or because it looks to the future to compensate for the disappointments of the present, or because the inertia of the mind urges it to slide down the easy slope of imagination, rather than to climb the steep slope of introspection. In reality, during those hours of crisis in which we would stake our whole life, in proportion as the woman upon whom it depends reveals more and more clearly the immensity of the place that she occupies for us, leaving nothing in the world that is not disrupted by her, so the image of that woman diminishes until it is no longer perceptible.

We find in everything the effect of her presence in the emotion that we feel; herself, the cause, we find nowhere. I was so incapable during those days of forming any picture of Albertine that I could almost have believed that I did not love her, just as my mother, in the moments of despair when she was incapable of ever picturing my grandmother (except once in the chance encounter of a dream, the importance of which she felt so strongly, although asleep, that she strove with all the strength that remained to her in her sleep to make it last), might have accused and did in fact accuse herself of not missing her mother, whose death had been a mortal blow to her but whose features eluded her memory.*

Why should I have supposed that Albertine did not care for women? Because she had said, especially of late, that she did not care for them: but did not our life rest upon a perpetual lie? Never once had she said to me: "Why can't I go out as and when I choose? Why do you always ask other people what I have been doing?" And yet, after all, the conditions of her life were so unusual that she must have asked me this had she not herself guessed the reason. And was it not understandable that my silence as to the causes of her confinement should be matched by a similar and constant silence on her part as to her perpetual desires, her innumerable memories, her countless hopes and longings? Françoise looked as though she knew that I was lying when I alluded to the imminence of Albertine's return. And her belief seemed to be founded upon something more than that truth which generally guided our old house-keeper, to the effect that masters do not like to be humiliated in front of their servants, and allow them to know only so much of the truth as does not depart too far from a flattering fiction calculated to maintain respect for themselves. This time, Françoise's belief seemed to be founded upon something else, as though she had herself aroused and fostered distrust in Albertine's mind, stimulated her anger, driven her, in short, to the point at which she could predict her departure as inevitable. If this was true, my version of a temporary absence, of which I had known and approved, could be received with nothing but incredulity by Françoise. But the idea that she had formed of Albertine's venal nature, the exasperation with which, in her hatred, she magnified the "profit" that Albertine was supposed to be making out of me, might to some extent belie that certainty. And so when in her hearing I made an allusion, as if to something perfectly natural, to

Albertine's imminent return, Françoise would look at my face to see whether I was making it up, in the same way as, when the butler teased her by pretending to read out some political news which she hesitated to believe, as for instance the closing of churches and the expulsion of the clergy, even from the other end of the kitchen, and without being able to read it, she would stare instinctively and greedily at the paper, as though she were capable of seeing whether the report was really written there.

But when Françoise saw that after writing a long letter I added the exact address of Mme Bontemps, her alarm that Albertine might return, hitherto quite vague, began to increase. It grew to the point of consternation when one morning she had to bring me with the rest of my mail a letter on the envelope of which she had recognised Albertine's handwriting. She wondered whether Albertine's departure had not been a mere sham, a supposition which distressed her twice over as finally ensuring Albertine's future presence in the house, and as constituting for me, and thereby, as I was her employer, for herself, the humiliation of having been tricked by Albertine. Impatient though I was to read the letter, I could not refrain from studying for a moment Françoise's eyes from which all hope had fled, inferring from this omen the imminence of Albertine's return, as a lover of winter sports concludes with joy that the cold weather is at hand when he sees the swallows fly south. At length Françoise left me, and when I had made sure that she had shut the door behind her, I opened, noiselessly so as not to appear anxious, the letter which ran as follows:

"Dear friend, thank you for all the nice things you wrote to me. I am at your disposal for the countermanding of the Rolls, if you think that I can help in any way, as I am sure I can. You have only to let me know the name of the agents. You would let yourself be taken for a ride by these people who are only interested in selling, and what would you do with a motor-car, you who never stir out of the house? I am deeply touched that you have kept a happy memory of our last outing. You may be sure that for my part I shall never forget that drive in a double twilight (since night was falling and we were about to part) and that it will be effaced from my thoughts only when the darkness is complete."

I felt that this last sentence was merely phrase-making and that Albertine could not possibly retain until death any such sweet memory of this drive from which she had certainly derived no pleasure since she had been impatient to leave me. But I was impressed also, when I thought of the cyclist, the golfer of Balbec, who had read nothing but *Esther* before she came to know me, to see how gifted she was and how right I had been in thinking that she had enriched herself in my house with new qualities which made her different and more complete. And thus, the words that I had said to her at Balbec: "I feel that my friendship would be of value to you, that I am just the person who could give you what you lack" (I had written by way of dedication on a photograph I gave her: "with the certainty of being providential"), words which I uttered without believing them and simply that she might derive some benefit from my society which would outweigh any possible boredom, these words turned out to have been true as well; as, for that matter, had been my remark to her that I did not wish to see her for fear of falling in love with her. I had said this because on the contrary I knew that in constant proximity my love became deadened and that separation kindled it, but in reality constant proximity had given rise to a need of her that was infinitely stronger than my love in the first weeks at Balbec, so that that remark too had proved true.

But Albertine's letter in no way advanced matters. She spoke to me only of writing to the agents. It was essential to break out of this situation, to hasten things on, and I had the following idea. I sent a letter at once to Andrée in which I told her that Albertine was at her aunt's, that I felt very lonely, that she would give me immense pleasure if she came and stayed with me for a few days and that, as I did not wish to make any mystery of it, I begged her to inform Albertine. And at the same time I wrote to Albertine as though I had not yet received her letter:

"Dear friend, forgive me for what I am sure you will understand. I have such a hatred of secrecy that I wanted you to be informed both by her and by myself. I have acquired, from having you staying so charmingly in the house with me, the bad habit of not being able to be alone. Since we have decided that you will not come back, it occurred to me that the person who would best fill your place, because she would make least change in my life, would remind me most of you, is Andrée, and I have asked her to come. So that all this should not appear too sudden, I have spoken to her only of a short visit, but between ourselves I am pretty certain that this time it will be a permanent thing. Don't you agree that I'm right? You know that your little group of girls at Balbec has always been the social unit that exerted the greatest influence upon me, in which I was most happy to be eventually included. No doubt this influence is still making itself felt. Since the fatal incompatibility of our characters and the mischances of life have decreed that my little Albertine can never be my wife, I believe that I shall nevertheless find a wife—less charming than herself but one whom greater natural affinities will enable perhaps to be happier with me—in Andrée."

But after I had sent off this letter, the suspicion occurred to me suddenly that, when Albertine had written to me to say: "I should have been only too glad to come back if you had written to me direct," she had said this only because I had not written to her, and that had I done so she would still not have come back, that she would be happy to know that Andrée was with me, and was to be my wife, provided that she herself remained free, because she could now, as already for a week past, stultifying the hourly precautions which I had taken during more than six months in Paris, abandon herself to her vices and do what, minute by minute, I had prevented her from doing. I told myself that she was probably making an improper use of her freedom down there, and no doubt this idea which I formed seemed to me sad but remained general, showing me no specific dctails, and, by the indefinite number of possible mistresses which it allowed me to imagine, prevented me from stopping to consider any one of them, drew my mind on in a sort of perpetual motion not untinged with pain, but with a pain which the absence of any concrete image rendered endurable. It ceased, however, to be endurable and became atrocious when Saint-Loup arrived.

Before I explain why the information that he gave me made me so unhappy, I must relate an incident which occurred immediately before his visit and the memory of which so disturbed me afterwards that it weakened, if not the painful impression made on me by my conversation with Saint-Loup, at any rate the practical effect of that conversation. This incident was as follows. Burning with impatience to see Saint-Loup, I was waiting for him on the staircase (a thing which I could not have done had my mother been at home, for it was what she most abominated, next to "talking out of the window") when I heard the following words: "What! you mean to say you don't know how to get a fellow you don't like sacked? It's not difficult. For instance, you need only hide the things he has to take in. Then, when they're in a hurry and ring for him, he can't find anything, he loses his head. My aunt will be furious with him, and will say to you: 'But what's the man doing?' When he does show his face, everybody will be raging, and he won't have what's wanted. After this has happened four or five times you may be sure that he'll be sacked, especially if you take care to dirty the things that he's supposed to bring in clean, and a dozen other tricks of that kind."

I remained speechless with astonishment, for these cruel, Machiavellian words were uttered by the voice of Saint-Loup. Now I had always regarded him as so kind, so tender-hearted a person that these words had the same effect on me as if he had been rehearsing the role of Satan for a play: it could not be in his own name that he was speaking.

"But, after all, a man has to earn his living," said the other person, of whom I then caught sight and who was one of the Duchesse de Guermantes's footmen.

"What the hell does that matter to you so long as you're all right?" Saint-Loup replied callously. "It will be all the more fun for you, having a whipping-boy. You can easily spill ink over his livery just when he has to go and wait at a big dinner-party, and never leave him in peace for a moment until he's only too glad to give notice. Anyhow, I can put a spoke in his wheel. I shall tell my aunt that I admire your patience in working with a great lout like that, and so dirty too."

I showed myself, and Saint-Loup came to greet me, but my confidence in him was shaken since I had heard him speak in a manner so different from anything that I knew. And I wondered whether a person who was capable of acting so cruelly towards some poor wretch might not have played the part of a traitor towards me on his mission to Mme Bontemps. This reflexion served mainly, after he had left, to help me not to regard his failure as a proof that I myself might not succeed. But while he was with me, it was still of the Saint-Loup of old, and especially of the friend who had just come from Mme Bontemps, that I thought. He began by saying: "You feel that I ought to have telephoned to you more often, but I was always told that you were engaged." But the point at which my pain became unendurable was when he said: "To begin where my last telegram left you, after going through a sort of shed, I went into the house and at the end of a long passage was shown into a drawing-room."

At these words, shed, passage, drawing-room, and before he had even finished uttering them, my heart was convulsed more instantaneously than by an electric current, for the force that circles the earth most times in a second is not electricity but pain. How I repeated to myself these words, shed, passage, drawing-room, renewing the shock at will, after Saint-Loup had left me! In a shed one girl can hide with another. And in that drawing-room, who knew what Albertine did when her aunt was not there? Had I then imagined the house in which she was living as incapable of possessing either a shed or a drawing-room? No, I had not imagined it at all, except as a vague dwelling. I had suffered first of all when the place where Albertine was had acquired a geographical identity, when I had learned that, instead of being in two or three possible places, she was in Touraine; those words uttered by her concierge had marked in my heart as upon a map the place where I must suffer. But once I had grown accustomed to the idea that she was in a house in Touraine, I had still not seen the house; never had there occurred to my imagination this appalling idea of a drawing-room, a shed, a passage, which struck me now, facing me in the retina of Saint-Loup's eyes which had seen them, as the rooms in which Albertine came and went, lived her life, as those rooms in particular and not an infinity of possible rooms which had cancelled one another out. With the words shed, passage, drawing-room, I became aware of my folly in having left Albertine for a week in that accursed place whose *existence* (instead of its mere possibility) had just been revealed to me. Alas! when Saint-Loup told me also that in this drawing-room he had heard someone singing at the top of her voice in an adjoining room and that it was Albertine who was singing, I realised with despair that, rid of me at last, she was happy! She had regained her freedom. And I had been thinking that she would come to take the place of Andrée! My grief turned to anger with Saint-Loup.

"That's the one thing in the world I asked you to avoid, that she should know of your coming."

"Do you think it was easy! They assured me that she wasn't in the house. Oh, I know very well that you're not pleased with me, I could tell that from your telegrams. But you're not being fair, I did what I could."

Set free once more, released from the cage in which, here at home, I used to leave her for days on end without letting her come to my room, Albertine had regained all her attraction in my eyes; she had become once more the girl whom everyone pursued, the marvellous bird of the earliest days.

"Anyhow, to sum up—as regards the money, I don't know what to say to you. I found myself addressing a woman who seemed to me to be so scrupulous that I was afraid of offending her. However, she didn't say a word when I mentioned the money. In fact, a little later she told me that she was touched to find that we understood one another so well. And yet everything that she said afterwards was so delicate, so refined, that it seemed to me impossible that she could have been referring to my offer of money when she said: 'We understand one another so well,' for after all I was behaving like a cad."

"But perhaps she didn't understand what you meant, perhaps she didn't hear. You ought to have repeated the offer, because then it would certainly have worked."

"But how could she possibly not have heard? I spoke to her as I'm speaking to you, and she's neither deaf nor mad."

"And she made no comment?"

"None."

"You ought to have repeated the offer."

"How do you mean, repeat it? As soon as we met I saw what sort of person she was. I said to myself that you'd been mistaken, that you were making me commit the most awful gaffe, and that it would be terribly difficult to offer her the money like that. I did it, however, to oblige you, convinced that she'd turn me out of the house."

"But she didn't. Therefore, either she hadn't heard you and you should have started afresh, or you could have pursued the subject."

"You say: 'She hadn't heard,' because you were here in Paris, but, I repeat, if you'd been present at our conversation, there wasn't a sound to interrupt us, I said it quite plainly, it's not possible that she failed to understand."

"But anyhow she's quite convinced that I've always wished to marry her niece?"

"No, as to that, if you want my opinion, she didn't believe that you had any intention of marrying the girl. She told me that you yourself had informed her niece that you wished to leave her. I'm not really sure that she's convinced even now that you want to marry."

This reassured me slightly by showing me that I was in a less humiliating position, and therefore more capable of being still loved, more free to take some decisive action. Nevertheless I was tormented.

"I'm sorry, because I can see you're not pleased," Saint-Loup went on.

"Well, I'm touched by your kindness, and I'm grateful to you, but it seems to me that you might have . . ."

"I did my best. No one else could have done more or even as much. Try sending someone else."

"No, no, as a matter of fact, if I had known I wouldn't have sent you, but the failure of your attempt prevents me from making another."

I heaped reproaches on him: he had tried to do me a service and had not succeeded.

On leaving the Bontemps' house he had met some girls arriving. I had already conjectured often enough that Albertine knew other girls in the neighbourhood; but this was the first time that I felt the pain of that conjecture. It would seem that nature has endowed the mind with the means of secreting a natural antidote which destroys the suppositions that we form unremittingly but without danger to ourselves; but nothing could immunise me against these girls whom Saint-Loup had met. But were not all these details precisely what I had sought to learn from everyone with regard to Albertine? Was it not I who, in order to learn them more fully, had begged Saint-Loup, summoned back to Paris by his colonel, to come and see me at all costs? Was it not I, therefore, who had desired them, or rather my famished grief, longing to feed and to wax fat upon them? Finally Saint-Loup told me that he had had the pleasant surprise of meeting down there—the only familiar face that had reminded him of the past—a former friend of Rachel, a pretty actress who was taking a holiday in the neighbourhood. And the name of this actress was enough to make me say to myself: "Perhaps it's with her"; was enough to make me see, in the very arms of a woman whom I did not know, Albertine smiling and flushed with pleasure. And, after all, why should this not have been so? Had I myself refrained from thinking of other women since I had known Albertine? On the evening of my first visit to the Princesse de Guermantes, when I returned home, had I not been thinking far less of her than of the girl of whom Saint-Loup had told me, who frequented houses of assignation, and of

Mme Putbus's maid? Was it not for the latter that I had returned to Balbec? More recently, had I not longed to go to Venice? Why then might Albertine not have longed to go to Touraine? Only, when it came to the point, as I now realised, I would not have left her, I would not have gone to Venice. Indeed, in my heart of hearts, when I said to myself: "I shall leave her soon," I knew that I would never leave her, just as I knew that I would never settle down to work, or live a healthy life, or do any of the things which, day after day, I vowed to do on the morrow. Only, whatever I might feel in my heart, I had thought it more adroit to let her live under the perpetual threat of a separation. And no doubt, thanks to my detestable adroitness, I had convinced her only too well. In any case, things could not now go on like this; I could not leave her in Touraine with those girls, with that actress; I could not endure the thought of that life which eluded me. I would await her reply to my letter: if she was doing wrong, alas! a day more or less made no difference (and perhaps I said this to myself because, being no longer in the habit of taking note of every minute of her life, a single one of which wherein she was unobserved would formerly have thrown me into a panic, my jealousy no longer observed the same time-scale). But as soon as I received her answer, if she was not coming back I would go and fetch her; willy-nilly, I would tear her away from her women friends. Besides, was it not better for me to go down in person, now that I had discovered Saint-Loup's hitherto unsuspected duplicity? Might he not, for all I knew, have organised a plot to separate me from Albertine?

Was it because I had changed, or because I had been incapable of imagining then that natural causes would bring me one day to this unprecedented pass? At all events, how I should have lied now had I written to her, as I had said to her in Paris, that I hoped that no accident might befall her! Ah! if some accident had happened to her, my life, instead of being poisoned for ever by this incessant jealousy, would at once regain, if not happiness, at least a state of calm through the suppression of suffering.

The suppression of suffering? Can I really have believed it, have believed that death merely strikes out what exists, and leaves everything else in its place, that it removes the pain from the heart of him for whom the other's existence has ceased to be anything but a source of pain, that it removes the pain and puts nothing in its place? The suppression of pain! As I glanced at the news items in the papers, I regretted that I had not had the courage to form the same wish as Swann. If Albertine could have been the victim of an accident, were she alive I should have had a pretext for hastening to her bedside, were she dead I should have recovered, as Swann said, my freedom to live. Did I believe this? He had believed it, that subtlest of men who thought that he knew himself well. How little do we know of what we have in our hearts! How clearly, a little later, had he been still alive, I could have proved to him that his wish was not only criminal but absurd, that the death of the woman he loved would have delivered him from nothing!

I forsook all pride with regard to Albertine, and sent her a despairing telegram begging her to return on any terms, telling her that she could do whatever she liked, that I asked only to be allowed to take her in my arms for a minute three times a week, before she went to bed. And if she had said once a week only, I would have accepted the restriction.

She never came back. My telegram had just gone off to her when I myself received one. It was from Mme Bontemps. The world is not created once and for all for each of us individually. There are added to it in the course of our lives things of which we have never had any suspicion. Alas! it was not a suppression of suffering that the first two lines of the telegram produced in me: "My poor friend, our little Albertine is no more. Forgive me for breaking this terrible news to you who were so fond of her. She was thrown by her horse against a tree while she was out riding. All our efforts to restore her to life were unavailing. If only I had died in her stead!" No, not the suppression of suffering, but a suffering until then unimagined, that of realising that she would not come back. But had I not told myself many times that she might not come back? I had indeed done so, but now I saw that I had never believed it for a moment. As I needed her presence, her kisses, to enable me to endure the pain that my suspicions caused me, I had formed, since Balbec, the habit of being always with her. Even when she had gone out, when I was alone, I was kissing her still. I had continued to do so since her departure for Touraine. I had less need of her fidelity than of her return. And if my reason might with impunity cast doubt upon it now and again, my imagination never ceased for an instant to picture it for me. Instinctively I drew my hand over my throat, over my lips, which felt themselves kissed by her lips still after she had gone away, and would never be kissed by them again; I drew my hand over them, as Mamma had caressed me at the time of my grandmother's death, saying to me: "My poor boy, your grandmother who was so fond of you will never kiss you again." All my life to come seemed to have been wrenched from my heart. My life to come? Had I not, then, thought at times of living it without Albertine? Of course not! Had I then for a long time past pledged her every minute of my life until my death? I had indeed! This future indissolubly blended with hers was something I had never had the vision to perceive, but now that it had just been demolished, I could feel the place that it occupied in my gaping heart. Françoise, who still knew nothing, came into my room. In a sudden fury I shouted at her: "What do you want?" Then (sometimes there are words that set a different reality in the same place as that which confronts us; they bewilder us in the same way as a fit of dizziness) she said to me: "Monsieur has no need to look cross. On the contrary he's going to be pleased. Here are two letters from Mademoiselle Albertine."

I felt, afterwards, that I must have stared at her with the eyes of a man whose mind has become unhinged. I was not even glad, nor was I incredulous. I was like a person who sees the same place in his room occupied by a sofa and by a grotto: nothing seeming real to him any more, he collapses on the floor. Albertine's two letters must have been written shortly before the fatal ride. The first said:

"My dear, I must thank you for the proof of your confidence which you give me when you tell me of your intention to bring Andrée to live with you. I am sure that she will be delighted to accept, and I think that it will be a very good thing for her. Gifted as she is, she will know how to make the most of the companionship of a man like yourself, and of the admirable influence which you manage to exert over other people. I feel that you have had an idea from which as much good may spring for her as for yourself. And so, if she should make the slightest difficulty (which I do not believe she will), telegraph to me and I will undertake to bring pressure to bear upon her."

The second was dated the following day. (In fact she must have written them both within a few minutes of one another, perhaps at the same time, and must have predated the first. For, all the time, I had been forming absurd ideas of her intentions, which had simply been to return to me, and which anyone not directly interested in the matter, a man without imagination, the negotiator of a peace treaty, the merchant who has to examine a transaction, would have judged more accurately than myself.) It contained only these words:

"Is it too late for me to return to you? If you have not yet written to Andrée, would you be prepared to take me back? I shall abide by your decision, but I beg you not to be long in making it known to me; you can imagine how impatiently I shall be waiting. If it is to tell me to return, I shall take the train at once. Yours with all my heart, Albertine."

For the death of Albertine to have been able to eliminate my suffering, the shock of the fall would have had to kill her not only in Touraine but in myself. There, she had never been more alive. In order to enter into us, another person must first have assumed the form, have adapted himself to the framework of time; appearing to us only in a succession of momentary flashes, he has never been able to reveal to us more than one aspect of himself at a time, to present us with more than a single photograph of himself. A great weakness no doubt for a person, to consist merely of a collection of moments; a great strength also: he is a product of memory, and our memory of a moment is not informed of everything that has happened since; this moment which it has recorded endures still, lives still, and with it the person whose form is outlined in it. And moreover, this disintegration does not only make the dead one live, it multiplies him or her. In order to be consoled I would have to forget, not one, but innumerable Albertines. When I had succeeded in bearing the grief of losing this Albertine, I must begin again with another, with a hundred others.

So then my life was entirely altered. What had constituted its sweetness—not because of Albertine, but concurrently with her, when I was alone—was precisely the perpetual resurgence, at the bidding of identical moments, of moments from the past. From the sound of pattering raindrops I recaptured the scent of the lilacs at Combray; from the shifting of the sun's rays on the balcony the pigeons in the Champs-Elysées; from the muffling of sounds in the heat of the morning hours, the cool taste of cherries; the longing for Brittany or Venice from the noise of the wind and the return of Easter. Summer was at hand, the days were long, the weather was warm. It was the season when, early in the morning, pupils and teachers repair to the public gardens to prepare for the final examinations under the trees, seeking to extract the sole drop of coolness vouchsafed by a sky less ardent than in the midday heat but already as sterilely pure. From my darkened room, with a power of evocation equal to that of former days but capable now of evoking only pain, I felt that outside, in the heaviness of the atmosphere, the setting sun was plastering the vertical fronts of houses and churches with a tawny distemper. And if Françoise, when she came in, accidentally disturbed the folds of the big curtains, I stifled a cry of pain at the rent that had just been made in my heart by that ray of long-ago sunlight which had made beautiful in my eyes the modern façade of Marcouville-l'Orgueilleuse when Albertine had said to me: "It's restored." Not knowing how to account to Françoise for my groan, I said to her: "Oh, I'm so thirsty." She left the room, then returned, but I turned sharply away under the impact of the painful discharge of one of the thousand invisible memories which continuously exploded around me in the darkness: I had noticed that she had brought me cider and cherries, things which a farm-lad had brought out to us in the carriage, at Balbec, "kinds" in which I should have made the most perfect communion, in those days, with the prismatic gleam in shuttered dining-rooms on days of scorching heat. Then I thought for the first time of the farm called Les Ecorres, and said to myself that on certain days when Albertine had told me, at Balbec, that she would not be free, that she was obliged to go somewhere with her aunt, she had perhaps been with one or another of her girlfriends at some farm to which she knew that I was not in the habit of going, and, while I waited desperately for her at Marie-Antoinette where they told me: "No, we haven't seen her today," had been saying to her friend the same words as she used to say to me when we went out together: "He'll never think of looking for us here, so there's no fear of our being disturbed." I told Françoise to draw the curtains together, so that I would no longer see that ray of sunlight. But it continued to filter through, just as corrosively, into my memory. "It doesn't appeal to me, it's been restored, but tomorrow we'll go to Saint-Mars-le-Vêtu, and the day after to . . ." Tomorrow, the day after, it was a prospect of life together, perhaps for ever, that was opening up; my heart leapt towards it, but it was no longer there, Albertine was dead.

I asked Françoise the time. Six o'clock. At last, thank God, that oppressive heat, of which in the past I used to complain to Albertine and which we so enjoyed, was about to die down. The day was drawing to its close. But what did that profit me? The cool evening air was rising; it was sunset; in my memory, at the end of a road which we had taken, she and I, on our way home, I saw it now, beyond the furthest village, like some distant place, inaccessible that evening, which we would spend at Balbec, still together. Together then; now I must stop short on the brink of that same abyss; she was dead. It was not enough now to draw the curtains; I tried to stop the eyes and ears of my memory in order not to see that band of orange in the western sky, in order not to hear those invisible birds responding from one tree to the next on either side of me who was then so tenderly embraced by her who was now dead. I tried to avoid those sensations that are produced by the dampness of leaves in the evening air, the rise and fall of humpback roads. But already those sensations had gripped me once more, carrying me far enough back from the present moment to give the necessary recoil, the necessary momentum to strike me anew, to the idea that Albertine was dead. Ah! never again would I enter a forest, never again would I stroll beneath the trees. But would the broad plains be less painful to me? How often had I crossed, on the way to fetch Albertine, how often had I retrodden, on the way back with her, the great plain of Cricqueville, sometimes in foggy weather when the swirling mists gave us the illusion of being surrounded by a vast lake, sometimes on limpid evenings when the moonlight, dematerialising the earth, making it appear from a few feet away as celestial as it is, in the daytime, in the distance only, enclosed the fields and the woods with the firmament to which it had assimilated them in the moss-agate of a universal blue!

Françoise must have been pleased by Albertine's death, and in fairness to her it should be said that by a sort of tact and decorum she made no pretence of sorrow. But the unwritten laws of her immemorial code and the tradition of the mediaeval peasant woman who weeps as in the romances of chivalry were older than her hatred of Albertine and even of Eulalie. Thus, on one of these late afternoons, as I was not quick enough in concealing my distress, she caught sight of my tears, prompted by her instinct as a former peasant girl which at one time had led her to catch and maltreat animals, to feel nothing but merriment in wringing the necks of chickens and in boiling lobsters alive, and, when I was ill, in observing, as it might be the wounds that she had inflicted on an owl, my suffering expression which she afterwards proclaimed in a sepulchral tone as a presage of coming disaster. But her Combray "unwritten law" did not permit her to treat tears and sorrow lightly—things which in her judgment were as fatal as shedding one's flannel vest or toying with one's food. "Oh, no, Monsieur, it doesn't do to cry like that, it isn't good for you." And in trying to stem my tears she looked as anxious as if they had been torrents of blood. Unfortunately I adopted a chilly air that cut short the effusions in which she was hoping to indulge and which might well have been sincere. Her attitude towards Albertine was perhaps akin to her attitude towards Eulalie, and, now that my mistress could no longer derive any profit from me, Françoise had ceased to hate her. She felt bound, however, to let me see that she was perfectly well aware that I was crying, and that, following the deplorable example set by my family, I did not wish to "show it." "You mustn't cry, Monsieur," she adjured me, in a calmer tone this time, and with the intention of proving her perspicacity rather than displaying her pity. And she added: "It was bound to happen; she was too happy, poor creature, she never knew how happy she was."

How slow the day is in dying on these interminable summer evenings! A pale ghost of the house opposite continued indefinitely to tinge the sky with its persistent whiteness. At last it was dark in the apartment; I stumbled against the furniture in the hall, but in the door that opened on to the staircase, in the midst of the darkness I had thought to be complete, the glazed panel was translucent and blue, with the blueness of a flower, the blueness of an insect's wing, a blueness that would have seemed to me beautiful had I not felt it to be a last glint, sharp as a steel blade, a final blow that was being dealt me, in its indefatigable cruelty, by the day. Finally, however, complete darkness came, but then a glimpse of a star behind the tree in the courtyard was enough to remind me of the times when we used to set out in a carriage, after dinner, for the woods of Chantepie, carpeted with moonlight. And even in the streets I might chance to isolate upon the back of a bench, to glean the natural purity of a moonbeam in the midst of the artificial lights of Paris—of Paris over which, by restoring the city for a moment, in my imagination, to a state of nature, with the infinite silence of the fields thus evoked, it enthroned the heart-rending memory of the walks that I had taken there with Albertine. Ah! when would the night end? But at the first coolness of dawn I shivered, for it had brought back to me the sweetness of that summer when, from Balbec to Incarville, from Incarville to Balbec, we had so many times escorted each other home until daybreak. I had now only one hope left for the future—a hope far more poignant than any fear—and that was that I might forget Albertine. I knew that I should forget her one day; I had forgotten Gilberte and Mme de Guermantes; I had forgotten my grand-mother. And it is our most just and cruel punishment for that forgetfulness, as total and as tranquil as the oblivion of the graveyard, through which we have detached ourselves from those we no longer love, that we should recognise it to be inevitable in the case of those we love still. In reality, we know that it is not a painful state but a state of indifference. But not being able to think at one and the same time of what I was and of what I would be, I thought with despair of all that integument of caresses, of kisses, of friendly slumber, of which I must presently let myself be stripped for ever. The influx of these tender memories, breaking against the idea that Albertine was dead, oppressed me with such a clash of warring currents that I could not remain still; I rose, but all of a sudden I stopped, overwhelmed; the same faint daybreak that I used to see when I had just left Albertine, still radiant and warm from her kisses, had just drawn above the curtains its now sinister blade whose whiteness, cold, implacable and compact, glinted like a dagger thrust into my heart.

Presently the sounds from the street would begin, enabling me to tell from the qualitative scale of their sonorities the degree of the steadily increasing heat in which they resounded. But in this heat which a few hours later would become saturated with the fragrance of cherries, what I found (as in a medicine which the substitution of one ingredient for another is sufficient to transform from the stimulant and tonic that it was into a depressant) was no longer the desire for women but the anguish of Albertine's departure. Besides, the memory of all my desires was as much impregnated with her, and with suffering, as the memory of my pleasures. Venice, where I had thought that her company would be irksome (doubtless because I had felt in a confused way that it would be necessary to me), no longer attracted me now that Albertine was no more. Albertine had seemed to me to be an obstacle interposed between me and all other things, because she was for me their container, and it was from her alone, as from a vase, that I could receive them. Now that this vase was shattered, I no longer felt that I had the courage to grasp things, and there was not one of them from which I did not now turn away, despondent, preferring not to taste it. So that my separation from her did not in the least throw open to me the field of possible pleasures which I had imagined to be closed to me by her presence. Besides, the obstacle which her presence had perhaps indeed been in the way of my travelling and enjoying life had merely (as always happens) concealed from me other obstacles which reappeared intact now that this one had been removed. Likewise, in the past, when some friendly call had prevented me from working, if on the following day I was left undisturbed I did not work any better. Let an illness, a duel, a runaway horse make us see death face to face, and how richly we should have enjoyed the life of pleasure, the travels in unknown lands, which are about to be snatched from us! And no sooner is the danger past than we resume once more the same dull life in which none of those delights existed for us.

No doubt these short summer nights last only for a brief season. Winter would at length return, when I should no longer have to dread the memory of drives with her until the too early dawn. But would not the first frosts bring back to me, preserved in their ice, the germ of my first desires, when at midnight I used to send for her, when the time seemed so long until I heard her ring at the door, a sound for which I might now wait everlastingly in vain? Would they not bring back to me the germ of my first anxieties, when twice I thought she would not come? At that time I saw her only rarely, but even those intervals between her visits which made her suddenly appear, after many weeks, from the heart of an unknown life which I made no attempt to possess, ensured my peace of mind by preventing the first inklings, constantly interrupted, of my jealousy from coagulating, from forming a solid mass in my heart. Soothing though they may have been at the time, in retrospect those intervals were stamped with pain since the unknown things she might have done in the course of them had ceased to be a matter of indifference to me, and especially now that no visit from her would ever occur again; so that those January evenings on which she used to come, and which for that reason had been so dear to me, would inject into me now with their biting winds an anxiety which was unknown to me then, and would bring back to me (but now grown pernicious) the first germ of my love. And when I thought how I would see the return of that cold season which, since the time of Gilberte and our games in the Champs-Elysées, had always seemed to me so melancholy, when I thought how evenings would come back like that snowy evening when I had waited in vain for Albertine far into the night, then, like an invalid—in his case physically, fearing for his chest, in my case mentally—what at such moments I still dreaded most, for my grief, for my heart, was the return of the intense cold, and I said to myself that what it would be hardest to live through was perhaps the winter.

Linked as it was to each of the seasons, in order for me to discard the memory of Albertine I should have had to forget them all, even if it meant having to get to know them all over again, like an old man learning to read again after a stroke; I should have had to renounce the entire universe. Nothing, I told myself, but a veritable extinction of myself would be capable (but that is impossible) of consoling me for hers. It did not occur to me that the death of oneself is neither impossible nor extraordinary; it is effected without our knowledge, even against our will, every day of our lives. And I should have to suffer from the recurrence of all sorts of days which not only nature, but adventitious circumstances, a purely conventional order, introduce into a season. Soon the date would return on which I had gone to Balbec, that last summer, and when my love, which was not yet inseparable from jealousy and did not concern itself with what Albertine was doing all day, was to undergo so many evolutions, before becoming that very different love of recent months, that this final year, in which Albertine's destiny had begun to change and had come to an end, appeared to me as full, as diverse and as vast as a whole century. Then it would be the memory of days more dilatory but dating from still earlier years, the rainy Sundays on which nevertheless everyone else had gone out, in the emptiness of the afternoon, when the sound of wind and rain would in the past have bidden me stay at home, to "philosophise in my garret"; with what anxiety would I see the hour approach at which Albertine, so little expected, had come to visit me, had caressed me for the first time, breaking off when Françoise had brought in the lamp, in that time now doubly dead when it had been Albertine who was curious about me, when my tenderness for her could legitimately cherish so many hopes! And even, later in the season, those glorious evenings when offices and girls' schools, half open like chapels, bathed in a golden dust, enable the street to crown itself with those demi-goddesses who, conversing not far from us with others of their kind, fill us with a feverish longing to penetrate into their mythological existence, now reminded me only of the tenderness of Albertine, whose presence by my side had been an obstacle to my approaching them.

Moreover, to the memory even of hours that were purely natural would inevitably be added the psychological background that makes each of them a thing apart. When, later on, I should hear the goatherd's horn, on a first fine almost Italian morning, that same day would blend alternately with its sunshine the anxiety of knowing that Albertine was at the Trocadéro, possibly with Léa and the two girls, then the homely, familial sweetness, almost that of a wife who seemed to me then an embarrassment and whom Françoise was bringing home to me. That telephone message from Françoise which had conveyed to me the dutiful homage of an Albertine returning with her had seemed to me then to be a matter for pride. I was mistaken. If it had exhilarated me, it was because it had made me feel that she whom I loved was really mine, lived only for me, and even at a distance, without my needing to occupy my mind with her, regarded me as her lord and master, returning home at a sign from me. And thus that telephone message had been a fragment of sweetness, coming to me from afar, sent out from that Trocadéro district where there happened to be, for me, sources of happiness directing towards me molecules of comfort, healing balms, restoring to me at length so precious an equanimity of mind that I need do no more—surrendering myself without the slightest qualm or reservation to Wagner's music—than await the certain arrival of Albertine, without anxiety, with an entire absence of impatience in which I had not had the perspicacity to recognise happiness. And the cause of this happiness at the knowledge of her returning home, of her obeying me and belonging to me, lay in love and not in pride. It would have been quite immaterial to me now to have at my behest fifty women returning, at a sign from me, not from the Trocadéro but from the Indies. But that day, thinking of Albertine coming dutifully home to me as I sat alone in my room making music, I had breathed in one of those substances, scattered like motes in a sunbeam, which, just as others are salutary to the body, do good to the soul. Then there had been, half an hour later, the arrival of Albertine, then the drive with Albertine, both of which had seemed to me boring because they were accompanied for me by certainty, but which, because of that very certainty, had, from the moment of Françoise's telephoning to me that she was bringing Albertine home, poured a golden calm over the hours that followed, had made of them as it were a second day, wholly unlike the first, because it had a very different emotional basis, an emotional basis which made it a uniquely original day, one to be added to the variety of the days that I had previously known, a day which I should never have been able to imagine— any more than we could imagine the delicious idleness of a summer day if such days did not exist in the calendar of those through which we have lived—a day of which I could not say absolutely that I recalled it, for to this calm I added now an anguish which I had not felt at the time. But much later, when I went back gradually, in reverse order, over the times through which I had passed before I had come to love Albertine so much, when my healed heart could detach itself without suffering from Albertine dead, then I was able to recall at length without suffering that day on which Albertine had gone shopping with Françoise instead of remaining at the Trocadéro; I recalled it with pleasure as belong- ing to an emotional season which I had not known until then; I recalled it at last exactly, no longer injecting it with suffering, but rather, on the contrary, as we recall certain days in summer which we found too hot while they lasted, and from which only after they have passed do we extract their unalloyed essence of pure gold and indestructible azure.

So that these few years imposed upon my memory of Albertine, which made them so painful, successive colourings, the different modulations, the embers, not only of their seasons or of their hours, from late afternoons in June to winter evenings, from moonlight on the sea to daybreak on the way home, from snow in Paris to fallen leaves at Saint-Cloud, but also of each of the particular ideas of Albertine that I successively formed, of the physical aspect in which I pictured her at each of those moments, the degree of frequency with which I had seen her during that season, which itself appeared consequently more or less dispersed or compact, the anxieties which she might have caused me by keeping me waiting, the desire which I had for her at such and such a moment, the hopes formed and then shattered—all this modified the character of my retrospective sadness fully as much as the impressions of light or of perfume which were associated with it, and complemented each of the solar years through which I had lived and which, simply with their springs, their autumns, their winters, were already so sad because of the inseparable memory of her, endowed it with a sort of sentimental counterpart in which the hours were defined not by the sun's position, but by the time spent waiting for a rendezvous, in which the length of the days or the changes in the temperature were measured by the soaring of my hopes, the progress of our intimacy, the gradual transformation of her face, the journeys she had made, the frequency and style of the letters she had written me during her absence, her eagerness, greater or lesser, to see me on her return. And lastly, if these changes of weather, these variegated days, each brought me back a different Albertine, it was not only through the evocation of similar moments. It will be remembered that always, even before I began to love, each season had made me a different person, having other desires because he had other perceptions, a person who, having dreamed only of cliffs and storms overnight, if the indiscreet spring daybreak had insinuated a scent of roses through the gaps in the ill-fitting enclosure of his sleep, would wake up on the way to Italy. Even in the course of my love, had not the volatile state of my emotional climate, the varying pressure of my beliefs, had they not one day reduced the visibility of the love that I was feeling, and the next day indefinitely extended it, one day embellished it to a smile, another day condensed it to a storm? We exist only by virtue of what we possess, we possess only what is really present to us, and many of our memories, our moods, our ideas sail away on a voyage of their own until they are lost to sight! Then we can no longer take them into account in the total which is our personality. But they know of secret paths by which to return to us. And on certain nights, having gone to sleep almost without missing Albertine any more—we can only miss what we remember—on awakening I found a whole fleet of memories which had come to cruise upon the surface of my clearest consciousness and which I could distinguish perfectly. Then I wept over what I could see so plainly, though the night before it had been non-existent to me. In an instant, Albertine's name, her death, had changed their meaning; her betrayals had suddenly resumed their old importance.

How could she have seemed dead to me when now, in order to think of her, I had at my disposal only those same images one or other of which I used to recall when she was alive? Either swift-moving and bent over the mythological wheel of her bicycle, strapped on rainy days inside the warrior tunic of her waterproof which moulded her breasts, her head turbaned and dressed with snakes, when she spread terror through the streets of Balbec; or else on the evenings when we had taken champagne into the woods of Chantepie, her voice provocative and altered, her face suffused with warm pallor, reddened only on the cheekbones, and when, unable to make it out in the darkness of the carriage, I drew her into the moonlight in order to see it more clearly, the face I was now trying in vain to recapture, to see again in a darkness that would never end. A little statuette on the drive to the island in the Bois, a still and plump face with coarse-grained skin at the pianola, she was thus by turns rain-soaked and swift, provoking and diaphanous, motionless and smiling, an angel of music. In this way each one was attached to a moment, to the date of which I found myself carried back when I saw again that particular Albertine. And these moments of the past do not remain still; they retain in our memory the motion which drew them towards the future—towards a future which has itself become the past—drawing us along in their train. Never had I caressed the waterproofed Albertine of the rainy days; I wanted to ask her to take off that armour, in order to experience with her the love of the tented field, the fraternity of travel. But this was no longer possible, for she was dead. Neither, for fear of corrupting her, had I ever shown any sign of comprehension on the evenings when she seemed to be offering me pleasures which, but for my self-restraint, she might not perhaps have sought from others, and which aroused in me now a frantic desire. I should not have found them the same in any other woman, but I might scour the whole world now without encountering the woman who was prepared to give them to me, for Albertine was dead. It seemed that I had to choose between two facts, to decide which of them was true, to such an extent was the fact of Albertine's death—arising for me from a reality which I had not known, her life in Touraine—in contradiction with all my thoughts of her, my desires, my regrets, my tenderness, my rage, my jealousy. So great a wealth of memories borrowed from the treasury of her life, such a profusion of feelings evoking, implicating her life, seemed to make it incredible that Albertine should be dead. Such a profusion of feelings, for my memory, in preserving my affection, left it all its variety. It was not Albertine alone who was a succession of moments, it was also myself. My love for her was not simple: to a curiosity about the unknown had been added a sensual desire, and to a feeling of almost conjugal sweetness, at one moment indifference, at another a furious jealousy. I was not one man only, but as it were the march-past of a composite army in which there were passionate men, indifferent men, jealous men—jealous men not one of whom was jealous of the same woman. And no doubt it would be from this that one day would come the cure for which I had no wish. In a composite mass, the elements may one by one, without our noticing it, be replaced by others, which others again eliminate, until in the end a change has been brought about which it would be impossible to conceive if we were a single person. The complexity of my love, of my person, multiplied and diversified my sufferings. And yet they could still be ranged in the two categories whose alternation had made up the whole life of my love for Albertine, swayed alternately by trust and by jealous suspicion.

If I found it difficult to imagine that Albertine, so alive in me (wearing as I did the double harness of the present and the past), was dead, perhaps it was equally paradoxical in me that this suspicion of the misdeeds which Albertine, stripped now of the flesh that had enjoyed them, of the mind that had conceived the desire for them, was no longer either capable of or responsible for, should excite in me such suffering, which I should only have blessed could I have seen it as the token of the spiritual reality of a person materially non-existent, instead of the reflexion, destined itself to fade, of impressions that she had made on me in the past. A woman who could no longer experience pleasures with others ought no longer to have excited my jealousy, if only my tenderness had been able to come to the surface. But it was precisely this that was impossible, since it could not find its object, Albertine, except among memories in which she was still alive. Since, merely by thinking of her, I brought her back to life, her infidelities could never be those of a dead woman, the moment at which she had committed them becoming the present moment, not only for Albertine, but for that one of my various selves thus suddenly evoked who happened to be thinking of her. So that no anachronism could ever separate the indissoluble couple, in which each new culprit was immediately mated with a jealous lover, pitiable and always contemporaneous. I had, during the last months, kept her shut up in my own house. But in my imagination now, Albertine was free; she was abusing her freedom, was prostituting herself to this person or that. Formerly, I used constantly to think of the uncertainty of the future that stretched before us, and endeavour to read its message. And now, what lay ahead of me, like a counterpart of the future—as worrying as the future because it was equally uncertain, equally difficult to decipher, equally mysterious, and crueller still because I did not have, as with the future, the possibility, or the illusion, of influencing it, and also because it would go on unfolding throughout the whole length of my life without my companion's being present to soothe the anguish that it caused me—was no longer Albertine's future, it was her past. Her past? That is the wrong word, since for jealousy there can be neither past nor future, and what it imagines is invariably the present.

Atmospheric changes, provoking other changes in the inner man, awaken forgotten selves, counteract the torpor of habit, restore their old force to certain memories, to certain sufferings. How much more so with me if this change of weather recalled to me the weather in which Albertine, at Balbec, in the lashing rain, had set out, heaven knows why, on long rides, in the clinging tunic of her waterproof! If she had lived, no doubt today, in this so similar weather, she would be setting out on a comparable expedition in Touraine. Since she could do so no longer, I ought not to have suffered from the thought; but, as with people who have lost a limb, the slightest change in the weather revived the pain I felt in the limb that no longer existed.

Then a recollection that had not come back to me for a long time—for it had remained dissolved in the fluid and invisible expanse of my memory—suddenly crystallised. Many years ago, when somebody mentioned her bath-wrap, Albertine had blushed. At that time I was not jealous of her. But since then I had intended to ask her if she could remember that conversation, and why she had blushed. It had preoccupied me all the more because I had been told that the two girls who were friends of Léa's frequented the bathing establishment of the hotel, and, it was said, not merely for the purpose of taking showers. But, for fear of annoying Albertine, or else pending some more opportune moment, I had always put off mentioning it to her and in time had ceased to think about it. And all of a sudden, some time after Albertine's death, I recalled this memory, stamped with the character, at once tormenting and solemn, of puzzles left for ever insoluble by the death of the one person who could have explained them. Might I not at least try to find out whether Albertine had ever done anything wrong or even behaved suspiciously in that bathing establishment? By sending someone to Balbec, I might perhaps succeed in doing so. Had she been alive, I should doubtless have been unable to learn anything. But tongues become strangely loosened and will readily talk about a misdeed when the culprit's resentment need no longer be feared. As the constitution of our imagination, which has remained rudimentary and oversimplified (not having undergone the countless transformations which improve upon the primitive models of human inventions, whether it be the barometer, the balloon, the telephone, or anything else, which become barely recognisable in their ultimate perfection), allows us to see only a very few things at one time, the memory of the bathing establishment occupied the whole field of my inner vision. It was as though nothing else had ever happened in the whole of Albertine's life.

Sometimes I came into collision in the dark lanes of sleep with one of those bad dreams which are not very serious because for one thing the sadness they engender lasts for barely an hour after we awake, like the faintness caused by an artificial soporific, and for another we encounter them only very rarely, no more than once in two or three years. And, moreover, it remains uncertain whether we have encountered them before, whether they have not rather that aspect of not being seen for the first time which is projected on to them by an illusion, a subdivision (for duplication would not be a strong enough term). Of course, since I entertained doubts as to the life and the death of Albertine, I ought long since to have begun to make inquiries, but the same lassitude, the same cowardice which had made me give way to Albertine when she was with me prevented me from undertaking anything since I had ceased to see her. And yet, from a weakness that has dragged on for years, a flash of energy sometimes emerges. I decided to make this investigation at least, partial though it was.

I wondered who I could best send down to make inquiries on the spot, at Balbec. Aimé seemed to me to be a suitable person. Apart from his thorough knowledge of the place, he belonged to that category of working-class people who have a keen eye to their own advantage, are loyal to those they serve and indifferent to any form of morality, and of whom—because, if we pay them well, they prove themselves, in their obedience to our will, as incapable of indiscretion, lethargy or dishonesty as they are devoid of scruples—we say: "They are excellent people." In such we can have absolute confidence. When Aimé had gone, I thought how much more to the point it would have been if I could now interrogate Albertine herself about what he was going to try to find out down there. And at once the thought of this question which I would have liked to put, which it seemed to me that I was about to put to her, having brought Albertine to my side, not by dint of a conscious effort of resuscitation but as though by one of those chance encounters which, as is the case with photographs that are not posed, with snapshots, always make the person appear more alive, at the same time as I imagined our conversation I became aware of its impossibility; I had just approached from a new angle the idea that Albertine was dead, Albertine who inspired in me that tenderness we feel for absent ones the sight of whom does not come to correct the embellished image, inspiring also sorrow at the thought that this absence was eternal and that the poor child had been deprived for ever of the joys of life. And immediately, by an abrupt transposition, from the torments of jealousy I passed to the despair of separation.

What filled my heart now, instead of odious suspicions, was the affectionate memory of hours of confiding tenderness spent with the sister that her death had really deprived me of, since my grief was related not to what Albertine had been to me, but to what my heart, anxious to participate in the most general emotions of love, had gradually persuaded me that she was; then I became aware that the life that had bored me so (or so I thought) had been on the contrary delightful; the briefest moments spent in talking to her about even the most trivial things were now augmented, blended with a pleasure which at the time—it is true—had not been perceived by me, but which was already the cause of my having sought those moments so persistently to the exclusion of any others; the most trivial incidents which I recalled, a movement she had made in the carriage by my side, or when sitting down to dinner facing me in her room, sent through my heart a surge of sweet sadness which gradually overwhelmed it altogether.

That room in which we used to dine had never seemed to me attractive; I had told Albertine that it was, merely in order that she should be content to live in it. Now, the curtains, the chairs, the books, had ceased to be a matter of indifference to me. Art is not alone in imparting charm and mystery to the most insignificant things; pain is endowed with the same power to bring them into intimate relation with ourselves. At the time I had paid no attention to the dinner which we had eaten together after our return from the Bois, before I went to the Verdurins', and towards the beauty, the solemn sweetness of which I now turned with my eyes full of tears. An impression of love is out of proportion to the other impressions of life, but when it is lost in their midst we are incapable of appreciating it. It is not from immediately below, in the tumult of the street and amid the thronging houses nearby, but when we have moved away, that, from the slope of a neighbouring hill, at a distance from which the whole town seems to have vanished or forms only a confused heap at ground level, we can appreciate, in the calm detachment of solitude and dusk, the towering splendour of a cathedral, unique, enduring and pure. I tried to embrace the image of Albertine through my tears as I thought of all the serious and sensible things that she had said that evening.

One morning, I thought I saw the oblong shape of a hill swathed in mist, and sniffed the warm odour of a cup of chocolate, while my heart was horribly wrung by the memory of the afternoon on which Albertine had come to see me and I had kissed her for the first time: the fact was that I had heard the hiccuping of the hot-water system which had just been turned on. And I flung angrily away an invitation which Françoise brought me from Mme Verdurin. How much more forcibly the impression I had felt when I went to dine for the first time at La Raspelière, that death does not strike us all at the same age, overcame me now that Albertine had died so young, while Brichot continued to dine with Mme Verdurin who was still entertaining and would perhaps continue to entertain for many years to come! At once the name of Brichot recalled to me the close of that same evening when he had accompanied me home, when I had seen from the street below the light of Albertine's lamp. I had already thought of it many times, but I had not approached this memory from the same angle. For, if our memories do indeed belong to us, they do so after the fashion of those country properties which have little hidden gates of which we ourselves are often unaware, and which someone in the neighbourhood opens for us, so that from one direction at least which is new to us, we find ourselves back in our own house. Then, when I thought of the void which I should now find on returning home, when I realised that never again would I see Albertine's window from below, that its light was extinguished for ever, I remembered how that evening, on leaving Brichot, I had felt irritated and regretful at my inability to roam the streets and make love elsewhere, and I saw how greatly I had been mistaken, that it was only because the treasure whose reflexions came down to me from above had seemed to be entirely in my possession that I had failed to appreciate its value, so that it appeared necessarily inferior to pleasures, however slight, whose value I estimated in seeking to imagine them. I understood how much this light, which seemed to me to issue from a prison, contained for me a plenitude of life and sweetness, this light which had intoxicated me for a moment, and then on the evening when Albertine had slept under the same roof as me, at Balbec, had appeared for ever impossible. I was perceiving that this life I had led in Paris, in a home of mine which was also a home of hers, was precisely the realisation of that profound peace I had dreamt of.

Remembering the conversation I had had with Albertine after our return from the Bois before that last party at the Verdurins', I would have been inconsolable had I felt that it had never occurred, that conversation which had to some extent involved Albertine in my intellectual life and in certain respects had made us one. For no doubt, if I returned with tender emotion to her intelligence and her sweetness to me, it was not because they had been any greater than those of other persons whom I had known; had not Mme de Cambremer said to me at Balbec: "What! you could be spending your days with Elstir, who is a genius, and you spend them with your cousin!" Albertine's intelligence pleased me because, by association, it reminded me of what I called her sweetness, as we call the sweetness of a fruit a certain sensation which exists only in our palate. And in fact, when I thought of Albertine's intelligence, my lips instinctively protruded and savoured a memory of which I preferred that the reality should remain external to me and should consist in the objective superiority of a person. There could be no denying that I had known people whose intelligence was greater. But the infinitude of love, or its egoism, brings it about that the people whom we love are those whose intellectual and moral physiognomy is least objectively defined in our eyes; we alter them incessantly to suit our desires and fears, we do not separate them from ourselves, they are simply a vast, vague arena in which to exteriorise our emotions. We do not have as clear an outline of our own body, into which so many sensations of pain and pleasure perpetually flow, as we have of a tree or a house or a passer-by. And where I had been wrong was perhaps in not making a greater effort to know Albertine in herself. Just as, from the point of view of her charm, I had long considered only the different positions that she occupied in my memory on the plane of the years, and had been surprised to see that she had become spontaneously enriched with modifications which were not due merely to the difference of perspective, so I ought to have sought to understand her character as that of an ordinary person, and thus perhaps, grasping the reason for her persistence in keeping her secret from me, might have avoided prolonging between us, through that strange tenacity, the conflict which had led to her death. And I then felt, together with an intense pity for her, a shame at having survived her. It seemed to me indeed, in the hours when I suffered least, that I had somehow benefited from her death, for a woman is of greater utility to our life if, instead of being an element of happiness in it, she is an instrument of suffering, and there is not a woman in the world the possession of whom is as precious as that of the truths which she reveals to us by causing us to suffer. In these moments, juxtaposing the deaths of my grandmother and of Albertine, I felt that my life was defiled by a double murder from which only the cowardice of the world could absolve me. I had dreamed of being understood by Albertine, of not being misjudged by her, thinking that it was for the great happiness of being understood, of not being misjudged, when so many other people could have done it better. One wants to be understood because one wants to be loved, and one wants to be loved because one loves. The understanding of others is a matter of indifference to us and their love importunate. My joy at having possessed a little of Albertine's intelligence and of her heart arose not from their intrinsic worth, but from the fact that this possession was a stage further towards the complete possession of Albertine, a possession which had been my goal and my chimera ever since the day when I had first set eyes on her. When we speak of the "niceness" of a woman, we are doing no more perhaps than project outside ourselves the pleasure that we feel in seeing her, like children when they say: "My dear little bed, my dear little pillow, my dear little hawthorns." Which explains, incidentally, why men never say of a woman who is not unfaithful to them: "She is so nice," and say it so often of a woman by whom they are betrayed.

Mme de Cambremer was right in thinking that Elstir's intellectual charm was greater. But one cannot judge in the same way the charm of a person who is external to oneself like every other person, painted upon the horizon of one's mind, and that of a person who, as a result of an error in localisation consequent upon certain accidents but nevertheless tenacious, has lodged herself in one's own body to the point where wondering retrospectively whether or not she looked at a woman on a particular day in the corridor of a little seaside railway-train causes one the same pain as would a surgeon probing for a bullet in one's heart. A simple slice of bread, but one that we eat, gives us more pleasure than all the ortolans, leverets and rock-partridges that were set before Louis XV, and the blade of grass quivering a few inches in front of our eyes as we lie on the hillside may conceal from us the vertiginous summit of a mountain if the latter is several miles away.

Moreover, our error does not lie in prizing the intelligence and amiability of a woman whom we love, however slight they may be. Our error is to remain indifferent to the amiability and intelligence of others. Falsehood begins to cause us the indignation, and kindness the gratitude, which they ought always to arouse in us, only if they come from a woman whom we love, and physical desire has the marvellous faculty of giving intelligence its true value and providing solid foundations for the moral life. Never should I find again that divine thing, a person with whom I could talk freely of everything, in whom I could confide. Confide? But did not others offer me greater confidence than Albertine? With others, did I not have more extensive conversations? The fact is that confidence and conversation are ordinary things in themselves, and what does it matter if they are less than perfect if only there enters into them love, which alone is divine. I could see Albertine now, seated at her pianola, pink-faced beneath her dark hair; I could feel against my lips, which she would try to part, her tongue, her maternal, incomestible, nutritious, hallowed tongue, whose secret dewy flame, even when she merely ran it over the surface of my neck or my stomach, gave to those caresses of hers, superficial but somehow imparted by the inside of her flesh, externalised like a piece of material reversed to show its lining, as it were the mysterious sweetness of a penetration.

I cannot even say that what I felt at the loss of all those moments of sweetness which nothing could ever restore to me was despair. To feel despair, we must still be attached to that life which can no longer be anything but unhappy. I had been in despair at Balbec when I saw the day break and realised that none of the days to come could ever be a happy one for me. I had remained just as selfish since then, but the self to which I was now attached, the self which constituted those vital reserves that bring the instinct of self-preservation into play, this self was no longer alive; when I thought of my inner strength, of my vital force, of what was best in me, I thought of a certain treasure which I had possessed (which I had been alone in possessing since others could not know exactly the feeling, hidden within myself, that it had inspired in me) and which no one could ever again take from me since I possessed it no longer. And in fact I had only ever possessed it because I had wanted to imagine myself as possessing it. I had not merely committed the imprudence, in looking at Albertine with my lips and lodging the treasure in my heart, of making it live within me, and that other imprudence of combining a domestic love with the pleasure of the senses. I had sought also to persuade myself that our relations were love, that we were mutually practising the relations that are called love, because she obediently returned the kisses that I gave her. And through having acquired the habit of believing this, I had lost not merely a woman whom I loved but a woman who loved me, my sister, my child, my tender mistress. And on the whole I had had a happiness and a misfortune which Swann had not experienced, for, after all, during the whole of the time in which he had loved Odette and had been so jealous of her, he had barely seen her, having found it so difficult, on certain days when she put him off at the last moment, to gain admission to her. But afterwards he had had her to himself, as his wife, and until the day of his death. I, on the contrary, while I was so jealous of Albertine, more fortunate than Swann, had had her with me in my own house. I had experienced in actuality what Swann had so often dreamed of and had experienced only when he had become indifferent to it. But, after all, I had not managed to keep Albertine as he had kept Odette. She had gone, she was dead. For nothing ever repeats itself exactly, and the most analogous lives which, thanks to kinship of character and similarity of circumstances, we may select in order to represent them as symmetrical, remain in many respects opposed. By losing my life I should not have lost very much; I should have lost only an empty form, the empty frame of a work of art. Indifferent as to what I might henceforth put into it, but happy and proud to think of what it had contained, I dwelt upon the memory of those hours of sweetness, and this moral support gave me a feeling of well-being which the approach of death itself would not have disturbed.

How she used to hasten to see me at Balbec when I sent for her, lingering only to sprinkle scent on her hair to please me! These images of Balbec and Paris which I loved thus to see again were the pages, still so recent, and so quickly turned, of her short life. All this, which for me was only memory, had been for her action, action speeding headlong, as in a tragedy, towards a swift death. For people develop in one way inside us, but in another way outside us (I had felt this strongly on those evenings when I remarked in Albertine an enrichment of qualities which was due not only to my memory), and these two ways inevitably react upon each other. Although, in seeking to know Albertine, then to possess her entirely, I had merely obeyed the need to reduce by experiment to elements meanly akin to those of our own ego the mystery of every being, I had been unable to do so without in my turn influencing Albertine's life. Perhaps my wealth, the prospect of a brilliant marriage, had attracted her; my jealousy had kept her; her kindness, or her intelligence, or her sense of guilt, or her shrewd cunning, had made her accept, and had led me on to make harsher and harsher, a captivity in chains forged simply by the internal development of my mental toil, but which had none the less had repercussions on Albertine's life, themselves destined, by a natural backlash, to pose new and ever more painful problems to my psychology, since from my prison she had escaped to go and kill herself on a horse which but for me she would not have owned, leaving me, even after she was dead, with suspicions the verification of which, if it was to come, would perhaps be more painful to me than the discovery at Balbec that Albertine had known Mlle Vinteuil, since Albertine would no longer be there to soothe me. So that the long plaint of the soul which thinks that it is living shut up within itself is a monologue in appearance only, since the echoes of reality alter its course, and a given life is like an essay in subjective psychology spontaneously pursued, but providing from a distance the "plot" for the purely realistic novel of another reality, another existence, the vicissitudes of which come in their turn to inflect the curve and change the direction of the psychological essay. How highly geared had been the mechanism, how rapid had been the evolution of our love, and, notwithstanding a few delays, interruptions and hesitations at the start, as in certain of Balzac's tales or Schumann's ballads, how sudden the dénouement! It was in the course of this last year, as long as a century to me—so often had Albertine changed position in relation to my thoughts between Balbec and her departure from Paris, and also, independently of me and often without my knowing it, changed in herself—that I must place the whole of that happy life of tenderness which had lasted so short a while and which yet appeared to me with an amplitude, almost an immensity, which now was for ever impossible and yet was indispensable to me. Indispensable without perhaps having been in itself and at the outset something necessary, since I should not have known Albertine had I not read in an archaeological treatise a description of the church at Balbec, had not Swann, by telling me that this church was almost Persian, directed my taste to the Byzantine Norman, had not a financial syndicate, by erecting at Balbec a hygienic and comfortable hotel, made my parents decide to grant my wish and send me to Balbec. To be sure, in that Balbec so long desired, I had not found the Persian church of my dreams, nor the eternal mists. Even the famous 1.22 train had not corresponded to my mental picture of it. But in exchange for what our imagination leads us to expect and we give ourselves so much futile trouble trying to find, life gives us something which we were very far from imagining. Who would have told me at Combray, when I lay waiting for my mother's good-night with so heavy a heart, that those anxieties would be healed, and would then break out again one day, not for my mother, but for a girl who would at first be no more, against the horizon of the sea, than a flower upon which my eyes would daily be invited to gaze, but a thinking flower in whose mind I was so childishly anxious to occupy a prominent place that I was distressed by her not being aware that I knew Mme de Villeparisis? Yes, it was for the good-night kiss of such an unknown girl that, in years to come, I was to suffer as intensely as I had suffered as a child when my mother did not come up to my room. And yet if Swann had not spoken to me of Balbec, I should never have known this Albertine who had become so necessary, of love for whom my soul was now almost exclusively composed. Her life would perhaps have been longer, mine would have been devoid of what was now making it a martyrdom. And thus it seemed to me that, by my entirely selfish love, I had allowed Albertine to die just as I had murdered my grandmother. Even later, even after I had already got to know her at Balbec, it is possible that I might not have loved her as I eventually did. For, when I gave up Gilberte and knew that I might love another woman some day, I hardly dared entertain a doubt as to whether, at any rate as regards the past, I could have loved anyone else but Gilberte. Whereas in the case of Albertine I no longer even had any doubt, I was sure that it might well not have been her that

I loved, that it might have been someone else. It would have been enough that Mlle de Stermaria, on the evening when I was to dine with her on the island in the Bois, should not have cancelled the appointment. There was still time then, and it would have been upon Mlle de Stermaria that I would have directed that activity of the imagination which makes us extract from a woman so special a notion of individuality that she appears to us unique in herself and predestined and necessary for us. At the most, adopting an almost physiological point of view, I could say that I might have been able to feel that same exclusive love for another woman but not for *any* other woman. For Albertine, plump and dark, did not resemble Gilberte, slim and fair, and yet they were fashioned of the same healthy stuff, and above the same sensual cheeks there was a look in the eyes of both whose meaning was difficult to grasp. They were women of a sort that would not attract the attention of men who for their part would go mad about other women who "meant nothing" to me. A man has almost always the same way of catching cold, of falling ill; that is to say, he requires for it to happen a particular combination of circumstances; it is natural that when he falls in love he should love a certain type of woman, a type which for that matter is very widespread. The first glances from Albertine which had set me dreaming were not absolutely different from Gilberte's first glances. I could almost believe that the obscure personality, the sensuality, the wilful, cunning nature of Gilberte had returned to tempt me, incarnate this time in Albertine's body, a body quite different and yet not without analogies. In Albertine's case, thanks to a wholly different life shared with me where no fissure of distraction or obliviousness had been able to penetrate a block of thoughts in which a painful preoccupation maintained a permanent cohesion, her living body had not, like Gilberte's, ceased one day to be that in which I found what I subsequently recognised as being to me (what they would not have been to other men) the attributes of feminine charm. But she was dead. I would forget her. Who could say whether the same qualities of rich blood, of uneasy brooding would then return one day to create turmoil in me? But in what feminine form they would be embodied I could not foretell. The example of Gilberte would as little have enabled me to form an idea of Albertine and guess that I should fall in love with her, as the memory of Vinteuil's sonata would have enabled me to imagine his septet. Indeed, what was more, the first few times I had seen Albertine, I had even managed to believe that it was others I would love. Moreover, she might even have appeared to me, had I met her a year earlier, as dull as a grey sky in which dawn has not yet broken. If I had changed in relation to her, she herself had changed too, and the girl who had come and sat on my bed on the day of my letter to Mlle de Stermaria was no longer the same girl I had known at Balbec, whether by virtue of the explosion of womanhood which occurs at the age of puberty, or as a result of circumstances which I was never able to discover. In any case, even if the woman I was one day to love must to a certain extent resemble her, that is to say if my choice of a woman was not entirely free, this nevertheless meant that, directed in a manner that was perhaps predetermined, it was directed towards something more considerable than an individual, towards a type of woman, and this removed all necessitude from my love for Albertine.

We are well aware that the woman whose face we have before our eyes more constantly than light itself, since even with our eyes shut we never cease for an instant to adore her beautiful eyes, her beautiful nose, to arrange opportunities of seeing them again—that this woman who to us is unique might well have been another if we had been in a different town from the one in which we met her, if we had explored other quarters of the town, if we had frequented a different salon. Unique, we suppose? She is legion. And yet she is compact and indestructible in our loving eyes, irreplaceable for a long time to come by any other. The truth is that this woman has only raised to life by a sort of magic countless elements of tenderness existing in us already in a fragmentary state, which she has assembled, joined together, effacing every gap between them, and it is we ourselves who by giving her her features have supplied all the solid matter of the beloved object. Whence it arises that even if we are only one among a thousand to her and perhaps the last of them all, to us she is the only one, the one towards whom our whole life gravitates. It was, indeed, true that I had been quite well aware that this love was not inevitable, not only because it might have crystallised round Mlle de Stermaria, but even apart from that, through knowing the feeling itself, finding it to be only too like what it had been for others, and also sensing it to be vaster than Albertine, enveloping her, unconscious of her, like a tide swirling round a tiny rock. But gradually, by dint of living with Albertine, I was no longer able to fling off the chains which I myself had forged; the habit of associating

Albertine's person with the sentiment which she had not inspired made me none the less believe that it was peculiar to her, as habit gives to the mere association of ideas between two phenomena, according to a certain school of philosophy, the illusory force and necessity of a law of causation. I had thought that my connexions, my wealth, would dispense me from suffering, and only too effectively perhaps, since it seemed to dispense me from feeling, loving, imagining; I envied a poor country girl whom the absence of connexions, even by telegraph, allows to day-dream for months on end about a sorrow which she cannot artificially put to sleep. And now I began to realise that if, in the case of Mme de Guermantes, endowed with everything that must make the gulf between her and myself infinite, I had seen that gulf suddenly bridged by abstract opinion, for which social advantages are no more than inert and transmutable matter, so, in a similar albeit converse fashion, my social relations, my wealth, all the material means by which not only my own position but the civilisation of my age enabled me to profit, had done no more than postpone the day of reckoning in my hand-to-hand struggle against the contrary, inflexible will of Albertine, upon which no pressure had had any effect. True, I had been able to exchange telegrams and telephone messages with Saint-Loup, to remain in constant communication with the post-office at Tours, but had not the delay in waiting for them proved useless, the result nil? And country girls without social advantages or connexions, or human beings in general before these improvements of civilisation—do they not suffer less, because one desires less, because one regrets less what one has always known to be inaccessible, what for that reason has continued to seem unreal? One desires more the woman who has yet to give herself to us; hope anticipates possession; regret is an amplifier of desire. Mlle de Stermaria's refusal to come and dine with me on the island in the Bois was what had prevented her from becoming the object of my love. It might also have sufficed to make me love her if afterwards I had seen her again in time. As soon as I knew that she would not come, entertaining the improbable hypothesis—which had been proved correct—that perhaps she had a jealous lover who kept her away from other men and that therefore I should never see her again, I had suffered so intensely that I would have given anything in the world to see her, and it was one of the most desolating agonies that I had ever felt that Saint-Loup's arrival had assuaged. But after we have reached a certain age our loves, our mistresses, are begotten of our anguish; our past, and the physical lesions in which it is recorded, determine our future. In the case of Albertine in particular, the fact that it was not necessarily she that I was predestined to love was inscribed, even without those circumambient loves, in the history of my love for her, that is to say for herself and her friends. For it was not even a love like my love for Gilberte, but was created by division among a number of girls. Conceivably it was because of her and because they appeared to me more or less similar to her that I had been attracted to her friends. The fact remains that for a long time it was possible for me to waver between them all, for my choice to stray from one to another, and when I thought that I preferred one, it was enough that another should keep me waiting, should refuse to see me, to make me feel the first premonitions of love for her. Often it might have happened that when Andrée was coming to see me at Balbec, a little before her visit, if Albertine had let me down, my heart would beat without ceasing, I felt that I would never see her again and that it was she whom I loved. And when Andrée came it was quite truthfully that I said to her (as I said to her in Paris after I had learned that Albertine had known Mlle Vinteuil) what she might suppose me to be saying with an ulterior motive, insincerely, what I would indeed have said and in the same words had I been happy with Albertine the day before: "Alas! if you had only come sooner, now I love someone else." Even then, in this case of Andrée being replaced by Albertine after I learned that the latter had known Mlle Vinteuil, my love had alternated between them, so that after all there had been only one love at a time. But there had been previous cases where I had fallen out with two of the girls. The one who took the first step towards a reconciliation would restore my peace of mind, but it was the other that I would love if she remained hostile, which does not mean that it was not with the former that I would form a definitive tie, for she would console me—however ineffectually—for the harshness of the other, whom I would end by forgetting if she did not return to me. Now, it sometimes happened that, convinced though I was that one or the other at least would come back to me, for some time neither of them did so. My anguish was therefore twofold, and twofold my love; pending the likelihood of my ceasing to love the one who came back, in the meantime I continued to suffer on account of them both. It is our fate at a certain stage in life, which may come to us quite early, to be made less enamoured by a person than by a desertion, in which event we end by knowing one thing and one thing only about the person, her face being dim, her soul non-existent, our preference quite recent and unexplained: namely that what we need to make our suffering cease is a message from her: "May I come and see you?" My separation from Albertine on the day when Françoise had said to me: "Mademoiselle Albertine has gone" was like an allegory of countless other separations. For very often, in order that we may discover that we are in love, perhaps indeed in order that we may fall in love, the day of separation must first have come.

In these cases, when it is an unkept appointment, a letter of refusal, that dictates one's choice, one's imagination, goaded by suffering, sets about its work so swiftly, fashions with so frenzied a rapidity a love that had scarcely begun and remained inchoate, destined, for months past, to remain a rough sketch, that there are times when one's intelligence, which has been unable to keep pace with one's heart, cries out in astonishment: "But you must be mad. What are these strange thoughts that are making you so miserable? None of this is real life." And indeed at that moment, had one not been roused to action by the unfaithful one, a few healthy distractions that would calm one's heart physically would be sufficient to nip one's infatuation in the bud. In any case, if this life with Albertine was not in its essence necessary, it had become indispensable to me. I had trembled when I was in love with Mme de Guermantes because I said to myself that, with her too abundant means of seduction, not only beauty but position and wealth, she would be too much at liberty to belong to too many people, that I should have too little hold over her. Albertine, being penniless and obscure, must have been anxious to marry me. And yet I had not been able to possess her exclusively. Whatever our social position, however wise our precautions, when the truth is confessed we have no hold over the life of another person. Why had she not said to me: "I have those tastes"? I would have yielded, would have allowed her to gratify them. In a novel I had read there was a woman whom no objurgation from the man who was in love with her could induce to speak. When I read the book, I had thought this situation absurd; had I been the hero, I assured myself, I would first of all have forced the woman to speak, then we could have come to an understanding. What was the good of all those futile miseries? But I saw now that we are not free to refrain from forging the chains of our own misery, and that however well we may know our own will, other people do not obey it.

And yet how often we had expressed them, those painful, those ineluctable truths which dominated us and to which we were blind, the truth of our feelings, the truth of our destiny, how often we had expressed them without knowing it, without meaning it, in words which doubtless we ourselves thought mendacious but the prophetic force of which had been established by subsequent events. I remembered many words that each of us had uttered without knowing at the time the truth that they contained, which indeed we had said thinking that we were play-acting and yet the falseness of which was very slight, very uninteresting, wholly confined within our pitiable insincerity, compared with what they contained unbeknown to us—lies and errors falling short of the profound reality which neither of us perceived, truth extending beyond it, the truth of our natures, the essential laws of which escape us and require Time before they reveal themselves, the truth of our destinies also. I had believed myself to be lying when I said to her at Balbec: "The more I see you, the more I shall love you" (and yet it was that constant intimacy which, through the medium of jealousy, had attached me so strongly to her), "I feel that I could be of use to you intellectually"; and in Paris: "Do be careful. Remember that if you met with an accident, it would break my heart" (and she: "But I may meet with an accident"); in Paris too, on the evening when I had pretended that I wished to leave her: "Let me look at you once again since presently I shall not be seeing you again, and it will be for ever!" and she, when that same evening she had looked round the room: "To think that I shall never see this room again, those books, that pianola, the whole house, I cannot believe it and yet it's true." In her last letters again, when she had written (probably saying to herself that it was eyewash): "I leave you the best of myself" (and was it not now indeed to the fidelity, to the strength—also too frail, alas—of my memory that her intelligence, her kindness, her beauty were entrusted?) and: "That moment of double twilight, since night was falling and we were about to part, will be effaced from my thoughts only when the darkness is complete" (that sentence written on the eve of the day when her mind had indeed been plunged into complete darkness, and when, in those last brief glimmers which the anguish of the moment subdivides ad infinitum, she had indeed perhaps recalled our last drive together and in that instant when everything forsakes us and we create a faith for ourselves, as atheists turn Christian on the battlefield, she had perhaps summoned to her aid the friend whom she had so often cursed but had so deeply respected, who himself—for all religions are alike—was cruel enough to hope that she had also had time to see herself as she was, to give her last thought to him, to confess her sins at length to him, to die in him).

But to what purpose, since even if, at that moment, she had time to see herself as she was, we had both of us understood where our happiness lay, what we ought to do, only when, only because, that happiness was no longer possible, when and because we could no longer do it—whether it is that, so long as things are possible, we postpone them, or that they cannot assume that force of attraction, that apparent ease of realisation except when, projected on to the ideal void of the imagination, they are removed from their deadening and degrading submersion in physical being. The idea that one will die is more painful than dying, but less painful than the idea that another person is dead, that, becoming once more a still, plane surface after having engulfed a person, a reality extends, without even a ripple at the point of disappearance, from which that person is excluded, in which there no longer exists any will, any knowledge, and from which it is as difficult to reascend to the idea that that person has lived as, from the still recent memory of his life, it is to think that he is comparable with the insubstantial images, the memories, left us by the characters in a novel we have been reading.

At any rate I was glad that before she died she had written me that letter, and above all had sent me that final message which proved to me that she would have returned had she lived. It seemed to me that it was not merely more soothing, but more beautiful also, that the event would have been incomplete without that message, would not have had so markedly the form of art and destiny. In reality it would have been just as markedly so had it been different; for every event is like a mould of a particular shape, and, whatever it may be, it imposes, upon the series of incidents which it has interrupted and seems to conclude, a pattern which we believe to be the only possible one, because we do not know the other which might have been substituted for it.

Why, I repeated to myself, had she not said to me: "I have those tastes"? I would have yielded, would have allowed her to gratify them; at this moment I would be kissing her still. How sad it was to have to remind myself that she had lied to me thus when she swore to me, three days before she left me, that she had never had with Mlle Vinteuil's friend those relations which at the moment when she swore it her blush had confessed! Poor child, she had at least had the honesty to be reluctant to swear that the pleasure of seeing Mlle Vinteuil again had no part in her desire to go that day to the Verdurins'. Why had she not made her admission complete? Perhaps, however, it was partly my fault that she had never, despite all my entreaties which were powerless against her denial, been willing to say to me: "I have those tastes." It was perhaps partly my fault because at Balbec, on the day when, after Mme de Cambremer's visit, I had had things out with Albertine for the first time, and when I was so far from imagining that she could possibly have had anything more than a rather too passionate friendship with Andrée, I had expressed with undue violence my disgust at those proclivities, had condemned them too cat-egorically. I could not recall whether Albertine had blushed when I had naïvely expressed my horror of that sort of thing, for it is often only long afterwards that we long to know what attitude a person adopted at a moment when we were paying no attention to it, an attitude which, later on, when we think again of our con-versation, would elucidate an agonising problem. But in our memory there is a blank, there is no trace of it. And very often we have not paid sufficient attention, at the actual moment, to the things which might even then have seemed to us important, we have not properly heard a sentence, have not noticed a gesture, or else we have forgotten them. And when later on, eager to discover a truth, we work back from deduction to deduction, leafing through our memory like a sheaf of written evidence, when we arrive at that sentence, at that gesture, we find it impossible to remember, and we repeat the process a score of times, in vain: the road goes no further. Had she blushed? I do not know whether she had blushed, but she could not have failed to hear, and the memory of my words had pulled her up later on when perhaps she had been on the point of confessing to me. And now she no longer existed anywhere; I could have scoured the earth from pole to pole without finding Albertine; the reality which had closed over her was once more unbroken, had obliterated every trace of the being who had sunk without trace. She was now no more than a name, like that Mme de Charlus of whom people who had known her said with indifference: "She was charming." But I could not conceive for more than an instant the existence of this reality of which Albertine had no knowledge, for in me she existed only too vividly, in me whose every feeling, every thought, related to her life. Perhaps, if she had known, she would have been touched to see that her lover had not forgotten her, now that her own life was finished, and would have been sensitive to things which in the past had left her indifferent. But as we would choose to abstain from infidelities, however secret, so fearful are we that she whom we love is not abstaining from them, I was terrified by the thought that if the dead do exist somewhere, my grandmother was as well aware of my forgetfulness as Albertine of my remembrance. And when all is said, even in the case of a single dead person, can we be sure that the joy we should feel in learning that she knows certain things would compensate for our alarm at the thought that she knows them *all*; and, however agonising the sacrifice, would we not sometimes forbear to keep those we have loved as friends after their death, for fear of having them also as judges?

My jealous curiosity as to what Albertine might have done was unbounded. I suborned any number of women from whom I learned nothing. If this curiosity was so tenacious, it was because people do not die for us immediately, but remain bathed in a sort of aura of life which bears no relation to true immortality but through which they continue to occupy our thoughts in the same way as when they were alive. It is as though they were travelling abroad. This is a thoroughly pagan survival. Conversely, when we have ceased to love, the curiosity which people arouse dies before they themselves are dead. Thus I would no longer have taken a single step to find out with whom Gilberte had been strolling on a certain evening in the Champs-Elysées. Now, I was well aware that these two forms of curiosity were absolutely identical, had no value in themselves, were incapable of lasting. But I continued to sacrifice everything to the cruel satisfaction of this transient curiosity, although I knew in advance that my enforced separation from Albertine, by the fact of her death, would lead me to the same indifference as had resulted from my voluntary separation from Gilberte.

If she could have known what was going to happen, she would have stayed with me. But this simply amounted to saying that, once she saw herself dead, she would have preferred to remain alive with me. Because of the very contradiction that it implied, such a supposition was absurd. But it was not innocuous, for in imagining how glad Albertine would be, if she could know, if she could retrospectively understand, to come back to me, I saw her before me, I wanted to kiss her, and alas, it was impossible, she would never come back, she was dead.

My imagination sought for her in the sky, at nightfall when, still together, we had gazed at it; beyond that moonlight which she loved, I tried to raise up to her my tenderness so that it might be a consolation to her for being no longer alive, and this love for a being who was now so remote was like a religion; my thoughts rose towards her like prayers. Desire is powerful indeed: it engenders belief; I had believed that Albertine would not leave me because I desired that she should not do so. Because I desired it, I began to believe that she was not dead; I took to reading books about table-turning; I began to believe in the possibility of the immortality of the soul. But that did not suffice me. I required that, after my own death, I should find her again in her body, as though eternity were like life. Life, did I say? I was more exacting still. I should have liked not to be for ever deprived by death of the pleasures of which in any case it is not alone in robbing us. For without it they would eventually have lost their edge; indeed they had already begun to do so through the effect of long-established habit, of fresh curiosities. Besides, had she been alive, Albertine, even physically, would gradually have changed; day by day I would have adapted myself to that change. But my memory, calling up only detached moments of her life, demanded to see her again as she would already have ceased to be had she lived; what it wanted was a miracle that would satisfy the natural and arbitrary limitations of memory, which cannot escape from the past. And yet, with the naïvety of the old theologians, I imagined this living creature vouchsafing me not simply the explanations which she might possibly have given me but, by a final contradiction, those that she had always refused me during her life. And thus, her death being a sort of dream, my love would seem to her an unlooked-for happiness; all I retained of death was the comfort and the optimism of a dénouement which simplifies, which settles everything.

Sometimes it was not so far off, it was not in another world, that I imagined our reunion. Just as, in the past, when I knew Gilberte only from playing with her in the Champs-Elysées, at home in the evening I used to imagine that I was about to receive a letter from her in which she would confess her love for me, that she was about to come into the room, so a similar force of desire, no more troubled by the laws of nature which inhibited it than on the former occasion, in the case of Gilberte (when after all it had not been mistaken since it had had the last word), made me think now that I was about to receive a message from Albertine, informing me that she had indeed had a riding accident but that for romantic reasons (and as, after all, has sometimes happened with people whom we have long believed to be dead) she had not wished me to hear of her recovery and now, repentant, asked to be allowed to come and live with me for ever. And—giving me an insight into the nature of certain mild lunacies in people who otherwise appear sane—I felt co-existing in me the certainty that she was dead and the constant hope that I might see her come into the room.

I had not yet received news from Aimé, although he must by now have reached Balbec. No doubt my inquiry turned upon a secondary point, and one quite arbitrarily chosen. If Albertine's life had been really culpable, it must have contained many other things of far greater importance, which chance had not allowed me to consider as it had in the case of the conversation about the bathing-wrap and Albertine's blushes. But those things precisely did not exist for me since I had not seen them. But it was quite arbitrarily that I had hit upon that particular day and, several years later, was trying to reconstruct it. If Albertine had been a lover of women, there were thousands of other days in her life which I did not know how she had spent and about which it might be just as interesting for me to learn; I might have sent Aimé to many other places in Balbec, to many other towns besides Balbec. But these other days, precisely because I did not know how she had spent them, did not present themselves to my imagination, had no existence for it. Things and people did not begin to exist for me until they assumed in my imagination an individual existence. If there were thousands of others like them, they became for me representative of all the rest. If I had long felt a desire to know, in the matter of my suspicions with regard to Albertine, what exactly had happened in the baths, it was in the same manner in which, in the matter of my desires for women, and although I knew that there were any number of young girls and lady's-maids who could satisfy them and whom chance might just as easily have brought to my notice, I wished to know—since it was they whom Saint-Loup had mentioned to me, they who existed individually for me—the girl who frequented houses of ill-fame and Mme Putbus's maid. The difficulties which my health, my indecision, my "procrastination," as M. de Charlus called it, placed in the way of my carrying anything through, had made me put off from day to day, from month to month, from year to year, the elucidation of certain suspicions as well as the accomplishment of certain desires. But I retained them in my memory, promising myself that I would not forget to learn the truth of them, because they alone obsessed me (since the others had no form in my eyes, did not exist), and also because the very accident that had chosen them out of the surrounding reality gave me a guarantee that it was indeed in them that I should come in contact with a trace of the reality, of the true and coveted life. Besides, is not a single small fact, if it is well chosen, sufficient to enable the experimenter to deduce a general law which will reveal the truth about thousands of analogous facts? Although Albertine might exist in my memory only as she had successively appeared to me in the course of her life, that is, subdivided in accordance with a series of fractions of time, my mind, re-establishing unity in her, made her a single person, and it was on this person that I wished to arrive at a general judgment, to know whether she had lied to me, whether she loved women, whether it was in order to associate with them freely that she had left me. What the woman in the baths would have to say might perhaps put an end for ever to my doubts as to Albertine's proclivities.

My doubts! Alas, I had supposed that it would be immaterial to me, even agreeable, not to see Albertine again, until her departure had revealed to me my error. Similarly her death had shown me how greatly I had been mistaken in believing that I sometimes wished for her death and supposed that it would be my deliverance. So it was that, when I received Aimé's letter, I realised that if I had not until then suffered too painfully from my doubts as to Albertine's virtue it was because in reality they were not doubts at all. My happiness, my life required that Albertine should be virtuous; they had laid it down once and for all that she was. Armed with this self-protective belief, I could with impunity allow my mind to play sadly with suppositions to which it gave a form but lent no credence. I said to myself, "She is perhaps a woman-lover," as we say "I may die tonight"; we say it, but we do not believe it, we make plans for the following day. This explains why, believing mistakenly that I was uncertain whether Albertine did or did not love women, and believing in consequence that a proof of Albertine's guilt would not tell me anything that I had not

often envisaged, I experienced, in the face of the images, insignificant to anyone else, which Aimé's letter evoked for me, an
unexpected anguish, the most painful that I had ever yet felt, and
one that formed with those images, with the image, alas! of
Albertine herself, a sort of precipitate, as they say in chemistry, in
which everything was indivisible and of which the text of Aimé's
letter, which I isolate in a purely conventional fashion, can give no
idea whatsoever, since each of the words that compose it was
immediately transformed, coloured for ever by the suffering it
had just aroused.

"MONSIEUR,
    Monsieur will kindly forgive me for not having written sooner to
Monsieur. The person whom Monsieur instructed me to see had gone
away for a few days, and, anxious to justify the confidence which
Monsieur had placed in me, I did not wish to return empty-handed.
I have just spoken at last to this person who remembers (Mlle A.) very
well." (Aimé, who possessed certain rudiments of culture, meant to put
"Mlle A." in italics or between inverted commas. But when he meant to
put inverted commas he put brackets, and when he meant to put something in brackets he put it between inverted commas. In the same way
Françoise would say that someone *stayed* in my street meaning that he
dwelt there, and that one could *dwell* for a few minutes, meaning *stay*, the
mistakes of popular speech consisting merely, as often as not, in inter-
changing—as for that matter the French language has done—terms
which in the course of centuries have replaced one another.)
"According to her the thing that Monsieur supposed is absolutely certain.
For one thing, it was she who looked after (Mlle A.) whenever she came
to the baths. (Mlle A.) came very often to take her shower with a tall
woman older than herself, always dressed in grey, whom the shower-
attendant without knowing her name recognised from having often seen
her going after girls. But she took no notice of any of them after she met
(Mlle A.). She and (Mlle A.) always shut themselves up in the cabin,
remained there a very long time, and the lady in grey used to give at least
10 francs as a tip to the person I spoke to. As this person said to me, you
can imagine that if they were just stringing beads they wouldn't have
given a ten-franc tip. (Mlle A.) also used to come sometimes with a
woman with a very dark skin and a lorgnette. But (Mlle A.) came most
often with girls younger than herself, especially one with very red hair.
Apart from the lady in grey, the people (Mlle A.) was in the habit of
bringing were not from Balbec and must even quite often have come
from quite a distance. They never went in together, but (Mlle A.) would
come in, and ask for the door of her cabin to be left unlocked—as she was
expecting a friend, and the person I spoke to knew what that meant. This

person could not give me any other details as she did not remember very well, 'which is easy to understand after such a long time.' Besides, this person did not try to find out, because she is very discreet and it was to her advantage because (Mlle A.) brought her in a lot of money. She was quite sincerely touched to hear that she was dead. It is true that so young it is a great calamity for her and for her family. I await Monsieur's orders to know whether I may leave Balbec where I do not think that I can learn anything more. I thank Monsieur again for the little holiday that he has procured me, and which has been very pleasant especially as the weather is as fine as could be. The season promises well for this year. Everyone hopes that Monsieur will come and put in a little apparition.

"I can think of nothing else to say that will interest Monsieur," etc.

To understand how deeply these words penetrated my being, it must be remembered that the questions which I had been asking myself with regard to Albertine were not secondary, insignificant questions, questions of detail, the only questions in fact that one asks about anyone who is not oneself, whereby one is enabled to carry on, wrapped in the imperviousness of one's thoughts, through the midst of suffering, falsehood, vice and death. No, in Albertine's case they were essential questions: In her heart of hearts what was she? What were her thoughts? What were her loves? Did she lie to me? Had my life with her been as lamentable as Swann's life with Odette? Hence Aimé's reply, although it was not a general but a particular reply—indeed precisely because of that—struck home, in Albertine and in myself, to the very depths.

At last I saw before my eyes, in that arrival of Albertine at the baths along the narrow lane with the lady in grey, a fragment of that past which seemed to me no less mysterious, no less horrifying than I had feared when I imagined it enclosed in the memory, in the look in the eyes of Albertine. No doubt anyone but myself might have dismissed as insignificant these details on which, now that Albertine was dead, my inability to secure a denial of them from her conferred the equivalent of a sort of probability. It is indeed probable that for Albertine, even if they had been true, even if she had admitted them, her own misdeeds (whether her conscience had thought them innocent or reprehensible, whether her sensuality had found them exquisite or somewhat insipid) would not have been accompanied by that inexpressible sense of horror from which I was unable to detach them. I myself, with the help of my own love of women, and although they could not have meant the same thing to Albertine, could imagine a little of what she felt. And indeed there was already an initial pain in my picturing her to myself desiring as I had so often desired, lying to me as I had so often lied to her, preoccupied with this or that girl, putting herself out for her, as I had done for Mlle de Stermaria and so many others, for the peasant-girls I met on country roads. Yes, all my own desires helped me to a certain extent to understand hers; it was by this time an immense anguish in which all desires were transformed into torments that were all the more cruel the more intense they had been; as though in this algebra of sensibility they reappeared with the same coefficient but with a minus instead of a plus sign. To Albertine, so far as I was capable of judging her by my own standard, her misdeeds—however anxious she might have been to conceal them from me (which made me suppose that she considered herself guilty or was afraid of hurting me)— because she had planned them to suit her own taste in the clear light of the imagination in which desire operates, must after all have appeared as things of the same kind as the rest of life, pleasures for herself which she had not had the strength to deny herself, griefs for me which she had sought to avoid causing me by concealing them from me, but pleasures and griefs which might be numbered among the other pleasures and griefs of life. But for me, it was from the outside, without my having been forewarned, without my having been able myself to elaborate them, it was from Aimé's letter that there had come to me the visions of Albertine arriving at the baths and preparing her tip.

No doubt it was because in that silent and deliberate arrival of Albertine with the woman in grey I read the assignation they had made, that convention of going to make love in a shower-cabin, which implied an experience of corruption, the well-concealed organisation of a double life, it was because these images brought me the terrible tidings of Albertine's guilt, that they had immediately caused me a physical grief from which they would never be detached. But at once my grief had reacted upon them: an objective fact, an image, differs according to the internal state in which we approach it. And grief is as powerful a modifier of reality as intoxication. Combined with these images, my suffering had at once made of them something absolutely different from what might be for anyone else a lady in grey, a tip, a shower, the street where the purposeful arrival of Albertine with the lady in grey had taken place. All those images—a vista of a life of lies and iniquities such as I had never conceived—my suffering had immediately altered them in their very essence; I did not see them in the light that illuminates earthly spectacles, they were a fragment of another world, of an unknown and accursed planet, a glimpse of Hell. My Hell was the whole region of Balbec, all those neighbouring villages from which, according to Aimé's letter, she frequently collected girls younger than herself whom she took to the baths. That mystery which I had long ago imagined in the country around Balbec and which had been dispelled after I had lived there, which I had then hoped to grasp again when I knew Albertine because, when I saw her pass by on the beach, when I was mad enough to hope that she was not virtuous, I thought that she must be its incarnation—how fearfully now everything that related to Balbec was impregnated with it! The names of those watering-places, Toutainville, Epreville, Incarville, that had become so familiar, so soothing, when I heard them shouted at night as I returned from the Verdurins', now that I thought how Albertine had been staying at one, had gone from there to another, must often have ridden on her bicycle to a third, aroused in me an anxiety more cruel than on the first occasion, when I had observed them with such misgivings from the little local train with my grandmother before arriving at a Balbec which I did not yet know.

It is one of the faculties of jealousy to reveal to us the extent to which the reality of external facts and the sentiments of the heart are an unknown element which lends itself to endless suppositions. We imagine that we know exactly what things are and what people think, for the simple reason that we do not care about them. But as soon as we have a desire to know, as the jealous man has, then it becomes a dizzy kaleidoscope in which we can no longer distinguish anything. Had Albertine been unfaithful to me? With whom? In what house? On what day? On the day when she had said this or that to me, when I remembered that I had in the course of it said this or that? I could not tell. Nor did I know what her feelings were for me, whether they were inspired by self-interest or by affection. And all of a sudden I remembered some trivial incident, for instance that Albertine had wished to go to Saint-Mars-le-Vêtu, saying that the name interested her, and perhaps simply because she had made the acquaintance of some peasant-girl who lived there. But it was useless that Aimé should have informed me of what he had learned from the woman at the baths, since Albertine must remain eternally unaware that he had informed me, the need to know having always been exceeded, in my love for Albertine, by the need to show her that I knew; for this broke down the partition of different illusions that stood between us, without having ever had the result of making her love me more, far from it. And now, since she was dead, the second of these needs had been amalgamated with the effect of the first: the need to picture to myself the conversation in which I would have informed her of what I had learned, as vividly as the conversation in which I would have asked her to tell me what I did not know; that is to say, to see her by my side, to hear her answering me kindly, to see her cheeks become plump again, her eyes shed their malice and assume an air of melancholy; that is to say, to love her still and to forget the fury of my jealousy in the despair of my loneliness. The painful mystery of this impossibility of ever making known to her what I had learned and of establishing our relations upon the truth of what I had only just discovered (and would not have been able, perhaps, to discover but for her death) substituted its sadness for the more painful mystery of her conduct. What? To have so desperately desired that Albertine—who no longer existed—should know that I had heard the story of the baths! This again was one of the consequences of our inability, when we have to consider the fact of death, to picture to ourselves anything but life. Albertine no longer existed; but to me she was the person who had concealed from me that she had assignations with women at Balbec, who imagined that she had succeeded in keeping me in ignorance of them. When we try to consider what will happen to us after our own death, is it not still our living self which we mistakenly project at that moment? And is it much more absurd, when all is said, to regret that a woman who no longer exists is unaware that we have learned what she was doing six years ago than to desire that of ourselves, who will be dead, the public shall still speak with approval a century hence? If there is more real foundation in the latter than in the former case, the regrets of my retrospective jealousy proceeded none the less from the same optical error as in other men the desire for posthumous fame. And yet, if this impression of the solemn finality of my separation from Albertine had momentarily supplanted my idea of her misdeeds, it only succeeded in aggravating them by bestowing upon them an irremediable character. I saw myself astray in life as on an endless beach where I was alone and where, in whatever direction I might turn, I would never meet her.

Fortunately, I found most opportunely in my memory—as there are always all sorts of things, some noxious, others salutary, in that jumble from which recollections come to light only one by one—I discovered, as a craftsman discovers the object that will serve for what he wishes to make, a remark of my grandmother's. She had said to me, with reference to an improbable story which the bath-attendant had told Mme de Villeparisis: "She is a woman who must suffer from a disease of mendacity." This memory was a great comfort to me. What significance could there be in the story she had told Aimé? Especially as, after all, she had seen nothing. A girl can come and take a shower with her friends without necessarily meaning any harm. Perhaps the woman had exaggerated the size of the tip in order to boast. I had indeed heard Françoise maintain once that my aunt Léonie had said in her hearing that she had "a million a month to spend," which was utter nonsense; another time that she had seen my aunt Léonie give Eulalie four thousand-franc notes, whereas a fifty-franc note folded in four seemed to me scarcely probable. And thus I sought to rid myself—and gradually succeeded in ridding myself—of the painful certainty which I had taken such trouble to acquire, tossed to and fro as I still was between the desire to know and the fear of suffering. Then my tenderness could revive anew, but, simultaneously with it, a sorrow at being parted from Albertine which made me perhaps even more wretched than I had been during the recent hours when it had been jealousy that tormented me. But the latter suddenly revived at the thought of Balbec, because of the vision which all at once reappeared (and which until then had never made me suffer and indeed appeared one of the most innocuous in my memory) of the dining-room at Balbec in the evening, with all that populace crowded together in the dark on the other side of the window, as in front of the luminous wall of an aquarium, watching the strange creatures moving around in the light but (and this I had never thought of) in its conglomeration causing the fisher-girls and other daughters of the people to brush against girls of the bourgeoisie envious of that luxury, new to Balbec, from which, if not their means, at any rate parsimony and tradition excluded their parents, girls among whom there had certainly been almost every evening Albertine whom I did not know and who doubtless used to pick up some little girl whom she would meet a few minutes later in the dark, upon the sands, or else in a deserted bathing-hut at the foot of the cliff. Then my sadness would return as I heard like a sentence of banishment the sound of the lift, which instead of stopping at my floor went on higher. And yet the only person from whom I could have hoped for a visit would never come again, for she was dead. And in spite of this, when the lift did stop at my floor, my heart leapt, and for an instant I said to myself: "What if it was only a dream after all! Perhaps it's her—she's going to ring the bell, she has come back, Françoise will come in and say with more alarm than anger—for she's even more superstitious than vindictive, and would be less afraid of the living girl than of what she will perhaps take for a ghost—'Monsieur will never guess who's here.'" I tried not to think of anything, to take up a newspaper. But I found it impossible to read all those articles written by men who felt no real grief. Of a trivial song, one of them said: "It moves one to *tears*," whereas I myself would have listened to it with joy had Albertine been alive. Another, albeit a great writer, having been greeted with applause when he alighted from a train, said that he had received "an *unforgettable* welcome," whereas I, if it had been I who received that welcome, would not have given it even a moment's thought. And a third assured his readers that but for tiresome politics life in Paris would be "alto-gether delightful," whereas I knew well that even without politics that life could not but be odious to me, and would have seemed to me delightful, even with politics, if I had found Albertine again. The field sports correspondent said (we were in the month of May): "This season of the year is truly distressing, nay, catas-trophic, to the true sportsman, for there is nothing, absolutely nothing in the way of game," and the art critic said of the Salon: "Faced with this method of arranging an exhibition one is over-come by an immense discouragement, by an infinite gloom . . ." If the strength of my feelings made me regard as untruthful and colourless the expressions of men who had no true happiness or sorrow in their lives, on the other hand the most insignificant lines which could, however remotely, be related either to Normandy, or to Touraine, or to hydrotherapeutic establishments, or to Léa, or to the Princesse de Guermantes, or to love, or to absence, or to infidelity, at once brought back before my eyes the image of Albertine, without my having the time to turn away from it, and my tears started afresh. In any case, usually I could not even read these newspapers, for the mere act of opening one of them reminded me at once that I used to open them when Albertine was alive, and that she was alive no longer; and I let it drop without having the strength to unfold its pages. Each impression called up an impression that was identical but marred, because Albertine's existence had been excised from it, so that I never had the heart to live these mutilated minutes to the end. Even when she gradually ceased to be present in my thoughts and all-powerful over my heart, I felt a sudden pang if I had occasion, as in the time when she was there, to go into her room, to grope for the light, to sit down by the pianola. Divided into a number of little household gods, she dwelt for a long time in the flame of the candle, the doorknob, the back of a chair, and other domains more immaterial such as a night of insomnia or the emotion that was caused me by the first visit of a woman who had attracted me. In spite of this the few sentences which I read in the course of a day, or which my mind recalled that I had read, often aroused in me a cruel jealousy. To do this, they required not so much to supply me with a valid proof of the immorality of women as to revive an old impression connected with the life of Albertine. Transported then to a forgotten moment the force of which had not been blunted by the habit of thinking of it, and in which Albertine still lived, her misdeeds became more immediate, more painful, more agonising. Then I asked myself whether I could be certain that the bath-attendant's revelations were false. A good way of finding out the truth would be to send Aimé to Touraine, to spend a few days in the neigh-bourhood of Mme Bontemps's villa. If Albertine enjoyed the pleasures which one woman takes with others, if it was in order not to be deprived of them any longer that she had left me, she must, as soon as she was free, have sought to indulge in them and have succeeded, in a neighbourhood which she knew and to which she would not have chosen to withdraw had she not expected to find greater facilities there than with me. No doubt there was nothing extraordinary in the fact that Albertine's death had so little altered my preoccupations. When one's mistress is alive, a large proportion of the thoughts which form what one calls one's love comes to one during the hours when she is not by one's side. Thus one acquires the habit of having as the object of one's musings an absent person, and one who, even if she remains absent for a few hours only, during those hours is no more than a memory. Hence death does not make any great difference. When Aimé returned, I asked him to go down to Châtellerault, and thus by virtue not only of my thoughts, my sorrows, the emotion caused me by a name connected, however remotely, with a certain person, but also of all my actions, the inquiries that I undertook, the use that I made of my money, all of which was devoted to the discovery of Albertine's actions, I may say that throughout the whole of that year my life remained fully occupied with a love affair, a veritable liaison. And she who was its object was dead. It is often said that something may survive of a person after his death, if that person was an artist and put a little of himself into his work. It is perhaps in the same way that a sort of cutting taken from one person and grafted on to the heart of another continues to carry on its existence even when the person from whom it had been detached has perished.

Aimé took lodgings close to Mme Bontemps's villa; he made the acquaintance of a maidservant, and of a livery-stable keeper from whom Albertine had often hired a carriage by the day. These people had noticed nothing. In a second letter, Aimé informed me that he had learned from a young laundry-girl in the town that Albertine had a peculiar way of gripping her arm when she brought back the washing. "But," she said, "the young lady never did anything more." I sent Aimé the money to pay for his journey, to pay for the pain he had caused me by his letter, and meanwhile I was doing my best to heal it by telling myself that what he had described was a familiarity which gave no proof of any vicious desire, when I received a telegram from him: "Have learned most interesting things. Have heaps of news for Monsieur. Letter follows." On the following day came a letter the envelope of which was enough to make me tremble; I had recognised that it was from Aimé, for every person, even the humblest, has under his control those little familiar creatures, at once alive and reclining in a sort of torpor upon the paper: the characters of his handwriting which he alone possesses.

"At first the young laundry-girl refused to tell me anything, she assured me that Mlle Albertine had never done anything more than pinch her arm. But to get her to talk, I took her out to dinner and gave her plenty to drink. Then she told me that Mlle Albertine often used to meet her on the bank of the Loire, when she went to bathe, that Mlle Albertine, who was in the habit of getting up very early to go and bathe, was in the habit of meeting her by the water's edge, at a spot where the trees are so thick that nobody can see you, and besides there is nobody who can see you at that hour in the morning. Then the laundry-girl brought her girlfriends and they bathed and afterwards, as it is already very hot down there and the sun beats down on you even through the trees, they used to lie about on the grass drying themselves and playing and stroking and tickling one another. The young laundry-girl confessed to me that she enjoyed playing around with her girlfriends and that seeing that Mlle Albertine was always rubbing up against her in her bathing-wrap she made her take it off and used to caress her with her tongue along the throat and arms, even on the soles of her feet which Mlle Albertine held out to her. The laundry-girl undressed too, and they played at pushing each other into the water. After that she told me nothing more, but being always at your service and ready to do anything to oblige you, I took the young laundry-girl to bed with me. She asked me if I would like her to do to me what she used to do to Mlle Albertine when she took off her bathing-dress. And she said to me: (If you could have seen how she used to wriggle, that young lady, she said to me (oh, it's too heavenly) and she got so excited that she could not keep from biting me.) I could still see the marks on the laundry-girl's arms. And I can understand Mlle Albertine's pleasure, for that young wench is really a very good performer."

I had suffered indeed at Balbec when Albertine told me of her friendship with Mlle Vinteuil. But Albertine was there to console me. Then, when by my excessive curiosity as to her actions I had succeeded in making Albertine leave me, when Françoise informed me that she was no longer in the house and I found myself alone, I had suffered even more. But at least the Albertine whom I had loved remained in my heart. Now, in her place—to punish me for having pushed even further a curiosity to which, contrary to what I had supposed, death had not put an end—what I found was a different girl, heaping up lies and deceit there where the other had so sweetly reassured me by swearing that she had never tasted those pleasures, which in the intoxication of her recaptured liberty she had set out to enjoy to the point of fainting, to the point of biting that young laundress whom she used to meet at sunrise, on the bank of the Loire, and to whom she used to say "Oh, it's too heavenly." A different Albertine, not only in the sense in which we understand the word different when we apply it to other people. If people are different from what we have supposed, as this difference does not affect us deeply, and the pendulum of intuition cannot swing outward with a greater oscillation than that of its inward swing, it is only in superficial areas of their being that we situate these differences. Formerly, when I learned that a woman loved other women, she did not seem to me on that account to be a quintessentially different woman. But in the case of a woman one loves, in order to rid oneself of the pain one feels at the thought that such a thing is possible, one wants to know not only what she has done, but what she felt while she was doing it, what she thought of what she was doing; then, probing ever more deeply, through the intensity of one's pain one arrives at the mystery, the quintessence. I suffered to the very depths of my being, in my body and in my heart, far more than the pain of losing my life would have made me suffer, from this curiosity to which all the force of my intelligence and my unconscious contributed; and thus it was into the core of Albertine's own being that I now projected everything that I learned about her. And the pain that the revelation of her vice had thus driven into me to such a depth was to render me, much later, a final service. Like the harm that I had done my grandmother, the harm that Albertine had done me was a last bond between her and myself which outlived memory even, for with the conservation of energy which belongs to every-thing that is physical, suffering has no need of the lessons of memory. Thus a man who has forgotten the glorious nights spent by moonlight in the woods, suffers still from the rheumatism which he then contracted.

Those tastes which she had denied but which were hers, those tastes the discovery of which had come to me not by a cold process of reasoning but in the burning anguish I had felt on reading the words "Oh, it's too heavenly," an anguish that gave them a qualitative distinction, those tastes were not merely added to the image of Albertine as the new shell which it drags after it is affixed to the hermit crab, but rather as a salt which, coming in contact with another salt, alters not only its colour but its nature. When the laundry-girl must have said to her friends, "Just fancy, I'd never have believed it, but the young lady is one too," to me it was not merely a vice hitherto unsuspected by them that they added to Albertine's person, but the discovery that she was another person, a person like themselves, speaking the same language, and this, by making her the compatriot of others, made her even more alien to myself, proved that what I had possessed of her, what I carried in my heart, was only quite a small part of her, and that the rest, which was made so extensive by not being merely that thing which is already mysteriously important enough, an individual desire, but being shared with others, she had always concealed from me, had kept me away from, as a woman might conceal from me that she was a native of an enemy country and a spy, and far more treacherously even than a spy, for the latter deceives us only as to her nationality, whereas Albertine had deceived me as to her profoundest humanity, the fact that she did not belong to ordinary humankind, but to an alien race which moves among it, hides itself among it and never merges with it. I had as it happened seen two paintings by Elstir showing naked women in a thickly wooded landscape. In one of them, a girl is raising her foot as Albertine must have raised hers when she offered it to the laundress. With her other foot she is pushing into the water another girl who gaily resists, her thigh raised, her foot barely dipping into the blue water. I remembered now that the raised thigh made the same swan's-neck curve with the angle of the knee as was made by the line of Albertine's thigh when she was lying by my side on the bed, and I had often meant to tell her that she reminded me of those paintings. But I had refrained from doing so, for fear of awakening in her mind the image of naked female bodies. Now I saw her, side by side with the laundry-girl and her friends, recomposing the group which I had so loved when I was sitting among Albertine's friends at Balbec. And if I had been an art-lover responsive to beauty alone, I should have recognised that Albertine recomposed it a thousand times more ravishingly, now that its elements were the nude statues of goddesses like those which the great sculptors scattered among the groves of Versailles or arrayed round the fountains to be washed and polished by the caresses of their waters. Now, beside the laundry-girl, I saw her, a girl at the water's edge, in their twofold nudity of marble statues in the midst of a grove of vegetation and dipping into the water like aquatic bas-reliefs. Remembering Albertine as she lay on my bed, I seemed to see the curve of her thigh, I saw it as a swan's neck, seeking the other girl's mouth. Then I no longer even saw a thigh, but simply the bold neck of a swan, like the one in a stirring sketch seeking the mouth of a Leda who is seen in all the specific palpitation of feminine pleasure, because there is no one else with her but a swan, and she seems more alone, just as one discovers on the telephone the inflexions of a voice which one fails to perceive so long as it is not dissociated from a face in which one objectivises its expression. In this sketch, the pleasure, instead of reaching out to the woman who inspires it and who is absent, replaced by an inert swan, is concentrated in her who feels it. At moments the contact between my heart and my memory was interrupted. What Albertine had done with the laundry-girl was indicated to me now only by quasi-algebraic abbreviations which no longer meant anything to me; but a hundred times an hour the interrupted current was restored, and my heart was pitilessly scorched by a fire from hell, while I saw Albertine, resurrected by my jealousy, really alive, stiffen beneath the caresses of the young laundry-girl to whom she was saying: "Oh, it's too heavenly."

As she was alive at the moment when she committed her misdeed, that is to say at the moment at which I myself found myself placed, it was not enough for me to know of the misdeed, I wanted her to know that I knew. Hence, if at those moments I thought with regret that I should never see her again, this regret bore the stamp of my jealousy, and, very different from the lacerating regret of the moments when I loved her, was only regret at not being able to say to her: "You thought I'd never know what you did after you left me. Well, I know everything—the laundry-girl on the bank of the Loire, and your saying to her 'Oh, it's too heavenly,' and I've seen the bite." Of course I said to myself: "Why torment yourself? She who took her pleasure with the laundry-girl no longer exists, and consequently was not a person whose actions retain any importance. She isn't telling herself that you know. But neither is she telling herself that you don't know, since she isn't telling herself anything." But this line of reasoning convinced me less than the visual image of her pleasure which brought me back to the moment in which she had experienced it. What we feel is the only thing that exists for us, and we project it into the past, or into the future, without letting ourselves be stopped by the fictitious barriers of death. If my regret that she was dead was subjected at such moments to the influence of my jealousy and assumed such a peculiar form, that influence naturally extended to my thoughts about occultism and immortality, which were no more than an effort to realise what I desired. Hence, at those moments, if I could have succeeded in evoking her by table-turning as Bergotte had at one time thought possible, or in meeting her in the other life as the abbé X thought, I would have wished to do so only in order to say to her: "I know about the laundry-girl. You said to her: 'Oh, it's too heavenly,' and I've seen the bite."

What came to my rescue against this image of the laundry-girl—certainly when it had lasted for some time—was that image itself, because we only truly know what is new, what suddenly introduces into our sensibility a change of tone which strikes us, what habit has not yet replaced with its colourless facsimiles. But it was above all that fragmentation of Albertine into many parts, into many Albertines, that was her sole mode of existence in me. Moments recurred in which she had simply been kind, or intelligent, or serious, or even loving sport above all else. And was it not right, after all, that this fragmentation should soothe me? For if it was not in itself something real, if it arose from the continuously changing shape of the hours in which she had appeared to me, a shape which remained that of my memory as the curve of the projections of my magic lantern depended on the curve of the coloured slides, did it not in its own way represent a truly objective truth, this one, namely that none of us is single, that each of us contains many persons who do not all have the same moral value, and that if a vicious Albertine had existed, it did not mean that there had not been others, the Albertine who enjoyed talking to me about Saint-Simon in her room, the Albertine who on the night when I had told her that we must part had said so sadly: "This pianola, this room, to think that I shall never see any of these things again" and, when she saw the distress which I had finally communicated to myself by my lie, had exclaimed with sincere pity: "Oh, no, anything rather than make you unhappy, I promise that I shall never try to see you again." Then I was no longer alone; I felt the barrier that separated us vanish. As soon as this good Albertine had returned, I had found once more the only person who could provide me with the antidote to the sufferings which Albertine was causing me. True, I still wanted to speak to her about the story of the laundry-girl, but no longer in order to score a cruel triumph and to show her maliciously how much I knew. I asked her tenderly, as I should have asked her had she been alive, whether the story about the laundry-girl was true. She swore to me that it was not, that Aimé was not very truthful and that, wishing to appear to have earned the money I had given him, he had not liked to return empty-handed, and had made the girl tell him what he wished to hear. No doubt Albertine had never ceased to lie to me. And yet, in the ebb and flow of her contradictions, I felt that there had been a certain progression due to myself. That she had not, indeed, confided some of her secrets to me at the beginning (perhaps, it is true, involuntarily, in a remark that escaped her lips) I would not have sworn. I no longer remembered. And besides, she had such odd ways of naming certain things that they could be interpreted one way or the other. But the impression she had received of my jealousy had led her afterwards to retract with horror what at first she had complacently admitted. In any case,

Albertine had no need to tell me this. To be convinced of her innocence it was enough for me to embrace her, and I could do so now that the barrier that separated us was down, that impalpable but hermetic barrier which rises between two lovers after a quarrel and against which kisses would be shattered. No, she had no need to tell me anything. Whatever she might have done, whatever she might have wished to do, the poor child, there were sentiments in which, over the barrier that divided us, we could be united. If the story was true, and if Albertine had concealed her tastes from me, it was in order not to make me unhappy. I had the comfort of hearing this Albertine say so. Besides, had I ever known any other? The two chief causes of error in one's relations with another person are, having oneself a kind heart, or else being in love with that other person. We fall in love for a smile, a look, a shoulder. That is enough; then, in the long hours of hope or sorrow, we fabricate a person, we compose a character. And when later on we see much of the beloved being, we can no more, whatever the cruel reality that confronts us, divest the woman with that look, that shoulder, of the sweet nature and loving character with which we have endowed her than we can, when she has grown old, eliminate her youthful face from a person whom we have known since her girlhood. I recalled the kind and compassionate look in the eyes of that Albertine, her plump cheeks, the grainy texture of her neck. It was the image of a dead woman but, as this dead woman was alive, it was easy for me to do immediately what I should inevitably have done if she had been by my side in her living body (what I should do were I ever to meet her again in another life), I forgave her.

The moments which I had lived through with this Albertine were so precious to me that I did not want to let any of them escape me. And occasionally, as one recovers the remnants of a squandered fortune, I recaptured some of them which I had thought to be lost: for instance, tying a scarf behind my neck instead of in front, I remembered a drive which I had never thought of since, during which, in order that the cold air might not reach my throat, Albertine had arranged my scarf for me in this way after first kissing me. That simple drive, restored to my memory by so humble a gesture, gave me the same pleasure as the intimate objects belonging to a dead woman who was dear to us which are brought to us by her old servant and which we find so precious; my grief was enriched by it, all the more so as I had never given another thought to the scarf in question. As with the future, it is not all at once but grain by grain that one savours the past.

Moreover my grief assumed so many forms that at times I no longer recognised it; I wanted to experience a great love; I wanted to find a woman who would live with me; this seemed to me to be the sign that I no longer loved Albertine, whereas it meant that I loved her still. Now, freed, she had taken flight again; men, women followed her. But she lived in me. I realised that this need to experience a great love was, quite as much as the desire to kiss Albertine's plump cheeks, merely a part of my regret. And at heart I was happy not to fall in love with another woman; I realised that this continuing love for Albertine was like the ghost of the feeling I had had for her, reproducing its various stages and obeying the same laws as the sentimental reality which it reflected on the further side of death. For I was well aware that if I could extend the intervals between my thoughts of Albertine, I should have ceased to love her if the gap had been too wide; I should have become indifferent to her as I was now indifferent to my grandmother. Too much time spent without thinking of her would have broken, in my memory, the continuity which is the very principle of life, though it may recover and resume after a certain lapse of time. Had not this been the case with my love for Albertine when she was alive, a love which had been able to revive after a quite long interval during which I had not given her a thought? My memory must have been obedient to the same laws, must have been unable to endure longer intervals, for it simply went on reflecting, like an aurora borealis, after Albertine's death the feeling I had had for her; it was like the phantom of my love. It was when I had forgotten her that I might think it wiser and happier to live without love. Thus my regret for Albertine, because it was it that aroused in me the need of a sister, made that need unassuageable. And as my regret for Albertine grew fainter, the need of a sister, which was only an unconscious form of that regret, would become less imperious. And yet these two residues of my love did not follow the same rate of progress in their gradual decline. There were hours when I was determined to marry, so completely had the former been eclipsed, while the latter on the contrary remained very strong. And on the other hand, later on, my jealous memories having died away, suddenly at times a feeling of tenderness for Albertine would well up in my heart, and then, thinking of my own love affairs with other women, I told myself that she would have understood, would have shared them—and her vice became almost a reason for loving her. At times my jealousy revived in moments when I no longer remembered Albertine, although it was of her that I was jealous. I thought that I was jealous of Andrée, apropos of whom I heard at that time of an amorous adventure she was having. But Andrée was to me merely a substitute, a by-road, a connecting link which brought me indirectly to Albertine. So it is that in dreams we give a different face, a different name to a person as to whose underlying identity we are not mistaken. When all was said, notwithstanding the continuing ebb and flow which upset in these particular instances the general law, the sentiments that Albertine had bequeathed to me were more difficult to extinguish than the memory of their original cause. Not only the sentiments, but the sensations. Different in this respect from Swann who, when he had begun to cease to love Odette, had not even been able to re-create in himself the sensation of his love, I felt myself still reliving a past which was now no more than the story of another person; my personality was now somehow split in two, and while the upper part was already hard and chilled, it still burned at its base whenever a spark made the old current pass through it, even after my mind had long ceased to conceive of Albertine. And as no image of her accompanied the painful palpitations that were sub-stituted for it, and the tears that were brought to my eyes by a cold breeze blowing as at Balbec through apple-trees already pink with blossom, I came to wonder whether the renewal of my grief was not due to entirely pathological causes and whether what I took to be the revival of a memory and the final period of a lingering love was not rather the first stage of heart-disease.

There are in certain affections secondary symptoms which the sufferer is too apt to confuse with the malady itself. When they cease, he is surprised to find himself nearer to recovery than he had supposed. Of this sort had been the suffering caused me—the "complication" brought about—by Aimé's letters with regard to the bathing establishment and the laundry-girls. But a spiritual healer, had such a person visited me, would have found that, in other respects, my grief itself was on the way to recovery. Doubtless, since I was a man, one of those amphibious creatures who are plunged simultaneously in the past and in the reality of the present, there still existed in me a contradiction between the living memory of Albertine and my consciousness of her death. But this contradiction was in a sense the converse of what it had been before. The idea that Albertine was dead, which at first used to contest so furiously with the idea that she was alive that I was obliged to run away from it as children run away from an oncoming wave, by the very force of its incessant onslaughts had ended by capturing the place in my mind that a short while before was still occupied by the idea of her life. Without my being precisely aware of it, it was now this idea of Albertine's death—no longer the present memory of her life—that for the most part formed the basis of my unconscious musings, with the result that if I interrupted them suddenly to reflect upon myself, what surprised me was not, as during the first days, that Albertine, so alive in me, could be no longer existent upon the earth, could be dead, but that Albertine, who no longer existed upon the earth, who was dead, should have remained so alive in me. Built up and held together by the contiguity of the memories that followed one another, the black tunnel in which my thoughts had lain dreaming so long that they had even ceased to be aware of it was suddenly broken by an interval of sunlight, bathing in the distance a blue and smiling universe where Albertine was no more than a memory, insignificant and full of charm. Was it she, I wondered, who was the true Albertine, or was it the person who, in the darkness through which I had so long been travelling, seemed to me the sole reality? The person I had been so short a time ago, who lived only in the perpetual expectation of the moment when Albertine would come in to say good-night and kiss him, was now made to appear to me, by a sort of multiplication of myself, as no more than a faint fragment of me, already half stripped away, and, like a flower unfolding its petals, I felt the rejuvenating refreshment of an exfoliation. However, these brief illuminations succeeded perhaps only in making me more conscious of my love for Albertine, as happens with every idea that is too constant, needing opposition to make it affirm itself. People who were alive during the war of 1870, for instance, say that the idea of war ended by seeming to them natural, not because they did not think enough about the war, but because they thought of it all the time. And in order to understand how strange and momentous a fact war is, it was necessary that, something else wrenching them out of their permanent obsession, they should forget for a moment that a state of war prevailed and should find themselves once again as they had been in peacetime, until all of a sudden, against that momentary blank, there stood out clearly at last the monstrous reality which they had long ceased to see, since there had been nothing else visible.

If only this withdrawal of my different impressions of Albertine had at least been carried out not in echelon but simultaneously, evenly, frontally, along the whole line of my memory, the recollections of her infidelities receding at the same time as those of her sweetness, forgetting would have brought me solace. It was not so. As upon a beach where the tide recedes unevenly, I would be assailed by the onrush of one of my suspicions when the image of her tender presence had already withdrawn too far from me to be able to bring me its remedial balm.

The betrayals had made me suffer because, however remote the year in which they had occurred, to me they were not remote; but I suffered from them less when they became remote, that is to say when I pictured them to myself less vividly, for the remoteness of a thing is in proportion rather to the visual power of the memory that is looking at it than to the real duration of the intervening days, as the memory of last night's dream may seem to us more distant in its imprecision and dimness than an event which is many years old. But, although the idea of Albertine's death made some headway in me, the reflux of the sensation that she was alive, if it did not arrest that progress, obstructed it nevertheless and prevented its being regular. And I realise now that during this period (doubtless because of my having forgotten the hours in which she had been cloistered in my house, hours which, by dispelling my anguish at misdeeds which seemed to me almost unimportant because I knew that she was not committing them, had become tantamount to so many proofs of her innocence), I underwent the martyrdom of living in the constant company of an idea quite as novel as the idea that Albertine was dead (until then I had always started from the idea that she was alive), with an idea which I should have supposed it to be equally impossible to endure and which, without my noticing it, was gradually forming the basis of my consciousness, substituting itself for the idea that Albertine was innocent: the idea that she was guilty. When I thought I was doubting her, I was on the contrary believing in her; similarly I took as the starting-point of my other ideas the certainty—often proved false as the contrary idea had been—of her guilt, while continuing to imagine that I still felt doubts. I must have suffered a great deal during this period, but I realise that it had to be so. One is cured of suffering only by experiencing it to the full. By protecting Albertine from any contact with the outside world, by creating for myself the illusion that she was innocent, and also, later on, by adopting as the basis of my reasoning the thought that she was alive, I was merely postponing the hour of recovery, because I was postponing the long hours of necessary suffering that must precede it. Now with regard to these ideas of Albertine's guilt, habit, were it to come into play, would do so in accordance with the same laws as I had already experienced in the course of my life. Just as the name Guermantes had lost the significance and the charm of a road bordered with red and purple flowers and of the window of Gilbert the Bad, Albertine's presence that of the blue undulations of the sea, the names of Swann, of the lift-boy, of the Princesse de Guermantes and so many others, all that they had meant to me—that charm and that significance leaving me with a mere word which they considered big enough to stand on its own feet, as a man who comes to set a subordinate to work gives him his instructions and after a few weeks withdraws—similarly the painful knowledge of Albertine's guilt would be expelled from me by habit. Moreover between now and then, like an attack launched from both flanks at once, in this action undertaken by habit two allies would mutually lend a hand. It was because this idea of Albertine's guilt would become for me more probable, more habitual, that it would become less painful. But at the same time, because it would be less painful, the objections against my certainty of her guilt, which were inspired in my mind only by my desire not to suffer too acutely, would collapse one by one; and, one action precipitating another, I should pass quickly enough from the certainty of Albertine's innocence to the certainty of her guilt. I had to live with the idea of Albertine's death, with the idea of her misdeeds, in order for these ideas to become habitual, that is to say in order to be able to forget these ideas and in the end forget Albertine herself.

I had not yet reached this stage. At one time it was my memory, made clearer by some intellectual excitement—such as reading a book—which revived my grief; at other times it was on the contrary my grief—when it was aroused, for instance, by the anguish of a spell of stormy weather—which raised higher, brought nearer to the light, some memory of our love. Moreover these revivals of my love for Albertine might occur after an interval of indifference interspersed with other curiosities, as, after the long interval which had begun with her refusal to let me kiss her at Balbec and during which I had thought far more about Mme de Guermantes, about Andrée, about Mlle de Stermaria, it had revived when I had started seeing her regularly again. But even now various preoccupations could bring about a separation—from a dead woman, this time—in which she left me more indifferent. All this for the same reason, that she was a living person for me. And even later on, when I loved her less, it remained nevertheless for me one of those desires of which we quickly tire, but which revive when we have allowed them to lie dormant for a while. I pursued one living woman, then another, then I returned to my dead one. Often it was in the most obscure recesses of myself, when I could no longer form any clear idea of Albertine, that a name would come by chance to stimulate painful reactions which I supposed to be no longer possible, like those dying people whose brain is no longer capable of thought and who are made to contract their muscles by the prick of a needle. And, during long periods, these stimulations occurred to me so rarely that I was driven to seek for myself occasions for grief, for a pang of jealousy, in an attempt to re-establish contact with the past, to remember her better. For, since regret for a woman is only a recrudescence of love and remains subject to the same laws, the keenness of my regret was intensified by the same causes which in Albertine's lifetime had increased my love for her and in the front rank of which had always appeared jealousy and grief. But as a rule these occasions—for an illness or a war can always last far longer than the most prophetic wisdom has calculated—took me unawares and caused me such violent shocks that I thought far more of protecting myself against suffering than of appealing to them for a memory.

Moreover a word did not even need to be connected, like "Chaumont," with some suspicion (even a syllable common to two different names was sufficient for my memory—as for an electrician who is happy with any substance that is a good conductor—to restore the contact between Albertine and my heart) in order to reawaken that suspicion, to be the password, the "Open sesame" unlocking the door of a past which one had ceased to take into account because, having seen more than enough of it, literally one no longer possessed it; one had been shorn of it, had supposed that by this subtraction one's own personality had changed its form, like a geometrical figure which by the removal of an angle would lose one of its sides; certain phrases, for instance, in which there occurred the name of a street or a road where Albertine might have been, were sufficient to incarnate a potential, non-existent jealousy, in quest of a body, a dwelling, some physical location, some particular realisation.

Often it was simply during my sleep that these "reprises," these "da capos" of one's dreams, which turn back several pages of one's memory, several leaves of the calendar at once, brought me back, made me regress to a painful but remote impression which had long since given place to others but which now became present once more. As a rule, it was accompanied by a whole stage-setting, clumsy but striking, which, giving me the illusion of reality, brought before my eyes, voiced in my ears, what thenceforward dated from that night. Besides, in the history of a love affair and of its struggles against forgetfulness, do not our dreams occupy an even larger place than our waking state, since they take no account of the infinitesimal divisions of time, suppress transitions, oppose sharp contrasts, undo in an instant the web of consolation so slowly woven during the day, and contrive for us, by night, a meeting with her whom we would eventually have forgotten, provided always that we did not see her again? For whatever people may say, we can perfectly well have in a dream the impression that what is happening in it is real. It would be impossible only for reasons drawn from our waking experience, an experience which at that moment is hidden from us. With the result that this supposititious life seems to us real. Sometimes, by a defect in the internal lighting which spoiled the success of the play, my well-staged memories giving me the illusion of life, I really believed that I had arranged to meet Albertine, that I was seeing her again, but then I found myself incapable of advancing to meet her, of uttering the words which I meant to say to her, of relighting in order to see her the torch that had gone out—impossibilities which were simply in my dream the immobility, the dumbness, the blindness of the sleeper —as suddenly one sees a huge shadow which ought not to be visible obliterate the figures on the screen of a magic lantern, a shadow which is that of the lantern itself, or that of the operator. At other times Albertine was present in my dream, and proposed to leave me once again, without my being moved by her resolve. This was because a warning ray of light had managed to filter into the darkness of my sleep, and what deprived Albertine's future actions, her threatened departure, of any importance for me was the knowledge that she was dead. But often, even more clearly, this memory that Albertine was dead was combined, without destroying it, with the sensation that she was alive. I chatted to her, and while I was speaking my grandmother moved to and fro at the back of the room. Part of her chin had crumbled away like a corroded statue, but I found nothing unusual in that. I told Albertine that I had various questions to ask her with regard to the bathing establishment at Balbec, and to a certain laundress in Touraine, but I would put them off till later since we had plenty of time and there was no longer any urgency. She assured me that she was not doing anything wrong and that she had merely, the day before, kissed Mlle Vinteuil on the lips. "What? Is she here?" "Yes, in fact it's time for me to leave you, as I have to go and see her presently." And since, now that Albertine was dead, I no longer kept her a prisoner in my house as in the last months of her life, her visit to Mlle Vinteuil perturbed me. I did not want to show it; Albertine told me that she had done no more than kiss her, but she was evidently beginning to lie again as in the days when she used to deny everything. Presently, no doubt, she would not be content merely with kissing Mlle Vinteuil. Doubtless from a certain point of view I was wrong to let myself be disturbed like this, since, according to what we are told, the dead can feel nothing, can do nothing. People say so, but this did not alter the fact that my grandmother, who was dead, had continued nevertheless to live for many years, and at that moment was walking to and fro in my room. And no doubt, once I was awake, this idea of a dead woman who continued to live ought to have become as impossible for me to understand as it is to explain. But I had already formed it so many times in the course of those transient periods of madness which are our dreams, that I had become in time familiar with it; our memory of dreams may become lasting, if they repeat themselves often enough. And long after my dream had ended, I remained tormented by that kiss which Albertine had told me she had given in words which I thought I could still hear. And indeed they must have passed very close to my ear since it was I myself who had uttered them. All day long, I continued to talk to Albertine; I questioned her, I forgave her, I made up for my forgetfulness of the things which I had always meant to say to her during her life. And all of a sudden I was startled by the thought that the creature invoked by memory to whom all these remarks were addressed no longer bore any relation to reality, that death had destroyed the various parts of the face to which the continual thrust of the will to live, now abolished, had alone given the unity of a person.

At other times, without my having dreamed, as soon as I awoke I felt that the wind had changed in me; it was blowing coldly and steadily from another direction, issuing from the remotest past, bringing back to me the sound of a clock striking far-off hours, of the whistle of departing trains which I did not ordinarily hear. One day I tried to interest myself in a book. I reopened a novel by Bergotte of which I had been especially fond. Its congenial characters appealed to me greatly, and very soon, reconquered by the charm of the book, I began to hope, as for a personal pleasure, that the wicked woman might be punished, while my eyes grew moist when the happiness of the young lovers was assured. "But then," I exclaimed in despair, "I cannot conclude, from the fact that I attach so much importance to what Albertine may have done, that her personality is something real which cannot be destroyed, that I shall find her one day in her own likeness in heaven, if I invoke with so many entreaties, await with such impatience, welcome with tears the success of a person who has never existed except in Bergotte's imagination, whom I have never seen, whose appearance I am at liberty to imagine as I please!" Besides, in this novel, there were seductive girls, amorous correspondences, deserted paths in which lovers meet, and all this, reminding me that one may love clandestinely, revived my jealousy, as though Albertine had still been able to stroll along deserted paths. And the novel also pictured a man who after fifty years meets a woman whom he loved in her youth, fails to recognise her, is bored in her company. And this reminded me that love does not last for ever and distressed me as though I were destined to be parted from Albertine and to meet her again with indifference in my old age. If I caught sight of a map of France, my fearful eyes took care not to fall upon Touraine so that I might not be jealous, nor, so that I might not be miserable, upon Normandy, where would certainly be indicated at least Balbec and Doncières, between which I could situate all those places we had traversed so many times together. In the midst of other names of towns or villages of France, names which were merely visible or audible, the name of Tours, for instance, seemed to be differently composed, to be made up, not of intangible images, but of venomous substances which acted instantaneously on my heart, making it beat faster and more painfully. And if this force extended to certain names, making them so different from the rest, how, when I stayed closer to myself, when I confined myself to Albertine herself, could I be astonished that this force which I found irresistible, and to produce which any other woman might have served, had been the result of an entanglement, of a bringing into contact of dreams, desires, habits, affections, with the requisite conjunction of alternating pains and pleasures? And this continued her life in death, memory being sufficient to sustain the reality of life, which is mental. I recalled Albertine alighting from a railway carriage and telling me that she wanted to go to Saint-Mars-le-Vêtu, and I saw her again before that, with her "polo" pulled down over her cheeks; I thought of new possibilities of happiness, towards which I sprang, saying to myself: "We might have gone on together to Infreville, to Doncières." There was no watering-place in the neighbourhood of Balbec in which I did not see her, with the result that that country, like a mythological land which had been preserved, restored to me, living and cruel, the most ancient, the most charming legends, those that had been most obliterated by the sequel of my love. Ah, what anguish were I ever to have to sleep again in that bed at Balbec around whose brass frame, as around an immovable pivot, a fixed bar, my life had moved and evolved, bringing successively into its compass gay conversations with my grandmother, the nightmare of her death, Albertine's soothing caresses, the discovery of her vice, and now a new life into which, looking at the glazed book-cases in which the sea was reflected, I knew that Albertine would never come again! Was it not, that Balbec hotel, like the single set of a provincial theatre, in which for years past the most diverse plays have been performed, which has served for a comedy, for first one tragedy, then another, for a purely poetical drama, that hotel which already stretched quite far back into my past? The fact that this part alone, with its walls, its book-cases, its mirror, remained invariably the same throughout new epochs of my life, made me better aware that all in all it was the rest, it was myself, that had changed, and thus gave me that impression that the mysteries of life, of love, of death—which in their optimism children believe they have no share in—are not set apart, but one perceives with sorrowful pride that they have formed an integral part of one's own life through the course of the years.

I tried at times to take an interest in the newspapers. But I found the act of reading them repellent, and moreover by no means innocuous. The fact is that from each of our ideas, as from a crossroads in a forest, so many paths branch off in different directions that at the moment when I least expected it I found myself faced by a fresh memory. The title of Fauré's melody *Le Secret* had led me to the Duc de Broglie's *Secret du Roi*, the name Broglie to that of Chaumont;[2] or else the words "Good Friday" had made me think of Golgotha, Golgotha of the etymology of the word which is, it seems, the equivalent of *Calvus Mons*, Chaumont. But, whatever the path by which I had arrived at Chaumont, at that moment I received so violent a shock that I was far more concerned to ward off pain than to probe for memories. Some moments after the shock, my intelligence, which like the sound of thunder travels less rapidly, produced the reason for it. Chaumont had made me think of the Buttes-Chaumont, where Mme Bontemps had told me that Andrée used often to go with Albertine, whereas Albertine had told me that she had never seen the Buttes-Chaumont. After a certain age our memories are so intertwined with one another that what we are thinking of, the book we are reading, scarcely matters any more. We have put something of ourselves everywhere, everything is fertile, everything is dangerous, and we can make discoveries no less precious than in Pascal's *Pensées* in an advertisement for soap.

No doubt a fact such as the one about the Buttes-Chaumont, which at the time had appeared to me trifling, was in itself far less serious, far less decisive evidence against Albertine than the story of the bath-attendant or the laundry-girl. But in the first place, a memory which comes to us fortuitously finds in us an intact capacity for imagining, that is to say in this case for suffering, which we would have partly used up had it been, on the contrary, we who had deliberately applied our mind to re-creating a memory. And then to these latter memories (those that concerned the bath-attendant and the laundry-girl), ever present albeit obscured in my consciousness, like the furniture placed in the semi-darkness of a gallery which, without being able to see, one avoids knocking into, I had grown accustomed. Whereas it was a long time since I had given a thought to the Buttes-Chaumont, or, to take another instance, to Albertine's scrutiny of the mirror in the casino at Balbec, or to her unexplained delay on the evening when I had waited so long for her after the Guermantes party, or any of those parts of her life which remained outside my heart and which I would have liked to know in order that they might become assimilated, annexed to it, merged with the sweeter memories formed therein by an interior Albertine, an Albertine genuinely possessed. Lifting a corner of the heavy curtain of habit (stupefying habit, which during the whole course of our life conceals from us almost the whole universe, and in the dead of night, without changing the label, substitutes for the most dangerous or intoxicating poisons of life something anodyne that procures no delights), such memories would come back to me as at the time itself with that fresh and piercing novelty of a recurring season, of a change in the routine of our hours, which, in the realm of pleasures also, if we get into a carriage on the first fine day in spring, or leave the house at sunrise, makes us observe our own most trivial actions with a lucid exaltation which makes that intense minute worth more than the sum-total of the preceding days. Days in the past cover up little by little those that preceded them and are themselves buried beneath those that follow them. But each past day has remained deposited in us, as in a vast library where, even of the oldest books, there is a copy which doubtless nobody will ever ask to see. And yet should this day from the past, traversing the translucency of the intervening epochs, rise to the surface and spread itself inside us until it covers us entirely, then for a moment names resume their former meaning, people their former aspect, we ourselves our state of mind at the time, and we feel, with a vague suffering which however is endurable and will not last for long, the problems which have long ago become insoluble and which caused us such anguish at the time. Our ego is composed of the superimposition of our successive states. But this superimposition is not unalterable like the stratification of a mountain. Incessant upheavals raise to the surface ancient deposits. I found myself once more after the party at the Princesse de Guermantes's, awaiting Albertine's arrival. What had she been doing that evening? Had she been unfaithful to me? With whom? Aimé's revelations, even if I accepted them, in no way diminished for me the anxious, despairing interest of this unexpected question, as though each different Albertine, each new memory, set a special problem of jealousy, to which the solutions of the other problems could not apply.

But I would have liked to know not only with what woman she had spent that evening, but what special pleasure it represented to her, what was happening inside her at that moment. Sometimes, at Balbec, Françoise had gone to fetch her, and had told me that she had found her leaning out of her window with an anxious, quest-ing air, as though she were expecting somebody. Supposing I learned that the girl she was awaiting was Andrée—what was the state of mind in which Albertine awaited her, that state of mind concealed behind the anxious, questing gaze? How important were those tastes to Albertine? How large a place did they occupy in her thoughts? Alas, remembering my own agitation whenever I had caught sight of a girl who attracted me, sometimes when I had merely heard her spoken of without having seen her, my anxiety to look my best, to show myself to advantage, my cold sweats, I had only, in order to torture myself, to imagine the same voluptuous excitement in Albertine, as though by means of the apparatus which, after the visit of a certain practitioner who had shown some scepticism about her malady, my aunt Léonie had wished to see invented, and which would enable the doctor to undergo all the sufferings of his patient in order to understand better. And already it was enough to torture me, to tell me that, compared with this other thing, serious conversations with me about Stendhal and Victor Hugo must have counted for very little with her, to feel her heart being drawn towards other people, detaching itself from mine, implanting itself elsewhere. But even the importance which this desire must have for her and the reserve with which she surrounded it could not reveal to me what it was qualitatively, still less how she referred to it when she spoke of it to herself. In physical suffering, at least we do not have to choose our pain ourselves. The malady determines it and imposes it on us. But in jealousy we have, so to speak, to try out sufferings of every shape and size, before we arrive at the one which seems to fit. And how much more difficult this is in the case of a suffering such as that of feeling that she whom we loved is finding pleasure with beings who are different from us, who give her sensations which we are not capable of giving her, or who at least by their configuration, their aspect, their ways, represent to her something quite different from us! Ah, if only Albertine had fallen in love with Saint-Loup, how much less, it seemed to me, I should have suffered!

It is true that we are unaware of the particular sensibility of each of our fellow-creatures, but as a rule we do not even know that we are unaware of it, for this sensibility of other people is a matter of indifference to us. So far as Albertine was concerned, my misery or happiness would have depended upon the nature of this sensibility; I was well aware that it was unknown to me, and the fact that it was unknown to me was painful in itself. Once, I had the illusion of seeing these unknown desires and pleasures of Albertine's, another time, of hearing them. Of seeing them when, some time after her death, Andrée came to see me.

For the first time she seemed to me beautiful. I said to myself that her almost frizzy hair, her dark, shadowed eyes, were doubtless what Albertine had loved so much, the materialisation before my eyes of what she pictured in her amorous day-dreams, what she saw with the expectant eyes of desire on the day when she had so suddenly decided to leave Balbec. Like a strange, dark flower brought back to me from beyond the grave, from the innermost being of a person in whom I had been unable to discover it, I seemed to see before me, the unlooked-for exhumation of a priceless relic, the incarnate desire of Albertine which Andrée was to me, as Venus was the desire of Jove. Andrée regretted Albertine's death, but I sensed at once that she did not miss her. Forcibly removed from her friend by death, she seemed to have easily reconciled herself to a final separation which I would not have dared to ask of her while Albertine was alive, so afraid would I have been of failing to obtain her consent. She seemed on the contrary to accept this renunciation without difficulty, but precisely at the moment when it could no longer be of any advantage to me. Andrée abandoned Albertine to me, but dead, and having lost for me not only her life but retrospectively a little of her reality, now that I saw that she was not indispensable and unique to Andrée who had been able to replace her with others.

While Albertine was alive, I would not have dared to ask Andrée to confide in me about the nature of their friendship both mutually and with Mlle Vinteuil's friend, being uncertain, towards the end, whether Andrée did not repeat to Albertine everything I said to her. But now such an inquiry, even if it were to prove fruitless, would at least be unattended by danger. I spoke to Andrée, not in a questioning tone but as though I had known all the time, perhaps from Albertine, of the fondness that she herself, Andrée, had for women and of her own relations with Mlle Vinteuil. She admitted it all without the slightest reluctance, smiling as she spoke. I could not help drawing the most painful conclusions from this avowal; first of all because Andrée, so

affectionate and coquettish with many of the young men at
Balbec, would never have been suspected by anyone of practices
which she made no attempt to deny, so that by analogy, when
I discovered this new Andrée, I felt that Albertine would have
confessed them with the same ease to anyone other than myself,
whom she felt to be jealous. But at the same time, Andrée having
been Albertine's best friend, and the friend for whose sake she had
probably returned in haste from Balbec, and Andrée having
admitted to these tastes, the conclusion that was forced upon my
mind was that Albertine and Andrée had always indulged them
together. Of course, just as, in the presence of a stranger, we do not
always dare to examine the gift he has brought us, the wrapper of
which we shall not unfasten until the donor has gone, so long as
Andrée was with me I did not retire into myself to examine the
pain she had brought me. Although I could feel that it was already
causing my bodily servants, my nerves, my heart, the greatest
turmoil, out of good manners I pretended not to notice, chatting
away on the contrary with the utmost affability to the girl who was
my guest without diverting my gaze to these internal incidents. It
was especially painful to me to hear Andrée say of Albertine: "Oh,
yes, she always loved going to the Chevreuse valley." To the vague
and non-existent universe in which Albertine's excursions with
Andrée occurred, it seemed to me that the latter, by a subsequent
and diabolical act of creation, had just added to God's work an
accursed valley. I felt that Andrée was going to tell me everything
that she had been in the habit of doing with Albertine, and, as
I went on trying, from politeness, from canniness, from pride,
perhaps from gratitude, to appear more and more affectionate,
while the space that I had still been able to concede to Albertine's
innocence became smaller and smaller, it seemed to me that,
despite my efforts, I presented the paralysed aspect of an animal
round which a bird of prey is wheeling in steadily narrowing
circles, unhurriedly because it is confident of being able to
swoop on its helpless victim whenever it chooses. I gazed at her
nevertheless, and, with such liveliness, naturalness and assurance as
a person can muster who is trying to make it appear that he is not
afraid of being hypnotised by someone's stare, I said casually to
Andrée: "I've never mentioned the subject to you for fear of
offending you, but now that we both find pleasure in talking
about her, I may as well tell you that I found out long ago all
about the things of that sort that you used to do with Albertine.

And I can tell you something that you will be glad to hear although you know it already: Albertine adored you."

I told Andrée that it would be of great interest to me if she would allow me to see her (even if she simply confined herself to caresses which would not embarrass her unduly in my presence) performing such actions with those of Albertine's friends who shared her tastes, and I mentioned Rosemonde, Berthe, each of Albertine's friends, in the hope of finding out something.

"Apart from the fact that not for anything in the world would I do the things you mention in your presence," Andrée replied, "I don't believe that any of the girls whom you've named have those tastes."

Drawing closer in spite of myself to the monster that was mesmerising me, I answered: "What! You don't expect me to believe that of all your group Albertine was the only one with whom you did that sort of thing!"

"But I never did anything of the sort with Albertine."

"Come now, my dear Andrée, why deny things which I've known for at least three years? I see nothing wrong in them, far from it. For instance, that evening when she was so anxious to go with you the next day to Mme Verdurin's, you may remember perhaps..."

Before I had completed my sentence, I saw in Andrée's eyes, which it sharpened to a pinpoint like those stones which for that reason jewellers find it difficult to use, a fleeting, worried look, like the look on the face of a person privileged to go behind the scenes who draws back the edge of the curtain before the play has begun and at once withdraws in order not to be seen. This anxious look vanished and everything was back in place, but I sensed that whatever I saw from now on would have been artificially arranged for my benefit. At that moment I caught sight of myself in the mirror, and was struck by a certain resemblance between myself and Andrée. If I had not long since ceased to shave my upper lip and had had only a faint shadow of a moustache, this resemblance would have been almost complete. It was perhaps on seeing my moustache at Balbec when it had scarcely begun to grow again that Albertine had suddenly felt that impatient, furious desire to return to Paris.

"But I still can't say things that aren't true simply because you see no harm in them. I swear to you that I never did anything with Albertine, and I'm convinced that she detested that sort of thing.

The people who told you that were lying to you, probably with some ulterior motive," she said with a questioning, defiant air.

"Oh, very well then, since you won't tell me," I replied, pretending to appear to be unwilling to furnish a proof which in fact I did not possess. However, I mentioned vaguely and at random the Buttes-Chaumont.

"I may have gone to the Buttes-Chaumont with Albertine, but is it a place that has a particularly evil reputation?"

I asked her whether she could not raise the subject with Gisèle who had at one time been on intimate terms with Albertine. But Andrée told me that because of a vile thing that Gisèle had done to her recently, asking a favour of her was the one thing that she must absolutely decline to do for me. "If you see her," she went on, "don't tell her what I've said to you about her; there's no point in making an enemy of her. She knows what I think of her, but I've always preferred to avoid having violent quarrels with her which only have to be patched up afterwards. And besides, she's dangerous. But you must understand that when one has read the letter which I had in my hands a week ago, and in which she lied with such absolute treachery, nothing, not even the noblest actions in the world, can wipe out the memory of such a thing."

On the whole I felt that if, in spite of the fact that Andrée had those tastes to the extent of making no pretence of concealing them, and the fact that Albertine had felt for her the great affection which she undoubtedly had felt, Andrée had none the less never had any carnal relations with Albertine and had never been aware that Albertine had those tastes, this meant that Albertine did not have them, and had never enjoyed with anyone those relations which, rather than with anyone else, she would have enjoyed with Andrée. And so when Andrée had left me, I realised that her categorical assertion had brought me some peace of mind. But perhaps it had been dictated by a sense of the obligation, which Andrée felt that she owed to the dead girl whose memory still survived in her, not to let me believe what Albertine, while she was alive, had doubtless begged her to deny.

Having thought for a moment, contemplating Andrée, that I could actually see these pleasures of Albertine's which I had so often tried to imagine, on another occasion I received an intimation of them otherwise than through the eyes: I thought I heard them. I had had two young laundry-girls, from a district where Albertine had often gone, brought to a house of assignation. One of them, beneath the caresses of the other, suddenly began to utter sounds which at first I found difficult to identify; for one never understands precisely the meaning of an original sound expressive of a sensation which one does not experience oneself. Hearing it from a neighbouring room without being able to see, one may mistake for uncontrollable laughter the noise which is forced by pain from a patient being operated on without an anaesthetic; and as for the noise emitted by a mother who has just been told that her child has died, it can seem to us, if we are unaware of its origin, as difficult to translate into human terms as the noise emitted by an animal or by a harp. It takes us a little time to realise that those two noises express what, by analogy with the (very different) sensations we ourselves may have felt, we call pain; and it took me some time, too, to understand that *this* noise expressed what, by analogy with the (very different) sensations I myself had felt, I called pleasure; and the pleasure must have been very great to overwhelm to this extent the person who was expressing it and to extract from her this strange utterance which seemed to describe and comment on all the phases of the exquisite drama which the young woman was living through and which was concealed from my eyes by the curtain that is for ever lowered for other people over what happens in the mysterious intimacy of every human creature. In any case these two girls could tell me nothing, as they had no idea who Albertine was.

Novelists sometimes pretend in an introduction that while travelling in a foreign country they have met somebody who has told them the story of another person's life. They then withdraw in favour of this chance acquaintance, and the story that he tells them is nothing more or less than their novel. Thus the life of Fabrice del Dongo was related to Stendhal by a canon of Padua. How gladly would we, when we are in love, that is to say when another person's existence seems to us mysterious, find some such well-informed narrator! And undoubtedly he exists. Do we not ourselves frequently relate the story of some woman or other quite dispassionately to one of our friends, or to a stranger, who has known nothing of her love affairs and listens to us with keen interest? Such a person as I was when I spoke to Bloch about the Princesse de Guermantes or Mme Swann, such a person existed, who could have spoken to me of Albertine, such a person exists always . . . but we never come across him. It seemed to me that if I had been able to find women who had known her I should have learned everything I did not yet know. And yet to strangers it must have seemed that nobody could have known as much about her life as I did. Indeed, did I not know her dearest friend, Andrée? Thus one imagines that the friend of a minister must know the truth about some political affair or cannot be implicated in a scandal. From his own experience the friend has found that whenever he discussed politics with the minister the latter confined himself to generalisations and told him nothing more than what had already appeared in the newspapers, or that if he was in any trouble, his repeated attempts to secure the minister's help have invariably been met with an "It's not in my power" against which the friend is himself powerless. I said to myself: "If I could have known such and such witnesses!"—from whom, if I had known them, I should probably have been unable to extract anything more than from Andrée, herself the custodian of a secret which she refused to surrender. Differing in this respect also from Swann who, when he was no longer jealous, ceased to feel any curiosity as to what Odette might have done with Forcheville, I found that, even after my jealousy had subsided, the thought of making the acquaintance of Albertine's laundry-girl, of people in her neighbourhood, of reconstructing her life in it, her intrigues, alone had any charm for me. And as desire always springs from an initial glamour, as had happened to me in the past with Gilberte and with the Duchesse de Guermantes, it was the women of Albertine's background, in the districts in which she had formerly lived, that I sought to know, and whose presence alone I could have desired. Whether or not I could learn anything from them, the only women towards whom I felt attracted were those whom Albertine had known or whom she might have known, women of her own background or of the sort with whom she liked to associate, in a word those women who had in my eyes the distinction of resembling her or of being of the type that might have appealed to her. Recalling thus either Albertine herself or the type for which she doubtless had a predilection, these women aroused in me a painful feeling of jealousy or regret, which later, when my grief subsided, changed into a curiosity that was not devoid of charm. And among these last, especially girls of the working class, because of that life, so different from the life that I knew, which is theirs. No doubt it is only in one's mind that one possesses things, and one does not possess a picture because it hangs in one's dining-room if one is incapable of understanding it, or a landscape because one lives in it without even looking at it. But still, I had had in the past the illusion of recapturing Balbec, when in Paris Albertine came to see me and I held her in my arms, and similarly I established some contact, restricted and furtive though it might be, with Albertine's life, the atmosphere of work-rooms, a conversation across a counter, the spirit of the slums, when I embraced a seamstress. Andrée, and these other women, all of them in relation to Albertine—like Albertine herself in relation to Balbec—were to be numbered among those substitute pleas-ures, replacing one another in a gradual declension, which enable us to dispense with the pleasure to which we can no longer attain, a trip to Balbec or the love of Albertine, pleasures which (just as going to the Louvre to look at a Titian consoles us for not being able to go to Venice where it originally was), separated one from another by indistinguishable gradations, convert one's life into a series of concentric, contiguous, harmonic and graduated zones, encircling an initial desire which has set the tone, eliminated everything that does not combine with it, applied the dominant colour (as had, for instance, occurred to me also in the cases of the Duchesse de Guermantes and of Gilberte). Andrée and these women were to the desire, which I knew I could no longer gratify, to have Albertine by my side, what had been, one evening, before I knew Albertine except by sight and felt that she could never be mine, the writhing, sun-drenched freshness of a cluster of grapes.

Associated now with the memory of my love, Albertine's physical and social attributes, in spite of which I had loved her, oriented my desire on the contrary towards what at one time it would least readily have chosen: dark-haired girls of the lower middle class. Indeed what was beginning partially to revive in me was that immense desire which my love for Albertine had been unable to assuage, that immense desire to know life which I used to feel on the roads round Balbec, in the streets of Paris, that desire which had caused me so much suffering when, supposing it to exist in Albertine's heart also, I had sought to deprive her of the means of satisfying it with anyone but myself. Now that I was able to endure the idea of her desire, since that idea was at once aroused by my own desire, these two immense appetites coincided; I would have liked us to be able to indulge them together, saying to myself: "That girl would have appealed to her," and led by this sudden detour to think of her and of her death, I felt too unhappy to be able to pursue my own desire any further. As, long ago, the

Méséglise and Guermantes ways had laid the foundations of my taste for the countryside and prevented me thereafter from finding any real charm in a place where there was no old church, where there were no cornflowers or buttercups, so it was by linking them in my mind to a past full of charm that my love for Albertine made me seek out exclusively a certain type of woman; I was beginning once more, as before I loved her, to feel the need for overtones from her which would be interchangeable with a memory that had become gradually less exclusive. I could not have found pleasure now in the company of a golden-haired and haughty duchess, because she would not have aroused in me any of the emotions that sprang from Albertine, from my desire for her, from my jealousy of her love affairs, from my grief at her death. For our sensations, in order to be strong, need to release inside us something different from themselves, a sentiment which cannot find its satisfaction in pleasure, but which adds itself to desire, swells it, makes it cling desperately to pleasure. Gradually, as the love that Albertine may have felt for certain women ceased to cause me pain, it attached those women to my past, made them somehow more real, as the memory of Combray gave to buttercups and hawthorn blossom a greater reality than to unfamiliar flowers. Even of Andrée, I no longer said to myself with rage in my heart: "Albertine loved her," but on the contrary, in order to explain my desire to myself, in an affectionate tone: "Albertine was fond of her." I could now understand the widowers whom we suppose to have found consolation and who prove on the contrary that they are inconsolable because they marry their deceased wife's sister.

Thus my waning love seemed to make new loves possible for me, and Albertine, like those women long loved for themselves who later, feeling their lover's desire fade, preserve their power by contenting themselves with the role of procuresses, provided me, as the Pompadour provided Louis XV, with fresh damsels. In the past, my time had been divided into periods in which I desired this woman or that. When the violent pleasures afforded by one had subsided, I longed for the other who would give me an almost pure affection until the need of more sophisticated caresses brought back my desire for the first. Now these alternations had come to an end, or at least one of the periods was being indefinitely prolonged. What I would have liked was that the newcomer should take up her abode in my house, and should give me at night, before leaving me, a familial, sisterly kiss. So that I might have been able to believe—had I not had experience of the intolerable presence of another person—that I regretted a kiss more than a certain pair of lips, a pleasure more than a love, a habit more than a person. I would have liked also that the new-comer should be able to play Vinteuil's music to me like Albertine, to talk to me as she had talked about Elstir. All this was impossible. Her love would not match up to Albertine's, I thought; either because a love which embraced all those episodes, visits to picture galleries, evenings at concerts, a whole complicated existence which allows correspondence, conversations, a flirtation pre-liminary to the more intimate relations, a serious friendship after-wards, possesses more resources than love for a woman who can only offer herself, as an orchestra possesses more resources than a piano; or because, more profoundly, my need of the same sort of tenderness as Albertine used to give me, the tenderness of a girl of a certain culture who would at the same time be a sister to me, was—like my need for women of the same background as Albertine—merely a recrudescence of my memory of Albertine, of my memory of my love for her. And once again I discovered, first of all that memory has no power of invention, that it is powerless to desire anything else, let alone anything better, than what we have already possessed; secondly that it is spiritual, in the sense that reality cannot provide it with the state which it seeks; and lastly that, stemming from a dead person, the resurrection that it incarnates is not so much that of the need to love, in which it makes us believe, as that of the need for the absent person. So that even the resemblance to Albertine of the woman I had chosen, the resemblance of her tenderness, if I succeeded in winning it, to Albertine's, only made me the more conscious of the absence of what I had been unconsciously seeking, of what was indispensable to the revival of my happiness, that is to say, Albertine herself, the time we had lived together, the past in the search for which I was unwittingly engaged.

Certainly, on fine days, Paris seemed to me innumerably aflower with all the girls, not whom I desired, but who thrust down their roots into the obscurity of the desire and the unknown nocturnal life of Albertine. It was of one such that she had said to me at the outset, when she had not yet begun to be wary of me: "She's ravishing, that girl. What pretty hair she has!" All that I had wanted to know about her life in the past when I knew her only by sight, and at the same time all my desires in life, merged into this one sole curiosity, to know in what manner Albertine experienced pleasure, to see her with other women, perhaps because thus, when they had left her, I should have remained alone with her, the last and the master. And seeing her hesitations as to whether it would be worth her while to spend the evening with this or that girl, her satiety when the other had gone, perhaps her disappointment, I should have elucidated, I should have restored to its true proportions, the jealousy that Albertine inspired in me, because seeing her thus experience them I should have taken the measure and discovered the limit of her pleasures. Of how many pleasures, of what an agreeable life she deprived us, I said to myself, by that stubborn obstinacy in denying her tastes! And as once again I sought to discover what could have been the reason for that obstinacy, all of a sudden the memory came back to me of a remark that I had made to her at Balbec on the day when she gave me a pencil. As I reproached her for not having allowed me to kiss her, I had told her that I thought a kiss just as natural as I thought it revolting that a woman should have relations with another woman. Alas, perhaps Albertine had remembered it.

I took home with me the girls who would have appealed to me least, I stroked sleek virginal tresses, I admired a small and well-shaped nose or a Spanish pallor. True, in the past, even with a woman I had merely glimpsed on a road near Balbec or in a street in Paris, I had felt the individuality of my desire and that it would be adulterating it to seek to assuage it with another person. But life, by disclosing to me little by little the permanence of our needs, had taught me that failing one person we must content ourselves with another, and I felt that what I had demanded of Albertine could have been given to me by another, by Mlle de Stermaria. But it had been Albertine; and between the satisfaction of my need for tenderness and the distinctive characteristics of her body, such an inextricable network of memories had been woven that I could no longer detach all that embroidery from any new physical desire. She alone could give me that happiness. The idea of her uniqueness was no longer a metaphysical *a priori* based upon what was individual in Albertine, as in the case of the women I passed in the street long ago, but an *a posteriori* created by the contingent and indissoluble overlapping of my memories. I could no longer desire physically without feeling a need for her, without suffering from her absence. Hence the mere resemblance of the woman chosen, the caresses sought, to the happiness I had known only made me the more conscious of all that they lacked wherewith to revive it. The same vacuum that I had found in my room since Albertine had left, and had supposed that I could fill by taking women in my arms, I regained in them. They had never spoken to me, these women, of Vinteuil's music, of Saint-Simon's memoirs, they had not sprayed themselves with an overpowering scent before coming to see me, they had not played at intertwining their eyelashes with mine, all of which things are important because they seem to enable one to weave dreams round the sexual act itself and to give oneself the illusion of love, but in reality because they formed part of my memory of Albertine and it was she whom I wanted there. What these women had in common with Albertine made me feel all the more strongly what was lacking of her in them, which was everything, and would never exist again since Albertine was dead. And so my love for Albertine, which had drawn me towards these women, made me indifferent to them, and my regret for Albertine and the persistence of my jealousy, which had already outlasted my most pessimistic calculations, would perhaps never have altered appreciably if their existence, isolated from the rest of my life, had been subjected merely to the play of my memories, to the actions and reactions of a psychology applicable to immobile states, and had not been drawn into a vaster system in which souls move in time as bodies move in space.

As there is a geometry in space, so there is a psychology in time, in which the calculations of a plane psychology would no longer be accurate because we should not be taking account of Time and one of the forms that it assumes, forgetting—forgetting, the force of which I was beginning to feel and which is so powerful an instrument of adaptation to reality because it gradually destroys in us the surviving past which is in perpetual contradiction with it. And I really ought to have discovered sooner that one day I should no longer be in love with Albertine. When I had realised, from the difference that existed between what the importance of her person and of her actions was to me and what it was to other people, that my love was not so much a love for her as a love in myself, I might have drawn various conclusions from this subjective nature of my love and in particular deduced that, being a mental state, it might survive the person for some time, but also that, having no real connexion with that person, having no support outside itself, it must, like every mental state, even the most lasting, find itself one day obsolete, be "replaced," and that when that day came every-thing that seemed to attach me so sweetly, indissolubly, to the memory of Albertine would no longer exist for me. It is the tragedy of other people that they are merely showcases for the very perishable collections of one's own mind. For this very reason one bases upon them projects which have all the fervour of thought; but thought languishes and memory decays: the day would come when I would readily admit the first comer to Albertine's room, as I had without the slightest regret given Albertine the agate marble or other gifts that I had received from Gilberte.

CHAPTER TWO

MADEMOISELLE DE FORCHEVILLE

IT was not that I did not still love Albertine, but I no longer loved her in the same fashion as in the final phase. No, it was in the fashion of the earlier days, when everything connected with her, places or people, made me feel a curiosity in which there was more charm than suffering. And indeed I was well aware now that before I forgot her altogether, before I got back to the initial stage of indifference, I should have to traverse in the opposite direction, like a traveller who returns by the same route to his starting-point, all the sentiments through which I had passed before arriving at my great love. But these stages, these moments of the past are not immobile; they have retained the tremendous force, the happy ignorance of the hope that was then soaring towards a time which has now become the past, but which a hallucination makes us for a moment mistake retrospectively for the future. I read a letter from Albertine in which she had announced her intention of coming to see me that evening, and I felt for an instant the joy of expectation. In these return journeys along the same line from a place to which one will never return, when one recognises the names and the appearance of all the places through which one passed on the outward journey, it happens that, while one's train is halted at one of the stations, for an instant one has the illusion of setting off again, but in the direction of the place from which one has come, as on the first occasion. The illusion vanishes at once, but for an instant one had felt oneself being carried towards it once more: such is the cruelty of memory.

And yet if, before returning to the state of indifference from which one started, one cannot avoid covering in the reverse direction the distances one had traversed in order to arrive at love, the itinerary one follows, the line one takes, are not necessarily the same. They have this in common, that they are not direct, because the process of forgetting is no more regular than that of love. But they do not necessarily take the same routes. And on the route which I followed on my return journey there were three stages, when I was already well on the way towards my destination, which I remember particularly, doubtless because I perceived in them things that had no part in my love for Albertine, or at most were linked to it only to the extent to which what existed already in one's heart before a great love becomes associated with it, whether by fostering it, or by combating it, or by offering contrasts with it or images of it for one's intelligence to analyse.

The first of these stages began early one winter, on a fine Sunday, which was also All Saints' Day, when I had gone out. As I approached the Bois, I remembered sadly how Albertine had come back to join me from the Trocadéro, for it was the same day, only without Albertine. Sadly and yet not without pleasure all the same, for the repetition in the minor, in a melancholy key, of the same motif that had filled that earlier day, the very absence of Françoise's telephone message, of Albertine's return, which was not something negative but the suppression in reality of what I remembered, gave the day a certain sadness, made of it something more beautiful than a simple, unbroken day, because what was no longer there, what had been torn from it, remained as it were etched upon it. In the Bois, I hummed a few phrases of Vinteuil's sonata. The thought that Albertine had so often played it to me no longer saddened me unduly, for almost all my memories of her had entered into that secondary chemical state in which they no longer cause an anxious oppression of the heart, but rather a certain sweetness. From time to time, in the passages which she used to play most often, when she was in the habit of making some observation which at the time I thought charming, of suggesting some reminiscence, I said to myself: "Poor child," but not sadly, merely investing the musical phrase with an additional value, as it were a historical, a curiosity value, like that which the portrait of Charles I by Van Dyck, already so beautiful in itself, acquires from the fact that it found its way into the national collection because of Mme du Barry's desire to impress the King. When the little phrase, before disappearing altogether, dissolved into its various elements in which it floated still for a moment in scattered fragments, it was not for me, as it had been for Swann, a messenger from a vanishing Albertine. It was not altogether the same associations of ideas that the little phrase had aroused in me as in Swann. I had been struck most of all by the elaboration, the trial runs, the repetitions, the gradual evolution of a phrase which developed through the course of the sonata as that love had developed through the course of my life. And now, aware that, day by day, one element after another of my love was vanishing, the jealous side of it, then some other, drifting gradually back in a vague remembrance to the first tentative beginnings, it was my love that, in the scattered notes of the little phrase, I seemed to see disintegrating before my eyes.

As I followed the paths through thickets whose gauzy screen of leaves grew thinner each day, the memory of a drive during which Albertine was by my side in the carriage on the way home with me, and during which I felt that my life was wrapped up in her, now floated round about me, in the vague mist of the darkening branches in the midst of which the setting sun lit up the tenuous horizontal strips of golden foliage so that they seemed suspended in the empty air. My heart kept fluttering from moment to moment, as happens to anyone who is haunted by an obsession which gives to every woman standing at the end of a path the resemblance or even the possible identity with the woman he is thinking of. "Perhaps it is she!" One looks round, the carriage continues on its way, and one does not go back. I did not simply contemplate this foliage with the eyes of memory; it interested me, touched me, like those purely descriptive pages into which an artist, to make them more complete, introduces a fiction, a whole romance; and this work of nature thus assumed the sole charm of melancholy which was capable of reaching my heart. The reason for this charm seemed to me to be that I still loved Albertine as much as ever, whereas the true reason was on the contrary that oblivion was continuing to make such headway in me that the memory of Albertine was no longer painful to me, that is to say had changed; but however clearly we may discern our impressions, as I then thought that I could discern the reason for my melancholy, we are unable to trace them back to their more distant meaning. Like those symptoms which the doctor hears his patient describe to him and with the help of which he works back to a deeper cause of which the patient is unaware, similarly our impressions, our ideas, have only a symptomatic value. My jealousy being kept in abeyance by the impression of charm and sweet sadness which I was feeling, my senses reawakened. Once again, as when I had ceased to see Gilberte, the love of women arose in me, relieved of any exclusive association with a particular woman already loved, and floated like those essences that have been liberated by previous destructions and stray suspended in the springtime air, asking only to be reunited with a new creature. Nowhere do so many flowers, "forget-me-nots" though they be styled, germinate as in a cemetery. I looked at the girls with whom this fine day was so multitudinously aflower, as I would have looked at them long ago from Mme de Villeparisis's carriage or from the carriage in which, on a similar Sunday, I had come there with Albertine. At once, the glance which I now gave one or other of them was matched immediately by the curious, furtive, speculative glance, reflecting unimaginable thoughts, which Albertine would surreptitiously have cast at them and which, duplicating my own with a mysterious, swift, steel-blue wing, wafted along these paths, so natural until then, the tremor of an unknown life with which my own desire would not have sufficed to animate them had it remained alone, for it, to me, contained nothing that was unfamiliar. At times the reading of a novel that was at all sad carried me suddenly back, for certain novels are like great but temporary bereavements, abolishing habit, bringing us back into contact with the reality of life, but for a few hours only, like a nightmare, since the force of habit, the oblivion it creates, the gaiety it restores through the powerlessness of the brain to fight against it and to re-create the truth, infinitely outweigh the almost hypnotic suggestion of a good book which, like all such influences, has very transient effects.

At Balbec, when I had first longed to know Albertine, was it not because she had seemed to me representative of those girls the sight of whom had so often brought me to a standstill in the streets of towns or on country roads, and because she might epitomise their life for me? And was it not natural that now the waning star of my love in which they had been condensed should disperse once again in this scattered dust of nebulae? All of them seemed to me Albertines—the image that I carried inside me making me find her everywhere—and indeed, at the bend of an avenue, a girl getting into a motor-car recalled her so strongly, was so exactly of the same build, that I wondered for an instant whether it was not her that I had just seen, whether people had not been deceiving me when they sent me the report of her death. I recalled her thus at the corner of an avenue, perhaps at Balbec, getting into a car in the same way, at a time when she was so full of confidence in life. And I did not merely record with my eyes, as one of those superficial phenomena which occur so often in the course of a walk, this other girl's action in climbing into the car: become a sort of sustained action, it seemed to me to extend also into the past by virtue of the memory which had been superimposed upon it and which pressed so voluptuously, so sadly against my heart. But by this time the girl had vanished.

A little further on I saw a group of three girls, slightly older, young women perhaps, whose elegant and energetic appearance corresponded so closely with what had attracted me on the day when I first saw Albertine and her friends that I hastened in pursuit of them and, when they stopped a carriage, looked frantically in every direction for another. I found one, but it was too late. I failed to overtake them. A few days later, however, on coming home, I saw emerging from the portico of our house the three girls whom I had followed in the Bois. They were absolutely typical, the two dark ones especially, except that they were slightly older, of those well-born girls who so often, seen from my window or encountered in the street, had made me form countless plans, had given me a taste for life, but whom I had never succeeded in getting to know. The fair one had a rather more delicate, almost an invalid air, which appealed to me less. It was she, nevertheless, who was responsible for my not contenting myself with gazing at them for a moment, having stopped dead, with one of those looks which, by their fixed absorption, their application as to a problem, seem to be concerned with something far beyond what meets the eye. I should doubtless have allowed them to disappear, as I had allowed so many others, if, as they walked past me, the fair-haired one—was it because I was scrutinising them so closely?—had not darted a furtive glance at me and then, turning round after having passed me, a second one that set me aflame. However, as she ceased to pay attention to me and resumed her conversation with her friends, my ardour would doubtless have subsided, had it not been increased a hundredfold by the following discovery. When I asked the concierge who they were, "They asked for Mme la Duchesse," he informed me. "I think only one of them knows her and the others were simply accompanying her as far as the door. Here's the name, I don't know whether I've taken it down properly." And I read: "Mlle Déporcheville," which it was easy to correct to "d'Eporcheville," that is to say the name, more or less, so far as I could remember, of the girl of excellent family, vaguely connected with the Guermantes, whom Robert had told me that he had met in a disorderly house and with whom he had

had relations. I now understood the meaning of her glance, why she had turned round without letting her companions see. How often I had thought about her, trying to visualise her from the name that Robert had given me! And here I had just seen her, in no way different from her friends, but for that clandestine glance which established between herself and me a secret entry into the parts of her life which were evidently hidden from her friends and which made her appear more accessible—already almost half mine—and more soft-hearted than girls of the aristocracy usually are. In the mind of this girl, she and I now had in common the hours that we might have spent together if she was free to make an assignation with me. Was it not this that her glance had sought to express to me with an eloquence that was intelligible to me alone? My heart beat wildly. I could not have given an exact description of Mlle d'Eporcheville's appearance, I could only picture vaguely a fair-skinned face viewed from the side; but I was madly in love with her. All of a sudden I realised that I was reasoning as though, of the three girls, Mlle d'Eporcheville must be the fair one who had turned round and looked at me twice. But the concierge had not told me this. I returned to his lodge and questioned him again. He told me that he could not enlighten me on the subject, because they had come today for the first time and while he was not there. But he would ask his wife who had seen them once before. She was busy at the moment scrubbing the service stairs. Which of us has not experienced in the course of his life exquisite uncertainties more or less similar to this? A charitable friend, to whom one describes a girl one has seen at a ball, concludes from the description that she must be one of his friends and invites one to meet her. But among so many others, and on the basis of a mere verbal portrait, is there not a possibility of error? The girl you are about to see may well turn out to be a different girl from the one you desire. On the other hand, you may be about to see, holding out her hand to you with a smile, precisely the girl whom you hoped that she would be. This latter case is not infrequent, and, without being justified always by a reasoning as convincing as mine with respect to Mlle d'Eporcheville, arises from a sort of intuition as well as from that wind of fortune which favours us at times. Then, on seeing her, one says to oneself: "She was the one." I remembered that, among the little band of girls who used to parade along the beach, I had guessed correctly which was named Albertine Simonet. This memory caused me a sharp but transient pang, and while the concierge went in search of his wife, my chief anxiety—as I thought of Mlle d'Eporcheville, and since in those minutes spent waiting during which a name or piece of information which we have for some reason or other fitted to a face finds itself free for an instant and floats between several, ready, if it belongs to a new one, to make the original face to which it had applied retrospectively strange, innocent, elusive—was that the concierge was perhaps going to inform me that Mlle d'Eporcheville was, on the contrary, one of the two dark girls. In that event, the being in whose existence I believed would vanish, the being whom I already loved, whom I now thought only of possessing, that sly, blonde Mlle d'Eporcheville whom the fateful answer must then separate into two distinct elements, which I had arbitrarily united after the fashion of a novelist who blends diverse elements borrowed from reality in order to create an imaginary character, elements which, taken separately—the name failing to corroborate the supposed intention of the glance—lost all their meaning. In that case my arguments would be nullified, but how greatly, on the contrary, they found themselves strengthened when the concierge returned to tell me that Mlle d'Eporcheville was indeed the fair girl.

From then on I could no longer believe that it was a case of homonymy. It would have been too great a coincidence that of these three girls one should be named Mlle d'Eporcheville, that she should be precisely (and this was an initial, highly relevant corroboration of my supposition) the one who had looked at me in that way, almost smiling at me, and that it should not be she who frequented houses of assignation.

Then began a day of wild excitement. Even before setting out to buy everything in which I thought it proper to array myself in order to create a favourable impression when I went to call upon Mme de Guermantes two days later, when (the concierge had informed me) the young lady would be coming back to see the Duchess, in whose house I should thus find a willing girl with whom I would arrange a rendezvous (for I could easily find an opportunity of speaking to her alone in a corner of the drawing-room), I decided, to make assurance doubly sure, to telegraph Robert to ask him for the girl's exact name and description, hoping to have his reply within forty-eight hours (I did not think for an instant of anything else, not even of Albertine), for I was determined, whatever might happen to me in the meantime, even if I had to be carried down in a chair because I was too ill to walk, to pay a call on the Duchess at the appropriate hour. If I telegraphed to Saint-Loup it was not that I had any lingering doubt as to the identity of the person, it was not that the girl whom I had seen and the girl of whom he had spoken were still distinct personalities in my mind. I had no doubt whatever that they were the same person. But in my impatience at the enforced interval of forty-eight hours, it was a pleasure to me, it gave me already a sort of secret power over her, to receive a telegram concerning her, filled with detailed information. At the telegraph office, as I drafted my message with the animation of a man who is fired by hope, I remarked how much less helpless I was now than in my boy-hood, and in relation to Mlle d'Eporcheville than I had been in relation to Gilberte. I had merely had to take the trouble to write out my telegram, and thereafter the clerk had only to take it from me, and the swiftest channels of electric communication to trans-mit it, and the whole length and breadth of France and the Mediterranean, together with the whole of Robert's roistering life applied to the identification of the person I had just met, would be placed at the service of the romance which I had just sketched out and to which I need no longer give a thought, for they would undertake to bring it to a conclusion one way or the other before twenty-four hours had passed. Whereas in the old days, brought home by Françoise from the Champs-Elysées, brooding alone in the house over my impotent desires, unable to make use of the practical devices of civilisation, I loved like a savage, or indeed, for I was not even free to move about, like a flower. From this moment onwards I was in a continual fever; a request from my father to go away with him for a couple of days, which would have obliged me to forgo my visit to the Duchess, filled me with such rage and despair that my mother intervened and persuaded my father to allow me to remain in Paris. But for several hours my fury refused to be allayed, while my desire for Mlle d'Eporcheville was increased a hundredfold by the obstacle that had been placed between us, by the fear which I had felt for a moment that those hours of my visit to Mme de Guermantes, at the prospect of which I smiled in constant anticipation, as at an assured blessing of which nothing could deprive me, might not occur. Certain phil-osophers assert that the external world does not exist, and that it is within ourselves that we develop our lives. However that may be, love, even in its humblest beginnings, is a striking example of how little reality means to us. Had I been obliged to draw from memory a portrait of Mlle d'Eporcheville, to furnish a description of her, or even to recognise her in the street, I should have found it imposs-ible. I had glimpsed her in profile, on the move, and she had struck me as being simple, pretty, tall and fair; I could not have said more. But all the reflexes of desire, of anxiety, of the mortal blow struck by the fear of not seeing her if my father took me away, all these things, associated with an image of which on the whole I knew nothing, and as to which it was enough that I knew it to be agreeable, already constituted a state of love. At last, on the following morning, after a night of happy sleeplessness I received Saint-Loup's telegram: "De l'Orgeville, *de* particle, *orge* barley, like rye, *ville*, like town, small, dark, plump, is at present in Switzerland." It was not the girl.

A moment later my mother came into my room with the mail, put it down carelessly on my bed as though she were thinking of something else, and withdrew at once to leave me on my own. And I, who was familiar with my dear Mamma's little subterfuges and knew that one could always read the truth in her face without fear of being mistaken, if one took as a key to the cipher her desire to give pleasure to others, I smiled and thought: "There must be something interesting for me in the post, and Mamma assumed that indifferent, absent-minded air so that my surprise might be complete and so as not to be like the people who take away half your pleasure by telling you of it beforehand. And she didn't stay with me because she was afraid that out of pride I might conceal my pleasure and so feel it less keenly." Meanwhile, on reaching the door, my mother had run into Françoise who was coming into the room, and forcing her to turn back, had dragged her out with her, somewhat alarmed, offended and surprised; for Françoise consid-ered that her duties conferred upon her the privilege of entering my room at any hour of the day and of remaining there if she chose. But already, upon her features, astonishment and anger had vanished beneath a dark and sticky smile of transcendent pity and philosophical irony, a viscous liquid secreted, in order to heal her wound, by her outraged self-esteem. So that she might not feel herself despised, she despised us. Moreover she knew that we were masters, in other words capricious creatures, who, not being conspicuously intelligent, take pleasure in imposing by fear upon clever people, upon servants, in order to prove that they are the masters, absurd tasks such as boiling water in times of epidemic, washing down a room with a damp cloth, and leaving it at the very moment when you wanted to come into it. Mamma had placed the post by my side, so that I might not overlook it. I could see however that it consisted only of newspapers. No doubt there was some article by a writer whom I admired, which, as he wrote seldom, would be a surprise for me. I went to the window, and drew back the curtains. Above the pale and misty daylight, the sky glowed pink, like the stoves that are being lighted in kitchens at that hour, and the sight of it filled me with hope and with a longing to spend the night in a train and awake at the little country station where I had seen the milk-girl with the rosy cheeks.

I opened the *Figaro*. What a bore! The main article had the same title as the article which I had sent to the paper and which had not appeared. But not merely the same title . . . why, here were several words that were absolutely identical. This was really too bad. I must write and complain. Meanwhile I could hear Françoise who, indignant at having been banished from my room, into which she considered that she had the right of entry, was grumbling: "It's a proper shame, a kid I saw brought into the world. I didn't see him when his mother bore him, to be sure. But when I first knew him, to say the most, it wasn't five years since he was birthed!" But it wasn't merely a few words, it was the whole thing, and there was my signature . . . It was my article that had appeared at last! But my brain which, even at that period, had begun to show signs of age and to tire easily, continued for a moment longer to reason as though it had not understood that this was my article, like an old man who is obliged to complete a movement that he has begun even if it has become unnecessary, even if an unforeseen obstacle, in the face of which he ought at once to draw back, makes it dangerous. Then I considered the spiritual bread of life that a newspaper is, still warm and damp from the press and the morning fog in which it is distributed, at daybreak, to the house-maids who bring it to their masters with their morning coffee, a miraculous, self-multiplying bread which is at the same time one and ten thousand, which remains the same for each person while penetrating innumerably into every house at once.

What I was holding in my hand was not a particular copy of the newspaper, but one out of the ten thousand; it was not merely what had been written by me, but what had been written by me and read by everyone. To appreciate exactly the phenomenon which was occurring at this moment in other houses, it was essential that I read this article not as its author but as one of the readers of the paper; what I was holding in my hand was not only what I had written, it was the symbol of its incarnation in so many minds. But then came an initial anxiety. Would the reader who had not been forewarned see this article? I opened the paper carelessly as would such a reader, even assuming an air of not knowing what there was this morning in my paper, of being in a hurry to look at the social and political news. But my article was so long that my eye, which was avoiding it (in order to be absolutely fair and not load the dice in my favour, as a person who is waiting counts very slowly on purpose) picked up a fragment of it in passing. But many of those readers who notice the main article and even read it do not look at the signature; I myself would be quite incapable of saying who had written the main article of the day before. And I now made up my mind always to read them, and the author's name too; but, like a jealous lover who refrains from being unfaithful to his mistress in order to believe in her fidelity, I reflected sadly that my own future attention would not compel, had not compelled the reciprocal attention of other people. And besides, there were those who would have gone out shooting, and those who would have left the house too early. But still, a few people would read it. I did as they would do: I began. Although I was well aware that many people who read this article would find it detestable, at the moment of reading it the meaning that each word conveyed to me seemed to me to be printed on the paper, and I could not believe that every other reader on opening his eyes would not see directly the images that I saw, assuming—with the same naïvety as those who believe that it is the actual speech they have uttered that proceeds just as it is along the telephone wires—that the author's thought is directly perceived by the reader, whereas quite other thoughts form in the latter's mind; at the very moment in which I was trying to be an ordinary reader, my mind was rewriting my article while reading it. If M. de Guermantes did not understand some sentence which would appeal to Bloch, he might, on the other hand, be amused by some reflexion which Bloch would scorn. Thus, a fresh admirer presenting himself for each section which the previous reader seemed to disregard, the article as a whole was lifted to the skies by a swarm of readers and prevailed over my own self-distrust, since I no longer needed to bolster it. The truth of the matter is that the value of an article, however remarkable it may be, is like that of those passages in parliamentary reports in which the words "We shall see," uttered by the Minister, only take on their full consequence when read thus: THE PRIME MINISTER, MINISTER OF THE INTERIOR AND OF RELIGIOUS AFFAIRS: "We shall see!" (*Loud exclamations on the extreme Left. "Hear, hear," from some Left and Centre benches*)—an ending better than the middle and worthy of the beginning. Part of the beauty—and it is the original flaw in this type of literature, from which the famous *Lundis* are not exempt—lies in the impression made on the readers. It is a collective Venus, of which we have but one truncated limb if we confine ourselves to the thought of the author, for it is fully realised only in the minds of his readers. In them it finds completion. And since a crowd, even a select crowd, is not an artist, this final seal which it sets upon the article must always retain a trace of the commonplace. Thus Sainte-Beuve, on a Monday, could imagine Mme de Boigne in her four-poster bed reading his article in the *Constitutionnel*, and appreciating some pretty sentence which he had taken a long delight in composing and which might never, perhaps, have flowed from his pen had he not thought it opportune to stuff it into his article in order to make a more far-reaching impression. Doubtless the Chancellor,[3] reading it too, would mention it during the visit he would pay to his old friend and mistress a little later. And when he dropped him home in his carriage that evening, the Duc de Noailles in his grey trousers would tell him what had been thought of it in society, if a note from Mme d'Arbouville had not already informed him.

And setting my own self-distrust against the ten-thousand-fold approbation which now sustained me, I drew as much strength and hope for my talent from reading the article at this moment as I drew misgivings when what I had written was addressed only to myself. I saw at that same hour my thought—or at least, failing my thought for those who were incapable of understanding it, the repetition of my name and as it were an embellished evocation of my person—shine on countless people, colour their own thoughts in an auroral light which filled me with more strength and triumphant joy than the multiple dawn which at that moment was blushing at every window. I saw Bloch, the Guermantes, Legrandin, Andrée, extracting from every sentence the images that it enclosed at the very moment in which I was endeavouring to be an ordinary reader, while reading as author, but not only as author. In order that the impossible creature I was endeavouring

to be should combine all the opposites that might be most favourable to me, if I read as an author I judged myself as a reader,
without any of the qualms that may be felt about a written text by
him who compares it with the ideal which he has sought to express
in it. Those passages which, when I wrote them, were so colourless in comparison with my thought, so complicated and opaque in
comparison with my harmonious and transparent vision, so full of
gaps which I had not managed to fill, that the reading of them was
a torture to me, had only accentuated in me the sense of my own
impotence and of my incurable lack of talent. But now, in forcing
myself to be a reader, I transferred to others the painful duty of
judging me, and I succeeded at least in making a clean sweep of
what I had attempted to do in reading what I had written. I read
the article while forcing myself to imagine that it had been written
by someone else. Then all my images, all my reflexions, all my
epithets taken in themselves, untarnished by the memory of the
failure which they represented in relation to my aims, charmed me
by their brilliance, their unexpectedness, their profundity. And
when I became aware of too blatant a weakness, taking refuge in
the spirit of the ordinary and astonished reader, I said to myself:
"Bah! how could a reader possibly notice that? There may well be
something lacking there, but good heavens, they ought to be
pleased! There are enough good things in it to be getting on
with, more than they usually get."

And thus, no sooner had I finished this comforting perusal than
I who had not had the courage to re-read my manuscript wanted
to start again immediately, for there is nothing of which one can
say more aptly than of an old article by oneself that "it bears re-
reading." I made up my mind to send Françoise out to buy more
copies—in order to give them to my friends, I would tell her, but
in reality to feel at first hand the miracle of the multiplication of my
thought and to read, as though I were another person who had just
opened the *Figaro*, the same sentences in another copy. It was, as it
happened, a very long time since I had seen the Guermantes:
I would go and pay them a visit in order to find out what people
thought of my article.

I thought of some female reader into whose room I would have
loved to penetrate and to whom the newspaper would convey, if
not my thought, which she would be incapable of understanding,
at least my name, like a eulogy of me. But eulogies awarded to
somebody one doesn't love do not captivate the heart any more

than the thoughts of a mind one is unable to penetrate attract the mind. With regard to other friends, however, I told myself that if the state of my health continued to grow worse and I could no longer see them, it would be pleasant to continue to write, in order thus to have access to them still, to speak to them between the lines, to make them share my thoughts, to please them, to be received into their hearts. I told myself this because, social relations having hitherto had a place in my daily life, a future in which they would no longer figure alarmed me, and because this expedient which would enable me to remain in the thoughts of my friends, perhaps to arouse their admiration, until the day when I should be well enough to begin to see them again, was a solace to me; I told myself this, but I was well aware that it was not true, that although I chose to imagine their attention as the object of my pleasure, that pleasure was an internal, spiritual, self-generated pleasure which they could not give me and which I could find not in conversing with them, but in writing far away from them, and that if I began to write in the hope of seeing them indirectly, in the hope they might have a better idea of me, in the hope of preparing for myself a better position in society, perhaps writing would relieve me of the wish to see them, and I should no longer have any desire to enjoy the position in society which literature might have given me, because my pleasure would be no longer in society but in literature.

After lunch, when I went down to Mme de Guermantes, it was less for the sake of Mlle d'Eporcheville, who had been stripped, by Saint-Loup's telegram, of the better part of her personality, than in the hope of finding in the Duchess herself one of those readers of my article who would enable me to form an idea of the impression that it had made upon those members of the public who were subscribers to or purchasers of the *Figaro*. It was not, incidentally, without pleasure that I went to see Mme de Guermantes. Although I told myself that what made her house different to me from all the rest was the fact that it had for so long haunted my imagination, by knowing the reason for this difference I did not abolish it. Moreover, the name Guermantes existed for me in many forms. If the form which my memory had merely noted down as in an address-book was not accompanied by any poetry, older forms, those which dated from the time when I did not know Mme de Guermantes, were liable to renew themselves in me, especially when I had not seen her for some time and the glaring light of the person with human features did not quench the mysterious radiance of the name. Then once again I began to think of Mme de Guermantes's dwelling as of something that was beyond the bounds of reality, in the same way as I began to think again of the misty Balbec of my early day-dreams as though I had not since then made that journey, or of the 1.22 train as though I had never taken it. I forgot for an instant my own knowledge that none of this existed, as we think at times of a beloved friend forgetting for an instant that he is dead. Then the idea of reality returned as I entered the Duchess's hall. But I consoled myself with the reflexion that in spite of everything she was for me the real point of intersection between reality and dream.

On entering the drawing-room, I saw the fair girl whom I had supposed for twenty-four hours to be the girl of whom Saint-Loup had spoken to me. It was she who asked the Duchess to "reintroduce" me to her. And indeed, the moment I came into the room I had the impression that I knew her quite well, an impression which the Duchess however dispelled by saying: "Oh! so you've met Mlle de Forcheville before?" For, on the contrary, I was certain that I had never been introduced to any girl of that name, which would certainly have struck me, so familiar was it in my memory ever since I had been given a retrospective account of Odette's love affairs and Swann's jealousy. In itself my twofold error as to the name, in having remembered "de l'Orgeville" as "d'Eporcheville" and in having reconstructed as "d'Eporcheville" what was in reality "Forcheville," was in no way extraordinary. Our mistake lies in supposing that things present themselves as they really are, names as they are written, people as photography and psychology give an unalterable notion of them. But in reality this is not at all what we ordinarily perceive. We see, we hear, we conceive the world in a lopsided fashion. We repeat a name as we have heard it spoken until experience has corrected our mistake— something that does not always happen. Everyone at Combray had spoken to Françoise for twenty-five years of Mme Sazerat and Françoise continued to say "Mme Sazerin," not from that deliberate and proud perseverance in error which was habitual with her, which was strengthened by our contradictions, and which was all that she had added of the egalitarian principles of 1789 to the France of Saint-André-des-Champs in her make-up (she claimed only one civic right, that of not pronouncing words as we did and of maintaining that "hôtel," "été" and "air" were of the feminine gender), but because she really did continue to hear "Sazerin." This perpetual error, which is precisely "life," does not bestow its countless forms merely upon the visible and the audible universe, but upon the social universe, the sentimental universe, the historical universe, and so forth. The Princesse de Luxembourg is no better than a prostitute in the eyes of the judge's wife, which of course is of little consequence; what is of slightly more consequence is the fact that Odette is in Swann's eyes a difficult woman to conquer, whence he builds up a whole romance which becomes all the more painful when he discovers his error; what is of even more consequence still, the French are thinking only of revenge in the eyes of the Germans. We have of the universe only inchoate, fragmentary visions, which we complement by arbitrary associations of ideas, creative of dangerous illusions. I should therefore have had no reason to be surprised when I heard the name Forcheville (and I was already wondering whether she was related to the Forcheville of whom I had so often heard) had not the fair girl said to me at once, anxious no doubt to forestall, tactfully, questions which would have been disagreeable to her: "Don't you remember that you knew me well long ago . . . you used to come to our house . . . your friend Gilberte. I could see that you didn't recognise me. I recognised you at once." (She said this as if she had recognised me at once in the drawing-room, but the truth is that she had recognised me in the street and had greeted me, and later Mme de Guermantes informed me that she had told her, as something very comic and extraordinary, that I had followed her and brushed against her, mistaking her for a tart.) I did not discover until after her departure why she was called Mlle de Forcheville. After Swann's death, Odette, who astonished everyone by her profound, prolonged and sincere grief, found herself an extremely rich widow. Forcheville married her, after making a long round of country houses and ascertaining that his family would acknowledge his wife. (The family raised some difficulties at first, but yielded to the material advantage of no longer having to provide for the expenses of a needy relative who was about to pass from comparative penury to opulence.) Shortly after this, an uncle of Swann's, in whose hands the successive demise of innumerable relatives had accumulated an enormous inheritance, died, leaving the whole of his fortune to Gilberte who thus became one of the richest heiresses in France. But this was a time when in the aftermath of the Dreyfus case an anti-semitic trend had arisen parallel to a growing trend towards the penetration of society by Jews. The politicians had not been wrong in thinking that the discovery of the judicial error would be a severe blow to anti-semitism. But, temporarily at least, a form of social anti-semitism was on the contrary enhanced and exacerbated thereby. Forcheville, who, like every petty nobleman, had derived from conversations in the family circle the certainty that his name was more ancient than that of La Rochefoucauld, considered that, in marrying the widow of a Jew, he had performed a similar act of charity to that of a millionaire who picks up a prostitute in the street and rescues her from poverty and squalor. He was prepared to extend his bounty to Gilberte, whose prospects of marriage would be assisted by all her millions but hindered by that absurd name "Swann." He declared that he would adopt her. We know that Mme de Guermantes, to the astonishment of her friends—which she enjoyed and was in the habit of provoking—had refused, after Swann's marriage, to meet his daughter as well as his wife. This refusal had appeared all the more cruel inasmuch as what the possibility of marriage to Odette had long represented to Swann was the prospect of introducing his daughter to Mme de Guermantes. And doubtless he ought to have known, he who had already had so long an experience of life, that these scenes which we picture to ourselves are never realised for a diversity of reasons, among which there is one which meant that he seldom regretted his inability to effect that introduction. This reason is that, whatever the image may be—from the prospect of eating a trout at sunset, which makes a sedentary man decide to take the train, to the desire to be able to astonish the proud lady at a cash desk one evening by stopping outside her door in a magnificent carriage, which makes an unscrupulous man decide to commit murder or to long for the death of rich relatives, according to whether he is brave or lazy, whether he follows his ideas through or remains fondling the first link in the chain—the act which is destined to enable us to attain to it, whether the act be travel, marriage, crime or whatever, modifies us so profoundly that not merely do we cease to attach any importance to the reason which made us perform it, but the image conceived by the man who was not then a traveller, or a husband, or a criminal, or a recluse (who has set himself to work with the idea of fame and simultaneously lost all desire for fame), may perhaps never even once recur to his mind. Moreover, even if we are stubbornly determined to prove that our wish to act was not an idle one, it is probable that the sunset effect would fail to materialise, that feeling cold at that moment we would long for a bowl of soup by the fireside and not for a trout in the open air, that our carriage would fail to impress the cashier who perhaps for wholly different reasons had a great regard for us and in whom this sudden opulence would arouse suspicion. In short, we have seen Swann, once married, attach importance above all else to the relations of his wife and daughter with Mme Bontemps, etc.

To all the reasons, derived from the Guermantes way of looking at social life, which had made the Duchess decide never to allow Mme and Mlle Swann to be introduced to her, we may add also that happy complacency with which people who are not in love dissociate themselves from that which they condemn in lovers and which is explained by their love. "Oh! I don't get mixed up in all that. If it amuses poor Swann to behave idiotically and ruin his life, that's his affair, but I'm not going to be dragged into that sort of thing; it may end very badly; I leave them to get on with it." It is the *suave mari magno* which Swann himself recommended to me with regard to the Verdurins, when he had long ceased to be in love with Odette and no longer cared about the little clan. It is what makes so wise the judgments of third persons with regard to passions which they themselves do not feel and the complications of behaviour which those passions bring about.

Mme de Guermantes had in fact applied to the ostracism of Mme and Mlle Swann a perseverance that caused general surprise. When Mme Molé and Mme de Marsantes had begun to make friends with Mme Swann and to bring a quantity of society ladies to her house, Mme de Guermantes had not only remained intractable but had contrived to sabotage the lines of communication and to see that her cousin the Princesse de Guermantes followed her example. On one of the gravest days of the crisis during Rouvier's ministry when it was thought that there was going to be war with Germany, I dined at Mme de Guermantes's with M. de Bréauté and found the Duchess looking worried. I supposed that, since she was always dabbling in politics, this was a manifestation of her fear of war, as when, appearing at the dinner-table one evening looking similarly pensive and barely replying in monosyllables, upon somebody's inquiring timidly what was the cause of her anxiety, she had answered solemnly: "I'm worried about China." But a moment later Mme de Guermantes, herself volunteering an explanation of that preoccupied air which I had put down to fear of a declaration of war, said to M. de Bréauté: "I'm told that Marie-Aynard intends to launch the Swanns. I simply must go and see Marie-Gilbert tomorrow and get her to help me prevent it. Otherwise there'll be no society left. The Dreyfus case is all very well. But then the grocer's wife round the corner has only to call herself a nationalist and expect us to invite her to our houses in return." And this remark was in such frivolous contrast to the one I expected to hear that I felt the same astonishment as a reader who, turning to the usual column of the *Figaro* for the latest news of the Russo-Japanese war, finds instead the list of people who have given wedding-presents to Mlle de Mortemart, the importance of an aristocratic marriage having relegated the battles on land and sea to the back of the paper. Moreover the Duchess had come to derive from this immoderate perseverance of hers a self-satisfied pride which she lost no opportunity of expressing. "Babal," she said, "maintains that we are the two most elegant people in Paris because he and I are the only two people who do not allow Mme and Mlle Swann to greet us. For he assures me that elegance consists in not knowing Mme Swann." And the Duchess laughed heartily.

However, when Swann was dead, it happened that her determination not to know his daughter had ceased to provide Mme de Guermantes with all the satisfactions of pride, independence, "self-government" and cruelty which she was capable of deriving from it and which had come to an end with the passing of the man who had given her the exquisite sensation that she was resisting him, that he could not compel her to revoke her decrees. Then the Duchess had proceeded to the promulgation of other decrees which, being applied to people who were still alive, could make her feel that she was free to act as she thought fit. She did not think about the Swann girl, but, when anyone mentioned her, she would feel a certain curiosity, as about some place that she had never visited, which was no longer suppressed by the desire to stand out against Swann's pretensions. Besides, so many different sentiments may contribute to the formation of a single one that it could not be said that there was not a lingering trace of affection for Swann in this interest. No doubt—for at every level of society a worldly and frivolous life paralyses the sensibility and robs people of the power to resuscitate the dead—the Duchess was one of those people who require a personal presence—that presence which, like a true Guermantes, she excelled in protracting—in order to love truly, but also, and this is less common, in order to hate a little. So that often her friendly feeling for people, suspended during their lifetime by the irritation caused her by some action or other on their part, revived after their death. She then felt almost a longing to make reparation, because she pictured them now— though very vaguely—with only their good qualities, and stripped of the petty satisfactions, the petty pretensions, which had irritated her in them when they were alive. This imparted at times, not-withstanding the frivolity of Mme de Guermantes, something rather noble—mixed with much that was base—to her conduct. For, whereas three-quarters of the human race flatter the living and pay no attention to the dead, she often did after their deaths what those whom she had treated badly would have wished her to do while they were alive.

As for Gilberte, all the people who were fond of her and had a certain respect for her dignity could rejoice at the change in the Duchess's attitude towards her only by thinking that Gilberte, by scornfully rejecting advances coming after twenty-five years of insults, would be able to avenge them at last. Unfortunately, moral reflexes are not always identical with what common sense ima-gines. A man who, by an untimely insult, thinks that he has forfeited for ever all hope of winning the friendship of a person whom he cares about, finds that, on the contrary, he has thereby assured himself of it. Gilberte, who remained fairly indifferent to the people who were kind to her, never ceased to think with admiration of the insolent Mme de Guermantes, to ask herself the reasons for such insolence; once indeed (and this would have made all the people who were at all fond of her die of shame on her behalf) she had thought of writing to the Duchess to ask her what she had against a girl who had never done her any harm. The Guermantes had assumed in her eyes proportions which their birth would have been powerless to give them. She placed them not only above all the nobility, but even above all the royal houses.

Some of Swann's former women-friends took a great interest in Gilberte. When the aristocracy learned of her latest inheritance, they began to remark how well brought up she was and what a charming wife she would make. People said that a cousin of Mme de Guermantes, the Princesse de Nièvre, was thinking of Gilberte for her son. Mme de Guermantes hated Mme de Nièvre.

She spread the word that such a marriage would be a scandal. Mme de Nièvre took fright and swore that she had never considered such a thing. One day, after lunch, as the sun was shining and M. de Guermantes was going to take his wife for a drive, Mme de Guermantes was arranging her hat in front of the mirror, her blue eyes gazing at their own reflexion and at her still golden hair, her maid holding in her hand various sunshades among which her mistress might choose. The sun was flooding in through the window and they had decided to take advantage of the fine weather to pay a visit to Saint-Cloud, and M. de Guermantes, all ready to set off with his pearl-grey gloves and topper, said to himself: "Oriane is really astounding still; I find her delicious," and went on, aloud, seeing that his wife seemed to be in a good humour: "By the way, I have a message for you from Mme de Virelef. She wanted to ask you to the Opéra on Monday, but as she's having the Swann girl she didn't dare, and asked me to explore the ground. I don't express any opinion, I simply convey the message. But really, it seems to me that we might..." he added evasively, for, their attitude towards people being a collect- ive one, springing up identically in each of them, he knew from his own feelings that his wife's hostility to Mlle Swann had subsided and that she was curious to meet her. Mme de Guermantes settled her veil to her liking and chose a sunshade. "Just as you like. What difference do you suppose it makes to me? I see no objection to our meeting the child. You know quite well that I've never had anything *against* her. I simply didn't want us to appear to be countenancing the dubious establishments of our friends. That's all." "And you were perfectly right," replied the Duke. "You are wisdom incarnate, Madame, and you are more ravishing than ever in that hat." "You're very kind," said Mme de Guermantes with a smile at her husband as she made her way to the door. But, before entering the carriage, she insisted on giving him a further explana- tion: "Lots of people call on the mother now. Besides, she has the sense to be ill for nine months of the year ... Apparently the child is quite charming. Everybody knows that we were very fond of Swann. People will think it quite natural." And they set off together for Saint-Cloud.

A month later, the Swann girl, who had not yet taken the name of Forcheville, came to lunch with the Guermantes. They talked about a variety of things, and at the end of the meal, Gilberte said timidly: "I believe you knew my father quite well." "Why, of course we did," said Mme de Guermantes in a melancholy tone which proved that she understood the daughter's grief and with a spurious intensity as though to conceal the fact that she was not sure whether she did remember the father very clearly. "We knew him very well, I remember him *very well*." (As indeed she might, seeing that he had come to see her almost every day for twenty-five years.) "I know quite well who he was, let me tell you," she went on, as though she were seeking to explain to the daughter what sort of man her father had been and to provide her with some information about him, "he was a great friend of my mother-in-law and he was also very attached to my brother-in-law Palamède." "He used to come here too, in fact he used to come to luncheon here," added M. de Guermantes with ostentatious modesty and a scrupulous regard for accuracy. "You remember, Oriane. What a fine man your father was! One felt that he must come of a very decent family. As a matter of fact, I once saw his father and mother long ago. What excellent people they were, he and they!"

One felt that if Swann and his parents had still been alive, the Duc de Guermantes would not have hesitated to recommend them for jobs as gardeners. And this is how the Faubourg Saint-Germain speaks to any bourgeois about other bourgeois, either to flatter him with the exception being made in his favour (for as long as the conversation lasts) or rather, or at the same time, to humiliate him. Thus it is that an anti-semite, at the very moment when he is smothering a Jew with affability, will speak ill of Jews, in a general fashion which enables him to be wounding without being rude.

But, queen of the present moment, when she knew how to be infinitely amiable to you, and could not bring herself to let you go, Mme de Guermantes was also its slave. Swann might have managed at times to give the Duchess the illusion, in the excitement of conversation, that she was genuinely fond of him, but he could do so no longer. "He was charming," said the Duchess with a wistful smile, fastening upon Gilberte a soft and kindly gaze which would at least, if the girl should prove to be a sensitive soul, show her that she was understood and that Mme de Guermantes, had the two been alone together and had circumstances permitted, would have loved to reveal to her all the depth of her sensibility. But M. de Guermantes, whether because he was indeed of the opinion that the circumstances forbade such effusions, or because he considered that any exaggeration of sentiment was a matter for women and that men had no more part in it than in the other feminine attributions, except for food and wine which he had reserved to himself, knowing more about them than the Duchess, felt it incumbent upon him not to encourage, by taking part in it, this conversation to which he listened with visible impatience.

However, this burst of sensibility having subsided, Mme de Guermantes added with worldly frivolity, addressing Gilberte: "Why, he was not only a *gggreat* friend of my brother-in-law Charlus, he was also on very good terms with Voisenon" (the country house of the Prince de Guermantes), not only as though Swann's acquaintance with M. de Charlus and the Prince had been a mere accident, as though the Duchess's brother-in-law and cousin were two men with whom Swann had happened to become friendly through some fortuitous circumstance, whereas Swann had been on friendly terms with all the people in that set, but also as though Mme de Guermantes wanted to explain to Gilberte roughly who her father had been, to "place" him for her by means of one of those characteristic touches whereby, when one wants to explain how it is that one happens to know somebody whom one would not naturally know, or to point up one's story, one invokes the names of his particular social sponsors.

As for Gilberte, she was all the more glad to find the subject being dropped, in that she herself was only too anxious to drop it, having inherited from Swann his exquisite tact combined with a delightful intelligence that was recognised and appreciated by the Duke and Duchess, who begged her to come again soon. Moreover, with the passion for minutiae of people whose lives are purposeless, they would discern, one after another, in the people with whom they became acquainted, qualities of the simplest kind, exclaiming at them with the artless wonderment of a townsman who on going into the country discovers a blade of grass, or on the contrary magnifying as with a microscope, endlessly commenting upon and inveighing against the slightest defects, and often applying both processes alternately to the same person. In Gilberte's case it was first of all upon her agreeable qualities that the idle perspicacity of M. and Mme de Guermantes was brought to bear: "Did you notice the way she pronounces certain words?" the Duchess said to her husband after the girl had left them; "it was just like Swann, I seemed to hear him speaking." "I was just about to say the very same thing, Oriane." "She's witty, she has exactly the same cast of mind as her father." "I consider that she's even far superior to him. Think how well she told that story about the sea-bathing. She has a vivacity that Swann never had." "Oh! but he was, after all, quite witty." "I'm not saying that he wasn't witty, I'm saying that he lacked vivacity," said M. de Guermantes in a querulous tone, for his gout made him irritable, and when he had no one else upon whom to vent his irritation, it was to the Duchess that he displayed it. But being incapable of any clear understanding of its causes, he preferred to adopt an air of being misunderstood.

This friendly attitude on the part of the Duke and Duchess meant that from now on, if the occasion arose, they would have said to her "your poor father," but this would no longer do, since it was just about this time that Forcheville adopted the girl. She addressed him as "Father," charmed all the dowagers by her politeness and distinction, and it was generally acknowledged that, if Forcheville had behaved admirably towards her, the child was very good-hearted and more than recompensed him. True, since she was able at times and anxious to show a great deal of naturalness and ease, she had reintroduced herself to me and had spoken to me about her real father. But this was an exception and no one now dared utter the name Swann in her presence.

As it happened, on entering the drawing-room I had caught sight of two sketches by Elstir which formerly had been banished to a little room upstairs where I had seen them only by chance. Elstir was now in fashion. Mme de Guermantes could not forgive herself for having given so many of his pictures away to her cousin, not because they were in fashion, but because she now appreciated them. For fashion is composed of the collective infatuation of a number of people of whom the Guermantes are typical. But she could not think of buying other pictures by him, for they had now begun to fetch madly high prices. She was determined to have something at least by Elstir in her drawing-room and had brought down these two drawings which, she declared, she "preferred to his paintings."

Gilberte recognised the technique. "They look like Elstirs," she said. "Why, yes," replied the Duchess without thinking, "in fact it was your fa...some friends of ours who made us buy them. They're admirable. To my mind, they're superior to his paintings."

Not having heard this conversation, I went up to one of the drawings to examine it, and exclaimed: "Why, this is the Elstir that . . . " I saw Mme de Guermantes's desperate signals. "Ah, yes, the Elstir that I admired upstairs. It looks much better here than in that passage. Talking of Elstir, I mentioned him yesterday in an article in the *Figaro*. Did you happen to read it?"

"You've written an article in the *Figaro*?" exclaimed M. de Guermantes with the same violence as if he had exclaimed: "Why, she's my cousin."

"Yes, yesterday."

"In the *Figaro*, are you sure? I can't believe it. Because we each of us get our *Figaro*, and if one of us had missed it, the other would certainly have noticed it. That's so, isn't Oriane, there was nothing."

The Duke sent for the *Figaro* and only yielded to the evidence of his own eyes, as though up till then the probability had been that I had made a mistake as to the newspaper for which I had written.

"What's that? I don't understand. So you've written an article in the *Figaro*?" said the Duchess, making an obvious effort in speaking of something that did not interest her. "Come, Basin, you can read it afterwards."

"No, the Duke looks so nice like that with his great beard dangling over the paper," said Gilberte. "I shall read it as soon as I get home."

"Yes, he wears a beard now that everybody else is clean-shaven," said the Duchess. "He never does anything that other people do. When we were first married, he shaved not only his beard but his moustache as well. The peasants who didn't know him by sight thought that he couldn't be French. At that time he was called the Prince des Laumes."

"Is there still a Prince des Laumes?" asked Gilberte, who was interested in everything that concerned the people who had refused to acknowledge her existence during all those years.

"Why, no," the Duchess replied with a melancholy, caressing gaze.

"Such a charming title! One of the finest titles in France!" said Gilberte, a certain sort of banality springing inevitably, as a clock strikes the hour, to the lips of certain quite intelligent persons.

"Ah, yes, I'm sorry too. Basin would like his sister's son to adopt it, but it isn't the same thing; though it would be possible, since it doesn't have to be the eldest son, it can be passed to a younger brother. I was telling you that in those days Basin was clean-shaven. One day, at a pilgrimage—you remember, my dear," she turned to her husband, "that pilgrimage at Paray-le-Monial—my brother-in-law Charlus, who always enjoys talking to peasants, was saying to one after another: 'Where do you come from?' and as he's extremely generous, he would give them something, take them off to have a drink. For nobody was ever at the same time simpler and more haughty than Mémé. You'll see him refuse to bow to a Duchess whom he doesn't think duchessy enough, and heap kindnesses on a kennelman. So then I said to Basin: 'Come, Basin, say something to them too.' My husband, who is not always very inventive . . ." ("Thank you, Oriane," said the Duke, without interrupting his reading of my article in which he was immersed) " . . . went up to one of the peasants and repeated his brother's question in so many words: 'Where do you come from?' 'I'm from Les Laumes.' 'You're from Les Laumes? Why, I'm your Prince.' Then the peasant looked at Basin's hairless face and replied: 'That ain't true. *You're* an English.' "[4]

In these little anecdotes of the Duchess's, such great and eminent titles as that of Prince des Laumes seemed to stand out in one's mind's eye in their true setting, in their original state and their local colour, as in certain Books of Hours one recognises amid the mediaeval crowd the soaring steeple of Bourges.

Some visiting-cards were brought to her which a footman had just left at the door. "I can't think what's got into her, I don't know her. It's to you that I'm indebted for this, Basin. Although that sort of acquaintance hasn't done you much good, my poor dear," and, turning to Gilberte: "I really don't know how to explain to you who she is, you've certainly never heard of her, she's called Lady Rufus Israels."

Gilberte flushed crimson: "No, I don't know her," she said (which was all the more untrue in that Lady Israels and Swann had been reconciled two years before the latter's death and she addressed Gilberte by her Christian name), "but I know quite well, from hearing about her, who it is that you mean."

Gilberte was becoming very snobbish. Thus a girl having one day asked her out of tactlessness or malice what the name of her real, not her adoptive father was, in her confusion and as though to euphemise the name a little, instead of pronouncing it "Souann" she said "Svann," a change, as she soon realised, for the worse, since it made this name of English origin a German patronymic.

And she had even gone on to say, abasing herself with the object of self-enhancement: "All sorts of different stories have been told about my birth, but I'm not supposed to know anything about it."

Ashamed though Gilberte must have felt at certain moments, when she thought of her parents (for even Mme Swann represented for her, and was, a good mother), of such a way of looking at life, it must alas be borne in mind that its elements were doubtless borrowed from her parents, for we do not create ourselves of our own accord out of nothing. But to a certain quantity of egoism which exists in the mother, a different egoism, inherent in the father's family, is admixed, which does not invariably mean that it is superadded, nor even precisely that it serves as a multiple, but rather that it creates a fresh egoism infinitely stronger and more redoubtable. And ever since the world began, ever since families in which some defect exists in one form have been intermarrying with families in which the same defect exists in another, thereby creating a peculiarly complete and detestable variety of that defect in the offspring, the accumulated egoisms (to confine ourselves, for the moment, to this defect) must have acquired such force that the whole human race would have been destroyed, did not the malady itself engender natural restrictions, capable of reducing it to reasonable proportions, comparable to those which prevent the infinite proliferation of the infusoria from destroying our planet, the unisexual fertilisation of plants from bringing about the extinction of the vegetable kingdom, and so forth. From time to time a virtue combines with this egoism to produce a new and disinterested force. The combinations by which, in the course of generations, moral chemistry thus stabilises and renders innocuous the elements that were becoming too powerful, are infinite, and would give an exciting variety to family history. Moreover, with these accumulated egoisms, such as must have existed in Gilberte, there may coexist some charming virtue of the parents; it appears for a moment to perform an interlude by itself, to play its touching part with an entire sincerity. No doubt Gilberte did not always go so far as when she insinuated that she was perhaps the natural daughter of some great personage; but as a rule she concealed her origins. Perhaps it was simply too painful for her to confess them and she preferred that people should learn of them from others. Perhaps she really believed that she was concealing them, with that dubious belief which at the same time is not doubt, which leaves room for the possibility of what we wish to be true, of which Musset furnishes an example when he speaks of hope in God.

"I don't know her personally," Gilberte went on. Did she, in fact, when she called herself Mlle de Forcheville, expect that people would not know that she was Swann's daughter? Some people, perhaps, who, she hoped, would in time become everybody. She could not be under any illusion as to their number at the moment, and doubtless knew that many people must be whispering: "That's Swann's daughter." But she knew it only with that knowledge which tells us of people taking their lives in desperation while we are going to a ball, that is to say, a remote and vague knowledge for which we are at no pains to substitute a more precise knowledge based on direct observation. Gilberte belonged, during those years at least, to the most widespread variety of human ostriches, the kind that bury their heads not in the hope of not being seen, which they consider highly improbable, but in the hope of not seeing that they can be seen, which seems to them something to the good and enables them to leave the rest to chance. As distance makes things appear smaller, more indistinct, less dangerous, Gilberte preferred not to be near other people at the moment when they made the discovery that she was by birth a Swann. And as we are near the people whom we picture to ourselves, and we can picture people reading their newspaper, Gilberte preferred the newspapers to style her Mlle de Forcheville. It is true that with the writings for which she herself was responsible, her letters, she prolonged the transition for some time by signing herself "G. S. Forcheville." The real hypocrisy in this signature was made manifest by the suppression not so much of the other letters of the name "Swann" as of those of the name "Gilberte." For, by reducing the innocent Christian name to a simple "G," Mlle de Forcheville seemed to insinuate to her friends that the similar amputation applied to the name "Swann" was due equally to the necessity of abbreviation. Indeed she gave a special significance to the "S," extending it with a sort of long tail which ran across the "G," but which one felt to be transitory and destined to disappear like the tail which, still long in the monkey, has ceased to exist in man.

In spite of all this, there was something of Swann's intelligent curiosity in her snobbishness. I remember that, in the course of that same afternoon, she asked Mme de Guermantes whether she could meet M. du Lau, and that when the Duchess replied that he was an invalid and never went out, Gilberte asked what he was like, for, she added with a faint blush, she had heard a great deal about him. (The Marquis du Lau had in fact been one of Swann's most intimate friends before the latter's marriage, and Gilberte may perhaps even have caught a glimpse of him, but at a time when she was not interested in such people.) "Would M. de Bréauté or the Prince d'Agrigente be at all like him?" she asked. "Oh! not in the least," exclaimed Mme de Guermantes, who had a keen sense of these provincial differences and drew portraits that were sober and restrained but coloured by her husky, golden voice, beneath the gentle efflorescence of her violet-blue eyes. "No, not in the least. Du Lau was very much the Périgord squire, full of charm, with all the good manners and informality of his province. At Guermantes, when we had the King of England with whom du Lau was on the friendliest terms, we used to have a little meal after the men came in from shooting. It was the hour when du Lau was in the habit of going to his room to take off his boots and put on big woollen slippers. Well, the presence of King Edward and all the grand-dukes didn't disturb him in the least, he came down to the great hall at Guermantes in his woollen slippers. He felt that he was the Marquis du Lau d'Allemans who had no reason to stand on ceremony with the King of England. He and that charming Quasimodo de Breteuil, they were the two I liked best. Actually they were great friends of . . ." (she was about to say "your father" and stopped short). "No, there's no resemblance at all, either to Gri-gri or to Bréauté. He was the typical nobleman from Périgord. Incidentally, Mémé quotes a page from Saint-Simon about a Marquis d'Allemans, and it's just like him."

I recited the opening words of the portrait: "M. d'Allemans, who was a man of great distinction among the nobility of Périgord, through his own birth and through his merit, and was regarded by every soul alive there as a general arbiter to whom each had recourse because of his probity, his capacity and the suavity of his manners, as it were the cock of his province."

"Yes, that's it," said Mme de Guermantes, "all the more so as du Lau was always as red as a turkeycock."

"Yes, I remember hearing that description quoted," said Gilberte, without adding that it had been quoted by her father, who was, as we know, a great admirer of Saint-Simon.

She liked also to speak of the Prince d'Agrigente and of M. de Bréauté for another reason. The Prince d'Agrigente had inherited his title from the House of Aragon, but the family domains were in Poitou. As for his country house, the house, that is to say, in which he lived, it was not the property of his own family but had come to him from his mother's first husband, and was situated approximately halfway between Martinville and Guermantes. And so Gilberte spoke of him and of M. de Bréauté as of country neighbours who reminded her of her old home. Strictly speaking there was an element of falsehood in this attitude, since it was only in Paris, through the Comtesse Molé, that she had come to know M. de Bréauté, albeit he had been an old friend of her father's. As for her pleasure in speaking of the country round Tansonville, it may have been sincere. Snobbery is with certain people analogous to those beverages in which the agreeable is mixed with the beneficial. Gilberte took an interest in some lady of fashion because she possessed priceless books and portraits by Nattier which my former friend would probably not have taken the trouble to inspect in the Bibliothèque Nationale or the Louvre, and I imagine that, in spite of their even greater proximity, the magnetic influence of Tansonville would have had less effect in drawing Gilberte towards Mme Sazerat or Mme Goupil than towards M. d'Agrigente.

"Oh! poor Babal and poor Gri-gri," said Mme de Guermantes, "they're in a far worse state than du Lau. I'm afraid they haven't long to live, either of them."

When M. de Guermantes had finished reading my article, he complimented me in somewhat qualified terms. He regretted the slightly hackneyed style with its "turgid metaphors as in the antiquated prose of Chateaubriand"; on the other hand he congratulated me wholeheartedly for "keeping myself busy": "I like a man to do something with what God gave him. I don't like useless people who are always self-important or fidgety. A fatuous breed!"

Gilberte, who was acquiring the ways of society with extreme rapidity, declared how proud she would be to be able to say that she was the friend of an author. "You can imagine that I shall tell people that I have the pleasure, the *honour* of your acquaintance."

"You wouldn't care to come with us tomorrow to the Opéra-Comique?" the Duchess asked me; and it struck me that it would be doubtless in that same box in which I had first beheld her, and which had seemed to me then as inaccessible as the underwater realm of the Nereids. But I replied in a melancholy tone: "No, I'm not going to the theatre just now; I've lost a friend to whom I was greatly attached." I almost had tears in my eyes as I said this, and yet for the first time it gave me a sort of pleasure to speak about it. It was from that moment that I began to write to everyone saying that I had just experienced a great sorrow, and to cease to feel it.

When Gilberte had gone, Mme de Guermantes said to me: "You didn't understand my signals. I was trying to hint to you not to mention Swann." And, as I apologised: "But I absolutely sympathise: I was on the point of mentioning him myself, but I stopped short just in time, it was terrible. You know, it really is a great bore," she said to her husband, seeking to mitigate my own error by appearing to believe that I had yielded to a propensity common to everyone and difficult to resist.

"What am I supposed to do about it?" replied the Duke. "You'd better tell them to take those drawings upstairs again, since they make you think about Swann. If you don't think about Swann, you won't speak about him."

On the following day I received two congratulatory letters which surprised me greatly, one from Mme Goupil, the Combray lady, whom I had not seen for many years and to whom, even at Combray, I had scarcely ever spoken. A reading-room had given her the chance of seeing the *Figaro*. Thus, when anything occurs in one's life which makes some stir, messages come to one from people situated so far outside the zone of one's acquaintance, and one's memory of whom is already so remote, that they seem to be placed at a great distance, especially in the dimension of depth. A forgotten friendship of one's school-days, which has had a score of opportunities of recalling itself to one's mind, gives us a sign of life, if in a negative sense. Thus for instance Bloch, whose opinion of my article I should have loved to know, did not write to me. It is true that he had read the article and was to admit it later, but as it were backhandedly. For he himself contributed an article to the *Figaro* some years later, and was anxious to inform me immediately of the event. Since what he regarded as a privilege had fallen to him as well, the envy that had made him pretend to ignore my article ceased, as though by the lifting of a compressor, and he spoke to me about it, though not at all in the way in which he hoped to hear me talk about his: "I knew that you too had written an article," he told me, "but I didn't think I ought to mention it to you, for fear of hurting your feelings, because one oughtn't to speak to one's friends about the humiliating things that happen to them. And it's obviously humiliating to write in the organ of the sabre and the aspergillum, of afternoon tea, not to mention the holy-water stoup." His character remained unaltered, but his style had become less precious, as happens to certain people who shed their mannerisms, when, ceasing to compose symbolist poetry, they take to writing serial novels.

To console myself for his silence, I re-read Mme Goupil's letter; but it was lacking in warmth, for if the aristocracy employ certain formulas which form a sort of palisade, between them, between the initial "*Monsieur*" and the "*sentiments distingués*" of the close, cries of joy and admiration may spring up like flowers, and their clusters spill over the palisade their adoring fragrance. But bourgeois conventionality enwraps even the content of letters in a tissue of "your well-deserved success," at best "your great success." Sisters-in-law, faithful to their upbringing and tight-laced in their respectable stays, think that they have overflowed into the most distressing enthusiasm if they have written "my kindest regards." "Mother joins me" is a superlative with which one is rarely indulged.

I received another letter as well as Mme Goupil's, but the name of the writer, Sanilon, was unknown to me. It was in a plebeian hand and a charming style. I was distressed not to be able to discover who had written to me.

Two days later I found myself rejoicing at the thought that Bergotte was a great admirer of my article, which he had been unable to read without envy. But a moment later my joy subsided. For Bergotte had written me not a word. I had simply wondered whether he would have liked the article, fearing that he would not. As I was asking myself the question, Mme de Forcheville had replied that he admired it enormously and considered it the work of a great writer. But she had told me this while I was asleep: it was a dream. Almost all our dreams respond thus to the questions which we put to ourselves with complicated statements, stage productions with several characters, which however have no future.

As for Mlle de Forcheville, I could not help feeling saddened when I thought of her. What? Swann's daughter, whom he would have so loved to see at the Guermantes', whom the latter had refused to give their great friend the pleasure of inviting—to think that she was now spontaneously sought after by them, time having passed, time that renews all things, that infuses a new personality, based upon what we have been told about them, into people whom we have not seen for a long time, during which we ourselves have grown a new skin and acquired new tastes. But when, to this daughter of his, he used from time to time to say, taking her in his arms and kissing her: "How comforting it is, my darling, to have a daughter like you; one day when I'm no longer here, if people still mention your poor papa, it will be only to you and because of you," Swann, in thus pinning a timorous and anxious hope of survival on his daughter after his death, was as mistaken as an old banker who, having made a will in favour of a little dancer whom he is keeping and who has very nice manners, tells himself that though to her he is no more than a great friend, she will remain faithful to his memory. She had very nice manners while her feet under the table sought the feet of those of the old banker's friends who attracted her, but all this very discreetly, behind an altogether respectable exterior. She will wear mourning for the worthy man, will feel relieved to be rid of him, will enjoy not only the ready money, but the real estate, the motor-cars that he has bequeathed to her, taking care to remove the monogram of the former owner which makes her feel slightly ashamed, and will never associate her enjoyment of the gift with any regret for the giver. The illusions of paternal love are perhaps no less poignant than those of the other kind; many daughters regard their fathers merely as the old men who leave their fortunes to them. Gilberte's presence in a drawing-room, instead of being an occasion for people to speak of her father from time to time, was an obstacle in the way of their seizing the opportunities that might still have remained for them to do so, and that were becoming more and more rare. Even in connexion with the things he had said, the presents he had given, people acquired the habit of not mention- ing him, and she who ought to have kept his memory young, if not perpetuated it, found herself hastening and completing the work of death and oblivion.

And it was not only with regard to Swann that Gilberte was gradually completing the process of forgetting; she had accelerated in me that process with regard to Albertine. Under the influence of desire, and consequently of the desire for happiness which Gilberte had aroused in me during the few hours in which I had supposed her to be someone else, a certain number of miseries, of painful preoccupations, which only a little while earlier had obsessed my mind, had slipped away from me, carrying with them a whole block of memories, probably long since crumbling and precarious, with regard to Albertine. For if many memories, which were connected with her, had at the outset helped to keep alive in me my grief for her death, in return that grief had itself fixed those memories. So that the modification of my sentimental state, prepared for no doubt obscurely day by day by the continuous erosions of forgetfulness, but realised abruptly as a whole, gave me the impression, which I remember having felt that day for the first time, of a void, of the suppression in myself of a whole segment of my associations of ideas, such as a man feels in whose brain a long-impaired artery has burst, so that a whole section of his memory is abolished or paralysed. I no longer loved Albertine. At most, on certain days, when the weather was of the sort which, by modifying, by awakening one's sensibility, brings one back into relationship with the real, I felt painfully sad in thinking of her. I was suffering from a love that no longer existed. Thus does an amputee, in certain kinds of weather, feel pain in the limb that he has lost.

The disappearance of my suffering, and of all that it carried away with it, left me diminished, as recovery from an illness which has occupied a big place in one's life often does. No doubt it is because memories are not always true that love is not eternal, and because life is made up of a perpetual renewal of cells. But this renewal, in the case of memories, is nevertheless retarded by one's attention, which temporarily arrests and freezes what is bound to change. And since it is the case with grief as with the desire for women that one magnifies it by thinking about it, having plenty of other things to do should make it easier not only to be chaste but to forget.

By another reaction, if (though it was a distraction—the desire for Mlle d'Eporcheville—that had suddenly brought home to me the tangible reality of forgetting) it remains true that it is time that gradually brings forgetfulness, forgetfulness in its turn does not fail to alter profoundly our notion of time. There are optical errors in time as there are in space. The persistence within me of an old impulse to work, to make up for lost time, to change my way of life, or rather to begin to live, gave me the illusion that I was still as young as in the past; and yet the memory of all the events that had succeeded one another in my life (and also of those that had succeeded one another in my heart, for when one has greatly changed, one is misled into supposing that one has lived longer) in the course of those last months of Albertine's existence, had made them seem to me much longer than a year, and now this forgetfulness of so many things, separating me by gulfs of empty space from quite recent events which they made me think remote, because I had had what is called "the time" to forget them, by its fragmentary, irregular interpolation in my memory—like a thick fog at sea which obliterates all the landmarks—distorted, dislocated my sense of distances in time, contracted in one place, distended in another, and made me suppose myself now further away from things, now much closer to them, than I really was. And as in the new spaces, as yet unexplored, which extended before me, there would be no more trace of my love for Albertine than there had been, in the time lost which I had just traversed, of my love for my grandmother, my life appeared to me—offering a succession of periods in which, after a certain interval, nothing of what had sustained the previous period survived in that which followed—as something utterly devoid of the support of an individual, identical and permanent self, something as useless in the future as it was protracted in the past, something that death might as well put an end to at this point or that, without in the least concluding it, as those courses of French history in the sixth form at school which stop short indiscriminately, according to the whim of the curriculum or the professor, at the Revolution of 1830, or that of 1848, or the end of the Second Empire.

Perhaps then the fatigue and sadness that I felt arose not so much from my having loved in vain what I was already forgetting as from my beginning to enjoy the company of new living people, purely social figures, mere friends of the Guermantes, offering no interest in themselves. It was easier perhaps to reconcile myself to the discovery that she whom I had loved was no more, after a certain interval of time, than a pale memory, than to the rediscovery in myself of that futile activity which makes us waste time decorating our lives with a human vegetation which is robust but parasitic, which likewise will become nothing when it is dead, which already is alien to all that we have ever known, but which nevertheless our garrulous, melancholy, conceited senility seeks to cultivate. The newcomer who would find it easy to endure the prospect of life without Albertine had made his appearance in me, since I had been able to speak of her at Mme de Guermantes's in the language of grief without any real suffering. The possible advent of these new selves, which ought each to bear a different name from the preceding one, was something I had always dreaded, because of their indifference to the object of my love—

long ago in connexion with Gilberte when her father told me that if I went to live in Oceania I would never wish to return, quite recently when I had read with such a pang in my heart the memoirs of a mediocre writer who, separated by life from a woman whom he had adored when he was young, meets her as an old man without pleasure, without any desire to see her again. Yet he was bringing me on the contrary, this newcomer, at the same time as oblivion an almost complete elimination of suffering, a possibility of comfort—this newcomer, so dreaded yet so beneficent, who was none other than one of those spare selves which destiny holds in reserve for us, and which, paying no more heed to our entreaties than a clear-sighted and thus all the more authoritative physician, it substitutes in spite of us, by a timely intervention, for the self that has been too seriously wounded. This process, as it happens, automatically occurs from time to time, like the decay and renewal of our tissues, but we notice it only if the former self contained a great grief, a painful foreign body, which we are surprised to find no longer there, in our amazement at having become another person to whom the sufferings of his predecessor are no more than the sufferings of a stranger, of which we can speak with compassion because we do not feel them. Indeed we are unconcerned about having undergone all those sufferings, since we have only a vague remembrance of having suffered them. It may well be that likewise our nightmares are horrifying. But on waking we are another person, who cares little that the person whose place he takes has had to flee from a gang of cut-throats during the night.

No doubt this self still maintained some contact with the old, as a friend who is indifferent to a bereavement speaks of it nevertheless to the persons present in a suitable tone of sorrow, and returns from time to time to the room in which the widower who has asked him to receive the company for him may still be heard weeping. I too still wept when I became once again for a moment the former friend of Albertine. But it was into a new personality that I was tending to change altogether. It is not because other people are dead that our affection for them fades; it is because we ourselves are dying. Albertine had no cause to reproach her friend. The man who was usurping his name was merely his heir. We can only be faithful to what we remember, and we remember only what we have known. My new self, while it grew up in the shadow of the old, had often heard the other speak of Albertine;

through that other self, through the stories it gathered from it, it thought that it knew her, it found her lovable, it loved her; but it was only a love at second hand.

Another person in whom the process of forgetting, as far as Albertine was concerned, was probably more rapid at this time, and indirectly enabled me to register a little later a new advance which that process had made in myself (and this is my memory of my second stage before finally forgetting), was Andrée. I can scarcely indeed but cite this forgetting of Albertine as, if not the sole cause, if not even the principal cause, at any rate a conditioning and necessary cause of a conversation which occurred between Andrée and myself about six months after the conversation I have already reported, and in which her words were very different from those that she had used on the former occasion. I remember that it was in my room because at that moment I found pleasure in having semi-carnal relations with her, by reason of the collective aspect which my love for the girls of the little band had originally had and now assumed once more, a love that had long been undivided among them and only for a while associated exclusively with Albertine's person, during the months that had preceded and followed her death.

We were in my room for another reason as well which enables me to date this conversation quite accurately. This was that I had been banished from the rest of the apartment because it was Mamma's "at home" day. After some hesitation she had gone to lunch with Mme Sazerat, thinking that, since the latter always contrived, even at Combray, to invite one to meet boring people, she would be able without sacrificing any pleasure to return home in good time. And she had indeed returned in time and without regrets, Mme Sazerat having had nobody but the most deadly people who were in any case chilled by the special voice that she adopted when she had company, what Mamma called her Wednesday voice. My mother was none the less fond of her, and sympathised with her ill-fortune—the result of the indiscretions of her father who had been ruined by the Duchesse de X—which compelled her to live all the year round at Combray, with a few weeks at her cousin's house in Paris and a long "pleasure-trip" every ten years.

I remember that the day before this, after months of entreaty from me, and because the Princess was always begging her to come, Mamma had gone to call on the Princesse de Parme, who paid no calls herself and at whose house people as a rule contented themselves with signing their names, but who had insisted on my mother's coming to see her, since the rules of etiquette forbade Her Highness to come to us. My mother had come home thoroughly cross: "You sent me on a wild goose chase," she told me. "The Princesse de Parme barely greeted me. She turned back to the ladies she was talking to without paying any attention to me, and after ten minutes, as she hadn't addressed a word to me, I came away without her even offering me her hand. I was extremely annoyed. However, on the doorstep, as I was leaving, I met the Duchesse de Guermantes who was very kind and spoke to me a great deal about you. What a strange idea of yours to talk to her about Albertine! She told me that you'd said to her that her death had been a great blow to you." (I had in fact said this to the Duchess, but I didn't even recall it, and I had hardly made a point of it. But the most heedless of people often give remarkable attention to words we let slip, words which seem quite natural to us, and which excite their curiosity profoundly.) "I shall never go near the Princesse de Parme again. You've made me make a fool of myself."

The next day, which was my mother's "at home," Andrée came to see me. She did not have much time, as she had to go and call for Gisèle with whom she was very anxious to dine. "I know her faults, but she's after all my best friend and the person for whom I feel most affection," she told me. And she even appeared to be slightly alarmed at the thought that I might ask her to let me dine with them. She was hungry for people, and a third person who knew her too well, such as myself, by preventing her from letting herself go, would prevent her from enjoying herself to the full in their company.

It is true that I was not there when she came; she was waiting for me, and I was about to go through my small sitting-room to join her when I realised, on hearing a voice, that I had another visitor. Impatient to see Andrée, and not knowing who the other person was (who evidently did not know her since he had been put in another room), I listened for a moment at the door of the small sitting-room; for my visitor was not alone, he was speaking to a woman. "Oh, my darling, it is in my heart!" he warbled to her, quoting the verses of Armand Silvestre. "Yes, you will always remain my darling in spite of everything you've done to me:

> The dead are sleeping peacefully beneath earth's crust.
> And so must sleep the feelings time effaces.
> Those relics of the heart, they also have their dust;
> Do not lay hands upon their sacred traces.[5]

It's a bit outmoded, but how pretty it is! And also what I might have said to you from the first:

> You will make them weep, child beloved and lovely . . .

What, you don't know it?

> . . . All those urchins, men of the future,
> Already they hang their youthful reverie
> Upon your eyelashes caressing and pure.

Ah! for a moment I thought I could say to myself:

> The very first night that he came here
> I had for my pride no further fear.
> I told him: 'You will love me, dear,
> For just as long as you are able.'
> In his arms I slept like an angel."

Curious to see the woman to whom this deluge of poems was addressed, even though it meant postponing for a moment my urgent meeting with Andrée, I opened the door. They were being recited by M. de Charlus to a young soldier whom I soon recognised as Morel, and who was about to set off for his fortnight's training. He was no longer on friendly terms with M. de Charlus, but saw him from time to time to ask some favour of him. M. de Charlus, who usually gave a more masculine style to his love-making, also had his tender moments. Moreover, during his childhood, in order to be able to feel and understand the words of the poets, he had been obliged to imagine them as being addressed not to faithless beauties but to young men. I left them as soon as I could, although I sensed that paying visits with Morel was an immense satisfaction to M. de Charlus, to whom it gave the momentary illusion of having married again. And besides, he combined in his person the snobbery of queens with the snobbery of servants.

The memory of Albertine had become so fragmentary that it no longer caused me any sadness and was no more now than a transition to fresh desires, like a chord which announces a change of key. And indeed, any idea of a passing sensual whim being ruled out, in so far as I was still faithful to Albertine's memory, I was happier at having Andrée in my company than I would have been at having an Albertine miraculously restored. For Andrée could tell me more things about Albertine than Albertine herself had ever told me. Now the problems concerning Albertine still remained in my mind although my tenderness for her, both physically and emotionally, had already vanished. And my desire to know about her life, because it had diminished less, was now relatively greater than my need of her presence. Moreover, the idea that a woman had perhaps had relations with Albertine no longer aroused in me anything save the desire to have relations with that woman myself. I told Andrée this, caressing her as I spoke. Then, without making the slightest effort to make her words consistent with those of a few months earlier, Andrée said to me with a lurking smile: "Ah! yes, but you're a man. And so we can't do quite the same things as I used to do with Albertine." And whether because she felt that it would increase my desire (in the hope of extracting confidences, I had told her that I would like to have relations with a woman who had had them with Albertine) or my grief, or perhaps destroy a sense of superiority to herself which she might suppose me to feel at being the only person who had had relations with Albertine, she went on: "Ah! we spent many happy hours together; she was so caressing, so passionate. But it wasn't only with me that she liked to enjoy herself. She had met a handsome young fellow at Mme Verdurin's called Morel. They came to an understanding at once. He undertook—having her permission to enjoy them himself, for he liked little novices, and as soon as he had set them on the path of evil would abandon them—he undertook to entice young fisher-girls in remote vil-lages, or young laundry-girls, who would fall for a boy but might not have responded to a girl's advances. As soon as a girl was well under his control, he'd bring her to a safe place and hand her over to Albertine. For fear of losing Morel, who took part in it all too, the girl always obeyed, and yet she lost him all the same, because, as he was afraid of what might happen and also as once or twice was enough for him, he would run off leaving a false address. Once he had the nerve to bring one of these girls, with Albertine, to a brothel at Couliville, where four or five of the women had her together, or in turn. That was his passion, and Albertine's too. But Albertine suffered terrible remorse afterwards. I believe that when she was with you she had conquered her passion and put off indulging it from day to day. Besides, her affection for you was so great that she had scruples. But it was quite certain that if she ever left you she'd begin again. Only I think that after having left you, if she succumbed to that overpowering urge, her remorse must have been even greater. She hoped that you would rescue her, that you would marry her. She felt in her heart that her obsession was a sort of criminal lunacy, and I've often wondered whether it wasn't after an incident of that sort, which had led to a suicide in a family, that she killed herself on purpose. I must confess that in the early days of her stay with you she hadn't entirely given up her games with me. There were days when she seemed to need it, so much so that once, when it would have been so easy elsewhere, she couldn't bring herself to say good-bye without taking me to bed with her, in your house. We were out of luck, and were very nearly caught. She'd taken advantage of the fact that Françoise had gone out to do some shopping, and you weren't yet home. Then she'd turned out all the lights so that when you let yourself in with your key it would take you some time to find the switch; and she'd left the door of her room open. We heard you come upstairs, and I only just had time to tidy myself up and come down. Which was quite unnecessary as it happened, for by an incredible chance you'd left your key at home and had to ring the bell. But we lost our heads all the same, so that to conceal our embarrassment we both of us, without having a chance to consult each other, had the same idea: to pretend to dread the scent of syringa which as a matter of fact we adored. You were bringing a big branch of it home with you, which enabled me to turn my head away and hide my confusion. This didn't prevent me from telling you in the most idiotic way that perhaps Françoise had come back and would let you in, when a moment earlier I had told you the lie that we'd only just come in from our drive and that when we arrived Françoise hadn't yet left the house (which was true). But the big mistake we made—assuming that you had your key—was to turn out the light, for we were afraid that as you came upstairs you'd see it being turned on again; or at least we hesitated too long. And for three nights on end Albertine couldn't get a wink of sleep because she was constantly afraid that you might be suspicious and ask Françoise why she hadn't turned on the light before leaving the house. For Albertine was terribly afraid of you, and at times she maintained that you were treacherous and nasty and that you hated her really. After three days she gathered from your calm that you hadn't thought of asking Françoise, and she was able to sleep again. But she never resumed her relations with me after that, either from fear or from remorse, for she made out that she did really love you, or perhaps she was in love with someone else. At all events, nobody could ever mention syringa again in her hearing without her turning crimson and putting her hand over her face in the hope of hiding her blushes."

Like certain strokes of fortune, there are strokes of misfortune that come too late, and do not assume the magnitude they would have had in our eyes a little earlier. One such was the misfortune that Andrée's terrible revelation was to me. No doubt, even when a piece of bad news is bound to make us unhappy, it may happen that, in the involvement, the give and take of conversation, it will pass in front of us without stopping and, preoccupied as we are by all the things we have to say in reply, transformed into someone else by the desire to please our present interlocutors, protected for a few moments in this new context against the affections and the sufferings that we discarded upon entering it and will return to when the brief spell is broken, we do not have the time to take them in. However, if these affections and these sufferings are too predominant, we enter only distractedly into the zone of a new and momentary world, in which, too faithful to our sufferings, we are incapable of becoming other; and then the words that we hear said enter at once into relation with our heart, which has not been neutralised. But for some time past words that concerned Albertine, like a poison that has evaporated, had lost their toxic power. She was already too remote from me. As an afternoon stroller, seeing a misty crescent in the sky, thinks: "So that's the vast moon," I said to myself: "What, so that truth which I've sought for so long, which I've so dreaded, is nothing more than these few words uttered in the course of conversation, words to which one cannot even give one's whole attention because one isn't alone!" Besides, it took me at a serious disadvantage, as I had exhausted myself with Andrée. Really, I would have liked to have more strength to devote to a truth of such magnitude; it remained extraneous to me, but this was because I had not yet found a place for it in my heart. We would like the truth to be revealed to us by novel signs, not by a sentence, a sentence similar to those which we have constantly repeated to ourselves. The habit of thinking prevents us at times from experiencing reality, immunises us against it, makes it seem no more than another thought. There is no idea that does not carry in itself its possible refutation, no word that does not imply its opposite.

In any case, if it was true, it was by this time the sort of useless truth about the life of a dead mistress that rises up from the depths and reveals itself when we can no longer have any use for it. Then, thinking doubtless of some other woman whom we now love and with regard to whom the same thing may occur (for to her whom we have forgotten we no longer give a thought), we lament. We say to ourselves: "If she were alive!" We say to ourselves: "If she who is alive could only understand all this and realise that when she is dead I shall know everything that she is hiding from me!" But it is a vicious circle. If I could have caused Albertine to live, I should at the same time have caused Andrée to reveal nothing. It is to some extent the same thing as the everlasting "You'll see when I no longer love you," which is so true and so absurd, since one would indeed elicit much if one no longer loved, but one would no longer be interested in eliciting it. In fact it is precisely the same thing. For if the woman you see again when you no longer love her then tells you all, it is because it is no longer she, or because it is no longer you: the person who loved has ceased to exist. There too death has passed by, and has made everything simple and pointless. I pursued these reflexions basing myself on the assumption that Andrée was truthful—which was possible— and had been prompted to sincerity with me precisely because she had now had relations with me, from that Saint-André-des-Champs side of her nature which Albertine too had shown me at the start. She was encouraged in this case by the fact that she was no longer afraid of Albertine, for the reality of other people survives their death for only a short time in our minds, and after a few years they are like those gods of obsolete religions whom one offends without fear because one has ceased to believe in their existence. But the fact that Andrée no longer believed in the reality of Albertine might mean that she no longer feared (any more than to betray a secret which she had promised not to reveal) to concoct a lie which retrospectively slandered her alleged accomplice. Had this absence of fear permitted her to reveal the truth at last in telling me all that, or else to concoct a lie, if, for some reason, she supposed me to be full of happiness and pride and wished to cause me pain? Perhaps she was irritated with me (an irritation that had been held in abeyance so long as she saw that I was miserable, disconsolate) because I had had relations with

Albertine and she envied me, perhaps—supposing that I considered myself on that account more favoured than her—an advantage which she herself had never, perhaps, obtained, nor even sought. Thus it was that I had often heard her say how ill they were looking to people whose look of radiant health, and in particular their awareness of it, exasperated her, and add, in the hope of annoying them, that she herself was very well, a fact that she never ceased to proclaim when she was seriously ill until the day when, in the detachment of death, it no longer mattered to her that others should be well and should know that she herself was dying. But that day was still remote. Perhaps she was angry with me, for what reason I had no idea, as long ago she had been filled with rage against the young man so learned in sporting matters, so ignorant of everything else, whom we had met at Balbec, who since then had been living with Rachel, and on the subject of whom Andrée poured forth defamatory remarks, hoping to be sued for slander in order to be able to formulate discreditable accusations against his father the falseness of which he would be unable to prove. Quite possibly this rage against myself had simply revived, having doubtless ceased when she saw how miserable I was. For the very same people whom, her eyes flashing with rage, she had longed to disgrace, to kill, to send to prison, by false testimony if need be, had only to reveal themselves to be unhappy or humiliated, for her to cease to wish them any harm, and to be ready to overwhelm them with kindness. For she was not fundamentally wicked, and if her unapparent, slightly deeper nature was not the niceness which one assumed at first from her delicate attentions, but rather envy and pride, her third nature, deeper still, the true but not entirely realised nature, tended towards kindness and the love of her fellow-creatures. Only, like all those people who in a certain state desire a better one, but, knowing it only through desiring it, do not realise that the first condition is to break away from the former state—like neurasthenics or drug-addicts who are anxious to be cured, but at the same time not to be deprived of their neuroses or their drugs, or like those world-loving religious or artistic spirits who long for solitude but seek none the less to envisage it as not implying an absolute renunciation of their former existence—Andrée was prepared to love all her fellow-creatures, but on the condition that she should first of all have succeeded in not having to visualise them as triumphant, and to that end should have humiliated them in advance. She did not understand that one should love even the proud, and conquer their pride by love and not by an even more overweening pride. But the fact is that she was like those invalids who wish to be cured by the very means that prolong their disease, which they like and would cease at once to like if they renounced them. But people wish to learn to swim and at the same time to keep one foot on the ground.

As regards the young sportsman, the Verdurins' nephew, whom I had met during my two visits to Balbec, it may be recounted here, incidentally and prematurely, that, some time after Andrée's visit, the account of which will be resumed in a moment, certain events occurred which caused a great sensation. First of all, this young man (perhaps in memory of Albertine with whom I did not then know that he had been in love) became engaged to Andrée and married her, to the despair of Rachel, of which he took no notice. Andrée no longer said then (that is to say some months after the visit of which I have been speaking) that he was a wretch, and I realised later on that she had said so only because she was madly in love with him and felt that he did not want her. But another fact made an even greater impression. This young man produced certain sketches for the theatre, with settings and costumes designed by himself, which effected in contemporary art a revolution at least equal to that brought about by the Russian ballet. In fact, the best-qualified critics regarded his works as being of cardinal importance, almost works of genius, and indeed I agree with them, confirming thus, to my own astonishment, the opinion long held by Rachel. The people who had known him at Balbec, intent only on seeing whether the cut of the clothes of the men with whom he associated was elegant or not, spending all his time at baccarat, at the races, on the golf-course or on the polo-ground, who knew that at school he had always been a dunce and had even been expelled from the lycée (to annoy his parents, he had gone to live for two months in the smart brothel in which M. de Charlus had hoped to surprise Morel), thought that perhaps his productions were the work of Andrée, who was prepared out of love to allow him all the glory, or that more probably he was paying, out of his huge personal fortune at which his excesses had barely nibbled, some inspired but needy professional to create them (this kind of wealthy society, unpolished by contact with the aristocracy and having no idea of what constitutes an artist—who to them is either an actor whom they engage to recite monologues at their daughter's engagement party, handing him his fee discreetly there and then in another room, or a painter to whom they make her sit once she is married, before the children come and when she is still at her best—are apt to believe that all the society people who write, compose or paint have their work done for them and pay to obtain a reputation as a creative artist as other men pay to secure a seat in Parliament). But all this was untrue, and this young man was indeed the author of those admirable works. When I learned this, I found myself torn between a number of different suppositions. Either he had indeed been for long years the "thickhead" that he appeared to be, and some physiological cataclysm had awakened the dormant genius in him, like a Sleeping Beauty; or else at the time of his turbulent school-days, of his failures to matriculate, of his heavy gambling losses at Balbec, of his reluctance to get into the little "tram" with his aunt Verdurin's faithful because of their hideous clothes, he was already a man of genius, distracted perhaps from his genius, which he had left in abeyance in the effervescence of juvenile passions; or again, already a conscious man of genius, and at the bottom of his class only because, while the master was spouting platitudes about Cicero, he himself was reading Rimbaud or Goethe. True, there were no grounds for any such hypothesis when I met him at Balbec, where his interests seemed to me to be centred exclusively on turning out a smart carriage and pair and mixing cocktails. But even this is not an irrefutable objection. He may have been extremely vain—something that is not incompatible with gen-ius—and have sought to shine in the manner which he knew was best calculated to dazzle in the world in which he lived, that is to say, not by showing a profound knowledge of *Elective Affinities*, but far rather a knowledge of how to drive four-in-hand. Moreover, I am not at all sure that later on, when he had become the creator of those fine and original works, he would have cared greatly, outside the theatres in which he was known, to greet anyone who was not in evening dress, like the "faithful" in their earlier manner, which would be a proof in him not of stupidity but of vanity, and indeed of a certain practical sense, a certain percept-iveness in adapting his vanity to the mentality of the imbeciles whose esteem he valued and in whose eyes a dinner-jacket might perhaps shine with greater brilliance than the gaze of a thinker. Who can say whether, seen from without, some man of talent, or even a man devoid of talent but a lover of the things of the mind, myself for instance, would not have appeared, to anyone who met him at Rivebelle, in the hotel at Balbec, or on the esplanade, the most perfect and pretentious fool? Not to mention that for Octave matters of art must have been something so intimate, inhabiting the most secret recesses of his being, that doubtless it would never have occurred to him to speak of them, as Saint-Loup, for instance, would have done, Saint-Loup for whom the arts had all the glamour that horses and carriages had for Octave. And then he may have had a passion for gambling, and it is said that he retained it. But all the same, if the piety which brought to light the unknown work of Vinteuil emerged from the murky environment of Montjouvain, I was no less struck by the thought that what were perhaps the most extraordinary masterpieces of our day had emerged not from the *concours général*, from a model, academic education in the manner of the Broglie family, but from the frequentation of paddocks and fashionable bars. In any case, in those days at Balbec, the reasons which made me anxious to know him, and which made Albertine and her friends anxious that I should not know him, were equally extraneous to his merit, and could only have illustrated the eternal misunderstanding between an "intellectual" (represented in this instance by myself) and society (represented by the little band) with regard to a social personality (the young golfer). I had no inkling of his talent, and his prestige in my eyes—like that of Mme Blatin long ago—had been that of being, whatever they might say, the friend of my girlfriends, and more one of their band than myself. On the other hand, Albertine and Andrée, symbolising in this respect the incapacity of society people to bring a sound judgment to bear upon the things of the mind and their propensity to attach themselves in that connexion to false appearances, not only thought me almost idiotic because I took an interest in such an imbecile, but were astonished above all that, golfer for golfer, my choice should have fallen upon the poorest player of them all. If, for instance, I had chosen to make friends with young Gilbert de Belloeuvre, apart from golf he was a boy who had a certain amount of conversation, who had almost succeeded in the *concours général* and was an agreeable versifier (as a matter of fact he was the stupidest of them all). Or again, if my object had been to "make a study for a book," Guy Saumoy, who was completely insane, who had abducted two girls, was at least a singular type who might "interest" me. These two might have been allowed me, but the other, what attraction could I find in him? He was the epitome of the "great lout," of the "thickhead."

To return to Andrée's visit, after the disclosure that she had just made to me of her relations with Albertine, she added that the main reason for which Albertine had left me was concern about what her friends of the little band, and other people as well, might think of her living like that with a young man to whom she was not married: "Of course I know it was in your mother's house. But that makes no difference. You can't imagine what that sort of girls' community is like, what they conceal from one another, how they dread one another's opinion of them. I've seen some of them being terribly severe with young men simply because they knew their friends and they were afraid that certain things might be repeated, and then I've happened by chance to see those very same girls in a totally different light, much to their chagrin."

A few months earlier, this knowledge which Andrée appeared to possess of the motives that swayed the girls of the little band would have seemed to me the most precious thing in the world. What she said was perhaps sufficient to explain why Albertine, who had given herself to me afterwards in Paris, had refused to do so at Balbec where I was constantly meeting her friends, a fact which I had absurdly supposed to be so advantageous for being on better terms with her. Perhaps indeed it was because she had seen signs of my confiding in Andrée, or because I had rashly told the latter that she was coming to spend the night at the Grand Hotel, that Albertine, who an hour earlier was perhaps ready to let me enjoy certain favours as though that were the simplest thing in the world, had abruptly changed her mind and threatened to ring the bell. But then, she must have been accommodating to lots of others. This thought rekindled my jealousy and I told Andrée that there was something that I wished to ask her.

"You did those things in your grandmother's empty apartment?"

"Oh, no, never, we'd have been disturbed."

"Why, I thought . . . it seemed to me . . . "

"Besides, Albertine chiefly liked doing it in the country."

"Oh! where?"

"Originally, when she hadn't time to go very far, we used to go to the Buttes-Chaumont. She knew a house there. Or else we would lie under the trees, there's never anyone about. In the grotto of the Petit Trianon, too."

"There, you see; how am I to believe you? You swore to me, not a year ago, that you'd never done anything at the Buttes-Chaumont."

"I was afraid of hurting you."

As I have said, I thought (although not until much later) that on the contrary it was on this second occasion, the day of her confessions, that Andrée had sought to hurt me. And this thought would have occurred to me at once, because I should have felt the need of it, if I had still been as much in love with Albertine. But Andrée's words did not hurt me sufficiently to make it essential for me to dismiss them immediately as untrue. On the whole, if what Andrée said was true, and I did not doubt it at the time, the real Albertine whom I now discovered, after having known so many diverse forms of Albertine, differed very little from the young bacchante who had loomed up and at once been detected that first day, on the front at Balbec, and who had offered me so many different aspects in succession, as a town alters the disposition of its buildings one after the other as we approach it, to the point of crushing, obliterating the principal monument which alone we could see from a distance, until finally, when we know it well and can judge it exactly, its true proportions prove to be those which the perspective of the first glance had indicated, the rest, through which we passed, being no more than that succession of lines of defence which everything in creation raises against our vision, and which we must cross one after another, at the cost of how much suffering, before we arrive at the heart. If, however, I had no need to believe absolutely in Albertine's innocence because my suffering had diminished, I can say that conversely, if I did not suffer unduly at this revelation, it was because, some time since, the belief in Albertine's innocence that I had fabricated for myself had been gradually replaced, without my realising it, by the belief, ever present in my mind, in her guilt. Now if I no longer believed in Albertine's innocence, it was because I had already ceased to feel the need, the passionate desire to believe in it. It is desire that engenders belief, and if we are not as a rule aware of this, it is because most belief-creating desires—unlike the desire which had persuaded me that Albertine was innocent—end only with our own life. To all the evidence that corroborated my original version, I had stupidly preferred mere assertions by Albertine. Why had I believed them? Lying is essential to humanity. It plays as large a part perhaps as the quest for pleasure, and is moreover governed by that quest. One lies in order to protect one's pleasure, or one's honour if the disclosure of one's pleasure runs counter to one's honour. One lies all one's life long, even, especially, perhaps only, to those who love one. For they alone make us fear for our pleasure and desire their esteem. I had at first thought Albertine guilty, and it was only my desire, by utilising the powers of my intelligence to construct an edifice of doubt, that had put me on the wrong track. Perhaps we live surrounded by electric, seismic signs which we must interpret in good faith in order to know the truth about people's characters. If the truth be told, saddened as I was in spite of everything by Andrée's words, I thought it fitter that the reality should finally turn out to accord with what my instinct had originally foreboded rather than with the wretched optimism to which I had later so cravenly surrendered. I preferred that life should remain on the same level as my intuitions. Those, moreover, that I had had that first day on the beach, when I had believed that these girls were the incarnation of frenzied pleasure, of vice, and again on the evening when I had seen Albertine's governess leading that passionate girl home to the little villa, as one drives into its cage a wild animal which nothing, later on, despite appearances, will ever succeed in taming—did not those intuitions accord with what Bloch had told me when he had made the world seem so fair to my eyes by showing me, making me quiver with excitement on all my walks, at every encounter, the universality of desire? Perhaps, when all was said, it was better that I should not have found those first intuitions verified afresh until now. While the whole of my love for Albertine endured, they would have made me suffer too acutely and it was better that there should have subsisted of them only a trace, my perpetual suspicion of things which I did not see and which nevertheless happened continually so close to me, and perhaps another trace as well, earlier, vaster, which was *my love itself*. For was it not, despite all the denials of my reason, tantamount to knowing Albertine in all her hideousness, actually to choose her, to love her? And even in the moments when mistrust is stilled, is not love the persistence of that mistrust and a transformation of it, is it not a proof of clair-voyance (a proof unintelligible to the lover himself), since desire, reaching out always towards what is most opposite to oneself, forces one to love what will make one suffer? There is no doubt that, inherent in a woman's charm, in her eyes, her lips, her figure, are the elements, unknown to us, most calculated to make us unhappy, so much so that to feel attracted to her, to begin to love her, is, however innocent we may pretend it to be, to read already, in a different version, all her betrayals and her misdeeds. And may not those charms which, to attract me, corporealised thus the raw, dangerous, fatal elements of a person, have stood in a more direct relation of cause and effect to those secret poisons than do the seductive luxuriance and the toxic juice of certain venomous flowers? It was perhaps, I told myself, Albertine's vice itself, the cause of my future sufferings, that had produced in her that honest, frank manner, creating the illusion that one enjoyed with her the same loyal and unqualified comradeship as with a man, just as a parallel vice had produced in M. de Charlus a feminine delicacy of sensibility and mind. In the midst of the most complete blindness, perspicacity subsists in the form of predilection and tenderness; so that it is a mistake to speak of a bad choice in love, since as soon as there is a choice it can only be a bad one.

"Did those excursions to the Buttes-Chaumont take place when you used to call for her here?" I asked Andrée.

"Oh! no, from the day Albertine came back from Balbec with you, except the time I told you about, she never did anything again with me. She wouldn't even allow me to mention such things to her."

"But my dear Andrée, why go on lying to me? By the merest chance, for I never try to find out anything, I've learned in the minutest detail things of that sort which Albertine did, I can tell you exactly, on the bank of a river with a laundry-girl, only a few days before her death."

"Ah! perhaps after she'd left you, that I can't say. She felt that she'd failed, that she'd never again be able to regain your trust."

These last words shattered me. Then I thought again of the evening of the syringa, and remembered that about a fortnight later, as my jealousy kept changing its object, I had asked Albertine whether she had ever had relations with Andrée, and she had replied: "Oh! never! Of course, I adore Andrée; I have a deep affection for her, but as I might have for a sister, and even if I had the tastes which you seem to suppose, she's the last person I should have thought of in that connexion. I can swear to you by anything you like, the honour of my aunt, the grave of my poor mother." I had believed her. And yet even if my suspicions had not been aroused by the contradiction between her former partial admissions with regard to certain matters and the vehemence with which she had afterwards denied them as soon as she saw that I was not indifferent to them, I ought to have remembered Swann, convinced of the platonic nature of M. de Charlus's friendships and assuring me of it on the evening of the very day I had seen the tailor and the Baron in the courtyard; I ought to have reflected that there are two worlds one behind the other, one consisting of the things that the best, the sincerest people say, and behind it the world composed of the sequence of what those same people do; so that when a married woman says to you of a young man: "Oh! it's perfectly true that I have an immense affection for him, but it's something quite innocent, quite pure, I could swear it on the memory of my parents," one ought oneself, instead of feeling any hesitation, to swear to oneself that she has probably just come out of the bathroom into which, after every assignation she has with the young man in question, she rushes in order not to have a child. The spray of syringa made me profoundly sad, as did also the thought that Albertine could have believed, and said, that I was treacherous and hostile; and most of all perhaps, certain lies so unexpected that I had difficulty in grasping them. One day Albertine had told me that she had been to an aerodrome where one of the airmen was a friend of hers (this doubtless in order to divert my suspicions from women, thinking that I was less jealous of men), and that it had been amusing to see how dazzled Andrée was by the said airman, by all the compliments he paid Albertine, until finally Andrée had wanted to go up in his aeroplane with him. Now this was a complete fabrication; Andrée had never visited the aerodrome in question.

When Andrée left me, it was dinner-time. "You'll never guess who has been to see me and stayed at least three hours," said my mother. "I call it three hours, but it was perhaps longer. She arrived almost on the heels of my first visitor, who was Mme Cottard, sat still and watched everybody come and go—and I had more than thirty callers—and left me only a quarter of an hour ago. If you hadn't had your friend Andrée with you, I'd have sent for you."

"Well, who was it?"

"A person who never pays calls."

"The Princesse de Parme?"

"Why, I have a cleverer son than I thought. It's no fun making you guess a name; you hit on it at once."

"Did she apologise for her coldness yesterday?"

"No, that would have been stupid. The visit itself was her apology. Your poor grandmother would have thought it admirable. It seems that about two o'clock she sent a footman to ask whether I had an 'at home.' She was told that this was the very day and so up she came."

My first thought, which I did not dare mention to Mamma, was that the Princesse de Parme, surrounded the day before by people of rank and fashion with whom she was on intimate terms and enjoyed conversing, on seeing my mother come into the room had felt an annoyance which she had made no attempt to conceal. And it was quite in the style of the great ladies of Germany, which for that matter the Guermantes had largely adopted—that haughtiness for which they thought to atone by a scrupulous affability. But my mother believed, and I came in time to share her opinion, that the Princesse de Parme, having simply failed to recognise her, had not felt bound to pay any attention to her, and that she had learned after my mother's departure who she was, either from the Duchesse de Guermantes whom my mother had met below or from the list of her visitors, whose names were requested by the ushers before they entered her presence and inscribed in a register. She had felt that it would be ungracious to send word or to say to my mother: "I didn't recognise you," and instead—and this was no less in keeping with the code of manners of the German courts and with the ways of the Guermantes than my original version— had thought that a visit, an exceptional action on the part of a royal personage, and what was more a visit of several hours' duration, would convey the explanation to my mother in an indirect but no less convincing form, which is just what did happen.

But I did not stay to hear my mother's account of the Princess's visit, for I had just recalled a number of facts concerning Albertine as to which I had intended but had forgotten to question Andrée. How little, for that matter, did I know, would I ever know, of this story of Albertine, the only story that really interested me, or was at least beginning to interest me again at certain moments. For man is that ageless creature who has the faculty of becoming many years younger in a few seconds, and who, surrounded by the walls of the time through which he has lived, floats within them as in a pool the surface-level of which is constantly changing so as to bring him within range now of one epoch, now of another. I wrote to Andrée asking her to come again. She was unable to do so until a week later. Almost as soon as she entered the room I said to her:

"Very well, then, since you maintain that Albertine never did that sort of thing while she was staying here, according to you it was to be able to do it more freely that she left me, but for which of her friends?"

"Certainly not, it wasn't that at all."

"Then because I was too disagreeable?"

"No, I don't think so. I think she was forced to leave you by her aunt who had designs for her future upon that guttersnipe, you know, the young man you used to call 'I'm a wash-out,' the young man who was in love with Albertine and had asked for her hand. Seeing that you weren't marrying her, they were afraid that the shocking length of her stay in your house might prevent the young man from doing so. And so Mme Bontemps, on whom the young man was constantly bringing pressure to bear, summoned Albertine home. Albertine after all needed her uncle and aunt, and when she realised that they were forcing her hand she left you."

I had never in my jealousy thought of this explanation, but only of Albertine's desire for women and of my own surveillance of her; I had forgotten that there was also Mme Bontemps who might eventually regard as strange what had shocked my mother from the first. At least Mme Bontemps was afraid that it might shock this possible husband whom she was keeping in reserve for Albertine in case I failed to marry her.

So that it was possible that a long debate had gone on in Albertine's mind between staying with me and leaving me, but that her decision to leave me had been made on account of her aunt, or of that young man, and not on account of women to whom perhaps she had never given a thought. The most disturbing thing to my mind was that Andrée, who after all no longer had anything to conceal from me as to Albertine's morals, swore to me that nothing of the sort had ever occurred between Albertine on the one hand and Mlle Vinteuil or her friend on the other (Albertine herself was unconscious of her own proclivities when she first met them, and they, from the fear of being mistaken in the object of one's desire which breeds as many errors as desire itself, regarded her as extremely hostile to that sort of thing. Perhaps later on they had learned that her tastes were similar to their own, but by that time they knew Albertine and Albertine knew them too well for there to be any question of their doing those things together).

"But, my dear Andrée, you're lying again. Remember—you admitted it to me yourself when I telephoned to you the evening before, don't you remember?—that Albertine had been so anxious, and kept it from me as though it was something that I mustn't know about, to go to the afternoon party at the Verdurins' at which Mlle Vinteuil was expected."

"Yes, but Albertine hadn't the slightest idea that Mlle Vinteuil was to be there."

"What? You yourself told me that she'd met Mme Verdurin a few days earlier. Besides, Andrée, there's no point in our trying to deceive one another. I found a note one morning in Albertine's room, a note from Mme Verdurin urging her to come that afternoon."

And I showed her this note which, as a matter of fact, Françoise had taken care to bring to my notice by placing it on top of Albertine's belongings a few days before her departure, and, I regret to say, leaving it there to make Albertine suppose that I had been rummaging among her things, to let her know in any case that I had seen it. And I had often wondered whether Françoise's ruse had not been largely responsible for the departure of Albertine, who saw that she could no longer conceal anything from me, and felt disheartened, defeated. I showed Andrée the note: *I feel no compunction, on the strength of this genuine family feeling...* "You know very well, Andrée, that Albertine used always to say that Mlle Vinteuil's friend was indeed a mother, an elder sister to her."

"But you've misinterpreted this note. The person Mme Verdurin wished Albertine to meet that afternoon wasn't Mlle Vinteuil's friend at all, it was the young man you call 'I'm a wash-out,' and the family feeling is what Mme Verdurin felt for the brute, who is after all her nephew. However, I think Albertine did hear afterwards that Mlle Vinteuil was to be there—Mme Verdurin may have let her know incidentally. And of course the thought of seeing her friend again gave her pleasure, reminded her of happy times in the past, just as you'd be glad, if you were going somewhere, to know that Elstir would be there, but no more than that, not even as much. No, if Albertine was unwilling to say why she wanted to go to Mme Verdurin's, it was because it was a rehearsal to which Mme Verdurin had invited a very small party, including that nephew of hers whom you met at Balbec, to whom Mme Bontemps was hoping to marry Albertine off and to whom Albertine wanted to talk. He was a real black-guard . . ."

And so Albertine, contrary to what Andrée's mother used to think, had had after all the prospect of a wealthy marriage. And when she had wanted to visit Mme Verdurin, when she had spoken to her in secret, when she had been so annoyed that I should have gone there that evening without warning her, the intrigue between her and Mme Verdurin had had as its object her meeting not Mlle Vinteuil but the nephew who loved Albertine and for whom Mme Verdurin, with that satisfaction of working towards the realisation of one of those marriages which surprise one in some families into whose state of mind one does not enter completely, did not desire a rich bride. Now I had never given another thought to this nephew who had perhaps been the initiator thanks to whom I had received Albertine's first kiss. And for the whole structure of Albertine's anxieties which I had built up, I must now substitute another, or rather superimpose it, for perhaps it did not exclude the other, a taste for women not being incompatible with marriage. Was this marriage really the reason for Albertine's departure, and had she, out of self-respect, so as not to appear to be dependent on her aunt, or to force me to marry her, preferred not to mention it? I was beginning to realise that the system of multiple motives for a single action, of which Albertine showed her mastery in her relations with her friends when she allowed each of them to suppose that it was for her sake that she had come, was only a sort of symbol, artificial and premeditated, of the different aspects that an action assumes according to the point of view from which we look at it. It was not the first time I had felt astonishment and a sort of shame at never once having told myself that Albertine was in a false position in my house, a position that might give offence to her aunt; it was not the first, nor was it the last. How often has it happened to me, after having sought to understand the relations between two people and the crises that they entail, to hear all of a sudden a third person speak to me of them from his own point of view, for he has even closer relations with one of the two, a point of view which has perhaps been the cause of the crisis! And if people's actions remain so unpredictable, how should not the people themselves be equally so? Listening to the people who maintained that Albertine was a schemer who had tried to get one man after another to marry her, it was not difficult to imagine how they would have defined her life with me. And yet to my mind she had been a victim, a victim who perhaps was not altogether pure, but in that case guilty for other reasons, on account of vices which people did not mention.

But above all we must remember this: on the one hand, lying is often a trait of character; on the other hand, in women who would not otherwise be liars, it is a natural defence, improvised at first, then more and more organised, against that sudden danger which would be capable of destroying all life: love. Furthermore, it is not by mere chance that sensitive, intellectual men invariably give themselves to insensitive and inferior women, and moreover remain attached to them, and that the proof that they are not loved does not in the least cure them of the urge to sacrifice everything to keep such women with them. If I say that such men need to suffer, I am saying something that is accurate while suppressing the preliminary truths which make that need—involuntary in a sense—to suffer a perfectly understandable consequence of those truths. Not to mention the fact that, all-round natures being rare, a man who is highly sensitive and highly intellectual will generally have little will-power, will be the plaything of habit and of that fear of suffering in the immediate present which condemns to perpetual suffering—and that in these conditions he will never be prepared to repudiate the woman who does not love him. One may be surprised that he should be content with so little love, but one ought rather to picture to oneself the anguish that may be caused him by the love which he himself feels. An anguish which one ought not to pity unduly, for those terrible commotions that are caused by an unrequited love, by the departure or the death of a mistress, are like those attacks of paralysis which at first leave us helpless, but after which the muscles tend gradually to recover their vital elasticity and energy. What is more, this anguish does not lack compensation. These sensitive and intellectual persons are as a rule little inclined to falsehood. It takes them all the more unawares in that, however intelligent they may be, they live in the world of the possible, live in the anguish which a woman has just inflicted on them rather than in the clear perception of what she wanted, what she did, what she loved, a perception granted chiefly to self-willed natures which need it in order to prepare against the future instead of lamenting the past. And so these persons feel that they are betrayed without quite knowing how. Wherefore the mediocre woman whom we are astonished to see them loving enriches the universe for them far more than an intelligent woman would have done. Behind each of her words, they feel that a lie is lurking, behind each house to which she says that she has gone, another house, behind each action, each person, another action, another person. Of course they do not know what or whom, they do not have the energy, would not perhaps find it possible, to discover. A lying woman, by an extremely simple trick, can beguile, without taking the trouble to change her method, any number of people, and, what is more, the very person who ought to have discovered the trick. All this confronts the sensitive intellectual with a universe full of depths which his jealousy longs to plumb and which are not without interest to his intelligence.

Without being precisely a man of that category, I was going perhaps to learn, now that Albertine was dead, the secret of her life. Here again, do not these indiscretions which come to light only after a person's life on earth is ended prove that nobody really believes in a future life? If these indiscretions are true, one ought to fear the resentment of a woman whose actions one reveals fully as much in anticipation of meeting her in heaven as one feared it while she was alive and one felt bound to keep her secret. And if these indiscretions are false, invented because she is no longer present to contradict them, one ought to be even more afraid of the dead woman's wrath if one believed in heaven. But no one does believe in it.

On the whole, I did not understand any better than before why Albertine had left me. If the face of a woman can with difficulty be grasped by the eyes, which cannot take in the whole of its mobile surface, or by the lips, or still less by the memory, if it is shrouded in obscurity according to her social position, according to the level at which we are situated, how much thicker is the veil drawn between those of her actions which we see and her motives! Motives are situated at a deeper level, which we do not perceive, and moreover engender actions other than those of which we are aware and often in absolute contradiction to them. When has there not been some man in public life, regarded as a saint by his friends, who is discovered to have forged documents, robbed the State, betrayed his country? How often is a great nobleman robbed by a steward whom he has brought up from childhood, ready to swear that he was an excellent man, as possibly he was! And how much more impenetrable does it become, this curtain that screens another's motives, if we are in love with that person, for it clouds our judgment and also obscures the actions of one who, feeling that she is loved, ceases suddenly to set any store by what otherwise would have seemed to her important, such as wealth for example. Perhaps also it induces her to feign to some extent this scorn for wealth in the hope of obtaining more by making us suffer. The bargaining instinct may also enter into everything else; and even actual incidents in her life, an intrigue which she has confided to no one for fear of its being revealed to us, which many people might for all that have discovered had they felt the same passionate desire to know it as we ourselves while preserving a greater equanimity of mind and arousing fewer suspicions in the guilty party, an intrigue of which certain people have in fact not been unaware—but people whom we do not know and would not know how to find. And among all these reasons for her adopting an inexplicable attitude towards us, we must include those idiosyncrasies of character which impel people, whether from indifference to their own interests, or from hatred, or from love of freedom, or under the impulse of anger, or from fear of what certain people will think, to do the opposite of what we expected. And then there are the differences of environment, of upbringing, in which we refuse to believe because, when we are talking together, they are effaced by our words, but which return when we are apart to direct the actions of each of us from so opposite a point of view that no true meeting of minds is possible.

"Anyhow there's no need to seek out all these explanations," Andrée went on. "Heaven knows I was fond of Albertine, and she was a really nice creature, but, especially after she had typhoid (a year before you first met us all), she was an absolute madcap. All of a sudden she would get sick of what she was doing, all her plans would have to be changed that very minute, and she herself probably couldn't say why. You remember the year when you first came to Balbec, the year when you met us all? One fine day she got somebody to send her a telegram calling her back to Paris; she barely had time to pack her trunks. But there was absolutely no reason for her to go. All the pretexts she gave were false. Paris would be a deadly bore at that moment. We were all of us still at Balbec. The golf club wasn't closed, indeed the heats for the cup which she was so keen on winning weren't finished. She'd certainly have won it. It only meant staying on for another week. Well, off she went at a gallop. I often spoke to her about it later.

She said herself that she didn't know why she had left, that she felt homesick (the home being Paris, you can imagine how likely that was), that she didn't feel happy at Balbec, that she thought there were people there who sneered at her."

And I told myself there was this much truth in what Andrée said: that if differences between minds account for the different impressions produced upon one person and another by the same work, and differences of feeling account for the impossibility of captivating a person who does not love you, there are also differences between characters, peculiarities in a single character, which are also motives for action. Then I ceased to think about this explanation and said to myself how difficult it is to know the truth in this world.

I had indeed noticed Albertine's desire to go to Mme Verdurin's and her concealment of it: I had not been mistaken on that point. But then even if we do thus manage to grasp one fact, all the others, which we perceive only in their outward appearance, escape us, and we see only a succession of flat silhouettes of which we say to ourselves: it is this, it is that, it is because of her, or it is because of someone else. The revelation that Mlle Vinteuil was expected had seemed to me the true explanation, all the more so because Albertine, forestalling me, had spoken to me about it. And subsequently had she not refused to swear to me that Mlle Vinteuil's presence gave her no pleasure? And here, with regard to this young man, I remembered a point which I had forgotten. A short time before, while Albertine was living with me, I had met him, and he had been—in contrast to his attitude at Balbec— extremely friendly, even affectionate towards me, had begged me to allow him to call on me, a request which I had refused for a number of reasons. And now I realised that it was quite simply because, knowing that Albertine was living in my house, he had wanted to be on good terms with me so as to have every facility for seeing her and for carrying her off from me, and I concluded that he was a scoundrel. Some time later, when I attended the first performances of this young man's work, although I continued to think that if he had been so anxious to call on me, it was for Albertine's sake, and although I felt this to be reprehensible, I remembered that in the past, if I had gone down to Doncières to see Saint-Loup, it was really because I was in love with Mme de Guermantes. It is true that the two cases were not quite the same: Saint-Loup not being in love with Mme de Guermantes, there was in my display of affection for him a trace of duplicity perhaps, but no treason. But I reflected afterwards that this affection which one feels for the person who possesses the object of one's desire is something that one feels equally even if he himself also loves that object. No doubt, one ought in that case to resist a friendship which will lead one straight to betrayal. And I think that this is what I have always done. But in the case of those who lack the strength to resist, we cannot say that the friendship they affect for their rival is a mere sham; they feel it sincerely and for that reason display it with a fervour which, once the betrayal has been accomplished, can cause the betrayed husband or lover to say with amazed indignation: "If you had heard the protestations of affection that the wretch showered on me! That a person should come to rob a man of his treasure, that I can understand. But that he should feel the diabolical need to assure him of his friendship first of all strikes me as a degree of ignominy and perversity almost impossible to imagine." No, in fact, there is no perverse pleasure in it, nor even an absolutely conscious lie.

The affection of this sort which Albertine's pseudo-fiancé had manifested for me that day had yet another excuse, being more complex than a simple by-product of his love for Albertine. It was only a short time since he had known himself to be, confessed himself to be, been anxious to be proclaimed an intellectual. For the first time, values other than sporting or hedonistic existed for him. The fact that I enjoyed the esteem of Elstir and Bergotte, that Albertine had perhaps told him of the way I talked about writers, which had led her to imagine that I might myself be able to write, meant that all of a sudden I had become to him (to the new man whom he at last realised himself to be) an interesting person whose friendship he would have liked to cultivate, to whom he would have liked to confide his plans, whom he might perhaps have asked for an introduction to Elstir. So that he was in fact sincere when he asked if he might call on me, expressing a regard for me to which intellectual reasons as well as a reflexion of Albertine imparted a certain veracity. No doubt it was not *for that* that he was so anxious to come and see me and would have dropped everything in order to do so. But of this last reason, which did little more than raise to a sort of impassioned paroxysm the two other reasons, he was perhaps unaware himself, and the other two existed really, as might really have existed in Albertine, when she had been anxious to go to Mme Verdurin's on the afternoon of the rehearsal, the perfectly respectable pleasure that she would feel in meeting again friends of her childhood who in her eyes were no more depraved than she was in theirs, in talking to them, in showing them, by the mere fact of her presence at the Verdurins', that the poor little girl whom they had known was now invited to a noted salon, the pleasure also that she might perhaps have felt in listening to Vinteuil's music. If all this was true, the blush that had risen to Albertine's cheeks when I had mentioned Mlle Vinteuil was due to the fact that I had done so in the context of that afternoon party which she had tried to keep secret from me because of the marriage proposal of which I was not to know. Albertine's refusal to swear to me that she would have felt no pleasure in meeting Mlle Vinteuil again at that party had at the moment intensified my torment, strengthened my suspicions, but proved to me in retrospect that she had wanted to be sincere, even over an innocent matter, perhaps simply because it was an innocent matter. There nevertheless remained what Andrée had told me about her relations with Albertine. Perhaps, however, even without going so far as to believe that Andrée had invented them solely that I should not be happy, or able to feel superior to her, I could still suppose that she had slightly exaggerated her account of what she used to do with Albertine, and that Albertine, by a mental reservation, also minimised slightly what she had done with Andrée, making use Jesuitically of certain definitions which I had stupidly formulated on the subject, judging that her relations with Andrée did not fall into the category of what she was obliged to confess to me and that she could deny them without lying. But why should I believe that it was she rather than Andrée who was lying? Truth and life are very difficult to fathom, and I retained of them, without really having got to know them, an impression in which sadness was perhaps actually eclipsed by exhaustion.

CHAPTER THREE

SOJOURN IN VENICE

M Y mother had taken me to spend a few weeks in Venice, and—as beauty may exist in the most precious as well as in the humblest things—I received there impressions analogous to those which I had felt so often in the past at Combray, but transposed into a wholly different and far richer key. When, at ten o'clock in the morning, my shutters were thrown open, I saw blazing there, instead of the gleaming black marble into which the slates of Saint-Hilaire used to turn, the golden angel on the campanile of St Mark's. Glittering in a sunlight which made it almost impossible to keep one's eyes upon it, this angel promised me, with its outstretched arms, for the moment when I appeared on the Piazzetta half an hour later, a joy more certain than any that it could ever in the past have been bidden to announce to men of good will. I could see nothing else so long as I remained in bed, but as the whole world is merely a vast sundial, a single sunlit segment of which enables us to tell what time it is, on the very first morning I was reminded of the shops in the Place de l'Eglise at Combray, which, on Sunday mornings, were always on the point of shutting when I arrived for mass, while the straw in the marketplace smelt strongly in the already hot sunlight. But on the second morning, what I saw on awakening, what made me get out of bed (because they had taken the place in my memory and in my desire of the recollections of Combray), were the impressions of my first morning stroll in Venice, in Venice where everyday life was no less real than in Combray, where as in Combray on Sunday mornings one had the pleasure of stepping down into a festive street, but where that street was entirely paved with sapphire-blue water, cooled by warm breezes and of a colour so durable that my tired eyes might rest their gaze upon it in search of relaxation without fear of its blenching. Like the good folk of the Rue de l'Oiseau at Combray, so also in this strange town, the inhabitants actually emerged from houses lined up side by side along the main street, but the role played there by houses of casting a patch of shade at their feet was entrusted in Venice to palaces of porphyry and jasper, above the arched doors of which the head of a bearded god (breaking the alignment, like the knocker on a door at Combray) had the effect of darkening with its shadow, not the brownness of the earth, but the splendid blueness of the water. On the Piazza, the shadow that would have been produced at Combray by the awning over the draper's shop and the barber's pole was a carpet of little blue flowers strewn at its feet upon the desert of sun-scorched flag-stones by the relief of a Renaissance façade, which is not to say that, when the sun beat down, one was not obliged, in Venice as at Combray, to pull down the blinds, even beside the canal, but they hung between the quatrefoils and foliage of Gothic windows. Of this sort was the window in our hotel behind the balusters of which my mother sat waiting for me, gazing at the canal with a patience which she would not have displayed in the old days at Combray, at a time when, cherishing hopes for my future which had never been realised, she was unwilling to let me see how much she loved me. Nowadays she was well aware that an apparent coldness on her part would alter nothing, and the affection she lavished upon me was like those forbidden foods which are no longer withheld from invalids when it is certain that they are past recovery. True, the humble details which gave an individuality to the window of my aunt Léonie's bedroom seen from the Rue de l'Oiseau, the impression of asymmetry caused by its unequal distance from the windows on either side of it, the exceptional height of its wooden ledge, the angled bar which served to open the shutters, the two curtains of glossy blue satin tied back with loops—the equivalent of all these things existed in this hotel in Venice where I could hear also those words, so distinctive and so eloquent, which enable us to recognise from a distance the dwelling to which we are going home to lunch, and afterwards remain in our memory as testimony that, for a certain period of time, that dwelling was ours; but the task of uttering them had, in Venice, devolved not, as at Combray and most other places, upon the simplest, not to say the ugliest things, but upon the ogive, still half Arab, of a façade which is reproduced in all the architectural museums and all the illustrated art books as one of the supreme achievements of the domestic architecture of the Middle Ages; from a long way away and when I had barely passed San Giorgio Maggiore, I caught sight of this ogival window which had already seen me, and the thrust of its pointed arches added to its smile of welcome the distinction of a loftier, scarcely comprehensible gaze. And because, behind its multi-coloured marble balusters, Mamma was sitting reading while she waited for me to return, her face shrouded in a tulle veil as heart-rending in its whiteness as her hair to me who sensed that, hiding her tears, she had pinned it to her straw hat not so much with the idea of appearing "dressed" in the eyes of the hotel staff as in order to appear to me to be less in mourning, less sad, almost consoled for the death of my grandmother; because, not having recognised me at first, as soon as I called to her from the gondola, she sent out to me, from the bottom of her heart, a love which stopped only where there was no longer any corporeal matter to sustain it, on the surface of her impassioned gaze which she brought as close to me as possible, which she tried to thrust forward to the advanced post of her lips, in a smile which seemed to be kissing me, within the frame and beneath the canopy of the more discreet smile of the arched window lit up by the midday sun—because of this, that window has assumed in my memory the precious quality of things that have had, simultaneously with us, side by side with us, their share in a certain hour that struck, the same for us and for them; and however full of admirable tracery its mullions may be, that illustrious window retains in my eyes the intimate aspect of a man of genius with whom we have spent a month in some holiday resort, where he has acquired a friendly regard for us; and if, ever since then, whenever I see a cast of that window in a museum, I am obliged to hold back my tears, it is simply because it says to me the thing that touches me more than anything else in the world: "I remember your mother so well."

And as I went indoors to join my mother who by now had left the window, on leaving the heat of the open air I had the same sensation of coolness that I experienced long ago at Combray when I went upstairs to my room; but in Venice it was a breeze from the sea that kept the air cool, and no longer on a little wooden staircase with narrow steps, but on the noble surfaces of marble steps continually splashed by shafts of blue-green sunlight, which, to the valuable instruction in the art of Chardin acquired long ago, added a lesson in that of Veronese. And since, in Venice, it is works of art, things of priceless beauty, that are entrusted with the task of giving us our impressions of everyday life, it is to falsify the character of that city, on the grounds that the Venice of certain painters is coldly aesthetic in its most celebrated parts (let us make an exception of the superb studies of Maxime Dethomas), to represent only its poverty-stricken aspects, in the districts where nothing of its splendour is to be seen, and, in order to make Venice more intimate and more genuine, to give it a resemblance to Aubervilliers. It has been the mistake of some very great artists, from a quite natural reaction against the artificial Venice of bad painters, to concentrate exclusively on the Venice of the more humble *campi*, the little deserted *rii*, which they found more real.

It was this Venice that I used often to explore in the afternoon, when I did not go out with my mother. The fact was that it was easier to find there women of the people, match-sellers, pearl-stringers, glass or lace makers, young seamstresses in black shawls with long fringes, whom there was nothing to prevent me from loving, because I had to a large extent forgotten Albertine, and who seemed to me more desirable than others, because I still remembered her a little. Who, in any case, could have told me precisely, in this passionate quest of mine for Venetian women, how much there was of themselves, how much of Albertine, how much of my old, long-cherished desire to visit Venice? Our slightest desire, though unique as a chord, nevertheless includes the fundamental notes on which the whole of our life is built. And sometimes, if we were to eliminate one of them, even one that we do not hear, that we are not aware of, one that has no connexion with the object of our quest, we would nevertheless see our whole desire for that object disappear. There were many things that I made no attempt to identify in the excitement I felt as I went in search of Venetian women.

My gondola followed the course of the small canals; like the mysterious hand of a genie leading me through the maze of this oriental city, they seemed, as I advanced, to be cutting a path for me through the heart of a crowded quarter which they bisected, barely parting, with a slender furrow arbitrarily traced, the tall houses with their tiny Moorish windows; and as though the magic guide had been holding a candle in his hand and were lighting the way for me, they kept casting ahead of them a ray of sunlight for which they cleared a route. One felt that between the mean dwellings which the canal had just parted, and which otherwise would have formed a compact whole, no open space had been reserved; so that a campanile or a garden trellis vertically overhung the *rio*, as in a flooded city. But, for both churches and gardens, thanks to the same transposition as in the Grand Canal, the sea so readily served as means of communication, as substitute for street or alley, that on either side of the *canaletto* the belfries rose from the water in this poor and populous district like those of humble and much-frequented parish churches bearing the stamp of their necessity, of their use by crowds of simple folk, the gardens traversed by the canal cutting trailed their startled leaves and fruit in the water, and on the ledges of the houses whose crudely cut stone was still rough as though it had only just been sawn, urchins surprised by the gondola sat back trying to keep their balance and allowing their legs to dangle vertically, like sailors seated upon a swing-bridge the two halves of which have been swung apart, allowing the sea to pass between them. Now and again would appear a handsomer building that happened to be there like a surprise in a box which one has just opened, a little ivory temple with its Corinthian columns and an allegorical statue on its pediment, somewhat out of place among the ordinary surroundings in the midst of which, for all that we tried to make space for it, the peristyle with which the canal had provided it retained the look of a landing-stage for market gardeners. I had the impression, which my desire strengthened further, of not being outside, but of entering more and more into the depths of something secret, because each time I found something new which came to place itself on one side of me or the other, a small monument or an unexpected *campo*, keeping the surprised expression of beautiful things which one sees for the first time and of which one doesn't yet perfectly understand the intended purpose or the utility.

I returned on foot through narrow lanes; I accosted plebeian girls as Albertine perhaps had done, and I should have liked to have her with me. Yet these could not be the same girls; at the time when Albertine had been in Venice, they would have been children still. But, after having been unfaithful in the past, in a basic sense and out of cowardice, to each of the desires that I had conceived as unique—since I had sought an analogous object and not the same one, which I despaired of finding again—now I systematically sought women whom Albertine had not known, just as I no longer sought those that I had desired in the past. True, it often happened to me to recall, with an extraordinary violence of desire, some wench of Méséglise or Paris, or the milk-girl I had seen early in the morning at the foot of a hill during my first journey to Balbec. But alas! I remembered them as they were then, that is to say as they certainly would not be now. So that if in the past I had been led to qualify my impression of the uniqueness of a desire by seeking, in place of a convent-girl I had lost sight of, a similar convent-girl, now, in order to recapture the girls who had troubled my adolescence or that of Albertine, I had to consent to a further departure from the principle of the individuality of desire: what I must look for was not those who were sixteen then, but those who were sixteen today, for now, in the absence of that which was most distinctive in the person and which eluded me, what I loved was youth. I knew that the youth of those I had known existed no longer except in my impassioned recollection, and that it was not them, however anxious I might be to make contact with them when my memory recalled them to me, that I must cull if I really wished to harvest the youth and the blossom of the year.

The sun was still high in the sky when I went to meet my mother on the Piazzetta. We would call for a gondola. "How your poor grandmother would have loved this simple grandeur!" Mamma would say to me, pointing to the Doges' Palace which stood contemplating the sea with the thoughtful expression that had been bequeathed to it by its architect and that it faithfully retained in its mute attendance on its vanished lords. "She would even have loved those soft pink tints, because they are unmawkish. How she would have loved the whole of Venice, and what informality, worthy of nature itself, she would have found in all these beauties, this plethora of objects that seem to need no formal arrangement but present themselves just as they are—the Doges' Palace with its cubic shape, the columns which you say are those of Herod's palace, slap in the middle of the Piazzetta, and, even less deliberately placed, put there as though for want of anywhere better, the pillars from Acre, and those horses on the balcony of St Mark's! Your grandmother would have had as much pleasure seeing the sun setting over the Doges' Palace as over a mountain." And there was indeed an element of truth in what my mother said, for, as the gondola brought us back along the Grand Canal, we watched the double line of palaces between which we passed reflect the light and angle of the sun upon their pink flanks, and alter with them, seeming not so much private habitations and historic buildings as a chain of marble cliffs at the foot of which one goes out in the evening in a boat to watch the sunset. Seen thus, the buildings arranged along either bank of the canal made one think of objects of nature, but of a nature which seemed to have created its works with a human imagination. But at the same time (because of the always urban character of the impressions which Venice gives almost in the open sea, on those waters whose ebb and flow makes itself felt twice daily, and which alternately cover at high tide and uncover at low tide the splendid outside stairs of the palaces), as we should have done in Paris on the boulevards, in the Champs-Elysées, in the Bois, in any wide and fashionable avenue, we passed the most elegant women in the hazy evening light, almost all foreigners, who, languidly reclining against the cushions of their floating carriages, followed one another in procession, stopped in front of a palace where they had a friend to call on, sent to inquire whether she was at home, and while, as they waited for the answer, they prepared to leave a card just in case, as they would have done at the door of the Hôtel de Guermantes, turned to their guide-books to find out the period and the style of the palace, being shaken the while, as though upon the crest of a blue wave, by the wash of the glittering, swirling water, which took alarm on finding itself pent between the dancing gondola and the resounding marble. And thus any outing, even when it was only to pay calls or to leave visiting-cards, was threefold and unique in this Venice where the simplest social coming and going assumed at the same time the form and the charm of a visit to a museum and a trip on the sea.

Several of the palaces on the Grand Canal had been converted into hotels, and for the sake of a change or out of hospitality towards Mme Sazerat whom we had encountered—the unexpected and inopportune acquaintance whom one invariably meets when one travels abroad—and whom Mamma had invited to dine with us, we decided one evening to try a hotel which was not our own and in which we had been told that the food was better. While my mother was paying the gondolier and taking Mme Sazerat to the drawing-room which she had engaged, I slipped away to inspect the great hall of the restaurant with its fine marble pillars and walls and ceiling that were once entirely covered with frescoes, recently and badly restored. Two waiters were conversing in an Italian which I translate:

"Are the old people going to dine in their room? They never let us know. It's annoying; I never know whether I ought to keep their table for them (*non so se bisogna conserva loro la tavola*). Serve them right if they come down and find it's been taken! I don't understand how they can take in *forestieri* (foreigners) like that in such a smart hotel. They're not our sort of people."

Notwithstanding his scorn, the waiter was anxious to know what action he was to take with regard to the table, and was about to send the lift-boy upstairs to inquire when, before he had had time to do so, he received his answer: he had just caught sight of the old lady who was entering the room. I had no difficulty, despite the air of melancholy and weariness that comes with the weight of years, and despite a sort of eczema, of red leprosy that covered her face, in recognising beneath her bonnet, in her black jacket made by W—— but to the untutored eye exactly like that of an old concierge, the Marquise de Villeparisis. The place where I was standing, engaged in studying the remains of a fresco between two of the beautiful marble panels, happened by chance to be immediately behind the table at which Mme de Villeparisis had just sat down.

"Then M. de Villeparisis won't be long. They've been here a month now, and they've only once not eaten together," said the waiter.

I was wondering who could be the relative with whom she was travelling and who was named M. de Villeparisis, when a few moments later I saw her old lover, M. de Norpois, advance towards the table and sit down beside her.

His great age had weakened the resonance of his voice, but had in compensation imparted to his speech, formerly so reserved, a positive intemperance. The cause of this was perhaps to be sought in ambitions for the realisation of which he felt that little time remained to him and which filled him with all the more vehemence and ardour; perhaps in the fact that, cut off from a world of politics to which he longed to return, he imagined, in the naïvety of his desire, that he could turn out of office, by the savage criticisms which he launched at them, the men he was determined to replace. Thus do we see politicians convinced that the Cabinet of which they are not members cannot hold out for three days. It would, however, be an exaggeration to suppose that M. de Norpois had entirely forgotten the traditions of diplomatic speech. Whenever "important matters" were at issue, he became once more, as we shall see, the man whom we remember in the past, but for the rest of the time he would inveigh against this man and that with the senile violence which makes certain octogenarians hurl themselves at women to whom they are no longer capable of doing any serious damage.

Mme de Villeparisis preserved, for some minutes, the silence of an old woman who in the exhaustion of age finds it difficult to rise from recollection of the past to consideration of the present. Then, turning to one of those eminently practical questions that indicate the survival of a mutual affection:

"Did you call at Salviati's?"

"Yes."

"Will they send it tomorrow?"

"I brought the bowl back myself. You shall see it after dinner. Let us look at the menu."

"Did you send instructions about my Suez shares?"

"No; at the present moment the Stock Exchange is entirely taken up with oil shares. But there's no hurry, in view of the propitious state of the market. Here is the menu. As a first course there is red mullet. Shall we try them?"

"I shall, but you are not allowed them. Ask for a risotto instead. But they don't know how to cook it."

"Never mind. Waiter, some mullet for Madame and a risotto for me."

A fresh and prolonged silence.

"Here, I've brought you the papers, the *Corriere della Sera*, the *Gazzetta del Popolo*, and all the rest of them. Did you know that there is a strong likelihood of a diplomatic reshuffle in which the first scapegoat will be Paléologue, who is notoriously inadequate in Serbia. He may perhaps be replaced by Lozé, and there will be a vacancy at Constantinople. But," M. de Norpois hastened to add in a biting tone, "for an Embassy of such scope, in a capital where it is obvious that Great Britain must always, whatever happens, occupy the chief place at the council-table, it would be prudent to turn to men of experience better equipped to counter the subterfuges of the enemies of our British ally than are diplomats of the modern school who would walk blindfold into the trap." The angry volubility with which M. de Norpois uttered these last words was due principally to the fact that the newspapers, instead of suggesting his name as he had recommended them to do, named as a "hot favourite" a young minister of Foreign Affairs. "Heaven knows that the men of years and experience are far from eager to put themselves forward, after all manner of tortuous manoeuvres, in the place of more or less incapable recruits. I have known many of these self-styled diplomats of the empirical school who centred all their hopes in flying a kite which it didn't take me long to shoot down. There can be no question that if the Government is so lacking in wisdom as to entrust the reins of state to unruly hands, at the call of duty any conscript will always answer 'Present!' But who knows" (and here M. de Norpois appeared to know perfectly well to whom he was referring) "whether it would not be the same on the day when they came in search of some veteran full of wisdom and skill. To my mind, though everyone may have his own way of looking at things, the post at Constantinople should not be accepted until we have settled our existing difficulties with Germany. We owe no man anything, and it is intolerable that every six months they should come and demand from us, by fraudulent machinations and under protest, some full discharge or other which is invariably advocated by a venal press. This must cease, and naturally a man of high distinction who has proved his merit, a man who would have, if I may say so, the Emperor's ear, would enjoy greater authority than anyone else in bringing the conflict to an end."

A gentleman who was finishing his dinner bowed to M. de Norpois.

"Why, there's Prince Foggi," said the Marquis.

"Ah, I'm not sure that I know who you mean," muttered Mme de Villeparisis.

"But, of course you do—Prince Odo. He's the brother-in-law of your cousin Doudeauville. Surely you remember that I went shooting with him at Bonnétable?"

"Ah! Odo, is he the one who went in for painting?"

"Not at all, he's the one who married the Grand Duke N——'s sister."

M. de Norpois uttered these remarks in the cross tone of a schoolmaster who is dissatisfied with his pupil, and stared fixedly at Mme de Villeparisis out of his blue eyes.

When the Prince had drunk his coffee and was leaving his table, M. de Norpois rose, hastened towards him and with a majestic sweep of his arm, stepping aside himself, presented him to Mme de Villeparisis. And during the few minutes that the Prince was standing beside their table, M. de Norpois never ceased for an instant to keep his azure pupils trained on Mme de Villeparisis, with the mixture of indulgence and severity of an old lover, but principally from fear of her committing one of those verbal solecisms which he had relished but which he dreaded. Whenever she said anything to the Prince that was not quite accurate he corrected her mistake and stared into the eyes of the abashed and docile Marquise with the steady intensity of a hypnotist.

A waiter came to tell me that my mother was waiting for me. I went to join her and made my apologies to Mme Sazerat, saying that I had been amused to see Mme de Villeparisis. At the sound of this name, Mme Sazerat turned pale and seemed about to faint. Controlling herself with an effort: "Mme de Villeparisis who was Mlle de Bouillon?" she inquired.

"Yes."

"Couldn't I just get a glimpse of her for a moment? It has been the dream of my life."

"Then there's no time to lose, Madame, for she will soon have finished her dinner. But how do you come to take such an interest in her?"

"Because Mme de Villeparisis was, before her second marriage, the Duchesse d'Havré, beautiful as an angel, wicked as a demon, who drove my father to distraction, ruined him and then abandoned him immediately. Well, she may have behaved to him like the lowest prostitute, she may have been the cause of our having had to live, my family and myself, in humble circumstances at Combray, but now that my father is dead, my consolation is to think that he loved the most beautiful woman of his generation, and as I've never set eyes on her, it will be a sort of solace in spite of everything . . ."

I escorted Mme Sazerat, trembling with emotion, to the restaurant and pointed out Mme de Villeparisis.

But, like a blind person who looks everywhere but in the right direction, Mme Sazerat did not bring her eyes to rest upon the table at which Mme de Villeparisis was dining, but, looking towards another part of the room, said:

"But she must have gone, I don't see her where you say she is."

And she continued to gaze round the room in quest of the loathed, adored vision that had haunted her imagination for so long.

"Yes, there she is, at the second table."

"Then we can't be counting from the same point. At what I count as the second table there's only an old gentleman and a little hunchbacked, red-faced, hideous woman."

"That's her!"

Meanwhile, Mme de Villeparisis having asked M. de Norpois to invite Prince Foggi to sit down, a friendly conversation ensued among the three of them. They discussed politics, and the Prince declared that he was indifferent to the fate of the Cabinet and would spend another week at least in Venice. He hoped that by that time all risk of a ministerial crisis would have been avoided. Prince Foggi thought for a few moments that these political topics did not interest M. de Norpois, for the latter, who until then had been expressing himself with such vehemence, had become suddenly absorbed in an almost angelic silence which seemed capable of blossoming, should his voice return, only into some innocent and tuneful melody by Mendelssohn or César Franck. The Prince supposed also that this silence was due to the reserve of a Frenchman who naturally would not wish to discuss Italian affairs in the presence of an Italian. Now in this the Prince was completely mistaken. Silence and an air of indifference had remained, in M. de Norpois, not a sign of reserve but the habitual prelude to an intervention in important affairs. The Marquis had his eye upon nothing less (as we have seen) than Constantinople, after the prior settlement of the German question, with a view to which he hoped to force the hand of the Rome Cabinet. He considered, in fact, that an action on his part of international significance might be the worthy consummation of his career, perhaps even a prelude to fresh honours, to difficult tasks to which he had not relinquished his pretensions. For old age makes us incapable of doing but not, at first, of desiring. It is only in a third period that those who live to a very great age relinquish desire, as they have already had to forgo action. They no longer even present themselves as candidates in futile elections where they have so often tried to win success, such as that for the Presidency of the Republic. They content themselves with taking the air, eating, reading the newspapers; they have outlived themselves.

The Prince, to put the Marquis at his ease and to show him that he regarded him as a compatriot, began to speak of the possible successors to the Prime Minister then in office. Successors who would have a difficult task before them. When Prince Foggi had mentioned more than twenty names of politicians who seemed to him suitable for office, names to which the ex-Ambassador listened with his eyelids drooping over his blue eyes and without moving a muscle, M. de Norpois broke his silence at length to utter the words which were to provide the chancelleries with food for conversation for many years to come, and afterwards, when they had been forgotten, would be exhumed by some personage signing himself "One Who Knows" or "Testis" or "Machiavelli" in a newspaper in which the very oblivion into which they had fallen enabled them to create a fresh sensation. So, Prince Foggi had mentioned more than twenty names to the diplomat who remained as motionless and silent as a deaf-mute, when M. de Norpois raised his head slightly, and, in the form in which his most pregnant and far-reaching diplomatic interventions had been couched, albeit this time with greater audacity and less brevity, shrewdly inquired: "And has no one mentioned the name of Signor Giolitti?" At these words the scales fell from Prince Foggi's eyes; he could hear a celestial murmur. Then at once M. de Norpois began to speak about one thing and another, no longer afraid to make a noise, as, when the last note of a sublime aria by Bach has died away, the audience are no longer afraid to talk aloud, to go and look for their hats and coats in the cloakroom. He made the break even more marked by begging the Prince to pay his most humble respects to Their Majesties the King and Queen when next he should see them, a farewell phrase corresponding to the shout for a coachman at the end of a concert: "Auguste, from the Rue de Belloy." We cannot say what exactly were Prince Foggi's impressions. He must certainly have been delighted to have heard the gem: "And has no one mentioned Signor Giolitti's name?" For M. de Norpois, in whom age had extinguished or deranged his most outstanding qualities, had on the other hand, as he grew older, perfected his bravura, as certain aged musicians, who in all other respects have declined, acquire and retain until the end, in the field of chamber-music, a perfect virtuosity which they did not formerly possess.

However that may be, Prince Foggi, who had intended to spend a fortnight in Venice, returned to Rome that very night and was received a few days later in audience by the King in connexion with certain properties which, as we may perhaps have mentioned already, the Prince owned in Sicily. The Cabinet hung on for longer than might have been expected. When it fell, the King consulted various statesmen as to the most suitable leader of a new Cabinet. Then he sent for Signor Giolitti, who accepted. Three months later a newspaper reported Prince Foggi's meeting with M. de Norpois. The conversation was reported as we have given it here, with the difference that, instead of: "M. de Norpois shrewdly inquired," one read: "M. de Norpois said with that shrewd and charming smile which is so characteristic of him." M. de Norpois considered that "shrewdly" had in itself sufficient explosive force for a diplomat and that this addition was, to say the least, excessive. He had even asked the Quai d'Orsay to issue an official denial, but the Quai d'Orsay did not know which way to turn. For, ever since the conversation had been made public, M. Barrère had been telegraphing several times hourly to Paris complaining of this unofficial ambassador to the Quirinal and describing the indignation with which the incident had been received throughout the whole of Europe. This indignation was non-existent, but the other ambassadors were too polite to contradict M. Barrère's assertion that everyone was up in arms. M. Barrère, guided only by his own reaction, mistook this courteous silence for assent. Immediately he telegraphed to Paris: "I have just had an hour's conversation with the Marchese Visconti-Venosta," and so forth. His secretaries were worn out.

M. de Norpois, however, had at his disposal a French newspaper of very long standing, which already in 1870, when he was French Minister in a German capital, had been of great service to him. This paper (especially its leading article, which was unsigned) was admirably written. But the paper became a thousand times more interesting whenever this leading article (styled "premier-Paris" in those far-off days and now, no one knows why, "editorial") was on the contrary badly expressed, with endless repetitions of words. Everyone sensed then, with great excitement, that the article had been "inspired." Perhaps by M. de Norpois, perhaps by some other man of the hour. To give an anticipatory idea of the Italian incident, let us show how M. de Norpois made use of this paper in 1870, to no purpose, it may be thought, since war broke out nevertheless, but most efficaciously, according to M. de Norpois, whose axiom was that one ought first and foremost to prepare public opinion. His articles, every word in which was weighted, resembled those optimistic bulletins which are at once followed by the death of the patient. For instance, on the eve of the declaration of war in 1870, when mobilisation was almost complete, M. de Norpois (remaining, of course, in the background) had felt it his duty to send to this famous newspaper the following "editorial":

"The opinion seems to prevail in authoritative circles that, since the afternoon hours of yesterday, the situation, without of course being of an alarming nature, might well be envisaged as serious and even, from certain angles, as susceptible of being regarded as critical. M. le Marquis de Norpois would appear to have had several conversations with the Prussian Minister, with a view to examining, in a firm and conciliatory spirit, and in a wholly concrete fashion, the various existing causes of friction, if one may so put it. Unfortunately, we have not yet heard, at the time of going to press, whether Their Excellencies have been able to agree upon a formula that may serve as the basis for a diplomatic instrument."

Stop press: "It has been learned with satisfaction in well-informed circles that a slight slackening of tension seems to have occurred in Franco-Prussian relations. Particular importance would appear to be attached to the fact that M. de Norpois is reported to have met the British Minister 'unter den Linden' and to have conversed with him for fully twenty minutes. This report is regarded as highly satisfactory." (There was added, in brackets, after the word "satisfactory" its German equivalent "*befriedigend*.") And on the following day one read in the editorial: "It would appear that, notwithstanding all the dexterity of M. de Norpois, to whom everyone must hasten to render homage for the skill and energy with which he has defended the inalienable rights of France, a rupture is now, one might say, virtually inevitable."

The newspaper could not refrain from following an editorial couched in this vein with a selection of comments, furnished of course by M. de Norpois. The reader may perhaps have observed in these last pages that the conditional was one of the Ambassador's favourite grammatical forms in the literature of diplomacy. ("Particular importance would appear to be attached" for "Particular importance is attached.") But the present indicative employed not in its usual sense but in that of the old "optative" was no less dear to M. de Norpois. The comments that followed the editorial were as follows:

"Never has the public shown itself so admirably calm" (M. de Norpois would have liked to believe that this was true but feared that it was precisely the opposite of the truth). "It is weary of fruitless agitation and has learned with satisfaction that the Government of His Majesty the Emperor would assume their responsibilities whatever the eventualities that might occur. The public asks" (optative) "nothing more. To its admirable composure, which is in itself a token of success, we shall add a piece of intelligence eminently calculated to reassure public opinion, were there any need of that. We are assured that M. de Norpois who, for reasons of health, was ordered long ago to return to Paris for medical treatment, would appear to have left Berlin where he considered that his presence no longer served any purpose."

Stop press: "His Majesty the Emperor left Compiègne this morning for Paris in order to confer with the Marquis de Norpois, the Minister for War and Marshal Bazaine in whom public opinion has especial confidence. H. M. the Emperor has cancelled the banquet which he was to give for his sister-in-law the Duchess of Alba. This action created everywhere, as soon as it became known, a particularly favourable impression. The Emperor has held a review of his troops, whose enthusiasm is indescribable. Several corps, by virtue of a mobilisation order issued immediately upon the Sovereign's arrival in Paris, are, in any contingency, ready to move in the direction of the Rhine."*

Sometimes at dusk as I returned to the hotel I felt that the Albertine of long ago, invisible to my eyes, was nevertheless enclosed within me as in the lead-covered cells of an inner Venice, the tight lid of which some incident occasionally lifted to give me a glimpse of that past.

Thus for instance one evening a letter from my stockbroker reopened for me for an instant the gates of the prison in which Albertine dwelt within me, alive, but so remote, so profoundly buried that she remained inaccessible to me. Since her death I had ceased to indulge in the speculations that I had made in order to have more money for her. But time had passed; the wisest judgments of the previous generation had been belied by the next, as had occurred in the past to M. Thiers who had said that railways could never prove successful; and the stocks of which M. de Norpois had said to us: "The income from them may not be very great, but at least the capital will never depreciate," were, more often than not, those which had declined most in value. In the case of my English Consols and Raffineries Say shares alone, I had to pay out such considerable sums in brokers' commissions, as well as interest and contango fees, that in a rash moment I decided to sell out everything and found that I now possessed barely a fifth of what I had inherited from my grandmother and still possessed when Albertine was alive. This became known at Combray among the surviving members of our family and their friends who, knowing that I went about with the Marquis de Saint-Loup and the Guermantes family, said to themselves: "Pride goes before a fall!" They would have been greatly astonished to learn that it was for a girl of Albertine's modest background, almost a protégée of my grandmother's former piano-teacher, Vinteuil, that I had made these speculations. Besides, in that Combray world in which everyone is classified for ever, as in an Indian caste, according to the income he is known to enjoy, no one would have been capable of imagining the great freedom that prevailed in the world of the Guermantes, where no importance was attached to wealth and where poverty was regarded as being as disagreeable as, but no more degrading, having no more effect on a person's social position, than a stomach-ache. Doubtless people at Combray imagined, on the contrary, that Saint-Loup and M. de Guermantes must be ruined aristocrats with heavily mortgaged estates, to whom I had been lending money, whereas if I had been ruined they would have been the first to offer, unavailingly, to come to my assistance. As for my comparative penury, it was all the more awkward at the moment, inasmuch as my Venetian interests had been concentrated for some little time past on a young vendor of glassware whose blooming complexion offered to the delighted eye a whole range of orange tones and filled me with such a longing to see her daily that, realising that my mother and I would soon be leaving Venice, I had made up my mind to try to create some sort of position for her in Paris which would save me from being parted from her. The beauty of her seventeen years was so noble, so radiant, that it was like acquiring a genuine Titian before leaving the place. But would the scant remains of my fortune be enough to tempt her to leave her native land and come to live in Paris for my sole convenience?

But as I came to the end of the stockbroker's letter, a passage in which he said: "I shall look after your credits" reminded me of a scarcely less hypocritically professional expression which the bath-attendant at Balbec had used in speaking to Aimé of Albertine: "It was I who looked after her," she had said. And these words which had never recurred to my mind acted like an "Open sesame!" upon the hinges of the prison door. But a moment later the door closed once more upon the immured victim—whom I was not to blame for not wishing to join since I was no longer able to see her, to call her to mind, and since other people exist for us only through the idea that we have of them—but who for a moment had been rendered more touching by my desertion of her, albeit she was unaware of it, so that for the duration of a lightning-flash I had thought with longing of the time, already remote, when I used to suffer night and day from the companionship of her memory. Another time, in San Giorgio degli Schiavoni, an eagle accompanying one of the Apostles, and conventionalised in the same manner, revived the memory and almost the suffering caused by the two rings the similarity of which Françoise had revealed to me, and as to which I had never learned who had given them to Albertine.

One evening, however, an incident occurred of such a nature that it seemed as though my love must revive. No sooner had our gondola stopped at the hotel steps than the porter handed me a telegram which the messenger had already brought three times to the hotel, for owing to the inaccurate rendering of the addressee's name (which I recognised nevertheless, through the corruptions introduced by the Italian clerks, as my own) the post-office required a signed receipt certifying that the telegram was indeed for me. I opened it as soon as I was in my room, and, glancing through the message which was filled with inaccurately trans-mitted words, managed nevertheless to make out: "My dear friend, you think me dead, forgive me, I am quite alive, I long to see you, talk about marriage, when do you return? Affectionately. Albertine." Then there occurred in me in reverse order a process parallel to that which had occurred in the case of my grandmother. When I had learned the fact of my grand-mother's death, I had not at first felt any grief. And I had been really grieved by her death only when certain involuntary mem-ories had brought her alive again for me. Now that Albertine no longer lived for me in my thoughts, the news that she was alive did not cause me the joy that I might have expected. Albertine had been no more to me than a bundle of thoughts, and she had survived her physical death so long as those thoughts were alive in me; on the other hand, now that those thoughts were dead, Albertine did not rise again for me with the resurrection of her body. And when I realised that I felt no joy at the thought of her being alive, that I no longer loved her, I ought to have been more shattered than a man who, looking at his reflexion in a mirror, after months of travel or sickness, discovers that he has white hair and a different face, that of a middle-aged or an old man. This is shattering because its message is: "the man that I was, the fair-haired young man, no longer exists, I am another person." And yet, was not the impression that I now felt the proof of as profound a change, as total a death of my former self and of the no less complete substitution of a new self for that former self, as the sight of a wrinkled face topped with a white wig instead of the face of long ago? But one is no more distressed at having become another person, after a lapse of years and in the natural sequence of time, than one is at any given moment by the fact of being, one after another, the incompatible persons, malicious, sensitive, refined, caddish, disinterested, ambitious which one can be, in turn, every day of one's life. And the reason why one is not distressed is the same, namely that the self which has been eclipsed—momentarily in this latter case and when it is a question of character, permanently in the former case and when the passions are involved—is not there to deplore the other, the other which is for the moment, or from then onwards, one's whole self; the caddish self laughs at his caddishness because one is the cad, and the forgetful self does not grieve about his forgetfulness precisely because he has forgotten.

I should have been incapable of resuscitating Albertine because I was incapable of resuscitating myself, of resuscitating the self of those days. Life, in accordance with its habit which is, by unceasing, infinitesimal labours, to change the face of the world, had not said to me on the morrow of Albertine's death: "Become another person," but, by changes too imperceptible for me to be conscious even that I was changing, had altered almost everything in me, with the result that my mind was already accustomed to its new master—my new self—when it became aware that it had changed; it was to this new master that it was attached. My feeling for Albertine, my jealousy, stemmed, as we have seen, from the irradiation, by the association of ideas, of certain pleasant or painful impressions, the memory of Mlle Vinteuil at Montjouvain, the precious good-night kisses that Albertine used to give me on the neck. But in proportion as these impressions had grown fainter, the vast field of impressions which they coloured with a hue that was agonising or soothing reverted to neutral tones. As soon as oblivion had taken hold of certain dominant points of suffering and pleasure, the resistance offered by my love was overcome, I no longer loved Albertine. I tried to recall her image to my mind. I had been right in my presentiment when, a couple of days after Albertine's flight, I was appalled by the discovery that I had been able to live for forty-eight hours without her. It had been the same as when I wrote to Gilberte long ago saying to myself: "If this goes on for a year or two, I shall no longer love her." And if, when Swann asked me to come and see Gilberte again, this had seemed to me as embarrassing as greeting a dead woman, in Albertine's case death—or what I had supposed to be death—had achieved the same result as a prolonged breach in Gilberte's. Death merely acts in the same way as absence. The monster at whose apparition my love had trembled, oblivion, had indeed, as I had feared, ended by devouring that love. Not only did the news that she was alive fail to revive my love, not only did it enable me to realise how far I had already proceeded along the road towards indifference, it at once and so abruptly accelerated that process that I wondered retrospectively whether the opposite report, that of Albertine's death, had not, conversely, by completing the effect of her departure, rekindled my love and delayed its decline. Yes, now that the knowledge that she was alive and the possibility of our reunion made her suddenly cease to be so precious to me, I wondered whether Françoise's insinuations, our rupture itself, and even her death (imaginary, but believed to be real) had not prolonged my love, to such an extent do the efforts of third persons, and even those of fate, to separate us from a woman succeed only in attaching us to her. Now it was the contrary process that had occurred. Anyhow, I tried to recall her image and perhaps because I had only to raise a finger for her to be mine once more, the memory that came to me was that of a somewhat stout and mannish-looking girl from whose faded features protruded already, like a sprouting seed, the profile of Mme Bontemps. What she might or might not have done with Andrée or with other girls no longer interested me. I no longer suffered from the malady which I had so long thought to be incurable, and really I might have foreseen this. Certainly, regret for a lost mistress and surviving jealousy are physical maladies fully as much as tuberculosis or leukaemia. And yet among physical maladies it is possible to distinguish those which are caused by a purely physical agency, and those which act upon the body only through the medium of the intelligence. Above all, if the part of the mind which serves as carrier is the memory—that is to say if the cause is obliterated or remote—however agonising the pain, however profound the disturbance to the organism may appear to be, it is very seldom (the mind having a capacity for renewal or rather an incapacity for conservation which the tissues lack) that the prognosis is not favourable. At the end of a given period after which someone who has been attacked by cancer will be dead, it is very seldom that the grief of an inconsolable widower or father is not healed. Mine was healed. Was it for this girl whom I saw in my mind's eye so bloated and who had certainly aged, as the girls whom she had loved had aged—was it for her that I must renounce the dazzling girl who was my memory of yesterday, my hope for tomorrow, to whom I could no longer give a sou, any more than to any other, if I married Albertine, that I must renounce this "new Albertine" whom I loved "not as Hades had beheld her . . . but faithful, but proud, and even rather shy"?[6] It was she who was now what Albertine had been in the past: my love for Albertine had been but a transitory form of my devotion to youth. We think that we are in love with a girl, whereas we love in her, alas! only that dawn the glow of which is momentarily reflected on her face.

The night went by. In the morning I gave the telegram back to the hotel porter explaining that it had been brought to me by mistake and that it was not for me. He told me that now it had been opened he might get into trouble, that it would be better if I kept it; I put it back in my pocket, but made up my mind to behave as though I had never received it. I had finally ceased to love Albertine. So that this love, after departing so greatly from what I had anticipated on the basis of my love for Gilberte, after obliging me to make so long and painful a detour, had ended too, after having proved an exception to it, by succumbing, like my love for Gilberte, to the general law of oblivion.

But then I thought to myself: I used to value Albertine more than myself; I no longer value her now because for a certain time past I have ceased to see her. My desire not to be parted from myself by death, to rise again after my death—that desire was not like the desire never to be parted from Albertine; it still persisted. Was this due to the fact that I valued myself more highly than her, that when I loved her I loved myself more? No, it was because, having ceased to see her, I had ceased to love her, whereas I had not ceased to love myself because my everyday links with myself had not been severed like those with Albertine. But if my links with my body, with myself, were severed also . . . ? Obviously, it would be the same. Our love of life is only an old liaison of which we do not know how to rid ourselves. Its strength lies in its permanence. But death which severs it will cure us of the desire for immortality.

After lunch, when I was not going to roam about Venice by myself, I went up to my room to get ready to go out with my mother and to collect the exercise books in which I would take notes for some work I was doing on Ruskin. In the abrupt angles of the walls I sensed the restrictions imposed by the sea, the parsimony of the soil. And when I went downstairs to join Mamma who was waiting for me, at that hour when at Combray it was so pleasant to feel the sun close at hand in the darkness preserved by the closed shutters, here, from top to bottom of the marble staircase where one could no more tell than in a Renaissance picture whether it was in a palace or on a galley, the same coolness and the same sense of the splendour of the scene outside were imparted thanks to the awnings which stirred outside the ever-open windows through which, upon an incessant stream of air, the warm shade and the greenish sunlight flowed as if over a liquid surface and suggested the mobile prox-imity, the glitter, the shimmering instability of the sea.

As often as not we would set off for St Mark's, with all the more pleasure because, since one had to take a gondola to go there, the church represented for me not simply a monument but the ter-minus of a voyage on these vernal, maritime waters, with which, I felt, St Mark's formed an indivisible and living whole. My mother and I would enter the baptistery, treading underfoot the marble and glass mosaics of the paving, in front of us the wide arcades whose curved pink surfaces have been slightly warped by time, thus giving the church, wherever the freshness of this col-ouring has been preserved, the appearance of having been built of a soft and malleable substance like the wax in a giant honeycomb, and, where on the contrary time has shrivelled and hardened the material and artists have embellished it with gold tracery, of being the precious binding, in the finest Cordoba leather, of the colossal Gospel of Venice. Seeing that I needed to spend some time in front of the mosaics representing the Baptism of Christ, and feeling the icy coolness that pervaded the baptistery, my mother threw a shawl over my shoulders. When I was with Albertine at Balbec, I felt that she was revealing one of those insubstantial illusions which clutter the minds of so many people who do not think clearly, when she used to speak of the pleasure—to my mind baseless—that she would derive from seeing works of art with me. Today I am sure that the pleasure does exist, if not of seeing, at least of having seen, a beautiful thing with a particular person. A time has now come when, remembering the baptistery of St Mark's—contemplating the waters of the Jordan in which St John immerses Christ, while the gondola awaited us at the landing-stage of the Piazzetta—it is no longer a matter of indifference to me that, beside me in that cool penumbra, there should have been a woman draped in her mourning with the respectful and enthusiastic fervour of the old woman in Carpaccio's *St Ursula* in the Accademia, and that that woman, with her red cheeks and sad eyes and in her black veils, whom nothing can ever remove from that softly lit sanctuary of St Mark's where I am always sure to find her because she has her place reserved there as immutably as a mosaic, should be my mother.

Carpaccio, as it happens, who was the painter we visited most readily when I was not working in St Mark's, almost succeeded one day in reviving my love for Albertine. I was seeing for the first time *The Patriarch of Grado exorcising a demoniac.* I looked at the marvellous rose-pink and violet sky and the tall encrusted chimneys silhouetted against it, their flared stacks, blossoming like red tulips, reminiscent of so many Whistlers of Venice. Then my eyes travelled from the old wooden Rialto to that fifteenth-century Ponte Vecchio with its marble palaces decorated with gilded capitals, and returned to the canal on which the boats are manoeuvred by adolescents in pink jackets and plumed toques, the spitting image of those avowedly inspired by Carpaccio in that dazzling *Legend of Joseph* by Sert, Strauss and Kessler. Finally, before leaving the picture, my eyes came back to the shore, swarming with the everyday Venetian life of the period. I looked at the barber wiping his razor, at the negro humping his barrel, at the Muslims conversing, at the noblemen in wide-sleeved brocade and damask robes and hats of cerise velvet, and suddenly I felt a slight gnawing at my heart. On the back of one of the *Compagni della Calza* identifiable from the emblem, embroidered in gold and pearls on their sleeves or their collars, of the merry confraternity to which they were affiliated, I had just recognised the cloak which Albertine had put on to come with me to Versailles in an open carriage on the evening when I so little suspected that scarcely fifteen hours separated me from the moment of her departure from my house. Always ready for anything, when I had asked her to come out with me on that melancholy occasion which she was to describe in her last letter as "a double twilight since night was falling and we were about to part," she had flung over her shoulders a Fortuny cloak which she had taken away with her next day and which I had never thought of since. It was from this Carpaccio picture that that inspired son of Venice had taken it, it was from the shoulders of this *Compagno della Calza* that he had removed it in order to drape it over the shoulders of so many Parisian women who were certainly unaware, as I had been until then, that the model for it existed in a group of noblemen in the foreground of the *Patriarch of Grado* in a room in the Accademia in Venice. I had recognised it down to the last detail, and, that forgotten cloak having restored to me as I looked at it the eyes and the heart of him who had set out that evening with Albertine for Versailles, I was overcome for a few moments by a vague and soon dissipated feeling of desire and melancholy.

There were days when my mother and I were not content with visiting the museums and churches of Venice only, and once, when the weather was particularly fine, in order to see the "Virtues" and "Vices" of which M. Swann had given me reproductions that were probably still hanging on the wall of the schoolroom at Combray, we went as far afield as Padua. After walking across the garden of the Arena in the glare of the sun, I entered the Giotto chapel, the entire ceiling of which and the background of the frescoes are so blue that it seems as though the radiant daylight has crossed the threshold with the human visitor in order to give its pure sky a momentary breather in the coolness and shade, a sky merely of a slightly deeper blue now that it is rid of the glitter of the sunlight, as in those brief moments of respite when, though no cloud is to be seen, the sun has turned its gaze elsewhere and the azure, softer still, grows deeper. This sky transplanted on to the blue-washed stone was peopled with flying angels which I was seeing for the first time, for M. Swann had given me reproductions only of the Vices and Virtues and not of the frescoes depicting the life of the Virgin and of Christ. Watching the flight of these angels, I had the same impression of actual movement, literally real activity, that the gestures of Charity and Envy had given me. For all the celestial fervour, or at least the childlike obedience and application, with which their minuscule hands are joined, they are represented in the Arena chapel as winged creatures of a particular species that had really existed, that must have figured in the natural history of biblical and apostolic times. Constantly flitting about above the saints whenever the latter walk abroad, these little beings, since they are real creatures with a genuine power of flight, can be seen soaring upwards, describing curves, "looping the loop," diving earth-wards head first, with the aid of wings which enable them to support themselves in positions that defy the laws of gravity, and are far more reminiscent of an extinct species of bird, or of young pupils of Garros practising gliding,[7] than of the angels of the Renaissance and later periods whose wings have become no more than emblems and whose deportment is generally the same as that of heavenly beings who are not winged.

On returning to the hotel I would meet young women, mainly Austrians, who came to Venice to spend the first fine days of this flowerless spring. There was one in particular whose features did not resemble Albertine's but who attracted me by the same fresh complexion, the same gay, light-hearted look. Soon I became aware that I was beginning to say the same things to her as I had said to Albertine at the start, that I concealed the same misery when she told me she would not be seeing me the following day because she was going to Verona, and that I immediately wanted to go to Verona too. It did not last—she was soon to leave for Austria and I would never see her again—but already, vaguely jealous as one is when one begins to fall in love, looking at her charming and enigmatic face I wondered whether she too loved women, whether what she had in common with Albertine, that clear complexion, that bright-eyed look, that air of friendly can-dour which charmed everyone and which stemmed more from the fact that she was not in the least interested in knowing about other people's actions, which interested her not at all, than that she was confessing her own, which on the contrary she concealed beneath the most puerile lies—I wondered whether all this con-stituted the morphological characteristics of the woman who loves other women. Was it this about her that, without my being able rationally to grasp why, exercised its attraction upon me, caused my anxieties (perhaps a deeper cause of my attraction towards her by virtue of the fact that we are drawn towards that which will make us suffer), gave me when I saw her so much pleasure and sadness, like those magnetic elements in the air of certain places which we do not see but which cause us such physical discomfort? Alas, I should never know. I should have liked, when I tried to read her face, to say to her: "You really should tell me, it would interest me as an example of human natural history," but she would never tell me. She professed an especial loathing for anything that resembled that vice, and was extremely distant towards her women friends. Perhaps indeed this was proof that she had something to hide, perhaps that she had been mocked or reviled for it, and the air that she assumed in order that people should not think such things of her was like an animal's instinctive and revealing recoil from someone who has beaten it. As for my finding out about her life, it was impossible; even in the case of Albertine, how long it had taken me to get to know anything! It had taken her death to loosen people's tongues, such prudent circumspection had Albertine, like this young woman, observed in all her conduct. And in any case, could I be certain that I had discovered anything about Albertine? Moreover, just as the conditions of life that we most desire become a matter of indifference to us if we cease to love the person who, without our realising it, made us desire them because they enabled us to be close to her, to be in a position to please her, so it is with certain kinds of intellectual curiosity. The scientific importance which I attached to knowing the particular kind of desire that lay hidden beneath the delicate pink petals of those cheeks, in the brightness, a sunless brightness as at daybreak, of those pale eyes, in those days that were never accounted for, would doubtless subside when I had entirely ceased to love Albertine or when I had entirely ceased to love this young woman.

After dinner, I went out alone, into the heart of the enchanted city where I found myself in the middle of strange purlieus like a character in the *Arabian Nights*. It was very seldom that, in the course of my wanderings, I did not come across some strange and spacious *piazza* of which no guide-book, no tourist had ever told me. I had plunged into a network of little alleys, or *calli*. In the evening, with their high bell-mouthed chimneys on which the sun throws the brightest pinks, the clearest reds, it is a whole garden blossoming above the houses, its shades so various that you would have said it was the garden of some tulip lover of Delft or Haarlem, planted on top of the town. Moreover, the extreme proximity of the houses made of every casement a frame from which a day-dreaming cook gazed out, or in which a seated girl was having her hair combed by an old woman whose face in the dark looked like a witch's—made of each humble quiet house, so close because of the narrowness of the *calli*, a display of a hundred Dutch paintings placed side by side. Packed tightly together, these *calli* divided in all directions with their furrows a chunk of Venice carved out between a canal and the lagoon, as if it had crystallised in accordance with these innumerable, tenuous and minute patterns. Suddenly, at the end of one of these alleys, it seemed as though a distension had occurred in the crystallised matter. A vast and splendid *campo* of which, in this network of little streets, I should never have guessed the scale, or even found room for it, spread out before me surrounded by charming palaces silvery in the moonlight. It was one of those architectural ensembles towards which, in any other town, the streets converge, lead you and point the way. Here it seemed to be deliberately concealed in an interlacement of alleys, like those palaces in oriental tales whither mysterious agents convey by night a person who, brought back home before daybreak, can never find his way back to the magic dwelling which he ends by believing that he visited only in a dream.

The next day, I set out in quest of my beautiful nocturnal *piazza*, following *calle* after *calle* which were exactly like one another and refused to give me the smallest piece of information, except such as would lead me further astray. Sometimes a vague landmark which I seemed to recognise led me to suppose that I was about to see appear, in its seclusion, solitude and silence, the beautiful exiled *piazza*. At that moment, some evil genie which had assumed the form of a new *calle* made me unwittingly retrace my steps, and I found myself suddenly brought back to the Grand Canal. And as there is no great difference between the memory of a dream and the memory of a reality, I finally wondered whether it was not during my sleep that there had occurred, in a dark patch of Venetian crystallisation, that strange mirage which offered a vast *piazza* surrounded by romantic palaces to the meditative eye of the moon.

But, far more than certain places, it was the desire not to lose for ever certain women that kept me while in Venice in a state of agitation which became febrile when, towards the end of the day on which my mother had decided that we should leave, and our luggage was already on the way to the station in a gondola, I read in the register of guests expected at the hotel: "Mme Putbus and attendants." At once, the thought of all the hours of casual pleasure of which our departure would deprive me raised this desire, which existed in me in a chronic state, to the level of a feeling, and drowned it in a vague melancholy. I asked my mother to put off our departure for a few days, and her air of not for a moment taking my request into consideration, of not even listening to it seriously, reawakened in my nerves, exacerbated by the Venetian springtime, that old desire to rebel against an imaginary plot woven against me by my parents, who imagined that I would be forced to obey them, that defiant spirit which drove me in the past to impose my will brutally upon the people I loved best in the world, though finally conforming to theirs after I had succeeded in making them yield. I told my mother that I would not leave Venice, but she, thinking it wiser not to appear to believe that I was saying this seriously, did not even answer. I went on to say that she would soon see whether I was serious or not. The porter brought us three letters, two for her, and one for me which I put in my wallet among several others without even looking at the envelope. And when the hour came at which, accompanied by all my belongings, she set off for the station, I ordered a drink to be brought out to me on the terrace overlooking the canal, and settled down there to watch the sunset, while from a boat that had stopped in front of the hotel a musician sang *O sole mio.*

The sun continued to sink. My mother must be nearing the station. Soon she would be gone, and I should be alone in Venice, alone with the misery of knowing that I had distressed her, and without her presence to comfort me. The hour of the train's departure was approaching. My irrevocable solitude was so near at hand that it seemed to me to have begun already and to be complete. For I felt myself to be alone; things had become alien to me; I no longer had calm enough to break out of my throbbing heart and introduce into them a measure of stability. The town that I saw before me had ceased to be Venice. Its personality, its name, seemed to me to be mendacious fictions which I no longer had the will to impress upon its stones. I saw the palaces reduced to their basic elements, lifeless heaps of marble with nothing to choose between them, and the water as a combination of hydrogen and oxygen, eternal, blind, anterior and exterior to Venice, oblivious of the Doges or of Turner. And yet this unremarkable place was as strange as a place at which one has just arrived, which does not yet know one, or a place which one has left and which has forgotten one already. I could no longer tell it anything about myself, I could leave nothing of myself imprinted upon it; it contracted me into myself until I was no more than a beating heart and an attention strained to follow the development of *O sole mio.* In vain might I fix my mind despairingly upon the beautiful and distinctive curve of the Rialto, it seemed to me, with the mediocrity of the obvious, a bridge not merely inferior to but as alien to the notion I had of it as an actor of whom, in spite of his blond wig and black garments, we know quite well that in his essence he is not Hamlet. So it was with the palaces, the canal, the Rialto, divested of the idea that constituted their reality and dissolved into their vulgar material elements. But at the same time this mediocre place seemed distant to me. In the dock basin of the Arsenal, because of an element which itself also was scientific, namely latitude, there was that singularity in things whereby, even when similar in appearance to those of our own land, they reveal themselves to be alien, in exile beneath other skies; I felt that that horizon so close at hand, which I could have reached in an hour by boat, was a curvature of the earth quite different from that of France, a distant curvature which, by the artifice of travel, happened to be moored close to where I was; so that the dock basin of the Arsenal, at once insignificant and remote, filled me with that blend of distaste and alarm which I had felt as a child when I first accompanied my mother to the Deligny baths, where, in that weird setting of a pool of water reflecting neither sky nor sun, which nevertheless amid its fringe of cabins one felt to be in communication with invisible depths crowded with human bodies in swimming-trunks, I had asked myself whether those depths, concealed from mortal eyes by hutments which made their existence impossible to divine from the street, were not the entry to arctic seas which began at that point, in which the poles were comprised, and whether that narrow space was not indeed the open water that surrounds the pole; and in this lonely, unreal, icy, unfriendly setting in which I was going to be left alone, the strains of *O sole mio*, rising like a dirge for the Venice I had known, seemed to bear witness to my misery. No doubt I ought to have ceased to listen to it if I wished to be able to join my mother and take the train with her; I ought to have made up my mind to leave without losing another second. But this was precisely what I was powerless to do; I remained motionless, incapable not merely of rising, but even of deciding that I would rise from my chair. My mind, no doubt in order not to have to consider the decision I had to take, was entirely occupied in following the course of the successive phrases of *O sole mio*, singing them to myself with the singer, anticipating each surge of melody, soaring aloft with it, sinking down with it once more.

No doubt this trivial song which I had heard a hundred times did not interest me in the least. I could give no pleasure to myself or anyone else by listening to it religiously to the end. After all, none of the already familiar phrases of this sentimental ditty was capable of furnishing me with the resolution I needed; what was more, each of these phrases, when it came and went in its turn, became an obstacle in the way of my putting that resolution into effect, or rather it forced me towards the contrary resolution not to leave Venice, for it made me too late for the train. Wherefore this occupation, devoid of any pleasure in itself, of listening to *O sole mio* was charged with a profound, almost despairing melancholy. I was well aware that in reality it was the resolution not to go that I was making by remaining there without stirring, but to say to myself: "I'm not going," which in that direct form was impossible, became possible in this indirect form: "I'm going to listen to one more phrase of *O sole mio*"; but the practical significance of this figurative language did not escape me and, while I said to myself: "After all, I'm only listening to one more phrase," I knew that the words meant: "I shall remain by myself in Venice." And it was perhaps this melancholy, like a sort of numbing cold, that constituted the despairing but hypnotic charm of the song. Each note that the singer's voice uttered with a force and ostentation that were almost muscular stabbed me to the heart. When the phrase was completed down below and the song seemed to be at an end, the singer had still not had enough and resumed at the top as though he needed to proclaim once more my solitude and despair.

My mother must by now have reached the station. In a little while she would be gone. I was gripped by the anguish that was caused me by the sight of the Canal which had become diminutive now that the soul of Venice had fled from it, of that commonplace Rialto which was no longer the Rialto, and by the song of despair which *O sole mio* had become and which, bellowed thus beside the insubstantial palaces, finally reduced them to dust and ashes and completed the ruin of Venice; I looked on at the slow realisation of my distress, built up artistically, without haste, note by note, by the singer as he stood beneath the astonished gaze of the sun arrested in its course beyond San Giorgio Maggiore, with the result that the fading light was to combine for ever in my memory with the shiver of my emotion and the bronze voice of the singer in an equivocal, unalterable and poignant alloy.

Thus I remained motionless, my will dissolved, no decision in sight. Doubtless at such moments our decision has already been made: our friends can often predict it, but we ourselves are unable to do so, otherwise we should be spared a great deal of suffering.

But suddenly, from caverns darker than those from which flashes the comet which we can predict—thanks to the unsuspected defensive power of inveterate habit, thanks to the hidden reserves which by a sudden impulse it hurls at the last moment into the fray—my will to action arose at last; I set off in hot haste and arrived, when the carriage doors were already shut, but in time to find my mother flushed with emotion and with the effort to restrain her tears, for she thought that I was not coming. "You know," she said, "your poor grandmother used to say: It's curious, there's nobody who can be as unbearable or as nice as that child." Then the train started and we saw Padua and Verona come to meet us, to speed us on our way, almost on to the platforms of their stations, and, when we had drawn away from them, return—they who were not travelling and were about to resume their normal life—one to its plain, the other to its hill.

The hours went by. My mother was in no hurry to read her two letters, which she had merely opened, and tried to prevent me from pulling out my pocket-book at once to take from it the letter which the hotel porter had given me. She was always afraid of my finding journeys too long and too tiring, and put off as long as possible, so as to keep me occupied during the final hours, the moment at which she would seek fresh distractions for me, bring out the hard-boiled eggs, hand me the newspapers, untie the parcel of books which she had bought without telling me. We had long passed Milan when she decided to read the first of her two letters. At first I sat watching her, as she read it with an air of astonishment, then raised her head, her eyes seeming to come to rest upon a succession of distinct and incompatible memories which she could not succeed in bringing together. Meanwhile I had recognised Gilberte's handwriting on the envelope which I had just taken from my pocket-book. I opened it. Gilberte wrote to inform me that she was marrying Robert de Saint-Loup. She told me that she had sent me a telegram about it to Venice but had had no reply. I remembered that I had been told that the telegraphic service there was inefficient. I had never received her telegram. Perhaps she would refuse to believe this. All of a sudden I felt in my brain a fact, which was installed there in the guise of a memory, leave its place and surrender it to another fact. The telegram that I had received a few days earlier, and had supposed to be from Albertine, was from Gilberte. As the somewhat laboured originality of Gilberte's handwriting consisted chiefly, when she wrote a line, in introducing into the line above it the strokes of her *t*'s which appeared to be underlining the words, or the dots over her *i*'s which appeared to be punctuating the sentence above them, and on the other hand in interspersing the line below with the tails and flourishes of the words immediately above, it was quite natural that the clerk who dispatched the telegram should have read the loops of *s*'s or *y*'s in the line above as an "-ine" attached to the word "Gilberte." The dot over the *i* of Gilberte had climbed up to make a suspension point. As for her capital *G*, it resembled a Gothic *A*. The fact that, in addition to this, two or three words had been misread, had dovetailed into one another (some of them indeed had seemed to me incomprehensible), was sufficient to explain the details of my error and was not even necessary. How many letters are actually read into a word by a careless person who knows what to expect, who sets out with the idea that the message is from a certain person? How many words into the sentence? We guess as we read, we create; everything starts from an initial error; those that follow (and this applies not only to the reading of letters and telegrams, not only to all reading), extraordinary as they may appear to a person who has not begun at the same place, are all quite natural. A large part of what we believe to be true (and this applies even to our final conclusions) with an obstinacy equalled only by our good faith, springs from an original mistake in our premises.

CHAPTER FOUR

NEW ASPECT OF ROBERT DE SAINT-LOUP

"Oh, it's too incredible," said my mother. "You know at my age one has ceased to be astonished at anything, but I assure you that nothing could be more unexpected than the news I've just read in this letter."

"Well," I replied, "I don't know what it is, but however astonishing it may be, it can't be quite so astonishing as what I've learnt from mine. It's a marriage. Robert de Saint-Loup is marrying Gilberte Swann."

"Ah!" said my mother, "then that must be what's in the other letter, which I haven't yet opened, for I recognised your friend's hand."

And my mother smiled at me with that faint trace of emotion which, ever since she had lost her own mother, she felt at every event, however insignificant, that concerned human creatures who were capable of grief and recollection and who themselves also mourned their dead. And so my mother smiled at me and spoke to me in a gentle voice, as though she were afraid, by treating this marriage lightly, of belittling the melancholy feelings that it might arouse in Swann's widow and daughter, in Robert's mother who had resigned herself to being parted from her son, all of whom Mamma, in her kindness of heart, in her gratitude for their kindness to me, endowed with her own faculty of filial, conjugal and maternal emotion.

"Was I right in saying that you wouldn't produce anything as astonishing?" I asked her.

"On the contrary," she replied in a gentle tone, "it's I who have the most extraordinary news, I shan't say the greatest or the smallest, for that quotation from Sévigné which everyone produces who knows nothing else that she ever wrote used to sicken your grandmother as much as 'What a pretty thing hay-making is.'

We don't deign to collect such hackneyed Sévigné. This letter is to announce the marriage of the Cambremer boy."

"Oh!" I remarked with indifference, "to whom? But in any case the personality of the bridegroom robs this marriage of any sensational character."

"Unless the bride's personality supplies it."

"And who is the bride in question?"

"Ah, if I tell you straight away, that will spoil the fun. Come on, see if you can guess," said my mother who, seeing that we had not yet reached Turin, wished to keep something in reserve for me as meat and drink for the rest of the journey.

"But how do you expect me to know? Is it someone brilliant? If Legrandin and his sister are satisfied, we may be sure that it's a brilliant marriage."

"I can't answer for Legrandin, but the person who informs me of the marriage says that Mme de Cambremer is delighted. I don't know whether you will call it a brilliant marriage. To my mind, it suggests the days when kings used to marry shepherdesses, and in this case the shepherdess is even humbler than a shepherdess, charming as she is. It would have amazed your grandmother, but would not have displeased her."

"But who in the world is this bride?"

"It's Mlle d'Oloron."

"That sounds to me tremendous and not in the least shepherdessy, but I don't quite gather who she can be. It's a title that used to be in the Guermantes family."

"Precisely, and M. de Charlus conferred it, when he adopted her, upon Jupien's niece. It's she who's marrying the young Cambremer."

"Jupien's niece! It isn't possible!"

"It's the reward of virtue. It's a marriage from the last chapter of one of Mme Sand's novels," said my mother. ("It's the wages of vice, a marriage from the end of a Balzac novel," thought I.)

"After all," I said to my mother, "it's quite natural, when you think of it. Here are the Cambremers established in that Guermantes clan among which they never hoped to pitch their tent; what is more, the girl, adopted by M. de Charlus, will have plenty of money, which was indispensable since the Cambremers have lost theirs; and after all she's the adopted daughter, and in the Cambremers' eyes probably the real daughter—the natural daughter—of a person whom they regard as a Prince of the Blood. A bastard of a semi-royal house has always been regarded as a flattering alliance by the nobility of France and other countries. Indeed, without going so far back, to the Lucinges,[8] only the other day, not more than six months ago, you remember the marriage of Robert's friend and that girl whose only social qualification was that she was supposed, rightly or wrongly, to be the natural daughter of a sovereign prince."

My mother, without abandoning the caste ethos of Combray in the light of which my grandmother ought to have been scandalised by such a marriage, being anxious above all to show the validity of her mother's judgment, added: "Anyhow, the girl is worth her weight in gold, and your dear grandmother wouldn't have had to draw upon her immense goodness, her infinite tolerance, to keep her from condemning young Cambremer's choice. Do you remember how distinguished she thought the girl was, long ago, when she went into the shop to have a stitch put in her skirt? She was only a child then. And now, even if she has rather run to seed and become an old maid, she's a different woman, a thousand times more perfect. But your grandmother saw all that at a glance. She found the little niece of a jobbing tailor more 'noble' than the Duc de Guermantes."

But even more necessary than to extol my grandmother was it for my mother to decide that it was "better" for her that she had not lived to see the day. This was the culmination of her daughterly love, as though she were sparing my grandmother a final grief.

"And yet, can you imagine for a moment," my mother said to me, "what old Swann—not that you ever knew him, of course— would have felt if he could have known that he would one day have a great-grandchild in whose veins the blood of old mother Moser who used to say: 'Ponchour Mezieurs' would mingle with the blood of the Duc de Guise!"

"But you know, Mamma, it's much more surprising than that. Because the Swanns were very respectable people, and, given the social position that their son acquired, his daughter, if he himself had made a decent marriage, might have married very well indeed. But everything had to start again from scratch because he married a whore."

"Oh, a whore, you know, people were perhaps rather malicious. I never quite believed it all."

"Yes, a whore; indeed I shall let you have some . . . family revelations one of these days."

Lost in reverie, my mother said: "To think of the daughter of a woman whom your father would never allow me to greet marrying the nephew of Mme de Villeparisis on whom your father wouldn't allow me to call at first because he thought her too grand for me!" Then: "And the son of Mme de Cambremer to whom Legrandin was so afraid of having to give us a letter of introduction because he didn't think us smart enough, marrying the niece of a man who would never dare to come to our flat except by the service stairs! . . . All the same, your poor grandmother was absolutely right—you remember—when she said that the high aristocracy did things that would shock the middle classes and that Queen Marie-Amélie was spoiled for her by the overtures she made to the Prince de Condé's mistress to get her to persuade him to make his will in favour of the Duc d'Aumale. You remember too how it shocked her that for centuries past daughters of the house of Gramont who were veritable saints had borne the name Corisande in memory of Henri IV's liaison with one of their ancestresses. These things may perhaps also occur among the middle classes, but they conceal them better. Can't you imagine how it would have amused your poor grandmother!" Mamma added sadly, for the joys which it grieved us to think that my grandmother was deprived of were the simplest joys of life—an item of news, a play, or even something more trifling still, a piece of mimicry, which would have amused her. "Can't you imagine her astonishment! But still, I'm sure that your grandmother would have been shocked by these marriages, that they would have grieved her; I feel that it's better that she never knew about them," my mother went on, for, when confronted with any event, she liked to think that my grandmother would have received an utterly distinctive impression from it which would have stemmed from the marvellous singularity of her nature and have been uniquely significant. If anything sad or painful occurred which could not have been foreseen in the past—the disgrace or ruin of one of our old friends, some public calamity, an epidemic, a war, a revolution—my mother would say to herself that perhaps it was better that Grandmamma had known nothing about it, that it would have grieved her too much, that perhaps she would not have been able to endure it. And when it was a question of something shocking like these two marriages, my mother, by an impulse directly opposite to that of the malicious people who are pleased to imagine that others whom they do not like have suffered more than is generally supposed, would not, in her tenderness for my grandmother, allow that anything sad or diminishing could ever have happened to her. She always imagined my grandmother as being above the assaults even of any evil which might not have been expected to occur, and told herself that my grandmother's death had perhaps been a blessing on the whole, inasmuch as it had shut off the too ugly spectacle of the present day from that noble nature which could never have become resigned to it. For optimism is the philosophy of the past. The events that have occurred being, among all those that were possible, the only ones which we have known, the harm that they have caused seems to us inevitable, and we give them the credit for the slight amount of good that they could not help bringing with them, for we imagine that without them it would not have occurred. My mother sought at the same time to form a more accurate idea of what my grandmother would have felt when she learned these tidings, and to believe that it was impossible for our minds, less exalted than hers, to form any such idea. "Can't you imagine," she said to me first of all, "how astonished your poor grandmother would have been!" And I felt that my mother was distressed by her inability to tell her the news, regretting that my grandmother would never know it, and feeling it to be somehow unjust that the course of life should bring to light facts which my grandmother would never have believed, thus rendering erroneous and incomplete, retrospectively, the knowledge of people and society which my grandmother had taken to the grave, the marriage of the Jupien girl and Legrandin's nephew being calculated to modify her general notions of life, no less than the news—had my mother been able to convey it to her—that people had succeeded in solving the problems, which my grandmother had regarded as insoluble, of aerial navigation and wireless telegraphy. But as we shall see, this desire that my grandmother should share in the blessings of our modern science was soon, in its turn, to appear too selfish to my mother.

What I was to learn later on—for I had been unable to keep in touch with it all from Venice—was that Mlle de Forcheville's hand had been sought both by the Duc de Châtellerault and by the Prince de Silistrie, while Saint-Loup was seeking to marry Mlle d'Entragues, the Duc de Luxembourg's daughter. This is what had occurred. Mlle de Forcheville possessing a hundred million francs, Mme de Marsantes had decided that she would be an excellent match for her son. She made the mistake of saying that the girl was charming, that she herself had not the slightest idea whether she was rich or poor, that she did not wish to know, but that even without a dowry it would be a piece of good luck for the most exacting young man to find such a wife. This was going rather too far for a woman who was tempted only by the hundred million, which made her shut her eyes to everything else. People realised at once that she was thinking of the girl for her own son. The Princesse de Silistrie went round protesting loudly, expatiating on Saint-Loup's social grandeur, and proclaiming that if he should marry the daughter of Odette and a Jew then it was the end of the Faubourg Saint-Germain. Mme de Marsantes, sure of herself as she was, dared not proceed further and retreated before the indignant protests of the Princesse de Silistrie, who immediately made a proposal on behalf of her own son. She had protested only in order to keep Gilberte for herself. Meanwhile Mme de Marsantes, refusing to own herself defeated, had turned at once to Mlle d'Entragues, the Duc de Luxembourg's daughter. Having no more than twenty million, the latter suited her purpose less, but Mme de Marsantes told everyone that a Saint-Loup could not marry a Mlle Swann (there was no longer any mention of Forcheville). Some time later, somebody having thoughtlessly remarked that the Duc de Châtellerault was thinking of marrying Mlle d'Entragues, Mme de Marsantes, who was the most punctilious woman in the world, mounted her high horse, changed her tactics, returned to Gilberte, made a formal offer of marriage on Saint-Loup's behalf, and the engagement was immediately announced.

This engagement was to provoke keen comment in the most different social circles. Several of my mother's friends, who had met Saint-Loup in our house, came to her "day," and inquired whether the bridegroom was indeed the same person as my friend. Certain people went so far as to maintain, with regard to the other marriage, that it had nothing to do with the Legrandin-Cambremers. They had this on good authority, for the Marquise, *née* Legrandin, had denied it on the very eve of the day on which the engagement was announced. I, for my part, wondered why M. de Charlus on the one hand, Saint-Loup on the other, each of whom had had occasion to write to me shortly

before and had spoken in such friendly terms of various travel plans
the realisation of which must have precluded the wedding cere-
monies, had said nothing whatever to me about them. I came to
the conclusion, forgetting the secrecy which people maintain
until the last moment in affairs of this sort, that I was less their
friend than I had supposed, a conclusion which, so far as Saint-
Loup was concerned, saddened me. Though why, when I had
already remarked that the affability, the egalitarian, "man-to-
man" attitude of the aristocracy was all a sham, should I be
surprised to find myself left out of it? In the establishment for
women—where men were now to be procured in increasing
numbers—in which M. de Charlus had spied on Morel, and in
which the "assistant matron,"[9] a great reader of the *Gaulois*, used
to discuss the social gossip with her clients, this lady, while conversing with a stout gentleman who used to come to her to drink
bottle after bottle of champagne with young men, because, being
already very stout, he wished to become obese enough to be
certain of not being called up should there ever be a war, declared:
"It seems young Saint-Loup is 'one of those,' and young
Cambremer too. Poor wives! In any case, if you know these
bridegrooms, you must send them to us. They'll find everything
they want here, and there's plenty of money to be made out of
them." Whereupon the stout gentleman, albeit he was himself
"one of those," indignantly retorted, being something of a snob,
that he often met Cambremer and Saint-Loup at his cousins' the
Ardonvillers, and that they were great womanisers, and quite the
opposite of "those." "Ah!" the assistant matron concluded in a
sceptical tone, but possessing no proof of the assertion, and convinced that in our century the perversity of morals was rivalled
only by the absurd exaggeration of slanderous tittle-tattle.

Certain people whom I no longer saw wrote to me and asked
me "what I thought" of these two marriages, precisely as though
they were conducting an inquiry into the height of women's hats
in the theatre or the psychological novel. I had not the heart to
answer these letters. Of these two marriages I thought nothing at
all, but I felt an immense sadness, as when two parts of one's past
existence, which have been anchored near to one, and upon
which one has perhaps been basing idly from day to day an
unacknowledged hope, remove themselves finally, with a joyous
flapping of pennants, for unknown destinations, like a pair of ships.
As for the prospective bridegrooms themselves, their attitude

towards their own marriages was perfectly natural, since it was a question not of other people but of themselves—though hitherto they had never tired of mocking at such "grand marriages" founded upon some secret taint. And even the Cambremer family, so ancient in its lineage and so modest in its pretensions, would have been the first to forget Jupien and to remember only the unimaginable grandeur of the House of Oloron, had not an exception appeared in the person who ought to have been most gratified by this marriage, the Marquise de Cambremer-Legrandin. Being spiteful by nature, she reckoned the pleasure of humiliating her family above that of glorifying herself. And so, not being enamoured of her son, and having rapidly taken a dislike to her future daughter-in-law, she declared that it was a calamity for a Cambremer to marry a person who had sprung from heaven knew where, and had such bad teeth. As for young Cambremer, who had already shown a propensity towards the society of men of letters such as Bergotte and even Bloch, it may be imagined that so brilliant a marriage did not have the effect of making him more of a snob than before, but that, feeling himself to have become the successor of the Ducs d'Oloron—"sovereign princes" as the newspapers said—he was sufficiently persuaded of his own grand-eur to be able to mix with anyone he chose. And he deserted the minor nobility for the intelligent bourgeoisie on the days when he did not confine himself to royalty. The notices in the papers, especially when they referred to Saint-Loup, invested my friend, whose royal ancestors were endlessly enumerated, with a renewed grandeur which, however, could only sadden me, as though he had become someone else, the descendant of Robert the Strong rather than the friend who, only a little while since, had taken the folding seat in the carriage in order that I might be more com-fortable in the back; the fact that I had had no previous suspicion of his marriage with Gilberte—the prospect of which had appeared to me suddenly, in my letter, so different from anything that I could have expected of either of them the day before, as unex-pected as a chemical precipitate—pained me, whereas I ought to have reflected that he had had a great deal to do, and that moreover in the fashionable world marriages are often arranged thus all of a sudden, as a substitute for a different combination which has come to grief. And the gloom, as dismal as the depression of moving house, as bitter as jealousy, that these marriages caused me by the accident of their sudden impact was so profound that people used to remind me of it later, congratulating me absurdly on my perspicacity, as having been, quite contrary to what it was at the time, a twofold, indeed a threefold and fourfold presentiment.

The people in society who had taken no notice of Gilberte said to me with an air of solemn interest: "Ah! she's the one who's marrying the Marquis de Saint-Loup," and studied her with the attentive gaze of people who not only relish all the social gossip of Paris but are anxious to learn and believe in the profundity of their observation. Those who on the other hand had known only Gilberte gazed at Saint-Loup with the closest attention, asked me (these were often people who scarcely knew me) to introduce them, and returned from the presentation to the bridegroom radiant with the joys of the festivity saying to me: "He's a fine figure of a man." Gilberte was convinced that the name "Marquis de Saint-Loup" was a thousand times grander than "Duc d'Orléans," but since she was very much of her knowing genera-tion, she did not want to appear less witty than others, and delighted in saying *mater semita*, to which she would add in order to show herself wittier still: "In my case, however, it's my *pater*."

"It appears that it was the Princesse de Parme who arranged young Cambremer's marriage," Mamma said to me. And this was true. The Princess had known for a long time, through her charitable activities, on the one hand Legrandin whom she regarded as a distinguished man, on the other hand Mme de Cambremer who changed the subject whenever the Princess asked her whether it was true that she was Legrandin's sister. The Princess knew how deeply Mme de Cambremer regretted having remained on the threshold of aristocratic high society without ever being invited in. When the Princess, who had undertaken to find a husband for Mlle d'Oloron, asked M. de Charlus whether he knew anything about an amiable and culti-vated man called Legrandin de Méséglise (it was thus that M. Legrandin now styled himself), the Baron first of all replied in the negative, then suddenly the memory recurred to him of a man whose acquaintance he had made in the train one night and who had given him his card. He smiled a vague smile. "It's perhaps the same man," he said to himself. When he learned that the prospective bridegroom was the son of Legrandin's sister, he said: "Why, that would be really extraordinary! If he took after his uncle, it wouldn't alarm me; after all, I've always said that they made the best husbands." "Who are *they*?" inquired the Princess.

"Ah, madame, I could explain it all to you if we met more often. With you one can talk freely. Your Highness is so intelligent," said Charlus, seized by a desire to confide which, however, went no further. The name Cambremer pleased him, although he did not like the boy's parents; he knew that it was one of the four Baronies of Brittany and everything he could possibly have hoped for his adopted daughter; it was an old and respected name, with solid connexions in its native province. A prince would have been out of the question and, moreover, not altogether desirable. This was the very thing. The Princess then asked Legrandin to call. Physically he had changed considerably of late, on the whole for the better. Like those women who deliberately sacrifice their faces to the slimness of their figures and never stir from Marienbad, he had acquired the breezy air of a cavalry officer. He had taken up tennis at the age of fifty-five. In proportion as M. de Charlus had thickened and slowed down, Legrandin had become slimmer and brisker, the contrary effect of an identical cause. This velocity of movement had its psychological reasons as well. He was in the habit of frequenting certain low haunts where he did not wish to be seen going in or coming out: he would hurl himself into them.

When the Princesse de Parme spoke to him of the Guermantes family and of Saint-Loup, he declared that he had known them all his life, making a sort of compound of the fact that he had always known *by name* the proprietors of Guermantes and the fact that he had met *in person*, at my aunt's house, Swann, the father of the future Mme de Saint-Loup—although he had always refused to have anything to do with Swann's wife and daughter at Combray. "Indeed, I travelled quite recently with the brother of the Duc de Guermantes, M. de Charlus. It was he who spontaneously engaged me in conversation, which is always a good sign, for it proves that a man is neither a strait-laced fool nor a pretentious snob. Oh, I know all the things that people say about him. But I never pay any attention to gossip of that sort. Besides, the private life of other people is not my business. He gave me the impression of having a sensitive nature and a cultivated mind." Then the Princesse de Parme spoke of Mlle d'Oloron. In the Guermantes circle people waxed sentimental about the nobility of heart of M. de Charlus who, generous as always, was securing the future happiness of a penniless but charming girl. And the Duc de Guermantes, who suffered from his brother's reputation, let it be understood that, fine as this conduct was, it was wholly natural.

"I don't know if I make myself clear, but everything in the affair is natural," he said, with calculated maladroitness. His object was to indicate that the girl was a daughter of his brother whom the latter acknowledged. This accounted at the same time for Jupien. The Princesse de Parme hinted at this version of the story to show Legrandin that after all young Cambremer would be marrying something in the nature of Mlle de Nantes, one of those bastards of Louis XIV who were scorned neither by the Duc d'Orléans nor by the Prince de Conti.

These two marriages which my mother and I discussed in the train that was taking us back to Paris had quite remarkable effects upon several of the characters who have figured in the course of this narrative. First of all upon Legrandin; needless to say, he swept like a hurricane into M. de Charlus's town house, for all the world as though he were entering a house of ill-fame where he must on no account be seen, and also, at the same time, to display his mettle and to conceal his age—for our habits accompany us even into places where they serve no useful purpose—and scarcely anybody observed that M. de Charlus greeted him with a smile which was hard to detect and harder still to interpret; this smile was similar in appearance—though in fact it was precisely the opposite—to the smile which two men who are in the habit of meeting in the best society exchange if they happen to meet in what they regard as disreputable surroundings (such as the Elysée where General de Froberville, whenever he met Swann there in the old days, would assume, on catching sight of him, an expression of ironical and mysterious complicity appropriate between two habitués of the salon of the Princesse des Laumes who were compromising themselves by visiting M. Grévy). But what was rather remarkable was the genuine improvement in Legrandin's character. For a long time past—ever since the days when I used to go as a child to spend my holidays at Combray—he had been surreptitiously cultivating relations with the aristocracy, productive at the most of an isolated invitation to a sterile house party. All of a sudden, his nephew's marriage having supervened to join up these scattered fragments, Legrandin stepped into a social position to which, retroactively, his former relations with people who had known him only in private but had known him well, gave a sort of solidity. Ladies to whom people offered to introduce him revealed that for the last twenty years he had stayed with them in the country for a fortnight annually, and that it was he who had given them the beautiful old barometer in the small drawing-room. It also transpired that he had been photographed in "groups" which included dukes who were now related to him. But as soon as he had acquired this social position, he ceased to take advantage of it. This was not merely because, now that people knew that he was received everywhere, he no longer derived any pleasure from being invited, but because, of the two vices that had long struggled for mastery in him, the less natural, snobbishness, was now giving way to another that was less artificial, since it did at least show a sort of return, however circuitous, towards nature. No doubt the two are not incompatible, and a nocturnal prowl may be undertaken immediately after leaving a duchess's party. But the dampening effect of age discouraged Legrandin from combining too many pleasures, from venturing out except well advisedly, and also made his enjoyment of the pleasures of nature fairly platonic, consisting chiefly in friendships, in time-consuming conversations, which, making him spend almost all his time among the people, left him very little for the life of society.

Mme de Cambremer herself became almost indifferent to the friendly overtures of the Duchesse de Guermantes. The latter, obliged to see something of the Marquise, had noticed, as happens whenever we come to see more of our fellow-creatures, that is to say as combinations of good qualities which we eventually discover and defects to which we eventually grow accustomed, that Mme de Cambremer was a woman endowed with an intelligence and culture which were little to my taste but which appeared remarkable to the Duchess. And so she often went to see Mme de Cambremer in the late afternoon and paid her long visits. But the fabulous charm which her hostess imagined to exist in the Duchesse de Guermantes vanished as soon as she found herself sought after by her, and she received her out of politeness rather than pleasure.

A more striking change manifested itself in Gilberte, a change at once symmetrical with and different from that which occurred in Swann after his marriage. It is true that during the first few months Gilberte had been happy to open her doors to the most select society. It was doubtless only because of the inheritance that she invited the intimate friends to whom her mother was attached, but on certain days only when there was no one but themselves, segregated from the fashionable people, as though the contact of Mme Bontemps or Mme Cottard with the Princesse de

Guermantes or the Princesse de Parme might, like that of two unstable powders, have produced irreparable catastrophes. Nevertheless the Bontemps, the Cottards and such, although disappointed to find themselves dining among themselves, were proud to be able to say: "We dined with the Marquise de Saint-Loup," all the more so because she sometimes went so far as to invite with them Mme de Marsantes, who showed herself emphatically the "great lady" with her tortoiseshell and ostrich-feather fan—also in the interests of the legacy. She merely made a point of paying tribute from time to time to the discreet people whom one never sees except when they are invited, a word to the wise after which she could bestow upon the Cottards, the Bontemps and their ilk her most gracious and lofty salutation. Perhaps because of my "Balbec girlfriend," by whose aunt I liked to be seen in these surroundings, I should have preferred to be included in that group. But Gilberte, in whose eyes I was now principally a friend of her husband and of the Guermantes (and who—perhaps even from the Combray days, when my parents did not call upon her mother—at the age when we do not merely add this or that to the value of things but classify them according to their species, had endowed me with the sort of prestige which one never afterwards loses), regarded these evenings as unworthy of me, and would say to me as I left: "It's delightful to have seen you, but you must come the day after tomorrow; you'll find my aunt Guermantes, and Mme de Poix; today it was just a few of Mamma's friends, to please Mamma." But this state of things lasted for a few months only, and then everything was totally transformed. Was this because Gilberte's social life was fated to exhibit the same contrasts as Swann's? However that may be, Gilberte had been for only a short time the Marquise de Saint-Loup (in the process of becoming, as we shall see, Duchesse de Guermantes)[10] when, having attained to the most brilliant and most rarefied position, she decided that the name Guermantes was now embodied in her like a lustrous enamel and that, whatever the society she frequented, from now onwards she would remain for all the world the Duchesse de Guermantes—sharing, in short, the opinion of the character in the operetta who declares: "My name, I think, dispenses me from saying more."[11] Wherein she was mistaken, for the value of a title, like that of stocks and shares, rises with the demand and falls when it is offered in the market. Everything that seems to us imperishable tends towards decay; a position in society, like anything else, is not created once and for all, but, just as much as the power of an empire, is continually rebuilding itself by a sort of perpetual process of creation, which explains the apparent anomalies in social or political history in the course of half a century. The creation of the world did not occur at the beginning of time, it occurs every day. The Marquise de Saint-Loup said to herself, "I am the Marquise de Saint-Loup," and she knew that, the day before, she had refused three invitations to dine with duchesses. But if to a certain extent her name aggrandised the very unaristocratic people whom she entertained, by an inverse process the people whom she entertained diminished the name that she bore. Nothing can hold out against such trends; the greatest names succumb to them in the end. Had not Swann known a princess of the House of France whose drawing-room, because anyone at all was welcomed there, had fallen to the lowest rank? One day when the Princesse des Laumes had gone to pay a brief duty call on this Highness, in whose drawing-room she had found only nonentities, arriving immediately afterwards at Mme Leroi's, she had said to Swann and the Marquis de Modène: "At last I find myself upon friendly soil. I have just come from Mme la Comtesse de X——, and there weren't three faces I knew in the room." At all events, Gilberte suddenly began to flaunt her contempt for what she had once so ardently desired, to declare that all the people in the Faubourg Saint-Germain were idiots, simply not worth meeting, and, suiting her actions to her words, ceased to meet them. People who did not make her acquaintance until after this period, and who, in the first stages of that acquaintance, heard her, by that time Duchesse de Guermantes, being very funny at the expense of the society in which she could so easily have moved, never inviting a single person from that society, and, if any of them, even the most brilliant, should venture into her drawing-room, yawning openly in their faces, blush now in retrospect at the thought that they themselves could ever have seen any glamour in the fashionable world, and would never dare to confess this humiliating secret of their past weaknesses to a woman whom they assume to have been, by an essential loftiness in her nature, incapable from the beginning of understanding such things. They hear her poking such delicious fun at dukes, and see her (which is more significant) matching her behaviour so entirely to her mockery! No doubt they do not think of inquiring into the causes of the accident which turned Mlle Swann into Mlle de Forcheville, Mlle de Forcheville into the Marquise de Saint-Loup, and finally into the Duchesse de Guermantes. Possibly it does not occur to them either that the effects of this accident would serve no less than its causes to explain Gilberte's subsequent attitude, association with commoners not being regarded in quite the same light in which Mlle Swann would have regarded it by a lady who is addressed by all and sundry as "Madame la Duchesse" and, by other duchesses who bore her so much, as "cousin." One is always ready to despise a goal which one has not succeeded in attaining, or has finally attained. And this contempt seems to us to form part of the character of people whom one did not know before. Perhaps, if we were able to go back over the years, we should find them devoured, more savagely than anyone, by those same weaknesses which they have succeeded so completely in disguising or conquering that we reckon them incapable not only of ever having been infected by them themselves but even of ever excusing them in others, because of their inability to imagine them. At all events, very soon the drawing-room of the new Marquise de Saint-Loup assumed its permanent aspect (from the social point of view at least, for we shall see what troubles were brewing in it in other respects). Now this aspect was surprising for the following reason. People still remembered that the most grandiose and glittering receptions in Paris, as brilliant as those given by the Princesse de Guermantes, had been those of Mme de Marsantes, Saint-Loup's mother. At the same time, in recent years Odette's salon, infinitely lower in the social scale, had been no less dazzling in its elegance and splendour. Saint-Loup, however, happy to have, thanks to his wife's vast fortune, everything that he could desire in the way of comfort, wished only to rest quietly in his armchair after a good dinner with a musical entertainment by good performers. And this young man who had seemed at one time so proud and so ambitious invited to share his luxury old friends whom his mother would not have admitted to her house. Gilberte, for her part, put into practice Swann's maxim: "Quality doesn't matter, what I dread is quantity." And Saint-Loup, very much on his knees before his wife, both because he loved her and because it was to her that he owed this extreme luxury, took care not to interfere with tastes that were so similar to his own. With the result that the great receptions that had been given year after year by Mme de Marsantes and Mme de Forcheville, principally with an eye to the establishing of their children in ostentatious splendour, gave rise to no receptions by M. and Mme de Saint-Loup. They had the best of saddle-horses on which to go out riding together, the finest of yachts in which to cruise—but they never took more than a couple of guests with them. In Paris, every evening, they would invite three or four friends to dine, never more; with the result that, by an unforeseen but at the same time quite natural retrogression, the two vast maternal aviaries had been replaced by a silent nest.

The person who profited least by these two marriages was the young Mlle d'Oloron who, already stricken with typhoid on the day of the religious ceremony, was barely able to crawl to the church and died a few weeks later. In the letter of intimation that was sent out some time after her death, names such as Jupien's were juxtaposed with some of the greatest in Europe, such as those of the Vicomte and Vicomtesse de Montmorency, H.R.H. the Comtesse de Bourbon-Soissons, the Prince of Modena-Este, the Vicomtesse d'Edumea, Lady Essex, and so forth. No doubt, even to a person who knew that the deceased was Jupien's niece, this plethora of grand marriage connexions could cause no surprise. The great thing, after all, is to have a grand marriage. Then, the *casus foederis* coming into play, the death of a simple little seamstress plunges all the princely families of Europe into mourning. But many young people of the rising generation, who were not familiar with the real situation, might, apart from the possibility of their mistaking Marie-Antoinette d'Oloron, Marquise de Cambremer, for a lady of the noblest birth, have been guilty of many other errors had they read this communication. Thus, supposing their excursions through France to have given them some slight familiarity with the country round Combray, when they saw that Mme L. de Méséglise and the Comte de Méséglise figured among the first of the signatories, close to the Duc de Guermantes, they might not have been at all surprised: the Méséglise way and the Guermantes way are cheek by jowl. "Old nobility of the same region, perhaps interrelated for generations," they might have said to themselves. "Who knows? It's perhaps a branch of the Guermantes family which bears the title of Comte de Méséglise." As it happened, the Comte de Méséglise had no connexion with the Guermantes and was not even enrolled on the Guermantes side, but on the Cambremer side, since the Comte de Méséglise, who by a rapid advancement had remained Legrandin de Méséglise for only two years, was our old friend Legrandin. No doubt, if they had to choose between bogus titles, few could have been so disagreeable to the Guermantes as this one. They had been connected in the past with the authentic Comtes de Méséglise, of whom there survived only one female descendant, the daughter of obscure parents who had come down in the world, herself married to one of my aunt's tenant farmers named Ménager, who had become rich and bought Mirougrain from her and now styled himself "Ménager de Mirougrain," with the result that when it was said that his wife was born "de Méséglise" people thought that she must simply have been born at Méséglise and that she was "from Méséglise" as her husband was "from Mirougrain."

Any other sham title would have caused less annoyance to the Guermantes family. But the aristocracy knows how to tolerate such irritations, and many others as well, the moment a marriage is at stake which is deemed advantageous, from whatever point of view. Shielded by the Duc de Guermantes, Legrandin was, to part of that generation, and would be to the whole of the generation that followed it, the real Comte de Méséglise.

Yet another mistake which any young reader not acquainted with the facts might have been led to make was that of supposing that the Baron and Baronne de Forcheville figured on the list in the capacity of parents-in-law of the Marquis de Saint-Loup, that is to say on the Guermantes side. But on this side they had no right to appear since it was Robert who was related to the Guermantes and not Gilberte. No, the Baron and Baronne de Forcheville, despite these deceptive appearances, did figure on the wife's side, it is true, and not on the Cambremer side, not because of the Guermantes, but because of Jupien, who, the better informed reader knows, was Odette's first cousin.

All M. de Charlus's favour had been transferred after the marriage of his adopted daughter on to the young Marquis de Cambremer; the young man's tastes, which were similar to those of the Baron, since they had not prevented the Baron from choosing him as a husband for Mlle d'Oloron, naturally made him appreciate him all the more when he was left a widower. This is not to say that the Marquis did not have other qualities which made him a charming companion for M. de Charlus. But even in the case of a man of real merit, it is a quality not to be despised by the person who admits him into his private life, and one that makes him particularly useful if he can also play whist. The intelligence of the young Marquis was remarkable, and, as they had already begun to say at Féterne when he was barely out of his cradle, he "took" entirely after his grandmother, had the same enthusiasms, the same love of music. He reproduced also some of her idiosyncrasies, but these more by imitation, like all the rest of the family, than from atavism. Thus it was that, some time after the death of his wife, having received a letter signed "Léonor," a name which I did not remember as being his, I realised who it was that had written to me only when I had read the closing formula: "*Croyez à ma sympathie vraie.*" The placing of that *vraie* infallibly added to the Christian name Léonor the surname Cambremer.

The train reached Paris before my mother and I had finished discussing these two pieces of news, which, so that the journey might not seem to me too long, she had deliberately reserved for the latter part of it, not allowing me to learn about them until after Milan. My mother had soon reverted to the point of view which for her was the only possible one, that of my grandmother. Mamma had first of all said that my grandmother would have been surprised, then that she would have been saddened, which was simply a way of saying that such a surprising event would have given her pleasure, and my mother, unable to accept that my grandmother should have been deprived of a pleasure, preferred to think that all was for the best, this news being of the kind that could only have caused her sorrow. But no sooner had we reached home than my mother felt that it was still too selfish of her to regret being unable to share with my grandmother all the surprises that life brings. She preferred to believe that this news would not have surprised my grandmother, since it merely confirmed her predictions. She wanted to see it as a confirmation of my grandmother's foresight, proof that she had been even more profound, more perceptive, more sagacious than we had thought. And so, in order to arrive at this attitude of pure admiration, it was not long before my mother was adding: "And yet, who knows whether your grandmother wouldn't have approved? She was so kind and tolerant. And then you know, for her, social status meant nothing; natural distinction was what mattered. And curiously enough, don't you remember, she liked both of them. Remember that first visit of hers to Mme de Villeparisis, when she came back and told us how common she thought M. de Guermantes was, and by comparison how full of praise she was for those Jupiens. Poor Mamma, do you remember her saying about the father: 'If I had another daughter, I'd give her to him as a wife, and his daughter is even nicer.' And the little Swann girl! She used to say of her: '*I* think she's charming; you'll see that she'll marry well.' Poor Mamma, if only she'd lived to see how right she was! Right up to the end she'll go on giving us lessons in goodness and foresight and judgment." And since the joys which we suffered to see my grandmother deprived of were all the humble little joys of life— an actor's intonation which would have amused her, a dish she would have enjoyed, a new novel by a favourite author—Mamma said: "How surprised she would have been! How it would have interested her! What a lovely letter she would have written in reply!" And my mother went on: "Just imagine, poor Swann who so longed for Gilberte to be received by the Guermantes, how happy he would˘ be if he could see his daughter become a Guermantes!"

"Under another name than his, led to the altar as Mlle de Forcheville—do you think he would be so happy after all?"

"Ah, that's true, I hadn't thought of it."

"That's what makes it impossible for me to be happy for her sake, the thought that the little beast could have had the heart to give up her father's name, when he was so good to her."

"Yes, you're right; all things considered, it's perhaps just as well that he never knew." So difficult is it for us to know, with the dead as with the living, whether a thing would cause them joy or sorrow! "It appears that the Saint-Loups are going to live at Tansonville," my mother went on. "Old Swann, who was so anxious to show your poor grandfather his pond, could never have dreamed that the Duc de Guermantes would see it constantly, especially if he had known of his son's shameful marriage. And then, you've talked so often to Saint-Loup about the hawthorns and lilacs and irises at Tansonville, he'll see what you meant now. They'll be his property."

Thus there proceeded in our dining-room, in the lamp-light that is so congenial to them, one of those long chats in which the wisdom not of nations but of families, taking hold of some event, a death, a betrothal, an inheritance, a bankruptcy, and slipping it under the magnifying glass of memory, brings it into high relief, detaches, thrusts back, and places in perspective at different points in space and time things which to those who have not lived through it seem to be juxtaposed on a single plane, the names of the deceased, successive addresses, the origins of a fortune and its vicissitudes, transfers of property. It is the wisdom inspired by the

Muse whom it is best to ignore for as long as possible if we wish to retain some freshness of impressions, some creative power, but whom even those who have ignored her meet in the evening of their lives in the nave of an old country church, at a point when suddenly they feel less susceptible to the eternal beauty expressed in the carvings on the altar than to the thought of the vicissitudes of fortune which those carvings have undergone, passing into a famous private collection or a chapel, from there to a museum, then returning at length to the church, or to the feeling that as they walk around it they may be treading upon a flagstone almost endowed with thought, which is made of the ashes of Arnauld or Pascal, or simply to deciphering (forming perhaps a mental picture of a fresh-faced country girl) on the brass plate of the wooden prie-dieu the names of the daughters of the squire or the notable—the Muse who has gathered up everything that the more exalted Muses of philosophy and art have rejected, everything that is not founded upon truth, everything that is merely contingent, but that reveals other laws as well: the Muse of History.

Some old friends of my mother, who belonged more or less to Combray, came to see her to discuss Gilberte's marriage, which did not dazzle them in the least. "You know who Mlle de Forcheville is, she's simply Mlle Swann. And her witness at the marriage, the 'Baron' de Charlus, as he calls himself, is the old man who used to keep her mother at one time, under Swann's very nose, and no doubt to his advantage." "But what do you mean?" my mother protested; "in the first place, Swann was extremely rich." "One must assume that he wasn't as rich as all that if he needed other people's money. But what is there about that woman, that she hangs on to her old lovers like that? She managed to persuade the first to marry her, then the third, and she drags out the second when he has one foot in the grave to get him to be a witness at the marriage of the daughter she had by the first or by someone else—for how is one to tell who the father was? She can't be certain herself! I said the third, but I should have said the three hundredth. Mind you, even if the girl's no more a Forcheville than you or I, that puts her on the same level as the bridegroom who of course isn't noble at all. You can imagine that only an adventurer would marry a girl like that. It appears he's just a plain Monsieur Dupont or Durand or something. If it weren't that we have a Radical mayor now at Combray, who doesn't even lift his hat to the priest, I should know all about it. Because, you understand, when they published the banns, they were obliged to give the real name. It's all very nice, for the newspapers or for the stationer who sends out the invitations, to describe yourself as the Marquis de Saint-Loup. That does no harm to anyone, and if it can give any pleasure to those worthy people, I should be the last person in the world to object! What harm can it do me? As I shall never dream of going to call on the daughter of a woman who has let herself be talked about, she can have a string of titles as long as my arm for the benefit of her servants. But in an official document it's not the same thing. Ah, if my cousin Sazerat was still deputy-mayor, I'd have written to him, and he would certainly have let *me* know what name the man was registered under."

I saw a good deal of Gilberte at this time, as it happened, having renewed my friendship with her: for our life, in the long run, is not calculated according to the duration of our friendships. Let a certain period of time elapse, and you will see (just as, in politics, former ministries reappear, or, in the theatre, forgotten plays are revived) friendships renewed between the same persons as before, after long years of interruption, and renewed with pleasure. After ten years, the reasons which made one party love too passionately, the other unable to endure a too exacting despotism, no longer exist. The affinity alone survives, and everything that Gilberte would have refused me in the past, that had seemed to her intolerable, impossible, she granted me quite readily—doubtless because I no longer desired it. Although neither of us had ever mentioned the reason for this change, if she was always ready to come to me, never in a hurry to leave me, it was because the obstacle had vanished: my love.

Some time later, I went to spend a few days at Tansonville. This excursion was something of an inconvenience, for I was keeping a girl in Paris who slept in a bachelor flat which I had rented. As other people need the aroma of forests or the ripple of a lake, so I needed her sleep by my side during the night and, by day, to have her always by my side in the carriage. For even if one love has passed into oblivion, it may determine the form of the love that is to follow it. Already, even in the midst of the previous love, daily habits existed, the origin of which we did not ourselves remember; perhaps it was a moment of anguish early on that had made us passionately desire, then permanently adopt, like customs the meaning of which has been forgotten, the habit of those homeward drives to the beloved's door, or her residence in our home, our presence or the presence of someone we trust during all her outings. All these habits, which are like great uniform high-roads along which our love passes daily and which were forged long ago in the volcanic fire of an ardent emotion, nevertheless survive the woman, survive even the memory of the woman. They become the pattern, if not of all our loves, at least of certain of our loves which alternate among themselves. And thus my home had demanded, in memory of a forgotten Albertine, the presence of my mistress of the moment whom I concealed from visitors and who filled my life as Albertine had filled it in the past. And in order to go to Tansonville I had to obtain her consent to being looked after for a few days by one of my friends who did not care for women. I was going because I had heard that Gilberte was unhappy, in that Robert was unfaithful to her, though not in the fashion which everyone believed, which perhaps she herself still believed, which in any case she alleged. A belief that could be explained by pride, by the desire to hoodwink other people and to hoodwink oneself, not to mention the imperfect knowledge of infidelities which is all that betrayed spouses ever acquire, all the more so as Robert, a true nephew of M. de Charlus, went about openly with women whom he compromised, whom the world believed and whom Gilberte on the whole believed to be his mistresses. It was even thought in society that he was somewhat barefaced, never stirring, at a party, from the side of some woman whom he afterwards accompanied home, leaving Mme de Saint-Loup to return as best she could. Anyone who had said that the other woman whom he compromised thus was not really his mistress would have been regarded as a fool, incapable of seeing what was staring him in the face; but I had been pointed, alas, in the direction of the truth, a truth which caused me infinite distress, by a few words let fall by Jupien. A few months before my visit to Tansonville I had gone to inquire after M. de Charlus, in whom certain cardiac symptoms had been causing great anxiety, and having mentioned to Jupien, whom I found alone, some love-letters addressed to Robert and signed Bobette which Mme de Saint-Loup had discovered, I was stupefied to learn from the Baron's former factotum that the person who used the signature Bobette was none other than the violinist-journalist who had played so important a part in M. de Charlus's life![12] Jupien could not speak of him without indignation: "The boy was free to do whatever he liked. But if there was one direction in which he ought never to have looked, that was in the direction of the Baron's nephew. All the more so as the Baron loved his nephew like his own son. He has tried to break up the marriage—it's really shameful. And he must have gone about it with the most devilish cunning, for no one was ever more opposed to that sort of thing by nature than the Marquis de Saint-Loup. You've only to think of the follies he committed for the sake of his mistresses! No, however despicably—there's no other word for it—he deserted the Baron, that was his business. But to take up with the nephew! There are some things that just aren't done."

Jupien was sincere in his indignation; among so-called immoral people, moral indignation is quite as violent as among other people, only its object is slightly different. What is more, people whose own hearts are not directly involved always regard unfortunate entanglements, disastrous marriages, as though one were free to choose whom one loves, and do not take into account the exquisite mirage which love projects and which envelops so entirely and so uniquely the person with whom one is in love that the "folly" a man commits by marrying his cook or the mistress of his best friend is as a rule the only poetical action that he performs in the course of his existence.

I gathered that Robert and his wife had been on the brink of a separation (though Gilberte had not yet discovered the precise nature of the trouble) and that it was Mme de Marsantes, a loving, ambitious and philosophical mother, who had arranged and enforced their reconciliation. She belonged to a world in which perennial inbreeding and the impoverishment of patrimonies constantly bring out, in the realm of the passions as in that of pecuniary interest, inherited vices and compromises. It was with the same energy that in the past she had patronised Mme Swann, encouraged the marriage of Jupien's niece and arranged that of her own son to Gilberte, exercising thus on her own behalf, with a pained resignation, the same atavistic wisdom which she deployed for the benefit of the entire Faubourg. And perhaps what had made her at a certain moment expedite Robert's marriage to Gilberte—which had certainly caused her less trouble and fewer tears than making him break with Rachel—had been the fear of his forming with another harlot—or perhaps with the same one, for Robert took a long time to forget Rachel—a fresh attachment which might have been his salvation. Now I understood what Robert had meant when he said to me at the Princesse de Guermantes's: "It's a pity your Balbec girlfriend hasn't the fortune that my mother insists upon. I believe she and I would have got on very well together." He had meant that she belonged to Gomorrah as he belonged to Sodom, or perhaps, if he did not yet belong, that he had ceased to enjoy women whom he could not love in a certain fashion and together with other women. Gilberte, too, might have been able to enlighten me as to Albertine. If therefore, apart from rare moments of recollection, I had not lost all my curiosity as to the life of my dead mistress, I could have questioned not only Gilberte but her husband about her. And on the whole it was the same thing that had given both Robert and myself a desire to marry Albertine—to wit, the knowledge that she was a lover of women. But the causes of our desire, as for that matter its objects, were the reverse of each other. In my case, it was the despair in which I had been plunged by the discovery, in Robert's the satisfaction; in my case to prevent her, by perpetual vigilance, from indulging her predilection; in Robert's to cultivate it, and by granting her her freedom to make her bring her girlfriends to him.

If Jupien traced back to a quite recent origin the new orientation, so divergent from their original course, that Robert's carnal pleasures had assumed, a conversation which I had with Aimé and which made me extremely unhappy showed me that the head waiter at Balbec traced this divergence, this inversion, back to a far earlier date. The occasion of this conversation had been a brief visit I paid to Balbec, where Saint-Loup himself, on long leave, had also come with his wife, whom during this first phase he never allowed out of his sight. I had been struck by the extent to which Rachel's influence over Robert still made itself felt. Only a young husband who has long been keeping a mistress knows how to take off his wife's cloak as they enter a restaurant, how to treat her with due attentiveness. He has received, during the course of his liaison, the education which a good husband requires. Not far from him, at a table adjoining mine, Bloch, among a party of pretentious young academics, was assuming a spuriously relaxed air, and shouted at the top of his voice to one of his friends, as he ostentatiously passed him the menu with a gesture which upset two carafes of water: "No, no, my dear fellow, you order! Never in my life have I been able to make head or tail of these documents. I've never known how to order dinner!" he repeated with a pride that was obviously insincere and, blending literature with greed, decided at once upon a bottle of champagne which he liked to see "in a purely symbolic fashion" adorning a conversation. Saint-Loup, on the other hand, did know how to order. He was seated by the side of Gilberte—already pregnant (subsequently he did not fail to keep her continually supplied with offspring)[13]—as he slept by her side in their double bed in the hotel. He spoke to no one but his wife; the rest of the hotel appeared not to exist for him; but whenever a waiter came to take an order, and stood close beside him, he swiftly raised his blue eyes and darted a glance at him which did not last for more than two seconds, but in its limpid penetration seemed to indicate a kind of investigative curiosity entirely differ- ent from that which might have inspired any ordinary diner scrutinising, even at greater length, a page or waiter with a view to making humorous or other observations about him which he would communicate to his friends. This little glance, brief, disin- terested, showing that the waiter interested him in himself, would have revealed to anyone who intercepted it that this excellent husband, this once so passionate lover of Rachel, had another plane in his life, and one that seemed to him infinitely more interesting than the one on which he moved from a sense of duty. But it was not otherwise visible. Already his eyes had returned to Gilberte who had noticed nothing; he introduced her to a passing friend and left the room to stroll with her outside. It was then that Aimé spoke to me of a far earlier time, the time when I had made Saint-Loup's acquaintance through Mme de Villeparisis, in this same Balbec.

"Why, of course, Monsieur," he said to me, "it's common knowledge, I've known it for ever so long. The first year Monsieur came to Balbec, M. le Marquis shut himself up with my lift-boy, on the pretext of developing some photographs of Monsieur's grandmother. The boy made a complaint, and we had the greatest difficulty in hushing the matter up. And besides, Monsieur, Monsieur remembers the day, no doubt, when he came to lunch at the restaurant with M. le Marquis de Saint- Loup and his mistress, whom M. le Marquis was using as a screen. Monsieur doubtless remembers that M. le Marquis left the room, pretending that he had lost his temper. Of course I don't suggest for a moment that Madame was in the right. She was leading him a regular dance. But as to that day, no one will ever make me believe that M. le Marquis's anger wasn't put on, and that he hadn't a good reason to get away from Monsieur and Madame."

So far as that day was concerned, I am convinced that, if Aimé was not deliberately lying, he was entirely mistaken. I remembered too well the state Robert was in, the blow he had struck the journalist. And, for that matter, it was the same with the Balbec incident; either that lift-boy had lied, or it was Aimé who was lying. At least so I believed; I could not be absolutely certain, for we never see more than one aspect of things, and had it not been that the thought distressed me, I should have found a certain beauty in the fact that, whereas for me sending the lift-boy to Saint-Loup had been the most convenient way of conveying a letter to him and receiving his answer, for him it had meant making the acquaintance of a person who had taken his fancy. For everything is at least dual. On to the most insignificant action that we perform, another man will graft a series of entirely different actions. Certain it is that Saint-Loup's adventure with the lift-boy, if it occurred, no more seemed to me to be inherent in the commonplace dispatch of my letter than that a man who knew nothing of Wagner save the duet in *Lohengrin* would be able to foresee the prelude to *Tristan*. True, things offer men only a limited number of their innumerable attributes, because of the paucity of our senses. They are coloured because we have eyes; how many other epithets would they not merit if we had hundreds of senses? But this different aspect which they might present is made more comprehensible to us by the occurrence in life of even the most trivial event of which we know a part which we suppose to be the whole, and at which another person looks as through a window opened up on the other side of the house and offering a different view. Supposing that Aimé had not been mistaken, Saint-Loup's blush when Bloch spoke to him of the lift-boy had not perhaps been due after all to my friend's pronouncing the word as "lighft." But I was convinced that Saint-Loup's physiological evolution had not begun at that period and that he had then been still exclusively a lover of women. More than by any other sign, I could tell this retrospectively by the friendship that Saint-Loup had shown me at Balbec. It was only while he still loved women that he was really capable of friendship. Afterwards, for some time at least, to the men who did not attract him physically he displayed an indifference which was to some extent, I believe, sincere—for he had become very curt—but which he exaggerated as well in order to make people think that he was interested only in women. But I remember all the same that one day at Doncières, when I was on my way to dine with the Verdurins and he had just been staring rather hard at Morel, he had said to me: "Curious, that fellow reminds me in some ways of Rachel. Doesn't it strike you? They seem to me identical in some ways. Not that it can be of the slightest interest to me." And yet his eyes had afterwards remained for a long time gazing abstractedly at the horizon, as when we think, before returning to the card-table or going out to dinner, of one of those long journeys which we think we shall never make, but for which we have felt a momentary longing. But if Robert found something of Rachel in Charlie, Gilberte, for her part, sought to give herself some resemblance to Rachel in order to appear more attractive to her husband, wearing, like her, bows of scarlet or pink or yellow ribbon in her hair, which she dressed in a similar style, for she believed that her husband was still in love with Rachel, and so was jealous of her. That Robert's love may have hovered at times on the boundary which divides the love of a man for a woman from the love of a man for a man was quite possible. In any case, the memory of Rachel now played only an aesthetic role in this context. It is indeed improbable that it could have played any other. One day Robert had gone to her to ask her to dress up as a man, to leave a lock of hair hanging down, and nevertheless had contented himself with gazing at her, unsatisfied. He remained none the less attached to her and paid her scrupulously, though without pleasure, the enormous income which he had promised her and which did not prevent her from treating him in the most abominable fashion later on. This generosity towards Rachel would not have distressed Gilberte if she had known that it was merely the resigned fulfilment of a promise which no longer bore any trace of love. But love was, on the contrary, precisely what he pretended to feel for Rachel. Homosexuals would be the best husbands in the world if they did not put on an act of loving other women. Not that Gilberte made any complaint. It was the belief that Robert had been loved, and loved for so long, by Rachel that had made her desire him, had made her reject more glittering matches; it seemed that he was making a sort of concession to her in marrying her. And indeed, at first, any comparison between the two women (incommensurable though they were in charm and beauty) did not favour the delightful Gilberte. But the latter subsequently grew in her husband's esteem while Rachel visibly diminished.

There was another person, who changed her tune, namely Mme Swann. If, in Gilberte's eyes, Robert before their marriage was already crowned with the double halo conferred on him on the one hand by his life with Rachel, perpetually advertised by Mme de Marsantes's lamentations, and on the other hand by the prestige which the Guermantes family had always had in her father's eyes and which she had inherited from him, Mme de Forcheville for her part would have preferred a more brilliant, perhaps a princely marriage (there were impoverished royal families who would not have refused the money—which incidentally proved to be considerably less than the promised eighty million—laundered as it was by the name Forcheville) and a son-in-law less depreciated in value by a life spent outside the world of society. She had been unable to overcome Gilberte's determination, and had complained bitterly to all and sundry, denouncing her son-in-law. One fine day her attitude changed completely; her son-in-law had become an angel, and she no longer said anything against him except surreptitiously. The fact was that age had left Mme Swann (now Mme de Forcheville) with the taste she had always had for being kept, but, by the desertion of her admirers, had deprived her of the means. She longed every day for another necklace, a new dress studded with brilliants, a more sumptuous motor-car, but she had only a small income, Forcheville having squandered most of it, and—what Jewish strain influenced Gilberte in this?—she had an adorable but fearfully avaricious daughter, who counted every sou that she gave her husband, and naturally even more so her mother. Then suddenly she had sniffed out and found her natural protector in Robert. That she was no longer in her first youth mattered little to a son-in-law who was not a lover of women. All that he asked of his mother-in-law was to smooth down any little difficulty that might arise between Gilberte and himself, to obtain his wife's consent to his going on a trip with Morel. Odette, having applied herself thereto, was at once rewarded with a magnificent ruby. To pay for this, it was necessary for Gilberte to be more generous to her husband. Odette urged her in this direction with all the more fervour in that it was she herself who would benefit by her daughter's generosity. Thus, thanks to Robert, she was enabled, on the threshold of her fifties (some said her sixties), to dazzle every table at which she dined, every party at which she appeared, with an unparalleled splendour without needing to have, as in the past, a "friend" who now would no longer have coughed up, or even fallen for her. And so she had entered, permanently it seemed, into the period of final chastity, and yet she had never been so elegant.

It was not merely the malice, the rancour of the once poor boy against the master who has enriched him and has moreover (this was in keeping with the character and still more with the vocabulary of M. de Charlus) made him feel the difference of their positions, that had made Charlie turn to Saint-Loup in order to aggravate the Baron's sufferings. He may also have had an eye to his own profit. I had the impression that Robert must be giving him a great deal of money. After an evening party at which I had met Robert before I went down to Combray—and where the manner in which he flaunted himself by the side of a lady of fashion who was reputed to be his mistress, glued to her, never leaving her for a moment, enveloped publicly in the folds of her skirt, reminded me, but with something more hectic and jumpy about it, of a sort of involuntary repetition of an ancestral gesture which I had had an opportunity of observing in M. de Charlus, when he appeared to be wrapped in the finery of Mme Molé or some other lady, the banner of a gynophile cause which was not his own but which, without having any right to do so, he loved to sport thus, whether because he found it useful as a protection or aesthetically charming—I had been struck, as we came away, by the discovery that this young man, so generous when he was far less rich, had become so careful. That a man clings only to what he possesses, and that he who used to scatter money when he so rarely had any now hoards that with which he is amply supplied, is no doubt a common enough phenomenon, and yet in this instance it seemed to me to have assumed a more particular form. Saint-Loup refused to take a cab, and I saw that he had kept a tramway transfer-ticket. No doubt in so doing Saint-Loup was exercising, for different ends, talents which he had acquired in the course of his liaison with Rachel. A young man who has lived for years with a woman is not as inexperienced as the novice for whom the woman he marries is the first. One had only to see, on the rare occasions when Robert took his wife out to a restaurant, the adroit and considerate way he looked after her, his skill and poise in ordering dinner and giving instructions to waiters, the care with which he smoothed Gilberte's sleeves before she put on her jacket, to realise that he had been a woman's lover for a long time before being this one's husband. Similarly, having had to enter into the minutest details of Rachel's domestic economy, partly because she herself was useless as a housekeeper, and later because his jealousy made him determined to keep a firm control over her domestic staff, he was able, in the administration of his wife's property and the management of their household, to go on playing this skilful and competent role which Gilberte, perhaps, might have been unable to fulfil and which she gladly relinquished to him. But no doubt he did so principally in order to be able to give Charlie the benefit of his candle-end economies, maintaining him in affluence without Gilberte's either noticing it or suffering from it—and perhaps even assuming the violinist to be a spendthrift "like all artists" (Charlie styled himself thus without conviction and without conceit, in order to excuse himself for not answering letters and for a mass of other defects which he believed to form part of the undisputed psychology of the artist). Personally, I found it absolutely immaterial from a moral point of view whether one took one's pleasure with a man or with a woman, and only too natural and human that one should take it where one could find it. If, therefore, Robert had not been married, his liaison with Charlie ought not to have caused me pain. And yet I realised that the pain I felt would have been as acute if Robert had been a bachelor. In anyone else, his conduct would have left me indifferent. But I wept when I reflected that I had once had so great an affection for a different Saint-Loup, an affection which, I sensed all too clearly from the cold and evasive manner which he now adopted, he no longer felt for me, since men, now that they were capable of arousing his desires, could no longer inspire his friendship. How could these tastes have come to birth in a young man who had loved women so passionately that I had seen him brought to a state of almost suicidal despair because "Rachel when from the Lord" had threatened to leave him? Had the resemblance between Charlie and Rachel—invisible to me—been the plank which had enabled Robert to pass from his father's tastes to those of his uncle, in order to complete the physiological evolution which even in the latter had occurred fairly late? At times, however, Aimé's words came back to my mind to make me uneasy; I remembered Robert that year at Balbec; he had had a trick, when he spoke to the lift-boy, of not paying any attention to him which strongly resembled M. de Charlus's manner when he addressed certain men. But Robert might easily have derived this from M. de Charlus, from a certain hauteur and a certain physical posture peculiar to the Guermantes family, without for a moment sharing the Baron's heterodox tastes. For instance, the Duc de Guermantes, who was wholly innocent of such tastes, had the same nervous trick as M. de Charlus of turning his wrist, as though he were straightening a lace cuff round it, and also in his voice certain shrill and affected intonations, mannerisms to all of which, in the case of M. de Charlus, one might have been tempted to ascribe another meaning, to which he had given another meaning himself, the individual expressing his distinctive characteristics by means of impersonal and atavistic traits which are perhaps simply age-old characteristics ingrained in his gestures and voice. On this latter assumption, which borders upon natural history, it would not be M. de Charlus whom one described as a Guermantes affected with a blemish and expressing it to a certain extent by means of traits peculiar to the Guermantes stock, but the Duc de Guermantes who, in a perverted family, would be the exception whom the hereditary disease has so effectively spared that the external stigmata it has left upon him have lost all meaning. I remembered that on the day when I had seen Saint-Loup for the first time at Balbec, so fair-complexioned, fashioned of so rare and precious a substance, his monocle fluttering in front of him, I had found in him an effeminate air which was certainly not the effect of what I had now learned about him, but sprang rather from the grace peculiar to the Guermantes, from the fineness of that Dresden china in which the Duchess too was moulded. I recalled his affection for myself, his tender, sentimental way of expressing it, and told myself that this too, which might have deceived any-one else, meant at the time something quite different, indeed the direct opposite of what I had just learned about him. But when did the change date from? If from the year of my return to Balbec, how was it that he had never once come to see the lift-boy, had never once mentioned him to me? And as for the first year, how could he have paid any attention to the boy, passionately enam-oured as he then was of Rachel? That first year, I had found Saint-Loup unusual, as was every true Guermantes. Now he was even odder than I had supposed. But things of which we have not had a direct intuition, which we have learned only through other people, are such that we no longer have the means, we have missed the chance, of conveying them to our inmost soul; its communications with the real are blocked and so we cannot profit by the discovery, it is too late. Besides, upon any consideration, this discovery distressed me too deeply for me to be able to appreciate it intellectually. Of course, after what M. de Charlus had told me in Mme Verdurin's house in Paris, I no longer doubted that Robert's case was that of any number of respectable people, to be found even among the best and most intelligent of men. To learn this of anyone else would not have affected me, of anyone in the world except Robert. The doubt that Aimé's words had left in my mind tarnished all our friendship at Balbec and Doncières, and although I did not believe in friendship, or that I had ever felt any real friendship for Robert, when I thought about those stories of the lift-boy and of the restaurant in which I had had lunch with Saint-Loup and Rachel, I was obliged to make an effort to restrain my tears.

TIME REGAINED

I should have no occasion to dwell upon this visit which I paid to the neighbourhood of Combray at perhaps the moment in my life when I thought least about Combray, had it not, precisely for that reason, brought me what was at least a provisional confirmation of certain ideas which I had first conceived along the Guermantes way, and also of certain other ideas which I had conceived on the Méséglise way. I repeated every evening, in the opposite direction, the walks which we used to take at Combray, in the afternoon, when we went the Méséglise way. One dined now at Tansonville at an hour at which in the past one had long been asleep at Combray. And because of the seasonal heat, and also because Gilberte spent the afternoon painting in the chapel attached to the house, we did not go out for our walk until about two hours before dinner. The pleasure of those earlier walks, which was that of seeing, on the way home, the crimson sky framing the calvary or mirroring itself in the Vivonne, was now replaced by the pleasure of setting forth at nightfall, when one encountered nothing in the village but the blue-grey, irregular and shifting triangle of a flock of sheep being driven home. Over one half of the fields the sun had already set; above the other half the moon was already alight and would soon bathe them in their entirety. It sometimes happened that Gilberte let me go without her, and I set off, trailing my shadow behind me, like a boat gliding across enchanted waters. But as a rule Gilberte came with me. The walks that we took thus together were very often those that I used to take as a child: how then could I help but feel much more acutely even than in the past on the Guermantes way the conviction that I would never be able to write, reinforced by the conviction that my imagination and my sensibility had weakened, when I found how incurious I was about Combray? I was distressed to see how little I relived my early years. I found the Vivonne narrow and ugly alongside the tow-path. Not that

I noticed any great physical discrepancies from what I remembered. But, separated as I was by a whole lifetime from places I now happened to be passing through again, there was lacking between them and me that contiguity from which is born, even before we have perceived it, the immediate, delicious and total deflagration of memory. Having doubtless no very clear conception of its nature, I was saddened by the thought that my faculty of feeling and imagining things must have diminished since I no longer took any pleasure in these walks. Gilberte herself, who understood me even less than I understood myself, increased my melancholy by sharing my astonishment. "What," she would say, "you feel no excitement when you turn into this little footpath which you used to climb?" And she herself had changed so much that I no longer thought her beautiful, that she was no longer beautiful at all. As we walked, I saw the landscape change; we had to climb hills, followed by downward slopes. We chatted—very agreeably for me. Not without difficulty, however. In so many people there are different strata which are not alike: the character of the father, then of the mother; one traverses first one, then the other. But, next day, the order of their superimposition is reversed. And finally one does not know who will decide between the contestants, to whom one is to appeal for the verdict. Gilberte was like one of those countries with which one dare not form an alliance because of their too frequent changes of government. But in reality this is a mistake. The memory of the most multiple person establishes a sort of identity in him and makes him reluctant to go back on promises which he remembers, even if he has not countersigned them. As for intelligence, Gilberte's, in spite of certain absurdities inherited from her mother, was very acute. But, quite unrelated to this, I remember that, in the course of our conversations during these walks, on several occasions she surprised me a great deal. The first time was when she said to me: "If you were not too hungry and if it was not so late, by taking that road to the left and then turning to the right, in less than a quarter of an hour we should be at Guermantes." It was as though she had said to me: "Turn to the left, then bear right, and you will touch the intangible, you will reach the inaccessibly remote tracts of which one never knows anything on this earth except the direction, except" (what I thought long ago to be all that I could ever know of Guermantes, and perhaps in a sense I had not been mistaken) "the 'way.'" One of my other surprises was that of seeing the "source of the Vivonne," which I imagined as something as extra-terrestrial as the Gates of Hell, and which was merely a sort of rectangular basin in which bubbles rose to the surface. And the third occasion was when Gilberte said to me: "If you like, we might after all go out one afternoon and then we can go to Guermantes, taking the road by Méséglise, which is the nicest way," a sentence which upset all the ideas of my childhood by informing me that the two "ways" were not as irreconcilable as I had supposed. But what struck me most forcibly was how little, during this stay, I relived my childhood years, how little I desired to see Combray, how narrow and ugly I thought the Vivonne. But where Gilberte corroborated some of my childhood imaginings along the Méséglise way was during one of those walks which were more or less nocturnal even though they occurred before dinner—for she dined so late. Before descending into the mystery of a deep and flawless valley carpeted with moonlight, we stopped for a moment like two insects about to plunge into the blue calyx of a flower. Gilberte then uttered, perhaps simply out of the politeness of a hostess who is sorry you are going away so soon and would have liked to show you more of a countryside which you seem to appreciate, an avowal of the sort in which her practice as a woman of the world skilled in putting to the best advantage silence, simplicity, sobriety in the expression of her feelings, makes you believe that you occupy a place in her life which no one else could fill. Opening my heart to her suddenly with a tenderness born of the exquisite air, the fragrant evening breeze, I said to her: "You were speaking the other day of the little footpath. How I loved you then!" She replied: "Why didn't you tell me? I had no idea. I loved you too. In fact I flung myself twice at your head." "When?" "The first time at Tansonville. You were going for a walk with your family, and I was on my way home, I'd never seen such a pretty little boy. I was in the habit," she went on with a vaguely bashful air, "of going to play with little boys I knew in the ruins of the keep of Roussainville. And you will tell me that I was a very naughty girl, for there were girls and boys there of all sorts who took advantage of the darkness. The altar-boy from Combray church, Théodore, who, I must admit, was very nice indeed (goodness, how handsome he was!) and who has become quite ugly (he's the chemist now at Méséglise), used to amuse himself with all the peasant girls of the district. As I was allowed to go out by myself, whenever I was able to get away, I used to rush over there. I can't tell you how I longed for you to come there too; I remember quite well that, as I had only a moment in which to make you understand what I wanted, at the risk of being seen by your people and mine, I signalled to you so vulgarly that I'm ashamed of it to this day. But you stared at me so crossly that I saw that you didn't want to."

And suddenly I thought to myself that the true Gilberte, the true Albertine, were perhaps those who had at the first moment yielded themselves with their eyes, one through the hedge of pink hawthorn, the other on the beach. And it was I who, having been incapable of understanding this, having failed to recapture the impression until much later in my memory after an interval in which, as a result of my conversation, a dividing hedge of senti-ment had made them afraid to be as frank as in the first moments, had ruined everything by my clumsiness. I had "botched it" more completely than had Saint-Loup with Rachel—although in fact the relative failure with them was less absurd—and for the same reasons.

"And the second time," Gilberte went on, "was years later when I passed you in the doorway of your house, the day before I met you again at my aunt Oriane's. I didn't recognise you at first, or rather I did unconsciously recognise you because I felt the same attraction as I had felt at Tansonville."

"But in the meantime there'd been, after all, the Champs-Elysées."

"Yes, but there you were too fond of me. I felt you were prying into everything I did."

I did not think to ask her who the young man was with whom she had been walking along the Avenue des Champs-Elysées on the day when I had set out to call on her again, when I might have been reconciled with her while there was still time, that day which would perhaps have changed the whole course of my life, if I had not caught sight of those two shadowy figures strolling side by side in the dusk. If I had asked her, she would perhaps have confessed the truth, as would Albertine had she been restored to life. And indeed when we meet again after many years women whom we no longer love, is there not the abyss of death between them and us, quite as much as if they were no longer of this world, since the fact that our love exists no longer makes the people that they were or the person that we were then as good as dead? Perhaps, too, she might not have remembered, or she might have lied. In any case

I was no longer interested to know, since my heart had changed even more than Gilberte's face. This face gave me little pleasure, but above all I was no longer unhappy, and I should have been incapable of conceiving, had I thought about it again, that I could have been so unhappy at the sight of Gilberte tripping along by the side of a young man that I had said to myself: "It's all over, I shall never attempt to see her again." Of the state of mind which, in that far-off year, had been tantamount to a long-drawn-out torture for me, nothing survived. For in this world of ours where everything withers, everything perishes, there is a thing that decays, that crumbles into dust even more completely, leaving behind still fewer traces of itself, than beauty: namely grief.

And so I am not surprised that I did not ask her then with whom she had been walking in the Champs-Elysées, for I had already seen too many examples of the incuriosity that is brought about by Time, but I am a little surprised that I did not tell her that before I saw her that evening I had sold a Chinese porcelain bowl in order to buy her flowers. It had indeed, during the gloomy period that followed, been my sole consolation to think that one day I should be able with impunity to tell her of so tender an intention. More than a year later, if I saw another carriage about to crash into mine, my sole reason for wishing not to die was that I might be able to tell this to Gilberte. I consoled myself with the thought: "There's no hurry, I have a whole lifetime in which to tell her." And for this reason I was anxious not to lose my life. Now it would have seemed to me an unseemly, almost ridiculous thing to say, and a thing that would "involve consequences."

I did not ask then with whom she had been walking that evening. (I asked her later. It was Léa dressed as a man. Gilberte was aware that she knew Albertine, but could tell me nothing more. Thus it is that certain persons always reappear in one's life to herald one's pleasures or one's griefs.) What reality there had been beneath the appearance on that occasion had become quite immaterial to me. And yet for how many days and nights had I not tormented myself with wondering who it had been, had I not been obliged, even more perhaps than in the effort not to go downstairs to say good-night to Mamma in this very Combray, to control the beating of my heart! It is said, and this is what accounts for the gradual disappearance of certain nervous affec-tions, that our nervous system grows old. This is true not merely of our permanent self, which continues throughout the whole duration of our life, but of all our successive selves which, after all, to a certain extent compose it.

"Moreover," Gilberte went on, "even on the day when I passed you in the doorway, you were still just the same as at Combray; if you only knew how little you'd changed!"

I pictured Gilberte again in my memory. I could have drawn the rectangle of light which the sun cast through the hawthorns, the spade which the little girl was holding in her hand, the slow gaze that she fastened on me. Only I had supposed, because of the coarse gesture that accompanied it, that it was a contemptuous gaze because what I longed for it to mean seemed to me to be a thing that little girls did not know about and did only in my imagination, during my hours of solitary desire. Still less could I have supposed that so casually, so rapidly, almost under the eyes of my grandfather, one of them would have had the audacity to suggest it.

And so I was obliged, after an interval of so many years, to touch up a picture which I recalled so well—an operation which made me quite happy by showing me that the impassable gulf which I had then supposed to exist between myself and a certain type of little girl with golden hair was as imaginary as Pascal's gulf, and which I thought poetic because of the long sequence of years at the end of which I was called upon to perform it. I felt a stab of desire and regret when I thought of the dungeons of Roussainville. And yet I was glad to be able to tell myself that the pleasure towards which I used to strain every nerve in those days, and which nothing could restore to me now, had indeed existed elsewhere than in my mind, in fact so close at hand, in that Roussainville of which I used to speak so often, and which I could see from the window of the orris-scented closet. And I had known nothing! In short, the image of Gilberte summed up everything that I had desired during my walks to the point of being unable to make up my mind to return home, seeming to see the tree-trunks part asunder and take human form. What I had so feverishly longed for then she had been ready, if only I had been able to understand and to meet her again, to let me taste in my boyhood. More completely even than I had supposed, Gilberte had been in those days truly part of the Méséglise way.

And even on the day when I had passed her in a doorway, although she was not Mlle de l'Orgeville, the girl whom Robert had met in houses of assignation (and what an absurd coincidence that it should have been to her future husband that I had applied for information about her), I had not been altogether mistaken as to the meaning of her glance, nor as to the sort of woman that she was and confessed to me now that she had been. "All that is a long time ago," she said to me, "I've never given a thought to anyone but Robert since the day of our engagement. And even so, you see, it's not those childish whims that I feel most guilty about."[14]

All day long, in that slightly too countrified house which seemed no more than a place for a rest between walks or during a sudden downpour, one of those houses in which all the sitting-rooms look like arbours and, on the wall-paper in the bedrooms, here the roses from the garden, there the birds from the trees outside join you and keep you company, isolated from the world—for it was old wall-paper on which every rose was so distinct that, had it been alive, you could have picked it, every bird you could have put in a cage and tamed, quite different from those grandiose bedroom decorations of today where, on a silver background, all the apple-trees of Normandy display their outlines in the Japanese style to hallucinate the hours you spend in bed—all day long I remained in my room which looked over the fine greenery of the park and the lilacs at the entrance, over the green leaves of the tall trees by the edge of the lake, sparkling in the sun, and the forest of Méséglise. Yet I looked at all this with pleasure only because I said to myself: "How nice to be able to see so much greenery from my bedroom window," until the moment when, in the vast verdant picture, I recognised, painted in a contrasting dark blue simply because it was further away, the steeple of Combray church. Not a representation of the steeple, but the steeple itself, which, putting in visible form a distance of miles and of years, had come, intruding its discordant tone into the midst of the luminous verdure—a tone so colourless that it seemed little more than a preliminary sketch—and engraved itself upon my window-pane. And if I left my room for a moment, I saw at the end of the corridor, in a little sitting-room which faced in another direction, what seemed to be a band of scarlet—for this room was hung with a plain silk, but a red one, ready to burst into flames if a ray of sun fell upon it.

The love of Albertine had disappeared from my memory. But it seems that there exists too an involuntary memory of the limbs, a pale and sterile imitation of the other but longer-lived, just as there are animals or vegetables without intelligence which are longer-lived than man. Our legs and our arms are full of torpid memories. And once, when I had said good-night to Gilberte rather early, I woke up in the middle of the night in my room at Tansonville and, still half-asleep, called out: "Albertine!" It was not that I had thought of her or dreamt of her, nor that I was confusing her with Gilberte, but a memory in my arm, opening like a flower, had made me fumble behind my back for the bell, as though I had been in my bedroom in Paris. And not finding it, I had called out: "Albertine!", thinking that my dead mistress was lying by my side, as she had often done in the evening, and that we were both dropping off to sleep, and reckoning, as I woke up, that, because of the time it would take Françoise to reach my room, Albertine might without imprudence pull the bell which I could not find.

During our walks Gilberte intimated to me that Robert was turning away from her, but only in order to run after other women. And it is true that many women encumbered his life, yet always these associations, like certain masculine friendships in the lives of men who love women, had that quality of ineffectual resistance, of purposelessly filling an empty space that often in a house may be seen in objects which are not there to be used.

He came several times to Tansonville while I was there and I found him very different from the man I had known. His life had not coarsened him or slowed him down, as had happened with M. de Charlus; on the contrary, working in him an inverse change, it had given him, in a degree in which he had never had it before—and this although he had resigned his commission on his marriage—the grace and ease of a cavalry officer. Gradually, just as M. de Charlus had grown heavier, Robert (it is true that he was very much younger, but one felt that with age he would only get nearer and nearer to this ideal), had, like those women who resolutely sacrifice their faces to their figures and after a certain moment never stir from Marienbad (they realise that they cannot preserve more than one kind of youth and think that a youthful figure will serve best to represent youth in general), become slimmer and taken to moving more rapidly, a contrary effect of an identical vice. This swiftness of movement had, moreover, various psychological causes, the fear of being seen, the wish to conceal that fear, the feverishness which is generated by self-dissatisfaction and boredom. He was in the habit of visiting certain low haunts into which, as he did not wish to be seen going in or coming out, he would hurl himself in such a way as to present the

smallest possible target to the unfriendly glances of possible passers-by, like a soldier going into an attack.[15] And this manner of
moving like a gust of wind had become a habit. Perhaps also it
symbolised the superficial intrepidity of a man who wants to show
that he is not afraid and does not want to give himself time to
think. We must mention too, if our account is to be complete, a
desire, the older he grew, to appear young, and also the impatience
characteristic of those perpetually bored and perpetually cynical
men that people inevitably turn into when they are too intelligent
for the relatively idle lives they lead, in which their faculties do not
have full play. No doubt idleness, in these men as in others, may
express itself in inertia. But in these days especially, when physical
exercise is so much in favour, there exists also, even outside the
actual hours of sport, an athletic form of idleness which finds
expression not in inertia but in a feverish vivacity that hopes to
leave boredom neither time nor space to develop in.

Becoming—at any rate during this tiresome phase—much
harder in his manner, towards his friends, towards for example
myself, he now exhibited scarcely any trace of sensibility. Towards
Gilberte on the other hand he behaved with an affectation of
sentiment carried to the point of theatricality, which was most
disagreeable. Not that he was in fact indifferent to her. No, he
loved her. But he lied to her all the time and his untruthfulness, if
not the actual purpose of his lies, was invariably detected; and then
he thought that the only way to extricate himself was to exaggerate
to a ridiculous degree the genuine distress which he felt at having
hurt her. He would arrive at Tansonville, obliged, he said, to leave
again the next morning because of some business with a certain
neighbouring landowner who was supposed to be waiting for him
in Paris; but the neighbour, when they happened to meet him near
Combray the same evening, would unintentionally expose the lie,
of which Robert had neglected to inform him, by saying that he
had come to the country for a month's rest and would not be going
back to Paris during his stay. Robert would blush, would observe
Gilberte's melancholy and knowing smile, get rid of the blunder-
ing friend with a few sharp words, go home before his wife, send
her a desperate note saying that he had told this lie in order not to
hurt her, so that she should not think, when she saw him go off for
a reason which he could not avow to her, that he did not love her
(and all this, though Robert thought that he was lying when he
wrote it, was in substance true), and then would ask permission to

come to her room and there—part genuine distress, part the
nervous strain of the life he led, part a pretence which became
every day more brazen—would sob, plunge his head into cold
water, talk about his imminent death, sometimes throw himself on
the floor as though he had been taken ill. Gilberte did not know
how far she should believe him, supposed that in each particular
case he was lying but that in a general way he loved her, and was
worried by this presentiment of an imminent death, thinking that
he perhaps had some illness she did not know of, so that for that
reason she did not dare to thwart him or ask him to give up his
travels. All this, however, did not help me to understand why
Robert insisted on Morel's being accepted as the son of the
house—as much a part of it as Bergotte,[16] wherever the Saint-
Loups were, in Paris or at Tansonville. Morel imitated Bergotte
marvellously. It was even unnecessary, after a while, to ask him for
an impersonation. Like those hysterics whom one doesn't have to
hypnotise to make them become such or such a person, he entered
spontaneously and immediately into the character.

Françoise, who had seen all that M. de Charlus had done for
Jupien and saw now all that Robert de Saint-Loup was doing for
Morel, did not conclude that this was a characteristic which
reappeared from generation to generation in the Guermantes
family. She, who was so moral and so full of prejudices, had
come rather to believe—as Legrandin too was so kind to
Théodore—that this was a custom rendered respectable by its
universality. She would say of a young man, whether Morel or
Théodore: "He has found a gentleman who takes an interest in
him and has done a great deal to help him." And as in such cases it
is the protectors who love and suffer and forgive, Françoise, faced
with a choice between the "gentlemen" and the youths whom
they seduced, did not hesitate to award her sympathy to the
seducers, to decide that it was they who "really had hearts." She
blamed Théodore for all the tricks he played on Legrandin—and
yet it seemed scarcely possible that she could have any doubt about
the nature of their relations, for she would add: "Then the boy
realised that it was his turn to make a move and said: 'Take me with
you, I will love you, I will do my best to please you,' and upon my
word the gentleman has such a heart that I'm sure Théodore is sure
to do well with him. Perhaps much better than he deserves, for
he's a proper madcap, but the gentleman is so good that I've often
said to Jeannette (Théodore's fiancée): 'My girl, if ever you're in

trouble, go to the gentleman. He'd give you his bed rather than let you sleep on the floor. He's been too fond of that lad (Théodore) to turn him out. You can be sure he'll never desert him.'" Out of politeness I inquired what was the surname of Théodore, who was now living somewhere in the south of France, and she told me that it was Sanilon. "Then that's who it was," I exclaimed, "who wrote to me about my article in *Le Figaro*."

In the same way Françoise had a higher esteem for Saint-Loup than for Morel and gave it as her opinion that, in spite of all the tricks the lad (Morel) had played, the Marquis would always come to his rescue if he were in trouble, for he was a man with a real heart—or if he didn't, it would only be because he himself had suffered some great disaster.

Saint-Loup insisted that I should stay on at Tansonville and once, although he never now visibly sought to give me pleasure, let slip the remark that my coming had been so great a joy to his wife that it had caused her, as she had told him, a transport of happiness which lasted a whole evening, an evening when she had been feeling so miserable that my unexpected arrival had miraculously saved her from despair, "Perhaps from something worse," he added. He asked me to try to persuade her that he loved her and told me that, though he loved another woman, he loved her less than his wife and would soon break with her. "And yet," he continued, with such self-satisfaction and such an evident need to confide that there were moments when I thought the name of Charlie would, for all Robert's efforts, "come up" like a number in a lottery, "I had something to be proud of. This woman who has given me so many proofs of her affection and whom I am about to sacrifice to Gilberte, had never looked at a man before, she even thought herself incapable of falling in love. I am the first man in her life. I knew that she had refused offers right and left, so that when I received the marvellous letter in which she told me that there would be no happiness for her except with me, I just could not get over it. Obviously, there would be something here for me to lose my head about, were it not that the thought of seeing poor Gilberte in tears is intolerable to me. Don't you see something of Rachel in her?" he went on. And indeed I had been struck by a vague resemblance which one could, if one tried, now find between them. Perhaps it was due to a real similarity of certain features (owing possibly to the Jewish origin of both, though of this there was little evidence in Gilberte) which had caused

Robert, when his family had insisted that he should marry, to feel himself more attracted to Gilberte than to any other girl who was equally rich. But it was due also to the fact that Gilberte, having come across some hidden photographs of Rachel, whose name even had been unknown to her, tried to please Robert by imitating certain habits dear to the actress, such as always wearing a red ribbon in her hair and a black velvet ribbon on her arm, and by dyeing her hair in order to look dark. Then, feeling that her unhappiness was spoiling her looks, she tried to do something about it. Sometimes she went a great deal too far. One day, when Robert was coming to Tansonville for a single night, I was astounded to see her take her place at table looking so strangely different, not merely from what she had been in the past, but from her present self of every day, that I sat dumbfounded as if I had before my eyes an actress, a sort of Empress Theodora. I felt that in spite of myself I was staring at her, so curious was I to know what it was that was changed. My curiosity was soon satisfied when she blew her nose—in spite of all the precautions with which she did this. For from the many colours which were left on her handkerchief, turning it into a sumptuous palette, I saw that she was heavily made up. This it was that gave her that blood-red mouth which she tried hard to control into laughter in the belief that it was becoming to her, while the thought that the time of her husband's train was approaching and still she did not know whether he would really come or whether he would send one of those telegrams of which M. de Guermantes had wittily fixed the formula: "Cannot come, lie follows," turned her cheeks pale beneath the violet sweat of her grease-paint and drew dark rings round her eyes.

"Ah! don't you see?" he would say to me—in an artificially affectionate manner which contrasted painfully with his spontaneous affection of the old days, with the voice of an alcoholic and an actor's intonations—"Gilberte happy, there is nothing I would not give to see that. She has done so much for me. You can't possibly know." And the most disagreeable part of all this was once again his vanity, for he was flattered at being loved by Gilberte and, without daring to say that it was Charlie whom he loved, gave, nevertheless, of the love which the violinist was supposed to feel for him, details which he, the Saint-Loup from whom Charlie every day demanded more and more money, knew to be wildly exaggerated if not invented from start to finish. And so, entrusting

Gilberte to my care, he would go off to Paris again. In Paris (to anticipate a little, for I am still at Tansonville) I once had an opportunity of observing him at a party and from a distance and on this occasion, though the way in which he spoke was still alive and charming and enabled me to rediscover the past, I was struck by the great changes taking place in him. More and more he resembled his mother: the haughtily elegant manner which he had inherited from her and which she, by means of the most elaborate training, had perfected in him was now freezing into exaggeration; the penetrating glance proper to him as a Guermantes gave him the air of inspecting every place in which he happened to be, but of doing this in an almost unconscious fashion, as though from habit, in obedience to a sort of animal characteristic. Even when he was at rest, the colouring which he possessed in a greater degree than any other Guermantes—that air of being merely the solidified sunniness of a golden day—gave him as it seemed a plumage so strange, made of him a species so rare and so precious, that one would have liked to acquire him for an ornithological collection; but when, in addition, this ray of light, metamorphosed into a bird, set itself in motion, when for instance I saw Robert de Saint-Loup enter this evening party at which I was present, the way in which he tossed back his head, so silkily and proudly crested with the golden tuft of his slightly moulting hair, and moved his neck from side to side, was so much more supple, so much more aloof and yet more delicate than anything to be expected of a human being that, fired by the sight with curiosity and wonder, half social and half zoological, one asked oneself whether one was really in the Faubourg Saint-Germain and not rather in the Zoological Gardens, whether one was watching the passage of a great nobleman through a drawing-room or a bird pacing its cage. And if one was prepared to exercise a little imagination, the twittering lent itself just as well to this second interpretation as the plumage. For he was beginning to use phrases which he thought redolent of the age of Louis XIV, and though in this he was simply imitating the manners of the Guermantes, in him some indefinable nuance was turning them into the manners of M. de Charlus. "I must leave you for a moment," he said to me for instance, at this party, at which Mme de Marsantes was standing a little way away from us. "I have to pay my respects to my mother."

To return to this "love," of which he could not stop talking to me, it was not only love for Charlie, although this was the only one that counted for him. Whatever the nature of a man's loves, one always makes mistakes as to the number of people with whom he has affairs, partly from wrongly interpreting friendships as love affairs, an error which exaggerates the total, but also through believing that one proved love affair excludes another, which is an error of a contrary kind. Two people may say: "X's mistress, yes, I know her," they may pronounce two different names and neither of them may be mistaken. A woman whom we love seldom satisfies all our needs and we deceive her with a woman whom we do not love. As to the species of loves that Saint-Loup had inherited from M. de Charlus, a husband who is that way inclined usually makes his wife happy. This is a general rule to which the Guermantes contrived to be an exception, because those of them who had this taste wanted it to be believed that on the contrary they were fond of women. So they made themselves conspicuous with one woman or another and drove their own wives to despair. The Courvoisiers were more sensible. The young Vicomte de Courvoisier thought he was the only man alive, perhaps the only man since the beginning of the world, to be tempted by someone of his own sex. Supposing this inclination to come to him from the devil, he struggled against it, married an extremely pretty wife and had children by her. Then one of his cousins taught him that the tendency is fairly widespread and was even so kind as to take him to places where he could indulge it. M. de Courvoisier became fonder than ever of his wife and redoubled his philoprogenitive zeal, and he and she were quoted as the happiest couple in Paris. That could not possibly be said of the Saint-Loups, because Robert, instead of being content with inversion, made his wife ill with jealousy by keeping mistresses without pleasure to himself.

It is possible that Morel, being excessively dark, was necessary to Saint-Loup in the way that shadow is necessary to the sunbeam. Can one not imagine some golden-haired aristocrat sprung from an ancient family such as his, intelligent and endowed with every kind of prestige, concealing within him, unbeknown to all his friends, a secret taste for negroes?

Robert never allowed the conversation to touch upon his own species of loves. If I said a word about it, "Oh! I don't know," he would reply, with a detachment so profound that it caused him to drop his monocle, "I am utterly ignorant about those things. If you want information about them, my dear boy, I advise you to go elsewhere. I am a soldier, that's all I can say for myself. The things you speak of leave me cold. What I *am* interested in, passionately, is the course of the Balkan war. That sort of thing interested you too once, the 'etymology' of battles. I told you in those days that we should see again, even in greatly changed circumstances, battles conforming to certain types, for example the great exercise in lateral envelopment, the battle of Ulm. Well! However special these Balkan wars may be, Lüleburgaz is Ulm all over again: lateral envelopment. These are the subjects you can talk to me about. As for the sort of thing you allude to, it means about as much to me as Sanskrit."

While Robert thus expressed his disdain for the subject, Gilberte on the contrary, after he had left, was very willing to raise it in the conversation which I had with her. Not with reference to her husband certainly, for she knew, or pretended to know, nothing. But she liked to discuss it at length in so far as other men were concerned, whether because she saw in this a sort of indirect excuse for Robert or because he, divided like his uncle between an austere silence with regard to the subject and a need to let himself go and talk slander, had opened her eyes in many directions. M. de Charlus was one of those who were not spared, doubtless because Robert, without mentioning Charlie to Gilberte, could not help, when he was with her, repeating in one form or another what the violinist had told him; and the latter pursued his former benefactor with unrelenting hate. These conversations, and Gilberte's evident liking for them, gave me a chance to ask her whether, in a parallel category, Albertine, whose name I had first heard from Gilberte herself when they were attending the same classes, had comparable tastes. Gilberte could not give me any information on this point. And in any case it had long ceased to be of interest to me. But I continued to make inquiries mechanically, as an old man with a failing memory from time to time asks for news of the son he has lost.

What is odd, though I cannot here enlarge upon the topic, is the degree to which, at that time, all the people whom Albertine loved, all those who might have been able to persuade her to do what they wanted, asked, entreated, I will even say begged to be allowed to have, if not my friendship, at least some sort of acquaintance with me. No longer should I have had to offer money to Mme Bontemps as an inducement to send Albertine back to me. But this turn of fortune's wheel, taking place when it was no longer of the slightest use, merely saddened me profoundly, not because of Albertine, whom I would have received without pleasure had she been brought back not from Touraine but from the other world, but because of a young woman with whom I was in love and whom I could not contrive to meet. I told myself that, if she died, or if I no longer loved her, all those who might have brought us together would suddenly be at my feet. Meanwhile, I tried in vain to work upon them, not having been cured by experience, which ought to have taught me—if ever it taught anybody anything—that loving is like an evil spell in a fairy-story against which one is powerless until the enchantment has passed.

"As a matter of fact the book I'm reading at the moment talks about that sort of thing," Gilberte said to me. "It is an old Balzac which I am swotting up so as to be as well-informed as my uncles, *La Fille aux Yeux d'Or*. But it is absurd, improbable, nightmarish. For one thing, I suppose a woman might be kept under surveillance in that way by another woman, but surely not by a man." "You are wrong, I once knew a woman who was loved by a man who in the end literally imprisoned her; she was never allowed to see anybody, she could only go out with trusted servants." "Well, you who are so kind must be horrified at the idea. By the way, we were saying, Robert and I, that you ought to get married. Your wife would improve your health and you would make her happy." "No, I have too bad a character." "How absurd!" "I mean it. Besides, I was engaged once. But I couldn't quite make up my mind to marry the girl—and anyhow she thought better of it herself, because of my undecided and cantankerous character." This was, in fact, the excessively simple light in which I regarded my adventure with Albertine, now that I saw it only from outside.

Back in my bedroom again, I thought sadly that I had not once been back to revisit Combray church, which seemed to be waiting for me amidst green foliage in a violet-tinted window. "Never mind," I said to myself, "that can wait for another year, if I don't die in the meanwhile," seeing no other possible obstacle but my own death and not envisaging that of the church which must, as I supposed, endure for centuries after my death as it had for centuries before my birth.

One day I spoke to Gilberte about Albertine, and asked her whether Albertine loved women. "Not in the least!" "But you used to say that you didn't approve of her." "I said that? No, I'm sure you're mistaken. In any case, if I said it—but you're wrong about that—what I was referring to was flirtations with young men. And anyhow, at her age, it probably didn't go very far." Did Gilberte say this in order to conceal from me that she herself—or so Albertine had told me—loved women and had made advances to Albertine? Or did she (for other people are often better informed about our life than we think) know that I had loved and been jealous of Albertine, and did she (since, though others may know more of the truth about us than we think, they may also stretch it too far and fall into the error of supposing too much, whereas we had hoped that they made the mistake of supposing nothing at all) imagine that this was still the case, was she, out of kindness, placing over my eyes that bandage with which we are always ready to blindfold the jealous? In any case, Gilberte's remarks, from the "disapproval" of the old days to the present certificate of respectability, were pursuing an opposite course to the statements of Albertine, who in the end had almost admitted some sort of relations with Gilberte. In this Albertine had astonished me, just as I had been astonished by what Andrée had told me, for with all the girls in the little band, if I had at first believed, before knowing them, in their perversity, I had come round to the view that my suspicions were false, as must often happen when one finds a virtuous girl, almost ignorant of the facts of love, in surroundings which one had wrongly supposed to be extremely depraved. Then later I had travelled the same road in the opposite direction, back to a belief in the truth of my original suspicions. But perhaps Albertine had told me this because she wanted to appear more experienced than she was and to dazzle me in Paris with the prestige of her depravity, as on the earlier occasion at Balbec with that of her virtue; or quite simply, when I had talked about women who loved women, had not wanted to appear not to know what I meant, just as, if Fourier or Tobolsk is mentioned in a conversation, one tries to look as if one understood even if one has no idea what they are. She had perhaps lived, though in proximity to Mlle Vinteuil's friend and to Andrée, yet separated from them by a watertight partition, so that they thought that she was "not one," and had perhaps only got to know about the subject later—in the spirit of a woman who marries a man of letters and tries to improve her mind—in order to please me by making herself capable of answering my questions, until the day when she realised that the questions were inspired by jealousy, when she had hastily gone into reverse. Unless it was Gilberte who was lying to me. It even occurred to me that it was because he had learnt from Gilberte, while flirting with her with an eye all the while on his real interests, that she did not altogether dislike women, that Robert had married her, hoping for pleasures which, since he now went elsewhere for them, he must have failed to obtain from her. None of these hypotheses was absurd, for with women like Odette's daughter or the girls of the little band there is such a diversity, such an accumulation of alternating if not actually simultaneous tastes, that they pass easily from an affair with a woman to a great love for a man, so that to define the real and dominating taste must always be difficult.

I did not want to borrow Gilberte's copy of *La Fille aux Yeux d'Or* as she was reading it herself. But she lent me to read in bed, on that last evening of my stay with her, a book which produced on me a strong but mixed impression, which did not, however, prove to be lasting. It was a newly published volume of the Journal of the Goncourts. And when, before putting out my candle, I read the passage which I am about to transcribe, my lack of talent for literature, of which I had had a presentiment long ago on the Guermantes way and which had been confirmed during the stay of which this was the last evening—one of those evenings before a departure when we emerge from the torpor of habits about to be broken and attempt to judge ourselves—struck me as something less to be regretted, since literature, if I was to trust the evidence of this book, had no very profound truths to reveal: and at the same time it seemed to me sad that literature was not what I had thought it to be. At the same time, the state of ill-health which was soon to shut me up in a sanatorium seemed to me also less to be regretted, if the beautiful things of which books speak were not more beautiful than what I had seen myself. And yet, by an odd contradiction, now that they were being spoken of in this book I had a desire to see them. Here are the pages that I read before fatigue closed my eyes . . .

"The day before yesterday Verdurin drops in here to carry me off to dine with him—Verdurin, former critic of the *Revue*, author of that book on Whistler in which the workmanship, the painterly coloration, of the American eccentric is interpreted sometimes with great delicacy by the lover of all the refinements, all the *prettinesses* of the painted canvas, that Verdurin is. And while I am getting dressed to accompany him, he treats me to a long narrative, almost at moments a timidly stammered confession, about his renunciation of writing immediately after his marriage to Fromentin's 'Madeleine,' a renunciation brought about, he says, by his addiction to morphine and which had the result, according to Verdurin, that most of the frequenters of his wife's drawing-room did not even know that her husband had ever been a writer and spoke to him of Charles Blanc, of Saint-Victor, of Sainte-Beuve, of Burty, as individuals to whom they considered him, Verdurin, altogether inferior. 'Now, you Goncourts, you know—and Gautier knew too—that my *Salons* were on a different plane from those pitiful *Maîtres d'Autrefois* which are deemed a master-piece in my wife's family.' Then, through a dusk in which, as we pass the towers of the Trocadéro, the last glimmer of a gleam of daylight makes them positively resemble those towers of red-currant jelly that pastry-cooks used to make, the conversation continues in the carriage on its way to the Quai Conti, where their mansion is, which its owner claims was once the mansion of the Venetian ambassadors and in which there is a room used as a smoking-room which Verdurin tells me was transported lock, stock and barrel, as in a tale of the *Arabian Nights*, from a celebrated *palazzo* whose name I forget, a *palazzo* boasting a well-head decorated with a Coronation of the Virgin which Verdurin main-tains is positively one of Sansovino's finest things and which now, he says, their guests find useful as a receptacle for cigar-ash. And upon my word, when we arrive, in the watery shimmer of a moonlight really just like that in which the paintings of the great age enwraps Venice, against which the silhouetted dome of the Institute makes one think of the Salute in Guardi's pictures, I have almost the illusion of looking out over the Grand Canal. And the illusion is preserved by the way in which the house is built so that from the first floor one cannot see the quay, and by the evocative remark of its owner, who affirms that the name of the Rue du Bac—the devil if ever I'd thought of it—comes from the ferry which once upon a time used to take an order of nuns, the Miramiones, across to attend services in Notre-Dame. A whole quarter which my childhood used idly to explore when my aunt de Courmont lived there, and which I am inspired to *re-love* by rediscovering, almost next door to the Verdurin mansion, the sign of 'Little Dunkirk,' one of the rare shops surviving elsewhere than in the crayon and wash vignettes of Gabriel de Saint-Aubin, to which the eighteenth-century connoisseur would come to pass a few leisure moments in cheapening trinkets French and foreign and 'all the newest products of the arts,' as an invoice of this Little Dunkirk puts it, an invoice of which we two, Verdurin and myself, are, I believe, alone in possessing copies, one of those flimsy masterpieces of engraved paper upon which the reign of Louis XV made out its accounts, with a headpiece representing a billowy sea laden with vessels, a sea of billows which might be an illustration, in the Fermiers Généraux La Fontaine, to 'The Oyster and the Litigants.' The mistress of the house, who has placed me next to her at dinner, graciously tells me before we go in that she has decked out her table with nothing but Japanese chrysanthemums—but chrysanthemums displayed in vases which are the rarest masterpieces, one in particular of bronze on which petals of red-gold copper seem to have been shed by the living flower. Cottard, the doctor, is there, his wife, the Polish sculptor Viradobetski, Swann the collector, and an aristocratic Russian lady, a princess with a name ending in -off which I fail to catch (Cottard whispers in my ear that she is the woman who is supposed to have fired point-blank at the Archduke Rudolf), according to whom in Galicia and the whole of the north of Poland my reputation stands extraordinarily high, no young girl ever giving her consent to an offer of marriage without first ascertaining whether her fiancé is an admirer of *La Faustin*. 'You cannot understand that, you western Europeans'—this is thrown in as a sort of coda by the Princess, who, upon my word, strikes me as a person of a really superior intelligence—'that penetration by a writer of a woman's most intimate feelings.' A man with a close-shaven chin and lip and the side-whiskers of a butler, rolling out in a condescending tone the witticisms of a fifth-form school-master unbending among his prize pupils on the feast of St Charlemagne—this is Brichot, of the university. I am introduced to him by Verdurin but he utters not a word of reference to our books, and I am filled with a mixture of discouragement and anger at this conspiracy organised against us by the Sorbonne, which brings even into this pleasant dwelling where I am received as an honoured guest the contradiction, the hostility, of deliberate silence. We go in to dinner, and there follows an extraordinary cavalcade of plates which are nothing less than masterpieces of the porcelainist's art, that artist whose chatter, during an exquisite meal, is heard with more pleasure than any fellow-guest's by the titillated attention of the connoisseur—Yung-cheng plates with nasturtium-coloured borders and purple-blue irises, leafless and tumid, and those supremely decorative flights of kingfishers and cranes trailing across a dawn sky, a dawn that has just the early-morning tones glimpsed daily from Boulevard Montmorency by my awakening eyes—Dresden plates daintier and of more graceful workmanship, with drowsy, bloodless roses fading into violet, with ragged-edged tulips the colour of wine-lees, with the rococo elegance of a pink or a forget-me-not—Sèvres plates meshed with the close guilloche of their white fluting, whorled in gold, or knotted with a golden ribbon that stands in gallant relief upon the creamy smoothness of the paste—finally a whole service of silver plate arabesqued with those myrtles of Luciennes that were not unknown to the du Barry. And what is perhaps equally rare is the truly quite remarkable quality of the things served upon these plates, a meal most subtly concocted, a real spread such as Parisians, one cannot say it too emphatically, never have at their really grand dinner-parties and which reminds me of certain prize dishes of Jean d'Heurs. Even the foie gras bears no resemblance to the insipid mousse customarily served under that name; and I do not know many places in which a simple potato salad is made as it is here with potatoes firm as Japanese ivory buttons and patina'd like those little ivory spoons with which Chinese women sprinkle water over their new-caught fish. Into the Venetian glass which I have before me is poured, like a rich cascade of red jewels, an extraordinary Léoville bought at M. Montalivet's sale, and it is a delight to the imagination of the eye and also, I am not afraid to say it, of what used to be called the gullet, to see a brill placed before us which has nothing in common with those anything but fresh brills that are served at the most luxurious tables, which in the slow course of their journey from the sea have had the pattern of their bones imprinted upon their backs; a brill that is served not with the sticky paste prepared under the name of white sauce by so many chefs in great houses, but with a genuine white sauce, made with butter that costs five francs a pound; to see this brill brought in on a wonderful Chinese dish streaked with the purple rays of a sun setting above a sea upon which ludicrously sails a flotilla of large lobsters, their spiky stippling rendered with such extraordinary skill that they seem to have been moulded from living shells, with a border too depicting a little Chinese who plays with rod and line a fish whose silver and azure belly makes it a marvel of iridescent colour. When I remark to Verdurin what an exquisite pleasure it must be for him to eat this choice grub off a collection such as no prince today possesses in his show cases: 'It is easy to see that you don't know him,' gloomily interjects the mistress of the house. And she speaks to me of her husband as of an original and a crank, indifferent to all these dainties, 'a crank,' she repeats, 'yes, that is the only word for it,' a crank who would get more enjoyment from a bottle of cider drunk in the somewhat plebeian coolness of a Normandy farm. And this charming woman, whose speech betrays her positive adoration of local colouring, talks with over-flowing enthusiasm of the Normandy in which they once lived, a Normandy, so she says, like an immense English park, with the fragrance of tall woodlands that Lawrence might have painted, with the cryptomeria-coloured velvet of natural lawns bordered with the porcelain of pink hydrangeas, with crumpled sulphur-roses which, as they cascade over a cottage-door, above which the incrustation of two entwined pear-trees has the effect of a purely decorative sign over a shop, make one think of the free arabesque of a flowery branch of bronze in a candle-bracket by Gouthière, a Normandy absolutely unsuspected by the Parisian holiday-makers, protected by the iron gates of each of its little properties, gates which the Verdurins confessed to me that they did not scruple to open one and all. At the end of the day, in the drowsy extinguishment of all colours, when the only light was from an almost curdled sea, blue-white like whey ('No, not in the least like the sea you know,' frantically protests my neighbour, when I start to tell her that Flaubert once took us, my brother and me, to Trouville, 'not the slightest bit, you must come with me, other-wise you will never find out'), they would go home, through the forests—absolute forests abloom with pink tulle—of the great rhododendrons, quite drunk with the smell of the sardine fisheries which gave her husband terrible attacks of asthma—'Yes,' she insists, 'I mean it, real attacks of asthma.' Thereupon, the follow-ing summer, they returned, lodging a whole colony of artists in an old cloister which they rented for next to nothing, and which made an admirable mediaeval abode. And upon my word, as I listen to this woman who, in passing through so many social circles of real distinction, has nevertheless preserved in her speech a little of the freshness and freedom of language of a woman of the people, a language which shows you things with the colour which your imagination sees in them, my mouth waters at the life which she avows to me they lived down there, each one working in his cell and the whole party assembling before luncheon, in a drawing-room so vast that it had two fireplaces, for really intelligent conversation interspersed with parlour games, a life which makes me think of the one we read of in that masterpiece of Diderot, the *Lettres à Mademoiselle Volland*. Then, after luncheon, they would all go out, even on the days when the weather was unsettled, in a brief burst of sunshine or the diffused radiance of a shower, a shower whose filtered light sharpened the knotted outlines of a magnificent avenue of century-old beeches which began just behind the house and brought almost up to the iron grill that vegetable embodiment of 'the beautiful' so dear to eighteenth-century taste, and of the ornamental trees which held suspended in their branches not buds about to flower but drops of rain. They would stop to listen to the delicate splish-splash of a bullfinch, enamoured of coolness, bathing itself in the tiny dainty Nymphenburg bath made for it by the corolla of a white rose. And when I mention to Mme Verdurin Elstir's delicate pastel sketches of the landscapes and the flowers of that coast: 'But it is through me that he discovered all those things,' she bursts out, with an angry toss of the head, 'all of them, yes, all, make no mistake about it, the interesting spots, every one of his subjects—I threw it in his teeth when he left us, didn't I, Gustave?—every one of the subjects he has painted. *Things* he has always known about, there one must be fair, one must admit that. But as for flowers, he had never seen any, he couldn't tell a mallow from a hollyhock. It was I who taught him—you won't believe this—to recognise jasmine.' And one must admit that it is a curious thought that the artist who is cited by connoisseurs today as our leading flower-painter, superior even to Fantin-Latour, would perhaps never, without the help of the woman sitting beside me, have known how to paint jasmine. 'Yes, honestly, jasmine. And all the roses he has done have been painted in my house, or else it was I who took them to him. Among us he was always known simply as Monsieur Tiche; ask Cottard, ask Brichot, ask anybody here, whether we treated him as a great man. He would have laughed at the idea himself. I taught him to arrange his flowers; at first he couldn't manage it at all. He never learnt how to make a bouquet. He had no natural taste in selecting, I had to say to him: "No, don't paint that, that's no good, paint this." Ah! if he had listened to us about the arrangement of his life as he did about the arrangement of his flowers, and hadn't made that vile marriage!' And of a sudden, her eyes feverish from her absorption in thoughts of the past, plucking nervously at the silk sleeves of her bodice as she frenziedly tenses her fingers, she presents, in the distortion of her grief-stricken pose, an admirable picture which has, I think, never been painted, a picture in which one would see portrayed all the restrained revolt, all the passionate susceptibilities of a female friend outraged in the delicate feelings, the modesty of a woman. Thereupon she talks about the admirable portrait which Elstir did for her, the portrait of the Cottard family, which she gave to the Luxembourg at the time of her quarrel with the painter, confessing that it was she who gave him the idea of painting the man in dress-clothes in order to get all that splendid ebullition of fine linen, and she who chose the woman's velvet gown which forms a solid mass amid all the glitter of the bright tones of the carpets, the flowers, the fruit, the little girls' muslin dresses that look like dancers' tutus. It was she too, she tells me, who gave him the idea of the woman brushing her hair, an idea for which the artist was subsequently much praised and which consisted simply in painting her not as if she were on show but surprised in the intimacy of her everyday life. '"In a woman doing her hair," I used to say to him, "or wiping her face, or warming her feet, when she thinks she is not observed, there is a multitude of interesting movements, movements of a grace and charm that are positively Leonardesque!"' But at a sign from Verdurin indicating that the revival of these old indignations is dangerous for the health of his wife, who is really a mass of nerves, Swann points out to me the wonderful necklace of black pearls which the mistress of the house is wearing, which she bought, as a necklace of white pearls, at the sale of a descendant of Mme de La Fayette, to whom they were given by Henrietta of England, and which became black as the result of a fire which destroyed part of a house which the Verdurins had in a street whose name I do not remember, after which fire the casket containing these pearls was found, with the pearls completely black inside it. 'And I know the portrait of these pearls, on the shoulders of Mme de La Fayette herself, yes, positively their portrait,' insists Swann, checking the exclamations of the somewhat dumbfounded guests, 'their authentic portrait, in the collection of the Duc de Guermantes.'

A collection which has not its equal in the world, proclaims Swann, and which I ought to go and see, a collection inherited by the celebrated Duke, who was her favourite nephew, from his aunt Mme de Beausergent, who afterwards became Mme d'Hatzfeldt and was the sister of the Marquise de Villeparisis and of the Princess of Hanover, in whose house years ago my brother and I became so fond of him under the guise of the charming infant known as Basin, which is indeed the Duke's first name. Thereupon Doctor Cottard, with that keen intelligence which shows him to be a man of real distinction, harks back to the story of the pearls and informs us that catastrophes of this kind can produce changes in people's brains which are just like those that may be observed in inanimate matter, and, discoursing in a philosophical vein well beyond the powers of most doctors, quotes as an example Mme Verdurin's own valet, who from the terrible shock of this fire in which he very nearly lost his life became a changed man, with a handwriting so altered that when his master and mistress, then in Normandy, first received a letter from him with the news of the fire, they thought that someone was playing a practical joke upon them. And not only an altered handwriting, according to Cottard, who maintains that this man, hitherto always sober, became such an abominable sot that Mme Verdurin was obliged to get rid of him. And the Doctor's stimulating dissertation passes, upon a gracious sign from the mistress of the house, from the dining-room to the Venetian smoking-room, where he tells us that he has witnessed cases of what can only be called dual personality, citing as an instance one of his patients, whom he is so kind as to offer to bring to my house, whose temples he only has to touch, so he says, to awaken him to a second life, a life during which he remembers nothing of his first life and so different that, while he behaves most respectably in the first, he has more than once been arrested for thefts committed in the second, in which he is nothing more nor less than an abominable scoundrel. Whereupon Mme Verdurin acutely observes that medical science could provide the theatre with truer themes than those now in favour, themes in which the comicality of the plot would be based upon misunderstandings of a pathological kind, and this, by a natural transition, leads Mme Cottard to say that a very similar subject has been employed by a story-teller who is her children's favourite at bedtime, the Scotsman Stevenson, a name which brings from Swann the peremptory statement: 'But he is a really great writer, Stevenson, I assure you, M. de Goncourt, a very great writer, equal to the greatest.' Next, after I have admired the ceiling of the room where we are smoking, with its escutcheoned coffers from the old Barberini palace, when I intimate my regret at the progressive blackening of a certain stone basin by the ash of our 'Havanas' and Swann remarks that similar stains on books from the library of Napoleon which are now, despite his anti-Bonapartist opinions, in the possession of the Duc de Guermantes, bear witness to the fact that the Emperor chewed tobacco, Cottard, who evinces a truly penetrating curiosity in all things, declares that the stains do not come from that at all—'No, no, no, not at all,' he insists with authority—but from the habit the Emperor had of always, even on the field of battle, clutching in his hand the liquorice tablets which he took to relieve the pain in his liver. 'For he had a disease of the liver and that is what he died of,' concludes the Doctor."

There I stopped, for I was leaving the next morning; and besides it was the hour at which I was habitually summoned by that other master in whose service we spend, every day, a part of our time. The task which he assigns to us we accomplish with our eyes closed. Every morning he hands us back to the master who shares us with him, knowing that, unless he did so, we should be remiss in his own service. Curious, when our intelligence reopens its eyes, to know what we can have done under this master who first makes his slaves lie down and then puts them to work at full speed, the most artful among us try, the moment their task is finished, to take a covert glance. But sleep is racing against them to obliterate the traces of what they would like to see. And after all these centuries we still know very little about the matter.

I closed the Journal of the Goncourts. Prestige of literature! I wished I could have seen the Cottards again, asked them all sorts of details about Elstir, gone to look at the shop called Little Dunkirk, if it still existed, asked permission to visit the Verdurin mansion where I had once dined. But I felt vaguely depressed. Certainly, I had never concealed from myself that I knew neither how to listen nor, once I was not alone, how to look. My eyes were blind to the sort of necklace an old woman might be wearing, and the things I might be told about her pearls never entered my ears. All the same, I had known these people in daily life, I had dined with them often, they were simply the Verdurins and the

Duc de Guermantes and the Cottards, and each one of them I had found just as commonplace as my grandmother had found that Basin of whom she had no suspicion that he was the darling nephew, the enchanting young hero, of Mme de Beausergent, each one of them had seemed to me insipid; I could remember the vulgarities without number of which each of them was composed . . .

And that all this should make a star in the night![17]

But provisionally I decided to ignore the objections against literature raised in my mind by the pages of Goncourt which I had read on the evening before I left Tansonville. Even without taking into account the manifest naïvety of this particular diarist, I could in any case reassure myself on various counts. First, in so far as my own character was concerned, my incapacity for looking and listening, which the passage from the Journal had so painfully illustrated to me, was nevertheless not total. There was in me a personage who knew more or less how to look, but it was an intermittent personage, coming to life only in the presence of some general essence common to a number of things, these essences being its nourishment and its joy. Then the personage looked and listened, but at a certain depth only, without my powers of superficial observation being enhanced. Just as a geometer, stripping things of their sensible qualities, sees only the linear substratum beneath them, so the stories that people told escaped me, for what interested me was not what they were trying to say but the manner in which they said it and the way in which this manner revealed their character or their foibles; or rather I was interested in what had always, because it gave me specific pleasure, been more particularly the goal of my investigations: the point that was common to one being and another. As soon as I perceived this my intelligence—until that moment slumbering, even if sometimes the apparent animation of my talk might disguise from others a profound intellectual torpor—at once set off joyously in pursuit, but its quarry then, for instance the identity of the Verdurin drawing-room in various places and at various times, was situated in the middle distance, behind actual appearances, in a zone that was rather more withdrawn. So the apparent, copiable charm of things and people escaped me, because I had not the ability to stop short there—I was like a surgeon who beneath the smooth surface of a woman's belly sees the internal disease which is devouring it. If I went to a dinner-party I did not see the guests: when I thought I was looking at them, I was in fact examining them with X-rays.

The result was that, when all the observations I had succeeded in making about the guests during the party were linked together, the pattern of the lines I had traced took the form of a collection of psychological laws in which the actual purport of the remarks of each guest occupied but a very small space. But did this take away all merit from my portraits, which in fact I did not intend as such? If, in the realm of painting, one portrait makes manifest certain truths concerning volume, light, movement, does that mean that it is necessarily inferior to another completely different portrait of the same person, in which a thousand details omitted in the first are minutely transcribed, from which second portrait one would conclude that the model was ravishingly beautiful while from the first one would have thought him or her ugly, a fact which may be of documentary, even of historical importance, but is not necessarily an artistic truth?

Furthermore my frivolity, the moment I was not alone, made me eager to please, more eager to amuse by chattering than to acquire knowledge by listening, unless it happened that I had gone out into society in search of information about some particular artistic question or some jealous suspicion which my mind had previously been revolving. Always I was incapable of seeing any-thing for which a desire had not already been roused in me by something I had read, anything of which I had not myself traced in advance a sketch which I wanted now to confront with reality. How often—and I was well aware of this even without being apprised of it by these pages of Goncourt—have I remained incapable of bestowing my attention upon things or people that later, once their image has been presented to me in solitude by an artist, I would have travelled many miles, risked death to find again! Then and then only has my imagination been set in motion, has it begun to paint. And of something which a year before had made me yawn I have said to myself with anguish, longingly contemplating it in advance: "Shall I really be unable to see this thing? I would give anything for a sight of it!"

When one reads articles about people, perhaps mere fashionable people, who are described as "the last representatives of a society of which no eye-witness now exists," one may of course exclaim: "Fancy using such extravagant language about so insignificant a creature! This is what I should have lamented never having known if I had only read the newspapers and the monthly reviews and had not met the man!" But I was tempted rather, when I read such pages in the newspapers, to think: "How unfortunate that in those days when I was solely preoccupied with meeting Gilberte or Albertine again I did not pay more attention to this gentleman! I took him for a society bore, a mere dummy. On the contrary he was a Distinguished Figure!" The pages of Goncourt which I had read made me regret this tendency of mine. For though I might have inferred from them that life teaches us to cheapen the value of a book, and shows us that what a writer extols was in fact worth very little, it was equally possible for me to come to the contrary conclusion, that reading teaches us to take a more exalted view of the value of life, a value at the time we did not know how to appreciate and of whose magnitude we have only become aware through the book. We may, without too much difficulty, console ourselves for having taken little pleasure in the society of a Vinteuil, a Bergotte. But the prudish respectability of the one, the intolerable defects of the other, even the pretentious vulgarity of an Elstir in his early days—for I had discovered from the Goncourt Journal that he was none other than the "Monsieur Tiche" whose twaddle had once exasperated Swann in the Verdurins' drawing-room—prove nothing against them: their genius is manifested in their works. What man of genius has not in his conversation adopted the irritating mannerisms of the artists of his set, before attaining (as Elstir had eventually done, though this does not always happen) to a good taste that rises above them? Are not Balzac's letters, for instance, strewn with vulgar expressions which Swann would have suffered a thousand deaths rather than employ? Yet can one doubt that Swann, finely intelligent as he was, purged of all odious absurdities, would have been incapable of writing *La Cousine Bette* or *Le Curé de Tours*? As for the Vinteuils, the Bergottes, the Elstirs, the question whether it is we or the writers of memoirs who are at fault when they represent the society of these men as charming whereas we found it disagreeable, it is a question of slight importance, since even if our estimate were the correct one, this would be no argument against the value of a life that can produce such geniuses.

Right at the other pole of experience, when I saw that the most piquant anecdotes, which form the inexhaustible material of the Goncourt Journal and provide the reader with entertainment for many solitary evenings, had been related to the writer by these people whom he had met at dinner and who, though on the evidence of his pages we should certainly have wanted to meet them, had in my mind left no trace of any interesting recollection, that too was not altogether difficult to explain. In spite of the naïvety of Goncourt, who inferred from the interest of these anecdotes the probable distinction of the man who related them, it might well be that commonplace men had seen during their lives, or heard related, remarkable things which they in their turn had described. Goncourt knew how to listen, just as he knew how to see; I did not. Besides, all these facts needed to be considered and judged separately. Certainly M. de Guermantes had not given me the impression of that adorable model of the youthful graces which my grandmother so wished she had known and which she set before me, in the Memoirs of Mme de Beausergent, as an inimitable example. But one must remember that Basin was then seven years old, that the writer was his aunt, and that even a husband who within a few months will be suing for divorce will praise his wife to the skies. In one of his most delightful poems Sainte-Beuve describes an apparition beside a fountain—a little girl crowned with every gift and every grace, young Mlle de Champlâtreux, whose age at the time cannot have been ten. And in spite of all the affectionate respect which the poet of genius who is the Comtesse de Noailles bore for her husband's mother, the Duchesse de Noailles *née* Champlâtreux, one wonders whether, had she had occasion to portray her, the result might not have contrasted rather sharply with the portrait drawn by Sainte-Beuve fifty years earlier.

More puzzling perhaps were the people in between the two extremes, those in whom what the writer says of them implies more than a memory which has succeeded in retaining a piquant anecdote, with whom, nevertheless, one has not, as with the Vinteuils, the Bergottes, the resource of judging them on their work, for they have created none: they have only—to the great astonishment of us who found them so commonplace—inspired the work of others. I could, it is true, understand how the drawing-room which, seen on the walls of a museum, will give a greater impression of elegance than anything since the great paintings of the Renaissance, might be that of the ridiculous middle-class woman whom, had I not known her, I would have longed, as I stood before the picture, to be able to approach in reality, hoping to learn from her the most precious secrets of the painter's art which his canvas did not reveal to me, and how her lace and her stately train of velvet might have become a piece of painting as lovely as anything in Titian. For I had already realised long ago that it is not the man with the liveliest mind, the most well-informed, the best supplied with friends and acquaintances, but the one who knows how to become a mirror and in this way can reflect his life, commonplace though it may be, who becomes a Bergotte (even if his contemporaries once thought him less witty than Swann, less erudite than Bréauté), and could one not say as much, and with better reason, of a painter's models? The artist may paint anything in the world that he chooses, but when beauty is awakened within him, the model for that elegance in which he will find themes of beauty will be provided for him by people a little richer than he is himself, in whose house he will find what is not normally to be seen in the studio of an unrecognised man of genius selling his canvases for fifty francs: a drawing-room with chairs and sofas covered in old brocades, an abundance of lamps, beautiful flowers, beautiful fruit, beautiful dresses—people in a relatively modest position, or who would seem to be so to people of real social brilliance (who are not even aware of their existence), but who, for that reason, are more within reach of the obscure artist's acquaintance, more likely to appreciate him, to invite him, to buy his pictures, than men and women of the aristocracy who, like the Pope and Heads of State, get themselves painted by academicians. Will not posterity, when it looks at our time, find the poetry of an elegant home and beautifully dressed women in the drawing-room of the publisher Charpentier as painted by Renoir, rather than in the portraits of the Princesse de Sagan or the Comtesse de La Rochefoucauld by Cot or Chaplin? The artists who have given us the most splendid visions of elegance have gathered the materials for them from among people who were rarely the leaders of fashion in their age, for the leaders of fashion rarely commission pictures from the unknown bearer of a new type of beauty which they are unable to distinguish in his canvases, concealed as it is by the interposition of that formula of hackneyed charm which floats in the eye of the public like the subjective visions which a sick man supposes really to exist before his eyes. This, I say, I could understand; but that these commonplace models whom I had known should in addition have inspired and advised certain arrangements which had enchanted me, that the presence of one or another of them in a painting should be not merely that of a model but of a friend whom an artist wants to put into his pictures, this made me ask myself whether all the people whom we regret not having known because Balzac depicted them in his novels or dedicated books to them in homage and admiration, the people about whom Sainte-Beuve or Baudelaire wrote their loveliest poems, still more whether all the Récamiers, all the Pompadours, would not have seemed to me insignificant creatures, either owing to an infirmity of my nature, which, if it were so, made me furious at being ill and therefore unable to go back and see again all the people whom I had misjudged, or because they owed their prestige only to an illusory magic of literature, in which case I had been barking up the wrong tree and need not repine at being obliged almost any day now by the steady deterioration of my health to break with society, renounce travel and museums, and go to a sanatorium for treatment.

These ideas, tending on the one hand to diminish, and on the other to increase, my regret that I had no gift for literature, were entirely absent from my mind during the long years—in which I had in any case completely renounced the project of writing—which I spent far from Paris receiving treatment in a sanatorium, until there came a time, at the beginning of 1916, when it could no longer get medical staff. I then returned to a Paris very different from the city to which, as we shall see presently, I had come back once before in August 1914 for a medical consultation, after which I had withdrawn again to my sanatorium.

On one of the first evenings of my second return, in 1916, wanting to hear people talk about the only thing that interested me at the time, the war, I went out after dinner to call on Mme Verdurin, who was, with Mme Bontemps, one of the queens of this wartime Paris which made one think of the Directory. As if by the germination of a tiny quantity of yeast, apparently of spontaneous generation, young women now went about all day with tall cylindrical turbans on their heads, as a contemporary of Mme Tallien's might have done, and from a sense of patriotic duty wore Egyptian tunics, straight and dark and very "war," over very short skirts; they wore thonged footwear recalling the buskin as worn by Talma, or else long gaiters recalling those of our dear boys at the front; it was, so they said, because they did not forget that it was their duty to rejoice the eyes of these "boys at the front," that they still decked themselves of an evening not only in flowing dresses, but in jewellery which suggested the army by its choice of decorative themes, when indeed the actual material from which it was made did not come from, had not been wrought in the army; for instead of Egyptian ornaments recalling the campaign in Egypt, the fashion now was for rings or bracelets made out of fragments of exploded shells or copper bands from 75 millimetre ammunition, and for cigarette-lighters constructed out of two English pennies to which a soldier, in his dug-out, had succeeded in giving a patina so beautiful that the profile of Queen Victoria looked as if it had been drawn by the hand of Pisanello; and it was also because they never stopped thinking of the dear boys, so they said, that when one of their own kin fell they scarcely wore mourning for him, on the pretext that "their grief was mingled with pride," which permitted them to wear a bonnet of white English crêpe (a bonnet with the most charming effect, "authorising every hope" and "inspired by an invincible confidence in final victory") and to replace the cashmere of former days by satin and chiffon, and even to keep their pearls, "while observing the tact and propriety of which there is no need to remind Frenchwomen."

The Louvre and all the other museums were closed, and when one saw at the head of an article in a newspaper the words: "A sensational exhibition," one could be sure that the exhibition in question was not one of paintings but of dresses, of dresses moreover which aimed at reviving "those refined joys of art of which the women of Paris have for too long been deprived." So it was that fashion and pleasure had returned, fashion, in the absence of the arts, apologising for its survival as the arts had done in 1793, in which year the artists exhibiting in the revolutionary Salon proclaimed that, though "stern Republicans might find it strange that we should occupy ourselves with the arts when Europe united in coalition is besieging the soil of liberty," they would be wrong. The same sort of thing was said in 1916 by the dressmakers, who, with the self-conscious pride of artists, affirmed that "to create something new, to get away from banality, to assert an individual character, to prepare for victory, to evolve for the post-war generations a new formula of beauty, such was the ambition that tormented them, the chimera that they pursued, as would be apparent to anyone who cared to visit their salons, delightfully installed in the Rue de la . . ., where to efface by a note of luminous gaiety the heavy sadness of the hour seems to be the watchword, with the discretion, naturally, that circumstances impose."

"The sadness of the hour"—it was true—"might prove too strong for feminine energies, were it not that we have so many lofty examples of courage and endurance to contemplate. So, as we think of our warriors dreaming in their trenches of more comfort and more pretty things for the girl they have left behind them, we shall not pause in our ever more strenuous efforts to create dresses that answer to the needs of the moment. The vogue"—and what could be more natural?—"is for the fashion-houses of our English allies, and the rage this year is the barrel-dress, which, with its charming informality, gives us all an amusing little cachet of rare distinction. We may even say that one of the happiest consequences of this sad war will be," added the delight-ful chronicler (and one expected: "the return of our lost pro-vinces" or "the reawakening of national sentiment")—"one of the happiest consequences of this sad war will be that we have achieved some charming results in the realm of fashion, without ill-considered and unseemly luxury, with the simplest materials, that we have created prettiness out of mere nothings. To the dresses of the great designers, reproduced in a number of copies, women prefer just now dresses made at home, which affirm the intelligence, the taste and the personal preferences of the indi-vidual."

As for charity, the thought of all the miseries that had sprung from the invasion, of all the wounded and disabled, meant natur-ally that it was obliged to develop forms "more ingenious than ever before," and this meant that the ladies in tall turbans were obliged to spend the latter part of the afternoon at "teas" round a bridge-table, discussing the news from the "front," while their cars waited at the door with a handsome soldier in the driver's seat who chatted to the footman. It was, moreover, not only the headdresses with their strange cylinders towering above the ladies' faces that were new. The faces were new themselves. These ladies in new-fangled hats were young women who had come one did not quite know from where and had been the flower of fashion, some for six months, others for two years, others for four. And these differ-ences were of as much importance for them as had been, at the time when I took my first steps in society, for two families like the Guermantes and the La Rochefoucaulds a difference of three or four centuries of proven antiquity. The lady who had known the

Guermantes since 1914 looked upon the lady who had been introduced to them in 1916 as an upstart, greeted her with the air of a dowager, quizzed her with her lorgnette, and admitted with a little grimace that no one even knew for certain whether or no she was married. "It is all rather nauseating," concluded the lady of 1914, who would have liked the cycle of new admissions to have come to a halt after herself. These new ladies, whom the young men found pretty ancient and whom, also, certain elderly men, who had not moved exclusively in the best circles, thought that they recognised as being not so new as all that, did not merely recommend themselves to society by offering it its favourite amusements of political conversation and music in intimate sur-roundings; part of their appeal was that it was *they* who offered these amenities, for in order that things should appear new even if they are old—and indeed even if they are new—there must in art, as in medicine and in fashion, be new names. (New names indeed there were in certain spheres. For instance, Mme Verdurin had visited Venice during the war, but—like those people who cannot bear sad talk or display of personal feelings—when she said that "it" was "marvellous" she was referring not to Venice, or St Mark's, or the palaces, all that I had so loved and she thought so unimportant, but to the effect of the searchlights in the sky, of which searchlights she could give you a detailed account sup-ported by statistics. So from age to age is reborn a certain realism which reacts against what the previous age has admired.)

The Saint-Euverte salon was a faded banner now, and the presence beneath it of the greatest artists, the most influential ministers, would have attracted nobody. But people would run to listen to the secretary of one of these same artists or a subordin-ate official of one of the ministers holding forth in the houses of the new turbaned ladies whose winged and chattering invasion filled Paris. The ladies of the first Directory had a queen who was young and beautiful and was called Mme Tallien. Those of the second had two, who were old and ugly and were called Mme Verdurin and Mme Bontemps. Who could now hold it against Mme Bontemps that in the Dreyfus Affair her husband had played a role which the *Echo de Paris* had sharply criticised? The whole Chamber having at a certain moment become revisionist, it was inevitably from among former revisionists—and also from among former socialists—that the party of social order, of religious toler-ance, of military preparedness, had been obliged to enlist its recruits. Time was when M. Bontemps would have been abominated, because then the antipatriots bore the name of Dreyfusards. But presently this name had been forgotten and replaced by that of "opponent of the law of three years' military service." M. Bontemps, far from being its opponent, was one of the sponsors of this law; consequently he was a patriot.

In society (and this social phenomenon is merely a particular case of a much more general psychological law) novelties, whether blameworthy or not, excite horror only so long as they have not been assimilated and enveloped by reassuring elements. It was the same with Dreyfusism as with that marriage between Saint-Loup and the daughter of Odette which had at first produced such an outcry. Now that "everybody one knew" was seen at the parties given by the Saint-Loups, Gilberte might have had the morals of Odette herself but people would have "gone there" just the same and would have thought it quite right that she should disapprove like a dowager of any moral novelties that had not been assimilated. Dreyfusism was now integrated in a scheme of respectable and familiar things. As for asking oneself whether intrinsically it was good or bad, the idea no more entered anybody's head, now when it was accepted, than in the past when it was condemned. It was no longer *shocking* and that was all that mattered. People hardly remembered that it had once been thought so, just as, when a certain time has elapsed, they no longer know whether a girl's father was a thief or not. One can always say, if the subject crops up: "No, it's the brother-in-law, or someone else with the same name, that you're thinking of. There has never been a breath of scandal about her father." In the same way, there had undeniably been Dreyfusism and Dreyfusism, and a man who was received by the Duchesse de Montmorency and was helping to pass the three years law could not be bad. And then, as the saying goes, no sin but should find mercy. If Dreyfusism was accorded an amnesty, so, *a fortiori*, were Dreyfusards. In fact, there no longer were Dreyfusards in politics, since at one moment every politician had been one if he wanted to belong to the government, even those who represented the contrary of what at the time of its shocking novelty—the time when Saint-Loup had been getting into bad ways—Dreyfusism had incarnated: anti-patriotism, irreligion, anarchy, etc. So the Dreyfusism of M. Bontemps, invisible and constitutional like that of every other politician, was no more apparent than the bones beneath the skin. No one troubled to remember that he had been a Dreyfusard, for people in society are scatterbrained and forgetful and, besides, all *that* had been a very long time ago, a "time" which these people affected to think longer than it was, for one of the ideas most in vogue was that the pre-war days were separated from the war by something as profound, something of apparently as long a duration, as a geological period, and Brichot himself, that great nationalist, when he alluded to the Dreyfus case now talked of "those prehistoric days."

(The truth is that this profound change wrought by the war was in inverse ratio to the quality of the minds which it affected, at least above a certain level. At the very bottom of the scale the really stupid people, who lived only for pleasure, did not bother about the fact that there was a war. But, at the other end of the scale too, people who have made for themselves a circumambient interior life usually pay small regard to the importance of events. What profoundly modifies their system of thought is much more likely to be something that in itself seems to have no importance, something that reverses the order of time for them by making them contemporaneous with another epoch in their lives. And that this is so we may see in practice from the beauty of the writing which is inspired in this particular way: the song of a bird in the park at Montboissier, or a breeze laden with the scent of mignonette, are obviously phenomena of less consequence than the great events of the Revolution and the Empire; but they inspired Chateaubriand to write pages of infinitely greater value in his *Mémoires d'Outre-tombe*.) The words Dreyfusard and anti-Dreyfusard no longer had any meaning then. But the very people who said this would have been dumbfounded and horrified if one had told them that probably in a few centuries, or perhaps even sooner, the word Boche would have only the curiosity value of such words as *sans-culotte*, *chouan* and *bleu*.

Things had altered so little that people still found it quite natural to use the old catchwords "right-minded" and "not right-minded." And yet change of a kind there was, for, just as former partisans of the Commune had at a later date been against a retrial, so now the most extreme Dreyfusards of the old days wanted to shoot people right and left, and the generals supported them in this policy just as they had supported Galliffet's opponents at the time of the Affair.

M. Bontemps did not want there to be any question of peace until Germany had been broken up into tiny states as it had been in the Middle Ages, the fall of the House of Hohenzollern pronounced, and the Kaiser stood up against a wall and shot. In a word he was what Brichot called a *jusqu'au-boutiste*, and this was the highest certificate of patriotism that could be conferred upon him. Doubtless for the first three days Mme Bontemps had been a little bewildered in the midst of the people who had asked Mme Verdurin to introduce them to her, and it was in a tone of some slight asperity that Mme Verdurin had replied: "No, my dear, the Comte," when Mme Bontemps said to her "That was the Duc d'Haussonville you introduced to me just now, wasn't it?", either out of total ignorance and failure to associate the name Haussonville with any title whatsoever or, on the contrary, from excess of information and an association of ideas with the "Party of the Dukes," to which she had been told that in the Academy M. d'Haussonville belonged. But by the fourth day she had begun to be firmly installed in the Faubourg Saint-Germain. Sometimes there could still be seen around her the nameless fragments of a world that one did not know, which, in those who knew the egg from which Mme Bontemps had emerged, evoked no more surprise than the debris of shell around a chick. But after a fortnight she had shaken them off, and before the end of the first month, when she said: "I am going to the Lévis'," everybody understood, without her having to explain herself, that it was the Lévis-Mirepoix she meant, and not a duchess would have gone to bed without having inquired of Mme Bontemps or Mme Verdurin, at least by telephone, what there had been in the evening communiqué, what had been deliberately left out, how the Greek situation was developing, what offensive was being prepared, in a word all the news that the public would know only on the following day or later but of which the two ladies staged the equivalent of a dressmaker's private view. In conversation, when she was announcing news, Mme Verdurin would say "we" when she meant France. "Now listen: we demand of the King of Greece that he should withdraw from the Peloponnese, etc.; we send him, etc." And in all her stories there was constant mention of GHQ ("I telephoned to GHQ"), an abbreviation which gave her, as it fell from her lips, the pleasure that in former days women who did not know the Prince d'Agrigente had got from asking with a smile, when his name was mentioned, so as to show that they were in the swim: "Grigri?", a pleasure which in untroubled times is confined to the fashionable world but in great crises comes within the reach of the lower classes. Our butler, for instance, if the King of Greece was mentioned, was able, thanks to the newspapers, to say like the Kaiser Wilhelm: "Tino?", whereas hitherto his familiarity with kings had been of his own invention and of a more plebeian kind, as when at one time he had been in the habit of referring to the King of Spain as "Fonfonse." Another noticeable change was that, as more and more smart people made advances to Mme Verdurin, inversely the number of those whom she dubbed "bores" diminished. By a sort of magical transformation, every bore who had come to call on her and asked to be invited to her parties immediately became a charming and intelligent person. In short, at the end of a year, the number of bores had dwindled to such an extent that "the fear and awfulness of being bored," which had filled so large a place in the conversation and played so great a role in the life of Mme Verdurin, had almost entirely disappeared. In her latter days, it seemed, this awfulness of being bored (which anyhow, as she had formerly assured people, she had not known in her early youth) afflicted her less, just as certain kinds of migraine, certain nervous asthmatic conditions lose their force as one grows older. And the terror of being bored would doubtless, for want of bores, have entirely abandoned Mme Verdurin had she not, in some slight degree, replaced the vanishing bores by others recruited from the ranks of the former faithful.

Be that as it may, to conclude the subject of the duchesses who now frequented Mme Verdurin's house, they came, though they did not realise this, in search of exactly the same thing as the Dreyfusards had sought there in the old days, that is to say a social pleasure so compounded that their enjoyment of it at the same time assuaged their political curiosities and satisfied their need to discuss with others like themselves the incidents about which they had read in the newspapers. Mme Verdurin said: "Come at 5 o'clock to talk about the war" as she would have said in the past: "Come and talk about the Affair," or at an intermediate period: "Come to hear Morel."

Morel, incidentally, ought not to have been there, for the reason that he had not, as was supposed, been invalided out of the army. He had simply failed to rejoin his regiment and was a deserter, but nobody knew this.

One of the stars of the salon was "I'm a wash-out," who in spite of his sportive tastes had got himself exempted and whom I now thought of mainly as the author of remarkable works of art which were constantly in my thoughts. To such an extent had he assumed for me this new character that it was only by chance, when from time to time I established a transverse current linking two series of memories, that it crossed my mind that he was also the person who had brought about the departure of Albertine from my house. And even this transverse current ended, as far as these vestigial memories of Albertine were concerned, in a channel which petered out completely at a distance of several years from the present. For I never thought of her now. That was a channel of memories, a route, which I had quite ceased to take. Whereas the works of "I'm a wash-out" were recent and this route of memory was one perpetually visited and used by my mind.

I ought to say that the acquaintance of Andrée's husband was neither very easy nor very agreeable to make, and that any attempt to make friends with him was destined to numerous disappointments. He was, in fact, at this time already seriously ill and spared himself all fatigues except those which he thought likely to give him pleasure. Now in this category he included only meetings with people whom he did not yet know, whom his ardent imagination represented to him doubtless as being possibly different from others. When it came to people he was already acquainted with, he knew too well what they were like and what they would be like again and they no longer seemed to him worth the trouble of a fatigue that would be dangerous and might even be fatal to him. In short, he was a very poor friend. And perhaps in his taste for new people there was still something to be found of the frenzied daring which he had shown in the old days at Balbec, in sport, in gambling, in excesses of eating and drinking.

Whenever Andrée and I were there together Mme Verdurin tried to introduce me to her, being unable to accept the fact that we were already acquainted. Andrée did not often come with her husband, but she at least was an admirable and sincere friend to me. Faithful to the aesthetic ideas of her husband, who had reacted against the Russian Ballet, she was always saying of the Marquis de Polignac: "He's had his house decorated by Bakst. How can one sleep with all that round one? I would rather have Dubuffe." The Verdurins, too, swept along by the fatal progress of aestheticism which ends by eating its own tail, said now that they could not endure *art nouveau* (besides, it came from Munich) or white rooms; they cared only for old French furniture in a sombre colour-scheme.

I saw a lot of Andrée at this time. We did not know what to say to each other, and once there came into my mind that name, Juliette, which had risen from the depths of Albertine's memory like a mysterious flower. Mysterious then, but now it no longer stirred any feeling in me: many subjects that were indifferent to me I discussed but on this subject I was silent; not that it meant less to me than others, but a sort of supersaturation takes place when one has thought about a thing too much. Perhaps the epoch in my life when I saw so many mysteries in that name was the true one. But as these epochs will not last for ever, it is a mistake for a man to sacrifice his health and his fortune to the elucidation of mysteries which one day will no longer interest him.

Now that Mme Verdurin could get anyone she wanted to come to her house, people were very surprised to see her make indirect advances to someone she had completely lost sight of, Odette, the general opinion being that Odette could add nothing to the brilliant set that the little group had become. But a prolonged separation, which has the effect of appeasing resentments, in some cases also reawakens feelings of friendship. And then too the phenomenon of the dying man who pronounces none but familiar names from the past, or the old man who finds pleasure in his childhood memories, has its social equivalent. To succeed in the project of making Odette return to her, Mme Verdurin employed, naturally, not the "ultras" but the less faithful members of the group who had kept a foot in each of the two drawing-rooms. "I can't think why we no longer see her here," she said to them. "She may have fallen out with me, I haven't with her. After all, what harm have I done her? It was in my house that she met both her husbands. If she wants to come back, let her know that the door is open." These words, which would have involved a sacrifice of pride for the Mistress if they had not been dictated to her by her imagination, were passed on, but without success. Mme Verdurin waited in vain for Odette, until events which will come to our notice later brought about, for entirely different reasons, what the intercession of the "deserters," for all their zeal, had been unable to achieve. So rarely do we meet either with easy success or with irreversible defeat.

To these parties Mme Verdurin used to invite a few ladies of rather recent origin, known for their good works, who at first came magnificently dressed, with great pearl necklaces that Odette, who had a necklace just as beautiful the display of which she had herself formerly overdone, regarded, now that she was "dressed for war" in imitation of the ladies of the Faubourg, with some severity. But women know how to adapt themselves. After three or four appearances they realised that the clothes which they had thought smart were precisely the ones proscribed by people who were smart; they laid aside their gold dresses and resigned themselves to simplicity.

"It is too bad," Mme Verdurin would say. "I must telephone to Bontemps to get things put right for tomorrow, they have *blue-pencilled* the whole of the end of Norpois's article and just because he hinted that Percin had been *bowler-hatted*." For the idiocy of the times caused people to pride themselves on using the expressions of the times; in this way they hoped to show that they were in the fashion, like the middle-class woman who says, when M. de Bréauté or d'Agrigente or de Charlus is mentioned: "You mean Babal de Bréauté? Grigri? Mémé de Charlus?" As a matter of fact duchesses do this too, and duchesses felt the same pleasure in saying "bowler-hatted," for it is in their names that these ladies—for the commoner with a poetical imagination—are exceptional; in their language and their ideas they conform to the intellectual category to which they belong and to which also belong a vast number of middle-class people. The classes of the intellect take no account of birth.

All this telephoning that Mme Verdurin did was not, however, without its disadvantages. Although we have forgotten to mention the fact, the Verdurin "salon," if it continued to exist in spirit and in all essentials, had been temporarily transferred to one of the largest hotels in Paris, the lack of coal and light making it too difficult for the Verdurins to entertain in the former mansion of the Venetian ambassadors, which was extremely damp. But the new drawing-room was not altogether disagreeable. Just as, in Venice, the restrictions that water imposes upon a site dictate the shape of a palace, and in Paris a scrap of garden is more ravishing than a whole park in the country, so the narrow dining-room that Mme Verdurin had in the hotel, with the dazzling white walls of its irregular quadrilateral, made a sort of screen upon which figured every Wednesday, indeed almost every day of the week, all the most interesting men of every kind, all the smartest women in Paris, only too delighted to avail themselves of the luxury of the Verdurins, which went on increasing, with their wealth, at a time when other very rich people were economising, because part of their income was frozen. In their altered form the receptions had not ceased to enchant Brichot, who, as the circle of the Verdurins' acquaintance grew wider and wider, found in their parties ever new pleasures, packed tight together in a tiny space like surprises in a Christmas stocking. On some days the guests were so numerous that the dining-room of the private suite was too small and the dinner was given in the huge dining-room downstairs, where the faithful, if they feigned a hypocritical regret for the intimacy of upstairs, were at heart delighted—while keeping themselves to themselves, as in the old days on the little train—to be a spectacle and an object of envy for neighbouring tables. Doubtless, under normal peacetime conditions, a "society" note surreptitiously sent to *Le Figaro* or *Le Gaulois* would have informed a larger public than could be contained in the dining-room of the Majestic that Brichot had dined with the Duchesse de Duras. But since the war, the social reporters having suppressed this type of news (they made up for it, however, in funerals, "mentions in despatches" and Franco-American banquets), publicity could only be attained through a more embryonic, a more restricted medium, worthy of primitive ages and anterior to the discovery of Gutenberg: one had actually to be seen at Mme Verdurin's table. After dinner the guests went upstairs to the Mistress's reception-rooms, and then the telephoning began. But many large hotels were at this period peopled with spies, who duly noted the news announced over the telephone by Bontemps with an indiscretion which might have had serious consequences but for a fortunate lack of accuracy in his reports, which invariably were contradicted by events.

Before the hour at which the afternoon tea-parties came to an end, at the close of the day, in the still light sky one saw, far off, little brown dots which one might have taken, in the blue evening, for midges or birds. In the same way, when one sees a mountain at a great distance one can imagine it to be a cloud. But because one knows that this "cloud" is huge, solid and resistant one's emotions are stirred. And I too was moved by the thought that the brown dot in the summer sky was neither midge nor bird but an aeroplane with a crew of men keeping guard over Paris. (The memory of the aeroplanes which I had seen with Albertine on our last drive, near Versailles, played no part in this emotion, for the memory of that drive had become indifferent to me.)

When the time came for dinner, the restaurants were full; and if, passing in the street, I saw a wretched soldier on leave, escaped for six days from the constant danger of death and about to return to the trenches, halt his gaze for a moment upon the illuminated windows, I suffered as I had in the hotel at Balbec when fishermen used to watch us at dinner, but I suffered more now because I knew that the misery of the soldier is greater than that of the poor, since it combines in itself all miseries, and more touching still because more resigned, more noble, and because it was with a philosophical shake of the head, without hatred, that on the eve of setting out again for the war the soldier would say to himself, as he saw the shirkers jostling one another in their efforts to secure a table: "You'd never know there was a war on here." Then at half-past nine, before anyone had had time to finish dinner, the lights were all suddenly turned out because of the police regulations, so that at nine thirty-five the second jostling of shirkers snatching their overcoats from the page-boys of the restaurant where I had dined with Saint-Loup one evening when he was on leave took place in a mysterious half-darkness which might have been that of a room in which slides are being shown on a magic lantern, or of the auditorium, during the exhibition of a film, of one of those cinemas towards which the men and women who had been dining would presently rush.

But at any later hour for those who, like myself on the evening which I am going to describe, had had dinner at home and were going to see friends, Paris, at least in certain quarters, was even blacker than had been the Combray of my childhood; the visits that people paid one another were like the visits of country neighbours. Ah! if Albertine had been alive, how delightful it would have been, on the evenings when I had dined out, to arrange to meet her out of doors, under the arcades! At first I should have seen nothing, I should have had the pang of thinking that she had failed to turn up, when suddenly I should have seen one of her beloved grey dresses emerge from the black wall, then her smiling eyes which had already seen me, and we could have walked along with our arms round each other without any fear of being recognised or disturbed, and then at length gone home. But alas, I was alone and I felt as if I was setting out to pay a neighbourly visit in the country, like those that Swann used to pay us after dinner, without meeting more people on his way through the darkness of Tansonville, along the little tow-path and as far as the

Rue du Saint-Esprit, than I now met in the streets, transformed into winding rustic lanes, between Sainte-Clotilde and the Rue Bonaparte. Or again—since the effect of those fragments of landscape which travel in obedience to the moods of the weather was no longer nullified by surroundings which had become invisible—on evenings when the wind was chasing an icy shower of rain I had, now, much more strongly the impression of being on the shore of that raging sea of which I had once so longingly dreamed than I had had when I was actually at Balbec; and other natural features also, which had not existed in Paris hitherto, helped to create the illusion that one had just got out of the train and arrived to spend a holiday in the depth of the country: for example the contrast of light and shadow on the ground that one had all round one on evenings when the moon was shining. There were effects of moonlight normally unknown in towns, sometimes in the middle of winter even, when the rays of the moon lay outpoured upon the snow on the Boulevard Haussmann, untouched now by the broom of any sweeper, as they would have lain upon a glacier in the Alps. Against this snow of bluish gold the silhouettes of the trees were outlined clear and pure, with the delicacy that they have in certain Japanese paintings or in certain backgrounds of Raphael; and on the ground at the foot of the tree itself there was stretched out its shadow as often one sees trees' shadows in the country at sunset, when the light inundates and polishes to the smoothness of a mirror some meadow in which they are planted at regular intervals. But by a refinement of exquisite delicacy the meadow upon which were displayed these shadows of trees, light as souls, was a meadow of paradise, not green but of a whiteness so dazzling because of the moonlight shining upon the jade-like snow that it might have been a meadow woven entirely from petals of flowering pear-trees. And in the squares the divinities of the public fountains, holding a jet of ice in their hand, looked like statues wrought in two different materials by a sculptor who had decided to marry pure bronze to pure crystal. On these exceptional days all the houses were black. But in the spring, on the contrary, here and there, defying the regulations of the police, a private house, or simply one floor of a house, or even simply one room of one floor, had failed to close its shutters and appeared, mysteriously supported by dark impalpable shadows, to be no more than a projection of light, an apparition without substance. And the woman whom, if one raised one's eyes high above the street, one could distinguish in this golden penumbra, assumed, in this night in which one was oneself lost and in which she too seemed to be hidden away, the mysterious and veiled charm of an oriental vision. Then one passed on and nothing more interrupted the rustic tramp, wholesome and monotonous, of one's feet through the darkness.

I reflected that it was a long time since I had seen any of the personages who have been mentioned in this work. In 1914, it was true, during the two months that I had spent in Paris, I had caught a glimpse of M. de Charlus and seen something of Bloch and Saint-Loup, the latter only twice. The second occasion was certainly that on which he had been most himself; he had quite effaced that disagreeable impression of insincerity which he had made on me during the stay at Tansonville that I have described, and I had once more recognised in him all the fine qualities of his earlier days. On the earlier occasion, which was less than a week after the declaration of war, while Bloch made a display of the most chauvinistic sentiments, Saint-Loup, once Bloch had left us, was unashamedly cynical about the fact that he himself had not joined his regiment, and I had been almost shocked at the violence of his tone.

Saint-Loup had just come back from Balbec. I learnt later, indirectly, that he had made unsuccessful advances to the manager of the restaurant. The latter owed his position to the money he had inherited from M. Nissim Bernard. He was, in fact, none other than the young waiter whom in the past Bloch's uncle had "protected." But wealth in his case had brought with it virtue and it was in vain that Saint-Loup had attempted to seduce him. Thus, by a process of compensation, while virtuous young men abandon themselves in their later years to the passions of which they have at length become conscious, promiscuous youths turn into men of principle from whom any Charlus who turns up too late on the strength of old stories will get an unpleasant rebuff. It is all a question of chronology.

"No," he exclaimed, gaily and with force, "if a man doesn't fight, whatever reason he may give, it is because he doesn't want to be killed, because he is *afraid*." And with the same affirming gesture, even more energetic than that which he had used to underline the fear of others, he added: "And that goes for me too. If I haven't rejoined my regiment, it is quite simply from *fear*—so there!" I had already observed in more than one person that the affection of praiseworthy sentiments is not the only method of covering bad ones; another less obvious method is to make a display of these bad sentiments, so that at least one does not appear to be unaware of them. Moreover, in Saint-Loup this tendency was strengthened by his habit, when he had committed an indiscretion or made a blunder for which he expected to be blamed, of proclaiming it aloud and saying that it had been done on purpose. A habit which, I believe, must have come to him from some instructor at the Ecole de Guerre whom he had known well and greatly admired. I had, therefore, no hesitation in interpreting this outburst as the verbal confirmation of a sentiment which, since it had dictated the conduct of Saint-Loup and his non-participation in the war now beginning, he preferred to proclaim aloud.

"Have you heard the rumour," he asked, as he left me, "that my aunt Oriane is going to get a divorce? Personally I know nothing about it whatsoever. There have been rumours of the kind from time to time, and I have so often heard that it's imminent that I shall wait until it happens before I believe it. I must admit, it would be very understandable. My uncle is a charming man, not only socially but as a friend and in the family. He even, in a way, has much more heart than my aunt, who is a saint but makes him terribly aware of it. Only he is a dreadful husband, who has never ceased to be unfaithful to his wife, to insult her, to bully her, to keep her short of money. It would be so natural for her to leave him that that is a reason for the story to be true, but also a reason why it may not be true—the idea occurs to people and inevitably they talk about it. And then she has put up with him for so long! Of course I know quite well that there are lots of things which are reported falsely, and then denied, but later do become true." This put it into my head to ask him whether there had ever been any question of his marrying Mlle de Guermantes. He seemed amazed and assured me that there had not, that it was merely one of those rumours of the fashionable world which arise from time to time one does not know why and vanish in the same way, without their falsity causing those who believed them to be any more cautious when a new rumour arises, of an engagement or a divorce, or a political rumour, in giving credence to it and spreading it.

Forty-eight hours had not elapsed before certain facts which I learnt proved to me that I had been absolutely wrong in my interpretation of Robert's words: "If a man is not at the front, it is because he is afraid." Saint-Loup had said this in order to shine in conversation, to appear in the role of an original psychologist, so long as he was not sure that his own enlistment would be accepted. But meanwhile he was moving heaven and earth to bring this about and showing himself in this less "original," in the meaning that he thought it necessary to give to the word, but more profoundly a Frenchman of Saint-André-des-Champs, more in conformity with all that at this moment was best in the Frenchmen of Saint-André-des-Champs, lords, citizens and serfs—feudally respectful serfs and serfs in revolt, those two divisions, both equally French, of the same family, the Françoise branch and the Morel branch, from which two arrows were now converging upon a common target, the frontier. Bloch had been enchanted to hear a confession of cowardice from a nationalist (who was, as a matter of fact, so little of a nationalist) and when Saint-Loup had asked him whether he himself would soon be off, had assumed a high-priestly air and replied: "Short-sighted."

But Bloch had completely changed his mind about the war a few days later, when he came to see me in a state of frenzy. Although short-sighted, he had been passed fit for service. I was accompanying him home when we met Saint-Loup, who was on his way to an interview at the Ministry of War with a colonel to whom he was to be introduced by a retired officer—"M. de Cambremer," he said to me, and added: "Oh! but of course, he is an old acquaintance of yours. You know Cancan as well as I do." I replied that I did indeed know him and his wife too, and that I didn't have a particularly high opinion of them. But I was so much in the habit, ever since I had first met them, of considering the wife as in her way a remarkable woman, who knew her Schopenhauer and at least had access to an intellectual sphere which was closed to her boorish husband, that I was at first astonished to hear Saint-Loup reply: "His wife is idiotic, I won't try to defend her. But *he* is an excellent man—he was talented once and is still a very pleasant person." By the "idiocy" of the wife, Saint-Loup meant no doubt her desperate desire to move in grand society, which is the thing that grand society judges most severely; by the good qualities of the husband, he meant perhaps something of the qualities that were recognised in him by his mother when she declared that he was the best of the family. He, at least, did not worry about duchesses, though this it must be admitted is a form of "intelligence" which differs as much from the intelligence that characterises thinkers as the "intelligence" admired by the public in this or that rich man who has "been clever enough to make a fortune." However, Saint-Loup's words did not displease me, because they reminded me that pretentiousness is near akin to stupidity and that simplicity has a flavour which though it lies beneath the surface is agreeable. I had, it is true, had no opportunity to savour that of M. de Cambremer. But this was merely an instance of the law that a person is many different persons according to who is judging him, quite apart from the different standards by which different people judge. In the case of M. de Cambremer, I had known only the rind. His flavour, therefore, though avouched to me by others, was to me personally unknown.

Bloch left us outside his house, overflowing with bitterness against Saint-Loup and saying to his face that men of his sort, privileged dandies who strutted about at headquarters, ran no risks and that he, as a plain private soldier, had no wish to "get a hole in his skin just because of William." "It seems that the Emperor William is seriously ill," replied Saint-Loup. Bloch, like everybody connected with the Stock Exchange, was more than usually credulous of sensational reports. "Yes," he said, "there is even a strong rumour that he is dead." In Stock Exchange circles every monarch who is ill, whether it be Edward VII or William II, is dead, every town which is about to be besieged has already been captured. "It is only being kept secret," added Bloch, "in order not to damage the morale of the Boches. But he died the night before last. My father has it from an absolutely first-class source." Absolutely first-class sources were the only ones to which M. Bloch senior paid any attention, and it was always with such a source that thanks to his "important connexions" he was fortunate enough to be in touch, when he heard before anyone else that Foreign Bonds were going to go up or that De Beers were going to fall. However, if just at that moment De Beers had a rise or Foreign Bonds "came on offer," if the market in the former was "firm and active" and that in the latter "hesitant and weak, with a note of caution," the first-class source did not, for that reason, cease to be a first-class source. So Bloch informed us of the death of the Kaiser with an air of mystery and self-importance, but also of fury. He was exasperated beyond measure at hearing Robert say: "the Emperor William." I believe that under the blade of the guillotine

Saint-Loup and M. de Guermantes could not have spoken otherwise. Two men of "society," surviving alone on a desert island where they would have nobody to impress by a display of good manners, would recognise each other by these little signs of breeding, just as two Latinists in the same circumstances would continue to quote Virgil correctly. Saint-Loup, even under torture at the hands of the Germans, could never have used any other expression than "the Emperor William." And this good breeding, whatever else one may think of it, is a symptom of formidable mental shackles. The man who cannot throw them off can never be more than a man of the world. However, his elegant mediocrity—particularly when it is allied, as is often the case, with hidden generosity and unexpressed heroism—is a delightful quality in comparison with the vulgarity of Bloch, at once coward and braggart, who started now to scream at Saint-Loup: "Can't you simply say William? The trouble is you've got the wind up. Even in Paris you crawl on your belly before him! Pooh! we're going to have some fine soldiers at the frontier, they'll lick the boots of the Boches. You and your friends in fancy uniforms, you're fit to parade in a tournament and that's about all."

"Poor Bloch is absolutely determined that I am to do nothing but strut about on parade," said Saint-Loup to me with a smile, when we had left our friend. And I sensed that this was not at all what Robert wished to do, although at the time I did not realise what his intentions were as clearly as I did later when, as the cavalry remained inactive, he got leave to serve as an officer in the infantry and then in the light infantry, or when, later still, there came the sequel which the reader will learn in due course. But Robert's patriotism was something that Bloch was unaware of simply because Robert chose not to display it. If Bloch had treated us to a viciously anti-militarist profession of faith once he had been passed as "fit," he had previously made the most chauvinistic statements when he thought that he would be discharged on the grounds of short sight. But Saint-Loup would have been incapable of making these statements; in the first place from that sort of moral delicacy which prevents people from expressing sentiments that lie too deep within them and that seem to them quite natural. My mother, in the past, would not only not have hesitated for a second to die for my grandmother, but would have suffered horribly if anyone had prevented her from doing so. Nevertheless, I cannot retrospectively imagine on her lips any such phrase as "I would give my life for my mother." And the same reticence, in his love of France, was displayed by Robert, who at this moment seemed to me much more Saint-Loup (in so far as I could form a picture of his father) than Guermantes. And then Robert would also have been saved from expressing the chauvinistic sentiments of Bloch by the fact that his intelligence was in itself to some extent a moral quality. Among intelligent and genuinely serious workers there is a certain aversion for those who make literature out of the subject they are engaged on, those who use it for self-display. Robert and I had not been at the Lycée or at the Sorbonne together, but we had attended, independently, certain courses of lectures by the same teachers, and I remember the smile he had for the ones who—as happens sometimes when a man is giving a remarkable series of lectures—tried to pass themselves off as geniuses by giving their theories an ambitious name. We only had to mention them for Robert to burst out laughing. Our personal and instinctive preference was, naturally, not for the Cottards or the Brichots, but we had nevertheless a certain respect for any man with a really thorough knowledge of Greek or medicine who did not for that reason think himself entitled to behave as a charlatan. I have said that, if in the past all Mamma's actions had as their basis the sentiment that she would have given her life for her mother, she had yet never formulated this sentiment to herself, and that in any case it would have seemed to her not merely unnecessary and ridiculous but shocking and shameful to express it to others; in the same way it was impossible for me to imagine on the lips of Saint-Loup—talking to me about his equipment, the things he had to do in Paris, our chances of victory, the weakness of the Russian army, how England would act—it is impossible for me to imagine on his lips even the most eloquent phrase that even the most deservedly popular minister might have addressed to a wildly cheering Chamber of Deputies. I cannot, however, say that in this negativeness which checked him from expressing the noble sentiments that he felt, he was not to some extent influenced by the "Guermantes spirit," of which we have seen so many similar instances in Swann. For, if I found him more Saint-Loup than anything else, he was, nevertheless, also Guermantes, and consequently, among the numerous motives which animated his courage, there were some which did not exist for his friends of Doncières, those young men enamoured of their profession with whom I had dined night after night and of whom so many went to their deaths at the battle of the Marne or elsewhere, leading their men into action.

As for the young socialists who were at Doncières when I was there but whom I did not get to know because they did not belong to the same set as Saint-Loup, they could see now for themselves that the officers of that set were by no means "nobs," with the implications of haughty pride and base self-indulgence which the "plebs," the ex-ranker officers, the freemasons attached to that word. And conversely, this same patriotism was found by the officers of aristocratic birth to exist in full measure among the socialists whom I had heard them accuse, while I was at Doncières at the height of the Dreyfus case, of being "men without a country." The patriotism of the military caste, as sincere and profound as any other, had assumed a fixed form which the members of that caste regarded as sacrosanct and which they were infuriated to see heaped with "opprobrium," but the radical-socialists, who were independent and to some extent unconscious patriots without any fixed patriotic religion, had failed to perceive the profound and living reality that lay behind what they thought were empty and malignant formulas.

No doubt, like his friends, Saint-Loup had formed the habit of inwardly cultivating, as the truest part of himself, the search for and the elaboration of the best possible manoeuvres which would lead to the greatest strategic and tactical successes, so that, for him as for them, the life of the body was something relatively unimportant which could easily be sacrificed to this inner part of the self, the real vital core within them, around which their personal existence was of value only as a protective outer skin. But in Saint-Loup's courage there were also more individual elements, and amongst these it would have been easy to recognise the generosity which in its early days had constituted the charm of our friendship, and also the hereditary vice which had later awoken from dormancy in him and which, at the particular intellectual level which he had not been able to transcend, caused him not only to admire courage but to exaggerate his horror of effeminacy into a sort of intoxication at any contact with virility. He derived, chastely no doubt, from spending days and nights in the open with Senegalese soldiers who might at any moment be called upon to sacrifice their lives, a cerebral gratification of desire into which there entered a vigorous contempt for "little scented gentlemen" and which, however contrary it might seem, was not so very different from that which he had obtained from the cocaine in which he had indulged excessively at Tansonville and of which heroism—one drug taking the place of another—was now curing him. And another essential part of his courage was that double habit of courtesy which, on the one hand, caused him to bestow praise on others but where he himself was concerned made him content to do what had to be done and say nothing about it—the opposite of a Bloch, who had said to him just now "You—of course you'd funk it," and yet was doing nothing himself—and on the other hand impelled him to hold as of no value the things that he himself possessed, his fortune, his rank, and even his life, so that he was ready to give them away: in a word, the true nobility of his nature.

"Are we in for a long war?" I said to Saint-Loup. "No, I believe it will be very short," he replied. But here, as always, his arguments were bookish. "Bearing in mind the prophecies of Moltke, re-read," he said to me, as if I had already read it, "the decree of the 28th October, 1913, about the command of large formations; you will see that the replacement of peacetime reserves has not been organised or even foreseen, a thing which the authorities could not have failed to do if the war were likely to be a long one." It seemed to me that the decree in question could be interpreted not as a proof that the war would be short, but as a failure on the part of its authors to foresee that it would be long, and what kind of war it would be, the truth being that they suspected neither the appalling wastage of material of every kind that would take place in a war of stable fronts nor the interdependence of different theatres of operations.

Outside the limits of homosexuality, among the men who are most opposed by nature to homosexuality, there exists a certain conventional idea of virility, which the homosexual finding at his disposal proceeds, unless he is a man of unusual intelligence, to distort. This ideal—to be seen in certain professional soldiers, certain diplomats—can be singularly exasperating. In its crudest form it is simply the gruffness of the man with the heart of gold who is determined not to show his emotions, the man who at the moment of parting from a friend who may very possibly be killed has a secret desire to weep, which no one suspects because he conceals it beneath a mounting anger which culminates, at the actual moment of farewell, in a sort of explosion: "Well, now, damn it! Shake hands with me, you old ruffian, and take this purse, it's no use to me, don't be an idiot." The diplomat, the officer, the man who believes that nothing counts except a great task in the service of the nation but who was fond nevertheless of the "poor boy" in his legation or his battalion who has died from a fever or a bullet exhibits the same taste for virility in a form that is less clumsy, and more sophisticated, but at bottom just as odious. He does not want to mourn for the "poor boy," he knows that soon he and everybody else will forget him, just as a kind-hearted surgeon soon forgets though, for a whole evening after some little girl has died in an epidemic, he feels a grief which he does not express. Should the diplomat be a writer and describe this death, he will not say that he felt grief. No—first from "manly reticence," secondly from that skilled artistry which arouses emotion by dissembling it. With one of his colleagues he will watch by the side of the dying man. Not for one second will they say that they feel grief. They will talk of the affairs of the legation or the battalion and their remarks may be even more terse than usual: "B. said to me: 'Don't forget we have the general's inspection tomorrow. See to it that your men are well turned out.' Habitually so gentle, he spoke in a sharper tone than usual. I noticed that he avoided looking at me, I too felt myself to be overwrought." And the reader understands that this "sharp tone" is simply grief, showing itself in men who do not want to appear to feel grief, an attitude which might be ridiculous and nothing more but is in fact also wretched and ugly, because it is the manner of feeling grief of those who think that grief does not matter, that there are more serious things in life than being parted from one's friends, etc., so that when someone dies they give the same impression of false-hood, of nothingness, as on New Year's Day the gentleman who hands you a present of marrons glacés and just manages to say with a titter: "With the compliments of the season!"

To conclude the narrative of the officer or the diplomat watch-ing at the deathbed, his head covered because the wounded or sick man has been carried out of doors, the moment comes when all is over. " 'I must go back and get my kit cleaned,' I thought. But I do not know why, at the moment when the doctor let go the pulse, simultaneously B. and I, without any sign passing between us— the sun was beating vertically down, perhaps we were hot standing beside the bed—removed our caps." And the reader knows that it was not because of the heat of the sun but from emotion in the presence of the majesty of death that the two virile men, on whose lips the words grief and affection were almost unknown, now bared their heads.

In homosexuals like Saint-Loup the ideal of virility is not the same, but it is just as conventional and just as false. The falsehood consists for them in the fact that they do not want to admit to themselves that physical desire lies at the root of the sentiments to which they ascribe another origin. M. de Charlus had detested effeminacy. Saint-Loup admired the courage of young men, the intoxication of cavalry charges, the intellectual and moral nobility of friendships between man and man, entirely pure friendships, in which each is prepared to sacrifice his life for the other. War, which turns capital cities, where only women remain, into an abomination for homosexuals, is at the same time a story of passionate adventure for homosexuals if they are intelligent enough to concoct dream figures, and not intelligent enough to see through them, to recognise their origin, to pass judgment on themselves. So that while some young men were enlisting simply in order to join in the latest sport—in the spirit in which one year everybody plays diabolo—for Saint-Loup, on the other hand, war was the very ideal which he imagined himself to be pursuing in his desires (which were in fact much more concrete but were clouded by ideology), an ideal which he could serve in common with those whom he preferred to all others, in a purely masculine order of chivalry, far from women, where he would be able to risk his life to save his orderly and die inspiring a fanatical love in his men. And thus, though there were many elements in his courage, the fact that he was a great nobleman was one of them, and another, in an unrecognisable and idealised form, was M. de Charlus's dogma that it was of the essence of a man to have nothing effeminate about him. But just as in philosophy and in art ideas acquire their value only from the manner in which they are developed, and two analogous ones may differ greatly according to whether they have been expounded by Xenophon or by Plato, so, while I recognise how much, in his behaviour, the one has in common with the other, I admire Saint-Loup, for asking to be sent to the point of greatest danger, infinitely more than I do M. de Charlus for refusing to wear brightly coloured cravats.

I spoke to Saint-Loup about my friend the manager of the Grand Hotel at Balbec, who, it seems, had alleged that at the beginning of the war there had been in certain French regiments defections, which he called "defectuosities," and had accused what he called the "Prussian militariat" of having provoked them; he had even, at one moment, believed in a simultaneous landing by the Japanese, the Germans and the Cossacks at Rivebelle as threatening Balbec, and had said that the only thing to do was to "decramp." He also thought that the departure of the government and the ministries for Bordeaux was a little precipitate and declared that they were wrong to "decramp" so soon. This German-hater would say with a laugh of his brother: "He is in the trenches, twenty-five yards away from the Boches," until the authorities, having discovered that he was a "Boche" himself, put him in a concentration camp. "Talking of Balbec, do you remember the lift-boy who used to be in the hotel?" said Saint-Loup as he left me, in a tone suggesting that he did not quite know who the lift-boy was and was counting on me for enlightenment. "He is joining up and has written to ask me to get him into the flying corps." No doubt the young man was tired of going up in the captive cage of the lift, and the heights of the staircase of the Grand Hotel no longer sufficed him. He was going to "get his stripes" otherwise than by becoming a hall-porter, for our destiny is not always what we had supposed. "I shall certainly support his application," said Saint-Loup. "I was saying to Gilberte only this morning, we shall never have enough aeroplanes. It is aeroplanes that will enable us to see what the enemy is preparing, and aeroplanes that will rob him of the greatest advantage of attack, which is surprise. The best army will be, perhaps, the army with the best eyes."

(I had met this lift-boy airman a few days earlier. He had spoken to me about Balbec, and, curious to know what he would say about Saint-Loup, I brought the conversation round to the subject by asking whether it was true, as I had heard, that towards young men M. de Charlus had . . . etc. The lift-boy seemed surprised, he knew absolutely nothing about it. But on the other hand he made accusations against the rich young man, the one who lived with a mistress and three friends. As he seemed to lump all of them together, and as I knew from M. de Charlus who, it will be remembered, had informed me in front of Brichot that it was not so, I told the lift-boy that he must be mistaken. He met my doubts with the firmest avowals. It was the girlfriend of the rich man who had the job of picking up young men, and they all took their pleasure together. Thus M. de Charlus, the best-informed of men on the subject, had been entirely wrong, so fragmentary, secret, unpredictable is the truth. Afraid of reasoning like a bourgeois, and of seeing Charlusism where it was not, he had missed the fact that the woman was flushing out the game. "She came often enough to find me," said the lift-boy. "But she saw at once who it was she was dealing with. I refused categorically, I don't go in for that sort of monkey business. I told her I found it wholly objectionable. It's enough for one person to talk, word gets around, and you can't find another place anywhere." These last reasons weakened the virtuous declarations with which the lift-boy had begun, for they implied that he would have obliged had he been assured of discretion. Such must not have been the case where Saint-Loup was concerned. It is probable that even the rich man and his mistress and friends had been luckier, since the lift-boy quoted many conversations between him and them, held at various times, something that happens rarely when one has declined so categorically. For instance, the rich man's mistress had come to him to make the acquaintance of a page with whom he was close friends. "I don't think you know him, you weren't here then. Victor, they called him. Of course," the lift-boy added with the air of referring to inviolable and faintly secret laws, "you can't say no to a comrade who isn't well off." I remembered the invitation the rich man's noble friend had extended to me a few days before I left Balbec. But most likely this had nothing to do with it, and was dictated purely by amiability.)

"And tell me about poor Françoise, has she succeeded in getting her nephew exempted?" But Françoise, who for a long time had been making every effort to achieve this, and who, when she had been offered through the Guermantes a recommendation to General de Saint-Joseph, had replied in a tone of despair: "Oh no, that would be quite useless, there's nothing to be got from that old fogy, he's as bad as could be, he's patriotic," Françoise, as soon as there had been any question of war, however much she suffered at the thought of it, was of the opinion that it would be wrong to abandon the "poor Russians" since we were "allianced" to them. The butler, who in any case was convinced that the war would only last ten days and would end in a brilliant victory for France, would not have dared, for fear of being contradicted by events—and would not even have had enough imagination—to predict a long and indecisive war. But from this complete and immediate victory he tried at least to extract in advance the maximum of suffering for Françoise. "Things may well take an ugly turn, because it seems there are lots who refuse to march, boys of sixteen in floods of tears." And this habit of telling her disagreeable things in order to "vex" her was what he called "putting the wind up her," "making her flesh creep," "giving her a bit of a jolt." "Sixteen, Holy Mother!" said Françoise, and then suspicious for a moment: "But they said they only took them at twenty, at sixteen they're still children." "Naturally the papers have been told to say nothing about it. Anyhow, the young men, one and all, will be off to the front and there won't be many to come back. In one way it'll do some good. A good blood-letting, you know, is useful now and again. And then it will help trade. And I promise you, if there are any lads who are a bit soft and think twice about it, they'll be for the firing-squad, bang, bang, bang! I suppose it has to be done. And then, the officers, what does it matter to them? They get paid their screw, that's all they ask." Françoise turned so pale whenever one of these conversations took place that we were afraid the butler might cause her death from a heart attack.

But this did not mean that she had lost her old faults. Whenever I had a visit from a girl, however much her old servant's legs might be hurting her, if I happened to leave my room for a moment there she was at the top of a step-ladder in the dressing-room, searching, so she said, for some overcoat of mine to see if the moths had got into it, but really in order to eavesdrop. And she still, in spite of all my complaints, had her insidious manner of asking questions in an indirect way, the phrase she now used for this purpose being "because of course." Not daring to say to me: "Has this lady her own house?" she would say, her eyes timidly raised like the eyes of a good dog: "Because of course this lady has her own house . . . ," avoiding a blatant interrogative not so much in order to be polite as in order not to seem too curious. Then again, as the servants whom we love most—and this is particularly true when they have almost ceased to give us either the service or the respect proper to their employment—remain, unfortunately, servants and only make more clear the limitations of their caste, which we ourselves would like to do away with, when they imagine that they are penetrating most successfully into ours, Françoise often addressed me ("to get under my skin," as the butler would have said) with odd remarks which someone of my own class could not have made: for instance, with a joy carefully dissembled but as profound as if she had detected a serious illness, she would say to me if I was hot and there were beads of sweat which I had not noticed on my forehead: "But you're absolutely dripping," looking astonished as though this were some strange phenomenon and at the same time with that little smile of contempt with which we greet an impropriety ("Are you going out? You know you've forgotten to put your tie on") and also with the anxious voice which we assume when we want to alarm someone about the state of his health. One would have thought that no one in the world had ever been "dripping" before. Finally, she no longer spoke good French as she had in the past. For in her humility, in her affectionate admiration for people infinitely inferior to herself, she had come to adopt their ugly habits of speech. Her daughter having complained to me about her and having used the words (I do not know where she had heard them): "She's always finding fault with me because I don't shut the doors properly and *patatipatali* and *patatatipatala*," Françoise clearly thought that only her imperfect education had deprived her until now of this beautiful idiom. And from those lips which I had once seen bloom with the purest French I heard several times a day: "And *patatipatali* and *patatatipatala*." It is indeed curious how little not only the expressions but also the ideas of an individual vary. The butler, having got into the habit of declaring that M. Poincaré was a wicked man, not because he was after money but because he had been absolutely determined to have a war, repeated this seven or eight times a day to an audience which was always the same and always just as interested. Not a word was altered, not a gesture or an intonation. The performance only lasted two minutes, but it was unvarying, like that of an actor. And his faulty French was quite as much to blame as that of her daughter for corrupting the language of Françoise. He thought that what M. de Rambuteau had been so annoyed one day to hear the Duc de Guermantes call "Rambuteau shelters" were called "rinals." No doubt in his childhood he had failed to hear the "u" and had never realised his mistake, so every time he used the word—and he used it frequently—he mispronounced it. Françoise, embarrassed at first, ended by using it too, and liked to complain that the same sort of thing did not exist for women as well as for men. But as a result of her humility and her admiration for the butler she never said "urinals" but—with a slight concession to customary usage—"arinals."

She no longer slept, no longer ate. Every day she insisted on the bulletins, of which she understood nothing, being read to her by the butler who understood hardly more of them than she did, and in whom the desire to torment Françoise was frequently dominated by a patriotic cheerfulness: he would say, with a sympathetic laugh, referring to the Germans: "Things are hotting up for them, it won't be long before old Joffre puts salt on the tail of the comet." Françoise had no idea what comet he was alluding to, but this strengthened her conviction that the phrase was one of those amiable and original extravagances to which a well-bred person is required by the laws of courtesy to respond good-humouredly, so gaily shrugging her shoulders as if to say: "He's always the same," she tempered her tears with a smile. At least she was happy that her new butcher's boy, who in spite of his trade was anything but courageous (his first job nevertheless had been in the slaughterhouses), was not old enough to be called up. Otherwise she would have been quite capable of going to see the Minister of War to get him exempted.

The butler had not enough imagination to realise that the bulletins were not excellent and that we were not advancing towards Berlin, since he kept reading: "We have repulsed with heavy enemy losses, etc.," actions which he celebrated as a succession of victories. I, however, was alarmed at the speed with which the scene of these victories was approaching Paris, and was astonished that even the butler, having seen in one bulletin that an engagement had taken place near Lens, was not disturbed to read in the newspaper next day that it had been followed by satisfactory operations in the neighbourhood of Jouy-le-Vicomte, of which the approaches were firmly in our hands. Now the butler knew Jouy-le-Vicomte well by name, for it was not so very far from Combray. But we read the newspapers as we love, blindfold. We do not try to understand the facts. We listen to the soothing words of the editor as we listen to the words of our mistress. We are "beaten and happy" because we believe that we are not beaten but victorious.

I had, in any case, not remained long in Paris but had returned very soon to my sanatorium. Although in principle the doctor's treatment consisted in isolation, I had been allowed to receive, at different times, a letter from Gilberte and a letter from Robert. Gilberte wrote (this was in about September 1914) that, however much she would have liked to stay in Paris in order to get news of Robert more easily, the constant Taube raids on the city had caused her such alarm, particularly for her little girl, that she had fled by the last train to leave for Combray, that the train had not even got as far as Combray, and that it was only thanks to a peasant's cart, on which she had had an appalling journey of ten hours, that she had succeeded in reaching Tansonville! "And there, imagine what awaited your old friend," she concluded her letter. "I had left Paris to escape from the German aeroplanes, supposing that at Tansonville I should be perfectly safe. Before I had been there two days you will never imagine what turned up: the Germans, who having defeated our troops near La Fère, were overrunning the district. A German headquarters staff, with a regiment just behind it, presented itself at the gates of Tansonville and I was obliged to take them in, and not a hope of getting away, no more trains, nothing." Whether the German staff had really behaved well, or whether it was right to detect in Gilberte's letter the influence, by contagion, of the spirit of those Guermantes who were of Bavarian stock and related to the highest aristocracy of Germany, she was lavish in her praise of the perfect breeding of the staff-officers, and even of the soldiers who had only asked her for "permission to pick a few of the forget-me-nots growing near the pond," a good breeding which she contrasted with the disorderly violence of the fleeing French troops, who had pillaged everything as they crossed the property before the arrival of the German generals. In any case, if Gilberte's letter was in some ways impregnated with the spirit of the Guermantes—others would say the spirit of Jewish internationalism, which would probably have been unfair to her, as we shall see—the letter which I received several months later from Robert was, on the other hand, much more Saint-Loup than Guermantes and reflected in addition all the liberal culture which he had acquired. Altogether, it was a delightful letter. Unfortunately, he did not talk about strategy as he had in our conversations at Doncières, nor did he tell me to what extent he considered that the war confirmed or invalidated the principles which he had then expounded to me.

All he said was that since 1914 there had in reality been a series of wars, the lessons of each one influencing the conduct of the one that followed. For example, the theory of the "break-through" had been supplemented by a new idea: that it was necessary, before breaking through, for the ground held by the enemy to be com-pletely devastated by the artillery. But then it had been found that on the contrary this devastation made it impossible for the infantry and the artillery to advance over ground in which thousands of shell-holes created as many obstacles. "War," he wrote, "does not escape the laws of our old friend Hegel. It is in a state of perpetual becoming."

This was meagre in comparison with what I should have liked to know. But what was still more annoying was that he was forbidden to mention the names of generals. And anyhow, according to the little that the newspapers told me, the generals as to whom at Doncières I had been so eager to know which among them would prove most effective and courageous in a war, were not the ones who were now in command. Geslin de Bourgogne, Galliffet, Négrier were dead. Pau had retired from active service almost at the beginning of the war. Of Joffre, of Foch, of Castelnau, of Pétain, Robert and I had never spoken. "My dear boy," he wrote, "I recognise that expressions like *passeront pas* and *on les aura* are not agreeable; they have always set my teeth on edge as much as *poilu* and the rest, and of course it is tiresome to be composing an epic with words and phrases which are—worse than an error of grammar or of taste—an appalling contradiction in terms, a vulgar affectation and pretension of the kind that you and I abominate, as bad as when people think it clever to say 'coco' instead of 'cocaine.' But if you could see everybody here, particularly the men of the humbler classes, working men and small shop-keepers, who did not suspect what heroism they concealed within them and might have died in their beds without suspecting it—if you could see them running under fire to help a comrade or carry off a wounded officer and then, when they have been hit themselves, smiling a few moments before they die because the medical officer has told them that the trench has been recaptured from the Germans, I assure you, my dear boy, it gives you a magnificent idea of the French people, makes you begin to understand those great periods in history which seemed to us a little extraordinary when we learned about them as students. The epic is so magnificent that you would find, as I do, that words no longer matter. Cannot Rodin or Maillol create a masterpiece from some hideous raw material which he transforms out of all recognition? At the touch of such greatness, the word *poilu* has for me become something of which I no more feel that it may originally have contained an allusion or a joke than one does, for instance, when one reads about the *chouans*. But I do know that *poilu* is already waiting for great poets, like other words, 'deluge,' or 'Christ,' or 'barbarians,' which were already instinct with greatness before Hugo, Vigny and the rest made use of them. As I say, the people, the working men, are the best of all, but everybody is splendid. Poor young Vaugoubert, the Ambassador's son, was wounded seven times before he was killed, and each time he came back from a raid without having 'copped it' he seemed to want to apologise and to say that it was not his fault. He was a charming creature. We had become close friends. His parents were given permission to come to the funeral, on condition that they did not wear mourning and only stayed five minutes because of the shelling. The mother, a great horse of a woman whom I dare say you know, was no doubt deeply moved but showed no sign of it. But the poor father was in such a state that I assure you that I, who am now totally unfeeling because I have got used to seeing the head of the comrade who is talking to me suddenly ripped open by a landmine or even severed from its trunk, I could not contain myself when I saw the collapse of poor Vaugoubert, who was an utter wreck. The general tried to tell him that it was for France, that his son had behaved like a hero, but it was no use, this only redoubled the sobs of the poor man, who could not tear himself away from his son's body. The fact is, and that is why we must learn to put up with *passeront pas*, it is men like these, like my poor valet, like Vaugoubert, who have prevented the Germans from 'passing.' You may think we are not advancing much, but logic is beside the point, there is a secret inner feeling which tells an army that it is victorious—or a dying man that he is finished. We know that victory will be ours and we are determined that it shall be, so that we can dictate a just peace, I don't mean 'just' simply for ourselves, but truly just, just to the French and just to the Germans."

I do not wish to imply that the "calamity" had raised Saint-Loup's intelligence to a new level. But just as soldier heroes with commonplace and trivial minds, if they happened to write poems during their convalescence, placed themselves, in order to describe the war, at the level not of events, which in themselves are nothing, but of the commonplace aesthetic whose rules they had obeyed in the past, and talked, as they would have ten years earlier, of the "blood-stained dawn," "victory's tremulous wings," and so on, so Saint-Loup, by nature much more intelligent and much more of an artist, remained intelligent and an artist, and it was with the greatest good taste that he now recorded for my benefit the observations of landscape which he made if he had to halt at the edge of a marshy forest, very much as he would have done if he had been out duck-shooting. To help me to understand certain contrasts of light and shade which had been "the enchantment of his morning," he alluded in his letter to certain paintings which we both loved and was not afraid to cite a passage of Romain Rolland, or even of Nietzsche, with the independent spirit of the man at the front, who had not the civilian's terror of pronouncing a German name, and also—in thus quoting an enemy—with a touch of coquetry, like Colonel du Paty de Clam who, waiting among the witnesses at Zola's trial and chancing to pass Pierre Quillard, the violently Dreyfusard poet, whom he did not even know, recited some lines from his symbolist play, *La Fille aux Mains Coupées*. In the same way, if Saint-Loup had occasion in a letter to mention a song by Schumann, he never gave any but the German title, nor did he use any periphrasis to tell me that, when at dawn on the edge of the forest he had heard the first twittering of a bird, his rapture had been as great as though he had been addressed by the bird in that "sublime *Siegfried*" which he so looked forward to hearing after the war.

And now, on my second return to Paris, I had received, the day after I arrived, another letter from Gilberte, who had doubtless forgotten, or at least forgotten what she had said in, the letter I have described, for in this new letter her departure from Paris at the end of 1914 was presented retrospectively in a very different light. "Perhaps you do not know, my dear friend," she wrote, "that I have now been at Tansonville for nearly two years. I arrived here at the same time as the Germans. Everybody had tried to prevent me from leaving. I was regarded as mad. 'What,' my friends said, 'here you are safe in Paris and you want to go off to enemy-occupied territory just when everybody is trying to escape from it.' I was quite aware of the strength of this argument. But I can't help it; if I have one good quality, it is that I am not a coward, or perhaps I should say, I am loyal, and when I knew that my beloved Tansonville was threatened, I simply could not leave our old bailiff to defend it alone. I felt that my place was by his side. And it was, in fact, thanks to this decision that I succeeded in more or less saving the house when all the other big houses in the neighbourhood, abandoned by their panic-stricken owners, were almost without exception reduced to ruins—and in saving not only the house but the valuable collections too, which dear Papa was so fond of." In a word, Gilberte was now persuaded that she had gone to

Tansonville not, as she had written to me in 1914, in order to escape from the Germans and be in a safe place, but on the contrary in order to face them and defend her house against them. They had, as a matter of fact, not stayed long at Tansonville, but since then the house had witnessed a constant coming and going of soldiers, far more intensive than that marching up and down the streets of Combray which had once drawn tears to the eyes of Françoise, and Gilberte had not ceased, as she said, this time quite truly, to live the life of the front. So that the newspapers spoke with the highest praise of her wonderful conduct and there was some question of giving her a decoration. The end of the letter was absolutely truthful. "You have no idea what this war is like, my dear friend, or of the importance that a road, a bridge, a height can assume. How often have I thought of you, of those walks of ours together which you made so delightful, through all this now ravaged countryside, where vast battles are fought to gain possession of some path, some slope which you once loved and which we so often explored together! Probably, like me, you did not imagine that obscure Roussainville and boring Méséglise, where our letters used to be brought from and where the doctor was once fetched when you were ill, would ever be famous places. Well, my dear friend, they have become for ever a part of history, with the same claim to glory as Austerlitz or Valmy. The battle of Méséglise lasted for more than eight months; the Germans lost in it more than six hundred thousand men, they destroyed Méséglise, but they did not capture it. As for the short cut up the hill which you were so fond of and which we used to call the hawthorn path, where you claim that as a small child you fell in love with me (whereas I assure you in all truthfulness it was I who was in love with you), I cannot tell you how important it has become. The huge field of corn upon which it emerges is the famous Hill 307, which you must have seen mentioned again and again in the bulletins. The French blew up the little bridge over the Vivonne which you said did not remind you of your childhood as much as you would have wished, and the Germans have thrown other bridges across the river. For a year and a half they held one half of Combray and the French the other."

The day after I received this letter, that is to say two days before the evening on which, as I have described, I made my way through the dark streets with the sound of my footsteps in my ears and all these memories revolving in my mind, Saint-Loup, arrived from the front and very shortly to return to it, had come to see me for a few moments only, and the mere announcement of his visit had violently moved me. Françoise had been tempted to fling herself upon him, in the hope that he could obtain an exemption for the timid butcher's boy whose class was to be called up the following year. But she had been checked, without my saying anything to her, by the thought of the futility of this endeavour, for the timid slaughterer of animals had moved to another butcher's some time previously. And whether our butcher's wife was afraid of losing our custom, or whether she was telling the truth, she declared to Françoise that she did not know where the boy—who, in any case, would never make a good butcher—was working. Françoise had searched everywhere. But Paris is large and butchers' shops are numerous, and although she had visited a great many she had never succeeded in finding the timid and blood-stained young man.

When Saint-Loup came into my room I had gone up to him with that feeling of shyness, that impression of something super-natural which was in fact induced by all soldiers on leave and which one feels when one enters the presence of a man suffering from a fatal disease, who still, nevertheless, leaves his bed, gets dressed, goes for walks. It seemed (above all it had seemed at first, for upon those who had not lived, as I had, at a distance from Paris, there had descended Habit, which cuts off from things which we have witnessed a number of times the root of profound impression and of thought which gives them their real meaning), it seemed almost that there was something cruel in these leaves granted to the men at the front. When they first came on leave, one said to oneself: "They will refuse to go back, they will desert." And indeed they came not merely from places which seemed to us unreal, because we had only heard them spoken of in the news-papers and could not conceive how a man was able to take part in these titanic battles and emerge with nothing worse than a bruise on his shoulder; it was from the shores of death, whither they would soon return, that they came to spend a few moments in our midst, incomprehensible to us, filling us with tenderness and terror and a feeling of mystery, like phantoms whom we summon from the dead, who appear to us for a second, whom we dare not question, and who could, in any case, only reply: "You cannot possibly imagine." For it is extraordinary how, in the survivors of battle, which is what soldiers on leave are, or in living men hypnotised or dead men summoned by a medium, the only effect of contact with mystery is to increase, if that be possible, the insignificance of the things people say. Such were my feelings when I greeted Robert, who still had a scar on his forehead, more august and more mysterious in my eyes than the imprint left upon the earth by a giant's foot. And I had not dared to put a single question to him and he had made only the simplest remarks to me. Remarks that even differed very little from the ones he might have made before the war, as though people, in spite of the war, continued to be what they were; the tone of conversation was the same, only the subject-matter differed—and even that not so very much!

I guessed from what he told me that in the army he had found opportunities which had gradually made him forget that Morel had behaved as badly towards him as towards his uncle. However, he still felt a great affection for him and was seized by sudden cravings to see him again, though he always postponed doing this. I thought it kinder to Gilberte not to inform Robert that to find Morel he had only to pay a call on Mme Verdurin.

I remarked apologetically to Robert how little one felt the war in Paris. He replied that even in Paris it was sometimes "pretty extraordinary." This was an allusion to a Zeppelin raid which had taken place the previous night and he went on to ask me if I had had a good view, very much as in the old days he might have questioned me about some spectacle of great aesthetic beauty. At the front, I could see, there might be a sort of bravado in saying: "Isn't it marvellous? What a pink! And that pale green!" when at any moment you might be killed, but here in Paris there could be no question of any such pose in Saint-Loup's way of speaking about an insignificant raid, which had in fact looked marvellously beautiful from our balcony when the silence of the night was broken by a display which was more than a display because it was real, with fireworks that were purposeful and protective and bugle-calls that did more than summon on parade. I spoke of the beauty of the aeroplanes climbing up into the night. "And perhaps they are even more beautiful when they come down," he said. "I grant that it is a magnificent moment when they climb, when they fly off in *constellation*, in obedience to laws as precise as those that govern the constellations of the stars—for what seems to you a mere spectacle is the rallying of the squadrons, then the orders they receive, their departure in pursuit, etc. But don't you prefer the moment, when, just as you have got used to thinking of them as stars, they break away to pursue an enemy or to return to the ground after the all-clear, the moment of *apocalypse*, when even the stars are hurled from their courses? And then the sirens, could they have been more Wagnerian, and what could be more appropriate as a salute to the arrival of the Germans?—it might have been the national anthem, with the Crown Prince and the Princesses in the imperial box, the *Wacht am Rhein*; one had to ask oneself whether they were indeed pilots and not Valkyries who were sailing upwards." He seemed to be delighted with this comparison of the pilots to Valkyries, and went on to explain it on purely musical grounds: "That's it, the music of the sirens was a 'Ride of the Valkyries'! There's no doubt about it, the Germans have to arrive before you can hear Wagner in Paris." In some ways the simile was not misleading. The town from being a black shapeless mass seemed suddenly to rise out of the abyss and the night into the luminous sky, where one after another the pilots soared upwards in answer to the heart-rending appeal of the sirens, while with a movement slower but more insidious, more alarming—for their gaze made one think of the object, still invisible but perhaps already very near, which it sought—the searchlights strayed ceaselessly to and fro, scenting the enemy, encircling him with their beams until the moment when the aeroplanes should be unleashed to bound after him in pursuit and seize him. And squadron after squadron, each pilot, as he soared thus above the town, itself now transported into the sky, resembled indeed a Valkyrie. Meanwhile on ground-level, at the height of the houses, there were also scraps of illumination, and I told Saint-Loup that, if he had been at home the previous evening, he might, while contemplating the apocalypse in the sky, at the same time have watched on the ground (as in El Greco's *Burial of Count Orgaz*, in which the two planes are distinct and parallel) a first-rate farce acted by characters in night attire, whose famous names merited a report to some successor of that Ferrari whose society paragraphs had so often provided amusement to the two of us, Saint-Loup and myself, that we used also to amuse ourselves by inventing imaginary ones. And that is what we did once more on the day I am describing, just as though we were not in the middle of a war, although our theme, the fear of the Zeppelins, was very much a "war" one: "Seen about town: the Duchesse de Guermantes

magnificent in a night-dress, the Duc de Guermantes indescribable in pink pyjamas and a bath-robe, etc."

"I am sure," he said, "that in all the large hotels you would have
seen American Jewesses in their night-dresses, hugging to their
ravaged bosoms the pearl necklaces which will enable them to
marry a ruined duke. The Ritz, on these evenings when the
Zeppelins are overhead, must look like Feydeau's *Hôtel du libre
échange*."

"Do you remember," I said to him, "our conversations at
Doncières?"

"Ah! those were the days! What a gulf separates us from them!
Will those happy times ever re-emerge

> from the abyss forbidden to our plummets,
> As suns rejuvenated climb the heavens,
> Having washed themselves on deep sea-beds?"[18]

"But don't let's think about those conversations simply in order
to remind ourselves how delightful they were," I said. "I was
attempting in them to arrive at a certain kind of truth. What do
you think, does the present war, which has thrown everything
into confusion—and most of all, so you say, the idea of war—does
it render null and void what you used to tell me then about the
types of battle, the battles of Napoleon, for instance, which would
be imitated in the wars of the future?"

"Not in the least," he said, "the Napoleonic battle still exists,
particularly in this war, since Hindenburg is imbued with the
Napoleonic spirit. His rapid movements of troops, his feints—
the device, for instance, of leaving only a small covering force
opposite one of his enemies, while he falls with his united strength
upon the other (Napoleon in 1814) or the other stratagem of
pressing home a diversion so strongly that the enemy is compelled
to keep up his strength on a front which is not the really important
one (for example, Hindenburg's feint before Warsaw, which
tricked the Russians into concentrating their resistance there and
brought about their defeat at the Mazurian Lakes)—his tactical
withdrawals, analogous to those with which Austerlitz, Arcola,
Eckmühl began, everything in Hindenburg is Napoleonic, and we
haven't seen the end of him. I must add that if, when we are no
longer together, you try, as the war proceeds, to interpret its
events, you should not rely too exclusively on this particular aspect
of Hindenburg to reveal to you the meaning of what he is doing

and the key to what he is about to do. A general is like a writer who
sets out to write a certain play, a certain book, and then the book
itself, with the unexpected potentialities which it reveals here, the
impassable obstacles which it presents there, makes him deviate to
an enormous degree from his preconceived plan. You know, for
instance, that a diversion should only be made against a position
which is itself of considerable importance; well, suppose the
diversion succeeds beyond all expectation, while the principal
operation results in a deadlock: the diversion may then become
the principal operation. But there is one type of Napoleonic
battle which I am waiting to see Hindenburg attempt, and that is
the one which consists in driving a wedge between two allies, in
this case the English and ourselves."

I have said that the war had not altered the stature of Saint-
Loup's intelligence, but I ought to add that this intelligence,
developing in accordance with laws in which heredity counted
for much, had acquired a brilliancy which I had never seen in him
before. What a difference between the fair-haired boy who had
once been run after by smart women or women who were hoping
to become smart, and the voluble talker, the theorist who never
stopped juggling with words! In another generation, grafted upon
another stock, like an actor reinterpreting a part played years ago
by Bressant or Delaunay, he was like a successor—pink, fair and
golden, whereas the other had been half and half very dark and
quite white—of M. de Charlus. It was true that he did not agree
with his uncle about the war, since he had ranged himself with that
section of the aristocracy which put France above everything else
in the world while M. de Charlus was at heart defeatist, but
nevertheless he could demonstrate to anyone who had not seen
the "creator of the part" what a success could be made in the role
of verbal acrobat.

"It seems that Hindenburg is a revelation," I said to him.

"An old revelation," he retorted instantly, "or a future revolution. Instead of being soft with the enemy, we should have
supported Mangin in his offensive, then we might have smashed
Austria and Germany and europeanised Turkey instead of balk-
anising France."

"But soon we shall have the help of the United States," I said.

"Meanwhile, I see here only the spectacle of the disunited
states. Why refuse to make more generous concessions to Italy
for fear of dechristianising France?"

"How shocked your uncle Charlus would be to hear you!" I said. "The fact is that you would be only too pleased to give the Pope another slap in the face, while your uncle is in despair at the thought of the damage that may be done to the throne of Franz Josef. And in this he says that he is in the tradition of Talleyrand and the Congress of Vienna."

"The age of the Congress of Vienna is dead and gone," he replied; "the old secret diplomacy must be replaced by concrete diplomacy. My uncle is at heart an impenitent monarchist, who can be made to swallow carps like Mme Molé and scamps like Arthur Meyer provided that both carps and scamps are *à la Chambord*. He so hates the tricolour flag that I believe he would rather serve under the duster of the Red Bonnet, which he would take in good faith for the white flag of the Monarchists."

Admittedly, this was mere play on words and Saint-Loup was far from possessing the sometimes profound originality of his uncle. But he was as affable and agreeable in character as the other was jealous and suspicious. And he had remained charming and pink as he had been at Balbec beneath his shock of golden hair. And one family characteristic he possessed in at least as high a degree as his uncle, that attitude of mind of the Faubourg Saint-Germain which remains deeply implanted in the men of that world who fancy that they have most completely detached themselves from it, the attitude which combines respect for clever men who are not of good family (a respect which flourishes, truly, only among the aristocracy, and which makes revolutions so unjust) with a fatuous satisfaction with themselves. Through this mixture of humility and pride, of acquired intellectual curiosity and innate authority, M. de Charlus and Saint-Loup, by different paths, and with opposite opinions, had become, with the gap of a generation between them, intellectuals whom every new idea interested and talkers whom no interruption could silence. So that a not very intelligent person might, according to the humour in which he happened to be, have found both the one and the other either dazzling or insufferably tedious.

I had gone on walking as I turned over in my mind this recent meeting with Saint-Loup and had come a long way out of my way; I was almost at the Pont des Invalides. The lamps (there were very few of them, on account of the Gothas) had already been lit, a little too early because "the clocks had been put forward" a little too early, when the night still came rather quickly, the time having been "changed" once and for all for the whole of the summer just as a central heating system is turned on or off once and for all on a fixed date; and above the city with its nocturnal illumination, in one whole quarter of the sky—the sky that knew nothing of summer time and winter time and did not deign to recognise that half-past eight had become half-past nine—in one whole quarter of the sky from which the blue had not vanished there was still a little daylight. Over that whole portion of the city which is dominated by the towers of the Trocadéro the sky looked like a vast sea the colour of turquoise, from which gradually there emerged, as it ebbed, a whole line of little black rocks, which might even have been nothing more than a row of fishermen's nets and which were in fact small clouds—a sea at that moment the colour of turquoise, sweeping along with it, without their notic- ing, the whole human race in the wake of the vast revolution of the earth, that earth upon which they are mad enough to continue their own revolutions, their futile wars, like the war which at this very moment was staining France crimson with blood. But if one looked for long at the sky, this lazy, too beautiful sky which did not condescend to change its time-table and above the city, where the lamps had been lit, indolently prolonged its lingering day in these bluish tones, one was seized with giddiness: it was no longer a flat expanse of sea but a vertically stepped series of blue glaciers. And the towers of the Trocadéro which seemed so near to the tur- quoise steps must, one realised, be infinitely remote from them, like the twin towers of certain towns in Switzerland which at a distance one would suppose to be near neighbours of the upper mountain slopes.

I retraced my steps, but once I had left the Pont des Invalides there was no longer any trace of day in the sky and there was practically no light in the town, so that stumbling here and there against dustbins and mistaking one direction for another, I found to my surprise that, by mechanically following a labyrinth of dark streets, I had arrived on the boulevards. There, the impression of an oriental vision which I had had earlier in the evening came to me again, and I thought too of the Paris of an earlier age, not now so much of the Paris of the Directory as of the Paris of 1815. As in 1815 there was a march past of allied troops in the most variegated uniforms; and among them, the Africans in their red divided skirts, the Indians in their white turbans were enough to transform for me this Paris through which I was walking into a whole imaginary exotic city, an oriental scene which was at once meticulously accurate with respect to the costumes and the colours of the faces and arbitrarily fanciful when it came to the background, just as out of the town in which he lived Carpaccio made a Jerusalem or a Constantinople by assembling in its streets a crowd whose marvellous motley was not more rich in colour than that of the crowd around me. Walking close behind two zouaves who seemed hardly to be aware of him, I noticed a tall, stout man in a soft felt hat and a long heavy overcoat, to whose purplish face I hesitated whether I should give the name of an actor or a painter, both equally notorious for innumerable sodomist scandals. I was certain in any case that I was not acquainted with him; so I was not a little surprised, when his glance met mine, to see that he appeared to be embarrassed and deliberately stopped and came towards me like a man who wants to prove that you have not surprised him in an occupation which he would prefer to remain secret. For a second I asked myself who it was that was greeting me: it was M. de Charlus. One may say that for him the evolution of his malady or the revolution of his vice had reached the extreme point at which the tiny original personality of the individual, the specific qualities he has inherited from his ancestors, are entirely eclipsed by the transit across them of some generic defect or malady which is their satellite. M. de Charlus had travelled as far as was possible from himself, or rather he was himself but so perfectly masked by what he had become, by what belonged not to him alone but to many other inverts, that for a moment I had taken him for some other invert, as he walked behind these zouaves down the wide pavement of the boulevard, for some other invert who was not M. de Charlus, who was not a great nobleman or a man of imagination and intelligence, and whose only point of resemblance to the Baron was the look that was common to them all, which in him now, at least until one had taken the trouble to observe him carefully, concealed every other quality from view.

Thus it was that, having intended to call on Mme Verdurin, I had met M. de Charlus. And certainly I should not now as in the past have found him in her drawing-room; their quarrel had grown steadily more bitter and Mme Verdurin even took advantage of present events to discredit him further. Having said for years that she found him stale, finished, more out of date in his professed audacities than the dullest philistine, she now summed up this condemnation in such a way as to make him an object of general aversion, by saying that he was "pre-war." The war had set between him and the present, so the little clan declared, an abyss which left him stranded in the deadest of dead pasts. Besides—and this was addressed particularly to the political world, which was less well informed—she made him out to be just as "bogus," just as much an "outsider" from the point of view of social position as from that of intellectual merit. "He sees nobody, nobody invites him," she said to M. Bontemps, whom she easily convinced. Anyhow, there was an element of truth in these words. The position of M. de Charlus had changed. Caring less and less about society, having quarrelled, because of his cantankerous character, and having disdained, because of his high opinion of his own social importance, to reconcile himself with most of the men and women who were the flower of society, he lived in a relative isolation which was not caused, like that in which Mme de Villeparisis had died, by the fact that the aristocracy had ostracised him, but which nevertheless in the eyes of the public for two reasons appeared to be worse. The bad reputation which M. de Charlus was now known to enjoy made ill-informed people think that it was for this reason that his company was not sought by people whom in fact he himself made a point of refusing to see. So that what was really the result of his own spleen seemed to be due to the contempt of the people upon whom he vented it. Secondly, Mme de Villeparisis had had one great bulwark: the family. But between his family and himself M. de Charlus had multiplied quarrels. His family in any case—particularly the "old Faubourg" side of it, the Courvoisier side—had always seemed to him uninteresting. And he was far from suspecting, he who, from a spirit of opposition to the Courvoisiers, had made such audacious advances in the direction of art, that the feature in him which would most have interested, for example, a Bergotte, was precisely his kinship with the whole of this old Faubourg which he despised, and the descriptions he could have given of the almost provincial life led by his female cousins, in that district bounded by the Rue de la Chaise and the Place du Palais-Bourbon in one direction and the Rue Garancière in the other.

And then, considering the question from another point of view, less transcendent and more practical, Mme Verdurin affected to believe that he was not French. "What is his nationality exactly, isn't he an Austrian?" M. Verdurin would ask innocently. "No, certainly not," Comtesse Molé would reply, her first reaction being one rather of common sense than of resentment. "No, he is Prussian," the Mistress would say. "Yes, I know what I am talking about, he has told us countless times that he is a hereditary member of the Prussian Chamber of Peers and a Durchlaucht." "Still, the Queen of Naples told me . . ." "You know she is a dreadful spy," screamed Mme Verdurin, who had not forgotten how the fallen sovereign had behaved in her house one evening. "I know—there is absolutely no question about it—that that is what she has been living on. If we had a more energetic government, she and her kind ought all to be in a concentration camp. I mean it! In any case, you will be wise not to receive visits from that charming set, because I know that the Minister of the Interior has his eye on them, your house would be watched. I have not the slightest doubt that for two years Charlus did nothing but spy on us all." And thinking probably that there might be some doubt as to the interest that the German government would show in even the most circumstantial reports on the organisation of the little clan, Mme Verdurin went on, with a mild and perspicacious air, like someone who knows that the value of what she is saying will only seem greater if she does not raise her voice: "Let me tell you, I said to my husband the very first day: 'I don't like the way that man wormed his way into my house. There's something shady here.' We had a property which stood on very high ground, looking down over a bay. Quite obviously he had been sent by the Germans to prepare a base for their submarines. There were many things which surprised me at the time, but which I understand now. For instance, at first, he would not come by the train with my other regular guests. I was so kind as to offer to put him up in the house. But no, he preferred to stay at Doncières, which was swarming with soldiers. All this stank to high heaven of espionage."

About the first of the charges brought against the Baron de Charlus, that of being out of date, fashionable people were only too ready to agree with Mme Verdurin. In this they were ungrateful, for M. de Charlus was to some extent their poet, the man who had been able to extract from the world of fashion a sort of essential poetry, which had in it elements of history, of beauty, of the picturesque, of the comic, of frivolous elegance. But people in society, incapable of understanding this poetry, did not see that it existed in their own lives; they sought for it rather elsewhere, and placed on an infinitely higher peak than M. de Charlus men who were much stupider than him but who professed to despise "society" and liked instead to hold forth about sociology and political economy. M. de Charlus, for instance, took a delight in repeating unconsciously characteristic remarks of the Duchesse de Montmorency and in describing the studied charm of her clothes, and spoke of her as if she were something sublime, but this merely gave him the reputation of an utter idiot in the eyes of the sort of society women who thought that the Duchesse de Montmorency was an uninteresting fool, and that dresses are made to be worn but without the wearer appearing to give them a moment's attention, and who meanwhile gave proof of their own superior intelligence by running to hear lectures at the Sorbonne or Deschanel speak in the Chamber.

In short, people in society had become disillusioned about M. de Charlus, not from having penetrated too far, but without having penetrated at all, his rare intellectual merit. The reason why he was found to be "pre-war," old-fashioned, was that the people who are least capable of judging the worth of individuals are also the most inclined to adopt fashion as a principle by which to classify them; they have not exhausted, or even grazed the surface of, the talented men of one generation, when suddenly they are obliged to condemn them all *en bloc*, for here is a new generation with a new label which will be no better understood than its predecessor.

As for the second accusation, that of being pro-German, fashionable people because of their dislike of extreme views tended to reject it, but the charge had an unwearying and particularly cruel advocate in Morel, who, having managed to retain in the newspapers and even in society the position which M. de Charlus had first achieved for him and then tried equally hard, but without success, to undermine, pursued the Baron with a hatred that was all the more infamous since, whatever the precise relations between them had been, Morel had seen and known the side of him that he concealed from so many people: his profound kindness. M. de Charlus had shown such generosity, such delicacy towards the violinist, had been so scrupulous about fulfilling his promises to him that, when Charlie left him, the image of the Baron that remained in his mind was not at all that of a vicious man (at most he regarded the Baron's vice as a disease) but of a man with loftier ideas than any other he had ever known, a man with extraordinary capacity for feeling, a kind of saint. So little disposed was he to deny this that even after the quarrel he would say in all sincerity to a young man's parents: "You can trust your son to him, he can only have the most excellent influence on him." And so when by his articles in the papers he tried to make him suffer, it was in his imagination not vice but virtue incarnate that he was scourging. Not long before the war there had begun to appear short "pieces," transparent to the so-called initiated, in which M. de Charlus was most monstrously libelled. Of one, entitled *The Misfortunes of a Dowager ending in -us or the Latter Days of the Baroness*, Mme Verdurin had bought fifty copies in order to be able to lend it to her acquaintances and M. Verdurin, declaring that Voltaire himself did not write better, took to reading it aloud. Since the war the tone of these pieces had changed. Not only was the Baron's inversion denounced, but also his alleged Germanic nationality: "Frau Bosch," "Frau von den Bosch" were the names habitually used to designate M. de Charlus. A little composition of a poetic nature appeared with the title—borrowed from some of Beethoven's dances—*Une Allemande*. Finally two short stories, *The Uncle from America and the Aunt from Frankfurt* and *The Jolly Rear Admiral*, read in proof in the little clan, had delighted even Brichot himself, who exclaimed: "So long as the most high and puissant Lady Censorship does not blue-pencil us!" The articles themselves were cleverer than their ridiculous titles. Their style derived from Bergotte but in a way which, for the reason that follows, perhaps no one but myself perceived. Bergotte's *writings* had had not the slightest influence on Morel. The fertilisation had been effected in a most unusual way, which I record here only because of its rarity. I have described earlier the very special manner which Bergotte had, when he spoke, of choosing and pronouncing his words. Morel, who for a long time had been in the habit of meeting him at the Saint-Loups', had at that period done "imitations" of him, in which he exactly mimicked his voice, using just the words that Bergotte would have chosen. And now that he had taken to writing, Morel used to transcribe passages of "spoken Bergotte," but without first transposing them in the way which would have turned them into "written Bergotte." Not many people having known Bergotte as a talker, the tone of his voice was not recognised, since it differed from the style of his pen. This oral fertilisation is so rare that I have thought it worth mentioning here. The flowers that it produces are, however, always sterile.

Morel, who was in the Press Office, found after a while, his French blood boiling in his veins like the juice of the grapes of Combray, that there was not much to be said for being in an office during the war, and he ended by joining up, although Mme Verdurin did everything she could to persuade him to stay in Paris. Admittedly she was indignant that M. de Cambremer, at his age, should be on the general staff, and of every man who did not come to her parties she would say: "I can't think where the wretch has managed to hide himself all this time," and if someone assured her that the wretch had been in the front line since the first day, would reply, without any scruple about telling a lie or perhaps just because she was so used to getting things wrong: "Not at all, he has not budged from Paris, he's doing something about as dangerous as taking a minister for walks, I know what I am talking about, you can take my word for it, I was told by someone who has seen him at it"; but where the faithful were concerned it was not the same thing, she did not want to let them go off to the war, and looked upon it as a great "bore" that caused them to defect. And so she pulled every possible string to keep them in Paris, which would give her the double pleasure of having them at her dinner-parties and at the same time, before they arrived or after they left, making scathing remarks about their inactivity. However, the faithful in each case had to be made to agree to the soft job she had found for them and she was bitterly distressed to find Morel recalcitrant; in vain had she said to him over and over again: "But don't you see, you are *serving* in your office, and serving more than you would be at the front. The important thing is to be useful, to be really part of the war, to be in it. There are those who are in it, and there are the shirkers. Now you, you're in it, you have nothing to worry about, everybody knows this, nobody's going to throw stones at you." In the same way, in different circumstances, although men were at that time not so scarce and she had not been, as she was now, obliged to have a preponderance of women, if a man had lost his mother she had not hesitated to try and convince him that there was no objection to his continuing to come to her parties. "Grief is worn in the heart. If you wanted to go to a dance" (she never gave one) "I should be the first to advise you not to do it, but here, at my little Wednesdays, or in a box, nobody will be in the least surprised. We all know you have had a great grief..." Men were scarcer now and mourning more frequent though no longer needed to prevent men from going to parties, the war itself having put a stop to that. Mme Verdurin hung on to the survivors. She tried to persuade them that they were more useful to France if they stayed in Paris, just as in the past she would have assured them that the deceased would have been happy to see them enjoying themselves. In spite of all her efforts she did not have many men; perhaps sometimes she regretted that between herself and M. de Charlus she had brought about a rupture which left no hope of a return to their former relations.

But, if M. de Charlus and Mme Verdurin no longer saw one another, they continued nevertheless, Mme Verdurin to entertain, M. de Charlus to pursue his pleasures, very much as if nothing had changed. A few little differences there were, but of no great importance: Cottard, for instance, was now to be seen at Mme Verdurin's parties in a colonel's uniform which might have come out of Loti's *Ile du Rêve* (it bore a striking resemblance to that of a Haitian admiral and at the same time, with its broad sky-blue ribbon, recalled that of the "Children of Mary"); and M. de Charlus, finding himself in a town from which the mature men for whom he had hitherto had a taste had vanished, followed the example of those Frenchmen who, after being womanisers in France, go to live in the colonies: from necessity he had acquired first the habit of and then the taste for little boys.

But the first of these newly acquired characteristics was not in evidence for long: Cottard soon died "facing the enemy," so the newspapers said, though he had never left Paris—but it was true that he had exerted himself too much for his age—and he was soon followed by M. Verdurin, whose death caused grief to one person only and that, strangely enough, was Elstir. For whereas I had been able to study Elstir's work from a point of view which was to some extent objective, the painter himself, particularly as he grew older, linked it superstitiously to the society which had provided him with models and which had also, after thus transforming itself within him through the alchemy of impressions into a work of art, given him his public, his spectators. More and more he was inclined to believe materialistically that a not inconsiderable part of beauty is inherent in objects, and just as, at the beginning, he had adored in Mme Elstir the archetype of that rather heavy beauty which he had pursued and caressed in his paintings and in tapestries, so now in the death of M. Verdurin he saw the disappearance of one of the last relics of the social framework, the perishable framework—as swift to crumble away as the very fashions in clothes which form part of it—which supports an art and certifies its authenticity, and he was as saddened and distressed by this event as a painter of *fêtes galantes* might have been by the Revolution which destroyed the elegances of the eighteenth century, or Renoir by the disappearance of Montmartre and the Moulin de la Galette; but more than this, with M. Verdurin he saw disappear the eyes, the brain, which had had the truest vision of his painting, in which, in the form of a cherished memory, his painting was to some extent inherent. No doubt young men had come along who also loved painting, but painting of another kind; they had not, like Swann, like M. Verdurin, received lessons in taste from Whistler, lessons in truth from Monet, lessons which alone would have qualified them to judge Elstir with justice. So the death of M. Verdurin left Elstir feeling lonelier, although they had not been on speaking terms for a great many years: it was for him as though a little of the beauty of his own work had been eclipsed, since there had perished a little of the universe's sum total of awareness of its special beauty.

As for the change which had overtaken the pleasures of M. de Charlus, this was no more than intermittent: by maintaining a correspondence with numerous soldiers at the front, who sometimes came on leave, he did not altogether lack the company of mature men.

At the time when I believed what people said I should have been tempted, hearing Germany, or later Bulgaria or Greece, protest their pacific intentions, to give credence to these statements. But since life with Albertine and with Françoise had accustomed me to suspect in them thoughts and projects which they did not disclose, I now allowed no pronouncement, however specious, of William II or Ferdinand of Bulgaria or Constantine of Greece, to deceive my instinct and prevent it from divining what each one of them was plotting. Of course my quarrels with Françoise or with Albertine had been merely private quarrels, of interest only to the life of that little cell, endowed with mind, that a human being is. But just as there are animal bodies and human bodies, each one of which is an assemblage of cells as large in relation to a single cell as Mont Blanc, so there exist huge organised accumulations of individuals which are called nations: their life does no more than repeat on a larger scale the lives of their constituent cells, and anybody who is incapable of comprehending the mystery, the reactions, the laws of these smaller lives, will only make futile pronouncements when he talks about struggles between nations. But if he is master of the psychology of individuals, then these colossal masses of conglomerated individuals will assume in his eyes, as they confront one another, a beauty more potent than that of the struggle which arises from a mere conflict between two characters; and they will seem to him as huge as the body of a tall man would seem to the infusoria of which more than ten thousand would be required to fill the space of a cubic millimetre. So it had been now for some time past: the huge irregular geometric figure France, filled to its perimeter with millions of little polygons of various shapes, and another figure filled with an even greater number of polygons, Germany, had been engaged in one of these quarrels. And considered from this point of view, the body Germany and the body France, and the allied and enemy bodies, were behaving to some extent like individuals, and the blows which they were exchanging were governed by the innumerable rules of that art of boxing which Saint-Loup had expounded to me; but since, even if one chose to consider them as individuals, they were at the same time giant assemblages of individuals, the quarrel took on immense and magnificent forms, like the surge of a million-waved ocean which tries to shatter an age-old line of cliffs, or like gigantic glaciers which with their slow destructive oscillations attempt to break down the frame of mountains which surrounds them.

But in spite of this, life continued almost unchanged for many of these who have played a part in this story, and not least for M. de Charlus and the Verdurins, just as if the Germans had not been as near them as they were, since the threat of a danger momentarily checked but permanently alive leaves us absolutely indifferent if we do not picture it to ourselves. People, as they go about their pleasures, do not normally stop to think that, if certain moderating and weakening influences should happen to be suspended, the proliferation of infusoria would attain its maximum theoretical rate and after a very few days the organisms that might have been contained in a cubic millimetre would take a leap of many millions of miles and become a mass a million times greater than the sun, having in the process destroyed all our oxygen and all the substances on which we live, so that there would exist neither humanity nor animals nor earth, nor do they reflect that an irremediable and by no means improbable catastrophe may one day be generated in the ether by the incessant and frenzied activity which lies behind the apparent immutability of the sun; they busy themselves with their own affairs without thinking about these two worlds, the one too small, the other too large for us to be aware of the cosmic menaces with which they envelop us.

So it was that the Verdurins gave dinner-parties (then, after a time, Mme Verdurin gave them alone, for M. Verdurin died) and M. de Charlus went about his pleasures and hardly ever stopped to reflect that the Germans—immobilised, it is true, by a bloody barrier perpetually renewed—were only an hour by car from Paris. The Verdurins, one would imagine, did think about this fact, since they had a political salon in which every evening they and their friends discussed the situation not only of the armies but of the fleets. They thought certainly of these hecatombs of regiments annihilated and passengers swallowed by the waves; but there is a law of inverse proportion which multiplies to such an extent anything that concerns our own welfare and divides by such a formidable figure anything that does not concern it, that the death of unknown millions is felt by us as the most insignificant of sensations, hardly even as disagreeable as a draught. Mme Verdurin, who suffered even more from her headaches now that she could no longer get croissants to dip in her breakfast coffee, had eventually obtained a prescription from Cottard permitting her to have them specially made in a certain restaurant of which we have spoken. This had been almost as difficult to wangle with the authorities as the appointment of a general. The first of these special croissants arrived on the morning on which the newspapers reported the sinking of the *Lusitania*. As she dipped it in her coffee and gave a series of little flicks to her newspaper with one hand so as to make it stay open without her having to remove her other hand from the cup, "How horrible!" she said. "This is something more horrible than the most terrible stage tragedy." But the death of all these drowned people must have been reduced a thousand million times before it impinged upon her, for even as, with her mouth full, she made these distressful observations, the expression which spread over her face, brought there (one must suppose) by the savour of that so precious remedy against headaches, the croissant, was in fact one of satisfaction and pleasure.

As for M. de Charlus, his case was a little different, but worse even, for he went beyond not passionately desiring the victory of France: he desired rather, without admitting it to himself, that Germany should, if not triumph, at least not be crushed as everybody hoped she would be. And for this attitude of his the reason was, again, that the great collections of individuals called nations themselves behave to some extent like individuals. The logic that governs them is an inner logic, wrought and perpetually re-wrought by passions, like that of men and women at grips with one another in an amorous or domestic quarrel, the quarrel of a son with his father, or of a cook with her mistress, or a wife with her husband. The party who is in the wrong believes nevertheless that he is in the right—this was so in the case of Germany—and the party who is in the right sometimes supports his excellent cause with arguments which appear to him to be irrefutable only because they answer to his own passionate feelings. In these quarrels of individuals, the surest way of being convinced of the excellence of the cause of one party or the other is actually to be that party: a spectator will never to the same extent give his unqualified approval. Now within a nation the individual, if he is truly part of the nation, is simply a cell of the nation-individual. It is ridiculous to talk about the power of propaganda. Had the French been told that they were going to be beaten, no single Frenchman would have given way to despair any more than he would if he had been told that he was going to be killed by the Berthas. The real propaganda is what—if we are genuinely a living member of a nation—we tell ourselves because we have hope, hope being a symbol of a nation's instinct of self-preser-vation. To remain blind to the unjustness of the cause of the individual "Germany," to recognise at every moment the justness of the cause of the individual "France," the surest way was not for a German to be without judgment, or for a Frenchman to possess it, it was, both for the one and for the other, to be possessed of patriotism. M. de Charlus, who had rare moral qualities, who was susceptible to pity, generous, capable of affection and devo-tion, on the other hand for various reasons—among which the fact that his mother had been a Duchess of Bavaria may have played a part—did not have patriotism. He belonged, in consequence, no more to the body France than to the body Germany. Even I myself, had I been devoid of patriotism, had I not felt myself to be one of the cells of the body France, could not, it seems to me, have judged the quarrel in the manner in which I might have judged it in the past. In my adolescence, when I believed word for word what I was told, I should no doubt, hearing the German government protest its good faith, have been tempted to believe that this good faith existed; but I had learned long ago that our thoughts do not always accord with our words; not only had I one day, from the window on the staircase, discovered a Charlus whose existence I did not suspect; more important, in Françoise, and then, alas, in Albertine, I had seen the formation of opinions and projects so contrary to their words that now, even in the role of mere spectator, I should not have allowed any of the pronouncements of the Kaiser or the King of Bulgaria to deceive my instinct. But after all I can only conjecture what I might have done if I had not been an actor in the drama, if I had not been a part of the actor France in the same way as, in my quarrels with Albertine, my sad gaze and the choking feeling in my throat had been parts of the individual "me" who was passionately interested in my cause; I could not arrive at detachment. That of M. de Charlus was complete. And given that he was nothing more than a spectator, and that, without being genuinely French, he was living in France, there was every reason why he was likely to be pro-German. In the first place, he was very intelligent and in every country fools form the bulk of the population; no doubt, had he lived in Germany, the German fools defending foolishly and with passion an unjust cause would have irritated him; but living as he did in France, the French fools defending foolishly and with passion a just cause irritated him quite as much. The logic of passion, even if it happens to be in the service of the best possible cause, is never irrefutable for the man who is not himself passionate. Inevitably M. de Charlus with his critical intelligence seized on every weak point in the reasoning of the patriots. And then the complacency that an imbecile derives from the excellence of his cause, and the certainty of victory, are particularly irritating phenomena. Inevitably M. de Charlus was irritated by the triumphant optimism of people who did not know Germany and Germany's strength as he did, who believed every month in a crushing victory for the following month, and at the end of the year were as confident in making fresh predictions as though they had never, with equal confidence, made false ones—which they had, however, forgotten, saying, if they were reminded of them, that it "was not the same thing." (Yet M. de Charlus, profound as his intelligence was in some directions, would perhaps have failed to see that in art "This is not the same thing" is what the detractors of Manet return to those who tell them "People said the same thing about Delacroix."

Then again, M. de Charlus was merciful, the idea of a vanquished opponent caused him pain, he was always on the side of the underdog, he refrained from reading the law reports in the newspapers in order not to have to suffer in his own flesh from the anguish of the condemned man and from the impossibility of assassinating the judge, the executioner and the crowd that stood gloating to see "justice done." He was certain in any case that France could not be defeated now, and he knew on the other hand that the Germans were suffering from famine and would be obliged sooner or later to surrender unconditionally. And this idea too he more particularly disliked owing to the fact that he was living in France. His memories of Germany, after all, were distant, while the French who spoke of the crushing defeat of Germany with a joy which disgusted him, were people whose defects were known to him, their personalities unsympathetic. In such circumstances we pity more readily those whom we do not know, whom we merely imagine, than those who are near us in the vulgarity of daily life, unless—once again—we ourselves altogether are the latter and form but one flesh with them, since patriotism accomplishes the miracle that we are "for" our country as in a quarrel between lovers we are "for" ourself.

So the war for M. de Charlus was an extraordinarily fertile breeding-ground of those hatreds he was prone to which sprang up in him in a moment and had only a very brief existence, during which, however, he would have abandoned himself to any violent impulse. When he read the newspapers, the air of triumph with which day after day the journalists portrayed Germany as beaten— "the Beast at bay, reduced to impotence"—while the contrary was only too true, their cheerful and savage stupidity, intoxicated him with rage. The newspapers at this moment were written partly by well-known men who found this a means of "serving their country again," men such as Brichot, Norpois, Morel even, and Legrandin. M. de Charlus longed to meet them, to heap the most bitter sarcasms on their heads. Always particularly well-informed about sexual irregularities, he knew of some in individuals who, believing their own to be unknown, complacently denounced such things in the sovereigns of the "Empires of Prey," in Wagner, etc. He had a furious desire to find himself face to face with these men, to rub their noses in their own vice before the eyes of the world and leave them, these insulters of a vanquished opponent, dishonoured and gasping for breath.

Finally, M. de Charlus had also more particular reasons for being the pro-German that he was. One was that, himself a man of the world, he had lived much among men of the world, honourable men and men of honour, men who will not shake hands with a scoundrel; he was acquainted with their scruples and also with their hardness, he knew them to be insensible to the tears of a man whom they expel from a club or with whom they refuse to fight a duel, even if this act of "moral hygiene" should bring about the death of the black sheep's mother. And so in spite of himself, whatever admiration he might feel for England and for the admirable fashion in which she entered the war, nevertheless this impeccable England—incapable of falsehood but forbidding the entry of wheat and milk into Germany—was in his eyes a little too much the man of honour among nations, the professional second in duels, the arbiter of affairs of honour, whereas his experience told him that men of a different type, men with a blot upon their reputation, scoundrels like some of Dostoievsky's characters, may in fact be better—though I have never been able to understand why he identified the Germans with such men, since falsehood and deceit are in themselves no evidence of a kind heart, which is something the Germans do not seem to have displayed.

One last trait must be mentioned to complete this account of the pro-Germanism of M. de Charlus: he owed it, and through a most bizarre reaction, to his "Charlusism." He found the Germans very ugly, perhaps because they were rather too near to his own blood—it was the Moroccans he was mad about and even more the Anglo-Saxons, in whom he saw living statues by Phidias. Now in him pleasure was not unaccompanied by a certain idea of cruelty of which I had not at that time learned the full force: the man whom he loved appeared to him in the guise of a delightful torturer. In taking sides against the Germans he would have seemed to himself to be acting as he did only in his hours of physical pleasure, to be acting, that is, in a manner contrary to his merciful nature, fired with passion for seductive evil and helping to crush virtuous ugliness. This too was his reaction at the time of the murder of Rasputin, an event which, happening as it did at a supper-party *à la* Dostoievsky, caused a general surprise because people found in it so strong a Russian flavour (this impression would have been stronger still had the public not been unaware of aspects of the case that were perfectly well known to M. de

Charlus), because life disappoints us so often that in the end we come to believe that literature bears no relation to it and we are therefore astounded when we see the precious ideas that literature has revealed to us display themselves, without fear of getting spoiled, gratuitously, naturally, in the midst of daily life, when we see, for instance, that a supper-party and a murder taking place in Russia actually have something Russian about them.

The war dragged on indefinitely and those who, already several years earlier, had reported on good authority that negotiations for peace had been begun, even specifying the clauses of the treaty, were at no pains now, when they talked to you, to make excuses for their previous false rumours. They had forgotten them and were ready in all sincerity to propagate others which they would forget just as quickly. It was the period when there were constant Gotha raids; the air was perpetually buzzing with the vibration, vigilant and sonorous, of French aeroplanes. But at intervals the siren rang out like the heart-rending scream of a Valkyrie— the only German music to have been heard since the war—until the moment when the fire-engines announced that the alert was over, while beside them, like an invisible street-urchin, the all-clear at regular intervals commented on the good news and hurled its cry of joy into the air.

M. de Charlus was astonished to see that even men like Brichot who before the war had been militarists and had never ceased to reproach France for her lack of military preparedness, were not content now with reproaching Germany for the excesses of her militarism, but criticised even her admiration of the army. No doubt they expressed quite different opinions the moment there was any danger of slowing down the war against Germany and continued, for the best reasons, to denounce the pacifists of their own country. But Brichot, for example, having consented, in spite of his bad eyesight, to discuss in some lectures certain works which had appeared in neutral countries, gave high praise to a novel by a Swiss author which has a satirical passage about two children— militarists in embryo—who are struck dumb with symbolic admiration at the sight of a dragoon. There were other reasons why this satire was likely to displease M. de Charlus, who deemed that a dragoon may be a very beautiful thing. But above all he did not understand Brichot's admiration, if not for the book, which the Baron had not read, at least for its spirit, so different from that which had animated Brichot himself before the war. At that time everything that a military man did was right, even the irregularities of General de Boisdeffre, the disguises and strategies of Colonel du Paty de Clam, the forgery of Colonel Henry. By what extraordinary volte-face (it was in reality merely another aspect of the same very noble passion, the passion of patriotism, which, from being militarist when it was struggling against Dreyfusism, a phenomenon of anti-militarist tendencies, had been obliged itself to become almost anti-militarist now that the struggle was against the hyper-militaristic Germany) had Brichot come to exclaim: "O marvellous and mighty spectacle, fit lure for the youth of an age that is all brutality and knows only the cult of force: a dragoon! Well may one judge what the base soldiery will be of a generation reared in the cult of these manifestations of brutal force." He approved too of another Swiss novelist, Spitteler, who "wanting something to oppose to the hideous conception of the sword supreme, symbolically exiled to the depths of the forests the dreamy figure, mocked, calumniated and solitary, whom he calls the Mad Student, his delightful incarnation of the sweetness—unfashionable, alas, and perhaps soon to be forgotten if the grim rule of the ancient god of the militarists is not destroyed—the adorable sweetness of the times of peace."

"Now tell me," M. de Charlus said to me, "you know Cottard and you know Cambremer. Every time I see them, they talk to me about Germany's extraordinary lack of psychology. But between ourselves, do you think that hitherto they have cared much about psychology, or that even now they are capable of giving proof of any skill in it? You may be sure that I am not exaggerating. Even if he is talking about the very greatest of Germans, about Nietzsche or Goethe himself, you will hear Cottard say: 'with the habitual lack of psychology which characterises the Teutonic race.' Naturally there are things in the war which cause me greater distress, but you must admit that this is exasperating. Norpois is more intelligent, I grant you, although since the beginning of the war he has on every occasion been wrong. But what can one say of these articles of Brichot's which are arousing universal enthusiasm? You know as well as I do, my dear sir, the merit of the man, whom I like very much, even after the schism which has cut me off from his little church, which causes me to see much less of him than I used to. But still I have a certain regard for this usher with the gift of the gab and a vast amount of learning, and I confess that it is very touching that at his age—and with his strength failing as it clearly has been failing for some years past—he should, as he says, have taken it upon himself to 'serve again.' But after all, good intentions are one thing, talent is another, and talent Brichot has never had. I admit that I share his admiration for certain elements of greatness in the present war. I do, however, find it strange that a blind partisan of antiquity like Brichot, who could not be sarcastic enough about Zola for discovering more poetry in a working-class home or a coal-mine than in the famous palaces of history, or about Goncourt for elevating Diderot above Homer and Watteau above Raphael, should incessantly drum into our ears that Thermopylae and even Austerlitz were nothing compared with Vauquois. And this time, to make things worse, the public, after resisting the modernists of literature and art, is falling into line with the modernists of war, because it is an accepted fashion to think like this and also because little minds are crushed, not by the beauty, but by the hugeness of the action. It is true that *kolossal* is now spelt only with a *k*, but fundamentally, what people are bowing the knee to is simply the colossal. By the way, talking of Brichot, have you seen Morel? I am told that he wants to see me again. He has only to take the first step. I am the older man, it is not for me to make a move."

Unfortunately only the next day, to anticipate a little, M. de Charlus found himself face to face with Morel in the street; Morel, to inflame his jealousy, took him by the arm and told him various tales which were more or less true and which agitated M. de Charlus and made him feel that he needed Morel's presence beside him that evening, that he must not be allowed to go anywhere else. But the young man, catching sight of a friend of his own age, quickly said good-bye to M. de Charlus, whereupon the Baron, hoping that this threat—which naturally he would never carry out—would make Morel stay, said to him: "Take care, I shall have my revenge." Morel, however, went off with a laugh, giving his astonished young friend a pat on the neck and putting his arm round his waist.

No doubt the remark which M. de Charlus had just made to me about Morel's wishing to see him was proof of the extent to which love—and that of the Baron must have been extremely persistent—while it makes a man more imaginative and quicker to take offence, at the same time makes him more credulous and less proud. But when M. de Charlus went on: "He is a boy who is mad about women and thinks of nothing else," his words were truer than he thought. He said this out of vanity and out of love, so that people might suppose that Morel's attachment to him had not been followed by others of the same nature. I certainly did not believe a word of it, I who had seen, what M. de Charlus still did not know, that for fifty francs Morel had once given himself to the Prince de Guermantes for a night. And if, when he saw M. de Charlus pass in the street, Morel (except on the days when, from a need to confess, he would bump into him so as to have the opportunity to say gloomily: "Oh! I am so sorry, I quite see that I have behaved disgustingly towards you"), seated at a café on the pavement with his friends, would join them in noisily pointing at the Baron and making those little clucking noises with which people make fun of an old invert, I was persuaded that this was in order to conceal his own activities; and that likewise, taken aside by the Baron, each one of these public accusers would have done everything that the latter asked of him. I was wrong. If a strange development had brought to inversion—and in every social class—men like Saint-Loup who were furthest removed from it, a movement in the contrary direction had detached from these practices those in whom they were most habitual. In some the change had been wrought by tardy religious scruples, by the emotion they had felt when certain scandals had blazed into publicity, or by the fear of non-existent diseases in which they had been made to believe either, in all sincerity, by a relative who was often a concierge or a valet, or, disingenuously, by a jealous lover who had thought that in this way he would keep for himself alone a young man whom he had, on the contrary, succeeded in detaching from himself as well as from others. Thus it was that the former lift-boy at Balbec would now not have accepted for silver or gold propositions which he had come to regard as no less criminal than treasonable proposals from the enemy. In the case of Morel, however, his refusal of all offers without exception, as to which M. de Charlus had unwittingly spoken a truth which at one and the same time justified his illusions and destroyed his hopes, came from the fact that, two years after having left M. de Charlus, he had fallen in love with a woman whom he now lived with and that she, having the stronger will of the two, had managed to impose upon him an absolute fidelity. So that Morel, who at the time when M. de Charlus was showering so much money upon him had given a night to the Prince de Guermantes for fifty francs, would not now have accepted from the latter or from any other man whatever an offer even of fifty thousand. In default of honour and disinterestedness, his mistress had inculcated in him some concern for people's opinion of him, which made him not averse even to demonstrating, with a show of bravado, that all the money in the world meant nothing to him when it was offered on certain conditions. Thus, in the flowering of the human species, the interplay of different psychological laws operates always in such a way as to compensate for any process that might otherwise, in one direction or the other, through plethora or through rarefaction, bring about the annihilation of the race. And thus, too, among flowers, a similar wisdom, which Darwin was the first to bring to light, governs their different modes of fertilisation, opposing them successively one to another.

"It is a strange thing," M. de Charlus went on, in the shrill little voice with which he sometimes spoke, "I hear people who appear to be perfectly happy all day long and enjoy their cocktails, declare that they will never last until the end of the war, that their hearts won't stand it, that they can think of nothing else, that they will quite suddenly die. And what is really extraordinary is that this does in fact happen! How curious it is! Is it a question of nourishment, because the food they eat is all so badly prepared now, or is it because, to prove their zeal, they harness themselves to tasks which are useless but destroy the mode of life which kept them alive? Anyhow, I have noted an astonishing number of these strange premature deaths, premature at least from the point of view of the deceased. I forget what I was saying to you just now, about Norpois and his admiration for the war. But what a singular manner he has of writing about it! First, have you noticed the pullulation in his articles of new expressions which, when they have eventually worn themselves out by dint of being employed day after day—for really Norpois is indefatigable, I think the death of my aunt Villeparisis must have given him a second youth—are immediately replaced by yet other commonplaces? In the old days I remember you used to amuse yourself by recording the fashionable phrases which appeared and had their vogue and then disappeared: 'he who sows the wind reaps the whirlwind'; 'the dogs bark, but the caravan moves on'; 'give me a good policy and I will give you good finances, as Baron Louis said'; 'these are symptoms which it would be exaggerated to take tragically but wise to take seriously'; 'to work for the King of Prussia' (this last, inevitably, has come to life again). Well, since then, alas, how many of the species have I seen born and die! We have had 'the scrap of paper,' 'the Empires of Prey,' 'the famous *Kultur* which consists in massacring defenceless women and children,' 'victory belongs, as the Japanese say, to the side which can hold out for a quarter of an hour longer than the other,' 'the Germano-Turanians,' 'scientific barbarism,' 'if we want to win the war, as Mr Lloyd George has forcibly said' (but that's out of date now), and 'the fighting spirit of our troops' or 'the pluck of our troops.' Even the syntax of the excellent Norpois has undergone in consequence of the war as profound a change as the baking of bread or the speed of transport. Have you observed that the excellent man, wanting to proclaim his own desires as a truth on the verge of being realised, does not dare nevertheless to employ the future pure and simple, since this would run the risk of being contradicted by events, but has adopted as a sign of future tense the verb 'to know'?"

I confessed to M. de Charlus that I did not quite understand what he meant.

(I ought to mention here that the Duc de Guermantes by no means shared his brother's pessimism. Furthermore, he was as anglophile as M. de Charlus was anglophobe. And he regarded M. Caillaux as a traitor who deserved a thousand times over to be shot. When his brother asked him for proofs of the man's treason, M. de Guermantes replied that, if we were only to convict people who signed a statement saying "I am a traitor," the crime of treason would never be punished. But in case I should not have occasion to return to the subject, I will mention also that a few years later, when Caillaux was on trial, the Duc de Guermantes, animated as he was by the purest anti-Caillautism, met an English military attaché and his wife, an exceptionally cultivated couple with whom he made friends, as he had done at the time of the Dreyfus case with the three charming ladies; that on the first day of the acquaintance he was astounded, talking of Caillaux, whom he regarded as obviously guilty and certain to be convicted, to hear the cultivated and charming couple say: "But he will probably be acquitted, there is absolutely no evidence against him." M. de Guermantes tried to argue that M. de Norpois, in the witness box, had fixed the unhappy Caillaux with his gaze and said to him: "You are the Giolitti of France, yes, Monsieur Caillaux, you are the Giolitti of France." But the cultivated and charming couple had smiled, made fun of M. de Norpois, cited proofs of his senility and concluded that, though *Le Figaro* might have said that he had addressed these words to "the unhappy M. Caillaux," he had probably in fact addressed them to a highly amused M. Caillaux. The Duc de Guermantes lost no time in changing his opinions. That this change could be brought about by the influence of an Englishwoman is not so extraordinary as one might have supposed had it been foretold even as late as 1919, when the English still spoke of the Germans only as "the Huns" and demanded savage penalties for the guilty. For their opinions too had changed and now—less than a year later—they approved every decision which was likely to distress France and be of help to Germany.)

To return to M. de Charlus: "Yes," he said, in reply to my confession that I did not quite understand. "I mean exactly what I say: 'to know,' in the articles of Norpois, indicates the future, it indicates, that is to say, the desires of Norpois, and indeed the desires of us all," he added, perhaps without complete sincerity. "I am sure you will agree with me. If 'to know' had not become simply a sign of the future tense, one might just find it intelligible for the subject of this verb to be a country. For instance, every time Norpois says: 'America would not know how to remain indifferent to these repeated violations of international law,' 'the Dual Monarchy would not know how to fail to come to its senses,' it is clear that such phrases express the desires of Norpois (they are also mine, and yours)—but here nevertheless the verb can still just retain its original meaning, for a country can 'know,' America can 'know,' the Dual Monarchy itself can 'know' (in spite of its eternal 'lack of psychology'). But when Norpois writes: 'These systematic devastations would not know how to persuade the neutrals,' 'the region of the Lakes would not know how to fail to fall speedily into the hands of the Allies,' 'the results of these neutralist elections would not know how to reflect the opinion of the vast majority of the country,' there is no longer any possibility of doubt. For it is certain that these devastations, these regions, these electoral results are inanimate things which cannot 'know.' And in using this formula Norpois is simply addressing to the neutrals an injunction (which, I regret to say, they do not appear to be obeying) to abandon their neutrality, or to the region of the Lakes an injunction no longer to belong to the 'Boches'" (M. de Charlus gave the impression of having to pluck up courage to pronounce the word "Boche," very much as in the past, in the "tram" at Balbec, he had when he had talked about men whose taste is not for women).

"And then, have you noticed the wily fashion in which, ever since 1914, Norpois has begun his articles to the neutrals? He starts by declaring that of course it is not for France to interfere in the politics of Italy (or of Romania or Bulgaria or whatever country it may be). These powers alone must decide, in full independence and with only their own national interests in view, whether or no it is their duty to abandon neutrality. But if these opening statements of the article (what would once have been called the exordium) are disinterested, the sequel is generally much less so. 'Nevertheless'—this is the gist of what Norpois goes on to say—'it is quite clear that only those nations will derive a material benefit from the struggle which have ranged themselves on the side of Law and Justice. It cannot be expected that the Allies should reward, by bestowing upon them the territories which for centuries have resounded with the groans of their oppressed brethen, those peoples who, taking the line of least resistance, have not drawn their sword in the service of the Allies.' Once he has taken this first step towards a counsel of intervention, there is no holding Norpois, it is not only the principles but the moment of intervention as to which, with less and less attempt at disguise, he delivers advice. 'Certainly,' he says, sailing, as he himself would say, under false colours, 'it is for Italy, for Romania alone to decide when the hour has come to strike and what form their intervention shall take. They cannot, however, be unaware that, if they protract their tergiversations, they run the risk of losing their opportunity. Already the hoofs of the Russian cavalry are sending a shiver of unspeakable panic through the trapped millions of Germany. It must be evident that the peoples who have done nothing more than fly to the help of that victory of which already we see the resplendent dawn, will have no right or title to the reward that they may still, if they hasten, etc.' It is like the notices you see at the theatre: 'Book now. The last remaining seats will soon be sold.' And what makes this reasoning all the stupider is that Norpois has to revise it every six months, saying to Romania at regular intervals: 'The hour has come for Romania to determine whether or no she wishes to realise her national aspirations. Any further delay and it may be too late.' But though he has been saying this for three years, not only has the 'too late' not yet come, the offers that are made to Romania are constantly being improved. In the same way he invites France, etc., to intervene in Greece by virtue of her status as a protective power because the treaty that bound Greece to Serbia has not been observed. But, candidly, if France were not at war and did not desire the assistance or the benevolent neutrality of Greece, would she take it into her head to intervene as a protective power? Those moral sentiments which make France raise her voice in horror because Greece has not kept her engagements towards Serbia, are they not silent the moment it is a question of the equally flagrant violation of treaties by Romania or Italy, which countries—rightly I think, and the same is true of Greece—have failed to carry out their obligations (though these are less imperative and less far-reaching than they are said to be) as allies of Germany? The truth is that people see everything through the medium of their newspaper, and what else could they do, seeing that they are not personally acquainted with the men or the events under discussion? At the time of the Affair in which you took so passionate and so bizarre an interest, in that epoch from which it is now the convention to say that we are separated by centuries—for the philosophers of the war have spread the doctrine that all links with the past are broken—I was shocked to see men and women of my family express high esteem for anti-clericals with a Communard past whom their newspaper represented to them as anti-Dreyfusards, and at the same time severe disapproval of a Catholic general of good family who was in favour of a retrial. I am no less shocked now to see all Frenchmen execrate that same Emperor Franz Josef whom once they venerated—and rightly, I may say, I who have known him well and whom he is gracious enough to treat as his cousin. Ah! I haven't written to him since the war," he added, as if he were boldly confessing a fault for which he knew quite well he could not be blamed. "No, the first year I did write, but once only. But what would you have me do? My respect for him is unaltered, but I have many young relatives here fighting in our lines who would, I know, be most displeased were I to carry on a regular correspondence with the head of a nation that is at war with us. How could I? Criticise me who will," he continued, and again he seemed bravely to invite my reproaches, "but in these times I have not wanted a letter signed Charlus to arrive in Vienna. There only one point in the conduct of the old monarch that I would wish to criticise at all severely, and that is that a nobleman of his rank, head of one of the most ancient and illustrious houses of Europe, should have allowed himself to be led astray by a petty landowner—a very intelligent man, of course, but still a complete upstart—like

William of Hohenzollern. It is one of the more shocking anomalies of this war."

And as, the moment he returned to considerations of genealogy and precedence, which for him fundamentally dominated all others, M. de Charlus became capable of extraordinary childishness, he said to me, in the tone that he might have used in speaking of the Marne or Verdun, that there were important and extremely curious things which ought not to be omitted by anyone who came to write the history of this war. "For instance," he said, "everybody is so ignorant that no one has bothered to point out this very striking fact: the Grand Master of the Order of Malta, who is a pure Boche, continues none the less to live in Rome where, as Grand Master of our order, he enjoys the privilege of extraterritoriality. Most interesting," he added significantly, as if to say: "You see that you have not wasted your evening by meeting me." I thanked him, and he assumed the modest air of one who asks no reward for services rendered.

M. de Charlus still retained all his respect and all his affection for certain great ladies who were accused of defeatism, just as he had in the past for others who had been accused of Dreyfusism. He regretted only that by stooping to meddle in politics they had given a handle to the "polemics of the journalists." In his own attitude to them nothing had changed. So systematic was his frivolity that for him birth, combined with beauty and with other sources of prestige, was the durable thing and the war, like the Dreyfus case, merely a vulgar and fugitive fashion. Had the Duchesse de Guermantes been shot for trying to make a separate peace with Austria, he would still have considered her no less noble than before, no more dishonoured by this mischance than is Marie-Antoinette in our eyes from having been condemned to the guillotine. He was speaking seriously now and for a brief instant, with the noble air of a Saint-Vallier or a Saint-Mégrin, erect and stiff and solemn, he was free of all those mannerisms by which men of his sort betray themselves. And yet, why is it that not one of these men can ever have a voice which hits absolutely the right note? Even at this moment, when M. de Charlus's voice was so very near to solemnity, its pitch was still false, it still needed the tuning-fork to correct it. "Now, what was I saying to you?" he went on. "Ah! yes, that people hate Franz Josef now, because they take their cue from their newspaper. As for King Constantine of Greece and the Tsar of Bulgaria, the public has oscillated more than once between aversion and sympathy, according as it has been said turn and turn about that they would join the side of the Entente or of what Brichot calls the Central Empires. Brichot, by the way, is telling us at every moment that 'the hour of Venizelos will strike.' Now I do not doubt that M. Venizelos is a statesman of great capabilities, but who says that the Greeks are so particularly eager to have him? We are told that he wanted Greece to keep her engagements towards Serbia. Even so, it would be as well to know what these engagements were and whether they were more far-reaching than those which Italy and Romania did not scruple to violate. We display for the manner in which Greece implements her treaties and respects her constitution an anxiety which we certainly would not display were it not in our interest to do so. Had there been no war, do you think the 'guarantor' powers would even have noticed the dissolution of the Chambers? What I see is simply that one by one the supports of the King of Greece are being withdrawn from him, so that when the day arrives when he no longer has an army to defend him he can be thrown out of the country or put into prison. I was saying just now that the public judges the King of Greece and the King of the Bulgars only as it is told to judge them by the newspapers. But here again, what opinion of these monarchs could people have except that of their newspapers, seeing that they are not acquainted with them? I personally have seen a great deal of them both, I knew Constantine of Greece very well indeed when he was Diadoch, he is a really splendid man. I have always thought that the Emperor Nicholas had a great affection for him. Of course I mean to imply nothing dishonourable. Princess Christian used to talk openly about it, but she is a terrible scandalmonger. As for the Tsar of the Bulgars, he is an out-and-out nancy and a monstrous liar, but very intelligent, a remarkable man. He likes me very much."

M. de Charlus, who could be so delightful, became horrid when he touched on these subjects. He brought to them that same sort of complacency which we find so exasperating in the invalid who keeps drawing attention to his good health. I have often thought that in the "twister" of Balbec, the faithful who so longed to hear the admission which he avoided making, would in fact have been unable to endure any real display of his mania; ill at ease, breathing with difficulty as one does in a sick-room or in the presence of a morphine addict who takes out his syringe in public, they would themselves have put a stop to the confidences which they imagined they desired. It was, indeed, exasperating to hear the whole world accused, and often without any semblance of proof, by someone who omitted himself from the special category to which one knew perfectly well that he belonged and in which he so readily included others. In spite of all his intelligence, he had in this context fabricated for himself a narrow little philosophy (at the bottom of which there was perhaps just a spark of that interest in the curiousness of life which Swann had felt) which explained everything by reference to these special causes and in which, as always happens when a man stoops to the level of his own vice, he was not only unworthy of himself but exceptionally satisfied with himself. Thus it was that this dignified and noble man put on the most imbecile smile to complete the following little speech: "As there are strong presumptions of the same kind as for Ferdinand of Coburg in the case of the Emperor William, this may well be the reason why Tsar Ferdinand has joined the side of the 'Empires of Prey.' After all, it is very understandable, one is indulgent to a *sister*, one refuses her nothing. To my mind that would be a very pretty explanation of Bulgaria's alliance with Germany." And at this stupid explanation M. de Charlus pealed with laughter as though he really found it most ingenious—an explanation which, even had it been based upon true facts, was in the same puerile category as the observations which M. de Charlus made about the war when he judged it from the point of view of a feudal lord or a Knight of St John of Jerusalem. He ended with a more sensible remark: "What is astonishing," he said, "is that this public which judges the men and events of the war solely from the newspapers, is persuaded that it forms its own opinions."

In this M. de Charlus was right. I have been told that it was fascinating to see the moments of silence and hesitation, so exactly like those that are necessary not merely to the pronouncement but to the formation of a personal opinion, which Mme de Forcheville used to have before declaring, as though it were a heartfelt sentiment: "No, I do not think they will take Warsaw"; "I have the impression that it cannot last another winter"; "the worst thing that could happen is a patched-up peace"; "what alarms me, if you want to know, is the Chamber"; "yes, I believe all the same that we shall succeed in breaking through." And to make these statements Odette assumed a simpering air which became even more exaggerated when she said: "I don't say the German armies do not fight well, but they lack what is called pluck." In pronouncing the word "pluck" (and it was the same when she merely said "fighting spirit") she executed with her hand the sculptural gesture, and with her eyes the wink, of an art student employing a technical term of the studios. Her language now, however, even more than in the past bore witness to her admiration for the English, whom she was no longer obliged to call, as formerly, merely "our neighbours across the Channel," or at most "our friends the English": they were "our loyal allies." Needless to say she never failed, relevant or not, to quote the expression *fair play* (and to point out that in the eyes of the English the Germans were unfair players) and also: "the important thing is to win the war, as our brave allies say." She even had an unfortunate habit of associating the name of her son-in-law with the subject of English soldiers and of referring to the pleasure which he derived from living cheek by jowl with Australians and Scotsmen, New Zealanders and Canadians. "My son-in-law Saint-Loup has learned the slang of all the brave *tommies*, he can make himself understood by the ones from the most distant *dominions*—and I don't mean just the general in command of the base, he fraternises with the humblest *private*."

May this parenthesis on Mme de Forcheville serve as my excuse, while I am strolling along the boulevards side by side with M. de Charlus, for embarking upon another, of greater length but useful as an illustration of this era, on the relations of Mme Verdurin with Brichot. The truth is that if, as we have seen, poor Brichot was judged without indulgence by M. de Charlus (because the latter was both extremely intelligent and more or less unconsciously pro-German), he was treated still worse by the Verdurins. They no doubt were chauvinistic, and this ought to have made them appreciate Brichot's articles, which were in any case quite as good as many pieces of writing which delighted Mme Verdurin. But first, the reader may remember that already at La Raspelière Brichot had become for the Verdurins, instead of the great man that he had once been in their eyes, if not actually a scapegoat like Saniette at any rate a target for their scarcely disguised ridicule. Still, at that period he remained a faithful of the faithful and thus was entitled to a share in the advantages tacitly conferred by the statutes upon all the founding or associate members of the little group. But while, under cover of the war perhaps, or through the rapid crystallisation of a long-delayed social prestige, of which in fact all the necessary elements had for a long time existed in it, invisible and in a state of saturation, the drawing-room of the Verdurins had been opening itself to a new world and the faithful, at first the baits to attract this new world, had ended by being invited less and less themselves, at the same time a parallel phenomenon had been taking place in the life of Brichot. In spite of the Sorbonne, in spite of the *Institut*, before the war he had been a celebrity only inside the Verdurin drawing-room. But when he began to write, almost every day, articles adorned with that second-rate brilliance which we have so often seen him scatter open-handed in the presence of the faithful, yet enriched too with a perfectly genuine learning which, like a true man of the Sorbonne, he made no attempt to conceal however he might clothe it in agreeable forms, the "great world" was literally dazzled. And for once it had bestowed its favour upon someone who was far from being a nonentity, upon a man who could hold the attention of an audience by the fertility of his intelligence and the resources of his memory. So that now, while three duchesses spent the evening with Mme Verdurin, three other duchesses contested the honour of having the great man at their dinner-table, and one of these invitations the great man usually accepted, feeling all the freer to do this since Mme Verdurin, exasperated by the success of his articles with the Faubourg Saint-Germain, was careful never to ask him to her house when some smart woman was to be there whom he did not yet know and who would lose no time in luring him away. Thus journalism (into which he was really doing no more than pour belatedly, with applause and in return for a magnificent financial reward, what all his life he had squandered incognito and for nothing in the Verdurin drawing-room—for his articles, since he had so much knowledge and wrote with such ease, cost him no more trouble than his conversation) might have led, indeed at one moment seemed to be leading Brichot to an indefeasible glory, had it not been for Mme Verdurin. Admittedly, these articles were far from being as remarkable as fashionable people supposed. The vulgarity of the man was apparent in every line beneath the pedantry of the scholar. And side by side with images which had absolutely no meaning ("the Germans will no longer be able to look Beethoven's statue in the face; Schiller must have shuddered in his tomb; the ink which had guaranteed the neutrality of Belgium was scarcely dry; Lenin speaks, but his words are scattered on the winds of the steppe") there were trivialities such as: "twenty thousand prisoners, that is indeed a figure; our command will know how to keep a weather eye open; we mean to win, that sums it up in a nutshell." Yet mixed with all this, how much knowledge, how much intelligence, what just reasoning! Mme Verdurin, however, never began an article by Brichot without first dwelling upon the enjoyable thought that she was going to find ridiculous things in it, and she read it with the most sustained attention in order to be certain of not letting them escape her. And unfortunately it could not be denied that ridiculous things there were. But the faithful did not even wait until they had found them. The most felicitous quotation from an author who was really very little known, at least in the work to which Brichot referred, was seized upon as proof of the most insufferable pedantry, and Mme Verdurin could hardly wait for the hour of dinner when she would unloose the torrential laughter of her guests. "Well, what do you say to tonight's Brichot? I thought of you when I read the quotation from Cuvier. I honestly think the man is going mad." "I haven't read it yet," Cottard would say. "What, you haven't read it yet? But you don't know what delights you are missing. I promise you you will die of laughter." And pleased at heart that someone had not yet read the latest Brichot, since this meant that she herself could call attention to the ludicrous things in it, Mme Verdurin would tell the butler to bring *Le Temps* and would herself read the article aloud, lingering with emphasis on the most simple phrases. After dinner, for the whole of the evening, the anti-Brichot campaign would continue, but with hypocritical reservations. "I won't say it too loud because I am afraid that over there," she would say, indicating Comtesse Molé, "there is a good deal of admiration for this stuff. Fashionable people are more foolish than is generally supposed." In saying this she did her best, by speaking just loud enough, to let Mme Molé hear that she was being talked about, and at the same time to convey to her, by occasionally lowering her voice, that she did not want her to hear what she was saying. Mme Molé was cowardly enough to disown Brichot, whom in fact she thought the equal of Michelet. She said that of course Mme Verdurin was right, and so as to end by nevertheless saying something which seemed to her incontestably true, added: "What one must allow him, is that it is well written." "You call that well written?" said Mme Verdurin. "Personally, I consider that it might have been written by a pig"—an audacity which always made her fashionable guests laugh, particularly as Mme Verdurin, as though she herself were frightened by the word "pig," uttered it in a whisper, holding her hand to her lips. Her

rage against Brichot was still further increased by the naïve fashion
in which he displayed his pleasure at his success, in spite of the fits
of ill-humour provoked in him by the censorship every time that
it—as he expressed it, for he liked to employ new words in order
to show that he was not too donnish—"blue-pencilled" part of his
article. In his presence, however, Mme Verdurin did not reveal
too clearly, save by a certain grumpiness which might have been a
warning to a more perspicacious man, the poor opinion which she
had of the writings of "Chochotte." Only once did she criticise
him, for using the word "I" too often. And it was true that he was
in the habit of using it continually, firstly because, with his pro-
fessorial habits, he was constantly employing phrases like "I grant
that" and even (in the sense of "I am willing to admit that") "I am
willing that," as for instance: "I am willing that the vast development of the fronts should necessitate, etc.," but principally
because, as a militant anti-Dreyfusard of the old days who had
had suspicions of German preparations long before the war, he had
frequently had occasion to write: "Since 1897 I have been
denouncing"; "I pointed out in 1901"; "In my little pamphlet,
of the greatest rarity today (*habent sua fata libelli*) I drew attention,"
and the habit, once formed, had remained with him. He turned
crimson at Mme Verdurin's remark, which had been made with
acerbity. "You are right, Madame. A man who had no more love
for the Jesuits than M. Combes—although he never had the
honour of a preface from our sweet master of delicious scepticism,
Anatole France, who was, if I am not mistaken, my adversary ...
before the Flood—observed that the first person singular is always
odious."[19] From that moment Brichot replaced "I" by "one," but
one did not prevent the reader from seeing that the author was
speaking of himself, indeed it permitted him to speak of himself
more frequently than ever, to comment on the most insignificant
of his own phrases, to build a whole article round a single negative
statement, always behind the protective screen of *one*. If for
example Brichot had said, in another article perhaps, that the
German armies had lost some of their strength, he would begin
thus: "One does not camouflage the truth here. One has said that
the German armies have lost some of their strength. One has not
said that they do not still possess great strength. Still less will one
write that the ground gained, if it is not, etc." In short, simply by
enunciating all that he would not say and by recalling all that he
had said some years ago and all that Clausewitz, Jomini, Ovid,

Apollonius of Tyana and others had said in the more recent or more remote past, Brichot could easily have put together the material for a solid volume. It is to be regretted that he did not publish one, for these erudite articles are now difficult to come by. The Faubourg Saint-Germain, admonished by Mme Verdurin, began by laughing at Brichot in her drawing-room, but continued, after departing from the little clan, to admire him. Then after a while it became the fashion to scoff at him as it had previously been to admire him, and even those ladies who continued to find him dazzling in secret while they were actually reading his articles, checked themselves and mocked as soon as they were no longer alone, so as not to appear less clever than their friends. Never was Brichot so much discussed in the little clan as at this period, but in a spirit of derision. The criterion for judging the intelligence of a newcomer was simply his opinion of Brichot's articles, and if the first time he gave the wrong reply no pains were spared to instruct him how it was that you were recognised to be foolish or clever.

"Well, my poor friend," M. de Charlus went on, "all this is very dreadful, and tedious articles are not the only things we have to deplore. We hear talk of vandalism, of the destruction of statues. But the destruction of so many marvellous young men, who while they lived were incomparable polychrome statues, is that not also vandalism? Will not a town which has lost all its beautiful men be like a town of which all the sculpture has been smashed to pieces? What pleasure can I get from dining in a restaurant where I am served by moth-eaten old buffoons who look like Father Didon, if not by hags in mob-caps who make me think I have strayed into one of Duval's soup-kitchens? Yes, it's as bad as that, my boy, and I think I have the right to say these things, because beauty is still beauty when it exists in a living material. How delightful to be served by rachitic creatures with spectacles on their noses and the reason for their exemption from military service written all over their faces! In these changed times, if you wish to rest your eyes on someone nice-looking in a restaurant, you must look not among the waiters who are serving you but among the customers who are eating and drinking. And then in the old days one could always see a waiter a second time, although they frequently changed, but with some English lieutenant who has perhaps never been to the restaurant before and may well be killed tomorrow, what hope is there of finding out who he is and when he will return? When Augustus of Poland, as we are told by the charming Morand, the delightful author of *Clarisse*, exchanged one of his regiments for a collection of Chinese porcelain, it is my opinion that he made a bad bargain. To think that all those huge footmen six foot tall and more, who used to adorn the monumental staircases of the lovely hostesses whose houses we visited, have one and all been killed, and that most of them joined up because it was dinned into them that the war would last two months! Ah! they did not know as I do the strength of Germany, the courage of the Prussian race," he said, forgetting himself. And then, realising that he had revealed too much of his point of view, he went on: "It is not so much Germany that I fear for France as the war itself. People away from the front imagine that the war is no more than a gigantic boxing-match, of which, thanks to the newspapers, they are spectators at a comfortable distance. But it is nothing of the sort. It is an illness which, when it seems to have been defeated at one point, returns at another. Today Noyon will be recovered from the enemy, tomorrow there will be no bread or chocolate, the next day the man who thought he was safe and was prepared, if necessary, to face death on the battlefield because he had not imagined it, will be panic-stricken to read in the newspapers that his class has been called up. As for monuments, it is not so much the quality as the quantity of the destruction that appals me, I am less horrified at the disappearance of a unique monument like Rheims than at that of all the living entities which once made the smallest village in France instructive and charming."

My mind turned immediately to Combray, but in the past I had thought that I would lower myself in the eyes of Mme de Guermantes by confessing to the humble position which my family occupied there. I wondered now whether the facts had not been revealed to the Guermantes and to M. de Charlus, either by Legrandin or by Swann or Saint-Loup or Morel, and I said nothing, even this silence being less painful to me than a retrospective explanation. I only hoped that M. de Charlus would not mention Combray.

"I do not wish to speak ill of the Americans, Monsieur," he went on, "it seems that they are inexhaustibly generous, and as there has been nobody to conduct the orchestra in this war, as each performer has joined in a long time after the one before and the Americans only began when we had almost finished, they may possibly have an ardour which in us four years of war have succeeded in damping. Even before the war they were fond of our country and our art, they paid high prices for our masterpieces. They have taken many home with them. But this uprooted art, as M. Barrès would call it, is precisely the opposite of what once formed the delicious charm of France. The château explained the church, which itself, because it had been a place of pilgrimage, explained the *chanson de geste*. I need not dwell upon the illustriousness of my family and my connexions, which in any case is not the subject that concerns us. But recently I had occasion, to settle a matter of business, and in spite of a certain coolness that exists between the young couple and myself, to visit my niece Saint-Loup who lives at Combray. Combray was simply a small town like hundreds of others. But the ancestors of my family were portrayed as donors in some of the windows in the church, and in others our armorial bearings were depicted. We had our chapel there, and our tombs. And now this church has been destroyed by the French and the English because it served as an observation-post to the Germans. All that mixture of art and still-living history that was France is being destroyed, and we have not seen the end of the process yet. Of course I am not so absurd as to compare, for family reasons, the destruction of the church of Combray with that of the cathedral of Rheims, that miracle of a Gothic cathedral which seemed, somehow naturally, to have rediscovered the purity of antique sculpture, or of the cathedral of Amiens. I do not know whether the raised arm of St Firmin is still intact today or whether it has been broken. If so, the loftiest affirmation of faith and energy ever made has disappeared from this world."

"You mean its symbol, Monsieur," I interrupted. "And I adore certain symbols no less than you do. But it would be absurd to sacrifice to the symbol the reality that it symbolises. Cathedrals are to be adored until the day when, to preserve them, it would be necessary to deny the truths which they teach. The raised arm of St Firmin said, with an almost military gesture of command: 'Let us be broken, if honour requires.' Do not sacrifice men to stones whose beauty comes precisely from their having for a moment given fixed form to human truths."

"I understand what you mean," M. de Charlus replied, "and M. Barrès, who has sent us, alas, on too many pilgrimages to the statue of Strasbourg and the tomb of M. Déroulède, was both moving and graceful when he wrote that the cathedral of Rheims itself was less dear to us than the lives of our infantrymen. An assertion which makes nonsense of the wrath of our newspapers against the German general in command there who said that the cathedral of Rheims was less precious to him than the life of one German soldier. Indeed, the exasperating and depressing thing is that each country says the same. The reasons for which the industrialists of Germany declare the possession of Belfort indispensable for safeguarding their nation against our ideas of revenge, are the very same reasons as those which Barrès gives for demanding Mainz as a protection against the recurrent urge to invade which possesses the Boches. Why is it that the recovery of Alsace-Lorraine seemed to France an insufficient motive for embarking on a war, yet a sufficient motive for continuing one, for redeclaring it afresh year after year? You appear to believe that nothing can rob France of victory now and with all my heart I hope that you are right, you may be quite sure of that. But is it not a fact that since, rightly or wrongly, the Allies have come to believe that they are sure to win (for my part naturally I should be enchanted by this outcome, but what I see is mostly a profusion of victories on paper, Pyrrhic victories whose cost is not revealed to us) and the Boches no longer believe that they are sure to win, we see Germany striving to make peace quickly and France to prolong the war, France which is a just nation and does right to pronounce words of justice but is also sweet, gentle France and ought to pronounce words of mercy, were it only in order to spare her own children and to allow the flowers which bloom with each new spring to shed their lustre on other things than tombs? Be honest, my friend, you yourself once propounded a theory to me about things existing only in virtue of a creation which is perpetually renewed. The creation of the world did not take place once and for all, you said, it is, of necessity, taking place every day. Well, if you are sincere, you cannot except war from this theory. Never mind if the excellent Norpois has written (trotting out one of those oratorical phrases which are as dear to him as 'the dawn of victory' and 'General Winter'): 'Now that Germany has determined on war, the die is cast,' the truth is that every morning war is declared afresh. And the men who wish to continue it are as guilty as the men who began it, more guilty perhaps, for the latter perhaps did not foresee all its horrors.

"Besides, can we be sure that a war thus prolonged, even if it must eventually end in victory, is without danger? It is difficult to speak of things which have no precedent and of the repercussions upon an organism of an operation which is being attempted for the first time. Generally, it is true, novelties which people find alarming pass off very well. The most prudent republicans thought that it was mad to separate the Church from the State. It was as easy as sending a letter through the post. Dreyfus was rehabilitated, Picquart was made Minister of War, and nobody uttered a murmur. Yet what may we not fear from the stress and strain of a war which has continued without pause for several years? What will men do when they return from it? Will fatigue have broken them or will it have driven them mad? All this could have grave results, if not for France, at least for the government, perhaps even for the present form of government. You once made me read Maurras's excellent novel *Aimée de Coigny*. The original Aimée, you remember, was waiting for the collapse of the Empire to ensue from the war that it was waging in 1812, and I should be surprised if she has not her counterpart today. If a present-day Aimée de Coigny exists, will her hopes with regard to the Republic be fulfilled? I wouldn't want that.

"But to return to the war itself, can we say that the man who first began it was the Emperor William? I am very doubtful about that. And if it was, what has he done that Napoleon, for instance, did not do—something that I certainly find abominable, but that I am astonished to see also inspiring such horror in those who burn incense before Napoleon, those who on the day that war was declared exclaimed like General Pau: 'I have been waiting forty years for this day. It is the most glorious day of my life.' Heaven knows whether anyone protested with greater energy than myself at the time when a deference out of all proportion was paid by society to the nationalists and the military men, when every friend of the arts was accused of occupying himself with things of baleful import to France and all civilisation of an unwarlike nature was thought to be pernicious! In those days an authentic member of the best society hardly counted compared with a general. Some madwoman came within an inch of presenting *me* to M. Syveton, as if *I* were *his* inferior. You will tell me that the rules I was striving to maintain were merely social ones. But for all their apparent frivolity they might have prevented many excesses. I have always honoured the defenders of grammar or logic. We realise fifty years later that they have averted serious dangers. Today our nationalists are the most anti-German of men, the most determined to persevere to the bitter end. But in the last fifteen years their philosophy has completely changed. It is true that they are pressing for the continuation of the war. But they are doing this only in order to exterminate a warlike race, they are doing it from love of peace. The idea of a martial civilisation, which fifteen years ago they thought so beautiful, now fills them with horror; not only do they reproach the Prussians for having allowed the military element to predominate in their state, they claim that throughout the ages military civilisations have been destructive of all that they now hold precious, not only of the arts but also of chivalry towards women. And if any critic of their views is converted to nationalism he at the same moment becomes a friend of peace. He is persuaded that in all martial civilisations women have been humiliated and crushed. One dare not reply that the 'lady' of a knight in the Middle Ages or Dante's Beatrice was perhaps placed upon a throne as elevated as the heroines of M. Becque. Any day now I expect to see myself placed at table beneath a Russian revolutionary or simply beneath one of these generals of ours who wage war out of horror of war and in order to punish a people for cultivating an ideal which fifteen years ago they themselves regarded as the only one that could invigorate a nation. It is not many months since the unhappy Tsar was honoured for his part in assembling the conference at The Hague. But now that people hail the advent of a free Russia they forget his claim to glory. So turns the wheel of the world. Meanwhile Germany uses expressions so similar to those of France that one can hardly believe she is not quoting her, she never tires of saying that she is 'struggling for existence.' When I read: 'We shall struggle against an implacable and cruel enemy until we have obtained a peace which will give us guarantees for the future against all aggression and ensure that the blood of our brave soldiers shall not have flowed in vain,' or: 'he who is not for us is against us,' I do not know whether the words are the Emperor William's or M. Poincaré's, for they have both of them, with a few trifling differences, pronounced such phrases twenty times, although to be truthful I must admit that in this instance it is the Emperor who has copied the President of the Republic. France would perhaps have been less eager to prolong the war if she had remained weak, and Germany certainly would have been in less of a hurry to end it if she had not ceased to be strong. I should say, to be as strong as she was; for strong, as you will see, she still is."

He had got into the habit of talking at the top of his voice, from excitability, from the need to find an outlet for impressions of which, never having cultivated any art, he needed to unburden himself—as an airman unloads his bombs, if necessary in open country—even where his words could impinge upon nobody, particularly in society, where they fell completely at random and where people listened to him out of snobbishness, uncritically and (to such an extent did he tyrannise his audience) one may say under compulsion and even from fear. On the boulevards this loud harangue of his was also a mark of contempt for the passers-by, for whom he no more lowered his voice than he would have stepped aside to avoid them. But it struck a discordant note there and caused astonishment and, worse than that, rendered audible to the people who turned round to look at us remarks which might well have made them take us for defeatists. I pointed this out to M. de Charlus but succeeded only in arousing his mirth. "You must admit that that would be most amusing," he said. "After all, one never knows, every evening each one of us runs the risk of being part of the next day's news. Is there really any reason why I should not be shot in a ditch at Vincennes? That is what happened to my great-uncle the Duc d'Enghien. The thirst for noble blood maddens a certain rabble—and here they show a greater fastidiousness than lions, for those beasts, as you know, would throw themselves even upon Mme Verdurin if she had so much as a scratch upon her nose. Upon what in my youth we would have called her boko!" And he began to roar with laughter as if we had been alone in a room.

At moments, seeing suspicious-looking individuals drawn out of the shadows by the passage of M. de Charlus conglomerate at a little distance from him, I wondered whether it would be more agreeable to him if I left him alone or remained with him. In the same way, if you meet an old man who is subject to frequent epileptic fits and see from the incoherence of his gait that an attack is probably imminent, you may ask yourself whether your company is more desired by him as a support or dreaded as that of a witness from whom he would prefer to conceal the attack and whose mere presence may perhaps suffice to bring it on, whereas absolute calm might succeed in averting it. But in the case of the sick man the possibility of the event upon which you are uncertain whether or no you ought to turn your back is revealed by his walking in circles as if he were drunk; while in that of M. de Charlus the divagations—sign of a possible incident as to which I did not know whether he desired or feared that my presence should prevent its occurrence—were transferred, as in an ingenious stage production, from the Baron himself, who was walking straight ahead, to a whole circle of supernumerary actors. All the same, it is my belief that he preferred to avoid the encounter, for he dragged me down a side-street, darker than the boulevard but into which nevertheless the latter was incessantly discharging—or else like a tributary stream they were flowing towards it—soldiers of every arm and of every nation, a rising youthful tide, compensatory and consoling for M. de Charlus, the reverse of that ebb-tide of all men towards the frontier which in the first days of mobilisation had made a vacuum in the capital. At every moment M. de Charlus expressed his admiration for the brilliant uniforms which passed before us, which made of Paris a town as cosmopolitan as a port, as unreal as a stage setting designed by a painter who has simply put up a few scraps of architecture as an excuse for assembling the most variegated and glittering costumes.

Literally he did not know which way to turn his head; often he raised it, regretting that he did not have a pair of field-glasses (which would in fact have been of very little use to him), since because of the Zeppelin raid of two days earlier, which had caused the authorities to redouble their precautions, there were soldiers in greater numbers than usual even in the sky. The aeroplanes which a few hours earlier I had seen, like insects, as brown dots upon the surface of the blue evening, now passed like blazing fire-ships through the darkness of the night, which was made darker still by the partial extinction of the street-lamps. And perhaps the greatest impression of beauty that these human shooting stars made us feel came simply from their forcing us to look at the sky, towards which normally we so seldom raise our eyes. In this Paris, whose beauty in 1914 I had seen awaiting almost defenceless the threat of the approaching enemy, there was certainly, as there had been then, the ancient unalterable splendour of a moon cruelly and mysteriously serene, which poured down its useless beauty upon the still untouched buildings of the capital; but as in 1914, and more now than in 1914, there was also something else, there were lights from a different source, intermittent beams which, whether they came from the aeroplanes or from the searchlights of the Eiffel Tower, one knew to be directed by an intelligent will, by a friendly vigilance which gave one the same kind of emotion, inspired the same sort of gratitude and calm that I had felt in Saint-Loup's room at Doncières, in the cell of that military cloister where so many fervent and disciplined hearts were exercising themselves in readiness for the day when, without hesitation, in the midst of their youth, they would consummate their sacrifice.

After the raid of two days earlier, when it had been more full of movement than the earth, the sky had become calm again as the sea becomes calm after a storm. But like the sea after a storm, it had not yet recovered absolute tranquillity. Aeroplanes were still mounting like rockets to the level of the stars, and searchlights, as they quartered the sky, swept slowly across it what looked like a pale dust of stars, of errant milky ways. Meanwhile the aeroplanes took their places among the constellations and seeing these "new stars" one might well have supposed oneself to be in another hemisphere.

M. de Charlus spoke to me of his admiration for these airmen of ours, and went on, since he was no more capable of checking the flow of his pro-German feelings than of his other inclinations, even though at the same time he denied both the one and the other tendency: "I must add of course that I have just as much admiration for the Germans who go up in the Gothas. And when it comes to the Zeppelins, think of the courage that is needed! They are heroes, there is no other word for it. What difference can it make that they are attacking civilians, if guns are firing at them? Are you afraid of the Gothas and the bombardment?" I admitted that I was not, but perhaps I was wrong. No doubt, my idleness having given me the habit, when it was a question of my work, of putting it off from one day to another, I imagined that death too might be postponed in the same fashion. How should one be afraid of a bombardment when one is convinced that one will not be hit today? Anyhow, formed in isolation, the idea of bombs being dropped, the idea of the possibility of death, had added nothing tragic to the image which I had in my mind of the German flying machines, until from one of them, storm-tossed and partly hidden from my sight by the thick billowing mists of an agitated sky, from an aeroplane which, though I knew it to be murderous, I imagined only as stellar and celestial, I had one evening seen the gesture of a bomb dropped upon us. For the novel reality of a danger is perceived only through the medium of that new thing, not assimilable to anything that we already know, to which we give the name "an impression" and which is often, as in the present case, epitomised in a line, a line which defines an intention and possesses the latent potentiality of the action which has given it its particular form, like the invisible line described by this falling bomb or those other lines which I had seen at the same time from the Pont de la Concorde, on all sides of the threatening, hunted aeroplane, as though they had been reflexions in the clouds of the fountains of the Champs-Elysées and the Place de la Concorde and the Tuileries: the beams of the searchlights travelling through the sky like luminous jets of water, which also were lines full of intention, full of the provident and protective intentions of men of power and wisdom to whom, as on that night in the barracks at Doncières, I felt grateful for condescending to employ their strength, with this so beautiful precision, in watching over our safety.

The night was as beautiful as in 1914, and the threat to Paris was as great. The moonlight was like a soft and steady magnesium flare, by the light of which some camera might, for the last time, have been recording nocturnal images of those lovely groups of buildings like the Place Vendôme and the Place de la Concorde, to which my fear of the shells that were perhaps about to destroy them imparted by contrast, as they stood in their still intact beauty, a sort of plenitude, as if they were bending forward and freely offering their defenceless architecture to the blows that might fall. "You are not afraid?" M. de Charlus repeated. "The people of Paris don't realise the situation. I am told that Mme Verdurin gives parties every day. I know it only from hearsay, personally I know absolutely nothing about them, I have completely broken off relations," he added, lowering not only his eyes as if a telegraph boy had passed, but also his head and his shoulders and raising his arm with the gesture that signifies, if not "I wash my hands of them" at any rate "I can tell you nothing about them" (not that I had asked him anything). "I know that Morel still goes there a lot," he went on (it was the first time that he had mentioned him again). "It is rumoured that he much regrets the past and would like to make it up with me," he continued, exhibiting at one and the same time the credulity of a man of the Faubourg who says: "People say that there are more talks than ever going on between France and Germany, and even that negotiations have been started," and that of the lover whom the most cruel rebuffs are unable to convince. "In any case, if he wants it, he only has to say so. I am older than he, it is not for me to take the first step." And certainly there was no need to say this, so evident was it. But it was not even sincere, and this made one very embarrassed for M. de Charlus, for one felt that, by saying that it was not for him to take the first step, he was in fact making one and was waiting for me to offer to undertake a reconciliation.

Naturally I was familiar with the credulity, naïve or feigned, of people who love someone, or simply are not invited to someone's house, and attribute to that someone a desire of which, in fact, in spite of wearisome solicitations, he has given no hint. But from the sudden tremor of the voice with which M. de Charlus pronounced these words, from the anxious look which flickered in the depths of his eyes, I got the impression that there was something more here than an ordinary attempt at bluff. I was not mistaken, and I will relate straight away the two facts which proved subsequently that I was right. (I take a leap of many years for the second of these incidents, which was posterior to the death of M. de Charlus, who was not to die until a much later period and whom we shall have occasion to see again a number of times, greatly changed from what we have known him to be, particularly the last time of all, when he had come to forget Morel completely.) The first of these incidents took place only two or three years after the evening on which I walked down the boulevards with M. de Charlus. About two years after this evening, I met Morel. I thought immediately of M. de Charlus, of the pleasure it would give him to see the violinist again, and I urged Morel to go and see him, even if it were only once. "He has been good to you," I said, "he is an old man now, he may die, you should settle old scores and obliterate all trace of your quarrel." Morel appeared to be entirely of my opinion as to the desirability of making peace, but he none the less refused categorically to visit M. de Charlus even once. "You are wrong," I said. "Is it from obstinacy, from indolence, from spite, from misplaced vanity, from concern for your virtue (you may be sure that it will not be attacked), from coquettishness?" At this point the violinist, twisting his features as he forced himself to make an admission which no doubt was extremely painful, replied with a shudder: "No, it is from none of all those things. As for virtue, I don't give a damn for it. Spite? On the contrary, I am beginning to pity him. It is not from coquettishness, which could serve no purpose. It is not from having too much to do, for there are whole days when I stay at home and twiddle my thumbs. No, it is not for any of these reasons. It is—but never say this to anybody, I am mad to tell you—it is, it is . . . from fear!" He began to tremble in every limb. I confessed that I did not understand him. "No, don't ask me, don't let's talk about it, you do not know him as I do, I may say that you do not know him at all." "But what harm can he do you? In any case, he won't want to harm you if you put an end to the bitterness that exists between you. And then, you know that at heart he is very kind." "Good heavens, yes! I know he is kind. And wonderfully considerate, and honest. But let me alone, don't let's talk about it, I beseech you—it's a shameful admission, but I am afraid!"

The second incident dates from after the death of M. de Charlus. I was brought one or two things which he had left me as mementoes, and also a letter enclosed in three envelopes, which he had written at least ten years before his death. He had been seriously ill at the time and had put all his affairs in order, but then had recovered, only to fall later into the condition in which we shall see him on the day of an afternoon party given by the Princesse de Guermantes—and the letter, put aside in a strong-box with the objects which he was bequeathing to a few friends, had remained there for seven years, seven years during which he had completely forgotten Morel. It was written in a firm and delicate handwriting and was couched in the following terms:

"My dear friend, the ways of Providence are inscrutable. Sometimes a fault in a very ordinary man is made to serve its purposes by helping one of the just not to slip from his lofty eminence. You know Morel, you know the humbleness of his origin and the height (my own level, no less) to which I wished to raise him. You are aware that he preferred to return not to the dust and ashes from which every man—for man surely is the true phoenix—may be born again, but to the slime in which the viper crawls. He fell, and in so doing he saved me from falling from where I belong. You know that my arms contain the device of Our Lord himself: *Inculcabis super leonem et aspidem*, with the crest of a man having beneath the soles of his feet, as heraldic supporters, a lion and a serpent. Well, if I have succeeded as I have in crushing the lion proper that I am, it is thanks to the serpent and his prudence, which just now I was thoughtless enough to call a fault, for the profound wisdom of the Gospel makes a virtue of it, a virtue at least for other people. Our serpent, of the once harmonious and well-modulated hisses, was, when he had a charmer—a charmer charmed, moreover—not merely musical and reptilian, he had, to the point of cowardice, that virtue, prudence, which I now hold to be divine. This divine prudence it was that made him resist the appeals to come back and see me which I conveyed to him, and I shall have no peace in this world or hope of forgiveness in the next if I do not confess the truth to you. He was, in resisting my appeals, the instrument of divine wisdom, for I was resolved, had he come, that he should not leave my house alive. One of us two had to disappear. I had decided to kill him. God counselled him prudence to preserve me from crime. I do not doubt that the intercession of the Archangel Michael, my patron saint, played a great part in this and I beseech him to pardon me for having so neglected him over many years and for having so ill responded to the innumerable favours which he has conferred upon me, especially in my struggle against evil. I owe it to this Servant of God—I say the words in the plenitude of my faith and my understanding—that the heavenly Father inspired Morel not to come. And so it is I who am now about to die.

> Your faithfully devoted, *Semper idem*,
> P. G. Charlus.

Reading these words I understood Morel's fear. Certainly there was in the letter more than a small element of pride and of literature. But the confession was true. And Morel had known better than I that the "practically mad side" of her brother-in-law's character which Mme de Guermantes used to hint at was not confined, as until this revelation I had supposed, to his momentary exhibitions of superficial and ineffective rage.

But I must return to my narrative. I am walking down the boulevards by the side of M. de Charlus, who has just made a vague attempt to use me as an intermediary for overtures of peace between himself and Morel. Seeing that I made no reply, "Anyhow," he went on, "I do not know why it is that he no longer gives concerts. There is no music now on the pretext that there is a war on, but people dance and go out to dinner and women invent something called Ambrine for their skin. Social amusements fill what may prove, if the Germans continue to advance, to be the last days of our Pompeii. And if the city is indeed doomed, that in itself will save it from frivolity. The lava of some German Vesuvius—and their naval guns are no less terrible than a volcano—has only to surprise these good people at their toilet and to eternise their gestures by interrupting them, and in days to come it will be part of a child's education to look at pictures in his school-books of Mme Molé about to put on a last layer of powder before going out to dine with a sister-in-law, or Sosthène de Guermantes adding the final touches to his false eyebrows; these things will be the subject of lectures by the Brichots of the future, for the frivolity of an age, when ten centuries have passed over it, is matter for the gravest erudition, particularly if it has been embalmed by a volcanic eruption or by the substances akin to lava which a bombardment projects. What documents for the future historian if asphyxiating gases, like the fumes of Vesuvius, and the collapse of a whole city, like the catastrophe which buried Pompeii, should preserve intact all the imprudent dowagers who have not yet sent off their paintings and their statues to safety in Bayonne! And indeed, for the last year, have we not already seen fragments of Pompeii every evening: people burying themselves in their cellars, not in order to emerge with some old bottle of Mouton Rothschild or Saint-Emilion, but to conceal along with themselves their most treasured belongings, like the priests of Herculaneum whom death surprised in the act of carrying away the sacred vessels? Attachment to an object always brings death to its possessor. True, Paris was not, like Herculaneum, founded by Hercules. But how many points of resemblance leap to the eye! And this lucid vision that is given to us is not unique to ourselves, it has been granted to every age. If I reflect that tomorrow we may suffer the fate of the cities of Vesuvius, these in their turn sensed that they were threatened with the doom of the accursed cities of the Bible. On the wall of a house in Pompeii has been found the revealing inscription: *Sodoma, Gomora.*"

Perhaps it was this name of Sodom and the ideas that it evoked in him, or possibly the idea of the bombardment, that made M. de Charlus for an instant raise his eyes to heaven, but soon he brought them back to earth. "I admire all the heroes of this war," he said. "Why, my dear boy, those English soldiers whom at the beginning I rather thoughtlessly dismissed as mere football players presumptuous enough to measure themselves against professionals—and what professionals!—well, purely from the aesthetic point of view they are quite simply Greek athletes, you understand me, my boy, Greek athletes, they are the young men of Plato, or rather they are Spartans. I have a friend who has been to Rouen where their base is, he has seen marvels, marvels almost unimaginable. It is not Rouen any longer, it is another town. Of course the old Rouen still exists, with the emaciated saints of the cathedral. And naturally, that is beautiful too, but it is something quite different. And our *poilus*! I cannot tell you how deliciously full of character I find our *poilus*, the young Parisian boys, like that one there, for instance, who is passing us, with his knowing expression, his alert and humorous face. I often stop them for one reason or another and we chat for a moment or two, and what subtlety, what good sense! And the boys from the provinces, how amusing and nice they are, with the way they roll their *r*'s and their regional dialects! I have always lived a lot in the country, I have slept in farms, I know how to talk to them. Still, our admiration for the French must not make us depreciate our enemies, that would only be to disparage ourselves. And you don't know what a soldier the German soldier is; you haven't seen him, as I have, march past on parade, doing the goose-step, *unter den Linden*."

And returning to that ideal of virility which he had outlined to me at Balbec and which, with time, had assumed a more philosophical form in his mind, but using also absurd arguments which at moments, even just after he had said something out of the ordinary, gave his hearer a glimpse of the flimsiness of mental fabric of a mere society gentleman, albeit an intelligent one: "You see," he said to me, "that splendid sturdy fellow the Boche soldier is strong and healthy and thinks only of the greatness of his country, *Deutschland über Alles*, which is not so stupid as you might think, whereas we, while they were preparing themselves in a virile fashion, were hopelessly sunk in dilettantism." This word probably signified for M. de Charlus something analogous to literature, for immediately, remembering no doubt that I was fond of literature and had at one time intended to devote myself to it, he slapped me on the shoulder (taking the opportunity to lean so heavily upon me that the blow hurt as much as, in the days when I was doing my military service, the recoil of a "76" against my shoulder-blade) and said, as if to soften the reproach: "Yes, we were sunk in dilettantism, all of us, you too, you may remember. Like me you may say your *mea culpa*. We have been too dilettante." From astonishment at this reproach, from lack of readiness in repartee, from deference towards my interlocutor, and also because I was touched by his friendly kindness, I replied as though I too, as he suggested, had cause to beat my breast—an idiotic reaction, for I could not be accused of the slightest suggestion of dilettantism. "Well," he said to me, "I must leave you here" (the group which had escorted him at a distance had finally abandoned us), "I am going off to bed like a very old gentleman, particularly as, so it seems, the war has changed all our habits—isn't that one of the imbecile aphorisms which Norpois is so fond of?" I knew, as a matter of fact, that when he went home at night M. de Charlus did not cease to be surrounded by soldiers, for he had turned his house

into a military hospital and had done this, I believe, in obedience
to the dictates much less of his imagination than of his kind heart.

It was a transparent and breathless night; I imagined that the
Seine, flowing between the twin semicircles of the span and the
reflection of its bridges, must look like the Bosporus. And—a
symbol perhaps of the invasion foretold by the defeatism of
M. de Charlus, or else of the co-operation of our Muslim brothers
with the armies of France—the moon, narrow and curved like a
sequin, seemed to have placed the sky of Paris beneath the oriental
sign of the crescent.

M. de Charlus lingered a few moments more, while he said
good-bye to me with a shake of my hand powerful enough to
crush it to pieces—a Germanic peculiarity to be found in those
who think like the Baron. For several seconds he continued, as
Cottard would have said, to "knead" my hand, as if he had wished
to restore to my joints a suppleness which they had never lost. In
certain blind men the sense of touch makes good to a certain
extent the lack of sight. I do not exactly know what sense it was
taking the place of here. Perhaps he thought that he was merely
shaking my hand, as no doubt he thought that he was
merely seeing a Senegalese soldier who passed in the darkness
without deigning to notice that he was being admired. But in
each case the Baron was mistaken, the intensity of contact and of
gaze was greater than propriety permitted. "Don't you see all the
Orient of Decamps and Fromentin and Ingres and Delacroix in
this scene?" he asked me, still immobilised by the passage of the
Senegalese. "As you know, I for my part am interested in things
and in people only as a painter, a philosopher. Besides, I am too
old. But how unfortunate that to complete the picture one of us
two is not an odalisque!"

It was not the Orient of Decamps or even of Delacroix that began
to haunt my imagination when the Baron had left me, but the old
Orient of those *Arabian Nights* which I had been so fond of; losing
myself gradually in the network of these dark streets, I thought of
the Caliph Harun al-Rashid going in search of adventures in the
hidden quarters of Baghdad. The weather was warm and my walk
had made me hot and thirsty, but the bars had all closed long ago
and, because of the scarcity of petrol, the rare taxis which I met,
driven by Levantines or negroes, did not even take the trouble to
respond to my signs. The only place where I might have been able

to get something to drink and rest until I felt strong enough to walk home would have been a hotel. But in the street, rather remote from the centre of the town, to which I had penetrated, every hotel, since the Gothas had begun to drop their bombs on Paris, had closed. The same was true of almost all the shops, the shop-keepers, either owing to lack of staff or because they had taken fright themselves, having fled to the country and left on their door a hand-written notice announcing in some conventional phrase that they would reopen at a distant date (though even that seemed problematical). The few establishments which had managed to survive announced in the same fashion that they were open only twice a week. One felt that poverty, dereliction, fear inhabited the whole quarter. I was all the more surprised, therefore, to see that among these abandoned houses there was one in which life seemed, on the contrary, to have been victorious and terror and bankruptcy to have yielded to activity and wealth. Behind the closed shutters of each window the lights, dimmed on account of police regulations, revealed nevertheless a complete disregard for economy. And at every moment the door opened to allow some fresh visitor to enter or leave. It was a hotel which, because of the money its proprietors must be making, could not fail to have aroused the envy of all the neighbouring tradespeople; and I too became curious when, at a distance of fifteen yards, that is to say too far off for me to be able to make him out clearly in the profound darkness, I saw an officer come out and walk rapidly away.

Something, however, struck me: not his face, which I did not see, nor his uniform, which was disguised by a heavy greatcoat, but the extraordinary disproportion between the number of different points which his body successively occupied and the very small number of seconds within which he made good this departure which had almost the air of a sortie from a besieged town. So that my mind turned, if I did not explicitly recognise him—I will not say even to the build, nor to the slimness or the carriage or the swift movements of Saint-Loup—but to the sort of ubiquity which was so special to him. This military man with the ability to occupy so many different positions in space in such a short time disappeared down a side-street without seeing me, and I was left wondering whether it would be wise to enter a hotel whose modest appearance made me think that it could hardly have been Saint-Loup who had emerged. And yet I recalled involuntarily that he had—unjustly—been involved in a case of espionage because his name had been found in some letters captured on a German officer. He had, of course, been completely exonerated by the military authorities. But in spite of myself I associated this recollection with what I now saw. Was this hotel being used as a meeting-place of spies?

The officer had only just disappeared when I saw some private soldiers of various arms go in, which further strengthened my suspicions. I was now, however, extremely thirsty. I should probably be able to get something to drink inside and at the same time I might attempt, although I felt nervous at the prospect, to assuage my curiosity. And so, but not, I think, primarily from curiosity about the officer I had seen, I hesitated no longer but climbed the little staircase at the top of which the door of a sort of hall stood open, no doubt on account of the heat. I thought at first that I might fail to discover very much, for from the staircase, where I remained in shadow, I saw several people come and ask for a room and receive the answer that there were absolutely none left. The objection to these people, I guessed, was simply that they did not belong to the nest of espionage, for a moment later a common sailor presented himself and was promptly given room No. 28. From where I stood in the darkness I could, without being seen, observe a few soldiers and two men of the working classes who were chatting tranquilly in a stiflingly hot little room, gaudily decorated with coloured pictures of women cut from illustrated magazines and reviews.

These men, as they chatted quietly together, were expounding patriotic ideas: "After all, you've got to do what the other blokes do," said one. "Well, you can be jolly sure *I* don't mean to get killed," was the reply of another, who evidently was going off the next day to a dangerous post, to some expression of good wishes which I had not heard. "I reckon, at twenty-two, after only doing six months, it would be a bit hard," he exclaimed in a voice in which could be heard, even more plainly than the desire to go on living, the assurance that his reasoning was correct, as though the fact that he was only twenty-two could not fail to give him a better chance of survival, as though it were out of the question that he should be killed. "It's terrific in Paris," said another; "you'd never know there's a war on. How about you, Julot, d'you still mean to join up?" "Of course I do, I can't wait to take a pot-shot or two at these filthy Boches." "This Joffre, you know, he's just a man who sleeps with the politicians' wives, he's never done a thing himself." "That's a dreadful way to talk," said a slightly older man, an airman, and then, turning to the workman who had just made the statement: "I should advise you not to talk like that in the front line, the *poilus* would soon do you in." The banality of these scraps of conversation did not inspire me with any great wish to hear more, and I was about to make my entrance or go back down the stairs when I was jolted out of my indifference by hearing a series of remarks which made me shudder: "I'm amazed the boss isn't back yet, damn it, at this hour of the night I don't know where he's going to find any chains." "Anyhow, the chap's already tied up." "Tied up? Well, he is and he isn't. Tie me up like that and I'd soon untie myself." "But the padlock's closed." "Of course it's closed, but it's not so impossible to open it. The trouble is the chains aren't long enough. Don't you try and tell me, I was beating the stuffing out of him all last night until my hands were covered with blood." "Are you doing the beating tonight?" "No. It's not me, it's Maurice. But it'll be me on Sunday, the boss promised me." I understood now why the strong arm of the sailor had been needed. If peaceable citizens had been turned away, it was not because the hotel was a nest of spies. An appalling crime was about to be committed, unless someone arrived in time to discover it and have the criminals arrested. And yet the whole scene, in the midst of this peaceful and threatened night, was like a dream or a fairy-tale, so that it was at once with the pride of an emissary of justice and the rapture of a poet that I at length, my mind made up, entered the hotel.

I touched my hat lightly and the people in the room, without rising to their feet, replied more or less civilly to the greeting. "Can you tell me who is in charge here? I should like a room and something to drink sent up to it." "Will you wait a minute, the boss has gone out." "There's the director, he's upstairs," suggested one of the men who had taken part in the conversation. "But you know he can't be disturbed." "Do you think they will give me a room?" "Expect so." "43 must be free," said the young man who was sure he would not be killed because he was twenty-two years old. And he moved a little way along the sofa to make room for me. "Suppose we open the window a bit, you can cut the smoke with a knife in here!" said the airman; and indeed they all had their pipe or their cigarette. "Yes, but in that case close the shutters first, you know it's forbidden to show any light because of the

Zeppelins." "We've finished with the Zeppelins. There's even been something in the papers about their having all been shot down." "We've finished with this, we've finished with that, what d'you know about it? When you've done fifteen months at the front, as I have, and shot down your fifth Boche aeroplane, you'll be able to talk. What d'you want to believe the papers for? They were over Compiègne yesterday, they killed a mother and two children." "A mother and two children!" said the young man who hoped not to be killed, with blazing eyes and a look of profound compassion upon his energetic and open countenance, which I found very likeable. "There's been no news of big Julot lately. His 'godmother' hasn't had a letter from him for eight days, and it's the first time he's been so long without writing." "Who is she, his 'godmother'?" "The woman who looks after the toilets just beyond the Olympia." "Do they sleep together?" "What an idea! She's a married woman, she couldn't be more respectable. She sends him money every week out of pure kindness of heart. She's a real good sort." "Do you know him then, big Julot?" "Do I know him!" retorted scornfully the young man of twenty-two. "He's a close friend of mine and one of the best. There's not many I think as highly of as I do of him: a real pal, always ready to do you a good turn. Yes, it would be a catastrophe all right if anything had happened to him." Someone proposed a game of dice and, from the feverish haste with which the young man of twenty-two shook them and cried out the results, with his eyes starting out of his head, it was easy to see that he had the gambler's temperament. I did not quite catch the next remark that someone made to him, but he exclaimed with a note of profound pity in his voice: "Julot a ponce! You mean he *says* he's a ponce. But he's no more a ponce than I am. I've seen him with my own eyes paying his woman, yes, paying her. That's to say, I don't say Jeanne l'Algérienne didn't give him a little something now and then, but it was never more than five francs, and what's that from a woman in a brothel earning more than fifty francs a day? A present of five francs! Some men are just too stupid to live. And now she's at the front, well, her life may be hard, I grant you, but she can earn as much as she wants—and she sends him nothing. Bah, that chap a ponce? There's plenty who could call themselves a ponce at that rate. Not only is he not a ponce, in my opinion he's an imbecile." The oldest of the group, whom the boss had no doubt for that reason put in charge of the others, with instructions to make them behave with a certain restraint, had been to the lavatory for a moment and heard only the end of this conversation. But he could not help looking in my direction and seemed visibly upset at the impression such talk must have made on me. Without addressing himself specially to the young man of twenty-two, though it was he who had been expounding this theory of venal love, he said, in a general manner: "You're talking too much and too loud, the window is open, there are people asleep at this hour. You know quite well that if the boss came back and heard you talking like that, he wouldn't be at all pleased."

At that very moment the door was heard to open and everyone was silent, thinking it was the boss, but it was only a foreign chauffeur who was welcomed as an old friend by everybody in the room. But seeing a magnificent watchchain displayed upon the chauffeur's jacket, the young man of twenty-two threw him a questioning and amused glance, followed by a frown and a severe wink in my direction. I understood that the first look meant: "What's that, did you steal it? My congratulations." And the second: "Don't say anything, because of this fellow we don't know." Suddenly the boss came in, carrying several yards of heavy iron chains—sufficient to secure quite a number of convicts—and sweating. "What a weight!" he said. "If you weren't all so idle, I shouldn't be obliged to fetch them myself." I told him that I wanted a room. "Just for a few hours. I can't find a cab and I am rather unwell. But I should like something to drink sent up." "Pierrot, go and fetch some *cassis* from the cellar and tell them to get No. 43 ready. There's 7 ringing again. They say they're ill. Ill my foot, I wouldn't be surprised if they'd been doping themselves, they look half cracked, it's time they were shown the door. Has anybody put a pair of sheets in 22? Good! There goes 7 again, run and see what it is. Well, Maurice, what are you standing there for? You know someone's waiting for you, go up to 14b. And get a move on." And Maurice hurried out after the boss, who seemed a little annoyed that I had seen his chains and disappeared carrying them with him. "How is it you're so late?" the young man of twenty-two asked the chauffeur. "What do you mean, late? I'm an hour early. But it's too hot in the streets. My appointment's not till midnight." "Who have you come for then?" "Pretty Pamela," said the dark-skinned chauffeur, whose laugh uncovered a set of fine white teeth. "Ah!" said the young man of twenty-two.

Presently I was taken up to Room 43, but it was so unpleasantly stuffy and my curiosity was so great that, having drunk my *cassis*, I started to go downstairs again, then, changing my mind, turned round and went up past the floor of Room 43 to the top of the building. Suddenly from a room situated by itself at the end of a corridor, I thought I heard stifled groans. I walked rapidly towards the sounds and put my ear to the door. "I beseech you, mercy, have pity, untie me, don't beat me so hard," said a voice. "I kiss your feet, I abase myself, I promise not to offend again. Have pity on me." "No, you filthy brute," replied another voice, "and if you yell and drag yourself about on your knees like that, you'll be tied to the bed, no mercy for you," and I heard the noise of the crack of a whip, which I guessed to be reinforced with nails, for it was followed by cries of pain. At this moment I noticed that there was a small oval window opening from the room on to the corridor and that the curtain had not been drawn across it; stealthily in the darkness I crept as far as this window and there in the room, chained to a bed like Prometheus to his rock, receiving the blows that Maurice rained upon him with a whip which was in fact studded with nails, I saw, with blood already flowing from him and covered with bruises which proved that the chastisement was not taking place for the first time—I saw before me M. de Charlus.

Suddenly the door opened and a man came in who fortunately did not see me. It was Jupien. He went up to the Baron with an air of respect and a smile of understanding: "Well, you don't need me, do you?" The Baron asked Jupien to send Maurice out of the room for a moment. Jupien did so with perfect unconcern. "We can't be heard, can we?" said the Baron to Jupien, who assured him that this was the case. The Baron knew that Jupien, with an intelligence worthy of a man of letters, was yet quite lacking in practical sense and constantly talked about people in their presence with innuendoes which deceived nobody and nicknames which everybody understood.

"Just a second," interrupted Jupien, who had heard a bell ring in Room No. 3. It was a deputy of the Liberal Action party, who was about to leave. Jupien did not need to look at the bell-board, for he recognised the man's ring. Indeed the deputy came every day after lunch, but today he had been obliged to rearrange his time-table for at twelve o'clock he had given away his daughter in marriage at the church of Saint-Pierre-de-Chaillot. So he had come in the evening but was anxious to leave early on account of his wife, who very easily became nervous if he was late in getting home, particularly in these days of bombardment. Jupien always liked to accompany him downstairs in order to show his deference for the status of "honourable," and in this he was quite disinterested. For although this deputy (who repudiated the exaggerations of *L'Action Française* and would in any case have been incapable of understanding a line of Charles Maurras or Léon Daudet) stood well with the ministers, whom he flattered by inviting them to his shooting-parties, Jupien would not have dared to ask him for the slightest support in his difficulties with the police. He knew that, had he ventured to mention that subject to the affluent and apprehensive legislator, he would not have saved himself even the most harmless "raid" but would immediately have lost the most generous of his clients. After having escorted the deputy as far as the door, from which he set off with his hat pulled down over his eyes and his collar turned up and with a rapid gliding movement not unlike the style of his electoral manifestos, by which devices he hoped to render his face invisible, Jupien went upstairs again to M. de Charlus. "It was Monsieur Eugène," he said to him. In Jupien's establishment, as in a sanatorium, people were referred to only by their Christian names, though their real names, either to satisfy the curiosity of the visitor or to enhance the prestige of the house, were invariably added in a whisper. Sometimes, however, Jupien was unaware of the real identity of a client and imagined and said that he was some well-known financier or nobleman or artist—fleeting errors not without charm for the man to whom the wrong name was attached—and in the end had to resign himself to the idea that he still did not know who Monsieur Victor was. Sometimes too, to please the Baron, he was in the habit of inverting the procedure that is customary on certain social occasions ("Let me introduce you to M. Lebrun," then a whisper: "He wants to be called M. Lebrun but he is really Grand Duke X—— of Russia"). Jupien on the other hand felt that it was not quite sufficient to introduce M. de Charlus to a young milkman. He would murmur to him with a wink: "He's a milkman but he's also one of the most dangerous thugs in Belleville" (and it was with a superbly salacious note in his voice that Jupien uttered the word "thug"). And as if this recommendation were not sufficient, he would try to add one or two further "citations." "He has had several convictions for theft and burglary, he was in Fresnes for assaulting" (the same salacious note in his voice) "and practically murdering people in the street, and he's been in a punishment battalion in Africa. He killed his sergeant."

The Baron was slightly cross with Jupien for his lack of prudence, for he knew that in this house which he had instructed his factotum to purchase for him and to manage through a subordinate, everybody, thanks to the blunders of Mlle d'Oloron's uncle, was more or less aware of his identity and his name (many, however, thought that it was not a title but a nickname, and mispronounced and distorted it, so that their own stupidity and not the discretion of Jupien had served to protect the Baron). But he found it simpler to let himself be reassured by Jupien's assurances, and now, relieved to know that they could not be heard, he said to him: "I did not want to speak in front of that boy, who is very nice and does his best. But I don't find him sufficiently brutal. He has a charming face, but when he calls me a filthy brute he might be just repeating a lesson." "I assure you, nobody has said a word to him," replied Jupien, without perceiving how improbable this statement was. "And besides, he was involved in the murder of a concierge in La Villette." "Ah! that is extremely interesting," said the Baron with a smile. "But I'll tell you who I have here: the killer of oxen, the man of the slaughterhouses, who is so like this boy; he happened to be passing. Would you care to try him?" "Yes, certainly I should." I saw the man of the slaughterhouses enter the room; he was indeed a little like Maurice, but—and this was odder—they both had in them something of a type which I had never myself consciously observed in Morel's face but which I now clearly saw to exist there; they bore a resemblance, if not to Morel as I had seen him, at least to a certain countenance which eyes seeing Morel otherwise than I did might have constructed out of his features. No sooner had I, out of features borrowed from my recollections of Morel, privately made for myself this rough model of what he might represent to somebody else, than I realised that the two young men, one of whom was a jeweller's assistant while the other worked in a hotel, were in a vague way substitutes for Morel. Was I to conclude that M. de Charlus, at least in a certain aspect of his loves, was always faithful to a particular type and that the desire which had made him select these two young men one after the other was the identical desire which had made him accost Morel on the platform at Doncières station; that all three resembled a little the ephebe whose form, engraved in the sapphire-like eyes of M. de

Charlus, gave to his glance that strange quality which had alarmed me the first day at Balbec? Or that, his love for Morel having modified the type which he pursued, to console himself for Morel's absence he sought men who resembled him? A third hypothesis which occurred to me was that perhaps, in spite of appearances, there had never existed between him and Morel anything more than relations of friendship, and that M. de Charlus caused young men who resembled Morel to come to Jupien's establishment so that he might have the illusion, while he was with them, of enjoying pleasure with Morel himself. It is true that, if one thought of everything that M. de Charlus had done for Morel, this hypothesis was bound to seem most unlikely, did one not know that love drives us not only to the greatest sacrifices on behalf of the person we love, but sometimes even to the sacrifice of our desire itself, a desire which in any case we find all the harder to gratify if the loved person is aware of the strength of our love.

Something else that makes this hypothesis less unlikely than at first sight it appears (though probably it does not correspond to the reality) lies in the nervous temperament, in the profoundly passionate character of M. de Charlus—in this resembling Saint-Loup—which in the early days of his relations with Morel might have played the same part, in a more decent and negative way, as it did at the beginning of his nephew's relations with Rachel. A man's relations with a woman whom he loves (and the same may be true of love for a young man) may remain platonic for a reason which is neither the woman's virtue nor a lack of sensuality in the love which she inspires. The reason may be that the lover, too impatient from the very excess of his love, does not know how to wait with a sufficient show of indifference for the moment when he will obtain what he desires. Over and over again he returns to the charge, he writes incessantly to the woman, he tries constantly to see her, she refuses, he is in despair. Henceforth she understands that if she accords him her company, her friendship, this happiness in itself will seem so considerable to the man who thought he had lost it, that she may spare herself the trouble of giving him anything more and may take advantage of a moment when he can no longer endure not to see her, when he is determined at any price to end the war, to impose upon him a peace of which the first condition will be the platonic nature of their relations. In any case, during the period which preceded this treaty, the lover, always anxious, hoping all the time for a letter, a glance, has given up thinking of physical possession, which at first had been the object of the desire which had tormented him; that desire has withered away with waiting and its place has been taken by needs of another order, needs which can, however, if they remain unsatisfied, cause him yet greater pain. So that the pleasure which at the beginning he had hoped to obtain from caresses, he receives later not in its natural form but instead from friendly words, from mere promises of the loved woman's presence, which after the effects of uncertainty—sometimes after a single look, black with a heavy cloud of disdain, which has withdrawn her to such a distance that he thinks he will never see her again— bring with them a delicious relief from tension. A woman divines these things and knows that she can afford the luxury of never giving herself to a man who, because he has been too agitated to conceal it during the first few days, has allowed her to become aware of his incurable desire for her. She is only too pleased to receive, without giving anything in return, much more than she is accustomed to be given when she gives herself. Men with a nervous temperament believe therefore in the virtue of their idol. And the halo which they place round her is a product, but as we have seen an indirect one, of their excessive love. The woman then finds herself very much in the position—though she of course is conscious, while they are not—of those unwit- tingly crafty drugs like sleeping-draughts and morphine. It is not to the people to whom they bring the pleasure of sleep or a genuine well-being that these drugs are an absolute necessity; it is not by such people as these that they would be bought at any price, bartered against all the sick man's possessions, but by that other class of sick men (who may perhaps be the same individuals but become different with the passage of a few years), those whom the medicine does not send to sleep, to whom it gives no thrill of pleasure, but who, so long as they are without it, are prey to an agitation which at any price, even the price of their own death, they need desperately to end.

    In the case of M. de Charlus, which on the whole, with slight discrepancies due to the identity of sex, accords very well with the general laws of love, for all that he belonged to a family more ancient than the Capets, that he was rich and vainly sought after by fashionable society while Morel was nobody, he would have got nowhere by saying to Morel, as he had once said to me: "I am a prince, I want to help you"—it was still Morel who had the upper hand so long as he refused to surrender. And for him to persist in this refusal, it was perhaps enough that he should feel himself to be loved. The horror that grand people have for the snobs who move heaven and earth to make their acquaintance is felt also by the virile man for the invert, by a woman for every man who is too much in love with her. M. de Charlus possessed, and would have offered Morel a share in, immense advantages. But it is possible that all this might have hurled itself in vain against a determined will. And in that case, M. de Charlus would have suffered the same fate as the Germans—in whose ranks in fact his ancestry placed him—who in the war at that moment taking its course were indeed, as the Baron was a little too fond of repeating, victorious on every front. But of what use were their victories, since after every one they found the Allies yet more firmly resolved to refuse them the one thing that they, the Germans, wanted: peace and reconciliation? Napoleon too, as he advanced into Russia, had again and again magnanimously invited the authorities to meet him. But nobody came.

I made my way downstairs and went back into the little ante-room where Maurice, uncertain whether he would be sent for again (he had been told by Jupien to wait just in case), was engaged in a game of cards with one of his friends. There was a lot of excitement about a *croix de guerre* which had been found lying on the ground—nobody knew who had lost it and to whom it ought to be returned so that the owner should not be punished. Then there was talk of the generosity of an officer who had been killed trying to save his batman. "All the same, there are some good blokes among the rich. I'd gladly get myself killed for a chap like that," said Maurice, who evidently performed his terrible fustigations of the Baron simply from mechanical habit, as a result of a neglected education, from need of money and from a certain preference for making it in a manner which was supposed to be less trouble, and was perhaps really more trouble, than ordinary work. But as M. de Charlus had feared, he was perhaps really very kind-hearted and certainly, so it seemed, a young man of exemplary courage. He almost had tears in his eyes as he spoke of the death of this officer, and the young man of twenty-two was no less moved. "Yes, indeed, they're fine blokes. For poor chaps like us there's not much to lose, but when it's a toff who has a whole troop of flunkeys and can go to posh bars every night of his life, it's really terrific! You can scoff as much as you like, but when you see blokes like that dying, it really does something to you. Rich people like that, God shouldn't let them die—for one thing they're too useful to the working man. A death like that makes you want to kill every Boche to the last man. And then look what they did at Louvain, and cutting off the hands of little children! No, I don't know, I'm no better than the next man, but I'd rather face the music and be shot to bits than give in to barbarians like that; they're not men, they're real barbarians, don't you try and tell me anything else." All these young men were patriots at heart. One only, who had been slightly wounded in the arm but was soon going to have to return to the front, did not rise to the level of the others. "Darn it," he said, "it wasn't the right sort of wound" (the kind that gets you invalided out), very much as in the past Mme Swann would have said: "Somehow or other I've caught this most tiresome influenza."

The door opened to readmit the chauffeur, who had been taking the air for a moment. "What, finished already? You weren't long," he said, catching sight of Maurice, whom he supposed to be still engaged in beating the individual whom, in allusion to a newspaper which was appearing at that time, they had nicknamed "the Man in Chains." "It may not have seemed long to you out in the fresh air," replied Maurice, vexed that the others should see that he had failed to give satisfaction upstairs. "But if you'd been obliged to wallop away with all your might in this heat, like me! If it wasn't for the fifty francs he gives . . ." "And then, he's a man who talks well; you can see he's educated. Does he say it will soon be over?" "He says we'll never beat them, it will end without either side really winning." "Bloody hell, if he says that he must be a Boche . . ." "I've already told you you're talking too loud," said the oldest of the group to the others, seeing that I had returned, and then to me: "Have you finished with your room?" "Shut your trap, you're not the boss here." "Yes, I've finished, and I've come to pay." "It would be better if you paid the *patron*. Maurice, go and fetch him." "But I don't want to bother you." "It's no trouble." Maurice went upstairs, and came back saying: "The *patron* will be down in a second." I gave him two francs for his pains. He blushed with pleasure. "Oh! thank you very much. I'll send it to my brother who's a prisoner. No, he doesn't have a bad time. It depends a lot on the camp you're in."

Meanwhile, two very smart clients, in white tie and tails and wearing overcoats—two Russians, as I guessed from the very slight accent with which they spoke—were standing in the doorway and deliberating whether they should enter. It was visibly the first time that they had been to the place, to which no doubt they had come on somebody's recommendation, and they appeared torn between desire, temptation and extreme fright. One of the two—a good-looking young man—kept repeating every ten seconds to the other, with a smile that was half a question and half an attempt at persuasion: "Well! After all, what do we care?" But though no doubt he meant by this that after all they did not care about the consequences, it is probable that he cared rather more than he implied, for the remark was not followed by any movement to cross the threshold but by a further glance at his companion, followed by the same smile and the same "After all, what do we care?" And in this "After all, what do we care?" I saw a perfect example of that portentous language, so unlike the language we habitually speak, in which emotion deflects what we had intended to say and causes to emerge in its place an entirely different phrase, issued from an unknown lake wherein dwell these expressions alien to our thoughts which by virtue of that very fact reveal them. I remember an occasion when Françoise, whose approach we had not heard, was about to come into the room while Albertine was completely naked in my arms, and Albertine, wanting to warn me, blurted out: "Good heavens, here's the beautiful Françoise!" Françoise, whose sight was no longer very good and who was merely going to cross the room at some distance from us, would no doubt have noticed nothing. But the unprecedented phrase "the beautiful Françoise," which Albertine had never uttered before in her life, was in itself enough to betray its origin; Françoise sensed that the words had been plucked at random by emotion and had no need to look to understand what was happening; she went out muttering in her dialect the word *poutana*. On another occasion, many years later, after Bloch had become the father of a family and had married off one of his daughters to a Catholic, an ill-mannered gentleman said to the young woman that he thought he had heard that her father was a Jew and asked what his name was. Whereupon she, who had been Mlle Bloch with a *k* sound from the day she was born, replied "Bloch" with the Teutonic *ch* which the Duc de Guermantes would have used.

The *patron*, to return to the scene in the hotel (into which the two Russians had decided to penetrate—"After all, what do we care?"), had still not arrived when Jupien came in to say that they were talking too loud and that the neighbours would complain. But seeing me he was rooted to the spot in amazement. "Go out on to the landing all of you." They were all rising to their feet when I said to him: "It would be simpler if these young men stayed where they are and you and I went outside for a moment." He followed me, very agitated. I explained to him why I had come. Clients could be heard inquiring of the *patron* whether he could introduce them to a footman, a choir-boy, a negro chauffeur. Every profession interested these old lunatics, every branch of the armed forces, every one of the allied nations. Some asked particularly for Canadians, influenced perhaps unconsciously by the charm of an accent so slight that one does not know whether it comes from the France of the past or from England. The Scots too, because of their kilts and because dreams of a landscape with lakes are often associated with these desires, were at a premium. And as every form of madness is, if not in every case aggravated by circumstances, at least imprinted by them with particular characteristics, an old man in whom curiosity of every kind had no doubt been satisfied was asking insistently to be introduced to a disabled soldier. Slow footsteps were heard on the stairs. With the indiscretion that was natural to him, Jupien could not refrain from telling me that it was the Baron who was coming down, and at all costs he must not see me, but that if I liked to go into the bedroom adjoining the ante-room where the young men were, he would open the ventilator, a device which he had fixed up so that the Baron could see and hear without being seen, and which he said he would use in my favour against him. "Only don't move." And pushing me into the dark, he left me. In any case he had no other room to give me, his hotel, in spite of the war, being full. The one which I had just left had been taken by the Vicomte de Courvoisier who, having got away from the Red Cross at X—— for two days, had come to Paris for an hour's entertainment before going on to the Château de Courvoisier to be reunited with his wife, to whom he would explain that he had not been able to catch the fast train. He had no suspicion that M. de Charlus was a few yards away from him, and the latter would have been equally surprised to know that his cousin was there, never having met him in the establishment of Jupien, who was himself ignorant of the Vicomte's carefully concealed identity.

The Baron soon entered the ante-room, walking with difficulty on account of his injuries, though doubtless he must have been used to them. Although his pleasure was at an end and he had only come in to give Maurice the money which he owed him, he directed at the young men a tender and curious glance which travelled round the whole circle, promising himself with each of them the pleasure of a moment's chat, platonic but amorously prolonged. And in the sprightly frivolity which he exhibited before this harem which appeared almost to intimidate him, I recognised those jerky movements of the body and the head, those languishing glances which had struck me on the evening of his first visit to La Raspelière, graces inherited from some grand-mother whom I had not known, which in ordinary life were disguised by more virile expressions on his face but which from time to time were made to blossom there coquettishly, when circumstances made him anxious to please an inferior audience, by the desire to appear a great lady.

Jupien had recommended the young men to the Baron's favour by swearing that they were all pimps from Belleville and would sell you their own sisters for a few francs. And in this he was at the same time lying and telling the truth. Better, more soft-hearted than he made them out to be, they did not belong to a race of savages. But the clients who believed them to be thugs spoke to them nevertheless with complete truthfulness, a truthfulness which they imagined these terrible beings to share. For a man given to sadistic pleasures may believe that he is talking to a murderer but this will not alter his own purity of heart, he will still be astounded by the mendacity of his companion, who is not a murderer at all but wants to earn a little easy money and whose father or mother or sister alternately die, come to life, and die again as he contradicts himself in his conversation with the client whom he is attempting to please. The client, in his naïvety, is astounded, for with his arbitrary conception of the gigolo, while he gets a thrill of delight from the numerous murders of which he believes him to be guilty, he is horrified by any simple contradiction or lie which he detects in his words.

Everybody in the room seemed to know him, and M. de Charlus stopped for a long time before each one, talking to them in what he thought was their language, both from a pretentious affectation of local colour and because he got a sadistic pleasure from contact with a life of depravity. "You're disgusting, you are, I saw you outside the Olympia with two tarts. After a bit of brass, no doubt. Just shows how faithful you are to me." Luckily for the man to whom these remarks were addressed, he did not have time to declare that he would never have accepted "brass" from a woman, a claim which would have damped the Baron's ardour, but reserved his protest for the final phrase, which he answered by saying: "But of course I'm faithful to you." This remark gave M. de Charlus a lively pleasure, and as, in spite of himself, the kind of intelligence that was natural to him showed through the character which he affected, he turned to Jupien: "How nice of him to say that! And how well he says it! One would really think it was true. And after all, what does it matter whether it is true or not since he manages to make me believe it? What charming little eyes he has! There, I'm going to give you two big kisses for your trouble, my dear boy. You will think of me in the trenches. Things are not too bad there?" "Whew, there are some days, when a grenade just misses you . . ." And the young man proceeded to imitate the noise of the grenade, the aeroplanes, etc. "But one's got to do what the others do, and you can be absolutely sure that we will go on to the end." "To the end! If one only knew to what end!" said the Baron in a melancholy manner, giving rein to his "pessimism." "You haven't seen what Sarah Bernhardt said in the papers: 'France will go on to the end. If necessary, the French will let themselves be killed to the last man.'" "I do not doubt for a single moment that the French would bravely let themselves be killed to the last man," said M. de Charlus, as if this were the simplest thing in the world and although he himself had no intention of doing anything whatsoever, hoping by this remark to correct the impression of pacifism which he gave when he forgot himself. "That I do not doubt, but I ask myself to what extent *Madame* Sarah Bernhardt is qualified to speak in the name of France . . . But I don't think I have made the acquaintance of this charming, this delightful young man," he added, spying another whom he did not recognise or perhaps had not seen before. He greeted him as he would have greeted a prince at Versailles, and making the most of this opportunity to have a supplementary pleasure for nothing—just as, when I was little and my mother had finished giving an order at Boissier's or Gouache's, I would accept the offer of a sweet which one of the ladies behind the counter would invite me to select from those glass bowls over which she and her colleagues held sway—he took the hand of the charming young man and gave it a long squeeze, in the Prussian manner, smilingly fixing him with his eyes for the interminable time which photographers used to take to pose you when the light was bad. "Sir, I am charmed, I am enchanted to make your acquaintance. What pretty hair he has!" he said, turning to Jupien. Next he went up to Maurice to give him his fifty francs, but first, putting his arm round his waist: "You never told me that you had knifed an old hag of a concierge in Belleville." And M. de Charlus shrieked with ecstatic laughter and brought his face close to that of Maurice. "Oh! Monsieur le Baron," said the gigolo, who had not been warned, "how can you believe such a thing?" Whether the report was in fact false, or whether it was true and the perpetrator of the deed nevertheless thought it abominable and one of those things that it is better to deny, he went on: "Me touch a fellow-creature? A Boche, yes, because that's war, but a woman, and an old woman at that!" This declaration of virtuous principles had the effect of a douche of cold water upon the Baron, who brusquely moved away from Maurice, having first handed him his money, but with the disgusted air of someone who has been cheated, who pays because he does not want to make a fuss but is far from pleased. The bad impression made upon the Baron was accentuated by the manner in which the recipient thanked him, with the words: "I shall send this to the old folks and keep a bit for my brother at the front as well." By these touching sentiments M. de Charlus was almost as gravely disappointed as he was irritated by the rather conventional peasant's language in which they were expressed. Occasionally Jupien warned the young men that they ought to be more perverse. Then one of them, as if he were confessing to something diabolical, would hazard: "I say, Baron, you won't believe me, but when I was a kid I used to watch my parents making love through the key-hole. Pretty vicious, wasn't it? You look as if you think that's a cock and bull story, but I swear it's the truth." And M. de Charlus was driven at once to despair and to exasperation by this factitious attempt at perversity, the result of which was only to reveal such depths both of stupidity and of innocence. Yet even the most determined thief or murderer would not have satisfied him, for that sort of man does not talk about his crimes; and besides there exists in the sadist—however kind he may be, in fact all the more the kinder he is—a thirst for evil which wicked men, doing what they do not because it is wicked but from other motives, are unable to assuage.

The young man realised his mistake and tried to repair it by saying that he loathed the sight of a copper and by daringly inquiring of the Baron: "How about a date?"—but it was too late, the charm was dispelled. One had a distinct feeling of sham, as with the books of authors who force themselves to write slang. It was in vain that the young man described in detail all the "filthy things" that he did with his wife; M. de Charlus merely reflected that these "filthy things" amounted to very little. And in this he was not simply being insincere. Nothing is more limited than pleasure and vice. In that sense one may say truly, altering slightly the meaning of the phrase, that we revolve always in the same vicious circle.

If M. de Charlus was believed to be not a baron but a prince, there was, conversely, general regret in the establishment for the death of someone of whom the gigolos said: "I don't know his name, but it seems that he is a baron," and who was none other than the Prince de Foix (the father of Saint-Loup's friend). Supposed by his wife to spend a lot of time at his club, in reality he would sit for hours at Jupien's, retailing fashionable gossip to an audience from the underworld. Like his son, he was tall and good-looking. M. de Charlus, no doubt because he had always known him in society, remained strangely ignorant that the Prince shared his own tastes, to such a degree that he was even said to have had designs at one time upon his own son, Saint-Loup's friend, then still at school. This was probably untrue: on the contrary, excellently informed about activities whose existence many do not suspect, he watched with care over the company kept by his son. One day a man—and a man not of exalted origin—followed the young Prince de Foix as far as his father's house, where he threw a note in at the window, which the father picked up. But the follower, though genealogically this was not the case, from another point of view belonged to the same world as M. de Foix the father. He therefore had no difficulty in finding among those who shared their common secrets an intermediary who silenced M. de Foix by proving to him that it was his son who had himself provoked this rash act of an elderly man. And this was quite possible. For the Prince de Foix had succeeded in preserving his son from the external influence of bad company but not from heredity. The young Prince de Foix, however, remained, like his father, in this respect unknown to his social equals, although in a different world his behaviour was wild in the extreme.

"How simple he is! You would never say he was a baron," said some of the frequenters of the establishment when M. de Charlus had left, after being escorted to the street-door by Jupien, to whom he did not fail to complain of the young man's virtuousness. From the air of annoyance of Jupien, whose duty it was to have trained the young man in advance, it was clear that the fictitious murderer would presently get a terrific dressing-down. "The truth is exactly the opposite of what you told me," added the Baron, so that Jupien might profit by the lesson for another time. "He seems most good-natured, he expresses sentiments of respect for his family." "Still, he's on bad terms with his father," Jupien objected. "It's true they live together, but they work in different bars." Obviously this was not much of a crime compared with murder, but Jupien had been caught unprepared with an answer. The Baron said no more, for, if he wanted others to prepare his pleasures for him, he wanted to give himself the illusion that they were unprepared. "He is a real crook, he said all that to mislead you, you are too gullible," Jupien went on, in an attempt to exculpate himself which succeeded only in wounding the vanity of M. de Charlus.

"It seems that he has a million francs a day to spend," said the young man of twenty-two, who saw no improbability in this statement. The car which had come to fetch M. de Charlus was now heard to drive away. At the same moment there entered the room with a slow step, by the side of a soldier who had evidently emerged with her from a neighbouring bedroom, what appeared to me to be an elderly lady in a black skirt. I soon realised my mistake: it was a priest—that thing so rare, and in France altogether exceptional, a bad priest. Evidently the soldier was teasing his companion about the discrepancy between his conduct and his habit, for the other with a serious air, raising a finger towards his hideous face with the gesture of a doctor of theology, said sententiously: "What do you expect? I am not" (I expected him to say "a saint") "a good girl." He was, however, ready to depart and he said good-bye to Jupien, who had just come upstairs again after seeing the Baron to the door. But absentmindedly the bad priest had forgotten to pay for his room. Jupien, who had always a ready wit, shook the collecting-box in which he placed the contribution of each client and said, as he made it clink: "For the expenses of the church, Monsieur l'Abbé!" The horrid creature apologised, put in his coin and disappeared.

Jupien came to fetch me from the cave of darkness in which I had been standing without daring to move. "Come into the hall for a moment where my young men are sitting, while I go upstairs and lock up the bedroom; since you have taken a room, it's quite natural." The *patron* was there, so I paid him. At that moment a young man in a dinner-jacket came in and asked the *patron* with an air of authority: "Will I be able to have Léon at a quarter to eleven instead of eleven tomorrow morning, as I have a luncheon engagement?" "That will depend," replied the *patron*, "on how long the Abbé keeps him." This reply appeared not to satisfy the young man in a dinner-jacket, who seemed to be on the point of launching into abuse of the Abbé, but his fury was diverted when he caught sight of me. Going straight up to the *patron*: "Who is this? What does this mean?" he muttered in a quiet but angry voice. The *patron*, very put out, explained that my presence was quite harmless, that I had taken a room. The young man in a dinner-jacket appeared to be not in the slightest degree pacified by this explanation. He kept repeating: "This is extremely unpleasant, things of this sort ought not to happen, you know I detest them, if you are not careful I will never set foot here again." The execution of this threat did not, however, appear to be imminent, for he went off in a rage, but not without asking that Léon should try to be free at a quarter to eleven, or better still half-past ten. Jupien came back to fetch me and we went downstairs together and out into the street.

"I do not want you to misjudge me," he said to me. "This house does not bring me in as much profit as you might think. I am obliged to let rooms to respectable people, though of course if they were my only customers I should simply be throwing money down the drain. Here, contrary to the doctrine of the Carmelites, it is thanks to vice that virtue is able to live. No, if I took this house, or rather if I got the manager whom you have seen to take it, it was purely and simply in order to render a service to the Baron and amuse his old age." Jupien was here referring not merely to scenes of sadism like those which I had witnessed and to the actual vicious practices of the Baron. The latter, even for conversation, for company, for a game of cards, now only enjoyed the society of lower-class people who exploited him. No doubt the snobbery of the gutter may be understood as easily as snobbery of the other kind. The two had in fact long been united, alternating one with the other, in M. de Charlus, who thought no one was smart enough to be numbered among his social acquaintances, no one sufficiently a ruffian to be worth knowing in other ways. "I detest the intermediate style," he would say. "Bourgeois comedy is stiff and affected. Let me have either the princesses of classical tragedy or broad farce. No half-way houses—either *Phèdre* or *Les Saltimbanques*." But in the end the balance between the two forms of snobbery had been broken. Perhaps because he was an old man and tired, perhaps because sensuality had come to enter into even his trivial relationships, the Baron now lived only among his "inferiors," thus unintentionally taking his place as the successor of more than one among his great ancestors, the Duc de La Rochefoucauld, the Prince d'Harcourt, the Duc de Berry, whom we see in the pages of Saint-Simon passing their lives in the midst of their lackeys, who extracted enormous sums from them, and sharing their amusements, to such an extent that people who had to visit them were embarrassed, for their sakes, to find these great noblemen familiarly engaged in a game of cards or a drinking-bout with their domestic servants. "And above all," Jupien went on, "it is to keep him out of trouble, because the Baron, you know, is a big baby. Even now that he has here everything that he can desire, he still wanders about in search of sordid adventures. And with his generosity, that sort of thing could have disagreeable consequences in these days. Only the other day there was a page-boy from a hotel who was absolutely terrified because of all the money the Baron offered him if he would go to his house! (To his house, what imprudence!) The boy, who in fact only cares about women, was reassured when he understood what was wanted of him. Hearing all these promises of money, he had taken the Baron for a spy. And he was greatly relieved when he realised that he was being asked to sell not his country but his body, which is possibly not a more moral thing to do, but less dangerous and in any case easier." And listening to Jupien, I said to myself: "How unfortunate it is that M. de Charlus is not a novelist or a poet! Not merely so that he could describe what he sees, but because the position in which a Charlus finds himself with respect to desire causes scandals to spring up around him, and compels him to take life seriously, to load pleasure with a weight of emotion. He cannot get stuck in an ironical and superficial view of things because a current of pain is perpetually reawakened within him.

Almost every time he makes a declaration of love he is violently snubbed, if he does not run the risk of being sent to prison." A slap in the face or a box on the ear helps to educate not only children but poets. If M. de Charlus had been a novelist, the house which Jupien had set up for him, by reducing so greatly the risks—at least (for a raid by the police was always a possibility) the risk emanating from an individual casually encountered in the street, of whose inclinations the Baron could not have felt certain—would have been a misfortune for him. But in the sphere of art M. de Charlus was no more than a dilettante, who never dreamt of writing and had no gift for it.

"Besides, I may as well admit to you," Jupien continued, "that I have very few scruples about making money in this way. The actual thing that is done here is—I can no longer conceal the fact from you—something that I like, it is what I have a taste for myself. Well, is it forbidden to receive payment for things that one does not regard as wickedness? You are better educated than I am, and you will tell me no doubt that Socrates was of the opinion that he could not accept money for his lessons. But in our age professors of philosophy do not hold that view, nor do doctors or painters or playwrights or theatrical producers. Do not imagine that this trade of mine brings me into contact only with the dregs of society. No doubt the director of an establishment of this kind, like a great courtesan, receives only men, but he receives men who are conspicuous in every walk of life and who are generally, on their own level, among the most intelligent, the most sensitive, the most agreeable of their profession. In no time at all, I assure you, this house could be transformed into an information bureau or a school of wit." Nevertheless, I was still under the impression of the blows which I had seen inflicted upon M. de Charlus.

And the truth is that, when one knew M. de Charlus well—his pride, his satiety with social pleasures, his fancies which changed easily into passions for men of the lowest class and the worst character—one could very easily understand that the possession of a huge fortune, the charm of which, had he been an upstart, would have been that it enabled him to marry his daughter to a duke and invite Highnesses to his shooting-parties, pleased him simply because it allowed him to have at his disposal in this way one or perhaps several establishments with a permanent supply of young men whose company he enjoyed. And perhaps this might have come to pass even without his special vice, heir as he was to so many great noblemen, dukes or princes of the blood, of whom Saint-Simon tells us that they never associated with anybody "who could boast a name."

"Meanwhile," I said to Jupien, "this house is anything but what you say it might become. It is worse than a madhouse, since the mad fancies of the lunatics who inhabit it are played out as actual, visible drama—it is a veritable pandemonium. I thought that I had arrived, like the Caliph in the *Arabian Nights*, in the nick of time to rescue a man who was being beaten, and in fact it was a different tale from the *Arabian Nights* which I saw enacted before me, the one in which a woman who has been turned into a dog willingly submits to being beaten in order to recover her former shape." Jupien appeared to be very upset by my words, for he realised that I had seen the Baron being beaten. He was silent for a moment, while I stopped a cab which was passing; then suddenly, with that pretty wit which had so often struck me in this self-educated man when in the courtyard of our house he had greeted me or Françoise with some graceful phrase: "You have mentioned one or two of the tales in the *Arabian Nights*," he said. "But there is another I know of, not unrelated to the title of a book which I think I have seen at the Baron's" (he was alluding to a translation of Ruskin's *Sesame and Lilies* which I had sent M. de Charlus). "If ever you are curious, one evening, to see, I will not say forty but a dozen thieves, you have only to come here; to know whether I am in the house you have only to look up at that window; if I leave my little window open with a light visible it means that I am in the house and you may come in; it is my private Sesame. I say only Sesame. As for Lilies, if they are what you seek I advise you to go elsewhere." And with a somewhat offhand gesture of farewell— for an aristocratic clientele and the habit of ruling like a pirate chief over a gang of young men had imparted a certain lordliness to his manners—he was about to take his leave of me when the noise of an explosion—a bomb which had fallen before the sirens could give warning—made him advise me to stay with him for a moment. Soon the anti-aircraft barrage began, and with such violence that one could sense very near, just above our heads, the presence of the German aeroplane.

In an instant the streets became totally black. At moments only, an enemy aeroplane flying very low lit up the spot upon which it wished to drop a bomb. I set off, but very soon I was lost. I thought

of that day when, on my way to La Raspelière, I had met an
aeroplane and my horse had reared as at the apparition of a god.
Now, I thought, it would be a different meeting—with the god of
evil, who would kill me. I started to walk faster in order to escape,
like a traveller pursued by a tidal wave; I groped my way round
dark squares from which I could find no way out. At last the flames
of a blazing building showed me where I was and I got back on to
the right road, while all the time the shells burst noisily above my
head. But my thoughts had turned to another subject. I was
thinking of Jupien's house, perhaps by now reduced to ashes, for
a bomb had fallen very near me just after I had left it—that house
upon which M. de Charlus might prophetically have written
Sodoma, as the unknown inhabitant of Pompeii had done, with
no less prescience or perhaps when the volcano had already started
to erupt and the catastrophe had begun. But what mattered sirens
and Gothas to the men who had come to seek their pleasure? The
social setting or the natural scene which surrounds our love-
making barely impinges upon our thoughts. The tempest may
rage over the sea, the ship roll and plunge in every direction, the
sky pour down avalanches convulsed by the wind, and at most we
bestow the attention of a single second, forced from us by physical
discomfort, upon this immense scenic background against which
we ourselves are so insignificant, both we and the body which we
long to approach. The siren with its warning of bombs troubled
Jupien's visitors no more than an iceberg would have done.
Indeed, the threat of physical danger delivered them from the
fear which for long had morbidly harassed them. For it is wrong to
suppose that the scale of our fears corresponds to that of the
dangers by which they are inspired. A man may be afraid of not
sleeping and not in the least afraid of a serious duel, afraid of a rat
and not of a lion. For a few hours now the police would have their
hands full looking after something as trivial as the lives of the city's
inhabitants and their reputations were temporarily in no danger.
But if some, their fears allayed, remained in Jupien's establishment,
others were tempted not so much by the thought of recovering
their moral liberty as by the darkness which had suddenly settled
upon the streets. Some of these, like the Pompeians upon whom
the fire from heaven was already raining, descended into the
passages of the Métro, black as catacombs. They knew that they
would not be alone there. And darkness, which envelops all things
like a new element, has the effect, irresistibly tempting for certain

people, of suppressing the first halt on the road to pleasure—it permits us to enter without impediment into a region of caresses to which normally we gain access only after a certain delay. Whether the coveted object is a woman or a man, supposing even that the first approach is easy and that there is no need of the gallant speeches which in a drawing-room might run on for ever (at any rate in daylight), on a normal evening, even in the most dimly lit street, there is at least a preamble in which the eyes alone feed on the unripe fruit, and fear of passers-by, fear even of the coveted being, prevents us from doing more than look and speak. In the darkness this time-honoured ritual is instantly abolished—hands, lips, bodies may go into action at once. There is always the excuse of darkness, and of the mistakes that darkness engenders, if we are not well received. And if we are, this immediate response of a body which does not withdraw but approaches, gives us of the woman (or the man) whom we have selected the idea that she is without prejudices and full of vice, which adds an extra pleasure to the happiness of having bitten straight into the fruit without first coveting it with our eyes and without asking permission. Meanwhile the darkness persisted; plunged into the new element, imagining that they had travelled to a distant country and were witnessing a natural phenomenon like a tidal wave or an eclipse, that they were enjoying not an artificially prepared, sedentary pleasure but a chance encounter in the unknown, the men who had come away from Jupien's house celebrated, while the bombs mimicked the rumbling of a volcano, deep in the earth as in a Pompeian house of ill-fame, their secret rites in the shadows of the catacombs.

The Pompeian paintings of Jupien's house were admirably suited, recalling as they did the later days of the Revolution, to the age so similar to the Directory which was about to begin. Already, without waiting for peace, concealing themselves in the darkness so as not too openly to infringe the regulations of the police, everywhere new-fangled dances were being evolved and frenziedly danced by their devotees throughout the night. And at the same time certain artistic opinions less anti-German in tone than those of the first years of the war were coming into vogue, allowing suffocated minds to breathe once more—but still before you dared to present these ideas you needed to produce a certificate of your patriotism. A professor might write a remarkable book on Schiller and it would be reviewed in the newspapers. But before discussing the author of the book they would record, as a sort of *imprimatur*, that he had been at the Marne or Verdun, that he had been mentioned in despatches five times or had two sons killed. Then and then only did they praise the lucidity, the depth of his work on Schiller, whom it was permissible to describe as "great" provided that he was called not "that great German" but "that great Boche." This was the pass-word, and having passed this test the article was allowed to proceed.

The clients who had not wished to leave had collected together in one room in Jupien's house. They were not acquainted with one another, but one could see that they all belonged nevertheless roughly to the same world, rich and aristocratic. The appearance of each one had in it something repugnant, a reflexion, I pre-sumed, of their failure to resist degrading pleasures. One, an enormous man, had a face covered with red blotches like a drunkard. I was told that formerly he had not drunk much himself but had merely enjoyed making young men drunk. But, terrified at the idea of being called up (although he seemed to be in his fifties) and being very stout, he had started to drink without stopping in order to get his weight above a hundred kilos, as nobody over this limit was accepted for the army. And now, this calculation having transformed itself into a passion, the moment that he was left alone, wherever it might be, he would disappear and be found again in a wine-shop. But as soon as he spoke I saw that, though his intelligence was commonplace, he was a man with a good deal of knowledge, education and culture. Another man came in, very young and of great physical distinction. This one, who clearly belonged to the best society, had as yet it is true no external marks of vice, but—and this was more disturbing— the interior signs were there. Very tall, with a charming face, his speech revealed an intelligence of quite a different order from that of his alcoholic neighbour, an intelligence that might without exaggeration be called really outstanding. But to everything that he said there was added a facial expression which would have suited a different phrase. As though, while possessing the whole treasure-house of the expressions of the human countenance, he lived in some world of his own, he displayed these expressions in the wrong order, appearing to scatter smiles and glances at random without any connexion with the remarks that were being addressed to him. I hope for his sake—if, as he certainly is, he is still alive—that he was the victim not of a lasting malady but of a brief intoxication. Probably, had one asked all these men for their visiting-cards, one would have been surprised to see that they belonged to an exalted social class. But some vice or other, and that greatest of all vices, the lack of will-power which prevents a man from resisting any vice in particular, brought them together in this place, in isolated rooms it is true, but evening after evening so I was told, so that, though their names might be known to fashionable hostesses, the latter had gradually lost sight of their faces and no longer ever received their visits. Invitations might still be sent to them, but habit brought them back to their composite haunt of depravity. They made, moreover, little attempt at concealment, unlike the page-boys, young workmen, etc., who ministered to their pleasures. And this fact, for which a number of reasons could be given, is best explained by this one: for a man with a job, whether in industry or in domestic service, to go to Jupien's was much the same as for a woman supposed respectable to go to a house of assignation; some, while ready to admit that they had gone there, denied having gone more than once, and Jupien himself, lying to protect their reputations or to discourage competition, would declare: "Oh, no, he doesn't come to my establishment, he wouldn't go *there*." For men with a social position it was not so serious, particularly as other men with a social position who do not go *there* know nothing about the place and do not concern themselves with your life. But in an aeroplane factory, for instance, if one or two fitters have gone *there*, their comrades, who have spied on them, would not dream of following their example for fear of being found out.

As I made my way home, I reflected upon the speed with which conscience ceases to be a partner in our habits, which she allows to develop freely without bothering herself about them, and upon the astonishing picture which may consequently present itself to us if we observe simply from without, and in the belief that they engage the whole of the individual, the actions of men whose moral or intellectual virtues may at the same time be developing independently in an entirely different direction. Clearly it was a gross fault in their education, or a complete absence of education, combined with a propensity for making money in the way which, if not the least painful (for there were many forms of work which must in the long run be pleasanter—but then does not an invalid in the same way fabricate for himself, with fads, privations and remedies, an existence much more painful than the one imposed upon him by the often trivial disease against which he imagines himself to be fighting by these methods?), was at least less laborious than any other, which had led these ordinary young men to do, quite innocently one may almost say and for a very moderate reward, things which caused them no pleasure and which must in the beginning have inspired in them a lively disgust. On this evidence one might have supposed them to be fundamentally bad, but not only were they in the war splendid soldiers, men of incomparable courage, in civil life too they had often been kind-hearted and sometimes wholly admirable people. They had long ceased to speculate upon the morality or immorality of the life they led, because it was the life that was led by everybody round them. So it is that, when we study certain periods of ancient history, we are astonished to see men and women individually good participate without scruple in mass assassinations or human sacrifices which probably seemed to them natural things. And our own age no doubt, when its history is read two thousand years hence, will seem to an equal degree to have bathed men of pure and tender conscience in a vital element which will strike the future reader as monstrously pernicious, but to which at the time these men adapted themselves without difficulty. Similarly, I knew few men, I may even say I knew none, who in point of intelligence and sensibility were as gifted as Jupien; for the store of knowledge which gave such a delightful quality of wit to his conversation came to him not from that instruction at school or that liberal education at a university which might have made him indeed a remarkable man, but from which many fashionable youths derive no profit. It was simply his innate good sense, his natural taste, which had enabled him, from a few books read at random, with-out a guide, at odd moments, to construct that correct and elegant manner of speaking in which all the symmetries of language were revealed and their beauty displayed. Yet the trade that he followed might with good reason be regarded, though certainly as one of the most lucrative, as the lowest of all. As for M. de Charlus, whatever disdain his aristocratic pride may have given him for the thought of what people would say, how was it that some feeling of personal dignity and self-respect had not forced him to refuse his sensuality certain satisfactions for which the only imaginable excuse might seem to be complete insanity? But in him, as in Jupien, the practice of separating morality from a whole order of actions (and this is something that must also often happen to men who have public duties to perform, those of a judge for instance or a statesman and many others as well) must have been so long established that Habit, no longer asking Moral Sentiment for its opinion, had grown stronger from day to day until at last this consenting Prometheus had had himself nailed by Force to the rock of Pure Matter.

No doubt, as I saw clearly enough, a new stage had been reached in the malady of M. de Charlus, which since I had first observed it had, to judge from the diverse phases which had presented themselves to my vision, pursued its development with ever-increasing speed. The poor Baron could not now be very far from the malady's final term, from death itself, though this possibly would be preceded, in accordance with the predictions and prayers of Mme Verdurin, by an imprisonment which at his age could only hasten its coming. Yet I have perhaps been inaccurate in speaking of the rock of Pure Matter. In this Pure Matter it is possible that a small quantum of Mind still survived. This madman knew, in spite of everything, that he was the victim of a form of madness and during his mad moments he nevertheless was playing a part, since he knew quite well that the young man who was beating him was not more wicked than the little boy who in a game of war is chosen by lot to be "the Prussian," upon whom all the others hurl themselves in a fury of genuine patriotism and pretended hate. The victim of a madness, yet a madness into which there entered nevertheless a little of the personality of M. de Charlus. Even in these aberrations (and this is true also of our loves or our travels), human nature still betrays its need for belief by its insistent demands for truth. Françoise, if I spoke to her about a church in Milan, a town which she would probably never visit, or about the cathedral of Rheims—or even merely that of Arras!—which she would not be able to see since they had been more or less destroyed, spoke enviously of the rich who can afford to visit such treasures or else exclaimed with nostalgic regret: "Ah! how lovely it must have been!" although, after all these years that she had lived in Paris, she had never had the curiosity to go and see Notre-Dame. For Notre-Dame is part of Paris and Paris was the town in which the daily life of Françoise took its course, the town, in consequence, in which it was difficult for our old servant—as it would have been for me had not the study of architecture corrected in me at certain points the instincts of Combray—to situate the objects of her dreams. In the people whom we love, there is, immanent, a certain dream which we cannot always clearly discern but which we pursue. It was my belief in Bergotte and in Swann which had made me love Gilberte, my belief in Gilbert the Bad which had made me love Mme de Guermantes. And what a vast expanse of sea had been hidden away in my love—the most full of suffering, the most jealous, seemingly the most individual of all my loves—for Albertine! In any case, just because we are furiously pursuing a dream in a succession of individuals, our loves for people cannot fail to be more or less of an aberration. (And are not even the maladies of the body, at least those that are at all closely connected with the nervous system, in the nature of special tastes or special fears acquired by our organs or our joints, which indicate in this manner that they have conceived for certain climates a horror as inexplicable and as obstinate as the fondness which certain men betray for, it might be, women with an eye-glass or women on horseback? Who can say to what long-lived and unconscious dream is linked the desire that never fails to reawaken at the sight of a woman on horseback, an unconscious dream as mysterious as is, for example, for a man who has suffered all his life from asthma, the influence of a certain town, in appearance no different from any other town, in which for the first time he breathes freely?) And if there is something of aberration or perversion in all our loves, perversions in the narrower sense of the word are like loves in which the germ of disease has spread victoriously to every part. Even in the maddest of them love may still be recognised. If M. de Charlus insisted that his hands and feet should be bound with chains of proven strength, if he asked repeatedly for the "bar of justice" and, so Jupien told me, for other ferocious instruments which it was almost impossible to obtain even from sailors—for they served to inflict punishments which have been abolished even on board ship where discipline is more rigorous than anywhere else—at the bottom of all this there persisted in M. de Charlus his dream of virility, to be attested if need be by acts of brutality, and all that inner radiance, invisible to us but projecting in this manner a little reflected light, with which his mediaeval imagination adorned crosses of judgment and feudal tortures. It was the same sentiment that made him, every time he arrived, say to Jupien: "I hope there will be no alert this evening, for already I see myself consumed by this fire from heaven like an inhabitant of Sodom." And he affected to be nervous of the Gothas, not that they caused him the slightest shadow of fear, but so as to have a pretext, as soon as the sirens sounded, to rush into the shelters in the Métro, where he hoped for pleasure from brief contact with unseen figures, accompanied by vague dreams of mediaeval dungeons and oubliettes. In short his desire to be bound in chains and beaten, with all its ugliness, betrayed a dream as poetical as, in other men, the longing to go to Venice or to keep ballet-dancers. And M. de Charlus was so determined that this dream should give him the illusion of reality that Jupien was obliged to sell the wooden bed which was in Room 43 and replace it by an iron bed which went better with the chains.

The all-clear sounded at last as I was approaching my house. A little boy in the street told me what a noise the fire-engines had made. I met Françoise coming up from the cellar with the butler. She thought that I had been killed. She told me that Saint-Loup had looked in, with apologies, to see whether he had not, in the course of the visit he had paid me during the morning, dropped his *croix de guerre*. For he had just noticed that he had lost it, and as he had to rejoin his regiment the following morning he had wanted to see whether it was in our flat. He had searched everywhere with Françoise and had found nothing. Françoise thought that he must have lost it before coming to see me, for, she said, she was almost sure, in fact she could have sworn that he was not wearing it when she saw him. In this she was mistaken. So much for the value of evidence and memory! In any case it was of no great importance. Saint-Loup was as much esteemed by his officers as loved by his men, and the matter could easily be arranged.

However, I sensed immediately, from the unenthusiastic manner in which they spoke of him, that Saint-Loup had made a poor impression on Françoise and on the butler. True, whereas the butler's son and Françoise's nephew had made every effort to get themselves into safe jobs, Saint-Loup had made efforts of the opposite kind, and with success, to be sent to as dangerous a post as possible. But this, because they judged from their own natures, was something that Françoise and the butler were incapable of believing. They were convinced that the rich are always put where there is no danger. In any case, had they known the truth concerning the heroic courage of Robert, it would have left them unmoved. He did not say "Boches," he had praised the valour of the Germans, he did not attribute to treachery the fact that we had not been victorious from the first day. That is what they would have liked to hear, that is what would have seemed to them a sign of courage. So although they continued to search for the *croix de guerre*, I found them chilly on the subject of Robert. Having my suspicions as to where the cross had been forgotten, I advised Françoise and the butler to go to bed. (However, if Saint-Loup had amused himself that evening in the fashion which I suspected, it was only to pass the time of waiting, for he had been seized once more by the desire to see Morel and had made use of all his military connexions to find out in what regiment he was serving, so that he could go and see him, but so far had only received hundreds of contradictory answers.) But the butler was never in a hurry to leave Françoise now that, thanks to the war, he had found a means of torturing her even more efficacious than the expulsion of the nuns or the Dreyfus case. That evening, and every time I went near them during the few more days that I spent in Paris before leaving to go to a new sanatorium, I heard the butler say to a terrified Françoise: "They're not in a hurry of course, they're biding their time, but when the time is ripe they will take Paris, and on that day we shall see no mercy!" "Heavens above, Mother of God," cried Françoise, "aren't they satisfied to have conquered poor Belgium? She suffered enough, that one, at the time of her innovation." "Belgium, Françoise? What they did in Belgium will be nothing compared to this!" And as the war had flooded the conversation of working-class people with a quantity of terms with which they had become acquainted through their eyes alone, by reading the newspapers, and which they consequently did not know how to pronounce, the butler went on to say: "I cannot understand how everybody can be so stupid. You will see, Françoise, they are preparing a new attack with a wider *scoop* than all the others." At this I rebelled, if not in the name of pity for Françoise and strategic common sense, at least in that of grammar, and declared that the word should be pronounced "scope," but succeeded only in causing the terrible phrase to be repeated to Françoise every time I entered the kitchen, for to the butler the pleasure of alarming his companion was scarcely greater than that of showing his master that, though he had once been a gardener at Combray and was a mere butler, he was nevertheless a good Frenchman according to the rule of Saint-André-des-Champs and possessed, by virtue of the Declaration of the Rights of Man, the right to use the pronunciation "scoop" in full independence and not to let himself be dictated to on a point which formed no part of his service and upon which in consequence, since the Revolution had made us all equals, he need listen to nobody.

To my annoyance, therefore, I had to listen to him talking to Françoise about an operation of wide "scoop" with an emphasis which was intended to prove to me that this pronunciation was the result not of ignorance but of an act of will following upon ripe reflexion. He confounded the government and the newspapers in a single "they" full of mistrust, saying: "They tell us about the losses of the Boches, they don't tell us about our own, it seems that they are ten times as big. They tell us that the enemy are at the end of their tether, that they have nothing to eat, personally I believe they are a hundred times better off than we are for food. It's no use stuffing us with lies. If the enemy had nothing to eat, they wouldn't fight as they did the other day when they killed a hundred thousand of our young men not twenty years old." Thus at every moment he exaggerated the triumphs of the Germans, as in the past he had those of the Radicals; and at the same time he recounted their atrocities in order that these triumphs might be yet more painful to Françoise, who never stopped saying: "Ah! Holy Mother of the Angels! Ah! Mary, Mother of God!", and sometimes, in order to be disagreeable to her in a different way, he said: "Anyhow, we are no better than they are, what we're doing in Greece is no prettier than what they have done in Belgium. You will see that we shall turn everybody against us, we shall find ourselves fighting every nation in the world," whereas the truth was exactly the opposite. On days when the news was good he destroyed its effect by assuring Françoise that the war would last thirty-five years, and if there was talk of the possibility of an armistice, he declared that peace would not last more than a few months and would be followed by battles which would make the present ones look like child's play, such battles that after them there would be nothing left of France.

The victory of the Allies seemed, if not near at hand, at least more or less certain, and it must unfortunately be admitted that the butler was greatly distressed at the prospect. For he had reduced the "world" war, like everything else, to the war which he was secretly waging against Françoise (of whom, nevertheless, he was fond, just as one may be fond of the person whom one enjoys infuriating every day by beating him at dominoes) and victory in his eyes took the shape of the first conversation in which he would have the pain of hearing Françoise say: "Well, it's over at last, and

they'll have to give us more than we gave them in '70." He
believed, nevertheless, that this fatal day of reckoning was perpetually about to arrive, for an unconscious patriotism made him
suppose, like all Frenchmen, victims of the same mirage as myself
since my illness, that victory—like my recovery—was just round
the corner. This event he anticipated by announcing to Françoise
that victory might perhaps come, but that his heart bled at the
thought, for revolution would follow hard on its heels and then
invasion. "Ah! this blooming war, the Boches will be the only
ones to recover from it quickly, Françoise. They have already
made hundreds of thousands of millions out of it. But as for their
coughing up a *sou* to us, what nonsense! They will print that in the
newspapers perhaps," he added out of prudence and so as to be
ready for any eventuality, "in order to appease the people, just as
for three years now they have been saying that the war will be over
tomorrow." Françoise was only too easily disturbed by these
words, because, having at first believed the optimists rather than
the butler, she saw now that the war, which she had thought
would end in a fortnight in spite of "the *innovation* of poor
Belgium," was indeed still going on, that we were not advancing
(the phenomenon of fixed front warfare was beyond her comprehension) and that, according to one of the innumerable "godsons"
to whom she gave everything that she earned with us, "they" were
concealing various awkward facts. "It's the working man who will
have to pay," concluded the butler. "They will take your field
away from you, Françoise." "Ah! God in Heaven!" But to these
distant misfortunes he preferred nearer ones and devoured the
newspapers in the hope of being able to announce a defeat to
Françoise. He waited for pieces of bad news as eagerly as if they
had been Easter eggs, hoping that things would go badly enough
to terrify Françoise but not badly enough to cause him any
material suffering. Thus the prospect of a Zeppelin raid enchanted
him: he would have the spectacle of Françoise hiding in the cellars,
and at the same time he was persuaded that in a town as large as
Paris the bombs would never happen to fall just on our house.

Françoise meanwhile was beginning at moments to return to
her Combray pacifism. She almost had doubts about the "German
atrocities." "When the war started we were told that the
Germans were murderers, brigands, real bandits, Bbboches..."
(If she gave several *b*'s to Boche, it was because the accusation that
the Germans were murderers seemed to her quite plausible, but

the idea that they were Boches, because of the enormity of the accusation, improbable in the extreme. Only it was not at all easy to understand what mysteriously terrifying sense Françoise gave to the word Boche, since the period she was talking about was the very beginning of the war, and also on account of the air of doubt with which she pronounced the word. For a doubt whether the Germans were criminals might be ill-founded in fact but did not contain in itself, from the point of view of logic, any contradiction. But how was it possible to doubt that they were Boches, since the word, in the popular language, means nothing more nor less than German? Perhaps she was simply repeating in an indirect fashion the violent remarks she had heard at the time, in which the word Boche was emphasised with particular energy.) "I believed all that," she went on, "but I am wondering now whether we are not every bit as scoundrelly as they are." This blasphemous thought had been slyly prepared in Françoise's mind by the butler, who, seeing that she had a certain fondness for King Constantine of Greece, had not ceased to represent him to her as literally starved by us until the day when he would yield. So the abdication of this monarch had aroused strong feelings in Françoise, who went so far as to declare: "We are no better than they are. If we were in Germany, we would do just the same."

I saw little of her, in any case, during these few days, for she spent much time at the house of those cousins of whom Mamma had said to me one day: "But you know that they are richer than you are." These cousins had given an example of that beautiful conduct which was very frequent at this period throughout the country and which would bear witness, if there were a historian to perpetuate its memory, to the greatness of France, her greatness of soul, her greatness after the fashion of Saint-André-des-Champs, a kind of conduct displayed as much by thousands of civilians living in safety far from the front as by the soldiers who fell at the Marne. There had been killed at Berry-au-Bac a nephew of Françoise who was also a nephew of the millionaire cousins, former proprietors of a large café who had retired long since after making their fortune. The young man who was killed had been the owner of a very small café and quite poor; he had gone off, twenty-five years old, when the army was mobilised, leaving his young wife alone to look after the little bar to which he hoped to return in a few months. He had been killed. And then this is what happened. The millionaire cousins of Françoise, who were not related by blood to the young woman who was their nephew's widow, had left the home in the country to which they had retired ten years earlier and had set to work again as café proprietors, without putting a sou into their own pockets; every morning at six the millionairess, a real lady, was up and dressed together with Mademoiselle her daughter, ready to help their niece and cousin by marriage. And for nearly three years now they had been washing glasses and serving drinks from early morning until half-past nine at night, without a day's rest. In this book in which there is not a single incident which is not fictitious, not a single character who is a real person in disguise, in which everything has been invented by me in accordance with the requirements of my theme, I owe it to the credit of my country to say that only the millionaire cousins of Françoise who came out of retirement to help their niece when she was left without support, only they are real people who exist. And persuaded as I am that I shall not offend their modesty, for the reason that they will never read this book, it is both with childish pleasure and with a profound emotion that, being unable to record the names of so many others who undoubtedly acted in the same way, to all of whom France owes her survival, I transcribe here the real name of this family: they are called—and what name could be more French?—Larivière. If there were a few vile shirkers like the arrogant young man in a dinner-jacket whom I had seen in Jupien's establishment, whose only concern was to know whether he could have Léon at half-past ten "as he had a luncheon engagement," they are redeemed by the innumerable throng of all the Frenchmen of Saint-André-des-Champs, by all the sublime soldiers and by those whom I rank as their equals, the Larivières.

The butler, to sharpen the fears of Françoise, showed her an old copy of *Lectures pour tous* which he had found, with a picture on its cover (it dated from before the war) of the "imperial family of Germany." "There's our lord and master to be," said the butler to Françoise, showing her "William." She goggled, then pointed to the feminine personage who stood by his side and said: "And there's the Williamess!"

My departure from Paris was delayed by a piece of news which caused me such grief that I was for some time rendered incapable of travelling. This was the death of Robert de Saint-Loup, killed two days after his return to the front while covering the retreat of his men. Never had any man felt less hatred for a nation than he (and as for the Emperor, for particular reasons, very possibly incorrect, he thought that William II had tried rather to prevent the war than to bring it about). Nor had he hated Germanism; the last words which I had heard on his lips, six days before he died, were the opening words of a Schumann song which he had started to hum in German on my staircase, until I had made him desist because of the neighbours. Accustomed by supreme good breeding to eliminate from his conduct all trace of apology or invective, all rhetoric, he had avoided in face of the enemy, as he had at the time of mobilisation, the actions which would have ensured his survival, through that tendency to efface himself before others of which all his behaviour was symbolic, down to his manner of coming out into the street bare-headed to close the door of my cab, every time I visited him. For several days I remained shut up in my room, thinking of him. I recalled his arrival the first time at Balbec, when, in an almost white suit, with his eyes greenish and mobile like the waves, he had crossed the hall adjoining the great dining-room whose windows gave on to the sea. I recalled the very special being that he had then seemed to me to be, the being for whose friendship I had so greatly wished. That wish had been realised beyond the limits of what I should ever have thought possible, without, however, at the time giving me more than a very slight pleasure; and then later I had come to understand the many great virtues and something else as well which lay concealed behind his elegant appearance. All this, the good as well as the bad, he had given without counting the cost, every day, as much on the last day when he advanced to attack a trench, out of generosity and because it was his habit to place at the service of others all that he possessed, as on that evening when he had run along the backs of the seats in the restaurant in order not to disturb me. And the fact that I had seen him really so little but against such varied backgrounds, in circumstances so diverse and separated by so many intervals—in that hall at Balbec, in the café at Rivebelle, in the cavalry barracks and at the military dinners in Doncières, at the theatre where he had slapped the face of the journalist, in the house of the Princesse de Guermantes—only had the effect of giving me, of his life, pictures more striking and more sharply defined and for his death a grief more lucid than we are likely to have in the case of people whom we have loved more, but with whom our association has been so nearly continuous that the image we retain of them is no more than a sort of vague average between an infinity of imperceptibly different images and our affection, satiated, has not, as with those whom we have seen only for brief moments, during meetings prematurely ended against their wish and ours, the illusion that there was possible between us a still greater affection of which circumstances alone have defrauded us. A few days after the day on which I had seen him pursuing his monocle and supposed him to be so haughty, in that hall at Balbec, there was another living form which I had seen for the first time on the beach at Balbec and which now, like his, no longer existed except in the state of memory: Albertine, making her progress along the sand that first evening, indifferent to everybody around her, a marine creature, like a seagull. For her my love had come so swiftly that, in order to be free to go out with her every day, I had never during my stay at Balbec gone over to Doncières to see Saint-Loup. And yet the history of my relations with him bore witness also to the fact that at one period I had ceased to love Albertine, since if later I had installed myself for a while near Robert at Doncières, the reason lay in my unhappiness at seeing that the feeling which I had for Mme de Guermantes was not returned. His life and Albertine's, so late made known to me, both at Balbec, and so swiftly concluded, had scarcely crossed, though it was he, I told myself, perceiving that the nimble shuttles of the years weave links between those of our memories which seem at first most independent of each other, it was he whom I had sent to see Mme Bontemps after Albertine had left me. And then it had turned out that their two lives had each of them a parallel secret, which I had not suspected. Saint-Loup's secret caused me now more sadness perhaps than that of Albertine, whose life had become so alien to me. But I felt an inconsolable regret that her life as well as his had been so short. They had often said to me, both of them: "You who are ill . . . ," they had looked after me. And yet it was they who were dead, while I, both of the one and of the other, could set side by side, separated by an interval which after all was really not very long, the final image—before the trench, in the river-bed—and the first image, which even in the case of Albertine I valued now only because it was associated in my mind with that of the sun setting over the sea.

Saint-Loup's death was received by Françoise with more compassion than that of Albertine. Immediately she assumed her role of hired mourner and descanted upon the memory of the dead man with frenzied threnodies and lamentations. She paraded her grief and only put on an unfeeling expression, at the same time averting her head, when in spite of myself I betrayed mine, which she wished to appear not to have seen. For like many emotional people, she was exasperated by the emotions of others, which bore no doubt too great a resemblance to her own. She loved now to draw attention to her slightest rheumatic twinge, to a fit of giddiness, to a bump. But if I referred to one of my symptoms, in an instant she was stoical and grave again and pretended not to have heard. "Poor Marquis," she said, although she continued to believe that he would have done anything in the world in order not to go to the front and, once there, in order to run away from danger. "Poor lady," she said, thinking of Mme de Marsantes, "how she must have cried when she heard about her boy's death! If at least she had been able to see him again! But perhaps it's better that she didn't, because his nose was cut in two, he was completely disfaced." And the eyes of Françoise filled with tears, behind which, however, there was perceptible the cruel curiosity of the peasant woman. No doubt Françoise pitied the sorrow of Mme de Marsantes with all her heart, but she regretted not knowing the form which this sorrow had taken and not being able to enjoy the afflicting spectacle of it. And as she would dearly have loved to cry and to be seen by me to cry, she said, in order to work herself up: "This has really done something to me!" In me too she sought to detect the traces of grief, with an avidity which caused me to feign a certain indifference when I spoke of Robert. And, largely no doubt out of a spirit of imitation and because she had heard the phrase used—for there are clichés in the servants' hall as well as in social coteries—she kept repeating, not however without a poor man's smugness in her voice: "All his riches did not save him from dying like anybody else, and what use are they to him now?" The butler took advantage of the occasion to say to Françoise that of course it was sad, but that it hardly counted beside the millions of men who fell every day in spite of all the efforts which the government made to conceal the fact. But this time the butler did not succeed in augmenting the sorrow of Françoise as he had hoped. For she replied: "It is true that they also die for France, but they are nobodies; it is always more interesting when it is somebody whom one knows." And Françoise, who enjoyed crying, went on to add: "You must be sure to let me know if they talk about the death of the Marquis in the newspaper."

Robert had often said to me sadly, long before the war: "Oh! my life, don't let's talk about it, I am a condemned man from the start." Was he alluding to the vice which he had succeeded hitherto in concealing from the world, but of which he was himself aware and whose seriousness he perhaps exaggerated, just as children who make love for the first time, or merely before that age seek solitary pleasure, imagine themselves to be like a plant which cannot scatter its pollen without dying immediately afterwards? Perhaps this exaggeration, for Saint-Loup as for the children, came partly from the still unfamiliar idea of sin, partly from the fact that an entirely novel sensation has an almost terrible force which later will gradually diminish; or had he really, justifying it if need be by the death of his father at an early age, a presentiment of his own premature end? Such a presentiment would seem, no doubt, to be impossible. Yet death appears to be obedient to certain laws. Often for instance, one gets the impression that children of parents who have died very old or very young are almost compelled to disappear at the same age, the former protracting until their hundredth year their incurable miseries and ailments, the latter, in spite of a happy and healthy existence, swept away at the premature but inevitable date by an illness so opportune and so accidental (whatever deep roots it may have in the victim's temperament) that it appears to be merely the formality necessary for the realisation of death. And may it not be possible that accidental death too—like that of Saint-Loup, which was perhaps in any case linked to his character in more ways than I have thought it necessary to describe—is somehow recorded in advance, known only to the gods, invisible to men, but revealed by a peculiar sadness, half unconscious, half conscious (and even, in so far as it is conscious, proclaimed to others with that complete sincerity with which we foretell misfortunes which in our heart of hearts we believe we shall escape but which will nevertheless take place) to the man who bears and forever sees within himself, as though it were some heraldic device, a fatal date?

He must have been truly magnificent in those last hours. This man who throughout his life, even when sitting down, even when walking across a drawing-room, had seemed to be restraining an impulse to charge, while with a smile he dissembled the indomitable will which dwelt within his triangular head, at last had charged. Freed from the books which encumbered it, the feudal turret had become military once more. And this Guermantes had died more himself than ever before, or rather more a member of his race, into which slowly he dissolved until he became nothing more than a Guermantes, as was symbolically visible at his burial in the church of Saint-Hilaire at Combray, completely hung for the occasion with black draperies upon which stood out in red, beneath the closed circle of the coronet, without initials or Christian names or titles, the G of the Guermantes that he had again in death become.

Even before going to this burial, which did not take place immediately, I wrote to Gilberte. I ought perhaps to have written to the Duchesse de Guermantes, but I told myself that she would receive the death of Robert with the same indifference which I had seen her display towards the deaths of so many others who had seemed to be closely linked to her life, and that she would perhaps even, with her Guermantes wit, try to show that she did not share the superstition about ties of blood. And I was too unwell to write to everybody. In the past I had believed that she and Robert were fond of each other in the sense in which that phrase is used in society, that is to say that, when they were together, they said to each other tender things which at the moment they truly felt. But away from her, he did not hesitate to declare that she was an idiot, and if she sometimes derived an egotistical pleasure from seeing him, I had observed her on the other hand to be incapable of taking the slightest trouble, of making even the smallest use of her credit in order to render him a service or even to spare him an unpleasantness. Her unkindness in refusing to give Robert a recommendation to General de Saint-Joseph, at the time when he wanted to avoid returning to Morocco, proved surely that the devoted help which she had given him on the occasion of his marriage was no more than a sort of atonement which cost her almost nothing. So I was very astonished to hear—she was unwell at the moment when Robert was killed—that in order to spare her the shock which the news would cause her her family had thought it necessary to conceal from her for several days, under the most fallacious pretexts, the newspapers which would have informed her of his death. And my surprise increased when I heard that, after they had at last been obliged to tell her the truth, the Duchess wept for a whole day, fell sick and for a long time—more than a week, which was a long time for her—was inconsolable. When I heard of her grief, I was touched. It enabled society to say, and it enables me to vouch for the truth of the statement, that a great friendship existed between them. But then when I recall all the little malicious utterances, all the ill-natured refusals to help each other which this friendship had not excluded, I cannot help reflecting that in society a great friendship does not amount to much.

However, a little later, in circumstances which, if they touched my heart less, were historically more important, Mme de Guermantes showed herself, to my mind, in a yet more favourable light. This woman who as a girl, as the reader may remember, had behaved with such audacious impertinence towards the imperial family of Russia, and who after her marriage had addressed them always with a freedom which sometimes caused her to be charged with lack of tact, was perhaps alone, after the Russian Revolution, in giving proofs of a limitless devotion to the Grand Duchesses and the Grand Dukes. Only the year before the war she had not a little annoyed the Grand Duchess Vladimir by persistently referring to Countess Hohenfelsen, the morganatic wife of the Grand Duke Paul, as "the Grand Duchess Paul." Nevertheless, no sooner had the Russian Revolution broken out than our ambassador in St Petersburg, M. Paléologue ("Paléo" in diplomatic society, which like society at large has its supposedly witty abbreviations), was plagued with telegrams from the Duchesse de Guermantes asking for news of the Grand Duchess Maria Pavlovna. And for a long time the only marks of sympathy and respect which this Princess received came to her regularly and exclusively from Mme de Guermantes.

To various individuals Saint-Loup caused not so much by his death as by what he had done in the preceding weeks a distress greater than that which afflicted the Duchess. What happened was that, only the day after the evening on which I had seen him, and two days after the Baron had said to Morel "I will have my revenge," the inquiries which Saint-Loup had made about the whereabouts of Morel were successful; they succeeded, that is to say, in bringing to the notice of the general under whose command Morel should have been the fact that he was a deserter, whereupon the general had him searched for and arrested and, to apologise to Saint-Loup for the punishment which he was obliged to inflict upon someone in whom he took an interest, wrote to inform him how the matter stood. Morel did not doubt that his arrest had been brought about by the rancour of M. de Charlus. He remembered the words "I will have my revenge," thought that this was the threatened revenge, and asked to be allowed to make some disclosures. "It is quite true," he declared, "that I am a deserter. But if I have been led astray, is it altogether my fault?" He then told apropos of M. de Charlus and M. d'Argencourt, with whom also he had quarrelled, stories in which he had not in fact himself been directly involved, but which they, with the double expansiveness of lovers and of inverts, had related to him, and the result was the immediate arrest of both these gentlemen. But each of them suffered less perhaps at being arrested than at learning—what neither of them had known—that the other was his rival, and the judicial examination revealed that they had an enormous number of other obscure, quotidian rivals, picked up in the street. M. de Charlus and M. d'Argencourt were soon released. So was Morel, because the general's letter to Saint-Loup was returned to him with the information: "Deceased, killed in action." Out of respect for the dead man the general so arranged things that Morel was merely sent to the front. He conducted himself bravely there, survived every danger and returned, when the war was over, with the cross which M. de Charlus had in the past vainly solicited for him and which in this indirect fashion was procured for him by the death of Saint-Loup.

I have often thought since then, remembering the *croix de guerre* which went astray in Jupien's establishment, that if Saint-Loup had lived, he could easily have got himself elected a deputy in the elections which followed the armistice, thanks to the scum of universal fatuousness which the war left in its wake and the halo which still adhered to military glory. For at that time, if the loss of a finger could abolish centuries of prejudice and allow a man of humble birth to make a brilliant marriage into an aristocratic family, the *croix de guerre*, even one won by sitting in an office, sufficed for a triumphal election to the Chamber of Deputies, if not to the Académie Française. The election of Saint-Loup, because of his "holy family," would have caused M. Arthur Meyer to pour out floods of tears and ink. But perhaps he was too sincerely fond of the people to be good at winning their votes, although on account of his quarterings of nobility they would probably have forgiven him his democratic ideas. These he would no doubt have expounded with success before a Chamber composed of aviators. Certainly these heroes would have understood him, and a few other exceptionally intelligent and high-minded men. But thanks to the platitudinous mentality of the National Bloc, the old lags of politics who are invariably re-elected had also turned up again, and such of them as failed to enter a Chamber of aviators solicited, so that they might at least get into the Académie Française, the suffrages of the Marshals, of the President of the Republic, the President of the Chamber, etc. These men would have looked with less favour upon Saint-Loup than they did upon another of Jupien's habitués, the deputy of Liberal Action, who was once more returned unopposed and who continued to wear the uniform of a territorial officer long after the war had been over. His election was hailed with joy by all the newspapers which had agreed to put his name forward, as well as by the noble and wealthy ladies who now dressed only in rags from feelings of propriety and from fear of taxes, while the gentlemen of the Bourse never stopped buying diamonds, not for their wives but because, having lost all confidence in the credit of any nation, they were seeking refuge in this tangible wealth and as a result sending up the price of De Beers by a thousand francs. All this tomfoolery was not exactly popular, but there was less disposition to blame the National Bloc when suddenly there appeared on the scene the victims of bolshevism, those Grand Duchesses in tatters whose husbands had been assassinated in carts, while their sons, after being left to starve and then forced to work in the midst of abuse, had finally been thrown into wells and buried beneath stones because it was believed that they had the plague and might pass it on. Those of them who succeeded in escaping suddenly turned up in Paris.

The new sanatorium to which I withdrew was no more successful in curing me than the first one, and many years passed before I came away. During the train journey which eventually took me back to Paris, the thought of my lack of talent for literature—a defect which I had first discovered, so I supposed, long ago on the Guermantes way, which I had again recognised, and been still more saddened by, in the course of the daily walks that I had taken with Gilberte before returning to dine very late at night at Tansonville, and which on the eve of my departure from that house I had come very near to identifying, after reading some pages of the Goncourt Journal, with the vanity, the falsehood of literature—this thought, less painful perhaps but more melancholy still if I referred it not to a private infirmity of my own but to the non-existence of the ideal in which I had believed, this thought, which for a very long time had not entered my mind, struck me afresh and with a force more painful than ever before. The train had stopped, I remember, in open country. The sun was shining on a row of trees that followed the railway line, flooding the upper halves of their trunks with light. "Trees," I thought, "you no longer have anything to say to me. My heart has grown cold and no longer hears you. I am in the midst of nature. Well, it is with indifference, with boredom that my eyes register the line which separates your radiant foreheads from your shadowy trunks. If ever I thought of myself as a poet, I know now that I am not one. Perhaps in the new, the so desiccated part of my life which is about to begin, human beings may yet inspire in me what nature can no longer say. But the years in which I might have been able to sing *her* praise will never return." But in thus consoling myself with the thought that the observation of humanity might possibly come to take the place of an unattainable inspiration, I knew that I was merely seeking to console myself, I knew that I knew myself to be worthless. If I really had the soul of an artist, surely I would be feeling pleasure at the sight of this curtain of trees lit by the setting sun, these little flowers on the bank which lifted themselves almost to the level of the steps of my compartment, flowers whose petals I was able to count but whose colour I would not, like many a worthy man of letters, attempt to describe, for can one hope to transmit to the reader a pleasure that one has not felt? A little later I had noticed with the same absence of emotion the glitter of gold and orange which the sun splashed upon the windows of a house; and finally, as the evening advanced, I had seen another house which appeared to be built out of a strange pink substance. But I had made these various observations with the same absolute indifference as if, walking in a garden with a lady, I had seen a pane of glass, and a little further on an object of an alabaster-like material, the unusual colour of which had failed to draw me out of the most languorous boredom, but as if, nevertheless, out of politeness towards the lady, in order to say something and also in order to show that I had noticed these colours, I had pointed in passing to the tinted glass and the fragment of stucco. In the same way, to satisfy my conscience, I indicated to myself now as to someone who was travelling with me and might be able to extract from them more pleasure than I, the flame-like reflexions in the windows and the pink transparency of the house. But the companion whose attention I had drawn to these curious effects was evidently of a less enthusiastic nature than many more sympathetically disposed persons who are enraptured by such sights, for he had taken cognisance of the colours without any kind of joy.

My long absence from Paris had not prevented old friends from continuing, as my name remained on their lists, faithfully to send me invitations, and when on my return I found—together with one to a tea-party given by Berma for her daughter and her son-in-law—another to an afternoon party with music which was to take place the following day at the house of the Prince de Guermantes, the gloomy reflexions which had passed through my mind in the train were not the least of the motives which urged me to accept. Really, I said to myself, what point is there in forgoing the pleasures of social life if, as seems to be the case, the famous "work" which for so long I have been hoping every day to start the next day, is something I am not, or am no longer, made for and perhaps does not even correspond to any reality. This reasoning was, it is true, completely negative and merely deprived of their force those other reasons which might have dissuaded me from going to this fashionable concert. The positive reason that made me decide to go was the name of Guermantes, absent long enough from my mind to be able, when I read it upon the invitation card, to reawaken a ray of my attention, to draw up from the depths of my memory a sort of section of the past of the Guermantes, attended by all the images of seigniorial forest and tall flowers which at that earlier time of my life had accompanied it, and to reassume for me the charm and the significance which I had found in it at Combray when, passing along the Rue de l'Oiseau on my way home, I used to see from outside, like some dark lacquer, the window of Gilbert the Bad, Lord of Guermantes. For a moment the Guermantes had once more seemed to me to be totally different from people in society, comparable neither with them nor with any living being, even a reigning prince, creatures begotten of the union of the sharp and windy air of the dark town of Combray in which my childhood had been spent with the past which could be sensed there, in the little street, at the height of the stained-glass window. I had had a longing to go to the Guermantes party as if in going there I must have been brought nearer to my childhood and to the depths of my memory where my childhood dwelt. And I had continued to read and re-read the invitation until in the end, rising in revolt, the letters which composed this name at once so familiar and so mysterious, like that of Combray itself, resumed their independence and outlined before my tired eyes a name that I seemed never to have seen before. (Mamma happened to be going to a little tea-party of Mme

Sazerat's which she knew beforehand she would find extremely boring, so I had no scruples about going to the Princesse de Guermantes's.)

I took a cab to go to the Prince de Guermantes's house, which was no longer his former home but a magnificent mansion that he had recently built in the Avenue du Bois. One of the mistakes of society people is not to realise that, if they want us to believe in them, it is first necessary that they should believe in themselves, or at least should respect the essential elements of our belief. At the time when I believed, even if I knew the contrary to be true, that the Guermantes lived in this or that grand house in virtue of a hereditary right, to penetrate into the palace of the sorcerer or the fairy, to compel to open before me the doors which yield only when one has pronounced the magic formula, seemed to me as difficult as to obtain an interview with the sorcerer or the fairy themselves. To persuade myself that the old manservant engaged twenty-four hours earlier or supplied by Potel and Chabot was the son, the grandson, the scion of a whole line of menials who had been in the family's service since long before the Revolution was the easiest thing in the world, and I was only too happy to take for an ancestral portrait some painting which had been bought the previous month from Bernheim Jeune. But enchantment cannot be decanted from one vessel to another, memories are indivisible, and of the Prince de Guermantes, now that he had himself shattered the illusions of my belief by going to live in the Avenue du Bois, nothing much was left. The ceilings which I had once feared to see collapse upon the announcement of my name, those ceilings under which, for me, there would still have floated something of the enchantment and the fears of those early days, now looked down upon the parties of an American hostess in whom I took not the slightest interest. Intrinsically, material objects have in themselves no power, but, since it is our practice to bestow power upon them, doubtless at this moment some middle-class schoolboy was feeling, in front of the house in the Avenue du Bois, the same sentiments that I had once felt as I stood before the house where the Prince de Guermantes had lived in my youth. He, this schoolboy, was still at the age of beliefs, but I had passed beyond it, I had lost that privilege, just as after one's first years one loses the ability that a baby has to break up the milk which he ingests into digestible fragments, so that the prudent adult will drink milk only in small quantities whereas babies can continue to suck it in

indefinitely without pausing for breath. But at least the Prince de
Guermantes's change of residence had this advantage for me, that
the cab which had come to fetch me and in which, as it took me
to the party, I was making these reflexions, was obliged to traverse
the streets which lead to the Champs-Elysées. They were very
badly paved at this time, but the moment I found myself in them
I was, none the less, detached from my thoughts by that sensation
of extraordinary physical comfort which one has when suddenly a
car in which one is travelling rolls more easily, more softly, without noise, because the gates of a park have been opened and one is
gliding over alleys covered with fine sand or dead leaves; materially nothing of the sort had happened, but I felt suddenly that all
external obstacles had been eliminated, simply because I no longer
had to make that effort of adaptation or attention which we make,
sometimes without being conscious of it, in the presence of new
things: the streets through which I was passing at this moment
were those, so long forgotten, which I used once upon a time to
take with Françoise when we went to the Champs-Elysées. The
solid earth knew of its own accord where it had to go; its resistance
was vanquished. And like an airman who hitherto has progressed
laboriously along the ground, abruptly "taking off" I soared
slowly towards the silent heights of memory. Among all the streets
of Paris these streets will always stand out for me, as though they
were made of a different substance from the others. When we
reached the corner of the Rue Royale where once had stood the
open-air vendor of the photographs beloved by Françoise, it
seemed to me that the cab, feeling the pull of hundreds of former
turns, could not do otherwise than turn of its own accord. I was
not traversing the same streets as the people who were walking
about the town that day, I was traversing a past, gliding, sad and
sweet; a past which was moreover compounded of so many
different pasts that it was difficult for me to recognise the cause
of my melancholy, to know whether it was due to those walks in
which the hope of meeting Gilberte had co-existed with the fear
that she would not come, to the proximity of a certain house to
which I had been told that Albertine had gone with Andrée, or to
that vanity of all things which seems to be the significance of a
route which one has followed a thousand times in a state of passion
which has disappeared and which has borne no fruit, like the route
which I used to take on those expeditions of feverish haste after

luncheon to see, with the paste still damp upon them, the posters of *Phèdre* and *Le Domino noir*.

The cab turned into the Champs-Elysées and, as I did not particularly want to hear the whole of the concert which was being given at the Guermantes party, I stopped it and was preparing to get out in order to walk a few yards when I was struck by the spectacle presented by another cab which was also stopping. A man with staring eyes and hunched figure was placed rather than seated in the back, and was making, to keep himself upright, the efforts that might have been made by a child who has been told to be good. But his straw hat failed to conceal an unruly forest of hair which was entirely white, and a white beard, like those which snow forms on the statues of river-gods in public gardens, flowed from his chin. It was—side by side with Jupien, who was unremitting in his attentions to him—M. de Charlus, now convalescent after an attack of apoplexy of which I had had no knowledge (I had only been told that he had lost his sight, but in fact this trouble had been purely temporary and he could now see quite well again) and which, unless the truth was that hitherto he had dyed his hair and that he had now been forbidden to continue so fatiguing a practice, had had the effect, as in a sort of chemical precipitation, of rendering visible and brilliant all that saturation of metal which the locks of his hair and his beard, pure silver now, shot forth like so many geysers, so that upon the old fallen prince this latest illness had conferred the Shakespearean majesty of a King Lear. His eyes had not remained unaffected by this total convulsion, this metallurgical transformation of his head, but had, by an inverse phenomenon, lost all their brightness. But what was most moving was that one felt that this lost brightness was identical with his moral pride, and that somehow the physical and even the intellectual life of M. de Charlus had survived the eclipse of that aristocratic haughtiness which had in the past seemed indissolubly linked to them. To confirm this, at the moment which I am describing, there passed in a victoria, no doubt also on her way to the reception of the Prince de Guermantes, Mme de Saint-Euverte, whom formerly the Baron had not considered elegant enough for him. Jupien, who tended him like a child, whispered in his ear that it was someone with whom he was acquainted, Mme de Saint-Euverte. And immediately, with infinite laboriousness but with all the concentration of a sick man determined to show that he is capable of all the movements which are still difficult for him, M. de

Charlus lifted his hat, bowed, and greeted Mme de Saint-Euverte as respectfully as if she had been the Queen of France or as if he had been a small child coming timidly in obedience to his mother's command to say "How do you do?" to a grown-up person. For a child, but without a child's pride, was what he had once more become. Perhaps the very difficulty that M. de Charlus had in making these gestures was in itself a reason for him to make them, in the knowledge that he would create a greater effect by an action which, painful for an invalid, became thereby doubly meritorious on the part of the man who performed it and doubly flattering to the individual to whom it was addressed, invalids, like kings, practising exaggerated civility. Perhaps also there was in the movements of the Baron that lack of co-ordination which follows upon maladies of the spinal column and the brain, so that his gestures went beyond anything that he intended. What I myself saw in them was above all a sort of gentleness, an almost physical gentleness, and of detachment from the realities of life, phenomena so strikingly apparent in those whom death has already drawn within its shadow. And the exposure of the veins of silver in his hair was less indicative of profound alterations than this unconscious humility which turned all social relations upside down and abased before Mme de Saint-Euverte—as it would have abased before the most vulgar of American hostesses (who at last would have been able to congratulate herself on the hitherto unattainable politeness of the Baron)—what had seemed to be the proudest snobbishness of all. For the Baron still lived, still thought; his intellect was not impaired. And more than any chorus of Sophocles on the humbled pride of Oedipus, more than death itself or any funeral oration on the subject of death, the humble greeting, full of effort to please, which the Baron addressed to Mme de Saint-Euverte proclaimed the fragile and perishable nature of the love of earthly greatness and all human pride. M. de Charlus, who until this moment would never have consented to dine with Mme de Saint-Euverte, now bowed to the ground in her honour. To receive the homage of M. de Charlus had been, for her, the highest ambition of snobbery, just as, for the Baron, the central principle of snobbery had been to be rude to her. And now this inaccessible and precious essence which he had succeeded in making Mme de Saint-Euverte believe to be part of his nature, had at a single stroke been annihilated by M. de Charlus, by the earnest timidity, the apprehensive zeal with which he raised a hat from beneath which, all the while that his head remained deferentially uncovered, there streamed with the eloquence of a Bossuet the torrents of his silvery hair. Jupien helped the Baron to descend and I greeted him. He spoke to me very rapidly, in a voice so inaudible that I could not distinguish what he was saying, which wrung from him, when for the third time I made him repeat his remarks, a gesture of impatience that astonished me by its contrast with the impassivity which his face had at first displayed, which was no doubt an after-effect of his stroke. But when after a while I had grown accustomed to this pianissimo of whispered words, I perceived that the sick man retained the use of his intelligence absolutely intact.

There were, however, two M. de Charluses, not to mention any others. Of the two, one, the intellectual one, passed his time in complaining that he suffered from progressive aphasia, that he constantly pronounced one word, one letter by mistake for another. But as soon as he actually made such a mistake, the other M. de Charlus, the subconscious one, who was as desirous of admiration as the first was of pity and out of vanity did things that the first would have despised, immediately, like a conductor whose orchestra has blundered, checked the phrase which he had started and with infinite ingenuity made the end of his sentence follow coherently from the word which he had in fact uttered by mistake for another but which he thus appeared to have chosen. Even his memory was intact, and from it his vanity impelled him, not without the fatigue of the most laborious concentration, to drag forth this or that ancient recollection, of no importance, which concerned myself and which would demonstrate to me that he had preserved or recovered all his lucidity of mind. Without moving his head or his eyes, and without varying in the slightest degree the modulation of his voice, he said to me, for instance: "Look, there's a poster on that telegraph-pole like the one which I was standing near when I saw you for the first time at Avranches—no, I am mistaken, at Balbec." And it was in fact an advertisement for the same product.

I had found it difficult at first to understand what he was saying, just as one begins by seeing absolutely nothing in a room of which all the curtains are closed. But like one's eyes in half-darkness, my ears soon accustomed themselves to this pianissimo. The sound had in any case, I think, gradually grown in volume while the Baron was speaking, perhaps because the weakness of his voice was due in part to a nervous apprehension which was dispelled when he was distracted by the presence of another person and ceased to think about it, though possibly, on the other hand, the feeble voice corresponded to the real state of his health and the momentary strength with which he spoke in conversation was the result of an artificial, transient and even dangerous excitement, which might make strangers say: "He is much better, he must stop thinking about his illness," but in fact only aggravated the illness, which lost no time in resuming its sway. Whatever the explanation may be, the Baron at this moment (even making allowances for the improvement in my own hearing) was flinging down his words with greater force, as the tide, on days of bad weather, flings down its little contorted waves. And the traces of his recent attack caused one to hear at the back of his words a noise like that of pebbles dragged by the sea. Continuing to speak to me about the past, no doubt to prove to me that he had not lost his memory, he evoked it now—in a funereal fashion but without sadness—by reciting an endless list of all the people belonging to his family or his world who were no longer alive, less, it seemed, with any emotion of grief that they were dead than with satisfaction at having survived them. He appeared indeed, as he recalled their extinction, to enjoy a clearer perception of his own return towards health and it was with an almost triumphal sternness that he repeated, in a monotonous tone, stammering slightly and with a dull sepulchral resonance: "Hannibal de Bréauté, dead! Antoine de Mouchy, dead! Charles Swann, dead! Adalbert de Montmorency, dead! Boson de Talleyrand, dead! Sosthène de Doudeauville, dead!" And every time he uttered it, the word "dead" seemed to fall upon his departed friends like a spadeful of earth each heavier than the last, thrown by a grave-digger grimly determined to immure them yet more closely within the tomb.

The Duchesse de Létourville, who was not going to the Princesse de Guermantes's reception because she had just recovered from a long illness, passed near us at that moment on foot, and seeing the Baron, of whose recent attack she knew nothing, stopped to say good-day to him. But the effect of her own illness was to make her not more understanding but more impatient— with a nervous ill-humour that was nevertheless perhaps not without a large element of compassion—of the illnesses of others. Hearing the Baron pronounce certain words with difficulty and incorrectly and seeing the painful effort he had to make to move his arm, she cast her eyes first upon Jupien and then upon myself as though to demand an explanation of so shocking a phenomenon. As we said nothing, it was to M. de Charlus himself that she addressed a long look full of sadness but also of reproach. She seemed to think it very wrong of him to be out of doors and in her company in a condition as unusual as if he had come out without a tie or without shoes. And when yet another error in pronunciation was perpetrated by the Baron, augmenting both the distress and the indignation of the Duchess, she cried out to him: "Palamède!" in the interrogative and exasperated tone of those nervous people who cannot bear to be kept waiting for a single moment and will say to you sharply, if you let them come into your room before you are ready (with a word of apology for being still engaged upon your toilet), not so as to excuse themselves but in order to accuse you: "Oh, I'm disturbing you, am I?" as if it was your fault that you were being disturbed. Finally she left us, looking crosser and crosser and saying to the Baron: "Really, you ought to go home."

M. de Charlus said he would like to sit down on a chair to rest while Jupien and I went for a little walk, and with some difficulty pulled out of his pocket a book which looked to me like a prayer-book. I was not displeased to have an opportunity to learn from Jupien various details of the Baron's state of health. "I am very glad to talk to you, sir," said Jupien, "but we won't go further than the Rond-Point. Thank heaven, the Baron is better now, but I dare not leave him alone for long, he is always the same, he is too kind-hearted, he would give away everything he possesses: and then that's not the only thing, he still tries to pick people up as if he was a young man, and I have to keep my eyes open." "Particularly as he has recovered the use of his own eyes," I replied; "I was very distressed when I was told that he had lost his sight." "Yes, it's true that his eyes were affected by his stroke. For a time he could see nothing at all. Just imagine, during the cure, which as a matter of fact did him a great deal of good, he was for several months unable to see more than a man born blind." "At least that must have made your surveillance largely unnecessary?" "Not at all, no sooner had he arrived in a hotel than he would ask me what this or that individual on the staff was like. I used to assure him that they were all horrors. But he realised that that couldn't be universally true, that I must sometimes be lying. Little rascal that he is! And then he was extraordinarily good at guessing, from the voice perhaps, I don't know. He used to contrive to send me on urgent errands. One day—you will excuse my telling you this, but you came once by chance to the Temple of Shamelessness and I have nothing to hide from you" (in fact, it was a disagreeable feature of his character that he seemed always to enjoy revealing secrets in his possession)—"I was returning from one of these supposedly urgent errands, all the faster because I guessed it to have been arranged on purpose, when as I approached the Baron's room I heard a voice saying: 'What?' and the Baron reply: 'You don't mean that this has never happened to you before?' I went into the room without knocking, and imagine my terror! The Baron, misled by a voice which was in fact deeper than is usual at that age (remember that at this period he was completely blind and in the old days, as you know, he had always been partial to men who were not quite young), was with a little boy who could not have been ten years old."

I have been told since that at that time he suffered almost every day from severe fits of mental depression, during which, though his mind was not actually wandering, he used to proclaim aloud before people whose presence or whose strict views he forgot opinions which normally he concealed, his pro-Germanism for instance. The war had long since ended, but still he groaned over the defeat of the Germans, amongst whose number he counted himself, and would say proudly: "And yet, inevitably, we shall have our revenge. For we have proved that we are the nation with the greatest capacity for resistance, and the best organisation too." Or else his confidences would take another direction, and he would cry out angrily: "Lord X—— (or the Prince de XX——) had better not dare repeat what he said yesterday, it was all I could do not to reply: 'You know you're just as much one as I am.'" Needless to say, when, at the moments when he was "not quite all there," M. de Charlus made these avowals of his pro-German or other tendencies, anybody from his immediate circle who might be with him, whether it were Jupien or the Duchesse de Guermantes, would interrupt the imprudent remarks and interpret them for the benefit of others less intimately acquainted with the Baron and less discreet in a far-fetched but honourable sense.

"But, good heavens!" cried Jupien, "I was right not to want us to go too far. Look! He's already managed to get into conversation with a gardener's boy. I had better say good-bye to you, sir, I must not leave my invalid alone for a second, he is really just a big baby now."

I got out of my cab a second time just before it reached the house of the Princesse de Guermantes and I began once more to reflect upon the mood of lassitude and boredom in which I had attempted, the previous day, to note the characteristics of that line which, in a countryside reputed one of the loveliest of France, had separated upon the trunks of the trees the shadow from the light. Certainly the reasoned conclusions which I had drawn at the time did not cause me so much pain today. They were unchanged; but at this moment, as on every occasion when I found myself torn from my habits—in a new place, or going out at an unaccustomed hour—I was feeling a lively pleasure. The pleasure seemed to me today a purely frivolous one, that of going to an afternoon party given by Mme de Guermantes. But since I knew now that I could hope for nothing of greater value than frivolous pleasures, what point was there in depriving myself of them? I told myself again that I had felt, in attempting the description, not a spark of that enthusiasm which, if it is not the sole, is a primary criterion of talent. I tried next to draw from my memory other "snapshots," those in particular which it had taken in Venice, but the mere word "snapshot" made Venice seem to me as boring as an exhibition of photographs, and I felt that I had no more taste, no more talent for describing now what I had seen in the past, than I had had yesterday for describing what at that very moment I was, with a meticulous and melancholy eye, actually observing. In a few minutes a host of friends whom I had not seen for years would probably ask me to give up being a recluse and devote my days to them. And what reason had I to refuse their request, now that I possessed the proof that I was useless and that literature could no longer give me any joy whatever, whether this was my fault, through my not having enough talent, or the fault of literature itself, if it were true that literature was less charged with reality than I had once supposed?

When I thought of what Bergotte had said to me: "You are ill, but one cannot pity you for you have the joys of the mind," how mistaken he had been about me! How little joy there was in this sterile lucidity! Even if sometimes perhaps I had pleasures (not of the mind), I sacrificed them always to one woman after another; so that, had fate granted me another hundred years of life and sound health as well, it would merely have added a series of extensions to an already tedious existence, which there seemed to be no point in prolonging at all, still less for any great length of time. As for the "joys of the intelligence," could I call by that name those cold observations which my clairvoyant eye or my power of accurate ratiocination made without any pleasure and which remained always infertile?

But it is sometimes just at the moment when we think that everything is lost that the intimation arrives which may save us; one has knocked at all the doors which lead nowhere, and then one stumbles without knowing it on the only door through which one can enter—which one might have sought in vain for a hundred years—and it opens of its own accord.

Revolving the gloomy thoughts which I have just recorded, I had entered the courtyard of the Guermantes mansion and in my absent-minded state I had failed to see a car which was coming towards me; the chauffeur gave a shout and I just had time to step out of the way, but as I moved sharply backwards I tripped against the uneven paving-stones in front of the coach-house. And at the moment when, recovering my balance, I put my foot on a stone which was slightly lower than its neighbour, all my discouragement vanished and in its place was that same happiness which at various epochs of my life had been given to me by the sight of trees which I had thought that I recognised in the course of a drive near Balbec, by the sight of the twin steeples of Martinville, by the flavour of a madeleine dipped in tea, and by all those other sensations of which I have spoken and of which the last works of Vinteuil had seemed to me to combine the quintessential character. Just as, at the moment when I tasted the madeleine, all anxiety about the future, all intellectual doubts had disappeared, so now those that a few seconds ago had assailed me on the subject of the reality of my literary gifts, the reality even of literature, were removed as if by magic.

I had followed no new train of reasoning, discovered no decisive argument, but the difficulties which had seemed insoluble a moment ago had lost all importance. The happiness which I had just felt was unquestionably the same as that which I had felt when I tasted the madeleine soaked in tea. But if on that occasion I had put off the task of searching for the profounder causes of my emotion, this time I was determined not to resign myself to a failure to understand them. The emotion was the same; the difference, purely material, lay in the images evoked: a profound

azure intoxicated my eyes, impressions of coolness, of dazzling
light, swirled round me and in my desire to seize them—as afraid
to move as I had been on the earlier occasion when I had continued to savour the taste of the madeleine while I tried to draw
into my consciousness whatever it was that it recalled to me—
I continued, ignoring the evident amusement of the great crowd
of chauffeurs, to stagger as I had staggered a few seconds ago, with
one foot on the higher paving-stone and the other on the lower.
Every time that I merely repeated this physical movement,
I achieved nothing; but if I succeeded, forgetting the
Guermantes party, in recapturing what I had felt when I first
placed my feet on the ground in this way, again the dazzling and
indistinct vision fluttered near me, as if to say: "Seize me as I pass if
you can, and try to solve the riddle of happiness which I set you."
And almost at once I recognised the vision: it was Venice, of which
my efforts to describe it and the supposed snapshots taken by my
memory had never told me anything, but which the sensation
which I had once experienced as I stood upon two uneven stones
in the baptistery of St Mark's had, recurring a moment ago,
restored to me complete with all the other sensations linked on
that day to that particular sensation, all of which had been waiting
in their place—from which with imperious suddenness a chance
happening had caused them to emerge—in the series of forgotten
days. In the same way the taste of the little madeleine had recalled
Combray to me. But why had the images of Combray and of
Venice, at these two different moments, given me a joy which was
like a certainty and which sufficed, without any other proof, to
make death a matter of indifference to me?

Still asking myself this question, and determined today to find
the answer to it, I entered the Guermantes mansion, because
always we give precedence over the inner task that we have to
perform to the outward role which we are playing, which was, for
me at this moment, that of guest. But when I had gone upstairs, a
butler requested me to wait for a few minutes in a little sitting-
room used as a library, next to the room where the refreshments
were being served, until the end of the piece of music which was
being played, the Princess having given orders for the doors to be
kept shut during its performance. And at that very moment a
second intimation came to reinforce the one which had been
given to me by the two uneven paving-stones and to exhort me
to persevere in my task. A servant, trying unsuccessfully not to

make a noise, chanced to knock a spoon against a plate and again that same species of happiness which had come to me from the uneven paving-stones poured into me; the sensation was again of great heat, but entirely different: heat combined with a whiff of smoke and relieved by the cool smell of a forest background; and I recognised that what seemed to me now so delightful was that same row of trees which I had found tedious both to observe and to describe but which I had just now for a moment, in a sort of daze—I seemed to be in the railway carriage again, opening a bottle of beer—supposed to be before my eyes, so forcibly had the identical noise of the spoon knocking against the plate given me, until I had had time to remember where I was, the illusion of the noise of the hammer with which a railwayman had done something to a wheel of the train while we stopped near the little wood. And then it seemed as though the signs which were to bring me, on this day of all days, out of my disheartened state and restore to me my faith in literature, were thronging eagerly about me, for, a butler who had long been in the service of the Prince de Guermantes having recognised me and brought to me in the library where I was waiting, so that I might not have to go to the buffet, a selection of petits fours and a glass of orangeade, I wiped my mouth with the napkin which he had given me; and instantly, as though I had been the character in the *Arabian Nights* who unwittingly accomplishes the very rite which can cause to appear, visible to him alone, a docile genie ready to convey him to a great distance, a new vision of azure passed before my eyes, but an azure that this time was pure and saline and swelled into blue and bosomy undulations, and so strong was this impression that the moment to which I was transported seemed to me to be the present moment: more bemused than on the day when I had wondered whether I was really going to be received by the Princesse de Guermantes or whether everything round me would not collapse, I thought that the servant had just opened the window on to the beach and that all things invited me to go down and stroll along the promenade while the tide was high, for the napkin which I had used to wipe my mouth had precisely the same degree of stiffness and starchedness as the towel with which I had found it so awkward to dry my face as I stood in front of the window on the first day of my arrival at Balbec, and this napkin now, in the library of the Prince de Guermantes's house, unfolded for me—concealed within its smooth surfaces and its folds—the plumage of an ocean green and blue like the tail of a peacock. And what I found myself enjoying was not merely these colours but a whole instant of my life on whose summit they rested, an instant which had been no doubt an aspiration towards them and which some feeling of fatigue or sadness had perhaps prevented me from enjoying at Balbec but which now, freed from what is necessarily imperfect in external perception, pure and disembodied, caused me to swell with happiness.

The piece of music which was being played might end at any moment, and I might be obliged to enter the drawing-room. So I forced myself to try as quickly as possible to discern the essence of the identical pleasures which I had just experienced three times within the space of a few minutes, and having done so to extract the lesson which they might be made to yield. The thought that there is a vast difference between the real impression which we have had of a thing and the artificial impression of it which we form for ourselves when we attempt by an act of will to imagine it did not long detain me. Remembering with what relative indifference Swann years ago had been able to speak of the days when he had been loved, because what he saw beneath the words was not in fact those days but something else, and on the other hand the sudden pain which he had been caused by the little phrase of Vinteuil when it gave him back the days themselves, just as they were when he had felt them in the past, I understood clearly that what the sensation of the uneven paving-stones, the stiffness of the napkin, the taste of the madeleine had reawakened in me had no connexion with what I frequently tried to recall to myself of Venice, Balbec, Combray, with the help of an undifferentiated memory; and I understood that the reason why life may be judged to be trivial although at certain moments it seems to us so beautiful is that we form our judgment, ordinarily, on the evidence not of life itself but of those quite different images which preserve nothing of life—and therefore we judge it disparagingly. At most I noticed cursorily that the differences which exist between every one of our real impressions—differences which explain why a uniform depiction of life cannot bear much resemblance to the reality—derive probably from the following cause: the slightest word that we have said, the most insignificant action that we have performed at any one epoch of our life was surrounded by, and coloured by the reflexion of, things which logically had no connexion with it and which later have been separated from it by our intellect which could make nothing of them for its own rational purposes, things, however, in the midst of which—here the pink reflexion of the evening upon the flower-covered wall of a country restaurant, a feeling of hunger, the desire for women, the pleasure of luxury; there the blue volutes of the morning sea and, enveloped in them, phrases of music half emerging like the shoulders of water-nymphs—the simplest act or gesture remains immured as within a thousand sealed vessels, each one of them filled with things of a colour, a scent, a temperature that are absolutely different one from another, vessels, moreover, which being disposed over the whole range of our years, during which we have never ceased to change if only in our dreams and our thoughts, are situated at the most various moral altitudes and give us the sensation of extraordinarily diverse atmospheres. It is true that we have accomplished these changes imperceptibly; but between the memory which brusquely returns to us and our present state, and no less between two memories of different years, places, hours, the distance is such that it alone, even without any specific originality, would make it impossible to compare one with the other. Yes: if, owing to the work of oblivion, the returning memory can throw no bridge, form no connecting link between itself and the present minute, if it remains in the context of its own place and date, if it keeps its distance, its isolation in the hollow of a valley or upon the highest peak of a mountain summit, for this very reason it causes us suddenly to breathe a new air, an air which is new precisely because we have breathed it in the past, that purer air which the poets have vainly tried to situate in paradise and which could induce so profound a sensation of renewal only if it had been breathed before, since the true paradises are the paradises that we have lost.

And I observed in passing that for the work of art which I now, though I had not yet reached a conscious resolution, felt myself ready to undertake, this distinctness of different events would entail very considerable difficulties. For I should have to execute the successive parts of my work in a succession of different materials; what would be suitable for mornings beside the sea or afternoons in Venice would be quite wrong if I wanted to depict those evenings at Rivebelle when, in the dining-room that opened on to the garden, the heat began to resolve into fragments and sink back into the ground, while a sunset glimmer still illumined the roses on the walls of the restaurant and the last water-colours of the day were still visible in the sky—this would be a new and distinct material, of a transparency and a sonority that were special, compact, cool after warmth, rose-pink.

Over all these thoughts I skimmed rapidly, for another inquiry demanded my attention more imperiously, the inquiry, which on previous occasions I had postponed, into the cause of this felicity which I had just experienced, into the character of the certitude with which it imposed itself. And this cause I began to divine as I compared these diverse happy impressions, diverse yet with this in common, that I experienced them at the present moment and at the same time in the context of a distant moment, so that the past was made to encroach upon the present and I was made to doubt whether I was in the one or the other. The truth surely was that the being within me which had enjoyed these impressions had enjoyed them because they had in them something that was common to a day long past and to the present, because in some way they were extra-temporal, and this being made its appearance only when, through one of these identifications of the present with the past, it was likely to find itself in the one and only medium in which it could exist and enjoy the essence of things, that is to say: outside time. This explained why it was that my anxiety on the subject of my death had ceased at the moment when I had unconsciously recognised the taste of the little madeleine, since the being which at that moment I had been was an extra-temporal being and therefore unalarmed by the vicissitudes of the future. This being had only come to me, only manifested itself outside of activity and immediate enjoyment, on those rare occasions when the miracle of an analogy had made me escape from the present. And only this being had the power to perform that task which had always defeated the efforts of my memory and my intellect, the power to make me rediscover days that were long past, the Time that was Lost.

And perhaps, if just now I had been disposed to think Bergotte wrong when he spoke of the life of the mind and its joys, it was because what I thought of at that moment as "the life of the mind" was a species of logical reasoning which had no connexion with it or with what existed in me at this moment—an error like the one which had made me find society and life itself tedious because I judged them on the evidence of untrue recollections, whereas now, now that three times in succession there had been reborn within me a veritable moment of the past, my appetite for life was immense.

A moment of the past, did I say? Was it not perhaps very much more: something that, common both to the past and to the present, is much more essential than either of them? So often, in the course of my life, reality had disappointed me because at the instant when my senses perceived it my imagination, which was the only organ that I possessed for the enjoyment of beauty, could not apply itself to it, in virtue of that ineluctable law which ordains that we can only imagine what is absent. And now, suddenly, the effect of this harsh law had been neutralised, temporarily annulled, by a marvellous expedient of nature which had caused a sensation—the noise made both by the spoon and by the hammer, for instance—to be mirrored at one and the same time in the past, so that my imagination was permitted to savour it, and in the present, where the actual shock to my senses of the noise, the touch of the linen napkin, or whatever it might be, had added to the dreams of the imagination the concept of "existence" which they usually lack, and through this subterfuge had made it possible for my being to secure, to isolate, to immobilise—for a moment brief as a flash of lightning—what normally it never apprehends: a fragment of time in the pure state. The being which had been reborn in me when with a sudden shudder of happiness I had heard the noise that was common to the spoon touching the plate and the hammer striking the wheel, or had felt, beneath my feet, the unevenness that was common to the paving-stones of the Guermantes court-yard and to those of the baptistery of St Mark's, this being is nourished only by the essences of things, in these alone does it find its sustenance and delight. In the observation of the present, where the senses cannot feed it with this food, it languishes, as it does in the consideration of a past made arid by the intellect or in the anticipation of a future which the will constructs with frag-ments of the present and the past, fragments whose reality it still further reduces by preserving of them only what is suitable for the utilitarian, narrowly human purpose for which it intends them. But let a noise or a scent, once heard or once smelt, be heard or smelt again in the present and at the same time in the past, real without being actual, ideal without being abstract, and immedi-ately the permanent and habitually concealed essence of things is liberated and our true self, which seemed—had perhaps for long years seemed—to be dead but was not altogether dead, is awakened and reanimated as it receives the celestial nourishment that is brought to it. A minute freed from the order of time has re-created in us, to feel it, the man freed from the order of time. And one can understand that this man should have confidence in his joy, even if the simple taste of a madeleine does not seem logically to contain within it the reasons for this joy, one can understand that the word "death" should have no meaning for him; situated outside time, why should he fear the future?

But this species of optical illusion, which placed beside me a moment of the past that was incompatible with the present, could not last for long. The images presented to us by the voluntary memory can, it is true, be prolonged at will, for the voluntary memory requires no more exertion on our part than turning over the pages of a picture-book. On the day, for instance, long ago, when I was to visit the Princesse de Guermantes for the first time, I had from the sun-drenched courtyard of our house in Paris idly regarded, according to my whim, now the Place de l'Eglise at Combray, now the beach at Balbec, as if I had been choosing illustrations for that particular day from an album of water-colours depicting the various places where I had been; and with the egotistical pleasure of a collector, I had said to myself as I catalogued these illustrations stored in my memory: "At least I have seen some lovely things in my life." And of course my memory had affirmed that each one of these sensations was quite unlike the others, though in fact all it was doing was to make varied patterns out of elements that were homogeneous. But my recent experience of the three memories was something utterly different. These, on the contrary, instead of giving me a more flattering idea of myself, had almost caused me to doubt the reality, the existence of that self. And just as on the day when I had dipped the madeleine in the hot tea, in the setting of the place where I happened at the time to be—on that first day my room in Paris, today at this moment the library of the Prince de Guermantes, a few minutes earlier the courtyard of his house—there had been, inside me and irradiating a little area outside me, a sensation (the taste of the madeleine dipped in the tea, a metallic sound, a step of a certain kind) which was common both to my actual surroundings and also to another place (my aunt Léonie's bedroom, the railway carriage, the baptistery of St Mark's). And now again, at the very moment when I was making these reflexions, the shrill noise of water running through a pipe, a noise exactly like those long-drawn-out whistles which sometimes on summer evenings one heard the pleasure-steamers emit as they approached Balbec from the sea, made me feel—what I had once before been made to feel in Paris, in a big restaurant, by the sight of a luxurious dining-room, half-empty, summery and hot—something that was not merely a sensation similar to the one I used to have at the end of the afternoon in Balbec when, the tables already laid and glittering with linen and silver, the vast window-bays still open from one end to the other on to the esplanade without a single interruption, a single solid surface of glass or stone, while the sun slowly descended upon the sea and the steamers in the bay began to emit their cries, I had, if I had wished to join Albertine and her friends who were walking on the front, merely to step over the low wooden frame not much higher than my ankle, into a groove in which the whole continuous range of windows had been wound down so that the air could come into the hotel. (The painful recollection of having loved Albertine was, however, absent from my present sensation. Painful recollections are always of the dead. And the dead decompose rapidly, and there remains even in the proximity of their tombs nothing but the beauty of nature, silence, the purity of the air.) Besides, it was not only an echo, a duplicate of a past sensation that I was made to feel by the noise of the water in the pipe, it was that past sensation itself. And in this case as in all the others, the sensation common to past and present had sought to re-create the former scene around itself, while the actual scene which had taken the former one's place opposed with all the resistance of material inertia this incursion into a house in Paris of a Normandy beach or a railway embankment. The marine dining-room of Balbec, with its damask linen prepared like so many altar-cloths to receive the setting sun, had sought to shatter the solidity of the Guermantes mansion, to force open its doors, and for an instant had made the sofas around me sway and tremble as on another occasion it had done to the tables of the restaurant in Paris. Always, when these resurrections took place, the distant scene engendered around the common sensation had for a moment grappled, like a wrestler, with the present scene. Always the present scene had come off victorious, and always the vanquished one had appeared to me the more beautiful of the two, so beautiful that I had remained in a state of ecstasy on the uneven paving-stones or before the cup of tea, endeavouring to prolong or to reproduce the momentary appearances of the Combray or the

Balbec or the Venice which invaded only to be driven back, which rose up only at once to abandon me in the midst of the new scene which somehow, nevertheless, the past had been able to permeate. And if the present scene had not very quickly been victorious, I believe that I should have lost consciousness; for so complete are these resurrections of the past during the second that they last, that they not only oblige our eyes to cease to see the room which is near them in order to look instead at the railway bordered with trees or the rising tide, they even force our nostrils to breathe the air of places which are in fact a great distance away, and our will to choose between the various projects which those distant places suggest to us, they force our whole self to believe that it is surrounded by these places or at least to waver doubtfully between them and the places where we now are, in a dazed uncertainty such as we feel sometimes when an indescribably beautiful vision presents itself to us at the moment of our falling asleep.

Fragments of existence withdrawn from Time: these then were perhaps what the being three times, four times brought back to life within me had just now tasted, but the contemplation, though it was of eternity, had been fugitive. And yet I was vaguely aware that the pleasure which this contemplation had, at rare intervals, given me in my life, was the only genuine and fruitful pleasure that I had known. The unreality of the others is indicated clearly enough—is it not?—either by their inability to satisfy us, as is the case with social pleasures, the only consequence of which is likely to be the discomfort provoked by the ingestion of un-wholesome food, or with friendship, which is a simulacrum, since, for whatever moral reasons he may do it, the artist who gives up an hour of work for an hour of conversation with a friend knows that he is sacrificing a reality for something that does not exist (our friends being friends only in the light of an agreeable folly which travels with us through life and to which we readily accommodate ourselves, but which at the bottom of our hearts we know to be no more reasonable than the delusion of the man who talks to the furniture because he believes that it is alive), or else by the sadness which follows their satisfaction, a sadness which I had felt, for instance, on the day when I had been introduced to Albertine, at having taken pains (not even in fact very great pains) in order to achieve something—getting to know this girl—which seemed to me trivial simply because I had achieved it. And even a more profound pleasure, like the pleasure which I might have hoped to feel when I was in love with Albertine, was in fact only experienced inversely, through the anguish which I felt when she was not there, for when I was sure that she would soon be with me, as on the day when she had returned from the Trocadéro, I had seemed to experience no more than a vague dissatisfaction, whereas my exaltation and my joy grew steadily greater as I probed more and more deeply into the noise of the spoon on the plate or the taste of the tea which had brought into my bedroom in Paris the bedroom of my aunt Léonie and in its train all Combray and the two ways of our walks.

To this contemplation of the essence of things I had decided therefore that in future I must attach myself, so as somehow to immobilise it. But how, by what means, was I to do this? Naturally, at the moment when the stiffness of the napkin had restored Balbec to me and for an instant caressed my imagination not only with the sight of the sea as it had been that morning but with the smell of my room, the speed of the wind, the sensation of looking forward to lunch, of wondering which of the different walks I should take (all this being attached to the feel of the linen like those thousand wings of the angels which revolve a thousand times in a minute), or at the moment when the unevenness of the two paving-stones had extended in every direction and dimension the desiccated and insubstantial images which I normally had of Venice and St Mark's and of all the sensations which I had felt there, reuniting the piazza to the cathedral, the landing-stage to the piazza, the canal to the landing-stage, and to all that the eyes see the world of desires which is seen only by the mind—naturally at those moments I had been tempted, if not, because of the time of the year, to go and walk once more through the watery streets of Venice which for me were above all associated with the spring, at least to return to Balbec. But this thought did not for an instant detain me. I knew for one thing that countries were not such as their names painted them to my imagination, so that now it was scarcely ever except in my dreams, while I was asleep, that a place could lie spread before me wrought in that pure matter which is entirely distinct from the matter of the common things that we see and touch but of which, when I had imagined these common things without ever having seen them, they too had seemed to me to be composed: and I knew also that the same was true of that other species of image which is formed by the memory, so that not only had I failed to discover the beauty of Balbec as I had imagined it when I had gone there for the first time, I had failed also when I went back the second time to rediscover the remembered beauty which that first visit had left me. Experience had taught me only too well the impossibility of attaining in the real world to what lay deep within myself; I knew that Lost Time was not to be found again on the piazza of St Mark's any more than I had found it again on my second visit to Balbec or on my return to Tansonville to see Gilberte, and that travel, which merely dangled once more before me the illusion that these vanished impressions existed outside myself, could not be the means which I sought. And I did not want to let myself be side-tracked once more, for the task before me was to discover at long last whether or no it was possible to attain to what—disappointed as I had always been by the actuality of places and people—I had, although once the septet of Vinteuil had seemed to point to the contrary conclusion, come to think of as unrealisable. I did not intend, then, to make yet another experiment in a direction which I had long known could lead nowhere. Impressions such as those to which I wished to give permanence could not but vanish at the touch of a direct enjoyment which had been powerless to engender them. The only way to savour them more fully was to try to get to know them more completely in the medium in which they existed, that is to say within myself, to try to make them translucid even to their very depths. I had not known pleasure at Balbec any more than I had known pleasure when I lived with Albertine, for the pleasure of living with her had been perceptible to me only in retrospect. When I recapitulated the disappointments of my life as a lived life, disappointments which made me believe that its reality must reside elsewhere than in action, what I was doing was not merely to link different disappointments together in a purely fortuitous manner and in following the circumstances of my personal existence. I saw clearly that the disappointment of travel and the disappointment of love were not different disappointments at all but the varied aspects which are assumed, according to the particular circumstances which bring it into play, by our inherent powerlessness to realise ourselves in material enjoyment or in effective action. And thinking again of the extra-temporal joy which I had been made to feel by the sound of the spoon or the taste of the madeleine, I said to myself: "Was this perhaps that happiness which the little phrase of the sonata promised to Swann and which he, because he was unable to find it in artistic creation, mistakenly assimilated to the pleasures of love, was this the happiness of which long ago I was given a presentiment—as something more supraterrestrial even than the mood evoked by the little phrase of the sonata—by the call, the mysterious, rubescent call of that septet which Swann was never privileged to hear, having died like so many others before the truth that was made for him had been revealed? A truth that in any case he could not have used, for though the phrase perhaps symbolised a call, it was incapable of creating new powers and making Swann the writer that he was not."

And then, after I had dwelt for some little time upon these resurrections of the memory, the thought came to me that in another fashion certain obscure impressions, already even at Combray on the Guermantes way, had solicited my attention in a fashion somewhat similar to these reminiscences, except that they concealed within them not a sensation dating from an earlier time, but a new truth, a precious image which I had sought to uncover by efforts of the same kind as those that we make to recall something that we have forgotten, as if our finest ideas were like tunes which, as it were, come back to us although we have never heard them before and which we have to make an effort to hear and to transcribe. I remembered—with pleasure because it showed me that already in those days I had been the same and that this type of experience sprang from a fundamental trait in my character, but with sadness also when I thought that since that time I had never progressed—that already at Combray I used to fix before my mind for its attention some image which had compelled me to look at it, a cloud, a triangle, a church spire, a flower, a stone, because I had the feeling that perhaps beneath these signs there lay something of a quite different kind which I must try to discover, some thought which they translated after the fashion of those hieroglyphic characters which at first one might suppose to represent only material objects. No doubt the process of decipherment was difficult, but only by accomplishing it could one arrive at whatever truth there was to read. For the truths which the intellect apprehends directly in the world of full and unimpeded light have something less profound, less necessary than those which life communicates to us against our will in an impression which is material because it enters us through the senses but yet has a spiritual meaning which it is possible for us to extract. In fact both in the one case and in the other, whether I was concerned with impressions like the one which I had received from the sight of the steeples of Martinville or with reminiscences like that of the unevenness of the two steps or the taste of the madeleine, the task was to interpret the given sensations as signs of so many laws and ideas, by trying to think—that is to say, to draw forth from the shadow—what I had merely felt, by trying to convert it into its spiritual equivalent. And this method, which seemed to me the sole method, what was it but the creation of a work of art? Already the consequences came flooding into my mind: first, whether I considered reminiscences of the kind evoked by the noise of the spoon or the taste of the madeleine, or those truths written with the aid of shapes for whose meaning I searched in my brain, where—church steeples or wild grass growing in a wall—they composed a magical scrawl, complex and elaborate, their essential character was that I was not free to choose them, that such as they were they were given to me. And I realised that this must be the mark of their authenticity. I had not gone in search of the two uneven paving-stones of the courtyard upon which I had stumbled. But it was precisely the fortuitous and inevitable fashion in which this and the other sensations had been encountered that proved the trueness of the past which they brought back to life, of the images which they released, since we feel, with these sensations, the effort that they make to climb back towards the light, feel in ourselves the joy of rediscovering what is real. And here too was the proof of the trueness of the whole picture formed out of those contemporaneous impressions which the first sensation brings back in its train, with those unerring proportions of light and shade, emphasis and omission, memory and forgetfulness to which conscious recollection and conscious observation will never know how to attain.

As for the inner book of unknown symbols (symbols carved in relief they might have been, which my attention, as it explored my unconscious, groped for and stumbled against and followed the contours of, like a diver exploring the ocean-bed), if I tried to read them no one could help me with any rules, for to read them was an act of creation in which no one can do our work for us or even collaborate with us. How many for this reason turn aside from writing! What tasks do men not take upon themselves in order to evade this task! Every public event, be it the Dreyfus case, be it the war, furnishes the writer with a fresh excuse for not attempting to decipher this book: he wants to ensure the triumph of justice, he wants to restore the moral unity of the nation, he has no time to think of literature. But these are mere excuses, the truth being that he has not or no longer has genius, that is to say instinct. For instinct dictates our duty and the intellect supplies us with pretexts for evading it. But excuses have no place in art and intentions count for nothing: at every moment the artist has to listen to his instinct, and it is this that makes art the most real of all things, the most austere school of life, the true last judgment. This book, more laborious to decipher than any other, is also the only one which has been dictated to us by reality, the only one of which the "impression" has been printed in us by reality itself. When an idea—an idea of any kind—is left in us by life, its material pattern, the outline of the impression that it made upon us, remains behind as the token of its necessary truth. The ideas formed by the pure intelligence have no more than a logical, a possible truth, they are arbitrarily chosen. The book whose hieroglyphs are patterns not traced by us is the only book that really belongs to us. Not that the ideas which we form for ourselves cannot be correct in logic; that they may well be, but we cannot know whether they are true. Only the impression, however trivial its material may seem to be, however faint its traces, is a criterion of truth and deserves for that reason to be apprehended by the mind, for the mind, if it succeeds in extracting this truth, can by the impression and by nothing else be brought to a state of greater perfection and given a pure joy. The impression is for the writer what experiment is for the scientist, with the difference that in the scientist the work of the intelligence precedes the experiment and in the writer it comes after the impression. What we have not had to decipher, to elucidate by our own efforts, what was clear before we looked at it, is not ours. From ourselves comes only that which we drag forth from the obscurity which lies within us, that which to others is unknown.

(A level ray of the setting sun recalls to me instantaneously an episode in my early childhood to which I had never since that time given a thought: my aunt Léonie had a fever which Doctor Percepied feared might be typhoid and for a week I was made to sleep in Eulalie's little room looking out on the Place de l'Eglise, which had nothing but rush mats on the floor and over the window a muslin curtain that was always buzzing with a sunshine to which I was not accustomed. And seeing how the recollection of this little old-fashioned servant's bedroom suddenly added to my past life a long stretch of time so different from the rest and so delicious, I thought by contrast of the nullity of the impressions which had been contributed to it by the most sumptuous entertainments in the most princely mansions. The only thing at all sad about this room of Eulalie's was that at night, because the viaduct was so near, one heard the hooting of the trains. But as I knew that these were bellowings produced by machines under human control, they did not terrify me as, in a prehistoric age, I might have been terrified by the ululations of a neighbouring mammoth taking a free and unco-ordinated stroll.)

I had arrived then at the conclusion that in fashioning a work of art we are by no means free, that we do not choose how we shall make it but that it pre-exists us and therefore we are obliged, since it is both necessary and hidden, to do what we should have to do if it were a law of nature—to discover it. But this discovery which art obliges us to make, is it not, I thought, really the discovery of what, though it ought to be more precious to us than anything in the world, yet remains ordinarily for ever unknown to us, the discovery of our true life, of reality as we have felt it to be, which differs so greatly from what we think it is that when a chance happening brings us an authentic memory of it we are filled with an immense happiness? In this conclusion I was confirmed by the thought of the falseness of so-called realist art, which would not be so untruthful if we had not in life acquired the habit of giving to what we feel a form of expression which differs so much from, and which we nevertheless after a little time take to be, reality itself. I began to perceive that I should not have to trouble myself with the various literary theories which had at moments perplexed me—notably those which practitioners of criticism had developed at the time of the Dreyfus case and had taken up again during the war, according to which "the artist must be made to leave his ivory tower" and the themes chosen by the writer ought to be not frivolous or sentimental but rather such things as great working-class movements or—in default of crowds—at least no longer as in the past unimportant men of leisure ("I must confess that the depiction of these useless characters rather bores me," Bloch had been fond of saying), but noble intellectuals or men of heroic stature.

In any case, quite apart from what I might think of the logical propositions which they contained, these theories seemed to me to indicate very clearly the inferiority of those who upheld them— my reaction was that of the truly well-brought-up child who, lunching in a strange house and hearing his hosts say: "We are frank, we don't hide our light under a bushel here," feels that the remark indicates a moral quality inferior to right conduct pure and simple, which says nothing. Authentic art has no use for proclamations of this kind, it accomplishes its work in silence. Moreover, those who theorised in this way used hackneyed phrases which had a curious resemblance to those of the idiots whom they denounced. And it is perhaps as much by the quality of his language as by the species of aesthetic theory which he advances that one may judge of the level to which a writer has attained in the moral and intellectual part of his work. Quality of language, however, is something the critical theorists think that they can do without, and those who admire them are easily persuaded that it is no proof of intellectual merit, for this is a thing which they cannot infer from the beauty of an image but can recognise only when they see it directly expressed. Hence the temptation for the writer to write intellectual works—a gross impropriety. A work in which there are theories is like an object which still has its price-tag on it. (And as to the choice of theme, a frivolous theme will serve as well as a serious one for a study of the laws of character, in the same way that a prosector can study the laws of anatomy as well in the body of an imbecile as in that of a man of talent, since the great moral laws, like the laws of the circulation of the blood or of renal elimination, vary scarcely at all with the intellectual merit of individuals.) A writer reasons, that is to say he goes astray, only when he has not the strength to force himself to make an impression pass through all the successive states which will culminate in its fixation, its expression. The reality that he has to express resides, as I now began to understand, not in the superficial appearance of his subject but at a depth at which that appearance matters little; this truth had been symbolised for me by that clink of a spoon against a plate, that starched stiffness of a napkin, which had been of more value to me for my spiritual renewal than innumerable conversations of a humanitarian or patriotic or internationalist or metaphysical kind. "Enough of style," had been the cry, "enough of literature, let us have life!" And one may well imagine how since the beginning of the war even the simple theories of M. de Norpois, his denunciations of the "flute-players," had enjoyed a second vogue. For plenty of people who lack the artistic sense, who lack, that is to say, the faculty of submitting to the reality within themselves, may yet possess the ability to expatiate upon the theory of art until the crack of doom. And if they happen to be diplomats or financiers to boot, involved in the "realities" of the present age, they are likely to believe that literature is an intellectual game destined in the future to be progressively eliminated. (Some critics now liked to regard the novel as a sort of procession of things upon the screen of a cinematograph. This comparison was absurd. Nothing is further from what we have really perceived than the vision that the cinematograph presents.)

The idea of a popular art, like that of a patriotic art, if not actually dangerous seemed to me ridiculous. If the intention was to make art accessible to the people by sacrificing refinements of form, on the ground that they are "all right for the idle rich" but not for anybody else, I had seen enough of fashionable society to know that it is there that one finds real illiteracy and not, let us say, among electricians. In fact, an art that was "popular" so far as form was concerned would have been better suited to the members of the Jockey Club than to those of the General Confederation of Labour—and as for subject, the working classes are as bored by novels of popular life as children are by the books which are written specially for them. When one reads, one likes to be transported into a new world, and working men have as much curiosity about princes as princes about working men. At the beginning of the war M. Barrès had said that the artist (he happened to be talking about Titian) must first and foremost serve the glory of his country. But this he can do only by being an artist, which means only on condition that, while in his own sphere he is studying laws, conducting experiments, making discoveries which are as delicate as those of science, he shall think of nothing—not even his country—but the truth which is before him. Let us not imitate the revolutionaries who out of "civic sense" despised, if they did not destroy, the works of Watteau and La Tour, painters who have brought more honour upon France than all those of the Revolution. Anatomy is not perhaps the occupation that a kind-hearted man would choose, if he or any artist had the possibility of choice, and certainly it was not the kindness of a virtuous heart (though he was a truly kind man) that made Choderlos de Laclos write *Les Liaisons dangereuses*, nor was it any affection for the lower or upper bourgeoisie that made Flaubert choose the themes of *Madame Bovary* and *L'Education sentimentale*—but this is no valid criticism of the work of these writers.

Some people were also saying that the art of an age of haste would be brief, just as many people before the war had predicted that it would be short. The railway, according to this mode of thinking, was destined to kill contemplation and there was no sense in regretting the age of the diligence. But in fact the car has taken over its function and once more deposits tourists outside forgotten churches.

As I entered the library where I had been pursuing this train of thought I had remembered what the Goncourts say about the magnificent first editions which it contains and I had promised myself that I would look at them while I was waiting. And all this while, without paying very much attention to what I was doing, I had been taking first one and then another of the precious volumes from the shelves, when suddenly, at the moment when I carelessly opened one of them—it was George Sand's *François le Champi*—I felt myself unpleasantly struck by an impression which seemed at first to be utterly out of harmony with the thoughts that were passing through my mind, until a moment later, with an emotion so strong that tears came to my eyes, I recognised how very much in harmony with them it was. Imagine a room in which a man has died, a man who has rendered great services to his country; the undertaker's men are getting ready to take the coffin downstairs and the dead man's son is holding out his hand to the last friends who are filing past it; suddenly the silence is broken by a flourish of trumpets beneath the windows and he feels outraged, thinking that this must be some plot to mock and insult his grief; but presently this man who until this moment has mastered his emotions dissolves into tears, for he realises that what he hears is the band of a regiment which has come to share in his mourning and to pay honour to his father's corpse. Like this dead man's son, I had just recognised how completely in harmony with the thoughts in my mind was the painful impression which I had experienced when I had seen this title on the cover of a book in the library of the Prince de Guermantes, for it was a title which after a moment's hesitation had given me the idea that literature did really offer us that world of mystery which I had ceased to find in it. And yet the book was not a very extraordinary one, it was *François le Champi*. But that name, like the name Guermantes, was for me unlike the names which I had heard for the first time only in later life. The memory of what had seemed to me too deep for understanding in the subject of *François le Champi* when my mother long ago had read the book aloud to me, had been reawakened by the title, and just as the name of Guermantes, after a long period during which I had not seen the Guermantes, contained for me the essence of the feudal age, so *François le Champi* contained the essence of the novel, and for a second this memory substituted itself for the quite commonplace idea of "one of George Sand's novels about Berry." At a dinner-party, where thought always remains superficial, I might no doubt have been able to talk about *François le Champi* and the Guermantes without either the novel or the family being what they had been to me at Combray. But alone, as I was at this moment, I was plunged by these names to a greater depth. At such moments the idea that some woman whom I had met at parties was a cousin of Mme de Guermantes, a cousin that is to say of a personage of the magic lantern, seemed to me incomprehensible, and equally incomprehensible was the idea that the best books I had ever read might be—I will not say superior to, though that is in fact of course what they were—but even equal to this extraordinary *François le Champi*. This was a very deeply buried impression that I had just encountered, one in which memories of childhood and family were tenderly intermingled and which I had not immediately recognised. My first reaction had been to ask myself, angrily, who this stranger was who was coming to trouble me. The stranger was none other than myself, the child I had been at that time, brought to life within me by the book, which knowing nothing of me except this child had instantly summoned him to its presence, wanting to be seen only by his eyes, to be loved only by his heart, to speak only to him. And this book which my mother had read aloud to me at Combray until the early hours of the morning had kept for me all the charm of that night. Admittedly the "pen" of George Sand, to borrow a phrase from Brichot, who was so fond of saying that a book was written with a "lively pen," no longer seemed to me, as for so long it had seemed to my mother before she had gradually come to model her literary tastes upon mine, in the least a magic pen. But it was a pen which, unintentionally, like a schoolboy amusing himself with a real pen, I had charged with electricity, and now a thousand trifling details of Combray which for years had not entered my mind came lightly and spontaneously leaping, in follow-my-leader fashion, to suspend themselves from the magnetised nib in an interminable and trembling chain of memories.

Certain people, whose minds are prone to mystery, like to believe that objects retain something of the eyes which have looked at them, that old buildings and pictures appear to us not as they originally were but beneath a perceptible veil woven for them over the centuries by the love and contemplation of millions of admirers. This fantasy, if you transpose it into the domain of what is for each one of us the sole reality, the domain of his own sensibility, becomes the truth. In that sense and in that sense alone (but it is a far more important one than the other), a thing which we have looked at in the past brings back to us, if we see it again, not only the eyes with which we looked at it but all the images with which at the time those eyes were filled. For things—and among them a book in a red binding—as soon as we have perceived them are transformed within us into something immaterial, something of the same nature as all our preoccupations and sensations of that particular time, with which, indissolubly, they blend. A name read long ago in a book contains within its syllables the strong wind and brilliant sunshine that prevailed while we were reading it. And this is why the kind of literature which contents itself with "describing things," with giving of them merely a miserable abstract of lines and surfaces, is in fact, though it calls itself realist, the furthest removed from reality and has more than any other the effect of saddening and impoverishing us, since it abruptly severs all communication of our present self both with the past, the essence of which is preserved in things, and with the future, in which things incite us to enjoy the essence of the past a second time. Yet it is precisely this essence that an art worthy of the name must seek to express; then at least, if it fails, there is a lesson to be drawn from its impotence (whereas from the successes of realism there is nothing to be learnt), the lesson that this essence is, in part, subjective and incommunicable.

Nor is this all. A thing which we saw, a book which we read at a certain period does not merely remain for ever conjoined to what existed then around us; it remains also faithfully united to what we ourselves then were and thereafter it can be handled only by the sensibility, the personality that were then ours. If, even in thought, I pick from the bookshelf *François le Champi*, immediately there rises within me a child who takes my place, who alone has the right to spell out the title *François le Champi*, and who reads it as he read it once before, with the same impression of what the weather was like then in the garden, the same dreams that were then shaping themselves in his mind about the different countries and about life, the same anguish about the next day. Or if I see something which dates from another period, it is a young man who comes to life. So that my personality of today may be compared to an abandoned quarry, which supposes everything it contains to be uniform and monotonous, but from which memory, selecting here and there, can, like some sculptor of genius, extract innumerable different statues. And this is true of everything that we see again after a lapse of time, books in this respect behaving just like other things: the way in which the covers of a binding open, the grain of a particular paper, may have preserved in itself as vivid a memory of the fashion in which I once imagined Venice and of the desire that I had to go there as the actual phrases of a book. An even more vivid memory perhaps, for phrases sometimes are an obstruction, just as sometimes when we look at a photograph of a person we recollect him less clearly than we do when we are merely thinking about him. Certainly, there are many books which I read in my childhood, including even, I am sorry to say, some of those of Bergotte himself, which now, if I happen to be tired one evening, I take up merely in the spirit in which I might go for a train journey, with the hope, that is, of resting myself by the sight of objects that I do not see every day and by breathing the atmosphere of an earlier time. But it can happen that this deliberate attempt at evocation is actually thwarted by the prolonged reading of the book. There is, for instance, a book by Bergotte (there was a copy in the Prince's library, with a dedication both sycophantic and platitudinous in the extreme), which I read years ago one winter day when I was unable to see Gilberte and which I now search in vain for the phrases which I then thought wonderful. Certain words almost make me believe that I have found them, but it cannot be so, for of the beauty that I once saw in them there is no trace. But the volume itself still glistens with the snow that covered the Champs-Elysées on the day when I first read it— I open its pages and the scene is before my eyes.

So it is that, if I had been tempted to become a bibliophile like the Prince de Guermantes, I should only have been one in my own peculiar fashion, though I should not have despised that beauty, independent of the intrinsic value of a book, which attached to it in the eyes of collectors by their knowing the libraries through which it has passed, knowing for instance that it was given by such and such a sovereign, on the occasion of such and such an event, to such and such a famous man, by their having followed it from sale to sale through the course of its life—that beauty, which is in a certain sense the historic beauty of a book, would not be lost upon me. But it is rather in the history of my own life, and not simply as a connoisseur of the past in general, that I should seek this beauty; and I should attach it often not to a particular copy but to the work itself, to *François le Champi*, for instance, first contemplated by me in my little bedroom at Combray, during the night that was perhaps the sweetest and the saddest of my life, when I had alas! (at a time when the Guermantes still seemed to me mysterious and inaccessible) won from my parents that first abdication of their authority from which, later, I was to date the decline of my health and my will, and my renunciation, each day disastrously confirmed, of a task that daily became more difficult—and rediscovered by me today, in the library of these same Guermantes, on this most wonderful of all days which had suddenly illuminated for me not only the old groping movements of my thought, but even the whole purpose of my life and perhaps of art itself. As for particular copies of books, I should have been able to take an interest in them too, but in a living sense. The first edition of a work would have been more precious in my eyes than any other, but by this term I should have understood the edition in which I read it for the first time. I should seek out original editions, those, that is to say, in which I once received an original impression of a book. For the impressions that one has later are no longer original. In the case of novels I should collect old-fashioned bindings, those of the period when I read my first novels, those that so often heard Papa say to me: "Sit up straight!" Like the dress which a woman was wearing when we saw her for the first time, they would help me to rediscover the love that I then had, the beauty on which I have since super-imposed so many less and less loved images, they would help me to find that first image again, even though I am no longer the "I" who first beheld it, even though I must make way for the "I" that I then was if that "I" summons the thing that it once knew and that the "I" of today does not know.

The library which I should thus assemble would contain volumes of an even greater value; for the books which I read in the past at Combray or in Venice, enriched now by my memory with vast illuminations representing the church of Saint-Hilaire or the gondola moored at the foot of San Giorgio Maggiore and the

Grand Canal incrusted with sparkling sapphires, would have become the equals of those ancient "picture books"—illustrated bibles or books of hours—which the collector nowadays opens not to read their text but to savour once more the enchantment of the colours which some rival of Foucquet has added to it and which make these volumes the treasures that they are. And yet, even to open these books for the purpose merely of looking at the pictures with which, when I read them long ago, they were not yet adorned, would seem to me in itself so dangerous that, even in the sense which I have described, which is the only one that I can understand, I should not, I think, be tempted to become a bibliophile. I know very well how easily these images, deposited by the mind, can be effaced by the mind. For the old images it substitutes new ones which no longer have the same power of resurrection. And if I still possessed the *François le Champi* which Mamma unpacked one evening from the parcel of books which my grandmother was to have given me for my birthday, I should never look at it; I should be too afraid that I might gradually insinuate into it my impressions of today and smother my original impressions beneath them, that I might see it become so far a thing of the present that, when I asked it to evoke once more the child who spelt out its title in the little bedroom at Combray, the child, not recognising its voice, would no longer reply to its summons and would remain for ever buried in oblivion.

An image presented to us by life brings with it, in a single moment, sensations which are in fact multiple and heterogeneous. The sight, for instance, of the binding of a book once read may weave into the characters of its title the moonlight of a distant summer night. The taste of our breakfast coffee brings with it that vague hope of fine weather which so often long ago, as with the day still intact and full before us, we were drinking it out of a bowl of white porcelain, creamy and fluted and itself looking almost like vitrified milk, suddenly smiled upon us in the pale uncertainty of the dawn. An hour is not merely an hour, it is a vase full of scents and sounds and projects and climates, and what we call reality is a certain connexion between these immediate sensations and the memories which envelop us simultaneously with them—a connexion that is suppressed in a simple cinematographic vision, which just because it professes to confine itself to the truth in fact departs widely from it—a unique connexion which the writer has to rediscover in order to link for ever in his phrase the two sets of phenomena which reality joins together. He can describe a scene by describing one after another the innumerable objects which at a given moment were present at a particular place, but truth will be attained by him only when he takes two different objects, states the connexion between them—a connexion analogous in the world of art to the unique connexion which in the world of science is provided by the law of causality—and encloses them in the necessary links of a well-wrought style; truth—and life too—can be attained by us only when, by comparing a quality common to two sensations, we succeed in extracting their common essence and in reuniting them to each other, liberated from the contingencies of time, within a metaphor. Had not nature herself—if one considered the matter from this point of view— placed me on the path of art, was she not herself a beginning of art, she who, often, had allowed me to become aware of the beauty of one thing only in another thing, of the beauty, for instance, of noon at Combray in the sound of its bells, of that of the mornings at Doncières in the hiccups of our central heating? The link may be uninteresting, the objects trivial, the style bad, but unless this process has taken place the description is worthless.

But my train of thought led me yet further. If reality were indeed a sort of waste product of experience, more or less identical for each one of us, since when we speak of bad weather, a war, a taxi rank, a brightly lit restaurant, a garden full of flowers, everybody knows what we mean, if reality were no more than this, no doubt a sort of cinematograph film of these things would be sufficient and the "style," the "literature" that departed from the simple data that they provide would be superfluous and artificial. But was it true that reality was no more than this? If I tried to understand what actually happens at the moment when a thing makes some particular impression upon one—on the day, for instance, when as I crossed the bridge over the Vivonne the shadow of a cloud upon the water had made me cry: "Gosh!" and jump for joy; or the occasion when, hearing a phrase of Bergotte's, all that I had disengaged from my impression was the not specially relevant remark: "How splendid!"; or the words I had once heard Bloch use in exasperation at some piece of bad behaviour, words quite inappropriate to a very commonplace incident: "I must say that that sort of conduct seems to me absolutely fffantastic!"; or that evening when, flattered at the politeness which the Guermantes had shown to me as their guest and also a little intoxicated by the wines which I had drunk in their house, I could not help saying to myself half aloud as I came away alone: "They really are delightful people and I should be happy to see them every day of my life"—I realised that the words in each case were a long way removed from the impressions that I or Bloch had in fact received. So that the essential, the only true book, though in the ordinary sense of the word it does not have to be "invented" by a great writer—for it exists already in each one of us—has to be translated by him. The function and the task of a writer are those of a translator.

And if in some cases—where we are dealing, for instance, with the inaccurate language of our own vanity—the rectification of an oblique interior discourse (which deviates gradually more and more widely from the first and central impression) until it merges with the straight line which the impression ought to have produced is a laborious undertaking which our idleness would prefer to shirk, there are other circumstances—for example, where love is involved—in which this same process is actually painful. Here all our feigned indifferences, all our indignation at the lies of whoever it is whom we love (lies which are so natural and so like those that we perpetrate ourselves), in a word all that we have not ceased, whenever we are unhappy or betrayed, not only to say to the loved one but, while we are waiting for a meeting with her, to repeat endlessly to ourselves, sometimes aloud in the silence of our room, which we disturb with remarks like: "No, really, this sort of behaviour is intolerable," and: "I have consented to see you once more, for the last time, and I don't deny that it hurts me," all this can only be brought back into conformity with the felt truth from which it has so widely diverged by the abolition of all that we have set most store by, all that in our solitude, in our feverish projects of letters and schemes, has been the substance of our passionate dialogue with ourselves.

Even where the joys of art are concerned, although we seek and value them for the sake of the impression that they give us, we contrive as quickly as possible to set aside, as being inexpressible, precisely that element in them which is the impression that we sought, and we concentrate instead upon that other ingredient in aesthetic emotion which allows us to savour its pleasure without penetrating its essence and lets us suppose that we are sharing it with other art-lovers, with whom we find it possible to converse just because, the personal root of our own impression having been suppressed, we are discussing with them a thing which is the same for them and for us. Even in those moments when we are the most disinterested spectators of nature, or of society or of love or of art itself, since every impression is double and the one half which is sheathed in the object is prolonged in ourselves by another half which we alone can know, we speedily find means to neglect this second half, which is the one on which we ought to concentrate, and to pay attention only to the first half which, as it is external and therefore cannot be intimately explored, will occasion us no fatigue. To try to perceive the little furrow which the sight of a hawthorn-bush or of a church has traced in us is a task that we find too difficult. But we play a symphony over and over again, we go back repeatedly to see a church until—in that flight to get away from our own life (which we have not the courage to look at) which goes by the name of erudition—we know them, the symphony and the church, as well as and in the same fashion as the most knowledgeable connoisseur of music or archaeology. And how many art-lovers stop there, without extracting anything from their impression, so that they grow old useless and unsatis-fied, like celibates of Art! They suffer, but their sufferings, like the sufferings of virgins and of lazy people, are of a kind that fecundity or work would cure. They get more excited about works of art than real artists, because for them their excitement is not the object of a laborious and inward-directed study but a force which bursts outwards, which heats their conversations and empurples their cheeks; at concerts they will shout "Bravo, bravo" till they are hoarse at the end of a work they admire and imagine as they do so that they are discharging a duty. But demonstrations of this kind do not oblige them to clarify the nature of their admiration and of this they remain in ignorance. Meanwhile, like a stream which can find no useful channel, their love of art flows over into even their calmest conversations, so that they make wild gestures and grim-ace and toss their heads whenever they mention the subject. "I was at a concert the other day. They played the first piece and I must say it left me cold. Then they started on the quartet. By Jove, what a difference!" (At this moment the face of the music-lover expresses a sudden anxiety, as if he were thinking: "Don't I see sparks? And I smell burning! Something's on fire.") "It's the most exasperating thing I've ever heard, damn it! It's not exactly a good composition, but it's stunning, it's something quite out of the ordinary." And yet, ludicrous though they may be, such people are not altogether to be despised. They are the first attempts of nature in her struggle to create the artist, experiments as mis-shapen, as unviable as those first animals that came before the species of today and were so constituted that they could not survive for long. And, with their sterile velleities, the art-lovers are as touching to contemplate as those early machines which tried to leave the ground and could not, but which yet held within them, if not the secret, the still to be discovered means, at least the desire of flight. "You know, old boy," goes on the music-lover, as he takes you by the elbow, "this is the eighth time I've heard it, and I promise you it won't be the last." And indeed, since they fail to assimilate what is truly nourishing in art, they need artistic pleasures all the time, they are victims of a morbid hunger which is never satisfied. So they go to concert after concert to applaud the same work and think that they have a duty to put in an appearance whenever it is performed just as other people think they have a duty to attend a board meeting or a funeral. Then presently, whether it be in music or in literature or in painting, other works come along, works that may even be the very opposite of the ones which they supersede. For the ability to launch ideas and systems—and still more of course the ability to assimilate them—has always been much commoner than genuine taste, even among those who themselves produce works of art, and with the multi-plication of reviews and literary journals (and with them of facti-tious vocations as writer or artist) has become very much more widespread. Not so long ago, for instance, the best part of the younger generation, the most intelligent and the most disinter-ested of them, through a change of fashion admired nothing but works with a lofty moral and sociological, and even religious, significance. This they imagined to be the criterion of a work's value, renewing the old error of David and Chenavard and Brunetière and all those who in the past thought like them. Bergotte, whose prettiest phrases had in fact demanded much deeper reflexion on the part of the reader, was rated lower now than writers who seemed more profound simply because they wrote less well. The intricacy of his style was all right for fashion-able people but not for anybody else, said democratic critics, paying to fashionable people a tribute which they did not deserve. The truth is that as soon as the reasoning intelligence takes upon itself to judge works of art, nothing is any longer fixed or certain: you can prove anything you wish to prove. Whereas the reality of talent is something universal, whether it be a gift or an acquirement, and the first thing that a reader has to do is to find out whether this reality is present beneath a writer's superficial mannerisms of thought and style, it is upon just these superficial mannerisms that criticism seizes when it sets out to classify authors. Because he has a peremptory tone, because he parades his contempt for the school that preceded him, criticism hails as a prophet a writer who in fact has no message that is new. And so frequent are these aberrations of criticism that a writer might almost with reason prefer to be judged by the general public (were not the public incapable even of understanding what an artist has attempted in a realm of discovery which is outside its experience). For there is a closer analogy between the instinctive life of the public and the talent of a great writer, which is simply an instinct religiously listened to in the midst of a silence imposed upon all other voices, an instinct made perfect and understood, than between this same talent and the superficial verbiage and changing criteria of the established judges of literature. From decade to decade their wordy battles are renewed, for it is not only social groups that are kaleidoscopic but ideas too about society and politics and religion; refracted through large bodies they can assume a momentary amplitude but their life-span is the brief one of ideas which owe their success to their novelty and gain the adherence only of such minds as are not particular about proof. So it is that parties and schools follow upon one another's heels, attaching to themselves always the same minds, those men of moderate intelligence who are an easy prey to the successive enthusiasms into which others more scrupulous and less easily satisfied in the matter of proof will decline to plunge. And unfortunately, just because those in the first category are no more than half-minds, they need to buttress themselves in action, with the result that, being more active than the better minds, they draw the crowd after them and create around them not only inflated reputations and victims of undeserved contempt but wars too, both civil and foreign, which a little self-examination of an old-fashioned Jansenist kind might well have prevented.

As for the enjoyment which is derived by a really discerning mind and a truly living heart from a thought beautifully expressed in the writings of a great writer, this is no doubt an entirely wholesome enjoyment, but, precious though the men may be who are truly capable of enjoying this pleasure—and how many of them are there in a generation?—they are nevertheless in the very process reduced to being no more than the full consciousness of another. If, for instance, a man of this type has done everything in his power to make himself loved by a woman who could only have made him unhappy, but has not even succeeded, in spite of efforts redoubled over the years, in persuading her to meet him in private, instead of seeking to express his sufferings and the danger from which he has escaped, he reads over and over again, appending to it "a million words" and the most moving memories of his own life, this observation of La Bruyère: "Men often want to love where they cannot hope to succeed; they seek their own undoing without being able to compass it, and, if I may put it thus, they are forced against their will to remain free." Whether or no this is the meaning that the aphorism had for the man who wrote it (to give it this meaning, which would make it finer, he should have said "to be loved" instead of "to love"), there is no doubt that, with this meaning, the sensitive lover of literature reanimates it and swells it with meaning until it is ready to burst, he cannot repeat it to himself without overflowing with joy, so true and beautiful does he find it—but in spite of all this he has added to it nothing, it remains merely an observation of La Bruyère.

How could the literature of description possibly have any value, when it is only beneath the surface of the little things which such a literature describes that reality has its hidden existence (grandeur, for example, in the distant sound of an aeroplane or the outline of the steeple of Saint-Hilaire, the past in the taste of a madeleine, and so on) and when the things in themselves are without significance until it has been extracted from them? Gradually, thanks to its preservation by our memory, the chain of all those inaccurate expressions in which there survives nothing of what we have really experienced comes to constitute for us our thought, our life, our "reality," and this lie is all that can be reproduced by the art that styles itself "true to life," an art that is as simple as life, without beauty, a mere vain and tedious duplication of what our eyes see and our intellect records, so vain and so tedious that one wonders where the writer who devotes himself to it can have found the joyous and impulsive spark that was capable of setting him in motion and making him advance in his task. The greatness, on the other hand, of true art, of the art which M. de Norpois would have called a dilettante's pastime, lay, I had come to see, elsewhere: we have to rediscover, to reapprehend, to make ourselves fully aware of that reality, remote from our daily preoccupations, from which we separate ourselves by an ever greater gulf as the conventional knowledge which we substitute for it grows thicker and more impermeable, that reality which it is very easy for us to die without ever having known and which is, quite simply, our life. Real life, life at last laid bare and illuminated—the only life in consequence which can be said to be really lived—is literature, and life thus defined is in a sense all the time immanent in ordinary men no less than in the artist. But most men do not see it because they do not seek to shed light upon it. And therefore their past is like a photographic dark-room encumbered with innumerable negatives which remain useless because the intellect has not developed them. But art, if it means awareness of our own life, means also awareness of the lives of other people—for style for the writer, no less than colour for the painter, is a question not of technique but of vision: it is the revelation, which by direct and conscious methods would be impossible, of the qualitative difference, the uniqueness of the fashion in which the world appears to each one of us, a difference which, if there were no art, would remain for ever the secret of every individual. Through art alone are we able to emerge from ourselves, to know what another person sees of a universe which is not the same as our own and of which, without art, the landscapes would remain as unknown to us as those that may exist on the moon. Thanks to art, instead of seeing one world only, our own, we see that world multiply itself and we have at our disposal as many worlds as there are original artists, worlds more different one from the other than those which revolve in infinite space, worlds which, centuries after the extinction of the fire from which their light first emanated, whether it is called Rembrandt or Vermeer, send us still each one its special radiance.

This work of the artist, this struggle to discern beneath matter, beneath experience, beneath words, something that is different from them, is a process exactly the reverse of that which, in those everyday lives which we live with our gaze averted from ourselves, is at every moment being accomplished by vanity and passion and the intellect, and habit too, when they smother our true impressions, so as entirely to conceal them from us, beneath a whole heap of verbal concepts and practical goals which we falsely call life. In short, this art which is so complicated is in fact the only living art. It alone expresses for others and renders visible to ourselves that life of ours which cannot effectually observe itself and of which the observable manifestations need to be translated and, often, to be read backwards and laboriously deciphered. Our vanity, our passions, our spirit of imitation, our abstract intelligence, our habits have long been at work, and it is the task of art to undo this work of theirs, making us travel back in the direction from which we have come to the depths where what has really existed lies unknown within us. And surely this was a most tempting prospect, this task of re-creating one's true life, of rejuvenating one's impressions. But it required courage of many kinds, including the courage of one's emotions. For above all it meant the abrogation of one's dearest illusions, it meant giving up one's belief in the objectivity of what one had oneself elaborated, so that now, instead of soothing oneself for the hundredth time with the words: "She was very sweet," one would have to transpose the phrase so that it read: "I experienced pleasure when I kissed her." Certainly, what I had felt in my hours of love is what all men feel. One feels, yes, but what one feels is like a negative which shows only blackness until one has placed it near a special lamp and which must also be looked at in reverse. So with one's feelings: until one has brought them within range of the intellect one does not know what they represent. Then only, when the intellect has shed light upon them, has intellectualised them, does one distinguish, and with what difficulty, the lineaments of what one felt.

But I realised also that the suffering caused by the thought that our love does not belong to the person who inspires it, a suffering which I had first known in connexion with Gilberte, is for two reasons salutary. The first and the less important is that, brief though our life may be, it is only while we are suffering that we see certain things which at other times are hidden from us—we are, as it were, posted at a window, badly placed but looking out over an expanse of sea, and only during a storm, when our thoughts are agitated by perpetually changing movements, do they elevate to a level at which we can see it the whole law-governed immensity which normally, when the calm weather of happiness leaves it smooth, lies beneath our line of vision; perhaps only for a few great geniuses does this movement of thought exist all the time, uncontingent upon the agitations of personal grief, yet can we be sure, when we contemplate the ample and regular development of their joyous creations, that we may not too readily infer from the joyousness of their work that there was joy also in their lives, which perhaps on the contrary were almost continuously unhappy? But the principal reason is that, if our love is not only the love of a Gilberte (and this fact is what we find so painful), the reason is not that it is also the love of an Albertine but that it is a portion of our mind more durable than the various selves which successively die within us and which would, in their egoism, like to keep it to themselves, a portion of our mind which must, however much it hurts us (and the pain may in fact be beneficial), detach itself from individuals so that we can comprehend and restore to it its generality and give this love, the understanding of this love, to all, to the universal spirit, and not merely first to one woman and then to another with whom first one and then another of the selves that we have successively been has desired to be united.

I was surrounded by symbols (Guermantes, Albertine, Gilberte, Saint-Loup, Balbec, etc.) and to the least of these I had to restore the meaning which habit had caused them to lose for me. Nor was that all. When we have arrived at reality, we must, to express it and preserve it, prevent the intrusion of all those extraneous elements which at every moment the gathered speed of habit lays at our feet. Above all I should have to be on my guard against those phrases which are chosen rather by the lips than by the mind, those humorous phrases such as we utter in conversation and continue at the end of a long conversation with other people to address, factitiously, to ourselves although they merely fill our mind with lies—those, so to speak, purely physical remarks, which, in the writer who stoops so low as to transcribe them, are accompanied always by, for instance, the little smile, the little grimace which at every turn disfigures the spoken phrase of a Sainte-Beuve, whereas real books should be the offspring not of daylight and casual talk but of darkness and silence. And as art exactly reconstitutes life, around the truths to which we have attained inside ourselves there will always float an atmosphere of poetry, the soft charm of a mystery which is merely a vestige of the shadow which we have had to traverse, the indication, as precise as the markings of an altimeter, of the depth of a work. (For the quality of depth is not inherent in certain subjects, as those novelists believe who are spiritually minded only in a materialistic way: they cannot penetrate beneath the world of appearances and all their noble intentions, like the endless virtuous tirades of certain people who are incapable of the smallest act of kindness, should not blind us to the fact that they have lacked even the strength of mind to rid themselves of those banalities of form which are acquired through imitation.)

As for the truths which the intellectual faculty—even that of the greatest minds—gathers in the open, the truths that lie in its path in full daylight, their value may be very great, but they are like drawings with a hard outline and no perspective; they have no depth because no depths have had to be traversed in order to reach them, because they have not been re-created. Yet it happens to many writers that after a certain age, when more mysterious truths no longer emerge from their innermost being, they write only with their intellect, which has grown steadily in strength, and then the books of their riper years will have, for this reason, greater force than those of their youth but not the same bloom.

I felt, however, that these truths which the intellect educes directly from reality were not altogether to be despised, for they might be able to enshrine within a matter less pure indeed but still imbued with mind those impressions which are conveyed to us outside time by the essences that are common to the sensations of the past and of the present, but which, just because they are more precious, are also too rare for a work of art to be constructed exclusively from them. And—capable of being used for this purpose—I felt jostling each other within me a whole host of truths concerning human passions and character and conduct. The perception of these truths caused me joy; and yet I seemed to remember that more than one of them had been discovered by me in suffering, and others in very trivial pleasures (every individual who makes us suffer can be attached by us to a divinity of which he or she is a mere fragmentary reflexion, the lowest step in the ascent that leads to it, a divinity or an Idea which, if we turn to contemplate it, immediately gives us joy instead of the pain which we were feeling before—indeed the whole art of living is to make use of the individuals through whom we suffer as a step enabling us to draw nearer to the divine form which they reflect and thus joyously to people our life with divinities). And then a new light, less dazzling, no doubt, than that other illumination which had made me perceive that the work of art was the sole means of rediscovering Lost Time, shone suddenly within me. And I understood that all these materials for a work of literature were simply my past life; I understood that they had come to me, in frivolous pleasures, in indolence, in tenderness, in unhappiness, and that I had stored them up without divining the purpose for which they were destined or even their continued existence any more than a seed does when it forms within itself a reserve of all the nutritious substances from which it will feed a plant. Like the seed, I should be able to die once the plant had developed and I began to perceive that I had lived for the sake of the plant without knowing it, without ever realising that my life needed to come into contact with those books which I had wanted to write and for which, when in the past I had sat down at my table to begin, I had been unable to find a subject. And thus my whole life up to the present day might and yet might not have been summed up under the title: A Vocation. In so far as literature had played no part in my life the title would not have been accurate. And yet it would have been accurate because this life of mine, the memories of its sadnesses and its joys, formed a reserve which fulfilled the same function as the albumen lodged in the germ-cell of a plant, from which that cell starts to draw the nourishment which will transform it into a seed long before there is any outward sign that the embryo of a plant is developing, though already within the cell there are taking place chemical and respiratory changes, secret but extremely active. In the same way my life was linked to what, eventually, would bring about its maturation, but those who would one day draw nourishment from it would remain ignorant, as most of us do when we eat those grains that are human food, that the rich substances which they contain were made for the nourishment not of mankind but of the grain itself and have had first to nourish its seed and allow it to ripen.

In this context, certain comparisons which are false if we start from them as premises may well be true if we arrive at them as conclusions. The man of letters envies the painter, he would like to take notes and make sketches, but it is disastrous for him to do so. Yet when he writes, there is not a single gesture of his characters, not a trick of behaviour, not a tone of voice which has not been supplied to his inspiration by his memory; beneath the name of every character of his invention he can put sixty names of characters that he has seen, one of whom has posed for the grimaces, another for the monocle, another for the fits of temper, another for the swaggering movement of the arm, etc. And in the end the writer realises that if his dream of being a sort of painter was not in a conscious and intentional manner capable of fulfilment, it has nevertheless been fulfilled and that he too, for his work as a writer, has unconsciously made use of a sketch-book.

For, impelled by the instinct that was in him, the writer, long before he thought that he would one day become one, regularly omitted to look at a great many things which other people notice, with the result that he was accused by others of being absent-minded and by himself of not knowing how to listen or look, but all this time he was instructing his eyes and his ears to retain for ever what seemed to others puerile trivialities, the tone of voice in which a certain remark had been made, or the facial expression and the movement of the shoulders which he had seen at a certain moment, many years ago, in somebody of whom perhaps he knows nothing else whatsoever, simply because this tone of voice was one that he had heard before or felt that he might hear again, because it was something renewable, durable. There is a feeling for generality which, in the future writer, itself picks out what is general and can for that reason one day enter into a work of art. And this has made him listen to people only when, stupid or absurd though they may have been, they have turned themselves, by repeating like parrots what other people of similar character are in the habit of saying, into birds of augury, mouthpieces of a psychological law. He remembers only things that are general. By such tones of voice, such variations in the physiognomy, seen perhaps in his earliest childhood, has the life of other people been represented for him and when, later, he becomes a writer, it is from these observations that he composes his human figures, grafting on to a movement of the shoulders common to a number of people—a movement as truthfully delineated as though it had been recorded in an anatomist's note-book, though the truth which he uses it to express is of a psychological order—a move-ment of the neck made by someone else, each of many individuals having posed for a moment as his model.

(It may be that, for the creation of a work of literature, imagina-tion and sensibility are interchangeable qualities and that the latter may with no great harm be substituted for the former, just as in people whose stomach is incapable of digesting this function is relegated to the intestine. A man born with sensibility but without imagination might, in spite of this deficiency, be able to write admirable novels. For the suffering inflicted upon him by other people, his own efforts to ward it off, the long conflict between his unhappiness and another person's cruelty, all this, interpreted by the intellect, might furnish the material for a book not merely as beautiful as one that was imagined, invented, but also in as great a degree exterior to the day-dreams that the author would have had if he had been left to his own devices and happy, and as astonishing to himself, therefore, and as accidental as a fortuitous caprice of the imagination.)

The stupidest people, in their gestures, their remarks, the sentiments which they involuntarily express, manifest laws which they do not themselves perceive but which the artist surprises in them. Because he makes observations of this kind the writer is popularly believed to be ill-natured. But this belief is false: in an instance of ridiculous behaviour the artist sees a beautiful generality, and he no more condemns on this account the individual in whom he observes it than a surgeon would despise a patient for suffering from some quite common disorder of the circulation; the writer, in fact, is the least inclined of all men to scoff at folly. Unhappily, he is more unhappy than ill-natured: when it concerns his own passions, while well aware of their universality, he frees himself less easily from the personal sufferings which they cause. Naturally, when some insolent fellow insults us, we would rather he had paid us a compliment, and *a fortiori*, when a woman whom we adore betrays us, what would we not give for this not to have happened! But then the pain of an affront, the anguish of abandonment, would have been lands which we should never know, lands whose discovery, painful though it may be for the man, is nevertheless invaluable for the artist. And so, though it is neither his wish nor theirs, the ill-natured and the ungrateful find their place in his work. The writer who writes a pamphlet involuntarily associates with his glory the riff-raff whom he castigates in it, and in every work of art one can recognise those whom the artist has most hated and also, alas! those whom he has most loved. They indeed have quite simply been posing for the artist at the very moment when, much against his will, they made him suffer most. When I was in love with Albertine, I had realised very clearly that she did not love me and I had had to resign myself to the thought that through her I could gain nothing more than the experience of what it is to suffer and to love, and even, at the beginning, to be happy.

And when we seek to extract from our grief the generality that lies within it, to write about it, we are perhaps to some extent consoled for yet another reason apart from those that I have mentioned, which is that to think in terms of general truths, to write, is for the writer a wholesome and necessary function the fulfilment of which makes him happy, it does for him what is done for men of a more physical nature by exercise, perspiration, baths. This conclusion, I must admit, I was a little reluctant to accept. I was ready to believe that the supreme truth of life resides in art, and I could see, too, that I was no more capable by an effort of memory of being still in love with Albertine than I was of continuing to mourn my grandmother's death, and yet I asked myself whether a work of art of which they would not be conscious could really for them, for the destiny of these two poor dead creatures, be a fulfilment. My grandmother, whom with so little feeling I had seen agonise and die beside me! I longed that in expiation, when my work should be finished, I might, incurably stricken, suffer for long hours, abandoned by all, and then die! And there were others less dear to me, or for whom I had cared nothing at all, for whom I felt an infinite pity, all those whose sufferings, or merely whose follies, my thought, in its effort to understand their destinies, had used for its own selfish purpose. All those men and women who had revealed some truth to me and who were now no more, appeared again before me, and it seemed as though they had lived a life which had profited only myself, as though they had died for me. Saddening too was the thought that my love, to which I had clung so tenaciously, would in my book be so detached from any individual that different readers would apply it, even in detail, to what they had felt for other women. But had I a right to be shocked at this posthumous infidelity, shocked that strangers should find new and alien objects for my feelings in unknown women, when this infidelity, this division of love between a number of women, had begun in my lifetime and even before I had started to write? It was true that I had suffered successively for Gilberte, for Mme de Guermantes, for Albertine. But successively I had also forgotten them, and only the love which I dedicated to different women had been lasting. The profanation of one of my memories by unknown readers was a crime that I had myself committed before them. I felt something near to horror at myself, the self-horror that some nationalist party might come to feel after a long war fought in its name, from which it alone had profited and in which many noble victims had suffered and succumbed without ever knowing (and for my grandmother at least what a recompense this would have been!) what the outcome of the struggle would be. And my only consolation for the thought that she did not know that at last I was getting down to work was (such is the lot of the dead) that, if she could not enjoy my progress, she had at least long ceased to be conscious of my inactivity, of my wasted life, which had been such an unhappiness to her. And certainly there were others besides my grandmother and Albertine, there were many from whom I had been able to assimilate a single phrase or look although as individual human beings I had no recollection of them; a book is a huge cemetery in which on the majority of the tombs the names are effaced and can no longer be read. Sometimes on the other hand we remember a name well enough but do not know whether anything of the individual who bore it survives in our pages. That girl with the very deep-set eyes and the drawling voice, is she here? and if she is, in what part of the ground does she lie? we no longer know, and how are we to find her beneath the flowers? But since we live at a great distance from other human beings, since even our strongest feelings—and in this class had been my love for my grandmother and for Albertine—at the end of a few years have vanished from our hearts and become for us merely a word which we do not understand, since we can talk casually of these dead people with fashionable acquaintances whose houses we still visit with pleasure though all that we loved has died, surely then, if there exists a method by which we can learn to understand these forgotten words once more, is it not our duty to make use of it, even if this means transcribing them first into a language which is universal but which for that very reason will at least be permanent, a language which may make out of those who are no more, in their truest essence, a lasting acquisition for the minds of all mankind? And as for that law of change which made these loved words unintelligible to us, if we succeed at least in explaining it, is not even our infirmity transformed into strength of a new kind?

And so I had to resign myself, since nothing has the power to survive unless it can become general and since the mind's own past is dead to its present consciousness, to the idea that even the people who were once most dear to the writer have in the long run done no more than pose for him like models for a painter.

When we turn to our own future, the work in which our unhappiness has collaborated may be interpreted both as an ominous sign of suffering and as an auspicious sign of consolation. For, when we say that the loves and griefs of a poet have been useful to him, have helped him to construct his work, that the unknown women who had not the least idea what they were doing, have—

one through her cruelty to him, another through her mockery—
brought each their stone for the building of the monument which
they will never see, we do not sufficiently reflect that the life of the
writer does not come to an end with this particular work, that the
same nature which caused him to have certain sufferings, which
then entered into his work, will continue to live after the work has
been concluded and will cause him to love other women in
conditions which would be similar, were they not made slightly
to differ by the modifications that time brings about in circumstances, in the subject himself, in his appetite for love and in his
resistance to pain. And from this point of view this first work of his
must be considered simply as an unhappy love which fatally
presages others of the kind: his life will resemble his work and in
future the poet will scarcely need to write, for he will be able to
find in what he has already written the anticipatory outline of what
will then be happening. Thus it was that my love for Albertine,
however different the two might be, was already inscribed in my
love for Gilberte, in the midst of the happy days of which, for the
first time, I had heard the name of Albertine pronounced and her
character described by her aunt, without suspecting that this
insignificant seed would develop and would one day overshadow
the whole of my life.

But from another point of view the work is a promise of
happiness, because it shows us that in every love the particular
and the general lie side by side and it teaches us to pass from one to
the other by a species of gymnastic which fortifies us against
unhappiness by making us neglect its particular cause in order to
gain a more profound understanding of its essence. Indeed—as
I was to experience in the sequel—even at a time when we are in
love and suffer, if our vocation has at last been realised, we feel so
strongly during the hours in which we are at work that the
individual whom we love is being dissolved into a vaster reality
that at moments we succeed in forgetting her and we come to
suffer from our love merely as we might from some purely
physical disease in which the loved one played no part, some
kind of malady of the heart. It is true that this only happens at a
certain stage of our love and that if the work comes a little later its
effect may appear to be the opposite. For when once the women
whom we love, through their cruelty or their triviality, have
succeeded in spite of us in destroying our illusions, have reduced
themselves to nothing and become detached from the amorous

chimera which we had fabricated in our imagination—if at this point we set ourselves to work, our mind will exalt them once more and identify them, for the purposes of our self-analysis, with objects of our love, and in this case literature, recommencing the ruined work of amorous illusion, will give a sort of second life to sentiments which have ceased to exist. And certainly we are obliged to relive our individual suffering, with the courage of the doctor who over and over again practises on his own person some dangerous injection. But at the same time we have to conceptualise it in a general form which will in some measure enable us to escape from its embrace, which will turn all mankind into sharers in our pain, and which is even able to yield us a certain joy. Where life immures, the intelligence cuts a way out, for if there exists no remedy for a love that is not shared, the awareness of a state of suffering is something from which we can extricate ourselves, if only by deducing the consequences which it entails. The intelligence knows nothing of those closed situations of life from which there is no escape.

Sometimes, when a painful passage has remained in an inchoate state, a mere rough draft, a new tenderness and a new suffering come our way which enable us to complete it, to fill it out. And on the score of these great but useful unhappinesses we have little ground for complaint: they are plentiful and we seldom have to wait long for them. (In love, our fortunate rival, which is as much as to say our enemy, is our benefactor. To a woman who previously excited in us a mere paltry physical desire he instantly adds an immense value, foreign to her but confounded by us with her. If we had no rivals, pleasure would not transform itself into love. If we had none, or if we believed that we had none. For it is not necessary that rivals should really exist. The progress of our work requires only that they should have that illusory life which is conferred upon non-existent rivals by our suspicion, our jealousy.) Nevertheless one must make haste to take advantage of them when they come, for they do not last very long: either one consoles oneself or else, when they are too severe, if one's heart is no longer very robust one dies. For if unhappiness develops the forces of the mind, happiness alone is salutary to the body. But unhappiness, even if it did not on every occasion reveal to us some new law, would nevertheless be indispensable, since through its means alone we are brought back time after time to a perception of the truth and forced to take things seriously, tearing up each new

crop of the weeds of habit and scepticism and levity and indifference. Yet it is true that truth, which is not compatible with
happiness or with physical health, is not always compatible even
with life. Unhappiness ends by killing. At every new torment
which is too hard to bear we feel yet another vein protrude, to
unroll its sinuous and deadly length along our temples or beneath
our eyes. And thus gradually are formed those terrible ravaged
faces, of the old Rembrandt, the old Beethoven, at whom the
whole world mocked. And the pockets under the eyes and
the wrinkled forehead would not matter much were there not
also the suffering of the heart. But since strength of one kind can
change into a strength of another kind, since heat which is stored
up can become light and the electricity in a flash of lightning can
cause a photograph to be taken, since the dull pain in our heart can
hoist above itself like a banner the visible permanence of an image
for every new grief, let us accept the physical injury which is done
to us for the sake of the spiritual knowledge which grief brings; let
us submit to the disintegration of our body, since each new
fragment which breaks away from it returns in a luminous and
significant form to add itself to our work, to complete it at the
price of sufferings of which others more richly endowed have no
need, to make our work at least more solid as our life crumbles
away beneath the corrosive action of our emotions. Ideas come to
us as the substitutes for griefs, and griefs, at the moment when they
change into ideas, lose some part of their power to injure our
heart; the transformation itself, even, for an instant, releases suddenly a little joy. But substitutes only in the order of time, for the
primary element, it seems, is the idea, and grief is merely the
mode in which certain ideas make their first entry into us. But
within the tribe of ideas there are various families and some of
them from the very first moment are joys.

    These reflexions enabled me to give a stronger and more precise
meaning to the truth which I had often dimly perceived, particularly when Mme de Cambremer had expressed surprise that I could
give up seeing a remarkable man like Elstir for the sake of
Albertine. Even from an intellectual point of view I had felt that
she was wrong, but I did not know what it was that she had failed
to understand: the nature of the lessons through which one serves
one's apprenticeship as a man of letters. In this process the objective value of the arts counts for little; what we have to bring to light
and make known to ourselves is our feelings, our passions, that is

to say the passions and feelings of all mankind. A woman whom we need and who makes us suffer elicits from us a whole gamut of feelings far more profound and more vital than does a man of genius who interests us. It is for us later to decide, according to the plane upon which we are living, whether an infidelity through which some woman has made us suffer is of little or great account beside the truths which it has revealed to us and which the woman who exulted in our suffering would hardly have been able to understand. In any case these infidelities are not likely to be wanting. A writer need have no anxieties on that score when he embarks upon a long labour. Let his intellect begin the work and as he proceeds he will meet with griefs, enough or more than enough, which will undertake to finish it. As for happiness, that is really useful to us in one way only, by making unhappiness possible. It is necessary for us to form in happiness ties of confidence and attachment that are both sweet and strong in order that their rupture may cause us the heart-rending but so valuable agony which is called unhappiness. Had we not been happy, if only in hope, the unhappinesses that befall us would be without cruelty and therefore without fruit.

And more even than the painter, the writer, in order to achieve volume and substance, in order to attain to generality and, so far as literature can, to reality, needs to have seen many churches in order to paint one church and for the portrayal of a single sentiment requires many individuals. For if art is long and life is short, we may on the other hand say that, if inspiration is short, the sentiments which it has to portray are not of much longer duration. It is our passions which draw the outline of our books, the ensuing intervals of repose which write them. And when inspiration is born again, when we are able to resume our work, the woman who was posing for us to illustrate a sentiment no longer has the power to make us feel it. We must continue to paint the sentiment from another model, and if this means infidelity towards the individual, from a literary point of view, thanks to the similarity of our feelings for the two women, which makes a work at the same time a recollection of our past loves and a prophecy of our new ones, there is no great harm in these substitutions. And this is one reason for the futility of those critical essays which try to guess who it is that an author is talking about. A work, even one that is directly autobiographical, is at the very least put together out of several intercalated episodes in the life of the author—

earlier episodes which have inspired the work and later ones which resemble it just as much, the later loves being traced after the pattern of the earlier. For to the woman whom we have loved most in our life we are not so faithful as we are to ourself, and sooner or later we forget her in order—since this is one of the characteristics of that self—to be able to begin to love again. At most our faculty of loving has received from this woman whom we so loved a particular stamp, which will cause us to be faithful to her even in our infidelity. We shall need, with the woman who succeeds her, those same morning walks or the same practice of taking her home every evening or giving her a hundred times too much money. (A curious thing, this circulation of the money which we give to women who because of that make us unhappy, that is to say are the cause of our writing books: it almost seems as though a writer's works, like the water in an artesian well, mount to a height which is in proportion to the depth to which suffering has penetrated his heart.) These substitutions add then to our work something that is disinterested and more general and they convey also the austere lesson that it is not to individuals that we should attach ourselves, that it is not individuals who really exist and are, in consequence, capable of being expressed, but ideas. Nevertheless, while we have these models at our disposal we must make haste and lose no time; for those who pose for us as "happiness" can in general spare us only a few sittings, and the same may be true alas!—since grief, yes, grief too passes so quickly—of those who pose as "grief." Yet grief, even when it does not, by revealing it to us, provide the raw material of our writing, is valuable to us as an incitement to work. The imagination, the reflective faculty may be admirable machines in themselves but they may also be inert. Suffering sets them in motion. And then at least the woman who poses for us as grief favours us with an abundance of sittings, in that studio which we enter only in these periods and which lies deep within us. And they are, these periods, like an image of our life with its different griefs. For they too contain different griefs within themselves, and at the very moment when we thought that all had become calm a new one makes its appearance. New in every sense of the word: perhaps because an unforeseen situation forces us to enter more profoundly into contact with ourself, these painful dilemmas which love is constantly putting in our way teach us and reveal to us, layer after layer, the material of which we are made. So when Françoise, seeing that Albertine had the run of the flat and passed in and out of all the rooms like a dog creating disorder everywhere and that she was ruining me and causing me unhappiness of every kind, used to say (for at that time I had already written some articles and done a few translations): "Ah! if only, instead of this girl who makes him waste all his time, Monsieur had got himself a nicely brought up young secretary who could have sorted all Monsieur's paperies for him!", I had perhaps been wrong in thinking that she spoke wisely. By making me waste my time, by causing me unhappiness, Albertine had perhaps been more useful to me, even from a literary point of view, than a secretary who would have arranged my "paperies." But all the same, when a living creature is so faultily constituted (and perhaps, if such a creature exists in nature, it is man) that he cannot love without suffering, and that he has to suffer in order to apprehend truths, the life of such a creature becomes in the end extremely wearisome. The happy years are the lost, the wasted years, one must wait for suffering before one can work. And then the idea of the preliminary suffering becomes associated with the idea of work and one is afraid of each new literary undertaking because one thinks of the pain one will first have to endure in order to imagine it. And once one understands that suffering is the best thing that one can hope to encounter in life, one thinks without terror, and almost as of a deliverance, of death.

If I had had to admit, albeit I found the idea somewhat repugnant, that the writer plays with life and exploits other people for the purpose of his books, I could not fail to observe also that this is sometimes very far from being the case. The history and the circumstances of Werther, the noble Werther, had not alas! been mine. Without for a moment believing in Albertine's love I had twenty times wanted to kill myself for her, I had ruined myself, I had destroyed my health for her. For when it is a question of writing, one is scrupulous, one examines things meticulously, one rejects all that is not truth. But when it is merely a question of life, one ruins oneself, makes oneself ill, kills oneself all for lies. It is true that these lies are a lode from which, if one has passed the age for writing poetry, one can at least extract a little truth. Sorrows are servants, obscure and detested, against whom one struggles, beneath whose dominion one more and more completely falls, dire and dreadful servants whom it is impossible to replace and who by subterranean paths lead us towards truth and death. Happy are those who have first come face to face with truth, those for whom, near though the one may be to the other, the hour of truth has struck before the hour of death!

When I considered my past life, I understood also that its slightest episodes had contributed towards giving me the lesson in idealism from which I was going to profit today. My meetings with M. de Charlus, for instance, had they not, even before his pro-German tendencies taught me the same lesson, demonstrated to me, even better than my love for Mme de Guermantes or for Albertine, or Saint-Loup's love for Rachel, the truth of the axiom that matter is indifferent and that anything can be grafted upon it by thought; an axiom which in the phenomenon, so ill-understood and so needlessly condemned, of sexual inversion is seen to be of even greater scope than in that, in itself so instructive, of love? For love shows us Beauty fleeing from the woman whom we no longer love, and coming to take up her abode in a face which anybody else would find hideous and which to ourselves too might have seemed, as one day it will seem, unpleasing: but even more striking is the spectacle of the goddess, taking with her the reverent homage of a great nobleman who thereupon instantly abandons a beautiful princess, migrating to a new perch beneath the cap of an omnibus conductor. And my astonishment every time I had seen after an interval, in the Champs-Elysées or in the street or on the beach, the face of Gilberte or of Mme de Guermantes or of Albertine, was this not a proof that a memory is prolonged only in a direction which diverges from the impression with which originally it coincided but from which gradually it further and further departs?

The writer must not be indignant if the invert who reads his book gives to his heroines a masculine countenance. For only by the indulgence of this slightly aberrant peculiarity can the invert give to what he is reading its full general import. Racine himself was obliged, as a first step towards giving her a universal validity, for a moment to turn the antique figure of Phèdre into a Jansenist; and if M. de Charlus had not bestowed upon the "traitress" for whom Musset weeps in *La Nuit d'Octobre* or *Souvenir* the features of Morel, he would neither have wept nor have understood, since it was only along this path, narrow and indirect, that he had access to the verities of love. For it is only out of habit, a habit contracted from the insincere language of prefaces and dedications, that the writer speaks of "my reader." In reality every reader is, while he is reading, the reader of his own self. The writer's work is merely a kind of optical instrument which he offers to the reader to enable him to discern what, without this book, he would perhaps never have perceived in himself. And the recognition by the reader in his own self of what the book says is the proof of its veracity, the contrary also being true, at least to a certain extent, for the difference between the two texts may sometimes be imputed less to the author than to the reader. Besides, the book may be too learned, too obscure for a simple reader, and may therefore present to him a clouded glass through which he cannot read. And other peculiarities can have the same effect as inversion. In order to read with understanding many readers require to read in their own particular fashion, and the author must not be indignant at this; on the contrary, he must leave the reader all possible liberty, saying to him: "Look for yourself, and try whether you see best with this lens or that one or this other one."

If I had always taken so great an interest in dreams, was this not because, making up for lack of duration by their potency, they help us better to understand the subjective element in, for instance, love through the simple fact that they reproduce—but with miraculous swiftness—the process vulgarly known as getting a woman under one's skin, so effectively that within a sleep of a few minutes we can fall passionately in love with an ugly woman, a thing which in real life could only happen after years of habit and intimacy—as though they were intravenous injections of love discovered by some wonder-working doctor, of love and sometimes also of suffering? With the same speed the amorous suggestions which they have instilled into us are dissipated, and sometimes, when the loving nocturnal visitant has vanished from our sight and reappeared in her familiar shape of an ugly woman, there vanishes with her something more precious, a whole ravishing landscape of feelings of tenderness, of voluptuous pleasure, of vaguely blurred regrets, a whole embarkation for the Cythera of passion, of which we should like to note, for our waking state, the subtle and deliciously lifelike gradations of tone, but which fades away like a discoloured canvas that can no longer be restored. And it was perhaps also because of the extraordinary effects which they achieve with Time that dreams had fascinated me. Have we not often seen in a single night, in a single minute of a night, remote periods, relegated to those enormous distances at which we can no longer distinguish anything of the sentiments which we felt in them, come rushing upon us with almost the speed of light as though they were giant aeroplanes instead of the pale stars which we had supposed them to be, blinding us with their brilliance and bringing back to our vision all that they had once contained for us, giving us the emotion, the shock, the brilliance of their immediate proximity, only, once we are awake, to resume their position on the far side of the gulf which they had miraculously traversed, so that we are tempted to believe—wrongly, however—that they are one of the modes of rediscovering Lost Time?

I had realised before now that it is only a clumsy and erroneous form of perception which places everything in the object, when really everything is in the mind; I had lost my grandmother in reality many months after I had lost her in fact, and I had seen people present various aspects according to the idea that I or others possessed of them, a single individual being several different people for different observers (Swann, for instance, for my family and for his friends in society, the Princesse de Luxembourg for the judge at Balbec and for those who knew her identity) or even for the same observer at different periods over the years (the name of Guermantes, and the different Swanns, for me). I had seen that love places in a person who is loved what exists only in the person who loves, indeed I could hardly have failed to become aware of this when I had seen stretched to its maximum the distance between objective reality and love (in Rachel, for instance, as she appeared to Saint-Loup and to me, in Albertine as she appeared to me and to Saint-Loup, in Morel or the omnibus conductor as they appeared to other people and to M. de Charlus, who in spite of this showered delicate attentions upon them, recited Musset's poems to them, etc.). Finally, to a certain extent, the Germanophilia of M. de Charlus (like the expression on the face of Saint-Loup when he had looked at the photograph of Albertine) had helped me to free myself for a moment, if not from my Germanophobia, at least from my belief in the pure objectivity of this feeling, had helped to make me think that perhaps what applied to love applied also to hate and that, in the terrible judgment which at this time France passed on Germany—that she was a nation outside the pale of humanity—the most important element was an objectification of feelings as subjective as those which had caused Rachel and Albertine to appear so precious, the one to Saint-Loup and the other to me. What, in fact, made it possible that this perversity was not entirely intrinsic to Germany was that, just as I as an individual had had successive loves and at the end of each one its object had appeared to me valueless, so I had already seen in my country successive hates which had, for example, at one time condemned as traitors—a thousand times worse than the Germans into whose hands they were delivering France—those very Dreyfusards such as Reinach with whom today patriotic Frenchmen were collaborating against a race whose every member was of necessity a liar, a savage beast, a madman, excepting only those Germans who, like the King of Romania, the King of the Belgians, or the Empress of Russia, had embraced the French cause. It is true that the anti-Dreyfusards would have replied to me: "But it is not the same thing." But then it never is the same thing, any more than it is the same person with whom after an interval we fall in love; otherwise, faced with the same phenomenon as before, someone who was a second time taken in by it would have no alternative but to blame his own subjective condition, he could not again believe that the qualities or the defects resided in the object. And so, since the phenomenon, outwardly, is not the same, the intellect has no difficulty in basing upon each set of circumstances a new theory (that it is against nature to have schools directed by the religious orders, as the radicals believe, or that it is impossible for the Jewish race to be assimilated into a nation, or that there exists an undying hatred between the Teutonic and the Latin races, the yellow race having been temporarily rehabilitated). This subjective element in the situation struck one forcibly if one had any conversation with neutrals, since the pro-Germans among them had, for instance, the faculty of ceasing for a moment to understand and even to listen when one spoke to them about the German atrocities in Belgium. (And yet they were real, these atrocities: the subjective element that I had observed to exist in hatred as in vision itself did not imply that an object could not possess real qualities or defects and in no way tended to make reality vanish into pure relativism.) And if, after so many years had slipped away and so much time had been lost, I felt this influence to be dominant even in the sphere of international relations, had I not already had some notion of its existence right at the beginning of my life, when I was reading in the garden at Combray one of those novels by Bergotte which, even today, if I chance to turn over a few of its forgotten pages where I see the wiles of some villain described, I cannot put down until I have assured myself, by skipping a hundred pages, that towards the end this same villain is humiliated as he deserves to be and lives long enough to learn that his sinister schemes have failed? For I no longer have any clear recollection of what happened to these characters, though in this respect they are scarcely to be distinguished from the men and women who were present this afternoon at Mme de Guermantes's party and whose past life, in many cases at least, was as vague in my mind as if I had read it in a half-forgotten novel. The Prince d'Agrigente, for instance: had he ended by marrying Mlle X——? Or was it rather the brother of Mlle X—— who might have married the sister of the Prince d'Agrigente? Or was I confusing it all with something that I had read long ago or recently dreamed?

Dreams were another of the facts of my life which had always most profoundly impressed me and had done most to convince me of the purely mental character of reality, and in the composition of my work I would not scorn their aid. At a time when I was still living, in a rather less disinterested fashion, for love of one kind or another, a dream would come to me, bringing strangely close, across vast distances of lost time, my grandmother, or Albertine, whom briefly I began to love again because in my sleep she had given me a version, highly diluted, of the episode with the laundry-girl in Touraine. And I thought that in the same way dreams would bring sometimes within my grasp truths or impressions which my efforts alone and even the contingencies of nature failed to present to me; that they would reawaken in me something of the desire, the regret for certain non-existent things which is the necessary condition for working, for freeing oneself from the dominion of habit, for detaching oneself from the concrete. And therefore I would not disdain this second muse, this nocturnal muse who might sometimes do duty for the other one.

I had seen aristocrats turn into vulgar people when their intelligence was vulgar. ("Make yourself at home," for instance the Duc de Guermantes would say, using an expression that Cottard might have used.) I had seen everybody believe, during the Dreyfus Affair or during the war, and in medicine too, that truth is a particular piece of knowledge which cabinet ministers and doctors possess, a Yes or No which requires no interpretation, thanks to the possession of which the men in power *knew* whether Dreyfus was guilty or not and *knew*, without having to send Roques to make an inquiry on the spot, whether Sarrail in Salonika had or had not the resources to launch an offensive at the same time as the

Russians, in the same way that an X-ray photograph is supposed to indicate without any need for interpretation the exact nature of a patient's disease.

It occurred to me, as I thought about it, that the raw material of my experience, which would also be the raw material of my book, came to me from Swann, not merely because so much of it concerned Swann himself and Gilberte, but because it was Swann who from the days of Combray had inspired in me the wish to go to Balbec, where otherwise my parents would never have had the idea of sending me, and but for this I should never have known Albertine. Certainly, it was to her face, as I had seen it for the first time beside the sea, that I traced back certain things which I should no doubt include in my book. And in a sense I was right to trace them back to her, for if I had not walked on the front that day, if I had not got to know her, all these ideas would never have been developed (unless they had been developed by some other woman). But I was wrong too, for this pleasure which generates something within us and which, retrospectively, we seek to place in a beautiful feminine face, comes from our senses: but the pages I would write were something that Albertine, particularly the Albertine of those days, would quite certainly never have understood. It was, however, for this very reason (and this shows that we ought not to live in too intellectual an atmosphere), for the reason that she was so different from me, that she had fertilised me through unhappiness and even, at the beginning, through the simple effort which I had had to make to imagine something different from myself. Had she been capable of understanding my pages, she would, for that very reason, not have inspired them. But Swann had been of primary importance, for had I not gone to Balbec I should never have known the Guermantes either, since my grandmother would not have renewed her friendship with Mme de Villeparisis nor should I have made the acquaintance of Saint-Loup and M. de Charlus and thus got to know the Duchesse de Guermantes and through her her cousin, so that even my presence at this very moment in the house of the Prince de Guermantes, where out of the blue the idea for my work had just come to me (and this meant that I owed to Swann not only the material but also the decision), came to me from Swann. A rather slender stalk, perhaps, to support thus the whole development of my life, for the "Guermantes way" too, on this interpretation, had emanated from "Swann's way." But often this begetter of all the various aspects of a man's life is someone very much inferior to Swann, someone utterly insignificant. Suppose some school-friend who meant nothing to me had described an attractive girl who was to be enjoyed there (whom probably I should not in fact have met), would not that have been enough to send me to Balbec? Often, meeting years later some friend of our youth whom we never particularly liked, we scarcely trouble to shake hands with him, and yet, did we but think of it, it is from a casual remark which he made to us, "You ought to come to Balbec" or something of the kind, that our whole life and our work have originated. But if it does not occur to us to thank him, this is no proof of ingratitude. For when he uttered those words he had no thought of the huge consequences which they would have for us. It is our sensibility and our intelligence which have exploited the circumstances, which, once he has given them their first impulsion, have engendered one another as cause and effect without his having been able to foresee either—to return to my own story—my living with Albertine or the masked ball given by the Guermantes or anything else that had happened. No doubt the impulsion that he gave was necessary, and on that account the external form of our life and even the material which we shall use in our work derive from him. Without Swann, as I have said, my parents would never have had the idea of sending me to Balbec. (Yet Swann was not for this reason responsible for the sufferings which he himself had indirectly caused me: they sprang from my weakness, just as his own weakness had made him suffer through Odette.) But whoever it is who has thus determined the course of our life has, in so doing, excluded all the lives which we might have led instead of our actual life. If Swann had not talked to me about Balbec, I should not have known Albertine, the dining-room of the hotel, the Guermantes. I should have gone to some other town, I should have known other people, my memory and my books would be filled with quite different scenes, which I cannot even imagine and the novelty of which, their unknown-ness, I find so seductive that I almost regret that I was not directed instead towards them and that Albertine and the beach of Balbec and Rivebelle and the Guermantes did not for ever remain unknown to me.

Jealousy is a good recruiting-sergeant who, when there is a gap in our picture, goes out into the street and brings us in the desirable woman who was needed to fill it. Perhaps in our eyes she had ceased to be a beauty? She has become one again, for we are jealous of her and therefore she will fill the gap. Once we are dead, we shall have no joy that our picture was completed in this fashion. But this consideration does not in the least discourage us. We feel merely that life is a little more complicated than it is said to be, and circumstances too. And it is absolutely necessary that we should portray this complexity. The jealousy that is so useful is not necessarily born of a look, or an anecdote, or a retroflexion. It may be found, ready to sting us, between the leaves of a directory—what for Paris is called *Tout-Paris* and for the country the *Annuaire des Châteaux*. We had heard, for instance, but without paying any attention, some beauty to whom we have become indifferent say that she would have to go and see her sister for a few days in the Pas-de-Calais, near Dunkirk; we had also, in the past, but again without paying any attention, thought that perhaps the beauty had formerly been pursued by Monsieur E——, whom she had ceased to see, since she had ceased to go to the bar where she used to meet him. What could her sister be? A housemaid perhaps? Out of tact, we had never asked. And now suddenly, opening the *Annuaire des Châteaux* at random we find that Monsieur E—— has his country .house in the Pas-de-Calais, near Dunkirk. At once all is clear: to oblige the beauty he has taken her sister into his employment as a housemaid, and if the beauty no longer sees him in the bar, the reason is that he gets her to come and see him at home, either in Paris, where he lives most of the year, or in the Pas-de-Calais, since he cannot do without her even for the few weeks that he is there. Drunk with rage and love, we paint furiously away at the picture. And yet, suppose we are wrong? May not the truth be that Monsieur E—— no longer sees the beauty but, wanting to help her, has recommended her sister to a brother of his who lives all the year round in the Pas-de-Calais? And in that case she is going, perhaps quite by chance, to see her sister at a time when Monsieur E—— is not there, for they are no longer interested in each other. And then there is another possibility, that the sister is not a housemaid in the house near Dunkirk or anywhere else, but has relations in the Pas-de-Calais. Our anguish of the first moment gives way before these last hypotheses, which calm our jealousy. But it makes no difference. Jealousy, concealed between the leaves of the *Annuaire des Châteaux*, came at the right moment, and now the space that stood empty in our canvas is filled to abundance. And the whole composition takes shape, thanks to the presence, evoked by jealousy, of the beauty of whom already we are no longer jealous and whom we no longer love.

At this moment the butler came in to tell me that the first piece of music was finished, so that I could leave the library and go into the rooms where the party was taking place. And thereupon I remembered where I was. But I was not in the least disturbed in the train of thought upon which I had embarked by the fact that a fashionable gathering, my return to society, had provided me with that point of departure for a new life which I had been unable to find in solitude. There was nothing extraordinary about this fact, there was no reason why an impression with the power to resuscitate the timeless man within me should be linked to solitude rather than to society (as I had once supposed and as had perhaps once been the case for me, and perhaps ought still to have been the case, had I developed harmoniously instead of going through this long standstill which seemed only now to be coming to an end). For, as this impression of beauty came to me only when, an immediate sensation—no matter how insignificant—having been thrust upon my consciousness by chance, a similar sensation, spontaneously born again within me, somehow in a single moment diffused the first sensation over different periods of my life and succeeded in filling with a general essence the empty space which particular sensations never failed to leave in my mind, as this was how I came to experience beauty I might just as well receive sensations of the appropriate kind in a social as in a natural environment, since they are supplied by chance, aided no doubt by that special kind of excitement which, on the days when we happen to be jolted out of the normal routine of our lives, causes even the simplest things to begin once again to give us those sensations which habit, in its economical way, ordinarily begrudges our nervous system. Why it was that precisely and uniquely this kind of sensation should lead to the production of a work of art was a question to which I proposed to try and find an objective answer, by following up the thoughts which had come to me, linked in a continuous chain, in the library, and I felt that the impulse given to the intellectual life within me was so vigorous now that I should be able to pursue these thoughts just as well in the drawing-room, in the midst of the guests, as alone in the library; it seemed to me that, from this point of view, even in the midst of a numerous gathering I should be able to maintain my solitude. For just as great events that impinge upon us from without fail to influence the powers of our mind, so that a mediocre writer who lives in a heroic age does not cease to be a mediocre writer, for the same reason, I realised, what is dangerous in social life is merely the social and worldly inclinations with which one approaches it. In itself it can no more turn one into a mediocre writer than an epic war can turn a bad poet into a sublime one. In any case, whether or no it was a good plan, theoretically, for a work of art to be constructed in this fashion, and whatever might be the result of the examination of this point which I intended to make, I could not deny that, so far as I was concerned, whenever genuinely aesthetic impressions had come to me, they had always followed upon sensations of this kind. It is true that such impressions had been rather rare in my life, but they dominated it, and I could still rediscover in the past some of these peaks which I had unwisely lost sight of (a mistake I would be careful not to make again). And already I could say that this characteristic, though it might, in the exclusive importance that it assumed in my thinking, be personal to me, was nevertheless, as I was reassured to find, akin to characteristics, less marked but still perceptible and at bottom not at all dissimilar, of certain well-known writers. Is it not from a sensation of the same species as that of the madeleine that Chateaubriand suspends the loveliest episode in the *Mémoires d'Outre-tombe*: "Yesterday evening I was walking alone . . . I was roused from my reflexions by the warbling of a thrush perched upon the highest branch of a birch-tree. Instantaneously the magic sound caused my father's estate to reappear before my eyes; I forgot the catastrophes of which I had recently been the witness and, transported suddenly into the past, I saw again those country scenes in which I had so often heard the fluting notes of the thrush." And of all the lovely sentences in those memoirs are not these some of the loveliest: "A sweet and subtle scent of heliotrope was exhaled by a little patch of beans that were in flower; it was brought to us not by a breeze from our own country but by a wild Newfoundland wind, unrelated to the exiled plant, without sympathy of shared memory or pleasure. In this perfume, not breathed by beauty, not cleansed in her bosom, not scattered where she had walked, in this perfume of a changed sky and tillage and world there was all the diverse melancholy of regret and absence and youth." And in one of the masterpieces of French literature, Gérard de Nerval's *Sylvie*, just as in the book of the *Mémoires d'Outre-tombe* which describes Combourg, there figures a sensation of the same species as the taste of the madeleine and the warbling of the thrush. Above all in Baudelaire, where they are more numerous still, reminiscences of this kind are clearly less fortuitous and therefore, to my mind, unmistakable in their significance. Here the poet himself, with something of a slow and indolent choice, deliberately seeks, in the perfume of a woman, for instance, of her hair and her breast, the analogies which will inspire him and evoke for him

> the azure of the sky immense and round

and

> a harbour full of masts and pennants.

I was about to search in my memory for the passages in Baudelaire at the heart of which one may find this kind of transposed sensation, in order once and for all to establish my place in so noble a line of descent and thus to give myself the assurance that the work which I no longer had any hesitation in undertaking was worthy of the pains which I should have to bestow upon it, when, having arrived at the foot of the flight of stairs which led down from the library, I found myself suddenly in the main drawing-room, in the middle of a party which, as I soon discovered, was to seem to me very different from those that I had attended in the past, and was to assume a special character in my eyes and take on a novel significance. In fact, as soon as I entered the crowded room, although I did not falter in the project which I had gone so far towards formulating within me, I was witness of a spectacular and dramatic effect which threatened to raise against my enterprise the gravest of all objections. An objection which I should manage no doubt to surmount, but which, while I continued silently to reflect upon the conditions that are necessary to a work of art, could not fail, by presenting to my gaze in a hundred different forms a consideration more likely than any other to make me hesitate, constantly to interrupt my train of thought.

For a few seconds I did not understand why it was that I had difficulty in recognising the master of the house and the guests and why everyone in the room appeared to have put on a disguise—in most cases a powdered wig—which changed him completely. The Prince himself, as he stood receiving his guests, still had that genial look of a king in a fairy-story which I had remarked in him the first

time I had been to his house, but today, as though he too felt
bound to comply with the rules for fancy dress which he had sent
out with the invitations, he had got himself up with a white beard
and dragged his feet along the ground as though they were
weighted with soles of lead, so that he gave the impression of
trying to impersonate one of the "Ages of Man." (His moustaches
were white too, as though the hoarfrost of Hop o'my Thumb's
forest still lay thick upon them. They seemed to get in the way of
his mouth, which he had difficulty in moving, and one felt that
having made his effect he ought to have taken them off.) So
successful was this disguise that I recognised him only by a process
of logical deduction, by inferring from the mere resemblance of
certain features the identity of the figure before me. I do not know
what young Fezensac had put on his face, but, while others had
whitened either half their beard or merely their moustache, he had
not bothered to use a dye like the rest but had found some means
of covering his features with wrinkles and making his eyebrows
sprout with bristles; and all this did not suit him in the least, it had
the effect of making his face look hardened, bronzed, rigid and
solemn, and aged him to such an extent that one would no longer
have said he was a young man at all. Still greater was my surprise
when a moment later I heard the name Duc de Châtellerault
applied to a little elderly man with the silvery moustaches of an
ambassador, in whom, thanks to a tiny fragment which still survived of the look that I remembered, I was just able to recognise
the youth whom I had once met at Mme de Villeparisis's tea-party.
The first time that I thus succeeded in identifying somebody, by
trying to dismiss from my mind the effects of his disguise and
building up, through an effort of memory, a whole familiar face
round those features which had remained unaltered, my first
thought ought to have been—and perhaps for a fraction of a
second was—to congratulate him on having made himself up
with such wonderful skill that one had initially, before recognising
him, that hesitation which a great actor, appearing in a role in
which he is unlike himself, can cause an audience to feel when he
first comes on to the stage, so that knowing from the programme
what to expect, it yet, for a moment, remains silent and puzzled
before bursting into applause.

From the point of view of disguise, the most extraordinary of all
the guests, the real star turn of the afternoon, was my personal
enemy, M. d'Argencourt. Not only had he concealed his real

beard, which was hardly even pepper-and-salt in colour, beneath a fantastic bushy growth of a quite improbable whiteness, but altogether (such is the power of small physical changes to shrink or enlarge a human figure and, even more, to alter the apparent character, the personality of an individual) he had turned into a contemptible old beggarman, and the diplomat whose solemn demeanour and starched rigidity were still present to my memory acted his part of old dotard with such verisimilitude that his limbs were all of a tremble and the features of what had once been a haughty countenance were permanently relaxed in an expression of smiling idiocy. Disguise, carried to this extent, ceases to be a mere art, it becomes a total transformation of the personality. And indeed, although certain details assured me that it was really Argencourt who presented this ludicrous and picturesque spectacle, I had to traverse an almost infinite number of successive states of a single face if I wished to rediscover that of the Argencourt whom I had known and who was now, though he had had no other materials than his own body with which to effect the change, so different from himself. Clearly this was the last extremity to which that body could be brought without suffering utter disintegration; already the immobile face and the proudly arched chest were no more than a bundle of rags, twitching and convulsed. With difficulty, by recalling certain smiles with which in the past Argencourt had sometimes for a moment tempered his disdain, was I able to see in the man before me the Argencourt whom I had once known, to understand that this smile of a doddering old-clothes-man existed potentially in the correct gentleman of an earlier day. But even supposing that the same intention lay behind Argencourt's smile now as in the past, because of the prodigious transformation of his face the actual physical matter of the eye through which he had to express this intention was so different that the smile which resulted was entirely new and even appeared to belong to a new person. I was tempted to laugh aloud at the sight of this sublime old gaffer, as senile in his amiable caricature of himself as was, in a more tragic vein, M. de Charlus thunderstruck into humble politeness. M. d'Argencourt, in his impersonation of an aged man in a farce by Regnard rewritten in an exaggerated fashion by Labiche, was as easy of access, as affable as M. de Charlus in the role of King Lear, punctiliously doffing his hat to the most unimportant passer-by. Yet it did not occur to me to tell him how impressed I was by the extraordinary vision which he offered to my eyes. And this was not because of any survival of my old feeling of antipathy, for indeed he had so far become unlike himself that I had the illusion of being in the presence of a different person, as gentle, as kindly, as inoffensive as the other Argencourt had been hostile, overbearing, and dangerous. So far a different person that the sight of this hoary clown with his ludicrous grin, this snowman looking like General Dourakine[20] in his second childhood, made me think that it must be possible for human personality to undergo metamorphoses as total as those of certain insects. I had the impression that I was looking into a glass-case in a museum of natural history at an instructive example of a later phase in the life-cycle of what had once been the swiftest and surest of predatory insects, and before this flabby chrysalis, more subject to vibration than capable of movement, I could not feel the sentiments which in the past M. d'Argencourt had always inspired in me. However, I was silent, I refrained from congratulating him on presenting a spectacle which seemed to extend the boundaries within which the transformations of the human body can take place.

For whereas at a fancy dress ball or behind the scenes at a theatre civility leads one, if anything, to exaggerate the difficulty—to talk even of the impossibility—of recognising the person beneath the disguise, here on the contrary an instinct had warned me to do just the contrary; I felt that the success of the disguise was no longer in any way flattering because the transformation was not intentional. And I realised something that I had not suspected when I entered the room a few minutes earlier: that every party, grand or simple, which takes place after a long interval in which one has ceased to go into society, provided that it brings together some of the people whom one knew in the past, gives one the impression of a masquerade, a masquerade which is more successful than any that one has ever been to and at which one is most genuinely "intrigued" by the identity of the other guests, but with the novel feature that the disguises, which assumed long ago against their wearers' will, cannot, when the party is over, be wiped off with the make-up. Intrigued, did I say, by the identity of the other guests? No more, alas, than they are intrigued by one's own. For the difficulty which I experienced in putting a name to the faces before me was shared evidently by all those who, when they happened to catch sight of mine, paid no more attention to it than if they had never seen it before or else laboriously sought

to extract from my present appearance a very different recollection.

In performing this extraordinary "number," this brilliant study
in caricature which offered certainly the most striking vision
which I was likely to retain of him, M. d'Argencourt might be
likened to an actor who at the end of a play makes a final
appearance on the stage before the curtain falls for the last time
in the midst of a storm of laughter. And if I no longer felt any ill-
will towards him, it was because in this man who had rediscovered
the innocence of childhood there was no longer any recollection
of the contemptuous notions which he might once have had of
me, no longer any memory of having seen M. de Charlus suddenly
drop my arm, either because these sentiments had ceased to exist
in him or because in order to arrive at me they were obliged to pass
through physical refractors which so distorted them that in the
course of their journey they completely changed their meaning, so
that M. d'Argencourt appeared to be kind for want of the physical
means of expressing that he was still unkind, from inability to
repress his unfailingly friendly mirth. I have compared him to an
actor, but in fact, unencumbered as he was by any conscious soul,
it was rather as a puppet, a trembling puppet with a beard of white
wool, that I saw him being shakily put through his paces up and
down this drawing-room, in a puppet-show which was both
scientific and philosophical and in which he served—as though
it had been at the same time a funeral oration and a lecture at the
Sorbonne—both as a text for a sermon on the vanity of all things
and as an object lesson in natural history.

A puppet-show, yes, but one in which, in order to identify the
puppets with the people whom one had known in the past, it was
necessary to read what was written on several planes at once,
planes that lay behind the visible aspect of the puppets and gave
them depth and forced one, as one looked at these aged marion-
ettes, to make a strenuous intellectual effort; one was obliged to
study them at the same time with one's eyes and with one's
memory. These were puppets bathed in the immaterial colours
of the years, puppets which exteriorised Time, Time which by
habit is made invisible and to become visible seeks bodies, which,
wherever it finds them, it seizes upon, to display its magic lantern
upon them. As immaterial now as Golo long ago on the doorknob
of my room at Combray, the new, the unrecognisable Argencourt
was there before me as the revelation of Time, which by his

agency was rendered partially visible, for in the new elements which went to compose his face and his personality one could decipher a number which told one the years of his age, one could recognise the hieroglyph of life—of life not as it appears to us, that is to say permanent, but as it really is: an atmosphere so swiftly changing that at the end of the day the proud nobleman is portrayed, in caricature, as a dealer in old clothes.

There were other people in the room in whom these changes, these veritable alienations seemed to belong rather to the realm of human psychology than of natural history, so that one was astonished, when one heard certain names, to learn that the same individual could present, not like M. d'Argencourt the characteristics of a new and different species, but the external features of a different personality. From this young girl, for instance, as from M. d'Argencourt, time had extracted possibilities that one could never have suspected, but these possibilities, though it was through her physiognomy or her body that they had expressed themselves, seemed to be of a moral order. The features of the face, if they change, if they group themselves differently, if their oscillations take on a slower rhythm, assume with a different aspect a different significance. In a woman, for instance, whom one had known as stiff and prim, an enlargement out of all recognition of the cheeks, an unpredictable arching of the nose, caused one the same surprise—and often it was an agreeable surprise—as one would have felt at some sensitive and profound remark, some noble and courageous action that one would never have expected of her. On either side of this nose, this new nose, one saw opening out horizons which one would not have dared to hope for. With these cheeks kindness and delicate affection, once out of the question, had become possible. And in the presence of this chin one could utter sentiments that one would never have dreamed of voicing when confronted with its predecessor. All these new features of the face implied new features also of the character; the thin, severe girl had turned into a vast and indulgent dowager. And no longer in a zoological sense, as with M. d'Argencourt, but in a social and moral sense one could say of her that she was a different person.

For all these reasons a party like this at which I found myself was something much more valuable than an image of the past: it offered me as it were all the successive images—which I had never seen—which separated the past from the present, better still it showed me the relationship that existed between the present and the past; it was like an old-fashioned peepshow, but a peepshow of the years, the vision not of a moment but a person situated in the distorting perspective of Time.

As for the woman whose lover M. d'Argencourt had been, considering the length of time that had elapsed she had not changed very much, that is to say her face was not too utterly demolished for the face of a human creature subject, as we all are, to deformation at every moment of her trajectory into the abyss towards which she had been launched, that abyss whose direction we can express only by means of comparisons that are all equally invalid, since we can borrow them only from the world of space and their sole merit, whether we give them the orientation of height, length or depth, is to make us feel that this inconceivable yet apprehensible dimension exists. To find a name for the faces before me I had been obliged, in effect, to follow the course of the years back towards their source, and this forced me, by a necessary consequence, to re-establish, to give their real place to those years whose passage I had hardly noticed. And from this point of view, freeing me from the illusions produced in us by the apparent sameness of space, the totally changed aspect of, for instance, M. d'Argencourt was a striking revelation to me of that chronological reality which under normal conditions is no more than an abstract conception to us, just as the first sight of some strange dwarf tree or giant baobab apprises us that we have arrived in a new latitude.

Life at such moments seems to us like a theatrical pageant in which from one act to another we see the baby turn into a youth and the youth into a mature man, who in the next act totters towards the grave. And as it is through endless small changes that we feel that these beings, who enter our field of vision only at long intervals, can have become so different, we feel that we ourselves must have followed the same law in virtue of which they have been so totally transformed that, without having ceased to exist, indeed just because they have never ceased to exist, they no longer in any way resemble what we observed them to be in the past.

A young woman whom I had known long ago, white-haired now and compressed into a little old witch, seemed to suggest that it is necessary, in the final scene of a theatrical entertainment, for the characters to be disguised beyond all recognition. But her brother was still so straight-backed, so like himself, that one was surprised on his youthful face to see a bristling moustache dyed white. Indeed everywhere the patches of white in beards and moustaches hitherto entirely black lent a note of melancholy to the human landscape of the party, as do the first yellow leaves on the trees when one is still looking forward to a long summer, when before one has begun to enjoy the hot weather one sees that the autumn has arrived. So that at last I, who from childhood had lived from day to day and had received, of myself and of others, impressions which I regarded as definitive, became aware as I had never been before—by an inevitable inference from the meta-morphoses which had taken place in all the people around me—of the time which had passed for them, a notion which brought with it the overwhelming revelation that it had passed also for me. And their old age, in itself a matter of indifference to me, froze my blood by announcing to me the approach of my own. At this point, as though to proclaim the lesson aloud and drive it home, there came to my ears at brief intervals a series of remarks which struck them like the trump of the Last Judgment. The first of these was made by the Duchesse de Guermantes; I had just caught sight of her, passing between a double hedge of curious onlookers, who, not fully aware of the marvellous artifices of toilet and aesthetic which evoked these responses within them, yet feeling themselves moved by the sight of this fair, reddish head, this salmon-pink body almost concealed by its fins of black lace and throttled by jewels, gazed at it, with its hereditary sinuosity of line, as they might have gazed at some archaic sacred fish, loaded with precious stones, in which was incarnate the protective genius of the Guermantes family. "Ah! how wonderful to see you," she said to me, "you, my oldest friend!" And though the vanity of the some-time young man from Combray who had never for a moment thought that he might become one of her friends, really partici-pating in the real mysterious life that went on in the houses of the Guermantes, with the same title to her friendship as M. de Bréauté or M. de Forestelle or Swann or all those others who were now dead, might well have been flattered by these words, more than anything I was saddened by them. "Her oldest friend!" I said to myself. "Surely she exaggerates. One of the oldest perhaps, but can I really be . . . " At that moment a nephew of the Prince came up to me: "You, as a veteran Parisian . . . " he said to me, and while he was still speaking I was handed a note. Outside the house I had made the acquaintance of a young Létourville, who was related in some way which I had forgotten to the Duchess but who knew at least who I was. He had just left Saint-Cyr, and, telling myself that he would be a nice friend for me, like Saint-Loup, who could initiate me into military matters and explain the changes which had taken place in the army, I had told him that I would see him again at the party and that we might arrange to have dinner together one evening, and for this he had thanked me very civilly. But I had stayed too long lost in thought in the library and the note which he had left for me was to tell me that he had not been able to wait, and to leave me his address. The letter of this imagined comrade ended thus: "With the respectful wishes of your young friend, Létourville." "Young friend!" That was how in the past I had written to men thirty years older than myself, to Legrandin, for example. And now this second lieutenant, whom in my mind's eye I saw as my comrade after the fashion of Saint-Loup, called himself my "young friend"! Since the days of Doncières, it seemed, it was not only military methods that had changed; from this M. de Létourville, with whom I imagined myself sharing the pleasures of a youthful comradeship—and why not, since I appeared to myself to be youthful?—I was separated, it seemed, by an arc traced by an invisible compass whose existence I had not suspected, which removed me so far from the boyish second lieutenant that in the eyes of this "young friend" I was an old gentleman.

Almost immediately afterwards, hearing someone mention the name of Bloch, I asked whether he meant young Bloch or his father (who, though I was not aware of this, had died during the war, from grief, it was said, at seeing France invaded). "I didn't know he had any children," said the Prince, "I didn't even know he was married. But clearly it is the father we are talking about. He is not in the least like a young Bloch," he added with a laugh. "He is quite old enough to have grown-up sons." And I realised that it was my former school-friend who was being discussed. A moment later he came into the room. And indeed superimposed upon the features of Bloch I saw the mild but didactic countenance, the frail movements of the head quickly coming to rest like a piece of clockwork, in which I should have recognised the learned weariness of some amiable old man if at the same time I had not recognised my friend standing before me, so that at once my memories animated him with an uninterrupted flow of youthful enthusiasm which he now no longer seemed to possess. For me, who had known him on the threshold of life and had never ceased to see him thus, he was the friend of my boyhood, an adolescent whose youth I measured by the youth which unconsciously, not believing that I had lived since that time, I attributed to myself. I heard someone say that he quite looked his age, and I was astonished to observe on his face some of those signs which are indeed characteristic of men who are old. Then I understood that this was because he was in fact old and that adolescents who survive for a sufficient number of years are the material out of which life makes old men.

Someone, hearing that I had not been well, asked me whether I was not afraid of catching the influenza of which there was an epidemic at that moment, whereupon another well-wisher reassured me by saying: "Oh! no, it's usually only the young who get it. A man of your age has very little to fear." I was assured also that some of the servants had recognised me. They had whispered my name, and had even, as a lady informed me ("You know the expressions they use"), been heard by her to say: "Look, there's father . . . " (and then my surname), and as I had no children this could only be an allusion to my age.

"What do you mean, did I know the Marshal?" said the Duchess to me. "But I knew figures far more typical of the period: the Duchesse de Galliera, Pauline de Périgord, Monsignor Dupanloup." Hearing her, I naïvely regretted that I had not known what she described as relics of an earlier time. I ought to have reflected that what one calls an earlier time is the period of which one has oneself known only the end: things that we see on the horizon assume a mysterious grandeur and seem to us to be closing over a world which we shall not behold again; but meanwhile we are advancing, and very soon it is we ourselves who are on the horizon for the generations that come after us; all the while the horizon retreats into the distance, and the world, which seemed to be finished, begins again. "I even, when I was a girl," Mme de Guermantes went on, "once saw the Duchesse de Dino. But then, you know I'm no longer a chicken." These last words upset me. "She shouldn't have said that," I thought, "that's the way for an old woman to talk." And immediately I reflected that in fact she was an old woman. "As for you," she continued, "you are always the same, you never seem to change." And this remark I found almost more painful than if she had told me that I had changed, for it proved—if it was so extraordinary that there was so little sign of change in me—that a long time had elapsed. "Yes," she said, "you are astonishing, you look as young as ever," another melancholy remark, which can only mean that in fact, if not in appearance, we have grown old. There was worse to come, for she added: "I have always regretted that you never married. But, who knows, perhaps after all it is fortunate. You would have been old enough to have sons in the war, and if they had been killed, like poor Robert (I still often think of him), sensitive as you are, how would you ever have survived their loss?" And I was able to see myself, as though in the first truthful mirror which I had ever encountered, reflected in the eyes of old people, still young in their own opinion as I in mine, who, when I spoke of "an old man like myself" in the hope of being contradicted, showed in their answering looks, which saw me not as they saw themselves but as I saw them, not a glimmer of protest. For we failed to see our own appearance, our own age, but each one of us, as though it were a mirror that faced him, saw those of the others. And no doubt the discovery that they have grown old causes less sadness to many people than it did to me. But in the first place old age, in this respect, is like death. Some men confront them both with indifference, not because they have more courage than others but because they have less imagination. And then, a man who from his childhood on has aimed at one single idea and who, from idleness and perhaps also because of poor health, has perpetually put off its realisation, every evening striking out as though it had never existed the day that has slipped away and is lost, so that the illness which hastens the ageing of his body retards that of his mind, such a man is more surprised and more appalled to see that all the while he has been living in Time than one who lives little inside himself and, regulating his activities by the calendar, does not in a single horrifying moment discover the total of the years whose mounting sum he has followed day by day. But there was a more serious reason for my distress: I had made the discovery of this destructive action of Time at the very moment when I had conceived the ambition to make visible, to intellectualise in a work of art, realities that were outside Time.

In some of the guests at the party the successive replacement, accomplished in my absence, of each cell by other cells, had brought about a change so complete, a metamorphosis so entire that I could have dined opposite them in a restaurant a hundred times without suspecting that I had known them in the past any more than I would have guessed the royal identity of a sovereign travelling incognito or the hidden vice of a stranger. And even this comparison is hardly adequate to the cases in which I had heard the name of the person before me, for it is perhaps not so extraordinary that a stranger sitting opposite one should be a criminal or a king, but these were people whom I had once known, or rather I had known people who bore the same name and yet were so different that I could not believe that they were the same. Nevertheless, just as I would have tried to introduce into the stranger the idea of royalty or of vice, which in a very short time can give a new face to the unknown person towards whom one might so easily, when one's eyes were still blindfolded, have committed the gaffe of behaving with inappropriate insolence or civility, and in whose unchanged features, once one knows who he is, one discerns traces of distinction or of guilt, so now I set to work to introduce into the face of the unknown, utterly unknown, woman before me the idea that she was, let us say, Mme Sazerat, and I succeeded eventually in restoring the meaning that I had once known to reside in her face, which would, however, have remained for me utterly alienated from its owner—as much the face of another person, wanting in all the human attributes which I had once known it to possess, as that of a man turned back into a monkey—if the name and the affirmation of identity had not, in spite of the arduous nature of the problem, set me on the path of its solution. Sometimes, however, the old image came to light again in my mind with such precision that I was able to essay a confrontation; and then, like a witness brought face to face with a suspect, I was obliged, so great was the difference, to say: "No, I do not recognise this person."

But was I right to tell myself that these special characteristics of individuals would die? I had always considered each one of us to be a sort of multiple organism or polyp, not only at a given moment of time—so that when a speck of dust passes it, the eye, an associated but independent organ, blinks without having received an order from the mind, and the intestine, like an embedded parasite, can fall victim to an infection without the mind knowing anything about it—but also, similarly, where the personality is concerned and its duration through life, I had thought of this as a sequence of juxtaposed but distinct "I's" which would die one after the other or even come to life alternately, like those which at Combray took one another's place within me when evening approached. But I had seen also that these moral cells of which an individual is composed are more durable than the individual himself. I had seen the vices and the courage of the Guermantes recur in Saint-Loup, as also at different times in his life his own strange and ephemeral defects of character, and as in Swann his Semitism. And now I could observe the same phenomenon in Bloch. He had lost his father some years previously, and when I had written to him at the time, he had at first been unable to answer my letter, for, quite apart from the strong family sentiments which often exist in Jewish families, the idea that his father was an altogether exceptional man had imparted to his affection the character of a cult. He had found his loss unbearable and had had to take refuge in a sanatorium, where he stayed for nearly a year. To my condolences he replied in a tone of profound grief which was at the same time almost haughty, so enviable in his eyes was the privilege which I had enjoyed of approaching this exceptional man whose very ordinary two-horse carriage he would have liked to present to some historical museum. And now, as he sat at table in the midst of his family, he was animated by the same wrath against his father-in-law as had animated his own father against M. Nissim Bernard and even interrupted his meals to deliver the same tirades against him. So that just as, in listening to the conversation of Cottard and Brichot and so many others, I had felt that, through the influence of culture and fashion, a single undulation propagates identical mannerisms of speech and thought through a whole vast extent of space, it seemed to me now that throughout the whole duration of time great cataclysmic waves lift up from the depths of the ages the same rages, the same sadnesses, the same heroisms, the same obsessions, through one superimposed generation after another, and that each geological section cut through several individuals of the same series offers the repetition, as of shadows thrown upon a succession of screens, of a picture as unchanged—though often not so insignificant—as that of Bloch exchanging angry words with his father-in-law, M. Bloch the elder doing the same in the same fashion with M. Nissim Bernard, and many other pairs of disputants whom I had myself never known.

Gilberte de Saint-Loup[21] said to me: "Shall we go and dine together by ourselves in a restaurant?" and I replied: "Yes, if you don't find it compromising to dine alone with a young man." As I said this, I heard everybody round me laugh, and I hastily added:

"or rather, with an old man." I felt that the phrase which had made people laugh was one of those which my mother might have used in speaking of me, my mother for whom I was still a child. And I realised that I judged myself from the same point of view as she did. If in the end I had registered, as she had, certain changes which had taken place since my early childhood, these were, nevertheless, changes which were now very remote. I had not advanced beyond the particular one which, long ago, almost before the remark corresponded with the facts, had made people say: "He's almost a grown-up man now." I still thought that was what I was, but by now the description was absurdly out of date. I did not realise how much I had changed. And indeed, though these people just now had burst out laughing, what was it that made them so sure of the change? I had not a single grey hair, my moustache was black. I should have liked to ask them what the evidence was which revealed the terrible fact.

And now I began to understand what old age was—old age, which perhaps of all the realities is the one of which we preserve for longest in our life a purely abstract conception, looking at calendars, dating our letters, seeing our friends marry and then in their turn the children of our friends, and yet, either from fear or from sloth, not understanding what all this means, until the day when we behold an unknown silhouette, like that of M. d'Argencourt, which teaches us that we are living in a new world; until the day when a grandson of a woman we once knew, a young man whom instinctively we treat as a contemporary of ours, smiles as though we were making fun of him because to him it seems that we are old enough to be his grandfather—and I began to understand too what death meant and love and the joys of the spiritual life, the usefulness of suffering, a vocation, etc. For if names had lost most of their individuality for me, words on the other hand now began to reveal their full significance. The beauty of images is situated in front of things, that of ideas behind them. So that the first sort of beauty ceases to astonish us as soon as we have reached the things themselves, but the second is something that we understand only when we have passed beyond them.

The cruel discovery which I had just made could not fail to be of service to me so far as the actual material of my book was concerned. For I had decided that this could not consist uniquely of the full and plenary impressions that were outside time, and amongst those other truths in which I intended to set, like jewels, those of the first order, the ones relating to Time, to Time in which, as in some transforming fluid, men and societies and nations are immersed, would play an important part. I should pay particular attention to those changes which the aspect of living things undergoes, of which every minute I had fresh examples before me, for, whilst all the while thinking of my work, which I now felt to be launched with such momentum that no passing distractions could check its advance, I continued to greet old acquaintances and to enter into conversation with them. The process of ageing, I found, was not marked in them all by signs of the same sort. I saw someone who was inquiring after my name, and I was told that it was M. de Cambremer. He came up to me and to show that he had recognised me, "Do you still have your fits of breathlessness?" he asked, and, upon my replying in the affirmative, went on: "Well, at least you see that it is no bar to longevity," as if I were already a centenarian. While speaking to him, I fixed my eyes on two or three features which I was able, by an effort of thought, to reintegrate into that complex of my recollections—totally different though it was—which I called his personality. But for a brief moment he turned his head aside. And then I saw that he had been made unrecognisable by the attach-ment of enormous red pouches to his cheeks, which prevented him from opening his mouth or his eyes completely, and the sight of these startled me into silence, since I did not dare to look at what I took to be some form of anthrax which it seemed more polite not to refer to unless he mentioned it first. However, like a courageous invalid, he made no allusion to his malady but talked and laughed, and I feared to appear lacking in sympathy if I did not ask, no less than in tact if I did ask, what was its nature. "But surely they have become less frequent with age?" he continued, still on the subject of my fits of breathlessness. I replied that they had not. "Oh! but my sister has them much less than she used to," he said, in a tone of contradiction, as though what was true of his sister must also be true of me, and as though age were one of a number of remedies which had helped Mme de Gaucourt and which, therefore, he was quite certain must be beneficial to me. Mme de Cambremer-Legrandin joined us and I became more and more afraid that they must think me callous for failing to deplore the symptoms which I observed on her husband's face, yet still I could not pluck up courage to broach the subject myself. "I expect you're glad to see him again," she said. "Yes, but how is he?" I replied, as though doubtful what answer I should receive. "Why, pretty well, as you can see for yourself." She had not noticed the disfigurement which offended my eyes and which was merely one of the masks in the collection of Time, a mask which Time had fastened to the face of the Marquis, but gradually, adding layer to layer so slowly that his wife had perceived nothing. When M. de Cambremer had finished his questions about my breathlessness, it was my turn to inquire in a low voice of someone standing near whether the Marquis's mother was still alive. And now I was beginning to discover that, in the appreciation of the passage of time, the first step is the hardest. At first one finds it extremely difficult to imagine that so much time has elapsed, later the difficulty is to understand how the lapse can have been so slight. Similarly, when one first suddenly becomes aware of the distance separating the thirteenth century from the present, it is difficult to believe that churches built in that age can still exist—but in fact they are to be found all over France. Within a few minutes I had developed, though very much more rapidly, in the same fashion as those who, after finding it hard to believe that somebody they knew in their youth has reached the age of sixty, are very much more surprised fifteen years later to learn that the same person is still alive and is only seventy-five. Having been assured that M. de Cambremer's mother had not died, I asked him how she was. "She is wonderful still," he said, using to describe her an adjective which in certain families—by contrast with those tribes where aged parents are treated without pity—is applied to old people in whom the continued exercise of the most rudimentary and unspiritual faculties, such as hearing, going to mass on foot, sustaining the demise of their relatives with insensibility, is endowed in the eyes of their children with an extraordinary moral beauty.

If some of the women in the room had acknowledged the arrival of old age by starting to paint their faces, it was also manifested in a contrary fashion by the absence of make-up on the features of certain men, where I had never consciously observed it in the past and who yet seemed to me greatly changed since they had given up the hopeless attempt to please and ceased to use it. One of these was Legrandin. The suppression of the pink, which I had never suspected of being artificial, upon his lips and his cheeks gave to his countenance the greyish tinge and also the sculptural precision of stone, so that with his long-drawn and gloomy features he was like some Egyptian god. Or perhaps less like a god than a ghost. He no longer had the heart either to paint himself or to smile, to make his eyes sparkle, to elaborate his ingenious speeches. One was astonished to see him so pale and so dejected, opening his mouth only at rare intervals to make remarks as trivial as those uttered by the spirits of the dead when we summon them to our presence. One wondered what could be the cause that prevented him from being lively, eloquent, charming, as one does when a medium, putting questions that call for long and fascinating answers to the "double" of a man who in his lifetime was brilliant, elicits from him only the most uninteresting replies. And one told oneself that this cause, which had substituted for a Legrandin of rapid movements and rich colour a pale and melancholy phantom Legrandin, was old age.

There were some people whose hair had not turned white. I recognised for instance, when he came up to say a word to his master, the old valet of the Prince de Guermantes. The coarse hairs which bristled all over his cheeks as well as on his skull were still of a red that verged upon pink, yet one could hardly suspect him of using dye like the Duchesse de Guermantes. Nevertheless, he appeared old. One felt merely that in the human race there exist species, like the mosses and the lichens and a great many others in the vegetable kingdom, which do not change at the approach of winter.

Others again had preserved their faces intact and seemed merely to walk with difficulty; at first one supposed that they had something wrong with their legs; only later did one realise that age had fastened its soles of lead to their feet. A few, of whom the Prince d'Agrigente was one, seemed actually to have been embellished by age. His tall, thin figure, with its lacklustre eye and hair that seemed destined to remain a carroty red for all eternity, had turned, through a metamorphosis more appropriate to an insect, into an entirely different old man, whose red hair, too long exposed to view, had been taken out of service like a table-cloth too long in use and replaced by white. His chest had acquired a new corpulence, robust and almost military, which must have necessitated a positive explosion of the fragile chrysalis that I had known; a conscious gravity flooded his eyes, which were tinged also with a new kindliness which made him bow to right and left. And as, in spite of his altered appearance, a certain resemblance could be detected between the puissant prince before me and the portrait preserved in my memory, I marvelled at the power to renew in fresh forms that is possessed by Time, which can thus, while respecting the unity of the individual and the laws of life, effect a change of scene and introduce bold contrasts into two successive aspects of a single person; for many of these people could be identified immediately, but only as rather bad portraits of themselves hanging side by side in an exhibition in which an inaccurate and spiteful artist has hardened the features of one sitter, robbed another of her fresh complexion and her slender figure, spread a gloom over the countenance of a third. Comparing these effigies with those that the eyes of my memory could show me, I preferred the latter. Just as often, when asked by a friend to choose a photograph, one finds the one he offers less good than some other and would like to refuse it, so to each of these people, presented with the new image which they showed me of themselves, I should have liked to say: "No, not this one, it is not so good of you, it's not really like you." I would not have dared to add: "Instead of your own straight and handsome nose, it has given you your father's crooked nose, which I have never seen on you." And yet this was what had happened: the nose was new, but it was a family nose. If this was a portrait-gallery, Time, the artist, had made of all the sitters portraits that were recognisable; yet they were not likenesses, and this was not because he had flattered them but because he had aged them. He was an artist, moreover, who worked very slowly. That replica of Odette's face, for instance, which I had seen as the merest outline of a sketch in Gilberte's face on the day on which I first met Bergotte, Time had at long last now wrought into the most perfect likeness; he was one of those painters who keep a work by them for half a lifetime, adding to it year after year until it is completed.

In some of the guests I recognised after a while not merely themselves but themselves as they had been in the past. Ski, for instance, was no more altered than a flower or a fruit which had been dried. Aged but still immature, one of those first attempts which nature abandons in the rough, he was a living confirmation of the theory which I had been formulating about the bachelor devotees of art. "Marvellous!" he said, taking me by the arm. "I have heard it eight times..." There were others, too, who had not ripened with age, not only art-lovers like Ski but men who had spent their lives in society. Their faces might be surrounded with a first circle of wrinkles and a sweep of white hair but they were still the same babyish faces, with the naïve enthusiasm of an eighteen-year-old. They were not old men, they were very young men in an advanced stage of withering. The marks of life were not deeply scored here, and death, when it came, would find it as easy to restore to these features their youthfulness as it is to clean a portrait which only a little surface dirt prevents from shining with its original brilliance. These men made me think that we are victims of an illusion when, hearing talk of a celebrated old man, we instantly make up our minds that he is kind and just and gentle; for I felt that, forty years earlier, these elderly men had been ruthless young men and that there was no reason to suppose that they had not preserved their youthful arrogance and their vanity, their duplicity and their guile.

And yet, in complete contrast with these, I had the surprise of talking to men and women whom I remembered as unendurable and who had now, I found, lost almost every one of their defects, possibly because life, by disappointing or by gratifying their desires, had rid them of most of their conceit or their bitterness. A rich marriage, with the consequence that struggle and ostentation had ceased to be necessary, the influence perhaps of the wife herself, the slowly acquired knowledge of values beyond those that had formed the whole creed of a frivolous youth, had allowed them to relax the tensions in their character and to display their good qualities. Growing old, they seemed to have acquired a different personality, like those trees whose essential nature appears to be changed by the autumn which alters their colours; the essential marks of old age were manifested in them, but old age, here, was a moral phenomenon. In others, it was almost entirely physical, and so strange were its effects that a person (Mme d'Arpajon, for instance) seemed to me at the same time unknown and familiar. Unknown, for it was impossible to suspect that it was she and in spite of every effort I could not help showing signs, as I responded to her salutation, of the mental activity which made me hesitate between three or four individuals, not one of whom was Mme d'Arpajon and any one of whom I thought that I might be greeting, and greeting with a fervour which must have astonished her, for, fearing in my uncertainty to appear too chilly should she turn out to be an old and close friend, I had made up for the doubtful expression of my eyes by the warmth of my hand-shake and my smile. And yet, in a way, her new appearance was not unfamiliar to me. It was the appearance, often seen by me in the course of my life, of certain stout, elderly women, of whom at the time I had never suspected that, many years earlier, they could have looked like Mme d'Arpajon. So different was she to look at from the woman I had known that one was tempted to think of her as a creature condemned, like a character in a pantomime, to appear first as a young girl, then as a stout matron, with no doubt a final appearance still to come as a quavering, bent old crone. Like a swimmer in difficulties almost out of sight of the shore, she seemed with infinite effort scarcely to move through the waves of time which beat upon her and threatened to submerge her. Yet gradually, as I studied her face, hesitant and uncertain like a failing memory which has begun to lose the images of the past, I succeeded in rediscovering something of the face which I had known, by playing a little game of eliminating the squares and the hexagons which age had added to her cheeks. For in her case the material which the years had superimposed consisted of geometrical shapes, though on the cheeks of other women it might be of quite a different character. On those, for instance, of Mme de Guermantes, in many respects so little changed and yet composite now like a bar of nougat, I could distinguish traces here and there of verdigris, a small pink patch of fragmentary shell-work, and a little growth of an indefinable character, smaller than a mistletoe berry and less transparent than a glass bead.

Some men walked with a limp, and one was aware that this was the result not of a motor accident but of a first stroke: they had already, as the saying is, one foot in the grave. There were women too whose graves were waiting open to receive them: half paralysed, they could not quite disentangle their dress from the tombstone in which it had got stuck, so that they were unable to stand up straight but remained bent towards the ground, with their head lowered, in a curve which seemed an apt symbol of their own position on the trajectory from life to death, with the final vertical plunge not far away. Nothing now could check the momentum of this parabola upon which they were launched; they trembled all over if they attempted to straighten themselves, and their fingers let fall whatever they tried to grasp.

Certain faces, beneath their hood of white hair, had already the rigidity, the sealed eyelids of those who are about to die, and their lips, shaken by an incessant tremor, seemed to be muttering a last prayer. A countenance of which every line was unchanged needed only the substitution of white hair for black or fair to look totally different, for, as theatrical costumiers know, a powdered wig is in itself an adequate disguise which will make its wearer unrecognisable. The Marquis de Beausergent, whom I had seen, as a young lieutenant, in Mme de Cambremer's box on the day on which Mme de Guermantes had been with her cousin in hers, still had the same perfectly regular features, indeed they had become even more regular, since the pathological rigidity brought about by arteriosclerosis had even further exaggerated the impassive rectitude of his dandy's physiognomy and given to his features the intense hardness of outline, almost grimacing in its immobility, that they might have had in a study by Mantegna or Michelangelo. His complexion, once almost ribaldly red, was now solemnly pale; silvery hair, a slight portliness, the dignity of a Doge, an air of fatigue, even of somnolence, all combined to give him a new and premonitory impression of doomed majesty. The square light brown beard had gone and in its place was a square white beard, of the same trim proportions, which so totally transformed his appearance that, noticing that the second lieutenant whom I remembered now had five bands of braid on his sleeve, my first thought was to congratulate him, not on having been promoted colonel but on looking so well in the part of colonel, a disguise for which he seemed to have borrowed, together with the uniform, the lugubrious gravity of the senior officer that his father had been. But there was another guest whose face, in spite of the substitution of a white for a fair beard, had remained lively, smiling and boyish, so that the change of beard merely made him appear more rubicund and more pugnacious and enhanced the sparkle in his eye, giving to the still youthful man about town the inspired air of a prophet.

The transformations effected, in the women particularly, by white hair and by other new features, would not have held my attention so forcibly had they been merely changes of colour, which can be charming to behold; too often they were changes of personality, registered not by the eye but, disturbingly, by the mind. For to "recognise" someone, and, *a fortiori*, to learn someone's identity after having failed to recognise him, is to predicate two contradictory things of a single subject, it is to admit that what was here, the person whom one remembers, no longer exists, and also that what is now here is a person whom one did not know to exist; and to do this we have to apprehend a mystery almost as disturbing as that of death, of which it is, indeed, as it were the preface and the harbinger. I knew what these changes meant,

I knew what they were the prelude to, and that is why the white hair of these women, along with all the other changes, profoundly disquieted me. I was told a name and I was dumbfounded to think that it could be used to describe both the fair-haired girl, the marvellous waltzer, whom I had known in the past, and the massive white-haired lady making her way through the room with elephantine tread. Along with a certain rosiness of complexion, the name was perhaps the only thing common to these two women, the girl in my memory and the lady at the Guermantes party, who were more unlike one another than an *ingénue* and a dowager in a play. To have succeeded in giving to the waltzer this huge body, in encumbering and retarding her movements by the adjustment of an invisible metronome, in substituting—with perhaps as sole common factor the cheeks, larger certainly now than in youth but already in those days blotched with red—for the feather-light fair girl this ventripotent old campaigner, it must have been necessary for life to accomplish a vaster work of dismantlement and reconstruction than is involved in the replacement of a steeple by a dome, and when one considered that this work had been effected not with tractable inorganic matter but with living flesh which can only change imperceptibly, the overwhelming contrast between the apparition before me and the creature that I remembered pushed back the existence of the latter into a past that was more than remote, that was almost unimaginable. One was terrified, because it made one think of the vast periods which must have elapsed before such a revolution could be accomplished in the geology of a face, to see what erosions had taken place all the way along the nose, what huge alluvial deposits at the edge of the cheeks surrounded the whole face with their opaque and refractory masses. It was difficult to find a link between the two figures, past and present, to think of the two individuals as possessing the same name; for just as one has difficulty in thinking that a dead person was once alive or that a person who was alive is now dead, so one has difficulty, almost as great and of the same kind (for the extinction of youth, the destruction of a person full of energy and high spirits, is already a kind of annihilation), in conceiving that she who was once a girl is now an old woman when the juxtaposition of the two appearances, the old and the young, seems so totally to exclude the possibility of their belonging to the same person that alternately it is the old woman and then the girl and then again the old woman who seems to one to be a dream, so that one might well refuse to believe that *this* can ever have been *that*, that the material of *that* has not taken refuge elsewhere but has itself, thanks to the subtle manipulations of Time, turned into *this*, that it is the same matter incorporated in the same body, were it not for the evidence of the similar name and the corroborative testimony of friends, to which an appearance of verisimilitude is given only by the pink upon the cheeks, once a small patch surrounded by the golden corn of fair hair, now a broad expanse beneath the snow.

And often these fair-haired dancers had acquired, along with a wig of white hair, the friendship of duchesses whom in the past they had not known. Nor was this all: having in their youth done nothing but dance, they had been "touched" by art as once a noble lady might have been touched by grace. And as the seventeenth-century lady, when this happened, withdrew into a life of religion, so now her descendant lived in an apartment filled with cubist paintings, a cubist painter worked for her alone and she lived only for him.

As in a snowy landscape, the degree of whiteness attained by a person's hair seemed in general to be an indication of the depth of time through which he or she had lived, just as in a range of mountains the higher peaks, even though they appear to the eye to be on the same level as the rest, nevertheless reveal their greater altitude by the intensity of their snowy whiteness. But there were exceptions to this rule, particularly among the women. Thus the tresses of the Princesse de Guermantes, which, when they were grey and had the lustre of silk, seemed to surround her bulging temples with silver, having in the process of turning white acquired the mattness of wool or tow, seemed now on the contrary, for that reason, to be grey, like snow which has become dirty and lost its brilliance.

Some of the old men whose features had changed tried nevertheless to preserve, fixed upon them in a state of permanency, one of those fugitive expressions which one assumes for a second when posing for a photograph, either in order to show off some good point in one's appearance to the best effect or to conceal a deformity; they seemed to have become, once and for all, snapshots of themselves insusceptible of change.

All these people had taken so much time putting on their disguises that generally these passed unobserved by the men and women who saw them every day. Often they had even been granted a reprieve, thanks to which up to a very late hour they were able to remain themselves. But in these cases the disguise, when it finally came, was assumed more rapidly; for disguise, one way or another, was unavoidable. Mme X——, for instance, had never seemed to me to bear any resemblance to her mother, whom I had known only as an old woman, looking like a little hunched Turk. The daughter, on the other hand, I had always known as a charming woman with an upright carriage, and this for many years she had continued to be, for too many years, in fact, for like someone who must not forget, before night falls, to put on his Turkish disguise, she had left things late and had then been obliged precipitately, almost instantaneously, to hunch herself up so as faithfully to reproduce the appearance of an old Turkish woman that had once been presented by her mother.

Someone offered to reintroduce me to a friend of my youth, whom for ten years I had seen almost every day. As I went up to him he said, in a voice which I recognised very well: "How delightful to see you again after all these years!" But if he was delighted, I was astonished. The familiar voice seemed to be emitted by a gramophone more perfect than any I had ever heard, for, though it was the voice of my friend, it issued from the mouth of a corpulent gentleman with greying hair whom I did not know, and I could only suppose that somehow artificially, by a mechanical device, the voice of my old comrade had been lodged in the frame of this stout elderly man who might have been anybody. And yet I knew that this was my friend; the man who had reintroduced us after all these years was not someone one could suspect of playing a practical joke. My friend himself declared that I had not changed, and I realised that in his own eyes he had not changed. I looked at him more closely. And in fact, except that he had grown so much stouter, he had preserved many features of his former self. And yet I could not take it in that it was he. Then I made an effort to remember. In his youth he had had blue eyes, always laughing and perpetually mobile, in search evidently of something the nature of which I had not asked myself, but something no doubt entirely disinterested, Truth perhaps, pursued in perpetual uncertainty, with a sort of boyish irresponsibility and yet with a wavering respect for all the friends of his family. And now that he had become an important politician, able and masterful, his blue eyes, which in any case had not found what they were seeking, had lost their mobility, and this gave them a look of narrow concentration, as though the brow above them were constantly frowning. His expression was no longer one of gaiety, innocence and spontaneity but of guile and dissimulation. Decidedly, I thought, this must be somebody else, but then suddenly I heard, evoked by something that I had said, his laugh, his old loud, unforced laugh, the one that went with the perpetual gay mobility of his glance. Experienced concert-goers find that orchestrated by X—— the music of Z—— becomes absolutely different, a somewhat subtle distinction which the ignorant public does not comprehend—but to hear the wild, choking laugh of a boy emerge from beneath a look which was as pointed as a well-sharpened blue pencil though set slightly crooked in the face, was more than a mere difference of orchestration. He stopped laughing; I should have liked to recognise my friend, but, like Ulysses in the *Odyssey* when he rushes forward to embrace his dead mother, like the spiritualist who tries in vain to elicit from a ghost an answer which will reveal its identity, like the visitor at an exhibition of electricity who cannot believe that the voice which the gramophone restores unaltered to life is not a voice spontaneously emitted by a human being, I was obliged to give up the attempt.

Nobody was exempt from change, but I had to qualify this statement with the observation that for certain people the tempo of Time itself may be accelerated or retarded. By chance I had met in the street, some four or five years earlier, the Vicomtesse de Saint-Fiacre (the daughter-in-law of the one who had been a friend of the Guermantes). Her sculptural features seemed to assure her of eternal youth, and indeed she was still young. But I was quite unable to recognise her now, in spite of her smiles and her greetings, in the lady before me whose features were so eroded that the original lines of her face could no longer be restored. For three years she had been taking cocaine and other drugs. Her eyes, deeply ringed with black, were almost frantic, and her mouth opened in a ghastly grin. She spent months on end now, I was told, without leaving her bed or her *chaise longue*, and had got up just for this party. Time has, it seems, special express trains which bring their passengers swiftly to a premature old age. But on the parallel track trains almost as rapid may be moving in the opposite direction. I took M. de Courgivaux for his son, for he looked the younger of the two—though he must have been more than fifty, he seemed younger than he had when he was thirty. He had found an intelligent doctor and given up alcohol and salt, and the result was that he had returned to his early thirties and on this particular day looked even younger still, for the reason that, that very morning, he had had his hair cut.

A curious thing was that the phenomenon of old age seemed, in its different modes, to take into account particular social habits. Thus certain great noblemen, who had always worn the plainest alpaca cloth and on their heads old straw hats which a man of the lower middle class would have refused to put on, had aged in the same fashion as the gardeners and the peasants in whose society they had spent their lives. Patches of brown had begun to spread over their cheeks and their faces had turned yellower and darker like the pages of an old book.

I thought also of all those who were not at the party because they were too weak or too ill to be there, those whom their secretary, seeking to give the illusion of their survival, had excused by one of those telegrams which from time to time were handed to the Princess, those invalids, moribund for years, who no longer leave their beds, no longer move, and even in the midst of the frivolous attentions of visitors, drawn to them by the curiosity of a tourist or the pious hopes of a pilgrim, with their eyes closed and their rosaries clutched in hands which feebly push back the sheet that is already a mortuary shroud, are like monumental figures, carved by illness until the skeleton is barely covered by a flesh which is white and rigid as marble, lying stretched upon a tomb.

There were men in the room whom I knew to be related to each other without it ever having crossed my mind that they had a feature in common. In admiring, for instance, the old hermit with white hair who was Legrandin in a new guise, I suddenly observed, with the satisfaction almost of a zoologist when he makes a scientific discovery, in the transitions between the planes of his cheeks the same construction as in the cheeks of his young nephew, Léonor de Cambremer, who appeared nevertheless to bear no resemblance to him; and to this first common feature I added another which I had never yet noticed in Léonor de Cambremer, and then again others, none of which was included in the youthful synthesis of the nephew which habitually presented itself to me, until soon I had of him a caricature which was truer and more profound for not being a literal representation: his uncle now seemed to me simply a young Cambremer who to amuse himself had assumed the countenance of the old man that he would in fact one day be, so that now it was not merely what had become of the young men of my own youth but what would one day become of those of today that impressed upon me with such force the sensation of Time.

The women sought to remain in contact with whatever had been most individual in their charm, but often the new matter of their face no longer lent itself to this purpose. Those features upon which had been engraved, if not their youth, at least their beauty, had disappeared, and they had endeavoured, with the face that remained to them, to construct a new beauty for themselves. Displacing, if not the centre of gravity, at least the central point of the perspective of their face, and grouping their features around it in a new pattern, they began at the age of fifty to display a beauty of a new type, in the same way that late in life a man may embark on a new profession or a piece of ground which has become useless as a vineyard may be turned over to the production of sugar beet. And in the midst of these new features a second youth was made to bloom. The only women who failed to adjust themselves to this kind of transformation were the ones who were either too beautiful or too ugly. The former were like some block of marble, the lines in which, once it has been carved, are final and admit of no change; ageing, they merely crumbled away like a statue. The others, those who had some deformity of face, actually had certain advantages over the beautiful women. In the first place they were the only women whom one instantly recognised. One knew, for example, that in the whole of Paris there could only be one mouth like *that*, so that at this party, where I failed to recognise almost everybody, I could at least put a name to the possessor of the mouth. And then they did not even appear to have aged. Old age is something human; these were monsters, and they no more seemed to have "changed" than whales.

Others too, both men and women, seemed not to have aged; their figures were just as slim, their faces as young. But if, to speak to them, one approached rather near to the face with the smooth skin and the delicate contours it then appeared quite different, like the surface of a plant or a drop of water or blood when you look at it under a microscope. At close quarters I could distinguish numerous greasy patches on the skin which I had supposed to be smooth and which now, because of these marks, I found repulsive. Nor could the lines of the face stand up to this magnification. That of the nose was seen now to be broken and rounded, its regularity marred by the same oily patches as the rest of the face; and the eyes at short range retreated behind pockets of flesh which destroyed the resemblance of the person before me to the one whom I had known in the past and thought that I had met again. So that these particular guests were young when seen at a distance but their age increased with the enlargement of the face and the possibility of studying its different planes; it was dependent upon the spectator, who to see them as young had to place himself correctly and to view them only with that distant inspection which diminishes its object like the lens selected by an oculist for a long-sighted elderly person; old age here, like the presence of infusoria in a drop of water, was made apparent not so much by the advance of the years as by a greater degree of accuracy in the scale of the observer's vision.

Some women no doubt were still easily recognisable: their faces had remained almost the same and they had merely, out of pro-priety and in harmony with the season, put on the grey hair which was their autumn attire. But there were others, and there were men too, whose metamorphosis was so complete, their identity so impossible to establish—that old monk, for instance, in a corner of the room and the notorious rake whom one remembered, were they the same person?—that it was of the art not so much of the actor as of certain prodigiously gifted mimes, of whom the supreme example is Fregoli, that these fabulous transformations reminded one. The old woman whose charm had resided in her indefinable and melancholy smile would have liked to weep, at first, when she realised that this smile could no longer break through with its radiance to the surface of the plaster mask with which age had covered her face. Then suddenly, weary of trying to please and finding it more intelligent, more amusing to resign herself to the inevitable, she had started to use it like a mask in the theatre, as a way of making people laugh. But with few exceptions the women strained every nerve in a ceaseless struggle against old age and held out the mirror of their features towards beauty, as it receded, as to a setting sun whose last rays they longed passionately to preserve. To achieve this end some of them tried to plane away all the irregularities of their face, to enlarge its smooth, white surface, renouncing the piquancy of dimples that had not long to live, the archness of a smile condemned and already half disarmed, while others, seeing that beauty had vanished beyond recall and taking refuge perforce in expression, like an actress whose skill in the art of diction makes up for the loss of her voice, clung desperately to a pout, to a pretty crow's-foot, to a dreamy glance, to a smile sometimes which, because of the incoordination of muscles that no longer obeyed the brain, made them look as though they were in tears.

Even in the case of the men who had changed very little—those, for instance, whose moustaches had merely turned white—one felt that the changes were not strictly speaking material. One might have been looking at these men through a vapour which imparted its own colour to them, or through a tinted optical glass which altered the appearance of their faces and above all, by making them slightly blurred, showed one that what it enabled us to see "life-size" was in reality a long way away, separated from us, it is true, by a distance other than spatial but from the depths of which, nevertheless, as from a further shore, we felt that they had as much difficulty in recognising us as we them. Only perhaps Mme de Forcheville, as though she had been injected with some liquid, some sort of paraffin with the property of inflating the skin but protecting it from change, might have been an old-fashioned cocotte "stuffed" for the benefit of posterity. Setting out from the idea that people have remained unchanged, one finds them old. But once one starts with the idea that they are old, meeting them again one does not think that they look too bad. In the case of Odette one could say much more than this; her appearance, once one knew her age and expected to see an old woman, seemed a defiance of the laws of chronology, more miraculous even than the defiance of the laws of nature by the conservation of radium. If I failed at first to recognise her, this was, uniquely, not because she had but because she had not changed. I had learnt in the last hour to take into account the new items that are added to people by Time and that had to be subtracted by me if I wanted to find my friends again as I had known them in the past, and I now rapidly made this calculation, adding to the former Odette the number of years which had passed over her; but the result at which I arrived was a person who could not, it seemed, be the one before me, precisely because she, the woman at the party, was so like the Odette of old days. In part, of course, this effect was achieved by rouge and dye. Beneath her flat golden hair—a little like the ruffled chignon of a big mechanical doll, above a face with a fixed expression of surprise which might also have belonged to a doll—on top of which rested a straw hat that was also flat, she might well have been "The Exhibition of 1878" (of which she would without a doubt, above all had she then been as old as she was today, have been the most fantastic marvel) coming forward on to the stage to speak her two lines in a New Year revue, but the Exhibition of 1878 played by an actress who was still young.

Another figure from the same period, who had been a minister before the era of Boulangism and was now in the government again, passed beside us, wafting to the ladies a tremulous and remote smile, but with the air of being imprisoned in a thousand chains of the past, like a little phantom paraded up and down by an invisible hand or—diminished in stature and altered in substance—a reduced version of himself in pumice stone. This former Prime Minister, now so well received in the Faubourg Saint-Germain, had at one time been the object of criminal proceedings, and had been execrated both by society and by the people. But thanks to the renewal of the individuals who compose these two bodies and to the renewal, within the surviving individuals, of passions and even of memories, nobody now knew this and he was held in high honour. For the fact is that there is no humiliation so great that one should not accept it with unconcern, knowing that at the end of a few years our misdeeds will be no more than an invisible dust buried beneath the smiling and blooming peace of nature. The man whose reputation is momentarily under a cloud will soon find himself, thanks to the balancing mechanism of Time, caught and held between two new social levels which will have for him nothing but deference and admiration. But Time alone will achieve this result and at the moment of his downfall nothing can console him for the fact that the young dairy-maid across the street heard the crowd shout "Bribery and corruption!" at him and saw them shake their fists as he climbed into the Black Maria—for the dairy-maid does not see things in the perspective of Time and does not know that the men who receive the incense of praise from this morning's newspapers were yesterday in disgrace and that the fallen politician, who at this moment feels the shadow of prison bars upon him and yet perhaps, as he thinks of the dairy-maid, cannot find within himself the humble words which might win her sympathy, will one day be extolled by the press and sought after by duchesses. And Time in the same way makes family quarrels recede into the distance. At the Princesse de Guermantes's party, for instance, there was a couple, husband and wife, who were respectively nephew and niece of two men, now dead, who had once come to blows and—

worse still—one of them, still further to humiliate the other, had
sent him as seconds his concierge and his butler, indicating that in
his judgment gentlemen would have been too good for him. But
these stories slumbered in the pages of the newspapers of thirty
years ago and nobody now remembered them. And thus the
drawing-room of the Princesse de Guermantes—illuminated,
oblivious, flowery—was like a peaceful cemetery. Time in this
room had done more than decompose the living creatures of a
former age, it had rendered possible, had created new associations.

To return to the politician, in spite of his change of physical
substance, just as profound as the transformation of the moral ideas
which his name now connoted to the public, in spite (to say the
same thing more simply) of the lapse of so many years since he had
been Prime Minister, he was once again a member of the Cabinet,
whose leader had given him a portfolio in the recent reshuffle
rather in the way that a theatrical producer gives a part to an old
actress friend long since retired, whom he judges nevertheless to
be, even now, better able to interpret a part with subtlety than any
of her younger successors and whom he knows, also, to be in
financial straits, and who in the event, at the age of nearly eighty,
exhibits once more to the public almost the fullness of her talent,
with that continued vitality which one is later astonished to have
observed up to the very threshold of death.

But if the politician was extraordinary, Mme de Forcheville was
so miraculous that one could not even say that she had grown
young again—it was more as though, with all her carmines and her
russets, she had bloomed for a second time. Even more than the
embodiment of the Universal Exhibition of 1878, she might have
been the principal rarity and attraction of a flower show of today.
And indeed, for me she seemed to say, not so much: "I am the
Exhibition of 1878" as: "I am the Allée des Acacias of 1892." That
was where, it seemed, she still might have been. And just because
she had not changed she seemed scarcely to be alive. She looked
like a rose that has been sterilised. I greeted her and her eyes
travelled for a while over my face, searching for my name as a
schoolboy searches on the face of his examiner for the answer that
he might more easily have found in his own head. Then I told her
who I was and at once, as though the sound of my name had
broken a spell and I had lost the look of an arbutus-tree or a
kangaroo which age no doubt had given me, she recognised me
and started to talk to me in that strangely individual voice which

people who had admired her acting in some little theatre were astonished, when they were invited to meet her at a luncheon-party, to find again, throughout the whole conversation, for as long as they cared to listen, in each one of her remarks. It was a voice that had not changed, exaggeratedly warm, caressing, with a trace of an English accent. And yet, just as her eyes appeared to be looking at me from a distant shore, her voice was sad, almost suppliant, like the voice of the shades in the *Odyssey*. Odette would still have been able to act. I complimented her on her youthfulness. "How nice of you, *my dear*," she said, "thank you," and, as it was difficult for her to express a sentiment, even the most sincere, in a manner that was not rendered artificial by her anxiety to be what she supposed was smart, she repeated several times: "Thank you *so* much, thank you *so* much." I meanwhile, who had once walked miles to see her pass in the Bois, who the first time that I had visited her house had listened to the sound of her voice as it fell from her lips as though it were some priceless treasure, now found the minutes that I was obliged to pass in her company interminable simply because I did not know what on earth to say to her, and I withdrew, thinking to myself that not only had Gilberte's remark, "You take me for my mother" been true[22] but that the likeness could only be flattering to the daughter.

Gilberte, for that matter, was by no means the only guest at the party in whom family features had become apparent which hitherto had remained as invisible in their faces as the coiled and hidden parts of a seed which one day will burst out into growth in a manner that it is impossible to foresee. Thus, in this woman or that man, at about the age of fifty an enormous maternal hook had arrived to transform a nose which until then had been straight and pure. And the complexion of another woman, a banker's daughter, from being as fresh as that of a milkmaid grew first russet and then coppery and finally assumed as it were a reflexion of the gold which her father had so lovingly handled. Some people had even in the end come to resemble the district in which they lived, bearing on their faces a sort of replica of the Rue de l'Arcade or the Avenue du Bois or the Rue de l'Elysée. But most commonly they reproduced the features of their parents.

Alas, Mme de Forcheville's second flowering was not to last for ever. Less than three years later I was to see her at an evening party given by Gilberte, not quite in her dotage but showing signs of senility and grown incapable of concealing beneath a mask of immobility what she was thinking, or rather (for thinking is too elevated a term) what she was passively experiencing, nodding her head, compressing her lips, shaking her shoulders in response to every impression that she felt, like a drunkard or a small child or those poets who, unaware of their surroundings and seized by inspiration, compose verses in the midst of a social occasion and frown and pout as they proceed to the dinner-table with an astonished lady on their arm. The impressions of Mme de Forcheville—except that single sentiment which was the cause of her presence at the party: her tender affection for her beloved daughter and her pride that she should be giving so brilliant a party, a pride which, in the mother, could not disguise the melancholy of being herself now nothing—these impressions were not joyful, their message was merely that she must not relax her defence against the snubs which were showered upon her, a defence, however, as timorous as that of a child. On all sides one heard people say: "I don't know whether Mme de Forcheville recognises me, perhaps I ought to get someone to introduce me to her again." "You may as well spare yourself the trouble," a booming voice would reply, its owner not suspecting that Gilberte's mother could hear every word—or perhaps not caring if she could. "It's quite unnecessary. You wouldn't find her at all amusing! She's best left alone in her corner. She's bit gaga, you know." Furtively Mme de Forcheville shot a glance from her eyes which had remained so beautiful at the authors of these offensive remarks, then swiftly withdrew it for fear of having been rude, but was distressed nevertheless by the insult, and though she smothered her feeble indignation one saw her head shake and her breast heave until presently another glance was shot at another guest who had expressed himself just as discourteously—yet nothing of all this seemed to surprise her very much, for having felt extremely unwell for several days, she had covertly suggested to her daughter that she should put off her party, but her daughter had refused. Mme de Forcheville did not love her any the less: the sight of all the duchesses entering the room, the admiration of all the guests for the large new house, flooded her heart with joy, and when finally the Marquise de Sabran was announced, who was at that moment the lady at whom one arrived after laboriously ascending the topmost rungs of the social ladder, Mme de Forcheville felt that she had been a good and far-sighted mother and that her maternal task was accomplished. New guests arrived to titter at her and again she shot her glances and spoke to herself, if a mute language expressed only in gesture can be described as speech. Beautiful still, she had become—what she had never been in the past—infinitely pathetic; she who had been unfaithful to Swann and to everybody found now that the entire universe was unfaithful to her, and so weak had she become that, the roles being reversed, she no longer dared to defend herself even against men. And soon she would not defend herself even against death. But we have anticipated, and let us now go back three years, to the afternoon party which is being given by the Princesse de Guermantes.

I had difficulty in recognising my friend Bloch, who was now in fact no longer Bloch since he had adopted, not merely as a pseudonym but as a name, the style of Jacques du Rozier, beneath which it would have needed my grandfather's flair to detect the "sweet vale of Hebron" and those "chains of Israel" which my old schoolmate seemed definitively to have broken. Indeed an English chic had completely transformed his appearance and smoothed away, as with a plane, everything in it that was susceptible of such treatment. The once curly hair, now brushed flat, with a parting in the middle, glistened with brilliantine. His nose remained large and red, but seemed now to owe its tumescence to a sort of permanent cold which served also to explain the nasal intonation with which he languidly delivered his studied sentences, for just as he had found a way of doing his hair which suited his complexion, so he had found a voice which suited his pronunciation and which gave to his old nasal twang the air of a disdainful refusal to articulate that was in keeping with his inflamed nostrils. And thanks to the way in which he brushed his hair, to the suppression of his moustache, to the elegance of his whole figure—thanks, that is to say, to his determination—his Jewish nose was now scarcely more visible than is the deformity of a hunchbacked woman who skilfully arranges her appearance. But above all—and one saw this the moment one set eyes on him—the significance of his physiognomy had been altered by a formidable monocle. By introducing an element of machinery into Bloch's face this monocle absolved it of all those difficult duties which a human face is normally called upon to discharge, such as being beautiful or expressing intelligence or kindliness or effort. The monocle's mere presence even absolved an interlocutor, in the first place, from asking himself whether the face was pleasant to look at or not, just as, when a shop-assistant has told you that some object imported from

England is "the last word in chic," you no longer dare to ask yourself whether you really like it. In any case, behind the lens of this monocle Bloch was now installed in a position as lofty, as remote and as comfortable as if it had been the glass partition of a limousine and, so that his face should match the smooth hair and the monocle, his features never now expressed anything at all.

Bloch asked me to introduce him to the Prince de Guermantes, and this operation raised for me not a shadow of those difficulties which I had come up against on the day when I went to an evening party at his house for the first time, difficulties which had then seemed to me a part of the natural order, whereas now I found it the simplest thing in the world to introduce to the Prince a guest whom he had invited himself and I should even have ventured, without warning, to bring to his party and introduce to him someone whom he had not invited. Was this because, since that distant era, I had become an intimate member, though for a long time now a forgotten one, of that fashionable world in which I had then been so new? Was it, on the contrary, because I did not really belong to that world, so that all the imaginary difficulties which beset people in society no longer existed for me once my shyness had vanished? Was it because, having gradually come to see what lay behind the first (and often the second and even the third) artificial appearance of others, I sensed behind the haughty disdain of the Prince a great human avidity to know people, to make the acquaintance even of those whom he affected to despise? Was it also because the Prince himself had changed, like so many men in whom the arrogance of their youth and of their middle years is tempered by the gentleness of old age—particularly as the new men and the unknown ideas whose progress they had once resisted are now familiar to them, at least by sight, and they see that they are accepted all round them in society—a change which takes place more effectually if old age is assisted in its task by some good quality or some vice in the individual which enlarges the circle of his acquaintance, or by the revolution wrought by a political conversion such as that of the Prince to Dreyfusism?

Bloch started to question me, as years ago, when I first began to go to parties, I had questioned others—a habit which I had not quite lost—about the people whom I had known in society in the old days and who were as remote, as unlike anybody else, as those inhabitants of the world of Combray whom I had often sought to "place" exactly. But Combray for me had a shape so distinctive, so impossible to confuse with anything else, that it might have been a piece of a jigsaw puzzle which I could never succeed in fitting into the map of France. "So the Prince de Guermantes can give me no idea either of Swann or of M. de Charlus?" asked Bloch, whose manner of speaking I had borrowed long ago and who now frequently imitated mine. "None at all." "But what was so different about them?" "To know that, you would have had to hear them talk yourself. But that is impossible. Swann is dead and M. de Charlus is as good as dead. But the differences were enormous." And seeing Bloch's eyes shine at the thought of what these marvellous personages must have been, I wondered whether I was not exaggerating the pleasure which I had got from their company, since pleasure was something that I had never felt except when I was alone and the real differentiation of impressions takes place only in our imagination. Bloch seemed to guess what I was thinking. "Perhaps you make it out to be more wonderful than it really was," he said; "our hostess today, for instance, the Princesse de Guermantes, I know she is no longer young, still it is not so many years since you were telling me about her incomparable charm, her marvellous beauty. Well, I grant you she has a certain splendour, and she certainly has those extraordinary eyes you used to talk about, but I can't say I find her so fantastically beautiful. Of course, one sees that she is a real aristocrat, but still . . ." I was obliged to tell Bloch that the woman I had described to him was not the one he was talking about. The Princesse de Guermantes had died and the present wife of the Prince, who had been ruined by the collapse of Germany, was the former Mme Verdurin. "That can't be right, I looked in this year's Gotha," Bloch naïvely confessed to me, "and I found the Prince de Guermantes, living at this address where we are now and married to someone of the utmost grandeur, let me try to remember, yes, married to Sidonie, Duchesse de Duras, _née_ des Baux." This was correct. Mme Verdurin, shortly after the death of her husband, had married the aged and impoverished Duc de Duras, who had made her a cousin of the Prince de Guermantes and had died after two years of marriage. He had served as a useful transition for Mme Verdurin, who now, by a third marriage, had become Princesse de Guermantes and occupied in the Faubourg Saint-Germain a lofty position which would have caused much astonishment at Combray, where the ladies of the Rue de l'Oiseau, Mme Goupil's daughter and Mme Sazerat's stepdaughter, had during these last years, before she married for the third time, spoken with a sneer of "the Duchesse de Duras" as though this were a role which had been allotted to Mme Verdurin in a play. In fact, the Combray principle of caste requiring that she should die, as she had lived, as Mme Verdurin, her title, which was not deemed to confer upon her any new power in society, did not so much enhance as damage her reputation. For "to make tongues wag," that phrase which in every sphere of life is applied to a woman who has a lover, could be used also in the Faubourg Saint-Germain of women who write books and in the respectable society of Combray of those who make marriages which, for better or for worse, are "unsuitable." After the twice-widowed lady had married the Prince de Guermantes, the only possible comment was that he was a false Guermantes, an impostor. For me, in this purely nominal identity, in the fact that there was once again a Princesse de Guermantes and that she had absolutely nothing in common with the one who had cast her spell upon me, who now no longer existed and had been robbed of name and title like a defenceless woman of her jewels, there was something as profoundly sad as in seeing the material objects which the Princess Hedwige had once possessed—her country house and everything that had been hers—pass into the possession and enjoyment of another woman. The succession of a new individual to a name is melancholy, as is all succession, all usurpation of property; and yet for ever and ever, without interruption, there would come, sweeping on, a flood of new Princesses de Guermantes—or rather, centuries old, replaced from age to age by a series of different women, of different actresses playing the same part and then each in her turn sinking from sight beneath the unvarying and immemorial placidity of the name, one single Princesse de Guermantes, ignorant of death and indifferent to all that changes and wounds our mortal hearts.

Of course, even these external changes in the figures whom I had known were no more than symbols of an internal change which had been effected day by day. Perhaps these people had continued to perform the same actions, but gradually the idea which they entertained both of their own activities and of their acquaintances had slightly altered its shape, so that at the end of a few years, though the names were unchanged, the activities that they enjoyed and the people whom they loved had become different and, as they themselves had become different individuals, it was hardly surprising that they should have new faces.

But there were also guests whom I failed to recognise for the reason that I had never known them, for in this drawing-room, as well as upon individuals the chemistry of Time had been at work upon society. This coterie, within the specific nature of which, delimited as it was by certain affinities that attracted to it all the great princely names of Europe and by forces of an opposite kind which repelled from it anything that was not aristocratic, I had found, I thought, a sort of corporeal refuge for the name of Guermantes, this coterie, which had seemed to confer upon that name its ultimate reality, had itself, in its innermost and as I had thought stable constitution, undergone a profound transformation. The presence of people whom I had seen in quite different social settings and whom I would never have expected to penetrate into this one, astonished me less than the intimate familiarity with which they were now received in it, on Christian name terms; a certain complex of aristocratic prejudices, of snobbery, which in the past automatically maintained a barrier between the name of Guermantes and all that did not harmonise with it, had ceased to function. Enfeebled or broken, the springs of the machine could no longer perform their task of keeping out the crowd; a thousand alien elements made their way in and all homogeneity, all consistency of form and colour was lost. The Faubourg Saint-Germain was like some senile dowager now, who replies only with timid smiles to the insolent servants who invade her drawing-rooms, drink her orangeade, present their mistresses to her. However, the sensation of time having slipped away and of the annihilation of a small part of my own past was conveyed to me less vividly by the destruction of that coherent whole which the Guermantes drawing-room had once been than by the annihilation of even the knowledge of the thousand reasons, the thousand subtle distinctions thanks to which one man who was still to be found in that drawing-room today was clearly in his natural and proper place there while another, who rubbed shoulders with him, wore in these surroundings an aspect of dubious novelty. And this ignorance was not merely ignorance of society, but of politics, of everything. For memory was of shorter duration in individuals than life, and besides, the very young, who had never possessed the recollections which had vanished from the minds of their elders, now formed part of society (and with perfect legitimacy, even in the genealogical sense of the word), and the origins of the people whom they saw there being forgotten or unknown, they accepted them at the particular point of their elevation or their fall at which they found them, supposing that things had always been as they were today, that the social position of Mme Swann and the Princesse de Guermantes and Bloch had always been very great, that Clemenceau and Viviani had always been conservatives. And as certain facts have a greater power of survival than others, the detested memory of the Dreyfus case persisting vaguely in these young people thanks to what they had heard their fathers say, if one told them that Clemenceau had been a Dreyfusard, they replied: "Impossible, you are making a confusion, he is absolutely on the other side of the fence." Ministers with a tarnished reputation and women who had started life as prostitutes were now held to be paragons of virtue. (Among the guests was a distinguished man who had recently, in a famous lawsuit, made a deposition of which the sole value resided in the lofty moral character of the witness, in the face of which both judge and counsel had bowed their heads, with the result that two people had been convicted. Consequently, when he entered the room there was a stir of curiosity and of deference. This man was Morel. I was perhaps the only person present who knew that he had once been kept by Saint-Loup and at the same time by a friend of Saint-Loup. In spite of these recollections he greeted me with pleasure, though with a certain reserve. He remembered the time when we had seen each other at Balbec, and these recollections had for him the poetry and the melancholy of youth.) Someone having inquired of a young man of the best possible family whether Gilberte's mother had not formerly been the subject of scandal, the young nobleman replied that it was true that in the earlier part of her life she had been married to an adventurer of the name of Swann, but that subsequently she had married one of the most prominent men in society, the Comte de Forcheville. No doubt there were still a few people in the room—the Duchesse de Guermantes was one—who would have smiled at this assertion (which, in its denial of Swann's position as a man of fashion, seemed to me monstrous, although I myself, long ago at Combray, had shared my great-aunt's belief that Swann could not be acquainted with "princesses"), and others also not in the room, women who might have been there had they not almost ceased to leave their homes, the Duchesses of Montmorency and

Mouchy and Sagan, who had been close friends of Swann and had never set eyes on this man Forcheville, who was not received in society at the time when they went to parties. But it could not be denied that the society of those days, like the faces now drastically altered and the fair hair replaced by white, existed now only in the memories of individuals whose number was diminishing day by day. During the war Bloch had given up going out socially, had ceased to visit the houses which he had once frequented and where he had cut anything but a brilliant figure. On the other hand, he had published a whole series of works full of those absurd sophistical arguments which, so as not to be inhibited by them myself, I was struggling to demolish today, works without originality but which gave to young men and to many society women the impression of a rare and lofty intellect, a sort of genius. And so it was after a complete break between his earlier social existence and this later one that he had, in a society itself reconstituted, embarked upon a new phase of his life, honoured and glorious, in which he played the role of a great man. Young people naturally did not know that at his somewhat advanced age he was in fact making his first appearance on the social scene, particularly as, by sprinkling his conversation with the few names which he had retained from his acquaintance with Saint-Loup, he was able to impart to his prestige of the moment a sort of indefinite recession in depth. In any case he was regarded as one of those men of talent who in every epoch have flourished in the highest society, and nobody thought that he had ever frequented any other.

Survivors of the older generation assured me that society had completely changed and now opened its doors to people who in their day would never have been received, and this comment was both true and untrue. On the one hand it was untrue, because those who made it failed to take into account the curve of time which caused the society of the present to see these newly received people at their point of arrival, whilst they, the older generation, remembered them at their point of departure. And this was nothing new, for in the same way, when they themselves had first entered society, there were people in it who had just arrived and whose lowly origins others remembered. In society as it exists today a single generation suffices for the change which formerly over a period of centuries transformed a middle-class name like Colbert into an aristocratic one. And yet, from another point of view there was a certain truth in the comments; for, if the social position of individuals is liable to change (like the fortunes and the alliances and the hatreds of nations), so too are the most deeply rooted ideas and customs and among them even the idea that you cannot receive anybody who is not chic. Not only does snobbishness change in form, it might one day altogether disappear—like war itself—and radicals and Jews might become members of the Jockey. Some people, who in my own early days in society, giving grand dinner-parties with only such guests as the Princesse de Guermantes, the Duchesse de Guermantes and the Princesse de Parme, and themselves being entertained by these ladies with every show of respect, had been regarded, perhaps correctly, as among the most unimpeachable social figures of the time, yet they had passed away without leaving any trace behind them. Possibly they were foreign diplomats, formerly *en poste* in Paris and now returned to their own countries. Perhaps a scandal, a suicide, an elopement had made it impossible for them to reappear in society; perhaps they were merely Germans. But their name owed its lustre only to their own vanished social position and was no longer borne by anyone in the fashionable world: if I mentioned them nobody knew whom I was talking about, if I spelt out the name the general assumption was that they were some sort of adventurers. People, on the other hand, who according to the social code with which I had been familiar ought not to have been at this party, were now to my great astonishment on terms of close friendship with women of the very best families and the latter had only submitted to the boredom of appearing at the Princesse de Guermantes's party for the sake of these new friends. For the most characteristic feature of this new society was the prodigious ease with which individuals moved up or down the social scale.

If in the eyes of the younger generations the Duchesse de Guermantes seemed to be of little account because she was acquainted with actresses and such people, the elder, the now old ladies of her family, still considered her to be an extraordinary personage, partly because they knew and appreciated her birth, her heraldic pre-eminence, her intimate friendships with what Mme de Forcheville would have called *royalties*, but even more because she despised the parties given by the family and was bored at them and her cousins knew that they could never count upon her attendance. Her connexions with the theatrical and political worlds, in any case only vaguely known in the family, merely had the effect of enhancing her rarity and therefore her prestige. So that while in political and artistic society she was regarded as a creature whom it was hard to define, a sort of unfrocked priestess of the Faubourg Saint-Germain who consorted with Under-Secretaries of State and stars of the theatre, in the Faubourg Saint-Germain itself if one was giving an important evening party one would say: "Is it worth while even asking Oriane? She won't come. Perhaps one should, just for form's sake, but one knows what to expect." And if, at about half-past ten, in a dazzling costume and with a hard glint in her eyes which bore witness to her contempt for all her female cousins, Oriane made her entrance, pausing first on the threshold with a sort of majestic disdain, and remained for a whole hour, this was even more of a treat for the old and noble lady who was giving the party than it would have been in the past for a theatrical manager who had obtained a vague promise from Sarah Bernhardt that she would contribute something to a programme, had the great actress, contrary to all expectation, turned up and recited, in the most unaffected and obliging way, not the piece which she had promised but twenty others. For although all the women there were among the smartest in Paris, the presence of this Oriane who was addressed in a condescending manner by Under-Secretaries and continued none the less ("intelligence governs the world") to try to make the acquaintance of more and more of them, had had the effect which nothing could have achieved without her, of placing the dowager's evening party in a class apart from and above all the other dowagers' evening parties of the same *season* (to use another of those English expressions of which Mme de Forcheville was so fond) which she, Oriane, had not taken the trouble to attend.

As soon as I had finished talking to the Prince de Guermantes, Bloch seized hold of me and introduced me to a young woman who had heard a lot about me from the Duchesse de Guermantes and who was one of the most fashionable women of the day. Not only was her name entirely unknown to me, but it appeared that those of the various branches of the Guermantes family could not be very familiar to her, for she inquired of an American woman how it was that Mme de Saint-Loup seemed to be on such intimate terms with all the most aristocratic people in the room. Now the American was married to the Comte de Farcy, an obscure cousin of the Forchevilles, for whom Forcheville was the grandest name in the world. So she replied ingenuously: "Well, isn't she a Forcheville by birth? And what could be grander than that?" But at least Mme de Farcy, though she naïvely believed the name of Forcheville to be superior to that of Saint-Loup, knew something about the latter. But to the charming lady who was a friend of Bloch and the Duchesse de Guermantes it was utterly unknown, and, being somewhat muddle-headed, she replied in all good faith to a young girl who asked her how Mme de Saint-Loup was related to their host, the Prince de Guermantes: "Through the Forchevilles," a piece of information which the girl passed on as if she had known it all her life to one of her friends, a bad-tempered and nervous girl, who turned as red as a turkeycock the first time a gentleman said to her that it was not through the Forchevilles that Gilberte was connected with the Guermantes, with the result that the gentleman supposed that he had made a mistake, adopted the erroneous explanation himself and lost no time in propagating it. For the American woman dinner-parties and fashionable enter-tainments were a sort of Berlitz School. She heard the names and she repeated them, without having first learnt their precise value and significance. To someone who asked whether Tansonville had come to Gilberte from her father M. de Forcheville I heard the explanation given that, on the contrary, it was a property in her husband's family, that Tansonville was a neighbouring estate to Guermantes and had belonged to Mme de Marsantes, that it had been heavily mortgaged and the mortgage paid off with Gilberte's dowry. And finally, a veteran of the old guard having exchanged memories with me of Swann, friend of the Sagans and the Mouchys, and Bloch's American friend having asked me how I had known Swann, the old man declared that this must have been in the house of Mme de Guermantes, not suspecting that what Swann represented for me was a country neighbour and a young friend of my grandfather. Mistakes of this kind have been made by the most distinguished men and are regarded as particu-larly serious in any society of a conservative temper. Saint-Simon, wishing to show that Louis XIV was of an ignorance which "sometimes made him fall, in public, into the most gross absurd-ities," gives of this ignorance only two examples, which are that the King, not knowing either that Renel belonged to the family of Clermont-Gallerande or that Saint-Herem belonged to that of Montmorin, treated these two men as though they were of low extraction. But at least, in so far as concerns Saint-Herem, we have the consolation of knowing that the King did not die in error, for "very late in life" he was disabused by M. de La Rochefoucauld.

"Even then," adds Saint-Simon with a touch of pity, "it was necessary to explain to him what these houses were, for their names conveyed nothing to him."

This forgetfulness, which with its vigorous growth covers so rapidly even the most recent past, this encroaching ignorance, creates as its own counter-agent a minor species of erudition, all the more precious for being rare, which is concerned with genealogies, the true social position of people, the reasons of love or money or some other kind for which they have allied or misallied themselves in marriage with this family or that, an erudition which is highly prized in all societies where a conservative spirit rules, which my grandfather possessed in the highest degree with regard to the middle classes of Combray and of Paris and which Saint-Simon valued so highly that when he comes to celebrate the marvellous intelligence of the Prince de Conti, before speaking of the recognised branches of knowledge, or rather as though this were the first of them all, he praises him as "a man of a very fine mind, enlightened, just, exact, wide-ranging; vastly well read and of a retentive memory; skilled in genealogies, their chimeras and their realities; of a politeness variously accommodated to rank and merit, rendering all those courtesies that the princes of the blood owe but no longer render and even explaining why he acted as he did and how the other princes exceeded their rights. The knowledge which he had gained from books and from conversation afforded him material for the most obliging comments possible upon the birth, the offices, etc." In a less exalted sphere, in all that pertained to the bourgeois society of Combray and Paris, my grandfather possessed this same knowledge with no less exactitude and savoured it with no less relish. The epicures, the connoisseurs who knew that Gilberte was not a Forcheville, that Mme de Cambremer had not been born a Méséglise nor her nephew's young wife a Valentinois, were already reduced in number. Reduced in number and perhaps not even recruited from among the highest aristocracy (it is not necessarily among devout believers, or even among Catholics of any kind, that you will find those who are most learned on the subject of the *Golden Legend* or the stained glass of the thirteenth century), but often from a minor aristocracy, whose scions have a keener appetite for the high society which they themselves can seldom approach and which the little time that they spend in it leaves them all the more leisure to study. Still, they meet together from time to time and enjoy making each other's acquaintance and giving succulent corporate dinners, like those of the Society of Bibliophiles or the Friends of Rheims, at which the items on the menu are genealogies. To these feasts wives are not admitted, but the husbands, when they get home, remark: "A most interesting dinner. There was a M. de La Raspelière there who kept us spell-bound with his explanation of how that Mme de Saint-Loup with the pretty daughter is not really a Forcheville at all. It was as good as a novel."

The friend of Bloch and of the Duchesse de Guermantes was not only beautifully dressed and charming, she was also intelligent and conversation with her was agreeable, but for me rendered difficult by the novelty to my ears of the names not only of my interlocutress herself but also of most of the people she talked about, although they were the very people who formed the core of society today. The converse also was true: at her request I related various anecdotes of the past, and many of the names which I pronounced meant absolutely nothing to her, they had all sunk into oblivion (all those at least which had shone only with the individual brilliance of a single person and were not the surname, permanent and generic, of some famous aristocratic family, whose exact title even so the young woman seldom knew, having per-haps recently misheard a name at a dinner-party and proceeded to form quite wrong ideas about its pedigree) and she had for the most part never heard them mentioned, having, not merely because she was young but because she had not lived in France for long and when she first arrived had known nobody, only started to go into society some years after I myself had withdrawn from it. So that though for ordinary speech she and I used the same language, when it came to names our vocabularies had nothing in common. The name of Mme Leroi happened to fall from my lips, and by chance, thanks to some elderly admirer, himself an old friend of Mme de Guermantes, my interlocutress had heard of her. But only vaguely and inaccurately, as I saw from the contemptu-ous tone in which this snobbish young woman replied to me: "Yes, I know who you mean by Mme Leroi, an old friend of Bergotte's, I believe," a tone which barely concealed the com-ment: "a woman whom I should never have wished to have in my house." I realised at once that the old friend of Mme de Guermantes, as a perfect man of the world imbued with the Guermantes spirit, one of the essential elements of which was not to appear to attach too much importance to aristocratic friendships, had thought it too stupid, too anti-Guermantes to say: "Mme Leroi, who was a friend of every Royalty and Duchess in Paris," and had preferred to say: "She could be quite amusing. Let me tell you the retort she made to Bergotte one day." But for people who are not already in the know information gleaned in this way from conversation is equivalent only to that which is doled out to the masses by the press and which makes them believe alternatively, depending upon the views of their newspaper, either that M. Loubet and M. Reinach are brigands or that they are great patriots. In the eyes of my interlocutress Mme Leroi had been something like Mme Verdurin as she was before her social transformation, but with less brilliance and with a little clan consisting of one member only, Bergotte. But at least this young woman, by pure chance, had heard the name of Mme Leroi, and she is one of the last of whom so much can be said. Today that name is utterly forgotten, nor is there any good reason why it should be remembered. It does not figure even in the index to the posthumous memoirs of Mme de Villeparisis, whose mind was so much occupied with the lady who bore it. And if the Marquise has omitted to mention Mme Leroi, this is less because in her lifetime that lady had been less than friendly towards her than because, once she was dead, no one was likely to take any interest in her, it is a silence dictated less by the social resentment of a woman than by the literary tact of an author. My conversation with Bloch's fashionable friend was delightful, for she was an intelligent young woman; but this difference which I have described between our two vocabularies made it at the same time both awkward and instructive. For although we know that the years pass, that youth gives way to old age, that fortunes and thrones crumble (even the most solid among them) and that fame is transitory, the manner in which—by means of a sort of snapshot—we take cognisance of this moving universe whirled along by Time, has the contrary effect of immobilising it. And the result is that we see as always young the men and women whom we have known young, that those whom we have known old we retrospectively endow in the past with the virtues of old age, that we trust unreservedly in the credit of a millionaire and the influence of a reigning monarch, knowing with our reason, though we do not actually believe, that tomorrow both the one and the other may be fugitives stripped of all power. In a more restricted field, one that is purely social—as in a simpler problem which initiates a student into difficulties that are more complex but of the same order—the unintelligibility which, in my conversation with the young woman, resulted from the fact that the two of us had lived in the same world but with an interval of twenty-five years between us, gave me the impression, and might have strengthened within me the sense, of History.

And indeed this ignorance of people's true social position which every ten years causes the new fashionable elect to arise in all the glory of the moment as though the past had never existed, which makes it impossible for an American woman just landed in Europe to see that in an age when Bloch was nobody M. de Charlus was socially supreme in Paris and that Swann, who put himself out to please M. Bontemps, had himself been treated with every mark of friendship by the Prince of Wales, this ignorance, which exists not only in new arrivals but also in those who have always frequented adjacent but distinct regions of society, is itself also invariably an effect—but an effect operative not so much upon a whole social stratum as within individuals—of Time. No doubt we ourselves may change our social habitat and our manner of life and yet our memory, clinging still to the thread of our personal identity, will continue to attach to itself at successive epochs the recollection of the various societies in which, even if it be forty years earlier, we have lived. Bloch the guest of the Prince de Guermantes remembered perfectly well the humble Jewish environment in which he had lived at the age of eighteen, and Swann, when he was no longer in love with Mme Swann but with a waitress at that same Colombin's where at one time Mme Swann had thought it smart to go and drink tea (as she did also at the tea-room in the Rue Royale), Swann was very well aware of his own social value—he remembered Twickenham and had no doubt in his mind about the reasons for which he chose to go to Colombin's rather than to call on the Duchesse de Broglie, and he knew also that, had he been a thousand times less "smart" than he was, he would not have become the slightest bit smarter by frequenting Colombin's or the Ritz, since anybody can go to these places who pays. And no doubt the friends, too, of Bloch or of Swann remembered the little Jewish coterie or the invitations to Twickenham and thus, as though they, the friends, were other not very clearly defined "I's" of the two men, made no division in their memories between the fashionable Bloch of today and the sordid Bloch of the past, between the Swann who in his latter days could be seen at Colombin's and the Swann of Buckingham Palace. But these friends were to some extent Swann's neighbours in life, their own lives had developed along lines near enough to his own for their memories to be fairly full of him, whereas other men who were more remote from Swann—at a greater distance measured not perhaps socially but in terms of intimacy, which caused their knowledge of him to be vaguer and their meetings with him rarer—possessed of him recollections that were less numerous and in consequence conceptions that were less fixed. And after thirty years a comparative stranger of this kind no longer has any precise recollection with the power to change the value of the person whom he has before his eyes by prolonging him into the past. In the last years of Swann's life I had heard people, even people in society, say when his name was mentioned, as though this had been his title to fame: "You mean the Swann who goes to Colombin's?" And now, with reference to Bloch, even those who ought to have known better might be heard to inquire: "The Guermantes Bloch? The Bloch who is such a friend of the Guermantes?" These errors which split a life in two and, by isolating his present from his past, turn some man whom one is talking about into another, a different man, a creation of yesterday, a man who is no more than the condensation of his current habits (whereas the real man bears within himself an awareness, linking him to the past, of the continuity of his life), these errors, though they too, as I have said, are a result of the passage of Time, are not a social phenomenon but one of memory. And at that very moment I was presented with an example, of a different variety, it is true, but all the more impressive for that, of this forgetfulness which modifies for us our image of a human being. Long ago a young nephew of Mme de Guermantes, the Marquis de Villemandois, had behaved towards me with a persistent insolence which had obliged me to retaliate by adopting an equally insulting attitude towards him, so that tacitly we had become as it were enemies. This man, while I was engaged in my reflexions upon Time at the Princesse de Guermantes's party, asked someone to introduce him to me, saying that he thought that I had known some of his family, that he had read articles of mine and wanted to make, or remake, my acquaintance. Now it is true to say that with age he had become, like many others, serious instead of rude and frivolous and that he had lost much of his former arrogance, and it is also true that I was a good deal talked about now, though on the strength of some very slight articles, in the circles which he frequented. But these motives for his cordiality, for his making advances to me, were only secondary. The principal motive, or at least the one which permitted the others to come into play, was that—either because he had a worse memory than I or because in the past, since I was then for him a much less important personage than he for me, he had paid less attention to my ripostes than I to his attacks—he had completely forgotten our feud. At most my name recalled to him that he must have seen me, or some member of my family, in the house of one of his aunts. And being uncertain whether he was being introduced to me for the first time or whether we were old acquaintances, he made haste to talk to me about the aunt in whose house he was sure that we had met, remembering that my name had often been mentioned there and not remembering our quarrels. A name: that very often is all that remains for us of a human being, not only when he is dead, but sometimes even in his lifetime. And our notions about him are so vague or so bizarre and correspond so little to those that he has of us that we have entirely forgotten that we once nearly fought a duel with him but remember that, when he was a child, he used to wear curious yellow gaiters in the Champs-Elysées, where he, on the contrary, in spite of our assurances, has no recollection of ever having played with us.

Bloch had come bounding into the room like a hyena. "He is at home now," I thought, "in drawing-rooms into which twenty years ago he would never have been able to penetrate." But he was also twenty years older. He was nearer to death. What did this profit him? At close quarters, in the translucency of a face in which, at a greater distance or in a bad light, I saw only youthful gaiety (whether because it survived there or because I with my recollections evoked it), I could detect another face, almost frightening, racked with anxiety, the face of an old Shylock, waiting in the wings, with his make-up prepared, for the moment when he would make his entry on to the stage and already reciting his first line under his breath. In ten years, in drawing-rooms like this which their own feebleness of spirit would allow him to dominate, he would enter on crutches to be greeted as "the Master" for whom a visit to the La Trémoïlles was merely a tedious obligation. And what would this profit him?

From changes accomplished in society I was all the better able to extract important truths, worthy of being used as the cement which would hold part of my work together, for the reason that such changes were by no means, as at the first moment I might have been tempted to suppose, peculiar to the epoch in which we lived. At the time when I, myself only just "arrived"—newer even than Bloch at the present day—had made my first entry into the world of the Guermantes, I must have contemplated in the belief that they formed an integral part of that world elements that were in fact utterly foreign to it, recently incorporated and appearing strangely new to older elements from which I failed to distinguish them and which themselves, though regarded by the dukes of the day as members of the Faubourg from time immemorial, had in fact—if not themselves, then their fathers or their grandfathers—been the upstarts of an earlier age. So much so that it was not any inherent quality of "men of the best society" which made this world so brilliant, but rather the fact of being more or less completely assimilated to this world which out of people who fifty years later, in spite of their diverse origins, would all look very much the same, formed "men of the best society." Even in the past into which I pushed back the name of Guermantes in order to give it its full grandeur—with good reason, for under Louis XIV the Guermantes had been almost royal and had cut a more splendid figure than they did today—the phenomenon which I was observing at this moment had not been unknown. The Guermantes of that time had allied themselves, for instance, with the family of Colbert, which today, it is true, appears to us in the highest degree aristocratic, since a Colbert bride is thought an excellent match even for a La Rochefoucauld. But it is not because the Colberts, then a purely bourgeois family, were aristocratic that the Guermantes had sought them in a matrimonial alliance, it was because of this alliance with the Guermantes that the Colberts became aristocratic. If the name of Haussonville should be extinguished with the present representative of that house, it will perhaps owe its future renown to the fact that the family today is descended from Mme de Staël, regardless of the fact that before the Revolution M. d'Haussonville, one of the first noblemen of the kingdom, found it gratifying to his vanity to be able to tell M. de Broglie that he was not acquainted with the father of that lady and was therefore no more in a position to present him at court than was M. de Broglie himself, neither of the two men for one moment suspecting that their own grandsons would later marry one the daughter and the other the granddaughter of the authoress of *Corinne*. From the remarks of the Duchesse de Guermantes

I realised that it would have been in my power to play the role of the fashionable commoner in grand society, the man whom everybody supposes to have been from his earliest days affiliated to the aristocracy, a role once played by Swann and before him by M. Lebrun and M. Ampère and all those friends of the Duchesse de Broglie who herself at the beginning of her career had by no means belonged to the best society. The first few times I had dined with Mme de Guermantes how I must have shocked men like M. de Beauserfeuil, less by my actual presence than by remarks indicating how entirely ignorant I was of the memories which constituted his past and which gave its form to the image that he had of society! Yet the day would come when Bloch, as a very old man, with recollections from a then distant past of the Guermantes drawing-room as it presented itself to his eyes at this moment, would feel the same astonishment, the same ill-humour in the presence of certain intrusions and certain displays of ignorance. And at the same time he would no doubt have developed and would radiate around him those qualities of tact and discretion which I had thought were the special prerogative of men like M. de Norpois but which, when their original avatars have vanished from the scene, form themselves again for a new incarnation in those of our acquaintance who seem of all people the least likely to possess them. It was true that my own particular case, the experience that I had had of being admitted to the society of the Guermantes, had appeared to me to be something exceptional. But as soon as I got outside myself and the circle of people by whom I was immediately surrounded, I could see that this was a social phenomenon less rare than I had at first supposed and that from the single fountain-basin of Combray in which I had been born there were in fact quite a number of jets of water which had risen, in symmetry with myself, above the liquid mass which had fed them. No doubt, since circumstances have always about them something of the particular and characters something of the individual, it was in an entirely different fashion that Legrandin (through his nephew's strange marriage) had in his turn penetrated into this exalted world, a fashion quite different from that in which Odette's daughter had married into it or those in which Swann long ago and I myself had reached it. Indeed to me, passing by shut up inside my own life so that I saw it only from within, Legrandin's life seemed to bear absolutely no resemblance to my own, the two seemed to have followed widely divergent paths, and in this respect I was like a stream which from the bottom of its own deep valley does not see another stream which proceeds in a different direction and yet, in spite of the great loops in its course, ends up as a tributary of the same river. But taking a bird's-eye view, as the statistician does who, ignoring the reasons of sentiment or the avoidable imprudences which may have led some particular person to his death, counts merely the total number of those who have died in a year, I could see that quite a few individuals, starting from the same social milieu, the portrayal of which was attempted in the first pages of this work, had arrived finally in another milieu of an entirely different kind, and the probability is that, just as every year in Paris an average number of marriages take place, so any other rich and cultivated middle-class milieu might have been able to show a roughly equal proportion of men who, like Swann and Legrandin and myself and Bloch, could be found at a later stage in their lives flowing into the ocean of "high society." Moreover, in their new surroundings they recognised each other, for if the young Comte de Cambremer won the admiration of society for his distinction, his refinement, his sober elegance, I myself was able to recognise in these qualities—and at the same time in his fine eyes and his ardent craving for social success—characteristics that were already present in his uncle Legrandin, who in spite of his aristocratic elegance of bearing had been no more than a typical middle-class friend of my parents.

Kindness, a simple process of maturation which in the end sweetens characters originally more acid even than that of Bloch, is as widely disseminated as that belief in justice thanks to which, if our cause is good, we feel that we have no more to fear from a hostile judge than from one friendly towards us. And the grandchildren of Bloch would be kind and modest almost from birth. Bloch himself had perhaps not yet reached this stage of development. But I noticed that, whereas once he had pretended to think himself obliged to make a two hours' railway journey in order to visit someone who had scarcely even asked him to come, now that he was flooded with invitations not only to lunch and to dine but to stay for a fortnight here and a fortnight there, he refused many of them and did this without telling people, without bragging that he had received and refused them. Discretion, both in action and in speech, had come to him with social position and with age, with, if one may use the expression, a sort of social longevity. No doubt in the past Bloch had lacked discretion, just as he had been incapable of kindness and devoid of good sense. But certain defects, certain qualities are attached less to this or that individual than to this or that moment of existence considered from the social point of view. One may almost say that they are external to individuals, who merely pass beneath the radiance that they shed as beneath so many solstices, varying in their nature but all pre-existent, general and unavoidable. In the same way a doctor who is trying to find out whether some medicine diminishes or augments the acidity of the stomach, whether it activates or inhibits its secretions, will obtain results which differ not according to the stomach from whose secretions he has removed a small quantity of gastric juice, but according to the more or less advanced stage in the process of ingestion of the drug at which he conducts the experiment.

To return to the name of Guermantes, considered as an agglom-eration of all the names which it admitted into itself and into its immediate neighbourhood, at every moment of its duration it suffered losses and recruited fresh ingredients, like a garden in which from week to week flowers scarcely in bud and preparing to take the places of those that have already begun to wither are confounded with the latter in a mass which presents always the same appearance, except to the people who have not seen the newest blooms before and still preserve in their memories a precise image of the ones that are no longer there.

More than one of the men and women who had been brought together by this party, or of whose existence it had reminded me by evoking for me the aspects which he or she had in turn presented as from the midst of different, perhaps opposite circum-stances one after another they had risen before me, brought vividly before my mind the varied aspects of my own life and its different perspectives, just as a feature in a landscape, a hill or a large country house, by appearing now on the right hand and now on the left and seeming first to dominate a forest and then to emerge from a valley, reveals to a traveller the changes in direction and the differences in altitude of the road along which he is passing. As I followed the stream of memory back towards its source, I arrived eventually at images of a single person separated from one another by an interval of time so long, preserved within me by "I's" that were so distinct and themselves (the images) fraught with mean-ings that were so different, that ordinarily when I surveyed (as I supposed) the whole past course of my relations with that particular person I omitted these earliest images and had even ceased to think that the person to whom they referred was the same as the one whom I had later got to know, so that I needed a fortuitous lightning-flash of attention before I could re-attach this latter-day acquaintance, like a word to its etymology, to the original significance which he or she had possessed for me. Mlle Swann, on the other side of the hedge of pink hawthorn, throwing me a look of which, as a matter of fact, I had been obliged retrospectively to retouch the significance, having learnt that it was a look of desire; Mme Swann's lover—or the man who according to Combray gossip occupied that position—studying me from behind that same hedge with an air of disapproval which, in this case too, had not the meaning which I had ascribed to it at the time, and then later so changed that I had quite failed to recognise him as the gentleman at Balbec examining a poster outside the Casino, the man of whom, when once every ten years I happened to remember that first image, I would say to myself: "How strange! That, though I did not know it, was M. de Charlus!"; Mme de Guermantes at the marriage of Dr Percepied's daughter; Mme Swann in a pink dress in my great-uncle's study; Mme de Cambremer, Legrandin's sister, so fashionable that he was terrified that we might ask him to give us an introduction to her—all these images and many others associated with Swann, Saint-Loup and others of my friends were like illustrations which sometimes, when I chanced to come across them, I amused myself by placing as frontispieces on the threshold of my relations with these various people, but always with the feeling that they were no more than images, not something deposited within me by this particular person, not something still in any way linked to him. Not only do some people have good memories and others bad (without going so far as that perpetual forgetfulness which is the native element of such creatures as the Turkish Ambassadress, thanks to which—one piece of news having evaporated by the end of the week or the next piece having the power to exorcise its predecessor—they are always able to find room in their minds for the news that contradicts what they have previously been told), we find also that two people with an equal endowment of memory do not remember the same things. One of two men, for instance, will have paid little attention to an action for which the other will long continue to feel great remorse, but will have seized on the other hand upon some random remark which his friend let fall almost without thinking and taken it to be the key to a sympathetic character. Again, the fact that we prefer not to be proved wrong when we have uttered a false prophecy cuts short the duration of our memory of such prophecies and permits us very soon to affirm that we never uttered them. Finally, preferences of a more profound and more disinterested kind diversify the memories of different people, so that a poet, for example, who has almost entirely forgotten certain facts which someone else is able to recall, will nevertheless have retained—what for him is more important—a fleeting impression. The effect of all these causes is that after twenty years of absence where one expected to find rancour one finds often involuntary and unconscious forgiveness, but sometimes also we stumble upon a bitterness for which (because we have ourselves forgotten some bad impression that we once made) we can provide no reasonable explanation. Even where the people whom we have known best are concerned, we soon forget the dates of the various episodes in their lives. And because it was at least twenty years since she had first set eyes on Bloch, Mme de Guermantes would have sworn that he had been born in the world to which she herself belonged and had been dandled on the knees of the Duchesse de Chartres when he was two years old.

How often had all these people reappeared before me in the course of their lives, the diverse circumstances of which seemed to present the same individuals always, but in forms and for purposes that were shifting and varied; and the diversity of the points in my life through which had passed the thread of the life of each of these characters had finished by mixing together those that seemed the furthest apart, as if life possessed only a limited number of threads for the execution of the most different patterns. What, for instance, in my various pasts, could be more widely separated than my visits to my great-uncle Adolphe, the nephew of Mme de Villeparisis who was herself a cousin of the Marshal, Legrandin and his sister, and the former tailor who lived in our courtyard and was a friend of Françoise? And yet today all these different threads had been woven together to form the fabric, there of the married lives of Robert and Gilberte Saint-Loup, here of the young Cambremer couple, not to mention Morel and all the others whose conjunction had played a part in forming a set of circumstances of such a nature that the circumstances seemed to me to be the complete unity and each individual actor in them merely a constituent part of the whole. And by now my life had lasted so long that not infrequently, when it brought a person to my notice, I was able, by rummaging in quite different regions of my memory, to find another person, unlike though with the same identity, to add to and complete the first. Even to the Elstirs which I saw hanging here in a position which was itself an indication of his glory I was able to add very ancient memories of the Verdurins, the Cottards, my first conversation with the painter in the restaurant at Rivebelle, the tea-party in his studio at which I had been introduced to Albertine, and a host of other memories as well. Thus a connoisseur of painting who is shown one wing of an altar-piece remembers in what church or which museums or whose private collection the other fragments of the same work are dispersed and, in the same way as by studying the catalogues of sales and haunting the shops of the antique-dealers he finds, in the end, some object which is a twin to one he already possesses and makes a pair with it, he is able to reconstruct in his mind the predella and the whole altar as they once were. As a bucket hauled up on a winch comes to touch the rope several times and on opposite sides, so there was not a character that had found a place in my life, scarcely even a thing, which hadn't turn and turn about played in it a whole series of different roles. If after an interval of several years I rediscovered in my memory a mere social acquaintance or even a physical object, I perceived that life all this while had been weaving round person or thing a tissue of diverse threads which ended by covering them with the beautiful and inimitable velvety patina of the years, just as in an old park a simple runnel of water comes with the passage of time to be enveloped in a sheath of emerald.

It was not merely the outward appearance of these people that made one think of them as people in a dream. In their inward experience too life, which already when they were young, when they were in love, had been not far from sleep, had now more and more become a dream. They had forgotten even their resentments, their hatreds, and in order to be certain that the person before them was the one with whom ten years earlier they had not been on speaking terms they would have had to consult some mnemonic register, but one which, unfortunately, was as vague as a dream in which one has been insulted one does not quite know by whom. All these dreams together formed the substance of the apparent contradictions of political life, where one saw as colleagues in a government men who had once accused each other of murder or treason. And this dream like existence became as torpid as death in certain old men on the days that followed any day on which they had chanced to make love. During those days it was useless to make any demands on the President of the Republic, he had forgotten everything. Then, if he was left in peace for a day or two, the memory of public affairs slowly returned to him, as haphazard as the memory of a dream.

Sometimes it was not merely in a single vivid image that the stranger so unlike the man or woman whom I had later come to know had first appeared before me. For years I had thought of Bergotte as the sweet bard with the snowy locks, for years my limbs had been paralysed, as though I had seen a ghost, by the apparition of Swann's grey top-hat or his wife's violet cloak, or by the mystery with which, even in a drawing-room, the name of her race enveloped the Duchesse de Guermantes; with all these, and with others too, my relations, which in the sequel were to become so commonplace, had had their origin almost in legend, in a delightful mythology which still at a later date prolonged them into the past as into some Olympian heaven where they shone with the luminous brilliance of a comet's tail. And even those of my acquaintanceships which had not begun in mystery, that for instance with Mme de Souvré, so arid today, so purely social in its nature, had preserved among their earliest moments the memory of a first smile calmer and sweeter than anything that was to follow, a smile mellifluously traced in the fullness of an afternoon beside the sea or the close of a spring day in Paris, a day of clattering carriages, of dust rising from the streets and sunny air gently stirring like water. And perhaps Mme de Souvré, had she been removed from this frame, would have been of little significance, like those famous buildings—the Salute, for example—which, without any great beauty of their own, are so well suited to a particular setting that they compel our admiration, but she formed part of a bundle of memories which I valued "all in," as the auctioneers say, at a certain price, without stopping to ask exactly how much of this value appertained to the lady herself.

One thing struck me even more forcibly in all these people than the physical or social changes which they had undergone, and this was the modification in the ideas which they possessed of one another. Legrandin in the past had despised Bloch and never addressed a word to him. Now he went out of his way to be civil. And this was not because of the improvement which had taken place in Bloch's social position—were this the case the fact would scarcely be worthy of mention, for social changes inevitably bring in their train a new pattern of relationships among those who have been affected by them. No: the reason was that people—and in saying "people" I mean "what people are for us"—do not in our memory possess the unvariability of a figure in a painting. Oblivion is at work within us, and according to its arbitrary operation they evolve. Sometimes it even happens that after a time we confuse one person with another. "Bloch? Oh yes, he was someone who used to come to Combray," and when he says Bloch, the speaker is in fact referring to me. Conversely, Mme Sazerat was firmly persuaded that it was I who was the author of a certain historical study of Philip II which was in fact by Bloch. More commonly, you forget after a while how odiously someone has behaved towards you, you forget his faults of character and your last meeting with him when you parted without shaking hands, and you remember on the other hand an earlier occasion when you got on excellently together. And it was to an earlier occasion of this kind that the manners of Legrandin adverted in his new civility towards Bloch, whether because he had lost the recollection of a particular past or because he thought it was to be deliberately eschewed, from a mixture of forgiveness and for-getfulness and that indifference which is another effect of Time. And then, as we have seen, the memories which two people preserve of each other, even in love, are not the same. I had seen Albertine reproduce with perfect accuracy some remark which I had made to her at one of our first meetings and which I had entirely forgotten. Of some other incident, lodged for ever in my head like a pebble flung with force, she had no recollection. Our life together was like one of those garden walks where, at intervals on either side of the path, vases of flowers are placed symmetrically but not opposite to one another. And if this discrepancy of memories may be observed even in the relation of love, even more understandable is it that when your acquaintance with someone has been slight you should scarcely remember who he is or should remember not what you used to think of him but something different, perhaps something that dates from an earlier epoch or that is suggested by the people in whose midst you have met him again, who may only recently have got to know him and see him therefore endowed with good qualities and a social prestige which in the past he did not possess but which you, having forgotten the past, instantly accept.

No doubt life, by placing each of these people on my path a number of times, had presented them to me in particular circumstances which, enclosing them finally on every side, had restricted the view which I had of them and so prevented me from discovering their essence. For between us and other people there exists a barrier of contingencies, just as in my hours of reading in the garden at Combray I had realised that in all perception there exists a barrier as a result of which there is never absolute contact between reality and our intelligence. Even those Guermantes around whom I had built such a vast fabric of dream had appeared to me, when at last I had first approached two of them, one in the guise of an old friend of my grandmother and the other in that of a gentleman who had looked at me in a most disagreeable manner one morning in the gardens of the Casino. So that it was in each case only in retrospect, by reuniting the individual to the name, that my encounter with them had been an encounter with the Guermantes. And yet perhaps this in itself made life more poetic for me, the thought that the mysterious race with the piercing eyes and the beak of a bird, the unapproachable rose-coloured, golden race, had so often and so naturally, through the effect of blind and varied circumstances, chanced to offer itself to my contemplation, to admit me to the circle of its casual and even of its intimate friends, to such a point that when I had wanted to get to know Mlle de Stermaria or to have dresses made for Albertine, it was to one or another of the Guermantes, as being the most obliging of my friends, that I had appealed for help. Admittedly I was bored when I went to their houses, no less bored than I was in the houses of the other society people whom I had later come to know. And in the case of the Duchesse de Guermantes, as in that of certain pages of Bergotte, even her personal charm was visible to me only at a distance and vanished as soon as I was near her, for the reason that it resided in my memory and my imagination. But still, in spite of everything, the Guermantes—and in this respect Gilberte resembled them—differed from other society people in that they plunged their roots more deeply into my past life, down to a level at which I had dreamed more and had had more belief in individuals. Bored I may have been as I stood talking this afternoon to Gilberte or Mme de Guermantes, but at least as I did so I held within my grasp those of the imaginings of my childhood which I had found most beautiful and thought most inaccessible and, like a shop-keeper who cannot balance his books, I could console myself by forgetting the value of their actual possession and remembering the price which had once been attached to them by my desire. But with other people I had not even this consolation, people however with whom my relations had at one time been swollen to an immense importance by dreams that were even more ardent and formed without hope, dreams into which my life of those days, dedicated entirely to them, had so richly poured itself that I could scarcely understand how their fulfilment could be merely this thin, narrow, colourless ribbon of an indifferent and despised intimacy, in which I could rediscover nothing of what had once been their mystery, their fever and their sweetness.

"What has become of the Marquise d'Arpajon?" inquired Mme de Cambremer. "She died," replied Bloch. "Aren't you confusing her with the Comtesse d'Arpajon, who died last year?" The Princesse d'Agrigente joined in the discussion; as the young widow of an old husband who had been very rich and the bearer of a great name she was much sought in marriage, and this had given her great self-assurance. "The Marquise d'Arpajon is dead too," she said, "she died nearly a year ago." "A year ago!" exclaimed Mme de Cambremer, "that can't be right, I was at a musical evening in her house less than a year ago." Bloch was as incapable as any young man about town of making a useful contribution to the subject under discussion, for all these deaths of elderly people were at too great a distance, from the young men because of the enormous difference in age and from a man like Bloch, because of his recent arrival in an unfamiliar society, by way of an oblique approach, at a moment when it was already declining into a twilight which was for him illumined by no memories of its past. And even for people of the same age and the same social background death had lost its strange significance. Hardly a day passed without their having to send to inquire for news of friends and relations *in articulo mortis*, some of whom, they would be told, had recovered while others had "succumbed," until a point was reached where they no longer very clearly remembered whether this or that person who was no longer seen anywhere had "pulled through" his pneumonia or had expired. In these regions of advanced age death was everywhere at work and had at the same time become more indefinite. At this crossroads of two generations and two societies, so ill placed, for different reasons, for distinguishing death that they almost confused it with life, the former of these two conditions had been turned into a social incident, an attribute to be predicated of somebody to a greater or lesser degree, without the tone of voice in which it was mentioned in any way indicating that for the person in question this "incident" was the end of everything. I heard people say: "But you forget that so and so is dead," exactly as they might have said "he has had a decoration" or "he has been elected to the Academy" or—and these last two happenings had much the same effect as death, since they too prevented a man from going to parties—"he is spending the winter on the Riviera" or "his doctor has sent him to the mountains." Perhaps, where a man was well known, what he left behind him at his death helped others to remember that his existence had come to an end. But in the case of ordinary society people of an advanced age it was easy to make a mistake as to whether or no they were dead, not only because one knew little about their past or had forgotten it but because they were in no way whatever linked to the future. And the difficulty that was universally experienced in these cases in choosing from among the alternatives of illness, absence, retirement to the country and death the one that happened to be correct, sanctioned and confirmed not merely the indifference of the survivors but the insignificance of the departed.

"But if she is still alive, why is it that one never sees her anywhere now, nor her husband either?" asked a spinster who liked to make what she supposed was witty conversation. "For the obvious reason," replied her mother, who in spite of her years never missed a party herself, "that they are old; when you get to that age you stay at home." Before you got to the cemetery, it seemed, there was a whole closed city of the old, where the lamps always glimmered in the fog. Mme de Saint-Euverte cut short the debate by saying that the Comtesse d'Arpajon had died in the previous year after a long illness and that more recently the Marquise d'Arpajon had also died, very rapidly, "in some quite unremarkable way," a death which, in virtue of this latter characteristic, resembled the lives of all these people (its unremarkableness explained too why it had passed unnoticed and excused those who had been in doubt). When she heard that Mme d'Arpajon really had died, the spinster cast an anxious glance at her mother, for she feared that the news of the death of one of her "contemporaries" might "be a blow" to her—indeed she already imagined people talking about her mother's death and explaining it in this way: "Madame d'Arpajon's death had been a *great blow* to her." But the old lady on the contrary, far from justifying her daughter's fears, felt every time someone of her own age "disappeared" that she had gained a victory in a contest against formidable competitors. Their deaths were the only fashion in which she still for a moment became agreeably conscious of her own life. The spinster noticed that her mother, who had seemed not displeased to remark that Mme d'Arpajon was one of those tired old people whose days are spent in homes from which they seldom emerge, had been even less displeased to learn that the Marquise had entered the city of hereafter, the home from which none of us ever emerges at all. This observation of her mother's want of feeling amused the daughter's sarcastic mind. And to make her own contemporaries laugh she gave them afterwards a comical account of the gleeful fashion in which her mother had said, rubbing her hands: "Gracious me, it appears to be true that poor Madame d'Arpajon is dead." Even the people who did not need this death to make them feel any joy in being alive, were rendered happy by it. For every death is for others a simplification of life, it spares them the necessity of showing gratitude, the obligation of paying calls. And yet this was not the manner in which Elstir had received the news of the death of M. Verdurin.

A lady left the room, for she had other afternoon parties to attend, and had also received the commands of two queens to take tea with them. It was the Princesse de Nassau, that great courtesan of the aristocratic world whom I had known in the past. Were it not that she had shrunk in height (which gave her, her head being now situated at a much lower elevation than formerly, an air of having "one foot in the grave"), one could scarcely have said that she had aged. She had remained a Marie-Antoinette with an Austrian nose and an enchanting glance, preserved, one might almost say embalmed, by a thousand cosmetics adorably blended so as to compose for her a face that was the colour of lilac. Over this face there floated that confused and tender expression which I remembered, which was at once an allusion to all the fashionable gatherings where she was expected and an intimation that she was obliged to leave, that she promised sweetly to return, that she would slip away without any fuss. Born almost on the steps of a throne, three times married, richly kept for years at a time by great bankers, not to mention the countless whims in which she had permitted herself to indulge, she bore lightly beneath her gown, mauve like her wonderful round eyes and her painted face, the slightly tangled memories of the innumerable incidents of her life. As she passed near me, making her discreet exit, I bowed to her. She recognised me, took my hand and pressed it, and fixed upon me the round mauve pupils which seemed to say: "How long it is since we have seen each other! We must talk about all that another time." Her pressure of my hand became a squeeze, for she had a vague idea that one evening in her carriage, when she had offered to drop me at my door after a party at the Duchesse de Guermantes's, there might have been some dalliance between us. Just to be on the safe side, she seemed to allude to something that had in fact never happened, but this was hardly difficult for her since a strawberry tart could send her into an ecstasy and whenever she had to leave a party before the end of a piece of music she put on a despairing air of tender, yet not final, farewell. But she was uncertain what had passed between us in the carriage, so she did not linger long over the furtive pressure of my hand and said not a word. She merely looked at me in the manner which I have described, the manner which signified: "How long it is!" and in which one caught a momentary glimpse of her husbands and the men who had kept her and two wars, while her stellar eyes, like an astronomical clock cut in a block of opal, marked successively all those solemn hours of a so distant past which she rediscovered every time she wanted to bid you a casual good-bye which was always also an apology. And then having left me, she started to trot towards the door, partly so that her departure should not inconvenience people, partly to show me that if she had not stopped to talk it was because she was in a hurry, partly also to recapture the seconds which she had lost in pressing my hand and so arrive on time at the Queen of Spain's, where she was to have tea alone with the Queen. I even thought, when she got near the door, that she was going to break into a gallop. And indeed she was galloping towards her grave.

A stout lady came up to me and greeted me, and during the few moments that she was speaking the most diverse thoughts jostled each other in my mind. I hesitated an instant to reply to her, for I was afraid that possibly, recognising people no better than I did, she might have mistaken my identity, but then the assurance of her manner caused me on the contrary, for fear that she might be someone whom I had known extremely well, to exaggerate the amiability of my smile, while my eyes continued to scan her features for some trace of the name which eluded me. As a candidate for a degree fixes his eyes upon the examiner's face in the vain hope of finding there the answer that he would do better to seek in his own memory, so, still smiling, I fixed my eyes upon the features of the stout lady. They seemed to be those of Mme Swann, and there crept into my smile the appropriate shade of respect, while my indecision began to subside. But a moment later I heard the stout lady say: "You took me for Mamma, and it's quite true that I'm beginning to look very like her." And I recognised Gilberte.

We had a long talk about Robert, Gilberte speaking of him in an almost reverent tone, as though he had been a superior being whom she was anxious to show me that she had admired and understood. We recalled to one another the ideas which he had expounded in the past upon the art of war (for he had often repeated to her at Tansonville the theories that I had heard him develop at Doncières and elsewhere) and we marvelled how often, and on how many different points, his views had been proved correct by the events of the late war.

"I cannot tell you," I said, "how struck I am now by even the least of the things that I heard him say at Doncières and also during the war. Almost the last remark that he ever made to me, just before we said good-bye for the last time, was that he expected to see Hindenburg, a Napoleonic general, fight one of the types of Napoleonic battle, the one which aims at driving a wedge between two hostile armies—perhaps, he had added, the English and ourselves. Now scarcely a year after Robert was killed, a critic for whom he had a profound admiration and who manifestly exercised a great influence upon his military ideas, M. Henry Bidou, was saying that the Hindenburg offensive of March 1918 was 'the battle of separation fought by a single concentrated army against two armies in extended formation, a manoeuvre which the Emperor executed successfully in the Apennines in 1796 but in which he failed in Belgium in 1815.' In the course of the same conversation Robert had compared battles to plays in which it is not always easy to know what the author has intended, in which perhaps the author himself has changed his plan in mid-campaign. Now admittedly, to take this same German offensive of 1918, had Robert interpreted it in this fashion he would not have been in agreement with M. Bidou. But other critics believe that it was Hindenburg's success in the direction of Amiens, followed by his check there, then his success in Flanders and then another check, which, by virtue really of a series of accidents, made first of Amiens and then of Boulogne objectives which he had not fixed upon before the engagement began. And as every critic can refashion a play or a campaign in his own way, there are some who see in this offensive the prelude to a lightning attack upon Paris and others a succession of uncoordinated hammer-blows intended to destroy the English army. And even if the orders actually given by the commander do not fit in with this or that conception of his plan, the critics will always be at liberty to say, as the actor Mounet-Sully said to Coquelin when the latter assured him that *Le Misanthrope* was not the gloomy melodrama that he wanted to make it (for Molière himself, according to the evidence of contemporaries, gave a comical interpretation of the part and played it for laughs): 'Well, Molière was wrong.' "

"And when aeroplanes first started"—it was Gilberte's turn now—"you remember what he used to say (he had such charming expressions): 'Every army will have to be a hundred-eyed Argus'? Alas, he never lived to see his prediction fulfilled!" "Oh! yes, he did," I replied, "he saw the battle of the Somme and he knew that it began with blinding the enemy by gouging out his eyes, by destroying his aeroplanes and his captive balloons." "Yes, that is true. And then," she went on, for now that she "lived only for the mind" she had become a little pedantic, "he maintained that we return always to the methods of the ancients. Well, do you realise that the Mesopotamian campaigns of this war" (she must have read this comparison at the time in Brichot's articles) "constantly recall, almost without alteration, Xenophon's *Anabasis*? And that to get from the Tigris to the Euphrates the English command made use of the *bellum*, the long narrow boat—the gondola of the country— which was already being used by the Chaldeans at the very dawn of history." These words did indeed give me a sense of that stagnation of the past through which in certain parts of the world, by virtue of a sort of specific gravity, it is indefinitely immobilised, so that it can be found after centuries exactly as it was. But I must admit that, because of the books which I had read at Balbec at no great distance from Robert himself, I myself had been more impressed first in the fighting in France to come again upon those "trenches" that were familiar to me from the pages of Mme de Sévigné and then in the Middle East, apropos of the siege of Kut-el-Amara (Kut-of-the-Emir, "just as we say Vaux-le-Vicomte or Bailleau-l'Evêque," as the curé of Combray would have said had he extended his thirst for etymologies to the languages of the East), to see the name of Baghdad once more attended closely by that of Basra, which is the Bassorah so many times mentioned in the *Arabian Nights*, the town which, whenever he had left the capital or was returning thither, was used as his port of embarkation or disembarkation, long before the days of General Townshend and General Gorringe, when the Caliphs still reigned, by no less a personage than Sindbad the Sailor.

"There is one aspect of war," I continued, "which I think Robert was beginning to comprehend: war is human, it is something that is lived like a love or a hatred and could be told like the story of a novel, and consequently, if anyone goes about repeating that strategy is a science, it won't help him in the least to understand war, since war is not a matter of strategy. The enemy has no more knowledge of our plans than we have of the objective pursued by the woman whom we love, and perhaps we do not even know what these plans are ourselves. Did the Germans in their offensive of March 1918 aim at capturing Amiens? We simply do not know. Perhaps they did not know themselves, perhaps it was what happened—their advance in the west towards Amiens— that determined the nature of their plan. And even if war were scientific, it would still be right to paint it as Elstir painted the sea, by reversing the real and the apparent, starting from illusions and beliefs which one then slowly brings into line with the truth, which is the manner in which Dostoievsky tells the story of a life. Quite certainly, however, war is not strategic, it might better be described as a pathological condition, because it admits of accidents which even a skilled physician could not have foreseen, such as the Russian Revolution."

Throughout this conversation Gilberte had spoken of Robert with a deference which seemed to be addressed more to my sometime friend than to her late husband. It was as though she were saying to me: "I know how much you admired him. Please believe that I too understood what a wonderful person he was." And yet the love which she assuredly no longer had for his memory was perhaps the remote cause of certain features of her present life. Thus Gilberte now had an inseparable friend in Andrée. And although the latter was beginning, thanks largely to her husband's talent and her own intelligence, to penetrate, if not into the society of the Guermantes, at least into circles infinitely more fashionable than those in which she had formerly moved, people were astonished that the Marquise de Saint-Loup should condescend to be her closest friend. The friendship was taken to be a sign in Gilberte of her penchant for what she supposed was an artistic existence and for what was, unequivocally, a social decline. This explanation may be the true one. But another occurred to me, convinced as I had always been that the images which we see anywhere assembled are generally the reflexion, or in some indirect fashion an effect, of a first group of different images—quite unlike the second and at a great distance from it, though the two groups are symmetrical. If night after night one saw Andrée and her husband and Gilberte in each other's company, I wondered whether this was not because, so many years earlier, one might have seen Andrée's future husband first living with Rachel and then leaving her for Andrée. Very likely Gilberte at the time, in the too remote, too exalted world in which she lived, had known nothing of this. But she must have learned of it later, when Andrée had climbed and she herself had descended enough to be aware of each other's existence. And when this happened she must have felt very strongly the prestige of the woman for whom Rachel had been abandoned by the man—the no doubt fascinating man— whom she, Rachel, had preferred to Robert. So perhaps the sight of Andrée recalled to Gilberte the youthful romance that her love for Robert had been, and inspired in her a great respect for Andrée, who even now retained the affections of a man so loved by that Rachel whom Gilberte felt to have been more deeply loved by Saint-Loup than she had been herself. But perhaps on the contrary these recollections played no part in Gilberte's fondness for the artistic couple, and one would have been right to see in her conduct, as many people did, an instance merely of those twin tastes, so often inseparable in society women, for culture and loss of caste. Perhaps Gilberte had forgotten Robert as completely as I had forgotten Albertine, and, even if she knew that Rachel was the woman whom the man of many talents had left for Andrée, never when she saw them thought about this fact which had in no way influenced her liking for them. Whether my alternative explanation was not merely possible but true was a question that could be determined only by appeal to the testimony of the parties themselves, the sole recourse which is open in such a case—or would be if they were able to bring to their confidences both insight and sincerity. But the first of these is rare in the circumstances and the second unknown. Whatever the true explanation of this friendship might be, the sight of Rachel, now a celebrated actress, could not be very agreeable to Gilberte. So I was sorry to hear that she was going to recite some poetry at this party, the programme announced being Musset's *Souvenir* and some fables of La Fontaine.

In the background could be heard the Princesse de Guermantes repeating excitedly, in a voice which because of her false teeth was like the rattle of old iron: "Yes, that's it, we will forgather! We will summon the clan! I love this younger generation, so intelligent, so ready to join in! Ah!" (to a young woman) "what a mujishun you are!" And she fixed her great monocle in her round eye, with an expression half of amusement, half of apology for her inability to sustain gaiety for any length of time, though to the very end she was determined to "join in" and "forgather."

"But how do you come to be at a party of this size?" Gilberte asked me. "To find you at a great slaughter of the innocents like this doesn't at all fit in with my picture of you. In fact, I should have expected to see you anywhere rather than at one of my aunt's get-togethers, because of course she is my aunt," she added meaningly, for having become Mme de Saint-Loup at a slightly earlier date than that of Mme Verdurin's entry into the family, she thought of herself as a Guermantes from the beginning of time and therefore attainted by the misalliance which her uncle had contracted when he married Mme Verdurin, a subject, it is true, on which she had heard a thousand sarcastic remarks made in her presence by members of the family, while naturally it was only behind her back that they discussed the misalliance which Saint-Loup had contracted when he married her. The disdain that she affected for this pinchbeck aunt was not diminished by the fact that the new Princesse de Guermantes, from the sort of perversity which drives intelligent people to behave unconventionally, from the need also to reminisce which is common in old people, and in the hope lastly of conferring a past on her new fashionable status, was fond of saying when the name of Gilberte arose in conversation: "Of course I have known her for donkey's years, I used to see a lot of the child's mother; why, she was a great friend of my cousin Marsantes. And it was in my house that she got to know Gilberte's father. And poor Saint-Loup too, I knew all his family long before he married her, indeed his uncle was one of my dearest friends in the La Raspelière days." "You see," people would say to me, hearing the Princesse de Guermantes talk in this vein, "the Verdurins were not at all bohemian, they had always been friends of Mme de Saint-Loup's family." I was perhaps alone in knowing, through my grandfather, how true it was that the Verdurins were not bohemian. But this was hardly because they had known Odette. However, you can easily dress up stories about a past with which no one is any longer familiar, just as you can about travels in a country where no one has ever been. "But really," Gilberte concluded, "since you sometimes emerge from your ivory tower, wouldn't you prefer little intimate gatherings which I could arrange, with just a few intelligent and sympathetic people? These great formal affairs are not made for you at all. I saw you a moment ago talking to my aunt Oriane, who has all the good qualities in the world, but I don't think one is doing her an injustice, do you, if one says that she scarcely belongs to the aristocracy of the mind."

I was unable to acquaint Gilberte with the thoughts which had been passing through my mind for the last hour, but it occurred to me that, simply on the level of distraction, she might be able to minister to my pleasures, which, as I now foresaw them, would no more be to talk literature with the Duchesse de Guermantes than with Mme de Saint-Loup. Certainly it was my intention to resume next day, but this time with a purpose, a solitary life. So far from going into society, I would not even permit people to come and see me at home during my hours of work, for the duty of writing my book took precedence now over that of being polite or even kind. They would insist no doubt, these friends who had not seen me for years and had now met me again and supposed that I was restored to health, they would want to come when the labour of their day or of their life was finished or interrupted, or at such times as they had the same need of me as I in the past had had of Saint-Loup; for (as I had already observed at Combray when my parents chose to reproach me at those very moments when, though they did not know it, I had just formed the most praise-worthy resolutions) the internal timepieces which are allotted to different human beings are by no means synchronised: one strikes the hour of rest while another is striking that of work, one, for the judge, that of punishment when already for the criminal that of repentance and self-perfection has long since struck. But I should have the courage to reply to those who came to see me or tried to get me to visit them that I had, for necessary business which required my immediate attention, an urgent, a supremely important appointment with myself. And yet I was aware that, though there exists but little connexion between our veritable self and the other one, nevertheless, because they both go under the same name and share the same body, the abnegation which involves making a sacrifice of easier duties and even of pleasures appears to other people to be egotism.

Was it not, surely, in order to concern myself with them that I was going to live apart from these people who would complain that they did not see me, to concern myself with them in a more fundamental fashion than would have been possible in their presence, to seek to reveal them to themselves, to realise their potentialities? What use would it have been that, for a few more years, I should waste hour after hour at evening parties pursuing the scarcely expired echo of other people's remarks with the no less vain and fleeting sound of my own, for the sterile pleasure of a social contact which precluded all penetration beneath the surface? Was it not more worthwhile that I should attempt to describe the graph, to educe the laws, of these gestures that they made, these remarks that they uttered, their very lives and natures? Unfortunately, I should have to struggle against that habit of putting oneself in another person's place which, if it favours the conception of a work of art, is an obstacle to its execution. A habit this is which leads people, through a superior form of politeness, to sacrifice to others not only their pleasure but their duty, since from the standpoint of other people our duty, whatever it may be—and duty for a man who can render no good service at the front may be to remain behind the lines where he is useful—appears illusorily to be our pleasure.

And far from thinking myself wretched—a belief which some of the greatest men have held—because of this life without friends or familiar talk that I should live, I realised that our powers of exaltation are being given a false direction when we expend them in friendship, because they are then diverted from those truths towards which they might have guided us to aim at a particular friendship which can lead to nothing. Still, intervals of rest and society would at times be necessary to me and then, I felt, rather than those intellectual conversations which fashionable people suppose must be useful to writers, a little amorous dalliance with young girls in bloom would be the choice nutriment with which, if with anything, I might indulge my imagination, like the famous horse that was fed on nothing but roses. What suddenly I yearned for once more was what I had dreamed of at Balbec, when, still strangers to me, I had seen Albertine and Andrée and their friends pass across the background of the sea. But alas! I could no longer hope to find again those particular girls for whom at this moment my desire was so strong. The action of the years which had transformed all the individuals whom I had seen today, and among them Gilberte herself, had assuredly transformed those of the girls of Balbec who survived, as it would have transformed Albertine had she not been killed, into women too sadly different from what I remembered. And it hurt me to think that I was obliged to look for them within myself, since Time which changes human beings does not alter the image which we have preserved of them. Indeed nothing is more painful than this contrast between the mutability of people and the fixity of memory, when it is borne in upon us that what has preserved so much freshness in our memory can no longer possess any trace of that quality in life, that we cannot now, outside ourselves, approach and behold again what inside our mind seems so beautiful, what excites in us a desire (a desire apparently so individual) to see it again, except by seeking it in a person of the same age, by seeking it, that is to say, in a different person. Often had I had occasion to suspect that what seems to be unique in a person whom we desire does not in fact belong to her. And of this truth the passage of time was now giving me a more complete proof, since after twenty years, spontaneously, my impulse was to seek, not the girls whom I had known in the past, but those who now possessed the youthfulness which the others had then had. (Nor is it only the reawakening of our old sensual desires which fails to correspond to any reality because it fails to take into account the Time that has been Lost. Sometimes I found myself wishing that, by a miracle, the door might open and through it might enter—not dead, as I had supposed, but still alive—not just Albertine but my grandmother too. I imagined that I saw them, my heart leapt forward to greet them. But I had forgotten one thing, that, if in fact they had not died, Albertine would now have more or less the appearance that Mme Cottard had presented in the Balbec days and my grandmother, being more than ninety-five years old, would show me nothing of that beautiful face, calm and smiling, with which I still imagined her, but only by an exercise of the fancy no less arbitrary than that which confers a beard upon God the Father or, in the seventeenth century, regardless of their antiquity, represented the heroes of Homer in all the accoutrements of a gentleman of that age.)

I looked at Gilberte, and I did not think: "I should like to see her again." I said merely, in answer to her offer, that I should always enjoy being invited to meet young girls, poor girls if possible, to whom I could give pleasure by quite small gifts, without expecting anything of them in return except that they should serve to renew within me the dreams and the sadnesses of my youth and perhaps, one improbable day, a single chaste kiss. Gilberte smiled and then looked as though she were seriously giving her mind to the problem.

Just as Elstir loved to see incarnate before him, in his wife, that Venetian beauty which he had often painted in his works, so I excused myself by saying that there was an aesthetic element in the egotism which attracted me to the beautiful women who had the power to make me suffer, and I had a sentiment almost of idolatry for the future Gilbertes, the future Duchesses de Guermantes, the future Albertine whom I might meet and who might, I thought, inspire me as a sculptor is inspired when he walks through a gallery of noble antique marbles. I ought to have reflected, however, that prior to each of the women whom I had loved there had existed in me a sentiment of the mystery by which she was surrounded and that therefore, rather than ask Gilberte to introduce me to young girls, I should have done better to go to places where there were girls with whom I had not the slightest connexion, those places where between oneself and them one feels an insurmountable barrier, where at a distance of three feet, on the beach, for instance, as they pass one on their way to bathe, one feels separated from them by the impossible. It was in this fashion that a sentiment of mystery had attached itself for me first to Gilberte, then to the Duchesse de Guermantes, then to Albertine and to so many others. (Later no doubt the unknown, the almost unknowable, had become the known, the familiar, perhaps painful, perhaps indifferent, but retaining still from an earlier time a certain charm.) And to tell the truth, as in those calendars which the postman brings us in the hope of a New Year's gift, there was not one of the years of my life that did not have, as a frontispiece, or intercalated between its days, the image of a woman whom I had desired during that year; an image sometimes entirely arbitrary, for the reason that, often, I had never seen the woman in question, whether she were Mme Putbus's maid or

Mlle d'Orgeville or some young woman or other whose name had caught my eye on the society page of a newspaper, amongst "the swarm of charming waltzers." I guessed her to be beautiful, I fell in love with her and I constructed for her an ideal body which towered above some landscape in the region of France where I had read in the *Annuaire des Châteaux* that the estates of her family were situated. In cases, however, where I had met and known the woman, the landscape against which I saw her was, at the very least, double. First she rose, each one of these women, at a different point in my life, with the imposing stature of a tutelary local deity, in the midst of one of those landscapes of my dreams which lay side by side like some chequered network over my past, the landscape to which my imagination had sought to attach her; then later I saw her from the angle of memory, sur-rounded by the places in which I had known her and which, remaining attached to them, she recalled to me, for if our life is vagabond our memory is sedentary and though we ourselves rush ceaselessly forward our recollections, indissolubly bound to the sites which we have left behind us, continue to lead a placid and sequestered existence among them, like those friends whom a traveller makes for a brief while in some town where he is staying and whom, leaving the town, he is obliged to leave behind him, because it is there that they, who stand on the steps of their house to bid him good-bye, will end their day and their life, regardless of whether he is still with them or not, there beside the church, looking out over the harbour, beneath the trees of the promenade. So that the shadow of, for instance, Gilberte lay not merely outside a church in the Ile-de-France where I had imagined her, but also upon a gravelled path in a park on the Méséglise way, and the shadow of Mme de Guermantes not only on a road in a watery landscape beside which rose pyramid-shaped clusters of red and purple flowers but also upon the matutinal gold of a pavement in Paris. And this second image, the one born not of desire but of memory, was, for each of these women, not unique. For my friendship with each one had been multiple, I had known her at different times when she had been a different woman for me and I myself had been a different person, steeped in dreams of a different colour. And the law which had governed the dreams of each year polarised around those dreams my recollections of any woman whom I had known during that year: all that related, for instance, to the Duchesse de Guermantes in the time of my childhood was concentrated, by a magnetic force, around Combray, while all that concerned the Duchesse de Guermantes who would presently invite me to lunch was disposed around a quite different centre of sensibility; there existed several Duchesses de Guermantes, just as, beginning with the lady in pink, there had existed several Mme Swanns, separated by the colourless ether of the years, from one to another of whom it was as impossible for me to leap as it would have been to leave one planet and travel across the ether to another. And not merely separated but different, each one bedecked with the dreams which I had had at very different periods as with a characteristic and unique flora which will be found on no other planet; so much so that, having decided that I would not accept an invitation to lunch either from Mme de Forcheville or from Mme de Guermantes, I was only able to say to myself—for in saying this I was transported into another world— that one of these ladies was identical with the Duchesse de Guermantes who was descended from Geneviève de Brabant and the other with the lady in pink because a well-informed man within me assured me that this was so, in the same author-itative manner as a scientist might have told me that a milky way of nebulae owed its origin to the fragmentation of a single star. Gilberte, too, whom nevertheless a moment ago I had asked, without perceiving the analogy, to introduce me to girls who might be friends for me of the kind that she had been in the past, existed for me now only as Mme de Saint-Loup. No longer was I reminded when I saw her of the role which had been played long ago in my love for her by Bergotte, Bergotte whom she had forgotten as she had forgotten my love and who for me had become once more merely the author of his books, without my ever recalling now (save in rare and entirely unconnected flashes of memory) the emotion which I had felt when I was presented to the man, the disillusion, the astonishment wrought in me by his conversation, in that drawing-room with the white fur rugs and everywhere bunches of violets, where the footmen so early in the afternoon placed upon so many different consoles such an array of lamps. In fact all the memories that went to make up the first Mlle Swann were withdrawn from the Gilberte of the present day and held at a distance from her by the forces of attraction of another universe, where, grouped around a phrase of Bergotte with which they formed a single whole, they were drenched with the scent of hawthorn.

The fragmentary Gilberte of today listened to my request with a smile and then assumed a serious air as she gave it her consideration. I was pleased to see this, for it prevented her from paying attention to a group which it could hardly have been agreeable for her to observe. In this group was the Duchesse de Guermantes, deep in conversation with a hideous old woman whom I studied without being able to guess in the least who she was—she seemed to be a complete stranger to me. It was in fact to Rachel, that is to say to the actress, the famous actress now, who was going to recite some poems by Victor Hugo and La Fontaine in the course of this party, that Gilberte's aunt was talking. For the Duchess, too long conscious that she occupied the foremost social position in Paris and failing to realise that a position of this kind exists only in the minds of those who believe in it and that many newcomers to the social scene, if they never saw her anywhere and never read her name in the account of any fashionable entertainment, would suppose that she occupied no position at all, now scarcely saw— except when, as seldom as possible, and then with a yawn, she paid a few calls—the Faubourg Saint-Germain which, she said, bored her to death, and instead did what amused her, which was to lunch with this or that actress whom she declared to be enchanting. In the new circles which she frequented, having remained much more like her old self than she supposed, she continued to think that to be easily bored was a mark of intellectual superiority, but she expressed this sentiment now with a positive violence which turned her voice into a hoarse bellow. When, for instance, I mentioned Brichot, "Tedious man!" she broke in, "how he has bored me for the last twenty years!", and when Mme de Cambremer was heard to say: "You must re-read what Schopenhauer says about music," the Duchess drew our attention to this phrase by exclaiming: "*Re-read* is pretty rich, I must say. Who does she think she's fooling?" Old M. d'Albon smiled, recognising in this outburst a sample of the Guermantes wit. In Gilberte, who was more modern, it evoked no response. Daughter of Swann though she was, like a duckling hatched by a hen she was more romantically minded than her father. "I find that most touching," she would say, or: "He has a charming sensibility."

I told Mme de Guermantes that I had met M. de Charlus. She found him much more "altered" for the worse than in fact he was, for people in society make distinctions, in the matter of intelligence, not only between different members of their set between whom there is really nothing to choose in this respect, but also, in a single individual, between different phases of his life. Then she went on: "He has always been the image of my mother-in-law, but now the likeness is even more striking." There was nothing very extraordinary in this resemblance: it is well known that women sometimes so to speak project themselves into another human being with the most perfect accuracy, with the sole error of a transposition of sex. This, however, is an error of which one can scarcely say: "*felix culpa*," for the sex has repercussions upon the personality, so that in a man femininity becomes affectation, reserve touchiness and so on. Nevertheless, in the face, though it may be bearded, in the cheeks, florid as they are beneath their side-whiskers, there are certain lines which might have been traced from some maternal portrait. Almost every aged Charlus is a ruin in which one may recognise with astonishment, beneath all the layers of paint and powder, some fragments of a beautiful woman preserved in eternal youth. While we were talking, Morel came in. The Duchess treated him with a civility which disconcerted me a little. "I never take sides in family quarrels," she said. "Don't you find them boring, family quarrels?"

If in a period of twenty years, like this that had elapsed since my first entry into society, the conglomerations of social groups had disintegrated and re-formed under the magnetic influence of new stars destined themselves also to fade away and then to reappear, the same sequence of crystallisation followed by dissolution and again by a fresh crystallisation might have been observed to take place within the consciousness of individuals. If for me Mme de Guermantes had been many people, for Mme de Guermantes or for Mme Swann there were many individuals who had been a favoured friend in an era that preceded the Dreyfus Affair, only to be branded as a fanatic or an imbecile when the supervention of the Affair modified the accepted values of people and brought about a new configuration of parties, itself of brief duration, since later they had again disintegrated and re-formed. And what serves most powerfully to promote this renewal of old friendships, adding its influence to any purely intellectual affinities, is simply the passage of Time, which causes us to forget our antipathies and our disdains and even the reasons which once explained their existence. Had one analysed the fashionableness of the young Mme de Cambremer, one would have found that she was the niece of

Jupien, a tradesman who lived in our house, and that the additional circumstance which had launched her on her social ascent was that her uncle had procured men for M. de Charlus. But all this combined had produced effects that were dazzling, while the causes were already remote and not merely unknown to many people but also forgotten by those who had once known them and whose minds now dwelt much more upon her present brilliance than upon the ignominy of her past, since people always accept a name at its current valuation. So that these drawing-room transformations possessed a double interest: they were both a phenomenon of the memory and an effect of Lost Time.

The Duchess still hesitated, for fear of a scene with M. de Guermantes, to make overtures to Balthy and Mistinguett, whom she found adorable, but with Rachel she was definitely on terms of friendship. From this the younger generation concluded that the Duchesse de Guermantes, despite her name, must be some sort of demi-rep who had never quite belonged to the best society. There were, it was true, a few reigning princes (the honour of whose familiar friendship two other great ladies disputed with her) whom Mme de Guermantes still took the trouble to invite to luncheon. But on the one hand kings and queens do not often come to see you and their acquaintances are sometimes people of no social position, and then the Duchess, with the superstitious respect of the Guermantes for old-fashioned protocol (for while well-bred people bored her to tears, she was at the same time horrified by any departure from good manners), would put on her invitation cards: "Her Majesty has commanded the Duchesse de Guermantes," or "has deigned," etc. And newcomers to society, in their ignorance of these formulae, inferred that their use was simply a sign of the Duchess's lowly situation. From the point of view of Mme de Guermantes herself, this intimacy with Rachel signified perhaps that we had been mistaken when we supposed her to be hypocritical and untruthful in her condemnations of a purely fashionable life, when we imagined that in refusing to go and see Mme de Saint-Euverte she acted in the name not of intelligence but of snobbery, finding the Marquise stupid only because, not having yet attained her goal, she allowed her snobbery to appear on the surface. But the intimacy with Rachel might also signify that the intelligence of the Duchess was no more than commonplace, but had remained unsatisfied and at a late hour, when she was tired of society, had driven her,

totally ignorant as she was of the veritable realities of the intellectual life, to seek for intellectual fulfilment with a touch of that spirit
of fantasy which can cause perfectly respectable ladies, thinking to
themselves: "How amusing it will be!", to end an evening with a
prank which is in fact deadly dull: you go off and wake up some
acquaintance and then, when you are in his room, you don't know
what to say, so, after standing awkwardly by his bed for a few
moments in your evening clothes and realising how late it is, there
is nothing left to do but go home to bed yourself.

One must add that the antipathy which the changeable Duchess
had recently come to feel for Gilberte may have caused her to take
a certain pleasure in receiving Rachel, a course of conduct which
enabled her also to proclaim aloud one of the favourite
Guermantes maxims, to wit, that the family was too numerous
for its members to have to espouse one another's quarrels (or even,
some might have said, to take notice of one another's bereavements), an independence, a spirit of "I can't see that I am obliged"
which had been reinforced by the policy that it had been necessary
to adopt with regard to M. de Charlus, who, had you followed
him, would have involved you in hostilities with all your
acquaintances.

As for Rachel, if the truth was that she had taken very great
pains to form this friendship with the Duchesse de Guermantes
(pains which the Duchess had failed to detect beneath a mask of
simulated disdain and deliberate incivility, which had put her on
her mettle and given her an exalted idea of an actress so little
susceptible to snobbery), this was no doubt in a general fashion an
effect of the fascination which after a certain time the world of
high society exercise upon even the most hardened bohemians, a
fascination paralleled by that which the same bohemians themselves exercise upon people in society, flux and reflux which
correspond to—in the political order—the reciprocal curiosity,
the desire to form a mutual alliance, of two nations which have
recently been at war with each other. But Rachel's desire had
possibly a more particular cause. It was in Mme de Guermantes's
house, it was at the hands of Mme de Guermantes herself, that
she had in the past suffered the most terrible humiliation of her
life. This snub Rachel had with the passage of time neither
forgotten nor forgiven, but the singular prestige which the event
had conferred upon the Duchess in her eyes could never be
effaced.

The conversation from which I was anxious to divert Gilberte's attention was, in any case, presently interrupted, for the mistress of the house came in search of the actress to tell her that the moment for her recital had arrived. She left the Duchess and a little later appeared upon the platform.

Meanwhile at the other end of Paris there was taking place a spectacle of a very different kind. Mme Berma, as I have said, had invited a number of people to a tea-party in honour of her daughter and her son-in-law. But the guests were in no hurry to arrive. Having learnt that Rachel was to recite poetry at the Princesse de Guermantes's (which utterly scandalised Berma, who from her own lofty position as a great artist looked down on Rachel as still no more than a kept woman who, because Saint-Loup paid for the dresses which she wore on the stage, was allowed to appear in the plays in which she herself, Berma, took the leading roles—and scandalised her all the more because a rumour had run round Paris that, though the invitations were in the name of the Princesse de Guermantes, it was in effect Rachel who was acting as hostess in the Princess's house), Berma had written a second time to certain faithful friends to insist that they should not miss her tea-party, for she was aware that they were also friends of the Princesse de Guermantes, whom they had known when she was Mme Verdurin. And now the hours were passing, and still nobody arrived to visit Berma. Bloch, having been asked whether he meant to come, had ingenuously replied: "No, I would rather go to the Princesse de Guermantes's," and this, alas! was what everyone in his heart of hearts had decided. Berma, who suffered from a deadly disease which had obliged her to cut down her social activities to a minimum, had seen her condition deteriorate when, in order to pay for the luxurious existence which her daughter demanded and her son-in-law, ailing and idle, was unable to provide, she had returned to the stage. She knew that she was shortening her days, but she wanted to give pleasure to her daughter, to whom she handed over the large sums that she earned, and to a son-in-law whom she detested but flattered—for she feared, knowing that his wife adored him, that if she, Berma, did not do what he wanted, he might, out of spite, deprive her of the happiness of seeing her child. This child, with whom secretly the doctor who looked after her husband was in love, had allowed herself to be persuaded that these performances in *Phèdre* were not really dangerous for her mother. She had more or less forced the doctor to tell her this, or rather of all that he had said to her about her mother's health she had retained only this in her memory, the truth being that, in the midst of various objections of which she had taken no notice, he had remarked that he saw no grave harm in Berma's appearing on the stage. He had said this because he had sensed that in so doing he would give pleasure to the young woman whom he loved, perhaps also from ignorance and also because he knew that the disease was in any case incurable, since a man readily consents to cut short the agony of an invalid when the action that will have this effect will be advantageous to himself—and perhaps also from the stupid idea that acting made Berma happy and was therefore likely to do her good, a stupid idea which had appeared to him to be corroborated when, having been given a box by Berma's daughter and son-in-law and having deserted all his patients for the occasion, he had found her as extraordinarily charged with life on the stage as she seemed to be moribund if you met her off it. And indeed our habits enable us to a large degree, enable even the organs of our bodies, to adapt themselves to an existence which at first sight would appear to be utterly impossible. Have we not all seen an elderly riding-master with a weak heart go through a whole series of acrobatics which one would not have supposed his heart could stand for a single minute? Berma in the same way was an old campaigner of the stage, to the requirements of which her organs had so perfectly adapted themselves that she was able, by deploying her energies with a prudence invisible to the public, to give an illusion of good health troubled only by a purely nervous and imaginary complaint. After the scene in which Phèdre makes her declaration of love to Hippolyte Berma herself might be conscious only of the appalling night which awaited her as a result of her exertions, but her admirers burst into tumultuous applause and said that she was more wonderful than ever. She would go home in terrible pain, happy nevertheless because she brought back to her daughter the blue banknotes which, with the playfulness of a true child of the footlights, she had the habit of squeezing into her stockings, whence she would draw them out with pride, hoping for a smile, a kiss. Unfortunately these banknotes merely made it possible for her son-in-law and her daughter to make new embellishments to their house, which was next door to Berma's own: hence constant hammering, which interrupted the sleep of which the great actress was so desperately in need. According to the latest change in fashion, or to conform to the taste of M. de X—— or M. de Y—— whom they hoped to attract to their house, they altered every room in it. And Berma, realising that sleep, which alone would have deadened her pain, had gone for good, would resign herself to lying awake, not without a secret contempt for this determination to be smart which was hastening her death and making her last days an agony. That these were its consequences was no doubt in part the reason why she despised this social ambition, contempt being a natural form of revenge upon something that does us harm and that we are powerless to prevent. But there was another reason, which was that, conscious of her own genius and having learnt at a very early age the meaninglessness of all these decrees of fashion, she for her part had remained faithful to tradition, which she had always respected and of which she was herself an embodiment, and which caused her to judge things and people as she would have judged them thirty years earlier, to judge Rachel, for example, not as the well-known actress that she was today, but as the little tart that she had once been. Berma was, one must add, no better natured than her daughter, for it was from her mother that the young woman had derived, through heredity and through the contagion of an example which an only too natural admiration had rendered more than usually potent, her egotism, her pitiless mockery, her unconscious cruelty. But all this Berma had sacrificed to her daughter and in this way she had liberated herself from it. However, even if Berma's daughter had not incessantly had workmen in her house, she would have tired her mother out just the same, since inevitably youth with its powers of attraction, its ruthless and inconsiderate strength, tires out old age and ill-health, which overtax themselves in the effort to keep up with it. Every day there was yet another luncheon-party, and Berma would have been condemned as selfish had she deprived her daughter of this pleasure, or even had she refused to be present herself at entertainments where the prestige of the famous mother was counted upon as a means of drawing to the house, not without difficulty, certain recent acquaintances who needed to be coaxed. And even away from home her attendance at a social function might be "promised" to these same acquaintances as a way of doing them a civility. So that the poor mother, seriously engaged in her intimate dialogue with the death that was already installed within her, was compelled to get up early in the morning and drag

herself out of the house. Nor was this enough. At about this time
Réjane, in the full blaze of her talent, made some appearances on
the stage in foreign countries which had an enormous success, and
the son-in-law decided that Berma must not allow herself to be
put in the shade; determined that his own family should pick up
some of the same easily acquired glory, he forced his mother-in-
law to set out on tours on which she was obliged to have injections
of morphine, which might at any moment have killed her owing
to the condition of her kidneys.

This same ambition to be smart, this longing for social prestige,
for life, had on the day of the Princesse de Guermantes's reception
acted in the manner of a suction-pump, drawing to the latter's
house with the irresistible force of some such machine even
Berma's loyalest friends, so that at the actress's party there was, in
contrast and in consequence, an absolute and deathlike void. One
solitary young man had come, thinking that possibly Berma's party
might be just as fashionable as the other. When Berma saw the
hour pass for which she had issued the invitations and realised that
everybody had deserted her, she ordered tea to be served and the
four people in the room sat down at the table as though it had been
spread for a funeral feast. Nothing now in her face recalled the
countenance of which the photograph, one distant New Year's
Day, had so disturbed me. Death, as the saying goes, was written all
over her face, and she resembled nothing so much as one of the
marble figures in the Erechtheum. Her hardened arteries were
already almost petrified, so that what appeared to be long sculptural ribbons ran across her cheeks, with the rigidity of a mineral
substance. The dying eyes were still relatively alive, by contrast at
least with the terrible ossified mask, and glowed feebly like a snake
asleep in the midst of a pile of stones. But already the young man,
who had sat down only because it would have been rude to do
anything else, was incessantly looking at his watch, for he too felt
the attraction of the brilliant party in the Guermantes mansion.
Berma uttered not a word in reproach of the friends who had
deserted her and who were foolish enough to hope that she would
not discover that they had been to the Guermantes'. She mur-
mured only: "A Rachel giving a party in the Princesse de
Guermantes's house—that is something that could only happen
in Paris." And silently and with a solemn slowness she continued
to eat the cakes which the doctor had forbidden her, still with the
air of playing her part in a funerary rite. The gloom of the tea-party

was made more intense by the vile temper of the son-in-law, who was furious that Rachel, whom he and his wife knew very well, had not invited them. To crown his indignation the young man who had come told him that he knew Rachel so well that, if he went off to the Guermantes party straight away, he could even at this eleventh hour ask her to invite the frivolous couple. But Berma's daughter was too well aware of the low level at which her mother placed Rachel, she knew that she would die of despair at the thought of her daughter begging for an invitation from the former prostitute. So she told the young man and her husband that what he suggested was impossible. But she took her revenge as she sat at the tea-table by a series of little grimaces expressive of the desire for pleasure and the annoyance of being deprived of it by her killjoy mother. The latter pretended not to see her daughter's cross looks and from time to time, in a dying voice, addressed an amiable remark to the solitary guest. But soon the rush of air which was sweeping everything towards the Guermantes mansion, and had swept me thither myself, was too much for him; he got up and said good-bye, leaving Phèdre or death—one scarcely knew which of the two it was—to finish, with her daughter and her son-in-law, devouring the funeral cakes.

My conversation with Gilberte was interrupted by the voice of the actress which now made itself heard. Her style of recitation was intelligent, for it presupposed the existence of the poem whose words she was speaking as a whole which had been in being before she opened her mouth, a whole of which we were hearing merely a fragment, as though for a few moments, as the actress passed along a road, she had happened to be within earshot of us.

The announcement that she was to recite poems with which nearly everybody was familiar had been well received. But when the actress, before beginning to speak, was seen to shoot searching and bewildered glances in every direction, to lift her hands with an air of supplication and then to utter each word as though it were a groan, the general reaction was to feel embarrassed, almost shocked by this display of sentiment. Nobody had said to himself that a recital of poetry could be anything like this. Gradually, however, each member of an audience grows accustomed to what is taking place before him, he forgets his first sensation of discomfort, he picks out what is good in a performance, he mentally compares different ways of reciting and passes judgment:

"this is excellent, this is not so good." But for the first few moments, just as when, in a trivial case in a law-court, we see a barrister advance, raise a toga'd arm in the air and start to speak in a threatening tone, we hardly dare look at our neighbours. For our immediate reaction is that this is grotesque—but we cannot be sure that it is not in fact magnificent, so for the present we suspend judgment.

Nevertheless the audience was amazed to see this woman, before she had emitted a single sound, bend her knees, stretch out her arms to cradle an invisible body and then, to recite some very well-known lines of poetry, start to speak in a voice of entreaty. People looked at one another, not knowing what expression to put on their faces: a few bad-mannered young things giggled audibly; everyone glanced at his neighbour with that stealthy glance which at a smart dinner-party, when you find beside your plate an unfamiliar implement, a lobster-fork or sugar-grinder perhaps, of which you know neither what it is for nor how to use it, you cast at some more authoritative guest in the hope that he will pick it up before you and so give you a chance to imitate him—or with which, when someone quotes a line of poetry which you do not know but of which you do not wish to appear ignorant, you turn towards a man better read than yourself and relinquish to him, as though it were a favour, as though you were courteously letting him pass through a door before you, the pleasure of naming the author. With just this same glance, as they listened to the actress, each member of the audience waited, his head lowered but his eyes furtively prying, for others to take the initiative and decide whether to laugh or to criticise, to weep or to applaud. Mme de Forcheville, who had come back specially for the occasion from Guermantes, whence, as we shall see, the Duchess had been almost expelled, had assumed an expression that was attentive, concentrated, almost bad-tempered, either in order to show that she was a connoisseur of the drama and had not come merely for social reasons, or to present a hostile front to people who were less versed in literature and might have talked to her about other things, or from the intensity with which with all her faculties she strove to discover whether she "liked" or "did not like" the performance, or perhaps because, while she found it "interesting," she nevertheless "did not like" the manner in which certain lines were recited. This attitude might, one would have thought, have been more appropriate to the Princesse de

Guermantes. But as the recitation was taking place in her house and as, having become as avaricious as she was rich, she had decided that her payment to Rachel would consist of five roses, she chose rather to act as claque and gave the signal for a forced display of enthusiasm by a series of exclamations of delight. And here alone could her Verdurin past be recognised, for she had the air of listening to the poems for her own private enjoyment, of having felt a desire for someone to come and recite them to her alone, so that it seemed to be mere chance that there were in the room five hundred people, her friends, whom she had permitted to come unobtrusively and share in her pleasure.

Meanwhile I observed—without any satisfaction to my vanity, for she was old and ugly—that the actress, in a somewhat restrained fashion, was giving me the glad eye. All the time that she was reciting she allowed to flutter in and out of her eyes a smile that was both repressed and penetrating and that seemed to be the first hint of an acquiescence which she would have liked to see come from me. Certain elderly ladies meanwhile, little accustomed to the recitation of poetry, were saying to their neighbours: "Did you see?", a question which had reference to the solemn, tragic miming of the actress, which they had no words to describe. The Duchesse de Guermantes sensed the slight wavering of opinion and turned the scale of victory with a cry of "Admirable!", ejaculated at a pause in the middle of the poem which perhaps she mistook for the end. More than one guest thought it incumbent upon him to underline this exclamation with a look of approval and an inclination of the head, less perhaps to display his comprehension of the reciter's art than his friendly relations with the Duchess. When the poem was finished, I heard the actress thank Mme de Guermantes, who was standing near her, as I was myself, and at the same time, taking advantage of my presence beside the Duchess, she turned to me and greeted me with charming civility. At this point I realised that she was somebody whom I ought to have known and that, whereas long ago I had mistaken the passionate glances of M. de Vaugoubert for the salutation of someone who was confused as to my identity, today on the contrary what I had taken in the actress to be a look of desire was no more than a decorous attempt to make me recognise and greet her. I responded with a smile and a gesture. "I am sure he does not recognise me," said the reciter to the Duchess. "Of course I do," I said confidently, "I recognise you perfectly." "Well then, who am I?" I had not the slightest idea and my position was becoming awkward. But fortunately, if throughout one of La Fontaine's finest poems this woman who was reciting it with such conviction had, whether from good-nature or stupidity or embarrassment, thought of nothing but the difficulty of saying good-afternoon to me, throughout this same beautiful poem Bloch had been wondering only how to manoeuvre himself so as to be ready, the moment the poem ended, to leap from his seat like a beleaguered army making a sally and, trampling if not upon the bodies at least upon the feet of his neighbours, arrive and congratulate the reciter, perhaps from an erroneous conception of duty, perhaps merely from a desire to make people look at him. "How curious it is to see Rachel here!" he whispered in my ear. At once the magic name broke the enchantment which had given to the mistress of Saint-Loup the unknown form of this horrible old woman.[23] And once I knew who she was, I did indeed recognise her perfectly. "You were wonderful," Bloch said to Rachel, and having said these simple words, having satisfied his desire, he started on his return journey—but encountered so many obstacles and made so much noise in reaching his place that Rachel had to wait more than five minutes before beginning her second poem. This was *Les Deux Pigeons*, and at the end of it Mme de Morienval came up to Mme de Saint-Loup, whom she knew to be very well read without remembering that she had inherited the oblique and sarcastic wit of her father. "That *is* La Fontaine's fable, isn't it?" she asked, thinking that she had recognised it but not being absolutely certain, since she did not know the fables of La Fontaine at all well and in any case supposed them to be childish things which no one would recite at a fashionable gathering. To have such a success the entertainer had no doubt produced a pastiche of La Fontaine, thought the good lady. Unintentionally Gilberte confirmed her in this idea, for, disliking Rachel and wanting to say that with her style of diction there was nothing left of the fables, she said it in that over-subtle manner which had been her father's and which left simple people in doubt as to the speaker's meaning: "One quarter is the invention of the actress, a second is lunacy, a third is mean-ingless and the rest is La Fontaine," a remark which encouraged Mme de Morienval to maintain that the poem which had just been recited was not La Fontaine's *Les Deux Pigeons*, but an arrange-ment of which at most a quarter was by La Fontaine himself.

Given the extraordinary ignorance of all these people, this assertion caused no surprise whatever.

Meanwhile, one of his friends having arrived after the recital was over, Bloch had the satisfaction of asking him whether he had ever heard Rachel and of painting for his benefit an extraordinary picture of her art, exaggerating, indeed suddenly discovering, as he described and revealed this modernistic diction to another person, a strange pleasure of which he had felt nothing as he listened to it. Then, with exaggerated emotion, he again congratulated Rachel in a high-pitched voice which proclaimed his sense of her genius and introduced his friend, who declared that his admiration for her was unbounded. To this, Rachel, who was now acquainted with ladies of the best society and unwittingly copied them, replied: "Oh! I am most flattered, most honoured by your appreciation." Bloch's friend asked her what she thought of Berma. "Poor woman, it seems that she is living in the most abject poverty. She was once, I won't say not without talent, for what she possessed was not true talent—her taste was appalling—still, one must admit she had merit of a kind: she was more alive on the stage than most actresses, and then she had nice qualities, she was generous, she ruined herself for others. And as it is years now since she has earned a penny, because the public these days loathes the sort of thing she does . . . But of course," she added with a laugh, "I must admit that someone of my generation, naturally, only heard her right at the end of her career, and even then I was really too young to form an opinion." "She didn't recite poetry very well, did she?" hazarded Bloch's friend, to flatter Rachel. "Poetry!" she replied, "she had no idea how to recite a single line. It might have been prose, or Chinese, or Volapük—anything, rather than poetry."

In spite of Rachel's words I was thinking myself that time, as it passes, does not necessarily bring progress in the arts. And just as some author of the seventeenth century, who knew nothing of the French Revolution, or the discoveries of science, or the war, may be superior to some writer of today, just as perhaps Fagon was as great a doctor as du Boulbon (a superiority in genius compensating in this case for an inferiority in knowledge), so Berma was, as the phrase goes, head and shoulders above Rachel, and Time, when simultaneously it turned Rachel into a star and Elstir into a famous painter, had inflated the reputation of a mediocrity as well as consecrated a genius.

It was scarcely surprising that Saint-Loup's former mistress should speak maliciously about Berma. She would have done this when she was young, and even if she would not have done it then, she was bound to now. When a society woman becomes an actress, a woman even of the highest intelligence and the greatest goodness of heart, and in this unfamiliar occupation displays great talent and encounters nothing but success, one will be surprised, meeting her years later, to hear on her lips not her own individual language but that which is common to the theatrical profession, the special brand of obloquy that actresses have for their colleagues, those special qualities which are added to a member of the human race by the passage over him of "thirty years on the stage." These qualities Rachel inevitably had and her origin, as we know, was not in good society.

"You can say what you like, it was a wonderful performance, it had line, it had character, it was intelligent, one has never heard anyone recite poetry like that before," said the Duchess, for fear that Gilberte should make disparaging remarks. Gilberte wandered off towards another group, to avoid an argument with her aunt, whose comments upon Rachel were indeed of the most commonplace kind. But then, since even the best writers cease often, at the approach of old age or after producing too much, to have any talent, society women may well be excused if sooner or later they cease to have any wit. Swann already in the sharp-edged wit of the Duchesse de Guermantes found it difficult to recognise the gentle raillery of the young Princesse des Laumes. And now late in life, wearied by the least effort, Mme de Guermantes said a prodigious number of stupid things. It was true that at any moment, as happened more than once in the course of this party, she could re-become the woman whom I had known in the past and talk wittily on social topics. But alongside these moments there were others, and they were no less frequent, when beneath her beautiful eyes the sparkling conversation which for so many years, from its throne of wit, had held sway over the most distinguished men in Paris, shone, in so far as it still shone at all, in a meaningless way. When the moment came to make a joke, she would check herself for the same number of seconds as in the past, she would appear to hesitate, to have something within her that was struggling to emerge, but the joke, when at last it arrived, was pitifully feeble. But how few of her listeners noticed this! Because the procedure was the same they believed that the wit too had survived intact, like those people who, superstitiously attached to some particular make of confectionery, continue to order their petits fours from a certain shop without noticing that they have become almost uneatable. Already during the war the Duchess had shown signs of this decay. If someone pronounced the word "culture," she would stop him, smile, kindle a light in her beautiful eyes and ejaculate: "Kkkkultur," which raised a laugh among her friends, who saw in this remark the latest manifestation of the Guermantes wit. And certainly the mould was the same, and the intonation and the smile, the same that had once enchanted Bergotte, who for his part too had preserved the individual rhythm of his phrases, his interjections, his aposiopeses, his epithets, but with all this rhetorical apparatus no longer had anything to say. But newcomers, who did not know her, were surprised and said sometimes, unless they had chanced to encounter her on a day when she was amusing and "at her best": "What a stupid woman this is!"

As her life drew to its close, Mme de Guermantes had felt the quickening within her of new curiosities. Society no longer had anything to teach her. The idea that she occupied the first place in it was as evident to her as the altitude of the blue sky above the earth, and she saw no need to strengthen a position which she deemed to be unshakeable. On the other hand she read and she went to the theatre, and enjoying these activities she would have been glad to prolong them; just as in the past, in the little narrow garden where she sipped orangeade with her friends, all that was most choice in the world of grand society would come familiarly, among the scented breezes of the evening and the gusts of pollen, to sustain in her the pleasure that this grand world gave her and her appetite for it, so now a different appetite caused her to want to know the reasons behind this or that literary controversy, to want to meet the authors whose books she had read, to make friends with the actresses whom she had seen on the stage. Her tired mind required a new form of food, and in order to get to know theatrical and literary people she now made herself pleasant to women with whom formerly she would have refused to exchange cards but who, in the hope of getting the Duchess to come to their parties, could boast to her of their great friendship with the editor of some review. The first actress to be invited to her house thought that she was the only one of her kind in an exotic milieu, which however appeared more commonplace to the second when she saw that she had a predecessor. The Duchess, because on certain evenings she received reigning monarchs, thought that there was no change in her social position. But the truth was that she who alone could boast of a blood that was absolutely without taint, she who had been born a Guermantes and who when she did not sign herself "La Duchesse de Guermantes" had the right to put "Guermantes-Guermantes," she who even to her husband's sisters seemed to be something more precious than they were themselves, like a Moses saved from the waters or Christ escaped into Egypt or Louis XVII rescued from his prison in the Temple, she the purest of the pure had now, sacrificing no doubt to that hereditary need for spiritual nourishment which had brought about the social decline of Mme de Villeparisis, herself become a Mme de Villeparisis, in whose house snobbish women were afraid of meeting this or that undesirable and of whom the younger generation, observing the *fait accompli* and not knowing what had gone before it, supposed that she was a Guermantes from an inferior cask or of a less good vintage, a Guermantes *déclassée*.

If, however, the Duchess indulged a taste for the society of her inferiors, she was careful to confine this activity within strict limits and not allow it to contaminate those members of her family from whom she derived the gratification of an aristocratic pride. If at the theatre, for instance, in order to fill her role of patroness of the arts, she had invited a minister or a painter and her guest had been so ingenuous as to ask whether her sister-in-law or her husband were not in the audience, the Duchess, with a superb assumption of lofty indifference which concealed her alarm, would haughtily reply: "I have not the slightest idea. As soon as I leave my house, I know nothing of what my family is doing. For politicians, for artists, whoever they may be, I am a widow." In this way she sought to prevent the too eager social climber from drawing upon himself a snub and upon her a reprimand from Mme de Marsantes or from Basin.

"I can't tell you how pleased I am to see you," said the Duchess. "Good heavens, when was it that I saw you last?" "I believe it was at Mme d'Agrigente's—I was paying a call and I found you there, as I often did." "But of course, I was constantly going there, my dear boy, since Basin was in love with her in those days. And calling on Basin's sweetheart of the moment was always where my friends were most likely to find me, because he used to say: 'I shall expect you to visit her without fail.' I must admit that there seemed to me to be a slight impropriety in these 'digestive visits' on which he used to send me to thank the lady for her entertainment of him. But I quite soon grew accustomed to them. The tiresome thing was, however, that I was obliged to continue my relations with his mistress after he had broken off his own. I was always reminded of the line in Victor Hugo:

Take away the happiness and leave the boredom to *me*.

Naturally—you remember how the poem goes on—'I entered smiling none the less,' but it really was not fair, he ought to have left me the right to be inconstant, for in the end I accumulated so many of his discards that I had not a single afternoon to myself. Still, compared with the present that epoch now seems to me relatively agreeable. That he has started to be unfaithful again is, of course, something that I can only find flattering, it almost makes me feel younger. But I preferred his old way of doing it. Unfortunately, he was so out of practice that he had forgotten how to set about it. However, in spite of it all we are on excellent terms, we talk to each other, we are even quite fond of each other"—this the Duchess added because she was afraid that I might think that she and her husband were completely separated, rather as one says apropos of someone who is desperately ill: "But he is still able to speak, I read to him this morning for an hour." "I will tell him you are here," she continued, "he will be delighted to see you." And she went towards the Duke, who was sitting on a sofa in conversation with a lady. I observed with admiration that, except that his hair was whiter, he had scarcely changed, being still as majestic and as handsome as ever. But seeing his wife approach to speak to him he assumed an air of such fury that she had no alternative but to retreat. "I can't interrupt him just now, I don't know what he is doing, we shall see presently," said Mme de Guermantes, preferring to leave me to form my own conclusions.

Bloch now came up to us and on behalf of his American inquired the identity of a young duchess who was at the party. I replied that she was a niece of M. de Bréauté, which caused Bloch, as this name meant nothing to him, to ask for further explanations. "Bréauté!" the Duchess exclaimed, turning to me. "You remember all that, of course. How ancient it seems now, how far away! Well,"—this to Bloch—"Bréauté was a snob. They were people who lived near my mother-in-law in the country.

This couldn't possibly interest you, Monsieur Bloch—though it may amuse this young man, who knew all that world long ago when I was in the midst of it myself." This last remark referred to me, and by it Mme de Guermantes brought home to me in a number of different ways how long was the time that had elapsed. First, her own friendships and opinions had so greatly changed since that period that now, in retrospect, she looked upon her charming Babal as a snob. And then, not only was he now seen at the other end of a great vista of time, but—and of this I had been quite unaware when at my first entry into society I had supposed him to be one of the quintessential notabilities of Paris, who would for ever remain associated with its social history as Colbert with the history of the reign of Louis XIV—he too bore the stamp of a provincial origin, he was a country neighbour of the old Duchess and it was as such that the Princesse des Laumes had made his acquaintance. Moreover this Bréauté, stripped of his wit and relegated to a distant past for which he himself provided a date (which proved that between then and now he had been entirely forgotten by the Duchess) and to the countryside near Guermantes, was—and this too I would never have thought possible that first evening at the Opéra, when he had appeared to me in the guise of a marine deity dwelling in his glaucous cavern— a link between the Duchess and myself, because she remembered that I had known him and therefore had been a friend of hers, if not of the same social origin as herself at any rate an inhabitant of the same social world for very much longer than a great many people who were at the party today, she remembered this and yet remembered it so hazily that she had forgotten certain details which to me on the contrary had then seemed to be of prime importance, such as that I never went to Guermantes and at the time when she came to Mlle Percepied's nuptial mass was merely a boy of a middle-class Combray family, and that, in spite of all Saint-Loup's entreaties, throughout the year which followed her apparition at the Opéra she had never invited me to her house. To me this seemed to be of supreme importance, for it was precisely during this brief period that the life of the Duchesse de Guermantes had appeared to me to be a paradise into which I should never enter. But for her, her life then was merely a part like any other of her normal, commonplace life, and as from a certain moment onwards I had dined often at her house and had also, even before that date, been a friend of her aunt and of her nephew, she no longer knew exactly at what period our friendship had begun and was unaware of the grave anachronism that she was perpetrating in supposing that we had become friends a few years earlier than in fact we had. For this would have meant that I had known the Mme de Guermantes of the name of Guermantes, whose essence it was to be unknowable, that I had been permitted to enter the name of the golden syllables, had been received into the Faubourg Saint-Germain, whereas in fact I had merely been to dine at the house of a lady who was already nothing more in my eyes than a very ordinary woman and who had occasionally invited me, not to descend into the submarine kingdom of the Nereids, but to spend an evening with her in her cousin's box. "If you want to know anything more about Bréauté," Mme de Guermantes continued, still speaking to Bloch, "though there is no earthly reason why you should, ask our friend here, who is a hundred times more interesting than Bréauté ever was. He must have dined at my house with him fifty times. It was at my house, was it not, that you got to know Bréauté? In any case, it was there that you met Swann." And I was just as surprised that she should imagine that I might have met M. de Bréauté elsewhere than at her house (which could only have happened had I moved in that society before I became acquainted with her) as I was to see that she believed that it was through her that I had met Swann. Less untruthfully than Gilberte, who had been in the habit of saying of Bréauté: "He is an old country neighbour, I so enjoy talking to him about Tansonville," whereas in fact in the past he had never visited the Swanns at Tansonville, I might have said of Swann: "He was a country neighbour who often used to come round and see us in the evening," for indeed the memories which he recalled to my mind had nothing to do with the Guermantes. "I don't know how to describe him," she went on. "He was a man whose only subject of conversation was people with grand titles. He had a whole collection of curious anecdotes about my Guermantes relations and about my mother-in-law and about Mme de Varambon before she became a lady-in-waiting to the Princesse de Parme. But does anybody today know who Mme de Varambon was? Our friend here, yes, he knew all those people. But it is all ancient history, they are not even names today, and in any case they don't deserve to be remembered." And again it struck me that, in spite of the apparent unity of that thing which we call "society," in which, it is true, social relations reach their maximum of concentration (for all paths meet at the top) and in which there are no barriers to communication, there exist nevertheless within it, or at least there are created within it by Time, separate provinces which after a while change their names and are no longer comprehensible to those who arrive in society only when its pattern has been altered. "Mme de Varambon was a good lady who said things of an incredible stupidity," continued the Duchess, who failed to appreciate that poetry of the incomprehensible which is an effect of Time and chose rather to extract from every situation its element of ironic humour, the element that could be transformed into literature of the type of Meilhac or into the Guermantes brand of wit. "At one moment she had a mania for swallowing a certain kind of lozenge which people used to take in those days for coughs and which was called" (and she laughed as she pronounced a name that was so special, so well known formerly and so unknown today to everyone around her) "a Géraudel lozenge. 'Madame de Varambon,' my mother-in-law used to say to her, 'if you don't stop swallowing a Géraudel lozenge every five minutes, you will injure your stomach.' 'But Madame la Duchesse,' replied Mme de Varambon, 'how can they possibly injure the stomach when they go into the bronchial tubes?' And then it was she who made the remark: 'The Duchess has a most beautiful cow, so beautiful that it is always taken for a bull!' " And Mme de Guermantes would gladly have gone on relating anecdotes of Mme de Varambon, of which she and I knew hundreds, but we realised that in the ignorant memory of Bloch this name evoked none of those images which rose up for us as soon as there was mention of her or of M. de Bréauté or of the Prince d'Agrigente, though perhaps for this very reason all these names were endowed in his eyes with a glamour which I knew to be exaggerated but which I found comprehensible—though not because I myself had at one time felt its influence, for it is rarely that our own errors and absurdities, even when we have penetrated to the truth behind them, make us more indulgent to those of others.

The past had been so transformed in the mind of the Duchess (or else the distinctions which existed in my mind had been always so absent from hers that what had been an event for me had gone unnoticed by her) that she was able to suppose that I had first met Swann in her house and M. de Bréauté elsewhere, thus conferring upon me a past as man about town of which she exaggerated the remoteness from the present. For the notion of time elapsed which

I had just acquired was something that the Duchess had too, and, whereas my illusion had been to believe the gap between past and present shorter than in fact it was, she on the contrary actually overestimated it, she placed events further back than they really were, a notable consequence of this being her disregard of that supremely important line of demarcation between the epoch when she had been for me first a name and then the object of my love and the utterly different epoch when she had been for me merely a society woman like any other. It was of course only during this second period, when she had become for me a different person, that I had been to her house. But to her own eyes these differences were invisible and she would have seen nothing in the least odd in my going to her house two years earlier, for how was she to know that she had then been a different woman and even her door-mat a different door-mat, since her personality did not present to her that break in continuity which it presented to me?

"All this reminds me," I said to her, "of that first evening when I went to the Princesse de Guermantes's, when I wasn't sure that I had been invited to her party and half expected to be shown the door, and when you wore a red dress and red shoes." "Good heavens, how long ago all that was!" said the Duchesse de Guermantes, accentuating by her words my own impression of time elapsed. She seemed to be gazing into this remote past in a melancholy mood, and yet she laid a particular emphasis upon the red dress. I asked her to describe it to me, which she did most willingly. "One couldn't possibly wear a thing like that now. It was the sort of dress that was worn in those days." "But it was pretty, wasn't it?" I said. She was always afraid of giving away a point in conversation, of saying something that might depreciate her in the eyes of others. "Personally, I found it a charming fashion. If nobody wears those dresses today, it is simply because it isn't done. But they will come back, as fashions always do—in clothes, in music, in painting," she added with vigour, for she supposed there to be a certain originality in this philosophic reflexion. Then the sad thought that she was growing old caused her to resume her languid manner, which a smile, however, momentarily contradicted: "Are you sure that they were red shoes that I wore? I thought they were gold." I assured her that I had the most vivid recollection of the colour of her shoes, though I preferred not to describe the incident which made me so certain on this point. "How kind of you to remember that!" she said to me sweetly, for women call it kindness when you remember their beauty, just as painters do when you admire their work. And then, since the past, however remote it may be for a woman like the Duchess who has more head than heart, may nevertheless chance to have escaped oblivion, "Do you recall," she said, as though to thank me for remembering her dress and her shoes, "that Basin and I brought you home in our carriage? You couldn't come in with us because of some girl who was coming to see you after midnight. Basin thought it the funniest thing in the world that you should receive visits at such an hour." Indeed that was the evening when Albertine had come to see me after the Princesse de Guermantes's party and I recalled the fact just as clearly as the Duchess, I to whom Albertine was now as unimportant as she would have been to Mme de Guermantes had Mme de Guermantes known that the girl because of whom I had had to refuse their invitation was Albertine. (In fact, she was quite in the dark as to the identity of this girl, had never known it and only referred to the incident because of the circumstances and the singular lateness of the hour.) Yes, I recalled the fact, for, long after our poor dead friends have lost their place in our hearts, their unvalued dust continues to be mingled, like some base alloy, with the circumstances of the past. And though we no longer love them, it may happen that in speaking of a room, or a walk in a public park, or a country road where they were present with us on a certain occasion, we are obliged, so that the place which they occupied may not be left empty, to make allusion to them, without, however, regretting them, without even naming them or permitting others to identify them. Such are the last, the scarcely desirable vestiges of survival after death.

If the opinions which the Duchess expressed about Rachel were in themselves commonplace, they interested me for the reason that they too marked a new hour upon the dial. For Mme de Guermantes had no more completely forgotten than Rachel the terrible evening which the latter had endured in her house, but in the Duchess's mind too this memory had been transformed. "Of course," she said to me, "it interests me all the more to hear her, and to hear her acclaimed, because it was I who discovered her, who saw her worth and praised her and got people to listen when she was quite unknown and everybody thought her ridiculous. Yes, my dear boy, this will surprise you, but the first house in which she recited in public was mine! Yes, while all the so-called avant-garde, like my new cousin," she said, pointing ironically towards the Princesse de Guermantes, who for Oriane had remained Mme Verdurin, "would have allowed her to die of hunger rather than condescend to listen to her, I had made up my mind that she was interesting and I offered her a fee to come and act in my house in front of the most distinguished audience that I could muster. I may say, though the word is rather stupid and pretentious—for the truth is that talent needs nobody to help it—that I launched her. But I am not suggesting that she needed me." I made a vague gesture of protest, and I saw that Mme de Guermantes was quite prepared to accept the contrary thesis. "You don't agree? You think that talent needs a support, needs someone to bring it into the light of day? Well, perhaps you are right. Curiously enough, that is exactly what Dumas used to say to me. In this case I am extremely flattered if I have done anything, however little, to promote not of course the talent but the reputation of so fine an artist." Mme de Guermantes preferred to abandon her idea that talent, like an abscess, forces its way to the surface unaided, partly because the alternative hypothesis was more flattering for her, but also because for some time now, mixing with newcomers to the social scene and being herself fatigued, she had become almost humble, questioning others and asking them their opinion before she formed her own. "I don't need to tell you," she went on, "that that intelligent public which calls itself society understood absolutely nothing of her art. They booed and they tittered. It was no use my saying: 'This is strange, interesting, something that has never been done before,' nobody believed me, just as nobody has ever believed anything I have said. And it was exactly the same with the piece that she recited, which was a scene from Maeterlinck. Now, of course, it is very well known but in those days people merely thought it ridiculous—not I, however, I admired it. I must say I am surprised, when I think of it, that a mere peasant like myself, with no more education than all the other provincial girls around her, should from the very first moment have felt drawn to these things. Naturally I couldn't have said why, but I liked them, I was moved—indeed, even Basin, who can hardly be called hypersensitive, was struck by the effect that they had on me. 'I won't have you listening to these absurdities,' he said, 'it makes you ill.' And he was right, because although I'm supposed to be a woman without any feeling I'm really a bundle of nerves."

At this moment an unexpected incident occurred. A footman came up to Rachel and told her that the daughter and son-in-law of Berma were asking to speak to her. As we have seen, Berma's daughter had resisted the desire, to which her husband would have yielded, to ask Rachel for an invitation. But after the departure of the solitary guest the irritation of the young pair as they sat with their mother had increased. The thought that other people were enjoying themselves had become a torment to them and presently, profiting from a momentary absence of Berma, who had retired to her room spitting a little blood, they had thrown on some smarter clothes, called for a cab and come, without an invitation, to the Princesse de Guermantes's house. Rachel, guessing what had happened and secretly flattered, put on an arrogant air and told the footman that she could not be disturbed, the visitors must write a line to explain the object of their curious procedure. Soon the footman came back with a card on which Berma's daughter had scribbled a few words to the effect that she and her husband had not been able to resist the desire to hear Rachel—might they have her permission to come in? Rachel smiled at the naïvety of the pretext and at her own triumph. She sent back a reply that she was terribly sorry but she had finished her recital. In the ante-room, where the couple had now been waiting for an embarrass-ingly long time, the footmen were beginning to jeer at the two rejected petitioners.

But the ignominy of a rebuff, and the thought too of the worthlessness of Rachel in comparison with her mother, drove Berma's daughter to pursue to final victory an enterprise on which she had first embarked merely from an appetite for pleasure. She sent a message to Rachel, asking as a favour that, even if she had missed the privilege of hearing her, she should be allowed to shake her by the hand. Rachel was talking to an Italian prince, said to be not insensible to the attractions of her large fortune, the origin of which was now to some extent disguised by her partial acceptance in the world of society. And here at her feet were the daughter and the son-in-law of the illustrious Berma, a reversal of positions which she was able to savour to the full. After giving a ludicrous account of what had happened to everybody within earshot, she ordered the young couple to be admitted and in they came with-out waiting to be asked twice, thus at a single stroke ruining Berma's social position just as they had destroyed her health. Rachel had foreseen this; she knew that an amiable condescension on her part would do more than a refusal to win for herself a reputation in society for kindness of heart and for the young couple one for grovelling servility. So she welcomed them with a theatrical gesture of open arms and a few words spoken in the role of an exalted patroness momentarily laying aside her dignity: "Ah! here you are, it is so lovely to see you. The Princess will be delighted." Not knowing that in the world of the theatre it was generally believed that she had sent out the invitations herself, she had feared perhaps that, if she refused to let Berma's daughter and son-in-law come in, they might have doubts as to the extent, not so much of her good nature, which would scarcely have worried her, as of her influence. Instinctively the Duchesse de Guermantes drifted away, for in proportion as anyone betrayed a desire to seek out fashionable society, he or she sank in her esteem. At the moment she was uniquely impressed with Rachel's kindness, and had the daughter and son-in-law been presented to her she would have turned her back on them. Rachel meanwhile was already composing in her head the gracious phrase with which she would annihilate Berma when she saw her the following day backstage: "I was distressed and appalled that your poor daughter should be made to dance attendance on me. If I had only realised! She kept sending me card after card." Her spirits rose as she thought of this blow that she would deal to Berma. Yet perhaps she would have flinched had she known that it would be mortal. We like to have victims, but without putting ourselves clearly in the wrong: we want them to live. Besides, in what way had she done wrong? A few days later she was heard to say, with a laugh: "It's a bit much. I try to be kinder to her children than she ever was to me, and now I'm practically accused of murdering her. The Duchess will be my witness." So died Berma. It seems that the children of actors inherit from their parents all their ugly emotions and all the artificiality of theatrical life, but not, as a by-product of these, the stubborn will to work that their father or mother possessed, and Berma is not the only great tragic actress who has died as the victim of a domestic plot woven around her, repeating in her own person the fate that she so many times suffered in the final act of a play.

In spite of her new interests the life of the Duchess was now very unhappy, for the reason to which she had briefly alluded in her conversation with me, a reason which had, as a further consequence, a parallel degradation of the society which M. de

Guermantes frequented. The Duke was still robust, but with the advance of age his desires had grown less imperious and he had long ceased to be unfaithful to Mme de Guermantes, when suddenly, without anyone knowing quite how the liaison had begun, he had fallen in love with Mme de Forcheville. When one considered what her age must now be, this seemed extraordinary. But perhaps she had been very young when she started on her amatory career. And then there are women who, decade after decade, are found in a new incarnation, having new love affairs (sometimes long after one had thought they were dead) and causing the despair of young wives who are abandoned for them by their husbands. In any case, the Duke's liaison with Mme de Forcheville had assumed such proportions that the old man, imitating in this final love the pattern of those that he had had in the past, watched jealously over his mistress in a manner which, if my love for Albertine had, with important variations, repeated the love of Swann for Odette, made that of M. de Guermantes for this same Odette recall my own for Albertine. He insisted that she should lunch with him and dine with him and he was always in her house, so that she was able to show him off to friends who without her would never have made the acquaintance of a Duc de Guermantes and who came there to meet him rather as one might go to the house of a courtesan to meet a king, her lover. It was true that Mme de Forcheville had long ago become a society lady. But starting again late in life to be kept, and to be kept by an old man of such enormous pride who, in spite of the situation, was the important person in her house, she was herself not too proud to wear only those wraps which pleased him, to serve only the dishes that he liked, and to flatter her friends by telling them that she had spoken of them to her new lover just as in the old days she would tell my great-uncle that she had spoken of him to the Grand Duke who sent her cigarettes; in a word, in spite of all that she had accomplished in building up a social position, she was tending under pressure of new circumstances to become once more, as she had first appeared to me in my earliest childhood, the lady in pink. (It was, of course, many years since my uncle Adolphe had died, but the replacement of the old figures around us by new ones does not necessarily prevent us from beginning our old life again.) If Odette had yielded to the pressure of her new circumstances, this was no doubt partly from greed, but also because, having been much sought after in society as the mother of an eligible daughter and then ignored once Gilberte had married Saint-Loup, she foresaw that the Duc de Guermantes, who would have done anything for her, would rally to her side a number of duchesses who would perhaps be delighted to do an ill turn to their friend Oriane; and perhaps too she warmed to the game when she saw how it distressed the Duchess, in whose discomfiture a feminine sentiment of rivalry caused her to rejoice. Even among the Duke's relations she now had her partisans. Saint-Loup up to his death had continued loyally to visit her with his wife. Were not he and Gilberte heirs both to M. de Guermantes and to Odette, who would herself no doubt be the principal beneficiary of the Duke's will? And even Courvoisier nephews with the most exacting standards, even the Princesse de Trania and Mme de Marsantes, came to her house in the hope of a legacy, without worrying about the pain that this might cause the Duchess, of whom Odette, stung by past affronts, spoke in the most scurrilous fashion. As for the Duke's own social position, his liaison with Mme de Forcheville—this liaison which was merely a pale copy of earlier affairs of the same kind—had recently caused him for the second time in his life to lose his chance of the presidency of the Jockey and a vacant seat in the Académie des Beaux-Arts, just as the way of life of M. de Charlus and his public association with Jupien had cost him the presidency of the Union and that also of the Société des Amis du Vieux Paris when these were within his grasp. Thus the two brothers, so different in their tastes, had lost their reputations from a common indolence and a common lack of will, qualities already perceptible, but in a more agreeable fashion, in the Duc de Guermantes their grandfather, member of the Académie Française, but which, reappearing in his two grandsons, had permitted a natural taste in the one and what passes for an unnatural taste in the other to alienate their possessors from their proper social sphere.

The old Duke no longer went anywhere, for he spent his days and his evenings with Mme de Forcheville. But today, as he would find her here, he had come for a moment, in spite of the vexation of having to meet his wife. I had not seen him, and I would certainly have failed to recognise him, had he not been clearly pointed out to me. He was no more than a ruin now, a magnificent ruin—or perhaps not even a ruin but a beautiful and romantic natural object, a rock in a tempest. Lashed on all sides by the surrounding waves—waves of suffering, of wrath at being made to suffer, of the rising tide of death—his face, like a crumbling block

of marble, preserved the style and the poise which I had always
admired; it might have been one of those fine antique heads, eaten
away and hopelessly damaged, which you are proud nevertheless
to have as an ornament for your study. In one respect only was it
changed: it seemed to belong to a more ancient epoch than
formerly, not simply because of the now rough and rugged surfaces of what had once been a more brilliant material, but also
because to an expression of keen and humorous enjoyment had
succeeded one, involuntary and unconscious, built up by illness,
by the struggle against death, by passive resistance, by the difficulty
of remaining alive. The arteries had lost all suppleness and gave to
the once expansive countenance a hard and sculptural quality. And
though the Duke had no suspicion of this, there were aspects of his
appearance, of his neck and cheeks and forehead, which suggested
to the observer that the vital spirit within, compelled to clutch
desperately at every passing minute, was buffeted by a great tragic
gale, while the white wisps of his still magnificent but less luxuriant
hair lashed with their foam the half submerged promontory of his
face. And just as there are strange and unique reflexions which
only the approach of a supreme all-foundering storm can impart to
rocks that hitherto have been of a different colour, so I realised that
the leaden grey of the stiff, worn cheeks, the almost white, fleecy
grey of the drifting wisps of hair, the feeble light that still shone
from the eyes that scarcely saw, were not unreal hues and glimmers—they were only too real but they were fantastic, they were
borrowed from the palette and the illumination, inimitable in
their terrifying and prophetic sombreness, of old age and the
imminence of death.

The Duke stayed only for a few moments, long enough, however, for me to perceive that Odette, reserving her favours for
younger wooers, treated him with contempt. But curiously,
whereas in the past he had been almost ridiculous when he used
to behave like a king in a play, he had now assumed an appearance
of true grandeur, rather like his brother, whom old age, stripping
him of all unessential qualities, caused him to resemble. And—in
this too resembling his brother—he who had once been
proud, though not in his brother's fashion, seemed now almost
deferential, though again in a different fashion. He had not suffered quite the degradation of M. de Charlus, he was not obliged
by the unreliable memory of a sick man to greet with civility
people whom he would once have disdained. But he was very old

and when, wanting to leave, he passed laboriously through the doorway and down the stairs, one saw that old age, which is after all the most miserable of human conditions, which more than anything else precipitates us from the summit of our fortunes like a king in a Greek tragedy, old age, forcing him to halt in the *via dolorosa* which life must become for us when we are impotent and surrounded by menace, to wipe his perspiring brow, to grope his way forward as his eyes sought the step which eluded them, because for his unsteady feet no less than for his clouded eyes he needed support, old age, giving him without his knowing it the air of gently and timidly beseeching those near him, had made him not only august but, even more, suppliant.

Thus in the Faubourg Saint-Germain three apparently impregnable positions, of the Duc and the Duchesse de Guermantes and of the Baron de Charlus, had lost their inviolability, changing, as all things change in this world, under the action of an inherent principle which had at first attracted nobody's attention: in M. de Charlus his love for Charlie, which had enslaved him to the Verdurins, and then later the advent of senility; in Mme de Guermantes a taste for novelty and for art; in the Duke an exclusive amorous passion, of a kind of which he had had several in the course of his life, but one which now, through the feebleness of age, was more tyrannical than those that had gone before and of which the ignominy was no longer compensated by the opposing, the socially redeeming respectability of the Duchess's salon, where the Duke himself no longer appeared and which altogether had almost ceased to function. Thus it is that the pattern of the things of this world changes, that centres of empire, assessments of wealth, letters patent of social prestige, all that seemed to be for ever fixed is constantly being refashioned, so that the eyes of a man who has lived can contemplate the most total transformation exactly where change would have seemed to him to be most impossible.

Unable to do without Odette, always installed by her fireside in the same armchair, whence age and gout made it difficult for him to rise, M. de Guermantes permitted her to receive friends who were only too pleased to be presented to the Duke, to defer to him in conversation, to listen while he talked about the society of an earlier era, about the Marquise de Villeparisis and the Duc de Chartres. At moments, beneath the gaze of the old masters assembled by Swann in a typical "collector's" arrangement which enhanced the unfashionable and "period" character of the scene, with this Restoration Duke and this Second Empire courtesan swathed in one of the wraps which he liked, the lady in pink would interrupt him with a sprightly sally: he would stop dead and fix her with a ferocious glance. Perhaps he had come to see that she too, like the Duchess, sometimes made stupid remarks; perhaps, suffering from an old man's delusion, he imagined that it was an ill-timed witticism of Mme de Guermantes that had checked his flow of reminiscence, imagined that he was still in his own house, like a wild beast in chains who for a brief second thinks that it is still free in the deserts of Africa. And brusquely raising his head, with his little round yellow eyes which themselves had the glitter of the eyes of a wild animal, he fastened upon her one of those looks which sometimes in Mme de Guermantes's drawing-room, when the Duchess talked too much, had made me tremble. So for a moment the Duke glared at the audacious lady in pink. But she, unflinching, held him in her gaze, and after a few seconds which seemed interminable to the spectators, the old tame lion recollecting that he was not free, with the Duchess beside him, in that Sahara which one entered by stepping over a door-mat on a landing, but in Mme de Forcheville's domain, in his cage in the Zoological Gardens, he allowed his head, with its still thick and flowing mane of which it would have been hard to say whether it was yellow or white, to slump back between his shoulders and continued his story. He seemed not to have understood what Mme de Forcheville was trying to say, and indeed there was seldom any very profound meaning in her remarks. He did not forbid her to have friends to dinner with him, but, following a habit derived from his former love affairs which was hardly likely to surprise Odette, who had been used to the same thing with Swann, and which to me seemed touching because it recalled to me my life with Albertine, he insisted that these guests should take their leave early so that he might be the last to say good-night to her. Needless to say, the moment he was out of the house she went off to meet other people. But of this the Duke had no suspicion or perhaps preferred her to think that he had no suspicion. The sight of old men grows dim as their hearing grows less acute, their insight too becomes clouded and even their vigilance is relaxed by fatigue, and at a certain age, inevitably, Jupiter himself is transformed into a character in one of Molière's plays, and not even into the Olympian lover of Alcmène but into a ludicrous

Géronte. It must be added that Odette was unfaithful to M. de Guermantes in the same fashion that she looked after him, that is to say without charm and without dignity. She was commonplace in this role as she had been in all her others. Not that life had not frequently given her good parts; it had, but she had not known how to play them.

On several occasions after the Guermantes party I attempted to see her again, but each time I was unsuccessful, for M. de Guermantes, in order to satisfy the requirements not only of his jealous nature but also of his medical regime, allowed her to attend social functions only in the daytime and even then placed an embargo upon dances. This seclusion in which she was kept she frankly avowed to me when at last we met, for several reasons. The principal one was that, although I had only written a few articles and published some essays, she imagined me to be a well-known author, an idea which even caused her naïvely to exclaim, recalling the days when I used to go to the Allée des Acacias to see her pass by and later visited her in her home: "Ah! if I had only guessed that he would be a great writer one day!" And having heard that writers seek the society of women as a means of collecting material for their work and like to get them to describe their love affairs, she now, in order to interest me, reassumed the character of an unashamed tart. She would tell me stories of this sort: "And then once there was a man who was mad about me, and I was desperately in love with him too. We were having a heavenly life together. He had to go to America for some reason, and I was to go with him. The day before we were to leave I decided that, as our love could not always remain at such a pitch of intensity, it was more beautiful not to let it slowly fade to nothing. We had a last evening together—he of course believed that I was coming with him—and then a night of absolute madness, in which I was ecstatically happy in his arms and at the same time in despair because I knew that I should never see him again. A few hours earlier I had gone up to some traveller whom I did not know and given him my ticket. He wanted at least to buy it from me, but I replied: 'No, you are doing me a service by taking it, I don't want any money.'" Here was another: "One day I was in the Champs-Elysées and M. de Bréauté, whom I had only met once, began to stare at me so insistently that I stopped and asked him why he took the liberty of staring at me like that. He replied: 'I am looking at you because you are wearing a ridiculous hat.' This was quite true.

It was a little hat with pansies, the fashions were dreadful in those days. But I was furious and said to him: 'I cannot allow you to talk to me like that.' At that moment it started to rain. I said to him: 'I would only forgive you if you had a carriage.' 'But I have one,' he replied, 'and I will accompany you.' 'No, I want your carriage but I don't want you.' I got into the carriage and he walked off in the rain. But the same evening he arrived on my doorstep. For two years we were madly in love with each other. Come and have tea with me one day, and I will tell you how I made the acquaintance of M. de Forcheville. The truth is," she went on with a melancholy air, "that I have spent my life in cloistered seclusion because my great loves have all been for men who were horribly jealous. I am not speaking of M. de Forcheville, who was at bottom a commonplace man—and I have never really been able to love anyone who was not intelligent. But M. Swann for one was as jealous as the poor Duke here, for whose sake I renounce all enjoyment, because I know that he is so unhappy in his own home. With M. Swann it was different, I was desperately in love with him and it seems to me only reasonable to sacrifice dancing and society and all the rest of it for a life which will give pleasure to a man who loves you, or will merely prevent him from suffering. Poor Charles, how intelligent he was, how fascinating, just the type of man I liked." And perhaps this was true. There had been a time when she had found Swann attractive, which had coincided with the time when she to him had been "not his type." The truth was that "his type" was something that, even later, she had never been. And yet how he had loved her and with what anguish of mind! Ceasing to love her, he had been puzzled by this contradiction, which really is no contradiction at all, if we consider how large a proportion of the sufferings endured by men in their lives is caused to them by women who are "not their type." Perhaps there are many reasons why this should be so: first, because a woman is "not your type" you let yourself, at the beginning, be loved by her without loving in return, and by doing this you allow your life to be gripped by a habit which would not have taken root in the same way with a woman who was "your type," who, conscious of your desire, would have offered more resistance, would only rarely have consented to see you, would not have installed herself in every hour of your days with that familiarity which means that later, if you come to love her and then suddenly she is not there, because of a quarrel or because of a journey during which you are left without news of her, you are hurt by the severance not of one but of a thousand links. And then this habit, not resting upon the foundation of strong physical desire, is a sentimental one, and once love is born the brain gets much more busily to work: you are plunged into a romance, not plagued by a mere need. We are not wary of women who are "not our type," we let them love us, and if, subsequently, we come to love them we love them a hundred times more than we love other women, without even enjoying in their arms the satisfaction of assuaged desire. For these reasons and for many others the fact that our greatest unhappinesses come to us from women who are "not our type" is not simply an instance of that mockery of fate which never grants us our wishes except in the form which pleases us least. A woman who is "our type" is seldom dangerous, she is not interested in us, she gives us a limited contentment and then quickly leaves us without establishing herself in our life, and what on the contrary, in love, is dangerous and prolific of suffering is not a woman herself but her presence beside us every day and our curiosity about what she is doing every minute: not the beloved woman, but habit.

I was cowardly enough to say that it was kind and generous of her to talk to me in this way, but I knew how little truth there was in my remark, I knew that her frankness was mixed with all sorts of lies. And as she continued to regale me with adventures from her past life, I thought with terror how much there was that Swann had not known—though some of it he had guessed almost to the point of certainty, merely from the look in her eyes when she saw a man or a woman whom she did not know and whom she found attractive—and how much the knowledge of it would have made him suffer, because he had fastened his sensibility to this one individual. And why was she now so outspoken? Simply in order to give me what she believed were subjects for novels. In this belief she was mistaken. It was true that from my earliest years she had supplied my imagination with abundance of material to work on, but in a much more involuntary fashion, through an act which originated with myself when I sought, unbeknown to her, to deduce from my observation of her the laws which governed her life.

M. de Guermantes now reserved his thunderbolts solely for the Duchess, to whose somewhat indiscriminate associations Mme de Forcheville did not fail to draw his wrathful attention. And so Mme de Guermantes was very unhappy. It is true that M. de

Charlus, with whom I had once discussed the subject, maintained that the original transgressions had not been on his brother's side and that beneath the legendary purity of the Duchess there in fact lay skilfully concealed an incalculable number of love affairs. But I had never heard any gossip to this effect. In the eyes of almost all the world Mme de Guermantes was a woman of a very different kind, and the idea that she had always been irreproachable went unchallenged. Which of these two ideas accorded with the truth I was unable to determine, the truth being almost always something that to three people out of four is unknown. I well recalled certain blue and wandering glances, which I had intercepted as they shot from the eyes of the Duchesse de Guermantes down the nave at Combray, but I could not really say that either of the two ideas was disproved by these glances, since both the one and the other could give them meanings which, though different, were equally acceptable. In my foolishness, child as I then was, I had for a moment taken them to be glances of love directed at myself. Later I had realised that they were merely the gracious looks that a sovereign lady, like the one in the stained-glass windows of the church, bestows upon her vassals. Was I now to suppose that my first idea had been correct and that, if in the sequel the Duchess had never spoken to me of love, this was because she had been more afraid to compromise herself with a friend of her nephew and her aunt than with an unknown boy encountered by chance in the church of Saint-Hilaire at Combray?

Perhaps the Duchess had been pleased for a moment to feel that her past had more substance because it had been shared by me, but certain questions which I put to her on the provincialism of M. de Bréauté, whom at the time I had scarcely distinguished from M. de Sagan or M. de Guermantes, caused her to resume the normal point of view of a society woman, the point of view, that is to say, of a woman who affects to despise society. While we were talking, she took me on a tour of the house. In one or two smaller sitting-rooms we came upon special friends of our hostess who had preferred to get away from the crowd in order to listen to the music. One of these was a little room with Empire furniture, where a few men in black evening clothes were sitting about on sofas, listening, while beside a tall mirror supported by a figure of Minerva a *chaise longue*, set at right angles to the wall but with a curved and cradle-like interior which contrasted with the straight lines all round it, disclosed the figure of a young woman lying at

full length. The relaxation of her pose, from which she did not
even stir when the Duchess entered the room, was set off by the
marvellous brilliance of her Empire dress, of a flame-red silk
before which even the reddest of fuchsias would have paled and
upon whose nacreous texture emblems and flowers seemed to
have been imprinted in some distant past, for their patterns were
sunk beneath its surface. To acknowledge the presence of the
Duchess she made a slight bow with her beautiful, dark head.
Although it was broad daylight, she had asked for the curtains to be
drawn as an aid to the silence and concentration which the music
required and, to prevent people from stumbling over the furniture, an urn had been lit upon a tripod and from it came a faint,
iridescent glimmer. I inquired of the Duchess who the young
woman was, and she told me that her name was Mme de Saint-
Euverte. This led me to inquire further how she was related to the
Mme de Saint-Euverte whom I had known. Mme de Guermantes
said that she was the wife of one of old Mme de Saint-Euverte's
great-nephews and appeared to think it possible that her maiden
name had been La Rochefoucauld, but denied that she had ever
herself known any Saint-Euvertes. I recalled to her the evening
party (known to me, it is true, only from hearsay) at which, when
she was still Princesse des Laumes, she had unexpectedly met
Swann. Mme de Guermantes assured me that she had never
been at this party. The Duchess had never been very truthful and
now told lies more readily than ever. For her Mme de Saint-
Euverte was a hostess—and one whose reputation, with the passage of time, had sunk very low indeed—whom she chose to
disown. I did not insist. "No, someone you may perhaps have
seen in my house—because at least he was amusing—is the husband of the woman you are talking about, but I never had anything to do with his wife." "But she didn't have a husband." "That
is what you imagined, because they were separated. In fact he was
much nicer than she was." At length it dawned upon me that an
enormous man, of vast height and strength, with snow-white hair,
whom I used to meet in various houses and whose name I had
never known, was the husband of Mme de Saint-Euverte. He had
died in the previous year. As for the great-niece, I do not know
whether it was owing to some malady of the stomach or the nerves
or the veins, or because she was about to have or had just had a
child or perhaps a miscarriage, that she lay flat on her back to listen
to the music and did not budge for anyone. Very probably she was

simply proud of her magnificent red silks and hoped on her *chaise longue* to look like Mme Récamier. She could not know that for me she was giving birth to a new efflorescence of the name of Saint-Euverte, which recurring thus after so long an interval marked both the distance travelled by Time and its continuity. Time was the infant that she cradled in her cockle-shell, where the red fuchsias of her silk dress gave an autumnal flowering to the name of Saint-Euverte and to the Empire style. The latter Mme de Guermantes declared that she had always detested, a remark which meant merely that she detested it now, which was true, for she followed the fashion, even if she did not succeed in keeping up with it. To say nothing of David, whose work she hardly knew, when she was quite young she had thought M. Ingres the most boring and academic of painters, then, by a brusque reversal—which caused her also to loathe Delacroix—the most delectable of the masters revered by *art nouveau*. By what gradations she had subsequently passed from this cult to a renewal of her early contempt matters little, since these are shades of taste which the writings of an art critic reflect ten years before the conversation of clever women. After having delivered herself of some strictures upon the Empire style, she apologised for having talked to me about people of as little interest as the Saint-Euvertes and subjects as trivial as the provincial side of Bréauté's character, for she was as far from guessing why these things could interest me as was Mme de Saint-Euverte *née* La Rochefoucauld, seeking in her supine pose the well-being of her stomach or an Ingresque effect, from suspecting that her name—her married name, not the infinitely more distinguished one of her own family—had enchanted me and that I saw her, in this room full of symbolic attributes, as a nymph cradling the Infant Time.

"But how can I talk to you about this nonsense, how can it possibly interest you?" exclaimed the Duchess. She had uttered these words in an undertone and nobody had been able to hear what she was saying. But a young man (who interested me later when I discovered his name, which had been much more familiar to me at one time than that of Saint-Euverte) got up with an air of exasperation and moved away from us in order to listen undisturbed. For the Kreutzer Sonata was now being played, but having lost his place in the programme the young man thought that it was a piece by Ravel, which he had been told was as beautiful as Palestrina but difficult to understand. In his haste to move to another seat, he bumped violently against an escritoire which he had not seen in the half-dark, and the noise had the effect of slewing round the heads of several people, for whom the trifling physical exertion of looking over their shoulder was a welcome interruption to the torture of listening "religiously" to the Kreutzer Sonata. Mme de Guermantes and I, who had caused this unfortunate little incident, hurriedly left the room. "Yes," she went on, "how can these inanities interest a man of your talent? That is what I asked myself just now, when I saw you talking to Gilberte de Saint-Loup. You should not waste your time on her. For me that woman is quite literally nothing—she is not even a woman, merely the most artificial and bourgeois phenomenon that I have ever encountered" (for even when she was defending intellectualism the Duchess did not divest herself of her aristocratic prejudices). "What, in any case, are you doing in a house like this? I can just see that you might want to be here today, because there was this recitation by Rachel and naturally that interests you. But wonderful though she was, she does not give of her best before a public like this. You must come and have luncheon alone with her in my house. Then you will see what an extraordinary creature she is. She is worth a hundred times more than all this riff-raff. And after luncheon she will recite Verlaine for you. You will be amazed! But otherwise your coming to a great omnium gatherum like this is something I simply cannot understand. Unless perhaps your interest is professional . . . " she added with a doubtful and mistrustful air and without venturing to follow this speculation too far for she had no very precise ideas as to the nature of the improbable operations to which she alluded. She went on to tempt me with the glittering prospect of her "afternoons": every day after luncheon there was X—— and there was Y——, and I found that her views on these matters were now those of all women who preside over a salon, those women whom in the past (though she denied it today) she had despised and whose great superiority, whose sign of election lay, according to her present mode of thinking, in getting "all the men" to come to them. If I happened to say that some great lady with a salon had spoken with malice of Mme Howland when she was alive, the Duchess burst out laughing at my simplicity: "But of course, she had all the men and Mme Howland was trying to get them away from her."

"Don't you think," I said to the Duchess, "that it must be painful for Mme de Saint-Loup to have to listen, as she has just

been doing, to a woman who was once her husband's mistress?"
I saw form in Mme de Guermantes's face one of those oblique bars
which indicate that a train of thought is linking something a
person has just heard to some disagreeable subject of reflexion. A
train of thought, it is true, which usually remains unexpressed, for
seldom if ever do we receive any answer to the unpleasant things
that we say or write. Only a fool begs vainly ten times in succession
for a reply to a letter which was a blunder and which he ought
never to have written, for the only reply ever vouchsafed to this
sort of letter is in the form of action: the lady whom you suppose to
be merely an unpunctual correspondent addresses you as
"Monsieur" when she next meets you instead of calling you by
your Christian name. My reference to Saint-Loup's liaison with
Rachel was, however, not seriously unpleasant and could only
cause Mme de Guermantes a moment's annoyance by reminding
her that I had been Robert's closest friend and that he had perhaps
confided in me on the subject of the snubs which Rachel had
suffered when she gave her performance at the Duchess's party.
But Mme de Guermantes did not persist in these reflexions, the
stormy bar faded from her face and she replied to my question
concerning Mme de Saint-Loup: "Frankly, it is my belief that it
can matter very little to Gilberte, since she never loved her husband. She is a quite dreadful young woman. She loved the social
position and the name and being my niece and getting away from
the slime where she belonged, but then having done this her one
idea was to return to it. I don't mind telling you that I suffered a
great deal for poor Robert, because, though he was no genius, he
saw this perfectly well, and a lot of other things too. Perhaps
I shouldn't say it, because after all she is my niece and I have no
absolute proof that she was unfaithful to him, but there were any
number of stories. Oh! yes, there were, and I know for a fact there
was something between her and an officer at Méséglise. Robert
wanted to challenge him. It was because of all this that
Robert joined up—the war came to him as a deliverance from
the misery of his family life: if you want my opinion, he wasn't
killed, he got himself killed. Do you think she felt any grief? Not a
scrap, she even astonished me by the extraordinary cynicism with
which she displayed her indifference, and this distressed me very
much, because I was really extremely fond of poor Robert.
Perhaps this will surprise you, because people have a wrong idea
of my character, but even now I still think of him sometimes—I

never forget anybody. He never said a word to me, but he saw very clearly that I guessed everything. Do you suppose, if she had loved her husband the least little bit, that she could stoically endure like this to be in the same drawing-room as the woman with whom he was desperately in love for so many years—indeed one may say 'always,' for I am quite certain that he never gave her up, even during the war. Why, she would fly at her throat!" exclaimed the Duchess, forgetting that she herself, in arranging for Rachel to be invited and so setting the stage for the drama which she judged to be inevitable if it were true that Gilberte had loved Robert, had perhaps acted cruelly. "No, in my opinion," the Duchess concluded, "she is a bitch." Such an expression on the lips of the Duchesse de Guermantes was rendered possible by the downward path which she was following, from the polished society of the Guermantes to that of her new actress friends, and came to her all the more easily because she grafted it on to an eighteenth-century mode of speech which she thought of as broad and racy—and then had she not always believed that to her all things were permitted? But the actual choice of the word was dictated by the hatred which she felt for Gilberte, by an irresistible wish to strike her at least in effigy if she could not attack her with physical blows. And at the same time the Duchess thought that somehow the word justified the whole manner in which she conducted herself towards Gilberte, or rather conducted hostilities against Gilberte, in society and in the family and even where pecuniary interests were concerned such as the succession to Robert's estate.

This savage attack on Gilberte struck me as quite unwarranted, but sometimes we pronounce a judgment which receives later from facts of which we were ignorant and which we could not have guessed an apparent justification, and Mme de Guermantes's tirade perhaps belonged to this category. For Gilberte, who had no doubt inherited certain family characteristics from her mother (and I had perhaps unconsciously anticipated some such laxness of principle in her when I had asked her to introduce me to young girls), had now had time to reflect upon my request and, anxious no doubt that the profit should stay in the family, had reached a decision bolder than any that I would have thought possible. "Let me fetch my daughter for you," she said, "I should so like to introduce her to you. She is over there, talking to young Mortemart and other babes in arms who can be of no possible interest. I am sure that she will be a charming little friend for you."

I asked whether Robert had been pleased to have a daughter. "Oh! yes," she replied, "he was very proud of her. But naturally," she went on, with a certain naïvety, "I think that nevertheless, his tastes being what they were, he would have preferred a son." Years later, this daughter, whose name and fortune gave her mother the right to hope that she would crown the whole work of social ascent of Swann and his wife by marrying a royal prince, happening to be entirely without snobbery chose for her husband an obscure man of letters. Thus it came about that the family sank once more, below even the level from which it had started its ascent, and a new generation could only with the greatest difficulty be persuaded that the parents of the obscure couple had enjoyed a splendid social position. The names of Swann and Odette de Crécy came miraculously to life whenever anyone wanted to explain to you that you were wrong, that there had been nothing so very wonderful about the family, and it was generally supposed that Mme de Saint-Loup had really made as good a match for her daughter as could be expected and that the marriage of this daughter's grandfather to Mme de Crécy had been no more than an unsuccessful attempt to rise to a higher sphere—a view of Swann's marriage which would have astonished his fashionable friends, in whose eyes it had been rather the product of an idealistic theory like those which in the eighteenth century drove aristocratic disciples of Rousseau and other precursors of the Revolution to abandon their privileges and live according to nature.

My surprise at Gilberte's words and the pleasure that they caused me were soon replaced, while Mme de Saint-Loup left me and made her way into another drawing-room, by that idea of Time past which was brought home to me once again, in yet another fashion and without my even having seen her, by Mlle de Saint-Loup. Was she not—are not, indeed, the majority of human beings?—like one of those star-shaped cross-roads in a forest where roads converge that have come, in the forest as in our lives, from the most diverse quarters? Numerous for me were the roads which led to Mlle de Saint-Loup and which radiated around her. Firstly the two great "ways" themselves, where on my many walks I had dreamed so many dreams, both led to her: through her father Robert de Saint-Loup the Guermantes way; through Gilberte, her mother, the Méséglise way which was also "Swann's way." One of them took me, by way of this girl's mother and the Champs-Elysées, to Swann, to my evenings at Combray,

to Méséglise itself; the other, by way of her father, to those afternoons at Balbec where even now I saw him again near the sun-
bright sea. And then between these two high roads a network of
transversals was set up. Balbec, for example, the real Balbec where
I had met Saint-Loup, was a place that I had longed to go to very
largely because of what Swann had told me about the churches in
its neighbourhood, and especially about its own church in the
Persian style, and yet Robert de Saint-Loup was the nephew of the
Duchesse de Guermantes, and through him I arrived at Combray
again, at the Guermantes way. And Mlle de Saint-Loup led to
many other points of my life, to the lady in pink, for instance, who
was her grandmother and whom I had seen in the house of my
great-uncle. And here there was a new transversal, for this great-
uncle's manservant, who had opened the door to me that day and
who later, by the gift of a photograph, had enabled me to identify
the lady in pink, was the father of the young man with whom not
only M. de Charlus but also Mlle de Saint-Loup's father had been
in love, the young man on whose account he had made her
mother unhappy. And was it not Swann, the grandfather of Mlle
de Saint-Loup, who had first spoken to me of the music of
Vinteuil, just as it was Gilberte who had first spoken to me
of Albertine? Yet it was in speaking of this same music of
Vinteuil to Albertine that I had discovered the identity of her
great friend and it was with this discovery that that part of our lives
had commenced which had led her to her death and caused me
such terrible sufferings. And it was also Mlle de Saint-Loup's father
who had gone off to try and bring Albertine back. And indeed my
whole social life, both in the drawing-rooms of the Swanns and
the Guermantes in Paris and also that very different life which I had
led with the Verdurins in the country, was in some sense a
prolongation of the two ways of Combray, a prolongation
which brought into line with one way or the other places as far
apart as the Champs-Elysées and the beautiful terrace of La
Raspelière. Are there in fact among all our acquaintances any
who, if we are to tell the story of our friendship with them, do
not constrain us to place them successively in all the most different
settings of our own lives? A life of Saint-Loup painted by me
would have as its background the various scenes of my own life,
would be related to every part of that life, even those to which it
was apparently most foreign, such as my grandmother and
Albertine. And the Verdurins, though they might be diametrically

opposed to these other characters, were yet linked to Odette through her past and to Robert de Saint-Loup through Charlie—and in the Verdurins' house too what a role, what an all-important role had not the music of Vinteuil played! And then Swann had been in love with Legrandin's sister, and Legrandin had known M. de Charlus, whose ward Legrandin's nephew, young Cambremer, had married. Certainly, if he was thinking purely of the human heart, the poet was right when he spoke of the "mysterious threads" which are broken by life. But the truth, even more, is that life is perpetually weaving fresh threads which link one individual and one event to another, and that these threads are crossed and recrossed, doubled and redoubled to thicken the web, so that between any slightest point of our past and all the others a rich network of memories gives us an almost infinite variety of communicating paths to choose from.

At every moment of our lives we are surrounded by things and people which once were endowed with a rich emotional significance that they no longer possess. But let us cease to make use of them in an unconscious way, let us try to recall what they once were in our eyes, and how often do we not find that a thing later transformed into, as it were, mere raw material for our industrial use was once alive, and alive for us with a personal life of its own. All round me on the walls were paintings by Elstir, that Elstir who had first introduced me to Albertine. And it was in the house of Mme Verdurin that I was about to be presented to Mlle de Saint-Loup whom I was going to ask to be Albertine's successor in my life, in the house of that very Mme Verdurin whom I had so often visited with Albertine—and how enchanting they seemed in my memory, all those journeys that we had made together in the little train on the way to Douville and La Raspelière—and who had also schemed first to promote and then to break not only my own love for Albertine but, long before it, that of the grandfather and the grandmother of this same Mlle de Saint-Loup. And to complete the process by which all my various pasts were fused into a single mass Mme Verdurin, like Gilberte, had married a Guermantes.

I have said that it would be impossible to depict our relationship with anyone whom we have even slightly known without passing in review, one after another, the most different settings of our life. Each individual therefore—and I was myself one of these individuals—was a measure of duration for me, in virtue of the revolutions which like some heavenly body he had accomplished not only on his own axis but also around other bodies, in virtue, above all, of the successive positions which he had occupied in relation to myself. And surely the awareness of all these different planes within which, since in this last hour, at this party, I had recaptured it, Time seemed to dispose the different elements of my life, had, by making me reflect that in a book which tried to tell the story of a life it would be necessary to use not the two-dimensional psychology which we normally use but a quite different sort of three-dimensional psychology, added a new beauty to those resurrections of the past which my memory had effected while I was following my thoughts alone in the library, since memory by itself, when it introduces the past, unmodified, into the present—the past just as it was at the moment when it was itself the present—suppresses the mighty dimension of Time which is the dimension in which life is lived.

I saw Gilberte coming across the room towards me. For me the marriage of Saint-Loup and the thoughts which filled my mind at that date—and which were still there, unchanged, this very morning—might have belonged to yesterday, so that I was astonished to see at her side a girl of about sixteen, whose tall figure was a measure of that distance which I had been reluctant to see. Time, colourless and inapprehensible Time, so that I was almost able to see it and touch it, had materialised itself in this girl, moulding her into a masterpiece, while correspondingly, on me, alas! it had merely done its work. And now Mlle de Saint-Loup was standing in front of me. She had deep-set piercing eyes, and a charming nose thrust slightly forward in the form of a beak and curved, perhaps not in the least like that of Swann but like Saint-Loup's. The soul of that particular Guermantes had fluttered away, but his charming head, as of a bird in flight, with its piercing eyes, had settled momentarily upon the shoulders of Mlle de Saint-Loup and the sight of it there aroused a train of memories and dreams in those who had known her father. I was struck too by the way in which her nose, imitating in this the model of her mother's nose and her grandmother's, was cut off by just that absolutely horizontal line at its base, that same brilliant if slightly tardy stroke of design—a feature so individual that with its help, even without seeing anything else of a head, one could have recognised it out of thousands—and it seemed to me wonderful that at the critical moment nature should have returned, like a great and original sculptor, to give to the granddaughter, as she had given to her mother and her grandmother, that significant and decisive touch of the chisel. I thought her very beautiful: still rich in hopes, full of laughter, formed from those very years which I myself had lost, she was like my own youth.

The idea of Time was of value to me for yet another reason: it was a spur, it told me that it was time to begin if I wished to attain to what I had sometimes perceived in the course of my life, in brief lightning-flashes, on the Guermantes way and in my drives in the carriage of Mme de Villeparisis, at those moments of perception which had made me think that life was worth living. How much more worth living did it appear to me now, now that I seemed to see that this life that we live in half-darkness can be illumined, this life that at every moment we distort can be restored to its true pristine shape, that a life, in short, can be realised within the confines of a book! How happy would he be, I thought, the man who had the power to write such a book! What a task awaited him! To give some idea of this task one would have to borrow comparisons from the loftiest and the most varied arts; for this writer—who, moreover, must bring out the opposed facets of each of his characters in order to show its volume—would have to prepare his book with meticulous care, perpetually regrouping his forces like a general conducting an offensive, and he would have also to endure his book like a form of fatigue, to accept it like a discipline, build it up like a church, follow it like a medical regime, vanquish it like an obstacle, win it like a friendship, cosset it like a little child, create it like a new world without neglecting those mysteries whose explanation is to be found probably only in worlds other than our own and the presentiment of which is the thing that moves us most deeply in life and in art. In long books of this kind there are parts which there has been time only to sketch, parts which, because of the very amplitude of the architect's plan, will no doubt never be completed. How many great cathedrals remain unfinished! The writer feeds his book, he strengthens the parts of it which are weak, he protects it, but afterwards it is the book that grows, that designates its author's tomb and defends it against the world's clamour and for a while against oblivion. But to return to my own case, I thought more modestly of my book and it would be inaccurate even to say that I thought of those who would read it as "my" readers. For it seemed to me that they would not be "my" readers but the readers of their own selves, my book being merely a sort of magnifying glass like those which the optician at

Combray used to offer his customers—it would be my book, but with its help I would furnish them with the means of reading what lay inside themselves. So that I should not ask them to praise me or to censure me, but simply to tell me whether "it really is like that," I should ask them whether the words that they read within themselves are the same as those which I have written (though a discrepancy in this respect need not always be the consequence of an error on my part, since the explanation could also be that the reader had eyes for which my book was not a suitable instrument). And—for at every moment the metaphor uppermost in my mind changed as I began to represent to myself more clearly and in a more material shape the task upon which I was about to embark— I thought that at my big deal table, under the eyes of Françoise, who like all unpretentious people who live at close quarters with us would have a certain insight into the nature of my labours (and I had sufficiently forgotten Albertine to have forgiven Françoise anything that she might have done to injure her), I should work beside her and in a way almost as she worked herself (or at least as she had worked in the past, for now, with the onset of old age, she had almost lost her sight) and, pinning here and there an extra page, I should construct my book, I dare not say ambitiously like a cathedral, but quite simply like a dress. Whenever I had not all my "paperies" near me, as Françoise called them, and just the one that I needed was missing, Françoise would understand how this upset me, she who always said that she could not sew if she had not the right size of thread and the proper buttons. And then through sharing my life with me had she not acquired a sort of instinctive comprehension of literary work, more accurate than that possessed by many intelligent people, not to mention fools? Already years ago, when I had written my article for *Le Figaro*, while our old butler, with that sort of commiseration which always slightly exaggerates the laboriousness of an occupation which the sympathiser does not practise himself and does not even clearly visualise—or even of a habit which he does not have himself, like the people who say to you: "How tiring you must find it to sneeze like that!"—expressed his quite sincere pity for writers in the words: "That's a head-splitting job you've got there," Françoise on the contrary both divined my happiness and respected my toil. The only thing that annoyed her was my speaking about the article to Bloch before it appeared, for she was afraid that he might forestall me. "You're too trustful," she would say, "all those people are nothing but copiators." And it was true that, whenever I had outlined to Bloch something that I had written and that he admired, he would provide a retrospective alibi for himself by saying: "Why, isn't that curious, I have written something very similar myself, I must read it to you one day," from which I inferred that he intended to sit down and write it that very evening.

These "paperies," as Françoise called the pages of my writing, it was my habit to stick together with paste, and sometimes in this process they became torn. But Françoise then would be able to come to my help, by consolidating them just as she stitched patches on to the worn parts of her dresses or as, on the kitchen window, while waiting for the glazier as I was waiting for the printer, she used to paste a piece of newspaper where a pane of glass had been broken. And she would say to me, pointing to my note-books as though they were worm-eaten wood or a piece of stuff which the moth had got into: "Look, it's all eaten away, isn't that dreadful! There's nothing left of this bit of page, it's been torn to ribbons," and examining it with a tailor's eye she would go on: "I don't think I shall be able to mend this one, it's finished and done for. A pity, perhaps it has your best ideas. You know what they say at Combray: there isn't a furrier who knows as much about furs as the moth, they always get into the best ones."

And yet in a book individual characters, whether human or of some other kind, are made up of numerous impressions derived from many girls, many churches, many sonatas, and combined to form a single sonata, a single church, a single girl, so that I should be making my book in the same way that Françoise made that *boeuf à la mode* which M. de Norpois had found so delicious, just because she had enriched its jelly with so many carefully chosen pieces of meat.

Thus it was that I envisaged the task before me, a task which would not end until I had achieved what I had so ardently desired in my walks on the Guermantes way and thought to be impossible, just as I had thought it impossible, as I came home at the end of those walks, that I should ever get used to going to bed without kissing my mother or, later, to the idea that Albertine loved women, though in the end I had grown to live with this idea without even being aware of its presence; for neither our greatest fears nor our greatest hopes are beyond the limits of our strength—

we are able in the end both to dominate the first and to achieve the second.

Yes, upon this task the idea of Time which I had formed today told me that it was time to set to work. It was high time. But—and this was the reason for the anxiety which had gripped me as soon as I entered the drawing-room, when the theatrical disguises of the faces around me had first given me the notion of Lost Time—was there still time and was I still in a fit condition to undertake the task? For one thing, a necessary condition of my work as I had conceived it just now in the library was a profound study of impressions which had first to be re-created through the memory. But my memory was old and tired. The mind has landscapes which it is allowed to contemplate only for a certain space of time. In my life I had been like a painter climbing a road high above a lake, a view of which is denied to him by a curtain of rocks and trees. Suddenly through a gap in the curtain he sees the lake, its whole expanse is before him, he takes up his brushes. But already the night is at hand, the night which will put an end to his painting and which no dawn will follow. How could I not be anxious, seeing that nothing was yet begun and that though on the ground of age I could still hope that I had some years to live, my hour might on the other hand strike almost at once? For the fundamental fact was that I had a body, and this meant that I was perpetually threatened by a double danger, internal and external, though to speak thus was merely a matter of linguistic convenience, the truth being that the internal danger—the risk, for instance, of a cerebral haemorrhage—is also external, since it is the body that it threatens. Indeed it is the possession of a body that is the great danger to the mind, to our human and thinking life, which it is surely less correct to describe as a miraculous entelechy of animal and physical life than as an imperfect essay—as rudimentary in this sphere as the communal existence of protozoa attached to their polyparies or as the body of the whale—in the organisation of the spiritual life. The body immures the mind within a fortress; presently on all sides the fortress is besieged and in the end, inevitably, the mind has to surrender.

But—to accept provisionally the distinction which I have just made between the two sorts of danger that threaten the mind, and to begin with that which is in the fullest sense external—I recalled that it had often happened to me in the course of my life, in moments of intellectual excitement which coincided with a complete suspension of physical activity, as for example on those evenings when, half drunk, I had left the restaurant at Rivebelle in a carriage to go to some neighbouring casino, to feel very clearly within me the present object of my thought and at the same time to realise how much at the mercy of chance this intellectual activity was: how fortuitous it was that this particular thought had not entered my mind before, and how easily, through an accident to the carriage which was hurtling through the darkness, it might, along with my body, be annihilated. At the time this did not worry me. My high spirits knew neither forethought nor anxiety. The possibility that this joy might end in a second and turn into nothingness mattered to me scarcely at all. How different was my attitude now! The happiness which I was feeling was the product not of a purely subjective tension of the nerves which isolated me from the past, but on the contrary of an enlargement of my mind, within which the past was re-forming and actualising itself, giving me—but alas! only momentarily—something whose value was eternal. This I should have liked to bequeath to those who might have been enriched by my treasure. Admittedly, what I had experienced in the library and what I was seeking to protect was pleasure still, but no longer pleasure of an egotistical kind, or if there was egotism in it (for all the fruitful altruisms of nature develop in an egotistical manner and any human altruism which is without egotism is sterile, like that of the writer who interrupts his work to receive a friend in distress or to accept some public function or to write propaganda articles) it was an egotism which could be put to work for the benefit of other people. No longer was I indifferent to my fate as I had been on those drives back from Rivebelle; I felt myself enhanced by this work which I bore within me as by something fragile and precious which had been entrusted to me and which I should have liked to deliver intact into the hands of those for whom it was intended, hands which were not my own. And this feeling that I was the bearer of a work made me think in a changed way of an accident in which I might meet with death, as of something much more greatly to be feared and at the same time, to the extent to which this work of mine seemed to me necessary and durable, absurd because in contradiction with my desire, with the flight of my thought, yet none the less possible for that, since accidents, being produced by material causes, can perfectly well take place at the very moment when wishes of a quite different order, which they destroy without being aware of their existence, render them most bitterly regrettable (at a trivial level of existence such accidents happen every day: at the very moment, for instance, when you are trying your hardest not to make a noise because of a friend who is asleep, a carafe placed too near the edge of his table falls to the ground and awakens him). I knew that my brain was like a basin of rock rich in minerals, in which lay vast and varied ores of great price. But should I have time to exploit them? For two reasons I was the only person who could do this: with my death would disappear the one and only engineer who possessed the skill to extract these minerals and—more than that—the whole stratum itself. Yet presently, when I left this party to go home, it only needed a chance collision between the cab which I should take and another car for my body to be destroyed, thus forcing my mind, from which life instantly would ebb away, to abandon for ever and ever the new ideas which at this moment, not yet having had time to place them within the safety of a book, it anxiously embraced with the fragile protection of its own pulpy and quivering substance.

But by a strange coincidence, this rational fear of danger was taking shape in my mind at a moment when I had finally become indifferent to the idea of death. In the past the fear of being no longer myself was something that had terrified me, and this had made me dread the end of each new love that I had experienced (for Gilberte, for Albertine), because I could not bear the idea that the "I" who loved them would one day cease to exist, since this in itself would be a kind of death. But by dint of repetition this fear had gradually been transformed into a calm confidence. So that if in those early days, as we have seen, the idea of death had cast a shadow over my loves, for a long time now the remembrance of love had helped me not to fear death. For I realised that dying was not something new, but that on the contrary since my childhood I had already died many times. To take a comparatively recent period, had I not clung to Albertine more tenaciously than to my own life? Could I at the time when I loved her conceive my personality without the continued existence within it of my love for her? Yet now I no longer loved her, I was no longer the person who loved her but a different person who did not love her, and it was when I had become a new person that I had ceased to love her. And yet I did not suffer from having become this new person, from no longer loving Albertine, and surely the prospect of one day no longer having a body could not from any point of view seem to me as sad as had then seemed to me that of one day no longer loving Albertine, that prospect which now was a fact and one which left me quite unmoved. These successive deaths, so feared by the self which they were destined to annihilate, so painless, so unimportant once they were accomplished and the self that feared them was no longer there to feel them, had taught me by now that it would be the merest folly to be frightened of death. Yet it was precisely when the thought of death had become a matter of indifference to me that I was beginning once more to fear death, under another form, it is true, as a threat not to myself but to my book, since for my book's incubation this life that so many dangers threatened was for a while at least indispensable. Victor Hugo says:

> Grass must grow and children must die.

To me it seems more correct to say that the cruel law of art is that people die and we ourselves die after exhausting every form of suffering, so that over our heads may grow the grass not of oblivion but of eternal life, the vigorous and luxuriant growth of a true work of art, and so that thither, gaily and without a thought for those who are sleeping beneath them, future generations may come to enjoy their *déjeuner sur l'herbe*.

So much for the dangers from without; there were others, as I have said, that threatened me from within. Supposing that I were preserved from all accidents of an external kind, might I not nevertheless be robbed of the fruits of this good fortune by some accident occurring within myself, some internal catastrophe assailing me before the necessary months had passed and I had had time to write my book? When presently I made my way home through the Champs-Elysées, who was to say that I might not be struck down by that malady which had struck my grandmother one afternoon when she had gone there with me for a walk which, though of this she had no suspicion, was destined to be her last—so ignorant are we, as ignorant as the hand of a clock when it arrives at the point upon its dial where a spring will be released within the mechanism which will cause the hour to strike. And indeed perhaps the fear that I might already have traversed almost the whole of that last minute which precedes the first stroke of the hour, that minute during which the stroke is already preparing itself, perhaps the fear of the stroke that might already be moving into action within my brain was itself a sort of obscure awareness of something that was soon to happen, a sort of reflexion in the conscious mind of the precarious state of the brain whose arteries are about to give way, a phenomenon no more impossible than that sudden acceptance of death that comes to wounded men who, though the doctor and their own desire to live try to deceive them, say, realising the truth: "I am going to die, I am ready," and write their farewells to their wives.

Nor was anything so grave as a cerebral haemorrhage needed to hinder me in the execution of my task. Already the premonitory symptoms of the same malady, perceptible to me in a certain emptiness in the head and a tendency to forgetfulness thanks to which I now merely stumbled upon things in my memory by chance in the way in which, when you are tidying your belongings, you find objects which you had forgotten even that you had to look for, were making me resemble a miser whose strong-box has burst open and whose treasures little by little are disappearing. For a while there existed within me a self which deplored the loss of these treasures, then I perceived that memory, as it withdrew from me, carried away with it this self too.

And something not unlike my grandmother's illness itself happened to me shortly afterwards, when I still had not started to work on my book, in a strange fashion which I should never have anticipated. I went out to see some friends one evening and was told that I had never looked so well, and how wonderful it was that I had not a single grey hair. But at the end of the visit, coming downstairs, three times I nearly fell. I had left my home only two hours earlier; but when I got back, I felt that I no longer possessed either memory or the power of thought or strength or existence of any kind. People could have come to call on me or to proclaim me king, to lay violent hands on me or arrest me, and I should passively have submitted, neither opening my eyes nor uttering a word, like those travellers of whom we read who, crossing the Caspian Sea in a small boat, are so utterly prostrated by seasickness that they offer not even a show of resistance when they are told that they are going to be thrown into the sea. I had, strictly speaking, no illness, but I felt myself no longer capable of anything, I was in the condition of those old men who one day are in full possession of their faculties and the next, having fractured a thigh or had an attack of indigestion, can only drag on for a while in their bed an existence which has become nothing more than a preparation, longer or shorter, for a now ineluctable death. One of my selves, the one which in the past had been in the habit of going to those barbarian festivals that we call dinner-parties, at which, for the men in white shirt-fronts and the half-naked women beneath feathered plumes, values have been so reversed that a man who does not turn up after having accepted the invitation—or merely arrives after the roast has been served—is deemed to have committed an act more culpable than any of those immoral actions which, along with the latest deaths, are so lightly discussed at this feast which nothing but death or a serious illness is an acceptable excuse for failing to attend—and then only provided that one has given notice in good time of one's intention to die, so that there may be no danger for the other guests of sitting down thirteen to table—this one of my selves had retained its scruples and lost its memory. The other self, the one which had had a glimpse of the task that lay before it, on the contrary still remembered. I had received an invitation from Mme Molé and I had learnt that Mme Sazerat's son had died. I determined therefore to employ one of those few hours after which I could not hope even to pronounce another word or to swallow a mouthful of milk, since my tongue would be tied as my grandmother's had been during her agony, in addressing my excuses to the one lady and my condolences to the other. But a moment or two later I had forgotten that I had these things to do—most happily forgotten, for the memory of my real work did not slumber but proposed to employ the hour of reprieve which was granted me in laying my first foundations. Unfortunately, as I took up a note-book to write, Mme Molé's invitation card slipped out in front of my eyes. Immediately the forgetful self, which nevertheless was able to dominate the other—is this not always the case with those scrupulous barbarians who have learnt the lore of the dinner-party?—pushed away the note-book and wrote to Mme Molé (whose esteem for me would no doubt have been great had she known that I had allowed my reply to her invitation to take precedence over my labours as an architect). Then suddenly a word in my letter reminded me that Mme Sazerat had lost her son and I wrote to her as well, after which, having sacrificed a real duty to the factitious obligation to appear polite and sympathetic, I fell back exhausted and closed my eyes, not to emerge from a purely vegetal existence before a week had elapsed. During this time, however, if all my unnecessary duties, to which I was willing to sacrifice my true duty, vanished after a few moments from my head, the idea of the edifice that I had to construct did not leave me for an instant. Whether it would be a church where little by little a group of faithful would succeed in apprehending verities and discovering harmonies or perhaps even a grand general plan, or whether it would remain, like a druidic monument on a rocky isle, something for ever unfrequented, I could not tell. But I was resolved to devote to it all my strength, which ebbed, as it seemed, reluctantly and as though to leave me time to complete the periphery of my walls and close "the funeral gate." Before very long I was able to show a few sketches. No one understood anything of them. Even those who commended my perception of the truths which I wanted eventually to engrave within the temple, congratulated me on having discovered them "with a microscope," when on the contrary it was a telescope that I had used to observe things which were indeed very small to the naked eye, but only because they were situated at a great distance, and which were each one of them in itself a world. Those passages in which I was trying to arrive at general laws were described as so much pedantic investigation of detail. What, in any case, was I hoping to achieve? In my youth I had had a certain facility, and Bergotte had praised as "admirable" the pages which I wrote while still at school. But instead of working I had lived a life of idleness, of pleasures and distractions, of ill-health and cosseting and eccentricities, and I was embarking upon my labour of construction almost at the point of death, without knowing anything of my trade. I felt that I no longer possessed the strength to carry out my obligations to people or my duties to my thoughts and my work, still less to satisfy both of these claims. As for the first, my forgetfulness of the letters I had to write and of the other things I had to do, to some extent simplified my task. But suddenly, at the end of a month, the association of ideas brought back the painful recollection of these duties and I was momentarily overwhelmed by the thought of my impotence. To my astonishment I found that I did not mind, the truth being that, since the day when my legs had trembled so violently as I was going downstairs, I had become indifferent to everything, I longed only for rest, while waiting for the great rest which would come in the end. Amongst other things I was indifferent to the verdict which might be passed on my work by the best minds of my age, and this not because I relegated to some future after my death the admiration which it seemed to me that my work ought to receive. The best minds of posterity might think what they chose, their opinions mattered to me no more

than those of my contemporaries. The truth was that, if I thought
of my work and not of the letters which I ought to answer, this was
not because I attached to these two things, as I had during my years
of idleness and later, in that brief interval between the conception
of my book and the day when I had had to cling to the banister,
very different degrees of importance. The organisation of my
memory, of the preoccupations that filled my mind, was indeed
linked to my work, but perhaps simply because, while the letters
which I received were forgotten a moment later, the idea of my
work was inside my head, always the same, perpetually in process
of becoming. But even my work had become for me a tiresome
obligation, like a son for a dying mother who still, between her
injections and her blood-lettings, has to make the exhausting
effort of constantly looking after him. Perhaps she still loves him,
but it is only in the form of a duty too great for her strength that she
is aware of her affection. In me, in the same way, the powers of the
writer were no longer equal to the egotistical demands of the
work. Since the day of the staircase, nothing in the world, no
happiness, whether it came from friendship or the progress of my
book or the hope of fame, reached me except as a sunshine
unclouded but so pale that it no longer had the virtue to warm
me, to make me live, to instil in me any desire; and yet, faint
though it was, it was still too dazzling for my eyes, I closed them
and turned my face to the wall. When a lady wrote to me: "I have
been *very surprised* not to receive an answer to my letter," I must, it
seemed, to judge from the sensation of movement in my lips, have
twisted an infinitesimal corner of my mouth into a little smile.
Nevertheless, I was reminded of her unanswered letter and I wrote
her a reply. Not wishing to be thought ungrateful, I tried hard to
raise my tardy civilities to the level of those which I supposed that
other people, though I had forgotten it, had shown to me. And I
was crushed by the effort to impose upon my moribund existence
the superhuman fatigues of life. The loss of my memory helped me
a little by creating gaps in my obligations; they were more than
made good by the claims of my work.

The idea of death took up permanent residence within me in
the way that love sometimes does. Not that I loved death,
I abhorred it. But after a preliminary stage in which, no doubt,
I thought about it from time to time as one does about a woman
with whom one is not yet in love, its image adhered now to the
most profound layer of my mind, so completely that I could not

give my attention to anything without that thing first traversing the idea of death, and even if no object occupied my attention and I remained in a state of complete repose, the idea of death still kept me company as faithfully as the idea of my self. And, on that day on which I had become a half-dead man, I do not think that it was the accidents characterising this condition—my inability to walk downstairs, to remember a name, to get up from a chair—that had, even by an unconscious train of thought, given rise to this idea of death, this conviction that I was already almost dead; it seems to me rather that the idea had come simultaneously with the symptoms, that inevitably the mind, great mirror that it is, reflected a new reality. Yet still I did not see how from my present ailments one could pass, without warning of what was to come, to total death. Then, however, I thought of other people, of the countless people who die every day without the gap between their illness and their death seeming to us extraordinary. I thought also that it was only because I saw them from within—rather than because I saw them in the deceptive colours of hope—that certain of my ailments, taken singly, did not seem to me to be fatal although I believed that I would soon die, just as those who are most convinced that their hour has come are, nevertheless, easily persuaded that if they are unable to pronounce certain words, this is nothing so serious as aphasia or a stroke, but a symptom merely of a local fatigue of the tongue, or a nervous condition comparable to a stutter, or the lassitude which follows indigestion.

No doubt my books too, like my fleshly being, would in the end one day die. But death is a thing that we must resign ourselves to. We accept the thought that in ten years we ourselves, in a hundred years our books, will have ceased to exist. Eternal duration is promised no more to men's works than to men.

In my awareness of the approach of death I resembled a dying soldier, and like him too, before I died, I had something to write. But my task was longer than his, my words had to reach more than a single person. My task was long. By day, the most I could hope for was to try to sleep. If I worked, it would be only at night. But I should need many nights, a hundred perhaps, or even a thousand. And I should live in the anxiety of not knowing whether the master of my destiny might not prove less indulgent than the Sultan Shahriyar, whether in the morning, when I broke off my story, he would consent to a further reprieve and permit me to resume my narrative the following evening. Not that I had the slightest pretension to be writing a new version, in any way, of the *Arabian Nights*, or of that other book written by night, Saint-Simon's *Memoirs*, or of any of those books which I had loved with a child's simplicity and to which I had been as superstitiously attached as later to my loves, so that I could not imagine without horror any work which should be unlike them. But—as Elstir had found with Chardin—you can make a new version of what you love only by first renouncing it. So my book, though it might be as long as the *Arabian Nights*, would be entirely different. True, when you are in love with some particular book, you would like yourself to write something that closely resembles it, but this love of the moment must be sacrificed, you must think not of your own taste but of a truth which far from asking you what your preferences are forbids you to pay attention to them. And only if you faithfully follow this truth will you sometimes find that you have stumbled again upon what you renounced, find that, by forgetting these works themselves, you have written the *Arabian Nights* or the *Memoirs* of Saint-Simon of another age. But for me was there still time? Was it not too late?

And I had to ask myself not only: "Is there still time?" but also: "Am I well enough?" Ill-health, which by compelling me, like a severe director of conscience, to die to the world, had rendered me good service (for "except a corn of wheat fall into the ground and die, it abideth alone: but if it die, it bringeth forth much fruit"), and which, after idleness had preserved me from the dangers of facility, was perhaps going to protect me from idleness, that same ill-health had consumed my strength and as I had first noticed long ago, particularly when I had ceased to love Albertine, the strength of my memory. But was not the re-creation by the memory of impressions which had then to be deepened, illumined, transformed into equivalents of understanding, was not this process one of the conditions, almost the very essence of the work of art as I had just now in the library conceived it? Ah! if only I now possessed the strength which had still been intact on that evening brought back to my mind by the sight of *François le Champi*! Was not that the evening when my mother had abdicated her authority, the evening from which dated, together with the slow death of my grandmother, the decline of my health and my will? All these things had been decided in that moment when, no longer able to bear the prospect of waiting till morning to place my lips upon my mother's face, I had made up my mind, jumped out of bed and gone in my nightshirt to post myself at the window through which the moonlight entered my room until I should hear the sounds of M. Swann's departure. My parents had gone with him to the door, I had heard the garden gate open, give a peal of its bell, and close . . .

While I was asking myself these questions, it occurred to me suddenly that, if I still had the strength to accomplish my work, this afternoon—like certain days long ago at Combray which had influenced me—which in its brief compass had given me both the idea of my work and the fear of being unable to bring it to fruition, would certainly impress upon it that form of which as a child I had had a presentiment in the church at Combray but which ordinarily, throughout our lives, is invisible to us: the form of Time.

Many errors, it is true, there are, as the reader will have seen that various episodes in this story had proved to me, by which our senses falsify for us the real nature of the world. Some of these, however, it would be possible for me to avoid by the efforts which I should make to give a more exact transcription of things. In the case of sounds, for instance, I should be able to refrain from altering their place of origin, from detaching them from their cause, beside which our intelligence only succeeds in locating them after they have reached our ears—though to make the rain sing softly in the middle of one's room or, contrarily, to make the quiet boiling of one's tisane sound like a deluge in the courtyard outside should not really be more misleading than what is so often done by painters when they paint a sail or the peak of a mountain in such a way that, according to the laws of perspective, the intensity of the colours and the illusion of our first glance, they appear to us either very near or very far away, through an error which the reasoning mind subsequently corrects by, sometimes, a very large displacement. Other errors, though of a more serious kind, I might continue to commit, placing features, for instance, as we all do, upon the face of a woman seen in the street, when instead of nose, cheeks and chin there ought to be merely an empty space with nothing more upon it than a flickering reflexion of our desires. But at least, even if I had not the leisure to prepare—and here was a much more important matter—the hundred different masks which ought properly to be attached to a single face, if only because of the different eyes which look at it and the different meanings which they read into its features, not to mention, for the same eyes, the different emotions of hope and fear or on the contrary love and habit which for thirty years can conceal the changes brought about by age, and even if I did not attempt—though my love affair with Albertine was sufficient proof to me that any other kind of representation must be artificial and untruthful—to represent some of my characters as existing not outside but within ourselves, where their slightest action can bring fatal disturbances in its train, and to vary also the light of the moral sky which illumines them in accordance with the variations in pressure in our own sensibility (for an object which was so small beneath the clear sky of our certainty can be suddenly magnified many times over on the appearance of a tiny cloud of danger)—if, in my attempt to transcribe a universe which had to be totally redrawn, I could not convey these changes and many others, the needfulness of which, if one is to depict reality, has been made manifest in the course of my narrative, at least I should not fail to portray man, in this universe, as endowed with the length not of his body but of his years and as obliged—a task more and more enormous and in the end too great for his strength—to drag them with him wherever he goes.

Moreover, that we occupy a place, always growing, in Time is something everybody is conscious of, and this universality could only make me rejoice, it being the truth, the truth suspected by each of us, that I had to seek to elucidate. Not only does everybody feel that we occupy a place in Time, but the simplest of us measures this place approximately, as he would measure the one we occupy in space. People with no special perspicacity, seeing two men whom they do not know, both perhaps with black moustaches or both clean-shaven, will say that of the two one is about twenty and the other about forty years old, for the face of a young man cannot possibly be confused with that of a man of middle age, which in the eyes even of the most ignorant beholder is veiled by a sort of mist of seriousness. Of course, this evaluation of age that we make is often inaccurate, but the mere fact that we think ourselves able to make it indicates that we conceive of age as an entity which is measurable. And the second of the two men with black moustaches has, in effect, had twenty years added to his stature.

This notion of Time embodied, of years past but not separated from us, it was now my intention to emphasise as strongly as possible in my work. And at this very moment, in the house of the Prince de Guermantes, as though to strengthen me in my resolve, the noise of my parents' footsteps as they accompanied M. Swann to the door and the peal—resilient, ferruginous, interminable, fresh and shrill—of the bell on the garden gate which informed me that at last he had gone and that Mamma would presently come upstairs, these sounds rang again in my ears, yes, unmistakably I heard these very sounds, situated though they were in a remote past. And as I cast my mind over all the events which were ranged in an unbroken series between the moment of my childhood when I had first heard its sound and the Guermantes party, I was terrified to think that it was indeed this same bell which rang within me and that nothing that I could do would alter its jangling notes. On the contrary, having forgotten the exact manner in which they faded away and wanting to relearn this, to hear them properly again, I was obliged to block my ears to the conversations which were proceeding between the masked figures all round me, for in order to get nearer to the sound of the bell and to hear it better it was into my own depths that I had to redescend. And this could only be because its peal had always been there, inside me, and not this sound only but also, between that distant moment and the present one, unrolled in all its vast length, the whole of that past which I was not aware that I carried about within me. When the bell of the garden gate had pealed, I already existed and from that moment onwards, for me still to be able to hear that peal, there must have been no break in continuity, no single second at which I had ceased or rested from existing, from thinking, from being conscious of myself, since that moment from long ago still adhered to me and I could still find it again, could retrace my steps to it, merely by descending to a greater depth within myself. And it is because they contain thus within themselves the hours of the past that human bodies have the power to hurt so terribly those who love them, because they contain the memories of so many joys and desires already effaced for them, but still cruel for the lover who contemplates and prolongs in the dimension of Time the beloved body of which he is jealous, so jealous that he may even wish for its destruction. For after death Time withdraws from the body, and the memories, so indifferent, grown so pale, are effaced in her who no longer exists, as they soon will be in the lover whom for a while they continue to torment but in whom before long they will perish, once the desire that owed its inspiration to a living body is no longer there to sustain them. Profound Albertine, whom I saw sleeping and who was dead.

In this vast dimension which I had not known myself to possess, the date on which I had heard the noise of the garden bell at Combray—that far-distant noise which nevertheless was within me—was a point from which I might start to make measurements. And I felt, as I say, a sensation of weariness and almost of terror at the thought that all this length of Time had not only, without interruption, been lived, experienced, secreted by me, that it was my life, was in fact me, but also that I was compelled so long as I was alive to keep it attached to me, that it supported me and that, perched on its giddy summit, I could not myself make a movement without displacing it. A feeling of vertigo seized me as I looked down beneath me, yet within me, as though from a height, which was my own height, of many leagues, at the long series of the years.

I understood now why it was that the Duc de Guermantes, who to my surprise, when I had seen him sitting on a chair, had seemed to me so little aged although he had so many more years beneath him than I had, had presently, when he rose to his feet and tried to stand firm upon them, swayed backwards and forwards upon legs as tottery as those of some old archbishop with nothing solid about his person but his metal crucifix, to whose support there rushes a mob of sturdy young seminarists, and had advanced with difficulty, trembling like a leaf, upon the almost unmanageable summit of his eighty-three years, as though men spend their lives perched upon living stilts which never cease to grow until sometimes they become taller than church steeples, making it in the end both difficult and perilous for them to walk and raising them to an eminence from which suddenly they fall. And I was terrified by the thought that the stilts beneath my own feet might already have reached that height; it seemed to me that quite soon now I might be too weak to maintain my hold upon a past which already went down so far. So, if I were given long enough to accomplish my work, I should not fail, even if the effect were to make them resemble monsters, to describe men as occupying so considerable a place, compared with the restricted place which is reserved for them in space, a place on the contrary prolonged past measure, for simultaneously, like giants plunged into the years, they touch the distant epochs through which they have lived, between which so many days have come to range themselves—in Time.

NOTES · ADDENDA · SYNOPSIS

NOTES

THE FUGITIVE

1. (p. 22) "*Notre mal ne vaut pas un seul de ses regards*"—the line is from one of Ronsard's *Sonnets pour Hélène*.

2. (p. 118) Albert, Duc de Broglie, the grandson of Mme de Staël, was exiled by Napoleon I and retired to Chaumont-sur-Loire—whence the association of ideas.

3. (p. 144) *Le chancelier* Pasquier, friend of Mme de Boigne, who ran a famous salon under the July Monarchy and whose *Mémoires* (published in 1907) suggested those of Mme de Beausergent which the narrator's grandmother loved to read. The Duc de Noailles was a friend and patron of Sainte-Beuve. Mme d'Arbouville was the latter's mistress.

4. (p. 158) Mme de Guermantes has told this story before, at the expense of the Prince de Léon (see p. 524).

5. (p. 171) "The dead are sleeping peacefully" comes from Musset's *La Nuit d'Octobre*, "You will make them weep . . . All those urchins" from Sully-Prudhomme's *Aux Tuileries*, and "The very first night" from Charles Cros's *Nocturne*.

6. (p. 215) The reference is to *Phèdre*, Act II, Scene 5, in which Phèdre declares her love for Hippolyte in cryptic terms: she loves him as she loved Thésée, "*non point tel que l'ont vu les Enfers . . . mais fidèle, mais fier, et même un peu farouche.*"

7. (p. 219) Roland Garros: famous French aviator.

8. (p. 229) An illegitimate daughter of the Duc de Berry, son of Charles X, married a Lucinge-Faucigny.

9. (p. 233) *Sous-maîtresse*: euphemism for a brothel-keeper or "madam".

10. (p. 239) This passage is a little confusing. Proust never got round to marrying Gilberte to the Duc de Guermantes. In *Time Regained* she reappears as Saint-Loup's widow while Oriane is still alive and married to the aged Duke.

11. (p. 239) Agamemnon in Offenbach's *La Belle Hélène*.

12. (p. 248) This signature can be explained by the fact that

Charles Morel was Bobby Santois in Proust's original manuscript.

13. (p. 251) The widowed Gilberte, in *Time Regained*, appears to be the mother of an only daughter.

TIME REGAINED

14. (p. 267) Proust's manuscript adds at this point: "Cruelty on the death of her father (copy from the note-book where it is described)."

15. (p. 269) Legrandin has earlier been described in almost identical terms (see *The Fugitive*, p. 236).

16. (p. 270) Another chronological inconsistency. Bergotte's death was reported long before the marriage of Gilberte and Saint-Loup.

17. (p. 287) From Victor Hugo's *Les Contemplations*.

18. (p. 329) Quotation from Baudelaire's *Le Balcon*.

19. (p. 362) "Le moi est haïssable" (Pascal).

20. (p. 492) Eponymous hero of a novel by the Comtesse de Ségur.

21. (p. 501) And yet the narrator does not meet her until 50 pages later, failing to recognise her at first (see p. 552).

22. (p. 520) The remark occurs later: see preceding note.

23. (p. 574) This passage is also rather surprising, since Rachel has been identified several pages before. All such inconsistencies are attributable to Proust's endless additions to his original text. He died before he had time to resolve the resulting confusions.

ADDENDA

THE FUGITIVE

Page 48. *The Pléiade editors have inserted here as a footnote an additional passage which Proust placed a few pages later (clearly in error)*:

I was going to buy, in addition to the motor-cars, the finest yacht which then existed. It was for sale, but at so high a price that no buyer could be found. Moreover, once bought, even if we confined ourselves to four-month cruises, it would cost two hundred thousand francs a year in upkeep. We should be living at the rate of half a million francs a year. Would I be able to sustain it for more than seven or eight years? But never mind; when I had only an income of fifty thousand francs left, I could leave it to Albertine and kill myself. This was the decision I made. It made me think of *myself*. Now, since one's ego lives by thinking incessantly of all sorts of things, since it is no more than the thought of those things, if by chance, instead of being preoccupied with those things, it suddenly thinks of itself, it finds only an empty apparatus, something which it does not recognise and to which, in order to give it some reality, it adds the memory of a face seen in a mirror. That peculiar smile, that untidy moustache—they are what would disappear from the face of the earth. When I killed myself five years hence, I would no longer be able to think all those things which passed through my mind unceasingly, I would no longer exist on the face of the earth and would never come back to it; my thought would stop for ever. And my ego seemed to me even more null when I saw it as something that no longer exists. How could it be difficult to sacrifice, for the sake of the person to whom one's thought is constantly straining (the person we love), that other person of whom we never think: ourselves? Accordingly, this thought of my death, like the notion of my ego, seemed to me most strange, but I did not find it at all disagreeable. Then suddenly it struck me as being terribly sad; this was because, reflecting that if I did not have more money at my disposal it was because my parents were still alive, I suddenly thought of my mother. And I could not bear the idea of what she would suffer after my death.

Page 210. *Proust's manuscript has a different version of the Norpois–Villeparisis episode which the Pléiade editors print as an appendix. Passages that have become illegible are indicated by square brackets:*

Several of the palaces on the Grand Canal were transformed into hotels, and by way of a change from the one at which we were staying, we decided one evening to dine in another where the food was said to be better. While my mother was paying the gondolier, I entered a vast marble-pillared hall that had once been entirely covered with frescoes, [...]

One of the waiters asked if the "old couple" [...] were coming down [...], that they never gave any warning, and that it was most tiresome. Then he saw the lady appear. It was in fact Mme de Villeparisis [...] but bent towards the ground, with that air of dejection and bemusement produced by extreme fatigue and the weight of years. We happened by chance to be given a table immediately behind hers, up against the splendid marble walls of the palace, and fortunately, since my mother was tired and wanted to avoid introductions, we had our backs to the Marquise and could not be seen by her, and were moreover protected by the relief of a massive column with a [...] capital. Meanwhile I was wondering which of her relations was being referred to as M. de Villeparisis, when a few minutes later I saw her old lover, M. de Norpois, even more bent than she, sit down at her table, having just come down from their room. They still loved each other, and, now that he had given up his functions at the Ministry, as soon as the relative incognito which one enjoys abroad permitted, they lived together completely. In order to allow his old mistress a degree of respectability, he was careful not to give his name in hotels, and the waiters, ignorant at this distance of celebrated Parisian liaisons, and moreover seeing this old gentleman, even when he had gone out without her, invariably coming back to dine alone with the old lady, assumed that they were M. and Mme de Villeparisis. The matrimonial character of their relationship, which had been greatly accentuated by the carelessness of old age and travel, manifested itself at once in the fact that on sitting down to table M. de

Norpois evinced none of those courtesies one shows towards a woman who is not one's wife, any more than she herself made any effort for him. More lively than Mme de Villeparisis, he related to her with a familiarity that surprised me what he had learned that day from a foreign ambassador he had been to see. She let a fair proportion of his words go by without answering, either from fatigue, or lack of interest, or deafness and a desire to conceal it. From time to time she addressed a few words to him in a faint voice, as though overcome with exhaustion. It was obvious that she now lived almost exclusively for him, and had long since lost touch with the social world—from which, with considerable volubility and in a rather loud voice (perhaps to enable her to hear him), he brought her the latest news—for she put to him, in a low-pitched, weary voice, questions that seemed strange on the lips of a person who, even though excluded from it for a long time, nevertheless belonged to the highest society. After a long silence [. . .] asked: "So this Bisaccia you [. . .] this afternoon, is he one of Sosthène's sons?" "Yes, of course, he's the one who became Duc de Bisaccia when Arnaud took the name Doudeauville. He's charming; he's a bit like Carnot's youngest son, only better-looking." And once more there was silence. What seemed most of all to be preoccupying the old woman, whose charming eyes in that ruined face no one could have identified through the mists which the distance from Paris and the remoteness of age accumulated round her, was a war over Morocco. In spite of what the foreign ambassador had said to M. de Norpois, she did not seem reassured. "Ah, but you always see the black side," said M. de Norpois with some asperity. "I admit that Emperor William is often unfortunate in his choice of words and gestures. But the fact that certain things must be taken seriously doesn't mean that they should be taken tragically. It would be a case of Jupiter making mad those he wishes to destroy; for war is in nobody's interest, least of all Germany's. They're perfectly aware in the Wilhelmstrasse that Morocco isn't worth the blood of a single Pomeranian grenadier. You're alarming yourself about trifles." And again there was silence, prolonged indefinitely by Mme de Villeparisis, whose beauty, which was said to have been so striking, had been as thoroughly effaced as the frescoes that had decorated the ceiling of this magnificent hall with its broad red pillars, and whose personality was as well concealed, if not from the eyes of Parisians who might perhaps have identified her, at least from the hotel's Venetian staff, as if she had been wearing a carnival mask as in the old days in Venice. M. de Norpois addressed an occasional reproof to a waiter who had failed to bring something he had ordered. I noticed that he enjoyed good food as much as at the time when he used to dine with my family, and Mme de Villeparisis was as finicky as she had been at Balbec. "No no, don't ask them for a soufflé," M. de Norpois said, "they've no idea what it is. They'll bring you something that bears not the slightest resemblance to a soufflé. In any case it's your own fault, since you won't hear of Italian cooking." Mme de Villeparisis did not answer; then after a while, in a plaintive voice, as sad and faint as the murmur of the wind, she wailed: "No one knows how to make anything any more. I don't know whether you remember, in the old days at my mother's house, they used to bring off to perfection a dish called a *crème renversée*. Perhaps we could ask for one of those." "In fact it hadn't yet come to be called a *crème renversée*; it was called," said M. de Norpois, putting the phrase in inverted commas, "'creamed eggs'. What they give you here won't be up to much. Creamed eggs were so smooth and succulent, do you remember?" But, whether because she did not in fact remember, or because she had talked enough, Mme de Villeparisis said nothing. She relapsed into a long silence which did not offend M. de Norpois, presumably because it did not surprise him and because it must have been one of the characteristics, perhaps one of the charms, of his life with her. And while she laboriously cut up her beans, he went back to telling her how interesting, and on the whole optimistic, the foreign ambassador had been, meanwhile keeping an eye out for a waiter from whom he could order their dessert. Before this had been served, my mother and I rose from the table, and, while keeping my head turned away so as not to attract their attention, I could nevertheless still see the two aged lovers, seemingly indifferent to one another, but in reality bent by time like two branches which have developed the same tilt, which have drawn so close to each other that they almost touch, and which nothing will ever either straighten up or separate again.

This was perhaps what might have happened to me in the long run if Albertine had lived. And yet, comforting though it must after all be, since worldly men and women sacrifice social life and ambition for it, I felt no regret that what might have been had failed to come about, so impervious had I become to the memory of Albertine. I cannot however say that sometimes in the evening, when we returned to our hotel (for, since our encounter with the old Villeparisis–Norpois couple, my mother had decided against our dining elsewhere), I did not feel, in the nervous restlessness of nightfall, that the Albertine of long ago, invisible to myself . . . (*cf. p. 210*).

SYNOPSIS

THE FUGITIVE

Grieving and Forgetting. "Mlle Albertine has gone" (3). Albertine's letter (4). Hypotheses about the reasons for her departure (5). All my different "selves" must learn to live with my suffering (13). Albertine in Touraine (15). The little poor girl in my room (16).

Saint-Loup's mission to Touraine (19). His astonishment on seeing Albertine's photograph (21). Bloch's indiscretion and my anger (26). Summons from the Sûreté (26). First furtive hint of forgetting (30). My sleep is full of Albertine (31). First telegraph from Saint-Loup: mission delayed (31); second telegram: Albertine has seen him (34). Furious, I cable to him telling him to return (35). A letter from Albertine (35). My mendacious reply (37). The declaration scene in *Phèdre* (41). The mystery of Albertine's rings (44; cf. III 644). Another letter from Albertine (49). I ask Andrée to come and live with me, and tell Albertine (50). Saint-Loup's return; an overheard conversation shows him in a new light (51). His report on his mission (52).

A telegram from Mme Bontemps: Albertine's death in a riding accident (57). New and unprecedented suffering (57). Proliferation of memories (59–61). The baths at Balbec (71). Aimé's mission of inquiry (72). Alternation of odious suspicions and tender memories (73). Analogy between my love for Gilberte and my love for Albertine (81). Our mistresses are the daughters of our anguish (84). Lying words become prophetic truths (86). Aimé's letter confirming my suspicions (93). His mission to Touraine (100). Albertine and the laundry-girl (101); evocation of an Elstir painting (104). Revival in my memory of a sweet, kind and innocent Albertine (106).

Beginnings of recovery (109). I grow accustomed to the idea of Albertine's death (110). Intermittent revival of my love and my suffering (112 et sqq.). Andrée confesses her taste for women, but denies having had relations with Albertine (121). Renewal of desire for other women (127). The power of oblivion (131).

Mlle de Forcheville. Three stages on the road to indifference (134). A walk in the Bois on All Saints' Day (134). The three girls (137). Some days later, one of them gives me a look which rouses my passion (137). I identify her with Mlle d'Eporcheville, whom Robert had met in a house of assignation (137; cf. III 88). Robert, in reply to a cable from me, tells me it is the wrong girl (141). My article in the *Figaro* (142–6). Visit to the Guermantes' (146). The blonde girl: Mlle de Forcheville (147), in other words Gilberte (148). Mme de Guermantes's changed attitude towards Swann's wife and daughter after his death (151); she entertains Gilberte and talks to her about her father (153). The Duke reads my article (157). Gilberte's snobbery (158). Two congratulatory letters (163). Gilberte helps to bury the memory of her father (165) and hastens the process of forgetting in me as regards Albertine (165). A new social self replaces the one that loved Albertine (167).

Second stage on the road towards indifference: second conversation with Andrée (169); her relations with Albertine (172); Albertine and Morel (172); the evening of the syringa (173; cf. III 541). Andrée's different natures (176); her engagement to the Verdurins' nephew, "I'm a wash-out" (177), an artist of genius underneath his crude and frivolous exterior (177). The Princesse de Parme's visit to my mother (184). Third visit from Andrée (186); a new explanation for Albertine's departure (186). Albertine and "I'm a wash-out" (187). His attitude towards me (192).

Sojourn in Venice. Third stage towards indifference (195). Venice and Combray (195). Mme de Villeparisis and M. de Norpois, greatly aged (201–10). A telegram from Albertine telling me she is alive; it gives me no joy (212). The self that loved Albertine is dead (213). My outings in Venice, alone or with my mother (216). The Giotto chapel at Padua (218). Evening walks in Venice (220).

I ask my mother to postpone our departure (221); she refuses, and I decide to stay (222). Solitude, misery, *O sole mio* (222). The train (225). A letter from Gilberte announcing her engagement to Robert de Saint-Loup (225); the recent telegram was from her (226).

New Aspect of Saint-Loup. My mother tells me of another marriage, that of the Cambremers' son and Mlle d'Oloron, Jupien's niece (228). My mother's reflexions on the news, and thoughts of my grandmother (229). Ups and downs of Saint-Loup's engagement plans (231). Disapproval from Combray (232). Reactions of society people (234). Opposite effects of the same vice in Charlus and Legrandin (236). Roles of the Princesse de Parme, Charlus and Legrandin in Mlle d'Oloron's marriage (236). Change in Legrandin (237). Gilberte, at first happy in her new social position (238), becomes indifferent to it (240). Mlle d'Oloron's death (242). The Muse of History (246).

A visit to Tansonville (247). Saint-Loup's infidelity; his relations with Morel (248). Retrospective analysis of Robert's sexual tastes (250–4). Robert and Mme de Forcheville (254). My tarnished friendship (258).

TIME REGAINED

Tansonville. Walks with Gilberte (261). Disenchantment with the scenes of my childhood (262). Gilberte shows me that the Guermantes and the Méséglise ways are not irreconcilable (263; cf. I 547) and reveals the meaning of the sign she made to me years ago (264; cf. I 139).

Scene from the window of my room at Tansonville (267). Effects of Saint-Loup's vice on his behaviour (268). His lies (269). Françoise's esteem for him (271). His feelings towards Gilberte (271). The Guermantes type in Robert (273). The Guermantes' amatory tastes (274). Conversation with Gilberte about Albertine (277–8).

The Goncourt journal (278). Its description of the Verdurin salon (279–86). My lack of a bent for literature (287).

M. de Charlus during the war. My return to Paris in 1916 (292). Wartime Paris: changes in fashions and in society (292–7). News of the war in the Verdurin salon (298). The new "faithful"; Morel, a deserter, and "I'm a wash-out", Andrée's husband (299). Mme Verdurin's overtures to Odette (301).

Aircraft in the sky at nightfall (303). Walks in night-time Paris, reminiscent of Combray (304).

Meeting with Saint-Loup in 1914 (306); his secret efforts to get to the front (308). Bloch passed fit for military service (308). Bloch and Saint-Loup (309). Ideal of virility among homosexuals (312–15). The manager of the Grand Hotel and the lift-boy (316); the lift boy and the rich young man (316–17). Françoise and the war (317); tormented by the butler (317–20).

Return to the sanatorium (320). A letter from Gilberte: German occupation of Tansonville (321). A letter from Robert (321).

Second return to Paris: another letter from Gilberte, with news of the fighting round Combray (324). A visit from Saint-Loup, in Paris on leave (326). Beauty of nocturnal air-raids (327); reflexions on strategy (329).

Beauty of night-time Paris (332). Meeting with M. de Charlus (333); Mme Verdurin's malevolence towards him (334); Morel's ingratitude and scurrilous articles in the press (336). Mme Verdurin's croissant and the *Lusitania* (342). M. de Charlus's pro-Germanism (342–7). His sarcasm about Brichot's articles (348). Morel and women (350). Norpois's articles (351). Odette's remarks about the war (358). Brichot falls out of favour with the Verdurins (359). M. de Charlus's defeatist harangue on the boulevards (363–8). Aeroplanes in the night sky (370). M. de Charlus and Morel (372–5). Paris and Pompeii (375). M. de Charlus's admiration for Allied and German soldiers (376). His hand-clasp (378).

I look for a hotel (379) and find one open from which a familiar figure (Saint-Loup?) emerges (379). Conversation between soldiers and workers (380). The *patron* comes in with some chains (383). I see M. de Charlus being thrashed by a soldier (384). Jupien appears (384). Other clients of the hotel (384). The lost *croix de guerre* (389; cf. 409). M. de Charlus in the midst of the harem (393–7). Jupien's explanations (398–401).

An air-raid (401). Pompeians in the Métro or in Jupien's establishment (402). Reflexions on morality, on Jupien, on M. de Charlus and his aberrations (405). Françoise and the butler (409). The Larivières (413).

Saint-Loup's death (414). Recollections of his friendship (415). Parallel with Albertine (416). Françoise in the role of mourner (416). The Duchesse de Guermantes's unexpected grief (419).

Morel's arrest as a deserter (420); his revelations cause the arrest of M. de Charlus and M. d'Argencourt (421). If Saint-Loup had survived . . . (421).

Reception at the Princesse de Guermantes's. Return to Paris many years later (422). Train stops in the middle of the countryside (422). My incurable lack of literary talent (423). Invitation to the Princesse de Guermantes's musical afternoon (424). Cab-drive towards the Champs-Elysées (425); the silent heights of memory (426). Meeting with a greatly aged Charlus (427). His greeting to Mme de Saint-Euverte (428). His roll-call of dead friends and relations (430). The Duchesse de Létourville, shocked by his mumbling voice (430). Jupien speaks of the Baron's health, his Germanophilia, his persistent randiness (431).

The uneven paving-stones in the Guermantes courtyard (434); sensation of felicity similar to that of the madeleine, etc. (434); resurrection of Venice (435). Further exhilarating sensations (436). "The true paradises are the paradises that we have lost" (438). Impresions "outside time" (439). Reflexions on time, reality, memory, artistic creation (439 et sqq.). Futility of literary theories (449). Absurdity of popular art or patriotic art (451). *François le Champi* (452). Bibliophilia (455). Celibates of art (460). Aberrations of literary criticism (462).

Further reflexions on literary and artistic creation (463 et sqq.). The raw material for literature: my past life (467). A vocation? (468). The importance of dreams (480). The influence of Swann (484). The role of jealousy (485). Chateaubriand, Nerval and Baudelaire (488).

Back to the Guermantes reception: a *coup de théâtre* (489). M. d'Argencourt as an old beggar (490). Bloch (497). The Duchesse de Guermantes (498). The meaning of old age (502). M. de Cambremer (503). Legrandin (504). The Prince d'Agrigente (505). Various effects of Time (506). Odette: a challenge to the laws of chronology (517); "a sterilised rose" (519). Bloch's English chic (522); I introduce him to the Prince de Guermantes (523). Mme Verdurin has become the Princesse de Guermantes (524). Society and the chemistry of Time (526 et sqq.). Following the stream of memory back to its source (541 et sqq.). "Who's dead?" (548–50).

The Princesse de Nassau (550). Gilberte: "You took me for Mamma" (552). Conversation about Robert (552) and the art of war (552). Her friendship with Andrée (555). My determination to avoid social life (557). The Duchesse de Guermantes and Rachel (563).

Berma's tea-party (567). Her daughter and son-in-law (567). Rachel's performance (571). She runs down Berma (575). Mme de Guermantes in old age: her social decline (577). Berma's daughter and son-in-law received by Rachel (586).

The Duke's liaison with Odette (588). "A magnificent ruin" (589). Odette's amatory reminiscences (593). A new Mme de Saint-Euverte (597). Mme de Guermantes's malevolent remarks about Gilberte (599). Gilberte introduces her daugther (601, 605). Mlle de Saint-Loup and the idea of Time (602–5). A spur to me to begin my work (606). How to set about it (606); Françoise's help (607). Indifference to death, except in so far as my work was concerned (610). My social self and the self that conceived my book (613). The idea of death takes up permanent residence within me (616). Working by night (617). "Is there still time?" (618). The garden bell at Combray (619, 621, 622). "Profound Albertine ..." (622). Men in Time: my resolution (622).

ABOUT THE TRANSLATORS

CHARLES KENNETH SCOTT MONCRIEFF was born in Scotland in 1889 and studied Law and English at Edinburgh University. He trained as a professional soldier and spent World War I in France until wounded in 1917. While convalescing he turned to translating, and his English version of the *Chansons de Roland* was published in 1919. He translated Proust during the 1920s, along with Stendhal's *The Charterhouse of Parma*, *Scarlet and Black*, *Armance* and some of the *Chroniques italiennes*. He died in Rome in 1930.

TERENCE KILMARTIN translated selected letters of Proust in four volumes (together with his wife, Joanna), and wrote an exhaustive *Guide to Proust*. His other translations include de Gaulle's memoirs, and works by André Malraux and Henri de Montherlant. He was Literary Editor of the *Observer* from 1952 to 1987. After his death in 1991, the poet and translator D. J. ENRIGHT, who had worked closely with Kilmartin on the Scott Moncrieff version of *À la recherche du temps perdu*, continued the task of revising the translation.

This book is set in BEMBO which was cut
by the punch-cutter Francesco Griffo
for the Venetian printer-publisher
Aldus Manutius in early 1495
and first used in a pamphlet
by a young scholar
named Pietro
Bembo.

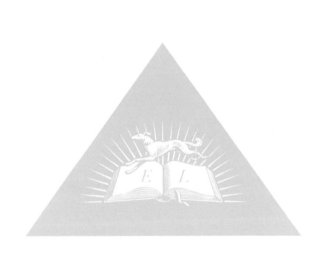